ABOUT THE AUTHOR

Joe Thomas is the author of *Paradise City* and *Gringa*. *Playboy* is the third novel in The São Paulo Quartet. The final part, *Brazilian Psycho*, will be published by Arcadia in 2020. He teaches English and Creative Writing at Royal Holloway, University of London. Prior to this, Joe lived and taught in São Paulo for ten years.

Arcadia Books Ltd
139 Highlever Road
London W10 6PH

www.arcadiabooks.co.uk

First published in the United Kingdom 2019
Copyright © Joe Thomas 2019

A catalogue record for this book is available from the British Library.

ISBN 978-1-911350-61-3

Typeset in Garamond by MacGuru Ltd
Printed and bound by T J International, Padstow PL28 8RW

ARCADIA BOOKS DISTRIBUTORS ARE AS FOLLOWS:

in the UK and elsewhere in Europe:
BookSource
50 Cambuslang Road
Cambuslang
Glasgow G32 8NB

in USA/Canada:
BookMasters
Baker & Taylor
30 Amberwood Parkway
Ashland, OH 44805
USA

in Australia/New Zealand:
NewSouth Books
University of New South Wales
Sydney NSW 2052

PLAYBOY

PLAYBOY

JOE THOMAS

A

For Martha Lecauchois

Author's note

Although based on actual events, this is a work of fiction. Certain names, dates, organisations, etc., have been changed for this purpose. A postscript and a glossary of Brazilian Portuguese follow the text.

Brasil is the only country where – in addition to whores cumming, pimps being jealous and drug dealers being addicted – poor people vote for the right wing

Tim Maia

A plague a' both your houses

William Shakespeare, *Romeo and Juliet*

Playboy, n., Brazilian Portuguese, slang: rich young man

Brasil, who pays for us to end up this way?

São Paulo, 2015 –
Year of the Goat.
Nem fodendo, cara. No fucking way. Year of the Snake.
The snake? President Dilma Rousseff. The boss. The head honcho. The Marxist with the mostest. The **Presidenta**, *she calls herself. It* burns.
Rumour has it she's been skimming off the Petrobras oil kickback scheme like a proper Russian oligarch. All power corrupts after all.
Cash-heavy bitch.
Yeah, Year of the Snake –
The snake? President Dilma Rousseff. Lula's prodigy. Leader of the Workers' Party. The balancer of one tricky-as-fuck left-centre coalition. A balance that has, for years, been achieved through very questionable means.
They don't like her in São Paulo.
Well, some do...

Article by Eleanor Boe

OLHA! Online magazine, 16 March 2016

What is Operação Lava Jato, Operation Car Wash?
(And why does this particular corruption scandal threaten to topple the government?)

It began in March 2014 as a routine federal investigation into money laundering through a car wash and garage complex in Brasilia, the country's capital. Two years later, and half a million people flooded the streets of São Paulo to call for President Dilma's impeachment. How did this happen? And where will it lead?

What started it all was the discovery of a Land Rover bought illegally by Alberto Youssef – a convicted money launderer of some distinction and considerable reach – for Paulo Roberto Costa, an executive at Petrobras, one of the biggest oil companies in the world, a company that accounts for an eighth of all investments in Brazil, and provides hundreds of thousands of jobs in construction, shipyards and refineries across the country.

And what this purchase led investigators to uncover was a far-reaching mechanism of corruption in which Petrobras overpaid on contracts to a cartel of construction companies, and, with the guaranteed business, this cartel channelled a percentage of each deal into offshore slush funds. Bribes, leaked documents have shown, were built into the contracts themselves, which made their illegality harder to spot.

So far, so your-basic-traditional-corruption model.

However, things might be about to change. Last week, on 8 March, Marcelo Odebrecht, CEO of the international Odebrecht construction conglomerate, was sentenced to nineteen years in jail for corruption, money laundering and criminal association. And it doesn't look like he wants to go quietly. To reduce his sentence, he's allegedly been outlining the epic scale of this kickback scheme. And exactly which politicians – and their parties – have benefited directly.

Last week, we saw the results of all of this: calls for Dilma's impeachment. On Sunday, we'll see the other side of the coin, as hundreds of thousands plan to march in solidarity, in her defence.

If nothing else, it appears that this unfolding scandal runs deep. And the question many people are asking is what's really more important: political ideology and policy-making, or being free of any association at all with corruption in a country in which it is considered systemic.

Brazil, quite clearly, is divided.

São Paulo, 20 March 2016

The thing about wealthy, or comfortable, Paulistanos when they first get a job – and this is something you English do better for once – is that they're not used to authority, don't know how to respond to a boss, how to behave professionally. In São Paulo, your first job is your career. You very rarely get the middle classes working through college, in a bar or restaurant, or doing something menial in the holidays to make a bit of pocket money. So when they turn up for work in their mid-twenties, in their first position, they don't know how to behave. They think they've made it. I'd make every upper- and middle-class Paulistano do a month in McDonald's. That'd be a start.

Camilla, 34, teacher

Leme sat at the counter, chopsticks poised. He was in the cop-friendly Chinaman's dumpling joint, deep down in Japa-town. Off duty and happy about it.

He angled his empty bottle of Chinese lager at the waitress and she brought him another. The TV was on with the sound down. Military Police in riot gear were hosing down troublemakers on Avenida Paulista, not a fifteen-minute walk away.

'An elegant business, Mario,' the Chinaman said, his hand on Leme's shoulder.

Leme had been coming to the Chinaman's for donkeys. He had spent time just across Avenida Vinte e Três de Maio in Bela Vista. Bixiga, as the neighbourhood was known by locals: the bladder of São Paulo. Leme's old man had a hard-on for crispy duck and took him on Sundays to feast. Everyone else was in the eye-talian canteens end of a weekend, but Leme was picking a fattened roast bird out of a line and watching the Chinaman tear into it with a machete. Habits, ne?

Leme nodded at the TV. 'Which side is this lot on?' he asked.

'Well, the nature of the affair seems to be more about the conflict than the ideology.'

Leme smiled. He thought of Renata, his late wife. It was her kind of an appraisal.

The Chinaman went on: 'But, shortly, we'll be engaged by the pro-Dilma rally and our chubby, gyppo fuckwit Lula will be pronouncing some political untruths.' He paused, took a pull at his own lager. 'So those young men getting their heads serviced by the Militars will be anti-Dilma, I'd wager, and God bless them for it.'

Leme laughed. He'd forgotten. The rally would cause him problems getting home. Since his run-ins a few years back, he no longer drank and drove for fear of angering the wrong Militar. He'd planned to walk across Paulista and down through Jardins until he got tired, then jump in a cab. This changed things.

'You not a fan then?' Leme asked, only half-serious.

'Dilma? Fuck no,' the Chinaman said. 'The puta don't got a noble bone. Sour-faced lefty cunt that's richer than God? On our dollar? No, Senhor. I form my political allegiances elsewhere.'

Leme grimaced. Nodded, slowly. 'It's your right as a citizen, my friend.'

'Yes, I know my rights,' the Chinaman said. 'Don't forget, young man, I was made by this town in the seventies. With your father.' He smiled. 'So, as you can imagine, I do know my rights.'

Leme raised his lager and they knocked bottles. 'So was Dilma,' he said.

The Chinaman chewed this over. 'Yes, I suppose so. It was a dishonourable time that affected many fine young minds. Though she seems reluctant to desist harping on about it. You know they tortured her when she *started* talking.' He paused, cracked a grin. Winked. 'It was the only way to shut her up!'

The Chinaman roared.

Leme winced. He smiled. Faz o que, ne? he thought. *What are you going to do?* Old-school Paulistanos have their reasons for being suspicious of the rise of the left.

He wondered what Renata would make of all this. He knew where she would be spending her afternoon. Which is what made up his mind.

He popped a prawn dumpling. He nailed the rest of his lager. He threw some notes on the counter.

'Ciao,' he said. 'I'm going to see what the gyppo and the slag have to say for themselves.'

He upped and left the restaurant. The bell rang as the door shut behind him. He turned left. Across the road, a man wheeled right and studied a window display in a Japanese supermarket. His arm was bent at the elbow. He flashed a look behind him as he spoke on his phone. The look seemed aimed at Leme. Was it? Leme slowed, eyed the man, couldn't place him – at least not from the back of his head.

It's not the paranoia that kills you, Leme thought.

He kept a slow pace. He didn't make the guy on his phone.

Leme hit Avenida Paulista twenty minutes later. There was a sea of red T-shirts. Cheap red baseball caps. Red balloons. A shit-tonne of them. And the odd, menacing black flag. Meaning: trouble ain't *too* far away.

Leme rubbernecked the crowd. The usual student rabble, the air around them hash-thick. A good number of workers: tough-skinned and gnarly men; grinning, dancing women. Lots of condo-dwellers eating out tonight, Leme thought, then felt a flash of repugnance that he had thought that. Some middle-class do-gooders, Renata's old mob, he expected. Gaggles of slouching anarchists in heavy metal slogans, bandana-ready. Standard. A textbook lefty bash, attendee-wise.

He bought a can of lager from a gawker with a cool box and worked his way slowly against the flow, aiming at the MASP building. Its outsized, red spider's legs fit right in. Even the museums were on Dilma's side today.

There were placards – everywhere.

Brave heart: there will be no coup

The Chinaman would have loved that one, Leme thought. There were placards with photos of a gurning Lula, '2018' emblazoned across his chest.

All Support

Leme studied the placards. All of them were stamped with #. His girlfriend Antonia had tried to explain to him what # meant only the other day.

'There's nothing more boring than a middle-aged man shrugging at the idiocy of the modern world,' she'd said. She'd gestured at their living room. 'An analogue throwback in a digital world. How original.'

He'd laughed at that.

The revolution is a click away, he thought. It's just a click away, click away. He smiled. Jagger-Richards it up a bit, entendeu?

He came up with his own little slogan: *vai tomar no coup*. Bilingual magic, that pun. Go take it up the... coup. He'd work on it.

He wormed through the crowds, south side of the avenue. It was a pertinent fucking contrast, the corporation towers flanking a marching band of anti-capitalists. Or pro-democrats. These days it was all so black and white it was hard to tell the difference.

Antonia let it wash over her: no nuance, no séance.

Or as the Chinaman was fond of saying: no barley, no parlay. Meaning: you wanna chat, we gonna drink.

There was a surge. Leme was pushed back against the Conjunto Nacional mall. The grill was down. A janitor peered through. Sensible positioning, son, Leme thought.

Then another man caught his eye, also just the other side of the grill. Leme, brow-furrowed, tensed. It was the guy from outside the Chinaman's – no doubt. Coincidence?

It's not the coincidence that kills you.

He gave the guy the sidelong fisheye. Definitely him. He was unshaven, hair unwashed, filthy little tache, corpse-pale, stick-thin, jittery.

Leme turned away so the guy wouldn't see his face, and tried to place him.

He acted crowd-curious.

He turned back to study the guy again. And he was right there, next to him, the grill separating them. Leme could feel the guy's heavy breath.

Bingo. Leme half-knew him. His detective partner in the Polícia Civil, Lisboa, knew him. His journo friend Silva *knew* him.

'Remember me?' the guy asked. 'Don't run now. Be cool, ne?'

Leme smiled, didn't look at him. He tiptoed and craned. Ah, Lula's on the stage. He couldn't see much beyond a bloated red shirt.

The sweat stains were *ominous*.

'I remember you. Fat João. Helluva joke that. You're even skinnier than I remember. Why are you following me?'

'Something for you.'

'What?'

'A tip. Something you want to see.'

Leme nodded. The guy was textbook-rat, informant-type working for chump change. He'd seen him once, twice, three times over the years, maybe. Never directly and never one to one. This was new.

OK.

'And what, I have to make it worth your while?' Leme asked.

'Not necessary – taken care of. I've just got a message for you.'

'Who from?'

'Not part of the deal.'

Leme weighed it. Lisboa, Silva – they can vouch for him. That's good enough.

'OK, shoot.'

'Know the dodgy little park in Praça Alexandre de Gusmão?'

Leme nodded.

'You might want to take a look. Like, *now*.'

Leme raised eyebrows. 'That the message?'

'Don't shoot the messenger, chief.'

Leme turned. The rat had skedaddled.

Leme let it marinate a moment.

It's not the curiosity that kills you.

He made up his mind. He could scoot over; pick up a cab nearby either way.

Leme edged further away, just catching a key line crackling through the inadequate PA: *Democracy is the only way to allow people to participate in the government's decisions.*

Leme wondered what that had to do with accusations of pilfering state funds and harvesting kickback money.

He tossed his beer can and got off the main drag.

Leme edged through Jardins towards the park. There was a taxi rank there he was sure would be freed up despite the rally. Old-school hardheads, no fans of The Snake.

It was Sunday-quiet. No real overspill from Paulista. Side-street dirty. Fast-food wrappers and empty cans blew about. Mangy dogs dug in. A group of drunk students let fly at them, laughing. Boot-heavy thumps turned to rib-cracking. The dogs yelped and whimpered. The students kicked cans and scarpered, singing.

Leme followed at a distance down Alameda Santos. They passed the Intercontinental Hotel and arrowed towards the square and Parque Tenente Siqueira Campos behind. Leme figured he'd pass by and boost a taxi down Peixoto or Azevedo if the rank was empty. At night, the park was a hotspot for hopheads and noias – paranoid crackheads – homeless bums and sex pests. It was getting dark. Leme wondered what exactly this tip was. Some Vice shit, he'd guess.

It's not the assumptions that kill you.

The students crossed the road in a drunk-spread, arms-wide traffic-taunt.

Though there were no cars.

It seemed the city was giving the Boss Bitch the swerve today, Leme thought.

Aside from the swarm of lefties just up the road.

He scoped the cab options. There were none. The students were gathered by the park railings. He watched them. They laughed and kicked jokes to and fro.

They sat on a moped that was propped against the gate.

Leme eyed them.

Something not quite right.

Ah, leave it, he thought. I'm off duty. Not my problem, no Senhor, not today.

Wide-berth it.

Kids, joshing.

Then a shout: 'Caralho, bicho!' Mate, look out!

And another: 'Puta, que isso?' What the fuck's going on?

A different, deeper voice. An instruction: 'Get the fuck off. Embora pentelho! Drive. Let's go. Vamos, vamos!'

The students jumped back.

The students fanned out.

The students turned and scrammed, five-ways.

Leme watched.

Two men in black T-shirts and black balaclavas jumped on the moped and gassed it the wrong way down the square. Then burned off up Jaú.

Leme looked – hard.

Number plate blacked out.

Leme waited.

Nothing.

He scanned the street both ways.

Nothing.

He cocked an ear.

Rally-traffic. Cracked voices and cheers.

He studied the buildings above street level and the shuttered shops.

Nothing. No obvious lights.

He crossed the road.

And he saw why the students had left in such a hurry.

At the bottom of the railings, poking out from beneath a bush –

A body.

Leme pulled his phone and began to spear in the emergency number.

He examined the body as he did.

A kid. A bloodied pink shirt. Sleeves rolled up. Smart pair of jeans. Slip-on black leather shoes. No socks.

Leme stopped dialling.

He got down on one knee. Looked more closely.

Chest wounds. Face untouched.

Good-looking lad. How old? About twenty-something. Hard to tell *exactly* these days.

Pink shirt.

No socks.

Aha.

The lad was rich. A playboy type.

Not the usual corpse to wash up on these shores.

Leme needed the cavalry and double-quick time.

He stood, turned, phone to his ear.

A blue-red flash.

Fuck.

'Good afternoon,' said an especially ferocious-looking member of the São Paulo Military Police.

These boys did not like Leme's mob, the Polícia Civil side of things, the *detectives*. Didn't like to get their hands dirty was one complaint. Cerebral and fresh with it. Bunch of fucking pussies was the general feeling.

The Militar had a sadistic look in his eye. 'And what the fuck do we have here then, old man?' he said.

'Less of the old, eh,' Leme said.

Leme hit the hang-up button and raised his hands.

Article by Eleanor Boe

OLHA! Online magazine, 20 March 2016

ONE HUNDRED THOUSAND ATTEND PRO-DILMA MARCH

Avenida Paulista turned red yesterday afternoon as a hundred thousand people took to the streets to show their support for President Dilma, who is battling calls for her impeachment.

Earlier in the day, Military Police dispersed crowds of anti-Dilma protestors. They used limited force, including tear gas and water cannons, justified, a statement issued late last night reads, to prevent the possibility of 'serious violence' between rival political factions.

As this took place, a Supreme Court Judge took the step of suspending former President Lula's ministerial nomination. Dilma's critics claim that by attempting to make her mentor part of the government, she is effectively shielding him from money laundering charges, charges he vigorously denies.

Many of the crowd waved red flags, defending the Workers' Party. Banners depicting Lula as a bodybuilder were among many creative displays of support, in stark contrast to only a few days before, when an anti-Dilma protest featured two huge inflatable dolls of Dilma and Lula – dressed as prisoners.

Lula, wearing a red shirt, addressed the crown to rapturous applause. 'There will not be a coup against Ms Rousseff,' he said, to cheers and raised fists. After he left the stage, the rally became a street party, with singing, dancing and pro-PT (Workers' Party) chanting.

The recent nationwide protests against corruption called for Dilma's removal due to 'economic mismanagement' and her alleged part in the far-reaching corruption scandal based around state-sponsored oil company Petrobras.

Dilma denies all wrongdoing.

More to follow

PART ONE: **FUCKHEADS**

Same day, same place:
São Paulo, 20 March 2016

My family is a political institution. I saw relatives arrested only to later host a former President of Brazil seeking support. People who didn't know me believed they had the right to judge me when they did not. My family wanted me to be someone I was not. São Paulo is a part of my family; my family is a part of São Paulo. We helped make it what it is. We helped build this city, build its infrastructure. Sometimes, I look at São Paulo with ambivalence; there are things you have to do to make a difference, politically, which are not always pretty. They say you can't choose your family; I wouldn't change mine.

Marina, 19, student

Junior

Less of the old?

Jesus, the fucking front on this guy. The *face* on the lad. Serious bolas. The cunt's caught leaning over a corpse by two Militars and he's got the garra and nouse to crack wise.

May not be the smartest move, however, thought the younger of the two, Junior. Old Assis had a temper on him, and there was no one around and they could easily make this an in flagrante-type scenario.

Bang, bang, medals and honour and all that jazz: just got to make sure the bullets are in the right place.

Junior scoped the street. Assis cuffed the guy.

Assis said, 'You going to tell us what the fuck you were doing, son?'

The guy smiled. Shook his head.

Assis nodded at Junior. Flicked his chin at the body. 'Have a look,' he said.

Junior did as he was told. He gloved up and examined the John. He could see he was a kid, about the same age as Junior, maybe a few years older. Who knew when a corpse flattened things out a touch. Different type of kid, though. Caucasian glint to him, for starters. Dressed rich.

The body wasn't too well hidden. A few leaves, a couple of branches, almost discarded, it seemed. It was the bottom end of the park and the slope down was steep enough the stiff wouldn't be seen too easily though. Like maybe he'd been rolled down the hill in the trees – good cover – and then pushed through the railings. There was a stillness to the air. Junior could hear the rally, but the distance pulled that stillness closer to him.

The park was deserted. Not a surprise. Normally was at that time of the day: the cusp of night. Any respectables well away by then, before the hopheads and noias, perverts and paedos turned up. Snide little line of underage rent-boy cocksuckers available to those who sought it. Drop-out schoolgirl pussy for hire for your less than discerning nonce, too, Junior had heard.

Takes all sorts.

Fuck knows what this lad was up to, but Junior guessed it wasn't pretty. He looked like he could afford a lot better.

'ID?' Assis called out.

Junior frisked the stiff. Not his first time and harder, in fact, than rifling the pockets of a real live human. Not called stiffs without reason. He was no medic, but Junior didn't think the kid had snuffed it too long ago.

In the pockets, he found:

Cigarettes – Marlboro Red

Lighter – a gold Zippo

Keys – house and car

A wallet – Louis Vuitton, brown

In the wallet, he found:

NADA.

Not a sausage. But it was old, well-thumbed, and recently emptied, Junior reckoned.

'Então?' Assis called out.

'Nothing, Senhor,' Junior replied.

'Cash?'

'Nope.'

'Shame.'

Junior raised an eyebrow. Assis continued, 'Rich kid gets robbed, gets merced. Textbook.' He pulled his radio.

Junior held tight.

'That how it usually works?' the guy asked.

Assis glared at him. 'Ask your opinion, did I?'

The guy smiled. 'Only it's an odd decision to take the poor cunt's ID and bank cards, as well as his cash, *and* button his coat while they're at it. Tad risky, entendeu? Somewhat incriminating, perhaps?'

Assis said nothing. Junior flanked the guy, wondering if the old temper might just kick in and kick off. Junior fingered his revolver, spread his legs a touch.

Assis got back on the radio. Assis barked some instructions.

Junior held tight. The air thinned, cooled, as the fat sun, once raw, hostile, sloped off.

Moments later, a Militar SUV pulled up. A colleague, Edu, hopped out. Assis bundled the guy into the back.

'You two stay with the stiff. There's people on their way.'

The SUV gunned, then squealed, then roared.

'Nasty business,' said Edu, nodding at the stiff.

Junior sighed. 'Pois é,' he said.

'What happened?'

'No idea, mate,' Junior said. 'We found that guy standing over him.' Junior gestured to where the SUV had been. 'It ain't even obvious how the kid was ironed out. He doesn't look that bad, to be fair.'

Edu smirked. 'That guy? Didn't you recognise him?'

Junior shook his head. 'Sure didn't. Nem fodendo, cara.' No fucking way.

'Ride-along in Paraisópolis couple of years ago. You were green as, proper rookie. Driving, I think you were. *That* guy was a mate of Big Carlos. Polícia Civil cunt, though I forget his name.'

Junior ran the ride-along in his mind. He remembered it well enough. He'd barely looked at the guy. Sensed something was messed up there, something best not to engage with. Alarm bells, it was personal, a fucked-up type of scene.

'Assis know, you think?' Junior asked.

'Meu, I don't doubt it.' Edu snorted. 'Good old Carlão. He's going to have to untangle a total clusterfuck.'

Junior shook his head. Laughed – rueful.

The blue-red flash of the Militar SUV lit the gloaming as it pulled away.

Junior worked his jaw hard – three fresh pieces of gum, tension thin.

They stood either side of the body. Motorbikes with their sirens flashing silently either side of them.

Junior narrowed his eyes as the sky darkened. He sniffed the air. He nodded up the hill towards Paulista.

'Fuckers had better turn up before the rally is over,' he said.

Edu turned to look at him. 'Ah, don't sweat it. Any minute now, no doubt.'

Junior nodded. Fact is he was nervous. Two Military Police standing over a dead body at a left-wing rally? There were better places to be stationed, sunshine, no fucking doubt about that, he thought. Their mob weren't exactly popular with the hundred or so thousand wankers just up the road. Automatic weapons or not, this was by no means a desirable stand-off.

'Know what?' Junior said.

Edu pulled a face – mock dumb. 'No. What?'

'Ha ha, yeah, very good. You're a hoot to work with. Know *that*?'

Edu laughed. 'Ah, don't be such a pussy. Please. Continue. Tell me what I should know.'

Junior shook his head, took a breath. 'OK,' he said. 'Something weird. About the body.' He angled his back towards it. 'Assis told me to search it, right? So I checked his wallet – no money, no ID, nada, entendeu?'

'Yeah,' Edu said. 'I'm following, mate. Complicated stuff.'

'OK, but I didn't think of this at the time. There was no phone on him.'

Edu sighed. 'Son, he was mugged. Pronto. Or looking for some dodgy action and misbehaved. Or his fucking boyfriend had enough of his whiny little backside and snuffed him himself.' Edu shook his head. 'Phone? Course there was no fucking phone.'

Junior – chastened. 'Alright, settle down, it was just a thought.'

'Piece of advice,' Edu said. 'When our boys turn up, you keep your thoughts to yourself. You've been with us, what, about four years?'

Junior nodded.

'So you don't know the different ways these things can go.'

'What does that mean?'

'It means, amigo, that you watch and fucking learn, entendeu?'

Junior shifted from foot to foot. He heard a siren.

'Anyway,' Edu said, 'they're here in moments, if you can hear that. So stand up straight and look sharp. I'll do the talking.'

The response vehicle pulled over and two uniforms jumped out the back with a stretcher.

The passenger door opened and a senior officer swung a leg out. He *glared* at the scene, like he was appalled and disgusted by it, like it was a personal affront to him, like it was nothing more than a monumental waste of his time, and anyone connected with it an equally monumental waste of his – and anyone else's – time.

Junior knew the sort.

He swung the other leg out and John Wayned it towards them, dead slow, legs wide, both hands resting on his belt buckle, just beneath his well-earned belly, residing there, firm, defiant, as if to say, 'Yep, my cock is exactly as big as my swagger suggests – you got a problem with that?'

Yeah, Junior knew the sort: classy guy. Proper swashbuckler.

The Swashbuckler took a deep breath and hoisted his trousers up. 'Right, cunthooks,' he said. 'What the fuck, eh? Talk.'

He looked away from them. The last of the sunlight flashed in his mirrored aviators.

Edu started. 'Junior here, and Assis, spotted a character acting suspiciously. They engaged and discovered the body. Assis apprehended the suspect, called for a tactical response unit and took the suspect into custody. My orders were to wait with Junior until the second unit arrived.'

'And here we are,' said the Swashbuckler.

He clicked his fingers and hissed something at the two uniforms. They rolled the body onto the stretcher, secured it, covered it and bundled it into the back of the vehicle. They checked the area, and, satisfied there was nothing else there, nodded at the Big Man and climbed into the car.

'Right, you two, jog on then.'

'But – ' Junior started.

The Swashbuckler grinned. 'But what, young man?'

'I – '

'I do hope you're not querying my methods, son.'

'No, I – '

'Insubordination is a serious charge, young man, *ta entendendo?*'

'Yes, I – '

The Swashbuckler hawked and spat. He looked at the two of them. Junior looked down.

'Now, you two are going to fucking jog on, and, while you're doing it, you're both going to think long and hard about where you got the fucking front to question a commanding officer, when said *commanding* officer is taking charge of and diffusing a potentially delicate, even, yes, even *dangerous* situation. You got that, sweethearts?'

They both nodded.

'So what are you going to do?'

'Jog on, sir,' Edu said.

The Swashbuckler smiled. 'Good lad.'

He turned and walked to the car, even slower, Junior thought, than when he'd ambled over towards them.

It seemed to take about five minutes.

'Nice one, dickhead,' Edu said.

Junior said nothing. What he was thinking: *isn't this a crime scene?*

'Come on,' Edu said. 'Let's fuck off, eh? Before something else goes wrong.'

And Junior could think of no reasonable argument against that idea.

Junior sat on his bed. Home.

He could hear his sisters and his mum in the kitchen down the corridor, arguing over something while they cooked. He could smell the onions and the thick drift of beans stewing with pork. He was hungry. He played with his rosary beads.

He heard the roar of his dad coming home. Laughter. He pictured his father lifting first his mother and then his two sisters off the floor in a bear hug, smothering them in dirty-lipped kisses, his helmet dropped where he stood, his orange, state-maintenance overalls tied at his waist, his vest oily, his breath sour with beer and cheap cachaça.

Don't judge, Junior, he told himself. Most people should be so lucky.

A shout – his mother. 'Junior! Vamos jantar, filho!'

'Coming, Mum,' he shouted. 'One second, eh?' he said to himself.

He studied the two text messages one last time before dinner. One from Assis and one from Edu. He didn't know what to make of them, mainly as it seemed there was nothing to make of them.

He read Edu's first:

cara, foi legal hoje, ne? really was cool. nice one. you did ok

This did not sound much like Edu at the best of times, let alone after Junior's misplaced comments to the Swashbuckler.

He swiped to Assis's message.

Today wasn't straightforward and you handled yourself and the situation very well. You did a good job. Your part is done. Get some rest. Tomorrow's another day.

He switched his phone off. His dad couldn't abide it at dinner.

Roberta

Idiota, Roberta thought. *Idiota!* It was typical of him, *typical*. It was typical of *her* too, and that made her angrier even than he did. *Why could she never control herself?*

She'd heard a phrase once: she's got a lot of buttons and he's got a lot of fingers. It was spot on.

Like every bloody argument they'd ever had. All she'd said was that there was no debate anymore, that this talk of impeachment *claimed* to be a debate, but that it was, in fact, the opposite, it was *closing down* the debate by polarising the country, dividing families, friends, colleagues. It was us and them now, and that is not democracy, not what politics is, should be, we no longer deserve the democracy we'd earned, and Dilma had been a part of achieving it, but now, who knows, ne? And she's either a snake in the grass or a terribly wronged woman in a society that is more misogynistic, conservative, backward-looking than ever.

'Settle down,' was all he'd said, but with that snide little smirk, and that had set her right off. Her last words to him: you can go and join your playboy, fuckhead friends and leave me well alone, you machista filho da puta, and then she'd stormed off, and there was no way she was going to find him, but she'd made the mistake of giving him her phone as she hadn't wanted to take a bag for fear of thieves, and the dress she was wearing was dead-on ripe for some ladrão, pickpocket.

So what now? Wait for Lula to get on the stage and speak? Listen to his pronouncement of support for Dilma on her own? Or go and find her old uni gang – they'd be there, for sure, and she'd likely spot the flags? Or go home and sulk. Pride, Roberta, pride. Don't let the man-child get you down. *He* should be looking for *her*.

Stay.

Yes, she thought. She'd see him later, yes, the fucker would likely turn up at her apartment with a swagger and a look of faux-contrition that would annoy the fuck out of her, but also likely make her laugh and he'd get back into her good books – the *fucker*.

Yes, *stay*. She decided to stay.

She needed to get a view of the march from above, or, at least, a little higher up, to see if any of the flags and banners were recognisable and she could find her friends. She snaked across Paulista in front of the Conjunto Nacional shopping mall, threading through the mass of bodies, which swayed to the music, and edged forwards and backwards in time to the whistles and horns. On the other side she climbed the steps of the Santander building and sat down at the top. If she looked too hard, she thought, she'd never see them. She rolled a cigarette. She lifted her sunglasses onto the top of her head. She closed her eyes as she drew hungrily, and the cigarette scratched, dry, harsh, at her throat, and the sun throbbed, pulsing, spreading its warmth in increments across her face, warmth which intensified as she breathed in and relaxed and let the sounds and excitement of the day settle into the background, acknowledging they were there, but allowing her feelings and calmness to be present too.

Fucking Antonio, she thought, after a moment or two of serenity, serenity that was short-lived precisely because she was aware she was having a moment or two of serenity. She'd been using a meditation app but she didn't want to pay the subscription after her ten trial 'lessons', and so she tried to remember them and do it herself from time to time. Perhaps, on reflection, she thought, the biggest political rally in years might not be the most conducive spot for achieving mindfulness.

The app was just the kind of thing Antonio mocked her for, the prick. His entitlement knew no bounds: a clear conscience, a clear head, an innate mindfulness, really, she supposed, were his for the taking. When you're brought up to believe everything you do is right, then you never understand when you're doing something wrong. Not quite a lack of empathy, but not far off.

'Guilt is for Catholics and the poor,' he'd once joked, adding: 'Actually that might be tautology.'

'You might want to try a literary elective, mate,' she said. 'But the sentiment is still deeply offensive.'

She sometimes wondered if they were right for each other.

'What does that even *mean*?' he'd asked. '*Right* for each other?'

He'd had a point. She couldn't answer that.

'Are *we right* for each other?' he'd mused. 'Right? *Right*. Funny word, when you examine it, ne?' He'd smiled, put his hand on her cheek. 'I think we're *good* for each other.'

He had these moments when he'd completely disarm her, see right through her, to the best version of herself, and she'd see the best version of him, and she'd believe that his playboy shtick was exactly that, bluster, nurture not nature, and that she could handle the rare-enough moments when it annoyed her.

She scanned the crowd, looking for the red-and-green flags her uni mob would be waving. There'd be the usual gang, all Masters and PhD students in political science and its various offshoots, most of them, like Roberta, interning at NGOs.

'All very Universidade de São Paulo, querida,' Antonio had said on first meeting some of them at a conference, spinning out the full name to add an extra layer of patronising, as nobody called it anything other than USP.

'Yeah,' she'd nodded across the courtyard where they were holding the drinks reception, 'and your pastel Polo-shirted, playboy crowd are very TAAP, entendeu?'

'Stereotypes everywhere.' He'd given her a wolfish grin. 'Who'd have thought it?' He'd leaned closer, his arm against a tree above her.

She'd kissed him then; that'd sealed it.

He was really good at kissing.

She spotted them.

The flags were huge, emblazoned with 'USP pra Dilma', and there was a fierceness to the chanting group beneath that marked them out.

That and a cloud of marijuana smoke thick enough to knock over even your most dedicated Bahia stoner. Roberta smiled and skipped down the steps and aimed herself at the biggest of the flags, and after a few minutes of tussling and being spun through gaps too small for her, squeezing her shoulder blades and pressing her arms together, trying to avoid touching anyone or being touched, she was with them.

'E aí, menina!' Roberta's friend Lis squealed as she grabbed her shoulder. 'How are you? Where have you been? Hanging with Antonio's boys, ne?'

Roberta laughed. 'Just him, but the malandro pissed me off so I'm all yours now, querida.'

'Ta, ta ótimo. That's great. Monica's here somewhere. Malô as well. Manu, over there, ta vendo, you see her? Ellie, you know, the gringa journalist? She's heading over too.'

Roberta saw Manu and nodded. 'And the speeches?' She pointed at Lis's hand. 'Give me that.' She'd had a smoke earlier with Antonio, something he rarely did, something she felt he did for *her*, and she needed a fucking top-up.

Lis passed the joint. 'Ah, I think soon, ne? But they're not really the point, right? It's about a show, não é? Main thing is we're *here*. *All* of us, entendeu?'

'Ta certo, cara.'

The noise level increased and Roberta craned to see why. There were cheers and arms raised in fists, or up and across one another in imitation of the sickle and hammer, solidarity. That was what this was all about, Lis was right.

'I mean,' she was saying, 'these attacks on Dilma cannot stand, sabe? Corrupt, old, right-wing white men accusing her of, like, what, ne? *Corruption*? Fuck off, know what I mean?'

'E isso ai,' Roberta said. That's exactly it. She agreed, of course she did, but they'd all had these discussions a million times and she was feeling a little looser after the hit, and her mind, if she was honest, was drifting away from politics and back to Antonio, and she was *here*, wasn't she, and so was he, *somewhere*, and isn't that the whole point?

She was aware of Lis and her friends shouting something, though she wasn't sure exactly what and suddenly it didn't really matter, and it was all a little bit too similar to the protests about the World Cup a few years before, and really what was the difference between shouting 'Fuck FIFA' or 'Fuck Temer'? Essentially, it was the same thing, 'Fuck the elite', and yet at least a dozen of the people standing closest to her were part of this elite, at least their families were, at least their paternal grandfather or whatever, and, yes, Antonio too, but *he was here.*

He was here.

And that meant something. She grabbed Lis's arm. She should go. She should.

'Oi, Lis, I think I'm going to head off.'

'You're going? Ah, vai. Why?'

'I'm not feeling great.' She pointed at the joint. 'Knocked me a little sideways, entendeu?'

Lis smiled. 'Fair enough, dude, you fuck off.' She gestured around her. 'There's plenty of us here.'

They embraced and Roberta wriggled through the tight space beside them, pushed past a group of students from a private university, forced her way through a group of manual labourers dressed in their orange overalls and white helmets, nailing their lagers with a certain grim efficiency, past a group of cleaners who were laughing, heads back, hips moving, and then she was on the other side of the road, and Lula was speaking, and she wasn't sure what to do next.

She headed up towards Paraíso, where she lived. It suddenly seemed important that she get home. She knew she could be a pain in the arse, and Antonio knew he could be too. They had been together two years. They made each other laugh.

'Laughter and orgasms,' he'd said, one weekend morning. 'It's a potent combination.'

It really was. It was around that time she began to understand properly the word *intoxicating*.

'It's high-low culture, querido,' she'd said. 'Philosophy and blow jobs, entendeu?'

He'd laughed. 'All the major food groups.'

'Nourishing, ne?'

'What's that joke? The brain: it's my second favourite organ.'

She smiled as she remembered the exchange. His friends were his friends and you can't escape your past and really his loyalty to them was admirable, and it *was* a trait he seemed to possess in spades. He wasn't your average rich-kid pussy-hound, that was for sure. And anyway, his friends *could* be fun, and they'd certainly had some good…

'Oi, Roberta! Roberta!'

She looked up. And there were his friends, about a dozen yards away. She smiled, shook her head, tried to refocus her dope-smudged brain, smiled again and fixed her grin in preparation. She would be nice.

'E aí,' she said. 'How are you lot getting on, eh?'

The guy who had called her name, Alexandre, narrowed his eyes. 'You're not with Tônico?'

'No, I thought he was with you.'

The noise of the crowd rose as someone shouted slogans through the tinny PA.

'Ah,' Alexandre said. 'I'll ring him.'

'Please. Idiot's walked off with my phone.'

Alexandre put his phone to his ear and lifted his finger to quiet her. Roberta seethed.

He took his phone from his ear and looked at the screen quizzically.

'Então?' Roberta said.

'Nada. Didn't even ring.' Alexandre raised his eyebrows. 'Huh,' he said.

'Ah, well, signal's likely jammed with all these people, ne?'

'Yeah, I guess.'

Alexandre fiddled with his phone and neither said anything for a moment. Roberta stood patiently, waited for him to finish.

She said, 'When you get hold of him, tell him I'm at home, certo?'

'Sure, of course,' Alexandre grinned. 'Getting the dinner on, right? Good girl.'

Roberta shook her head but found she was smiling, despite herself.

'Exactly,' she said. 'And tell him if he stays out too late with his good-for-nothing, layabout, playboy friends, he'll be *wearing* his fucking dinner.'

And with that, Alexandre laughing, she ducked down a road that led off Paulista and set off home, looking forward to, excited, even, about the evening ahead.

Roberta's apartment seemed even emptier than it normally did. Standing in a crowd of thousands will do that to your sparsely furnished, though sizeable, studio flat, with its bed, its piles of books and its wicker rocking chair that you 'borrowed' from your grandparents' farm years before. She put water to boil on the hob and jumped into the shower, immediately relieved to scrub off the dirt of the street, wash the smoke from her hair, feel the heat from the day rinse away from her. She was in the shower for what felt like a long time, and when she came out wearing only a towel, hair fresh and damp on her shoulders, the kettle was boiling ferociously, and clearly had been for some time. She'd burned through three of these kettles in exactly this way over the years. Amor fati, she thought, smiling at her pretentiousness, the love of one's fate, Nietzsche's eternal return. Meaning: we never fucking learn, querida.

She made a cup of mint tea, put on a sweatshirt, sweat pants, her slippers and a thick hair band, and thought about what she should do next. It was a little after seven, the light fading, the heat dissipating and the excitement of the day, which, at its beginning, had felt contained and trembling, like the coiled spring of the hick fazenda rifles her grandparents' farm workers used to carry to scare off intruders, had now settled, and she heard only the odd shout, the occasional firework and empty cans and rubbish blowing down the road below.

She sat in the wicker chair, her legs folded underneath her, feet crossed, and she sipped at her drink, both hands around the mug. She blew gently on the tea, closed her eyes and let its aroma and heat waft up her nose and into her eyes, a little like, she realised, her mother's ritual sinus cleanse with her bowl steaming a heavy menthol vapour. It felt calming, meditative, and she focused on her breathing – as the app had taught her – and tried to let go of any thoughts that interfered with this moment, with her sensual *awareness*, sensual appreciation of what she could smell and hear both in the immediate vicinity, and a little further away, where, she hoped, Antonio would be, laughing with his friends and preparing to set off to see her. The idea occurred to her that, as he had her phone, he had an excuse to stay out later, and she acknowledged it, understood where it had come from and why, refused to judge herself for having the thought, and then dismissed it, consigned it to the ether.

Minutes passed.

Her breathing settled as she focused on it again, counting to ten each time she exhaled, then starting again. She sipped at her tea. It was cheating, she knew that, to drink tea while trying to achieve mindfulness, but she'd always figured even Buddhists have to multi-task every now and then. All that infinite space had to be useful for something.

She stopped the counting and let her mind drift.

She saw his face, smiling, turning to look at her, tanned, hair salty and wet, his shoulders dusky, sitting next to each other on the beach at Camburi, watching the last of the surfers at the end of the afternoon, sharing a cold beer and a joint, talking about what happened next. This was eighteen months ago.

'I never thought I'd say the words "so where is this going then?"' he laughed. 'But there you are, I'm saying them, can't take it back.'

She was smiling then and she was smiling now. 'Ah, it's natural, Tônico. Don't sweat it. *Own* that shit, querido.'

'Natural why?'

'Six months, ne?' she said. 'Six months we've been seeing each other. We've had our wobble and we're through it, sabe? It's "shit or get out of the woods" time now, meu amor.'

He laughed. 'Que romantic, ne?'

She took the beer from his hand, placed it in the sand and kissed him.

Yeah, they'd had their wobble, their whole Gaugin moment, as she'd later called it: *Where do we come from? What are we? Where are we going?*

'Hiding behind your learning again, sweetheart, but I see your point,' he'd said.

They'd decided that the key was that wherever they were going, they'd be going there together, for the foreseeable.

Roberta let the memory settle, slowly opened her eyes and took a final deep breath.

And another.

A wave of panic, of guilt, seized her, stabbed her and she shuddered and stood up. He wasn't here. Why wasn't he here? Perhaps this time she really had fucked things up? Perhaps he was more patient with her than she had realised, and now was like, chega, querida, enough, entendeu? She might not blame him, she thought. Perhaps she had driven him away; that was her deepest fear – that her behaviour, prompted by her love for him and fuelled by her own inescapable nature, would mean he couldn't love her anymore, that he could no longer live with *her*.

'You knew what I was like when we got together,' he'd say when they disagreed on something, when they argued, or discussed anything that might provoke discord.

It was a supremely confident assertion –

I'm me and I will not be a different person just for you.

She respected, envied and resented him for that – and the truth that she knew was contained within the statement.

Oh yes, she had a lot of buttons and he had a lot of fingers and he knew just what to say – or not say – and do – or not do – to push those buttons and engineer a scenario where she was apologising, where she was chasing him to reconcile, to make things right, which meant, of course, to make him tell her she was forgiven and that he loved her.

And he did tell her –

Often. He told her he loved her every day.

She smiled, let go of her anxiety.

What was she supposed to do *now*?

She turned on her TV and got into bed, and hoped she'd find something inane enough to fall asleep to, so that when he arrived and woke her up, the fight would be nothing more than a distant memory, perhaps even funny, considering the context, where it took place, and they could get on with the getting on with.

She yawned and sighed, and she settled.

Mario

Leme leaned back. Shifted to give his wrists a little space. The seat was hard, blood-soaked to its core, no doubt. No point crying over spilt PCC, the unofficial Militar slogan. AC roaring. Leme's sweat cooled. Toxic shivers. All that. And fear. The Chinaman's beer dripping out of him – fast.

'Mate,' Leme said, 'take the cuffs off and I'll show you my fucking badge and we might be able to speed all this up a little, entendeu?'

The Militar snorted. 'I know who you are, son,' he said. 'And those cuffs are going nowhere.'

Interesting, Leme thought. That'll be the old Carlão connection. Which is either a relief, or very fucking worrying indeed.

Leme hadn't seen Carlos in donkeys. Not since they had agreed to go their separate ways after the incident with Ellie and all that Cracolândia land deal beef. Carlos got a decent wedge of dinheiro. Leme got –

Peace of mind.

No one'd find out he'd been part of the Militar gang that stomped the gold-toothed kid dealer to death, way up high in Paraisópolis. The gold-toothed kid dealer old Carlos had made as a dead cert for the triggerman in Renata's murder. She was killed by a stray bullet, a bala perdida, in a firefight between the Military Police and the PCC drug gang in the favela Paraisópolis where she ran a legal aid office. The community mourned her. The community was quite happy for the police to do whatever was necessary to bring about justice. Most of them, that is, the village elders, though they kept it quiet, of course, didn't let on to the big men with guns who ran the place. And what did Leme care, in the end? It'd troubled him – at first. He'd done the thing he'd said he'd never do and blah blah blah.

But, you know, menos um, as they say with a shrug, one less villain, entendeu?

Some kid dealer gets merced, no one gives a fuck.

But –

But this was a my-word your-word type of situation and Leme didn't trust old Carlos anymore. Not as far as he could wrestle him. And he certainly wasn't called Big Carlos for nothing.

'What's your name then, pal?' Leme asked. 'You know, let's even the scores here a little.'

The Militar laughed. 'You've trod on the ball here, son. My name ain't gonna make an ounce, entendeu?'

Leme decided to keep his counsel.

Leme hoped they were going somewhere official.

He didn't have a cat's chance if they weren't.

He playbooked it:

Fat João, the skinny rat copper's beak, tails him from the Chinaman's to the rally and tips him off –

Militars witness Leme poking about the corpse –

Leme causes a stir, uses his copper nouse and whatnot –

Leme's ironed out in a classic he-tried-to-do-one scenario.

Bullet in the back. Textbook Militar.

Leme had *better* hope they were going somewhere official. And if they were, he'd have to call Antonia. She wasn't the worrying kind, but he wasn't the stay-out-all-night-on-his-day-off kind either.

And after the Cracolândia land deal and her involvement –

Minor, of course, and forgivable, but it meant she had an insight into the workings of the mind of someone like Carlão, and she could handle him, yes, she *had* handled him, she had handled him better than Leme ever had, but she *knew* him now, and types like him, and she did *not* want anything to threaten, well, to threaten *them* –

Point is, it all worked in the end: they really did live happily ever after.

'I need to ring my bird,' Leme said. 'You going to let me?'

The Militar laughed again. 'Patience, lover boy. All in good tick-tock, entendeu?'

Leme noted where they were headed: Lapa-bound.

Could go either way: plenty of official buildings in Lapa. But only a stone's throw beyond and you're in bandit country.

'Hold tight, son,' the Militar said, laughing.

Leme thought he probably didn't have much choice.

Leme gave up wondering where the fuck they were going.

And guess what? Moments later they arrived.

They ghosted into the garage of a medium-sized condominium building in Lapa, a little way off the main drag, not far from the Polícia Federal building, not that that meant anything at all. Only bureaucracy boys in there.

Leme didn't like the idea of a private residence. But the condo was modern, slick, and they had lowered all the windows for the seguranças, the usual phalanx of condo security guards behind bulletproof glass, so there was no doubt they knew he was there. These seguranças didn't seem too bothered by the Militar SUV –

Cash-happy, no doubt.

The old aspirational-Militar-assist. The money's good and the hours are minimal. Zero contract: you're paid *not* to do anything.

So this felt like a could-go-either-way type of scene.

Leme thought he'd have taken that, an hour ago.

The cunt with no name bundled Leme out. A younger one flanked him.

They were elevator-whisked to the eighth floor.

Usual swank condo set-up.

Narrow corridor, one apartment either side of the lift.

No Name knocked once on the door to the right. He waited a beat and opened the door. Leme clocked the number: 8B.

The sala stretched out in front of them. Dark wood floors, a dining table and four chairs to the left, a black sofa to the right and two brown leather armchairs either side of a fireplace. A fucking fireplace, Leme thought. Antonia had friends who used theirs once a year. Get their polo-necked jumpers out and their wedding-present fondue set and play at being your sophisticate Alpine swingers for an evening. Leme quite enjoyed it. Never stayed late enough to drop his keys into the empty fondue pot, mind.

There were three men out on the balcony. All in uniform. All with guns in their belts. All huge men, wide around the middle, shoulders pinned back, straining to keep themselves upright.

Leme could see two faces. He recognised neither.

One of these two noticed Leme and his guard dogs and he nodded at the room. The third man turned. The third man shook his head, smiling.

Carlos.

Carlão. Big Carlos.

Not a surprise. Leme grinned back. Winked.

Why the fuck not? Not a great deal to lose at this point. Might as well go down swinging, entendeu?

Carlos stepped into the room. He examined the two Militars with Leme.

'Cuffs off, and fuck off, certo?' he said.

The younger one uncuffed Leme and the pair of them nodded at Carlão and skedaddled. Leme stretched his hands out.

Carlos nodded at Leme and smirked. 'You'd think they'd be used to a bit of work, your wrists,' he said. 'Kitchen.' He turned and pushed through a door at the end of the room.

Leme decided not to comment on this stain on his impeccable, and followed.

Carlos had his head in the fridge. He pulled a beer and tossed it to Leme. He pulled one for himself and they both cracked their cans.

'Saúde,' Carlos said, raising his can.

Leme nodded.

'Long time,' Carlos said.

'You miss me?'

Carlos smiled. 'Yes, mate. I brought you here to mata saudades, entendeu?'

Mata saudades. To kill the longing. Leme always liked the phrase.

But the word 'kill' escaping old Carlão's meaty chops wasn't too sweet.

'That's what I figured. A drink and a catch-up, ne? We've earned it.'

Carlos's expression shifted. He muttered, 'Cheeky cunt.'

'What was that?'

'You heard.'

They nailed their lagers. Carlos belched and popped the fridge. 'Another?'

'I got much choice?'

'Good point.'

He tossed Leme another can. They drank deeply and said nothing for a minute or two. The lager gave Leme a nice post-work glaze: a two-cans-by-the-fridge sort of deal, even before you've said hello to your missus. He felt good, but suddenly hungry.

'Any nibbles, Carlão?'

Carlos snorted. 'Turn it in, son. This is a safe house, not a fucking padaria.'

'So it *is* safe, then?'

'Vamos ver, ne, cara?' Let's see.

Leme was reassured – just. Safe house meant negotiation, deal, protection. It didn't mean an on-the-sly whack job. Might as well figure the next steps then.

'So what's the play, Carlão? I'm fairly sure I ain't here to help with the investigation, sabe?'

'The grand detective,' Carlos said. He tapped his right temple. 'Not just a hat rack, ne?'

Leme laughed. 'Então?'

'Então,' Carlos said, 'I brought you here as a reminder – and to give you a little info that you won't have worked out yourself, certo?'

'A reminder of what exactly?'

'You know very well, amigo.'

Leme did know very well.

It had been three years. And two since the Cracolândia land deal beef. It was a score draw at this point: 2–2.

They both had the death of Gold Teeth over each other.

Leme had Carlão over a barrel in terms of the dodgy Cracolândia resident benefits and the suitcase of cash and what all that meant.

Carlos had been running a protection and drug racket in Cracolândia, Crackland. It was a desperate place, a lawless area in downtown São Paulo where crack cocaine was openly sold and taken.

But Cracolândia was a part of the old, colonial centre. Leme remembered how his friend Ellie, the young English journalist had described the place, her foreigner's eye. You approached from Praça Julio Prestes. It smelled of urine baked in the heat. Palm trees swayed drunk in the breeze. Small groups of dark, defeated faces scurried about, occasionally words escaping their toothless mouths, either an offer or a request. Smashed windows and black, gaping doorways, toothless and dust-rinsed women and men. Groups of swollen-bellied women sat on the road, cackling. Dead-eyed, rail-thin men wrapped in dirty blankets, passed out on each other on sofas underneath streetlights. Couples in rags shuffled back and across the road, arm in arm, muttering. Carlos was clearing the nastier elements of the place, disappearing them, Leme heard, making the downtown neighbourhood palatable again for visitors in time for the World Cup.

And Carlos had, by association, implicated Antonia – her law firm was connected to the relocation aspects of it, so he had that over Leme.

So score draw, and extra time and pens if they weren't careful.

Complicated scene.

Or not, really. You scratch mine and I'll scratch yours seemed to be the order of the day. Until today, that is.

Aha –

Leme thought maybe he'd got it.

'So this,' he said, gesturing around them, 'is what, some sort of further insurance?'

Carlos smiled. 'Cookie-sharp, my son,' he said. 'What happens next is up to you.'

'Seems unlikely.'

'Well, you're in the frame, mate. At this point, there's a stiff and a man – *you* – poking around next to it.' He paused. 'We Military Police are always very grateful when a member of our Civil counterpart assists in an investigation. A real relief it was, when we found that Detective Leme was already on the scene, doing his job, asking the right kind of investigative questions.' He looked at Leme. 'That's one way this could go.'

'And the other?'

'Don't make me laugh.'

Leme nodded. 'You know who the kid was?'

'I told you not to make me laugh. Sleep on it. We'll be in touch. Assis downstairs will give you a lift home.'

'He's a real heartbreaker,' Leme said. Assis. He noted the name.

Carlos laughed. 'Total charmer. Now fuck off, eh?'

Leme did what he was told. He had about forty-five minutes in the car to decide what he was going to tell Antonia when he got home.

She'd be fucking delighted old Carlão was back in touch.

Article by Eleanor Boe

TIME OUT SÃO PAULO, 21 March 2016

OPINION: SEX AND THE MARCH IN MARCH

The colours of Brasil used to be yellow and green. Not anymore. These days they're black and white. Politically speaking, there isn't a single shade of grey; erotic fiction has never been less relevant in a country where nothing used to get in the way of the old horizontal samba. Not anymore.

It's us and them in every sphere now, *queridos*. Flirting has become a partisan activity; Dilma divides. You say the wrong thing on a first date, and you are *not* going to score, no *Senhor*. Oh, we'll lie about being in a relationship, about our jobs, about where we live, about who we know. But politics? Not anymore.

No right-thinking, left-leaning Dilma fan is going to put out for any member of the conservative elite calling for her impeachment, no matter how enticing they look. The whole swipe left / swipe right conundrum has got an edge to it now; alignment is everywhere!

And the march in March proved this beyond reasonable doubt. Yes, there was a fair amount of booze flying around, and the air was, ahem, pretty pungent, but I'd wager that a good number of the hook-ups that took place – both at the rally and in the evening that followed – were driven by solidarity, a we're-all-in-this-together, like-minded sexiness. A quick trawl of social media and you'll see it – good place to pull, a political event in this day and age.

The age of Black and White / Us and Them. Families and friends divided, the country *triste*, saddened by the lack of political discourse, debate, nuance, the abundance of hostility and anger.

There's got to be an upside, *ne*? Or as one of the placards I saw put it:

Progressive liberals are better lovers

And speaking as one myself, there's really no need to put that policy to a vote.

São Paulo, 21 March 2016

I'm very privileged. I've always had a very good life. But everything I've got out of life was obtained through dedication and a tremendous desire to achieve my goals… a great desire for victory, meaning victory in life, not as a driver. To all of you who have experienced this or are searching now, let me say that whoever you may be in your life, whether you're at the highest or most modest level, you must show great strength and determination and do everything with love and a deep belief in God. One day, you'll achieve your aim and you'll be successful.

Ayrton, deceased, driver

Junior

They used to do blow before work in the locker room, back in the day.

So Junior had heard. Get them good and jacked up for all the law-enforcing and strong-arming and head-banging they'd have to do. Level playing field, then, you see:

The villains were all up to their eyeballs in the stuff, after all.

Bit of Colombian courage, know what I mean? It was sanctioned from the top down, apparently. The headquarters of the *2°BPChq Anchieta*, the second battalion of shock troops in the São Paulo Military Police, was in Lapa, and Junior had arrived early.

He always did –

He'd grown up in the neighbourhood; it was fifteen minutes from home. He remembered the hopped-up Militars, blitzed and on the prowl. Quite a ruckus on some days when he was a kid. Muito heavy.

This morning, troubled by the day before, he sat in the locker room and reflected on his role, his job. He listed his responsibilities, his missions: control of civil commotions, policing in sports areas, policing during artistic and cultural events and ROCAM (ostensible patrol with motorcycles).

As he sat and waited for the day's tasks to come in, it occurred to him that dealing with a dead body was absolutely not something he was professionally supposed to be involved in.

He had been there in a different capacity. Civil commotion, he supposed –

Or would have been, had the anarchist Black Blocs turned up. There were a few in the battalion who had been well up for giving them a kicking, turning them over in a straightener for a change, instead of that snide form of terrorism they usually practised when no one was looking.

'It's going to be old school today, son,' an older Militar, Araken, had told him. 'Rocks and fists, shields and truncheons. About time we had a proper tear-up. Too much firepower with the old PCC. I fancy getting my hands dirty, know what I mean?'

Junior had said nothing. He didn't like the fact that the week before they'd been out for the anti-Dilma protest, and this week it was *her* supporters. What did that *mean*? If he was an instrument of the state, then what exactly was he protecting? And who?

And now, why could he not get that playboy kid's face out of his mind?

Fuck it.

Not your problem, Junior, seu filho da puta, he thought, forget about it.

The door swung open and smacked against the wall. A slight, damp echo. Boot heels clicked across the floor, slowly. Junior was alone; someone had come to see him. He readied himself –

The locker room was not well known as a venue for negotiating a promotion, after all.

Look sharp.

'Junior, isn't it?' Carlos said. 'Remember me?' He smiled and held out his hand. 'It's been a while, ne?'

'Sim, Senhor,' Junior said, standing up, feeling the firm clasp of Carlos's handshake.

'Quite a night that, wasn't it?' Carlos said. 'Please, sit down.'

Junior nodded and sat back on the bench. His first ride-along, a good four years ago. A gold-toothed dealer interrogated. A Civil police detective. He and Carlos had shared a burger when it was all done. Something of an initiation.

Carlos smiled again. He stood over Junior, put his left foot up on the bench next to him, leant his left elbow on his knee. 'Interesting few weeks we've been having,' he said. 'Civil unrest means we're busy as fuck. Difficult to get any perspective, though, you know, politi-cally speaking.'

'Sim, Senhor,' Junior said. He tried to keep Carlos's eye. Failed.

'At this point, the key thing is to remember what it is we do here, entendeu?'

Junior nodded.

'Our role is to keep the peace, that's all. To make sure things don't get out of hand. We don't judge, we don't take sides, certo? It's simple enough when you think of it like that. Make sense?'

Junior nodded. 'Sim, Senhor,' he said. 'Makes total sense.'

Carlos levered his leg off the bench and turned away slightly, rolled his bulky shoulders, clicked his bulldog neck first left, then right. He was a *biiiiig* unit, old Carlos –

Heavy man. His team were known inside as the Heavy Mob. Junior twitched, waited.

Carlos went on. 'You might have recognised the lad we boosted yesterday evening. Mario Leme, a detective in the Polícia Civil. Did you?'

Junior nodded.

Carlos pursed his meaty lips, grimaced, smiled again. 'Thought you might. He's an old friend. Helping us out, entendeu?'

Junior nodded. 'Sim, Senhor.'

'The John Doe is a young man, not much older than you. Wrongplace wrong-time type of scene. It's taken care of.' Carlos smiled again. 'It's done, ta ligado? No follow-up required. We're on it with the Civil lot now. Ta entendendo?'

Junior did know what he meant. Carlos meant –

Nothing to see here.

Junior nodded. 'Senhor, I understand,' he said.

'Good lad,' Carlos said, cracking another big smile, nodding his swollen head. 'You know what you're doing today?'

'Not yet, Senhor,' Junior said. 'Waiting orders.'

'Good lad. Fact is,' Carlos went on, 'things are a bit topsy-turvy right now, what with the corruption investigation, you know, this Lava Jato nonsense. And let's not forget this Dilma impeachment business.' He smiled. 'No official opinions on the slag, of course. Everything else is a bit on hold for now. We've just got to focus on doing what we're told, entendeu?'

Junior nodded.

'But hold tight. Play it straight, son, and there might be a place on my team in not too long.' He smiled again, his eyes danced. 'Benefits of a good set of peepers and a tight gob, know what I mean? I'll see to it that you come out with my lot today, certo?'

'Sim, Senhor.'

Carlos turned, walked a few paces towards the door. 'You're alright, son,' he said. 'Important that.' He laughed. 'Enjoy your moment's respite, young man. We'll call for you shortly.'

Junior said nothing. The door swung shut. He exhaled –

Yep, he thought, he knew his responsibilities, his missions.

And he knew not to think too much beyond that.

He'd have to try and forget this dead playboy, whoever he was –

And this Polícia Civil detective named Leme.

Though after that night in Paraisópolis, that night high up in the favela, and whatever the connection was with yesterday's palaver, he was pretty sure forgetting anything might be a fairly tough fucking assignment.

Half an hour later: Militar SUV, Carlos quarterbacking. 'Então, young man,' he said to Junior, 'we're going to be putting the wind up a few rich cunts today. That suit you alright?'

Carlos wolfed a mixto quente. He guzzled at a jug of foaming coffee. Grease dripped from the cheese and ham sandwich. He back-handed milk from his top lip. He levered his bulk around in the passenger seat of the Militar SUV and winked at Junior, who sat in the back, squashed between two of Carlos's boys. The Heavy Mob.

'Learning on the job, son,' Carlos barked between mouthfuls. 'Never fails.' He sprayed liquid, breadcrumbs.

'Sim, Senhor,' Junior said – with purpose. Sunglass-set expression, dead ahead.

Carlos laughed. 'That's enough lip from you, querido.'

They were, ostensibly, on a follow-up to the previous day's rally, wheedling out provocateur types. Junior wasn't sure what this meant exactly, but he had his suspicions. The phrase 'rich cunts' rang in his head like the long note of a bell. A warning bell, perhaps, he thought.

The SUV moved through the traffic like a shark. The Heavy Mob either side of Junior held their automatic weapons from their windows, showing their teeth.

They feathered through the posh part of the city, arrowed through the traffic: floored it.

A rush of images, of colour, as foreign to Junior, in the lives they represented, as Europe or Africa or, in fact, anywhere outside Brazil, outside São Paulo, outside *his* São Paulo –

Low-rise, light-brown, red-brick housing; green spaces; pedestrians in smart navy clothes, suits and shirts, well-cut jeans, shining black shoes, shining black Lycra sports kit, well-groomed dogs obediently trotting alongside; *dogs* in smart clothes; glass security booths with painted green doors; cars neatly parked, in lines of black and silver and white; black maids and nannies dressed in white, holding children's hands, while their white mothers and white fathers chatted to other white mothers and white fathers, laughing, making dinner plans outside expensive schools; black maids dressed in white carrying shopping bags from smart supermarkets, while white men and white women walk behind; white men and white women in suits and sunglasses, sitting at pavement tables, served at these tables by black waitresses and white waitresses in smart black and white clothes, drinking black coffee and sparkling water, talking on black mobile phones, tap-tapping on white mobile phones, stepping into chauffeur-driven black cars, cars that look like they were bought from the foreign concessions that line the roads with their foreign, sophisticated goods, concessions that scream their message in their simplicity, lines of expensive, foreign, sophisticated goods, concessions that a man like Junior has no place in, no more place in them than he does in –

No more place in them than he does anywhere else, he thought – anywhere else but home.

And driving through these wealthy neighbourhoods in a Militar

SUV with automatic weapons and an obvious show of force, of authority, Junior was still invisible. The men and the women chatting by the side of the road didn't notice them, and if they did, it was out of a sort of expectancy, an ownership: *oh good*, their expressions seemed to say, *here go the people that get their hands dirty to protect us*.

'Cinco minutinhos,' the driver said to Carlos. About five minutes.

The Heavy Mob grinned at each other. They grinned and nodded at Junior.

But five minutes until what?

'Young Junior here is technically on watch, that's all,' Carlos said. 'I mean, *technically*, sabe? It's not up to us to police his *every* move, entendeu?'

The driver laughed. The Heavy Mob laughed. Carlos winked, raised his eyebrows. Junior looked dead ahead, eyes on the road.

They stopped outside a bar in Itaim. The name: Vaca Veia. Clientele: young, good-looking, professional. Cash flow: heavy. Tables dotted inside and out. A lunchtime buzz. Some drinking. Plates of food picked at. Not much on them, Junior thought. Memorabilia on the walls, hanging from the ceiling.

'Vamos,' said Carlos.

The five of them bounced. They lined up in front of the bar in formation: Carlão at the head, a Heavy Mob flank, driver and Junior fanned out behind.

Heads turned. Heads looked up from tables. Eyes shot other eyes glances. Conversations stopped. Nerves: jangled. Junior could feel the equivocation – it throbbed. This sense of power, this ability to *impact*: he liked it. He was, for a moment, *seduced*.

They stood and waited for the bar's attention. It was quite a scene. It was quite a performance. *São Paulo is Shakespeare*. Junior had heard some smarmy fuck at the academy once say that. He understood, suddenly, the power of a show of strength, the power of a *show*.

Carlos grandstanded. He paraded. He *prowled*. He rested his fat hands on his fat hips, hoisted his fat belly up, scowled and swaggered. Another fucking John Wayne in the cavalry, Junior thought.

Another swashbuckler type. Except Carlos was far more dangerous. This was *not* just for show. The tension crackled. The air stank of it.

Carlos grinned. He prepared to speak. Silence.

Carlos scanned the bar. His eyes ran over the tables, they ran over a couple holding hands, over a group of men and women in smart work clothes, over another couple, but these two were not holding hands, they were sitting more stiffly than the first, backs straight, expressions strained. His eyes ran over a second group of colleagues, dressed the same, laughing. They ran, Carlos's eyes, over all these people before they landed on a table of three young men, three good-looking, healthy-looking, tanned, confident young men, three privileged young men dressed in expensive polo shirts and tailored shorts, wearing boat shoes, shoes with tassels and no socks, three young men who could absolutely be described as classic Paulistano playboys, three young men who –

'Mind if I join you?' Carlos said. He gestured at the empty chair at their table. 'This taken?'

The bar, it felt to Junior, held its breath.

'Not at all, it's yours,' one of the young men replied. 'Please, join us.'

The bar, with great relief, exhaled –

Except for the table of three young men where Carlos now towered.

Each of these three young men reacted in quite different ways to the situation, to the intrusion, to Carlos.

The young man who had spoken wore a look of pure nonchalance, casually, loosely, he wore this look, like a sweater tossed and knotted, casually, loosely around his neck.

Carlos raised his arm, clicked his fingers and whistled. A waiter appeared. 'Another round for my friends here,' Carlos said. 'And the same for me.'

Carlos sat, heavily, down. He sat opposite the young man who had spoken. The young man Carlos sat next to did not have the same breezy, casual disposition as the first.

In fact, Junior thought, the lad appeared to be shitting bricks.

Carlos spoke to this nervous-looking young man. 'I suspect you're wondering what this is all about,' he said. 'To what, exactly, you might owe this honour and whatnot.'

The young man nodded and looked down at the table. His hands fidgeted with each other, and the way that he examined his hands made Junior feel as if this nervous young man were looking down at some distinct object, something separate from himself, his volition, some entirely *foreign* object.

The waiter appeared and dumped four glasses of beer on the table. Not hanging around to see if they wanted to order anything else, he scuttled off sharpish.

A hubbub returned to the bar. The other customers, very self-consciously, were ignoring the drama being played out in front of them.

Junior looked them over –

They did not want to be there –

But nobody was going to be the first to leave.

The Heavy Mob jawed their gum. They scowled. They glowered. They did their best to keep the bar guessing. Driver slouched, leant against a lamp post, his hand by his side, close to his holster, but not too close, giving the impression of some quick-draw kid, like he should be chewing on a match and flirting, stone-faced, with a woman. How often, Junior thought, had they done this sort of thing before? Could *he* do this sort of thing, again and again, he thought, could he, *willingly*, really do this sort of thing?

Carlos nailed his beer in one long, thirsty gulp. 'Puta que pariu,' he said, 'that hit the spot.' He grinned at each of the three young men in turn.

They did not grin back –

They sipped at their beers. They tried not to look at each other.

Junior was, by now, sweating profusely. Even in the relatively leafy neighbourhood of Itaim, there were few trees, there was little cover, the concrete baked from all sides.

The heavy flak jacket, the boots, the weight of the weapons, the *accessories* –

It was quite a workout in this weather.

Carlos was speaking more quietly now. Junior tried, but failed, to follow the conversation. The confident young man remained confident. He drank his beer. His body language said: I'm doing *you* a favour, and it's fine, not a problem, entendeu? The nervous young man twitched and fidgeted. The third young man, Junior couldn't get a read on. But he sat, broadly speaking, involved –

Then things happened very fast.

Carlos placed his hand on the nervous-looking young man's shoulder – and it was definitely not a friendly gesture.

The Heavy Mob bristled.

Driver turned back to the vehicle.

The third young man pushed back his chair and bolted.

Carlos barked an order.

The Heavy Mob hotfooted it.

The lad managed about half a dozen yards before doing what he was told –

Arms up legs spread hands behind the head, son.

Carlos signalled for the other two to relaxa the fuck out and sit the fuck down, entendeu –

He signalled to Junior to keep an eye, and he walked, slowly, purposefully, down the road to where the Heavy Mob waited.

The bar gasped, then hushed.

The two other lads kept their hands where Junior could see them –

This was not common, boosting playboys like they were on a favela roust –

Carlos better know what he's doing, Junior thought. You can't fuck with these boys too much, you don't know who their old man went to school with.

Carlos instructed the Heavy Mob; they patted the lad down. They pulled his wallet. Carlos opened it up, rifled through it, flicking cards – credit and business, gym and loyalty – onto the pavement. He, quite obviously, quite deliberately, lifted the cash, held it in the air and pocketed it.

Then –

'Bingo,' Carlos sang. He held up, between thumb and forefinger, a small bag of something most definitely not sold at the bar.

The young man, resigned, nodded. He offered his wrists. Carlos laughed.

The Heavy Mob led him to the SUV. They ducked his head, pushed him in. They jammed themselves either side. Doors slammed, driver popped the siren and the car squealed off, screeched away in a blue-red flash.

Carlos, grinning again, pulled his phone and turned a circle, jabbering –

Junior held tight.

Carlos finished the call, waved at Junior, gestured for him to sit down at the table with the two other lads.

'Another round,' Carlos called out to the waiter. 'Rapido, ne?' He looked at the two young men. 'You two best fuck off then. If I need anything from either of you, your mate will tell me how to find you, certo?'

They nodded. The waiter returned. Carlos looked up. 'Second thoughts,' he said, 'it's just the two of us now.'

The waiter nodded and placed a beer in front of Carlos and one in front of Junior. The two young men scraped their chairs loudly, so eager were they to be up and away.

The bar watched them leave. There was audible relief, tangible fear that this wasn't quite over.

'Cheers.' Carlos raised his glass, knocked it against Junior's. 'Drink up,' he said. 'Car's on its way, we don't have long.' He grinned. His eyes sparkled. 'We'll go back and have a quiet word with young Scar-face, entendeu?'

Junior took a sip of his beer. Christ, he thought.

Here we go then.

The interrogation room buzzed. The stuffy, cramped interrogation room really fizzed. It *popped*. Carlos drove his hand into the wall with a smack, hard, flat palm, no more than an inch or so to the right of the young man's head.

The young man's name, it transpired, was Gabriel.

Junior watched. Gabriel's old man, Junior now knew, was *somebody*. And that was all they needed. Somebody, in fact, who was not going to appreciate his son on a little drug-possession beef. Best for everyone if young Gabriel here does what it is we want him to do, was the gist of Carlão's little opening speech, his opening *salvo*.

Junior learned.

'Now you listen to me, son,' Carlos spat, his right hand still pressed against the wall, his left now threatening to tighten up around young Gabriel's neck. 'We are not going to fuck around. I have you, in front of a bar-load of witnesses, not to mention four of our finest Militar officers, such as young Junior here, running away from a perfectly civilised meeting, *resisting arrest* even, you could call it, then apprehended, searched and discovered with a decent-sized bag's worth of high quality bugle, not the yellowing, sulphurous shit you'd find in a boca in Paraisópolis!'

He leant back off the wall. Indicated that Gabriel should sit back down at the interview table.

'Favela, you got it in the favela.' Carlos shook his head. 'You're having a fucking laugh, son.'

Gabriel said nothing. Carlos sat down in front of him and leaned across the table. Junior imagined his sour breath, his rancid tongue, his pores *alive* with rankness.

'Fact is, Gabriel, I don't give two fucks where you got this from.'

Gabriel looked confused.

'And by that I mean to say that if you *don't* do what I tell you, we'll be pursuing a particular line of enquiry that means the person you got this sample of expensive and exquisitely proficient cocaine from, is in fact, you!'

Carlos smiled. 'Do you know what I mean?'

'You're saying that the deal is I do something for you, all this disappears?'

Carlos winked. 'Clever boy.'

Gabriel processed this.

'Course,' Carlos added, 'you don't, and all this gets a hell of a lot worse.'

Junior watched as Gabriel fingered his jewellery, a silver bracelet on his left wrist, a gold signet ring on his right hand. Gabriel's expression was one Junior had seen before in these sorts of situations. It was one of *understanding*: there is no choice to be made; it is out of your control. So.

Gabriel nodded. 'What is it you want me to do exactly?'

'Good boy,' Carlos said. He stood. 'We know that you lot, you posh lot, you boys who went to the private international schools and the private universities and now work as lawyers and in finance and whatnot, you all know each other, certo?'

Gabriel nodded. 'Mais ou menos, sim, ne?' he said. More or less, that's true.

'OK, good, look like you want to help.'

'Sim, I do, yeah.'

Junior thought of the way that he himself agreed to Carlos's demands, the way he cowered – at least on the inside – always aware of who he was, where he came from, always a little favela fuck with a bit of luck, none of the bargaining or entitlement of this Gabriel, even with the violence in Carlos –

It was something.

'So, look,' Carlos said. 'We think at least one, if not two, of your sort of people might well be AWOL. Certo?'

Gabriel nodded.

'We don't know who or why or where, but we think this is the case.'

Junior clocked Carlos's shift in tone, shift in manner –

He was feigning ignorance to get the lad on side. Carlos was letting Gabriel feel like *he*, Gabriel, would be doing them all a very big favour indeed, and that in some way Gabriel was, in fact, the boss man here.

'OK,' Gabriel said.

'Here's my card.' Carlos placed one on the table and pushed it across with his finger. 'You're going to call me every three hours, from now, with any news you get, anything you find out. Entendeu?'

Gabriel nodded.

'Just ask around, that's all. No mention of anything else. We just want to know if anyone isn't where they should be, ta ligado?'

'Crystal.'

'But you call me, right? Through the night, too. One word: nada, if there's nothing. We'll talk if you find something.'

The air in the room thinned. Their limbs relaxed.

'One thing,' Gabriel asked. 'What's the timescale here, roughly?'

'You mean when are you free from this binding contract and no longer in danger of being made as a dope-hound and a pusher?'

Gabriel smiled. 'Yeah, I guess I mean that.'

Junior admired the balls on this kid, the *front*. Serious front. It comes with the knowledge that this whole thing is based on a bluff; he walks out the door, nothing will ever happen – legally. So essentially they've become partners. They're working together now.

Carlos stood up. 'Mate, we don't find out by tomorrow night tops, it'll be too late for everyone.' He moved to the door. 'See him out, Junior, will you?' he said.

Junior nodded. 'Sim, Senhor.' He moved from the back of the room closer to the table.

Gabriel keyed Carlos's number into his phone. When he was done, he holstered his mobile, smirking. He pushed the card towards Junior.

Junior pulled a pen. He pushed the card back towards Gabriel.

'Write your number on this, cara,' Junior said. 'Quick.'

Gabriel read Junior's expression, understood it, nodded:

He scribbled digits.

Junior pocketed the card.

'Vamos, ne?' he said, and they left the room, Junior's hand on Gabriel's arm, his tight, firm grip on Gabriel's now limp, exhausted arm, and Gabriel breathed a helluva sigh of relief, an enormous, deep breath of relief as the door banged behind them and they were on their way down the corridor and back towards the sunlight of the front entrance.

'You probably don't want to pick up a cab right outside the building,' Junior said.

Roberta

Roberta woke.

A whiff of him – just in the moment before her eyes opened, his hair product faint on the pillow next to her and she smiled and clutched it to her, and then her eyes did open and it was gone and she was alone.

She shook her head, shook herself awake, half-crawled, half-fell out of bed. She put water on to boil and took a shower, the same ritual she acknowledged each day.

In the shower, she'd decided what to do. For a start, she needed her fucking phone, Christ knows what she might have missed, and she needed to go into college and retrieve her laptop, and there were at least three or four people there who might know something, might know where the hell he was. Or, at least, she'd be able to try his or her phone; not for the first time she lamented how her generation never wrote anything down, never knew anyone's number or email address without checking their contacts, fucking millennials, she thought, laughing, generation sext. That was one of Antonio's jokes. He was funny, old Antonio. Good old Antonio. She felt happy, suddenly, knowing she'd see him soon.

She drove to the university. It felt, distinctly, a Monday.

Her head soupy with the draw she'd smoked the night before, traffic buzzing, an irritant to be swatted but just out of reach, streets lined with rubbish, the odd placard, socialist newspapers strewn about. Post-rally city-slump.

She weaved down through Jardins. Mid-morning quiet, which meant it only took about twenty minutes longer than it should. She feathered through the quieter side streets, coming out at Rebouças and the shopping centre, crossed the bridge and headed right, out towards Butanta and USP and she wound down her windows as the air thinned, felt immediately fresher, just a few kilometres out from the centre.

She negotiated the roundabout at Praça Vincente Rodrigues. It was unusually quiet. More often than not, Roberta found herself riding the horn; her car, and its staccato, jarring movements, would course through her, jerked this way then that by the awkward, selfish flow of the traffic, shunting forwards, jamming the brakes, gesturing with middle finger…

…not today. She glided around and along Avenida Afrânio Peixoto, circled the second of the three roundabouts before campus, then accelerated, her left arm hanging from the window feeling the sun and the breeze along Avenida Universidade.

She parked in front of the Economics department. There were hardly any cars about. She looked up at the clock tower in the central plaza, the Praça do Relogio, as she always did. Habits, even on a day like this, an uncertain day, held fast. The tower had always fascinated her. Its vast, concrete flat front and back, its jutting rectangle rising skyscraper-high from a circular pool of green brackish water, its modernist, yet indigenous etchings, and the clock itself, high up at the top, like an afterthought, so you had to squint to see the time.

It made a stark contrast with the functional, low-level brick-and-glass boxes that made up the departments and teaching and research areas. When Roberta was an undergraduate, her professor had showed her class – political economy – photos of New York projects and London council estates, to interrogate the distinction of the first world favela from their own; but many students were impressed at how their university didn't look so different.

She sat back for a moment, the engine off, the AC off, the driver's window wound down, and she closed her eyes and let herself listen to the noises around her. In the distance, faint but constant, the low hum of Marginal traffic by the river, coming into the city, leaving the city, *stretching* the city, it sometimes seemed; more immediately, the buzz and snap from the electricity cables that fed the medical and science facilities in the next buildings; and next to her, in the space she claimed as hers, nothing really at all.

She was calm, she acknowledged this, but there was something more, something persistent, which she couldn't identify, something that made her stomach shrink and her eyes narrow, something about powerlessness, she thought. She was proud of the way she'd handled it yesterday, practical and realistic given that she had no phone, no computer, no way of contacting anyone save going round to their house, and pleased too that she'd had the self-possession to manage all this without panic, without fear, without too much anxiety from the uncertainty, from, yes, she thought, the *powerlessness*.

She nodded to herself three times and, in three quick motions, wound up the window, grabbed her bag from the passenger seat and jumped out of the car, locking it remotely with a beep as she walked towards the Economics block and her on-campus locker.

She couldn't help but notice something: there didn't appear to be a single person around. Had she missed some sort of holiday, or strike? The building, too, looked empty, all the lights out, almost derelict in the muggy heat of the morning.

And yet, despite the heat, despite the clammy space between her shoulder blades, the tight wetness where her thighs had melted on the car's leather seats, she shivered as she keyed in the six-digit entry code.

Half an hour later: Roberta stood, confused, in front of the reception desk at Antonio's office. 'So what you're telling me is that I can't ask questions about employees unless I have a prior appointment?'

The receptionist gave her a thin smile. Actually, Roberta thought, thin was being generous. This woman's smile was a slit, knife-sharp; it was barely even an acknowledgement of Roberta, of her existence, let alone her presence.

'That's right. I believe I told you this over the phone.'

This was true, she had. Back at university, Roberta had picked up her laptop from her locker, gave it a quick charge, then set about getting some numbers, firstly hers and Antonio's, sitting easily as they were in her contacts folder. She scribbled them down. She then got online and found his work number; it made sense to call him there if the mobile phones were out of battery, even though she never had before, had never even possessed the number, nor, in fact, the desire to do so. She also noted the address; it would likely be her next destination.

'You did, of course,' Roberta said, smiling, though reluctantly, herself. 'But I really need to talk to him. He's my boyfriend. Can't we imagine I'm making an appointment with you now?'

The phone conversation had gone about as well. After jotting down what she needed, she'd headed to the Economics department admin office. There was no one there. She hadn't seen a soul since she'd arrived. But it was unlocked and there were telephones. She tried the two mobile numbers, and both went straight to voicemail. She didn't leave messages. No one did anymore, only parents. She was yet to decide what she felt about it. It used to be a pleasure to receive a message from a friend she wanted to hear from. Now it was a faff, pressing this number or that – or was it a faff, really? Had everyone simply become even *more* impatient? When friends didn't answer when she called and then sent her a text to see what she wanted, it made her furious.

Right now though she wanted to speak to Antonio. That was all that mattered.

'I'm not sure you've totally understood what it means to make an appointment?' the receptionist said. And that smile again, though a touch more joy in it this time, perhaps pleased with the joke, or retort, or witticism.

Roberta swore under her breath. 'Do you think you could at least tell me if he's here?' she said, and as she said it – as she was saying it – she realised quite how desperate or vulnerable or sad the question made her look, and she felt all at once miniscule and hot and mortified and enraged by the whole thing.

The receptionist arched an eyebrow, made a tight, ironic face.

'Please.'

Her expression softened. 'OK.'

'Thank you,' Roberta said.

She'd driven over from the university fast – and twitchy with nerves or confusion or uncertainty, she wasn't sure which, or, in fact, if she really thought that for her there was any difference between the three things. She had expected to see friends – or possibly even friends of his – and had hoped she would get some company, some support, if that wasn't too dramatic, and some good practical advice. Instead, it seemed that everyone had disappeared and she had no way of tracking them down bar actually going looking for them, which was sort of unthinkable, not something any of her generation ever really did.

She smiled in genuine relief as the receptionist fiddled first with her computer then with her headset earpiece. She turned away from Roberta and spoke in a whisper, nodded, spoke a little more. She looked up at Roberta and flashed another tight smile, but this one wasn't hostile, no, it was something else, something…

Roberta didn't know much about Antonio's work. This was not a reflection on their relationship, though, thinking about it, if it were, it was a positive one, she thought. There were several reasons why she didn't. The principal reason, it seemed to her, was that Antonio was basically ashamed of what he did, realised that it was an easy route from expensive school to private university to finance sector, that he had taken, knew that, yes, he was after money and status, and knew this to be a superficial approach to life, knew that he was in fact better than this, and so only spoke of it to her in ironic and dismissive tones. And she, realising all of this, *understanding* it, and not wanting to be judgemental or be seen to be pushing him, wanting him to improve, to *be a better man*, never really asked him any questions or asked him for any details beyond the very broad generic sketches he gave her of the world in which he moved.

Yes, she thought now – this was a good reflection of their relationship; they didn't *need* to know that much about each other's work.

She was a PhD student and an intern at an NGO; he worked in a small, but prestigious, private finance company, a hedge fund, she thought. These were not incompatible things. Not at all.

'So?' Roberta asked, sweating now that her body heat had cooled.

The receptionist kept her eyes on her screen. 'Antonio Neves, you said, ne?'

'Yes.'

She nodded. 'He's not here. He's not due in until Thursday. In his calendar it's marked off. I've spoken to his manager, I – ' She shook her head, gave Roberta a sympathetic, pleading look.

'You're sure?'

'Yes.'

Roberta nodded. 'Holiday… makes sense, of course,' she said. 'Absolutely. Thank you. You've been really kind.' She smiled again, but she felt the panic in her smile.

She drifted from the desk, tripping slightly as she gathered her things.

'I can call someone if you – '

Roberta moved away, shook her head, stumbled, called out, 'No, don't worry at all, thank you!'

She staggered through the revolving doors and out into the blistering midday sun, light-headed and alone.

Roberta swore to herself. She shook as she drank the herbal tea she'd just about managed to order in the café across the road from Antonio's office, order without quite bursting into tears, without embarrassing the poor girl who served her with a curious glance, a curious, not unsympathetic glance, a look, really, and it had taken all of her willpower not to burst into tears, to cry, freely, to *weep* –

And then she had an idea.

Well, she thought, not really an idea, as such, more of a realisation. And a pretty fucking simple one at that, but one that about twenty minutes before she was incapable of having.

She didn't have her phone, but she did have her laptop, which meant she had email. And she was in a café that had Wi-Fi. What a millennial genius.

You've gone on fucking holiday!? Without telling me!? You fucking prick! I can't believe you'd even think about doing that. And you've got my phone, caralho. I need it. You'd better reply to this – soon.

Sending that message had felt good. But where did it leave her? No closer to any sort of resolution, or closure, or, fuck, I don't know, she thought, *serenity.*

She read it again. She read it three times. And then she realised something else.

She looked at the words she had written: *I can't believe you'd even* think *about doing that.*

Interesting words to have chosen, she thought. Yes, she can close read it and see the indignation, the anger, the disbelief that he could ever be so insensitive –

I can't believe you'd even think *about doing that.*

But of course a close reading can be a psychological one too, and she slowly, on her fourth or fifth reading, realised that she'd used the words *I can't believe you'd even* think *about doing that* precisely because she couldn't believe he'd even *think* about doing that, she couldn't believe, she *didn't* believe he had done that, didn't believe he'd gone on holiday without her, let alone without telling her –

Which means what exactly? she thought.

And then she *did* start to cry.

Mario

Leme was smiling before he'd even opened his eyes.

Positively beaming, he was –

What a sop. This was getting to be something of a regular occurrence. What was it, contentment, is that what they call it? Quite the headline: man enjoys living with his girlfriend.

Two noises: the shower and the kitchen TV –

Morning routines. Antonia's pre-work rinse, then catching up on the latest skulduggery that Globo offered up as news over a pingado – a sweet milky coffee – and a little pão na chapa, bread fried in a hefty wallop of butter. Old-school Brazilian breakfast.

Leme breathed a rattle, cleared his throat, snorted like a horse. Lips buzzed. He swung his legs out of the bed and lumbered into the en suite. Antonia was hum-singing something that sounded like 'I'm in my little rowboat', which made his heart zoom and his grin widen. Naked, he pissed, heavily, straight into the bowl, no hands, back arched, scratching at his chest hair and clawing at the sleep in his eyes; it was a *proper* piss, a real *man's* piss, and he took great pleasure in doing it while Antonia showered.

'Mario, really, caralho,' she'd said the first time she'd seen him do it. Well, *yelped* the first time she'd seen him do it. 'Don't we have any mystery left?'

He'd laughed. 'Intimacy is what this is, querida. We don't share this with anyone else, after all.'

She'd shaken her head, smiling, and kissed at him through the glass of the shower, smudging the impression of her lips and mouth.

'At least put the seat up,' she said.

Antonia sang; Leme mooned. Leme swooned. He stood and watched her a moment then wrapped himself in his dressing gown and went through to the kitchen to make breakfast. He wanted to ask about her period. But he didn't want to ask about her period. He didn't want to be that guy. They were being consciously less careful. This was an agreed and agreeable position. He wanted to ask and he didn't want to ask. Most of all, he wanted her to want whatever it was that the answer was.

Leme flicked through the channels. TV news:

All pro-Dilma rally. Numbers of attendees smudged depending on the network. Connections to Lava Jato implicit or outright. Criticism, or congratulation, of the rabble. No one seemed to know much, though.

Nothing on the kid. *Nada* –

Thank fuck for that.

Not exactly a surprise though. He'd shelve it, for now – stick it in a box.

This was the thing about living with Antonia:

When he's with her, nothing else matters.

Leme cranked the coffee machine. It gurgled. He filled the milk frother and pressed play. It swirled. He whacked a heavy cast-iron frying pan onto the electric hob. It beeped heat immediately. He forked a wedge of butter into the pan. It slid and softened. He cut hard bread like wood, in a sawing motion. He tossed two slices into the pan from across the room.

Back of the net.

He mixed the coffee and milk, flipped the bread and pushed it down hard into the butter, the heat, then plated up on the breakfast bar.

Morning routines.

There was a time when he mixed a different kind of drink first thing. Or chased his pingado e pão com manteiga with a cachaça shot and a cigarette –

Old-school labourers' and night-shift breakfast, that one.

Two and a half years they'd lived together now. He was giddy with domesticity. It was a sharp contrast to the dope-fiends and gash-hounds and freaks and shooters and knife-men and balaclaved hoodlums he scouted and collared each day at work –

He was still stuck in that petty criminal rut:

Not exactly a surprise though. No senhor, no surprise *at all*, not given his last couple of run-ins with the big men and the Heavy Mob.

Suited him though. His partner Lisboa, too.

Quiet life, that's the goal, no drama.

Church.

Antonia breezed in. Perfume and lines. No real make-up. She kissed him. She smiled. 'Thanks, love,' she said.

They ate and the TV jabbered.

Antonia nodded at it. 'Anything?'

Leme shook his head. 'Same old, same old, entendeu?'

He'd arrived the night before and it wasn't too late. She was out with a friend and home not long after. They were both jazzed on a little too much booze. It was easy to shelve what had happened, to stick it all in a box. *When he's with her, nothing else matters.* To put Carlos and the playboy corpse in a box. *When he's with her, nothing else matters.* To put the consequences, for now, in a box. *When he's with her, nothing else matters.* They shared some leftovers and watched the news and then half of a film that Leme wouldn't have been able to pick out of a line this morning, if asked about it.

Antonia ate slowly. She drank slowly. She looked at her coffee. She nodded. She gestured with her chin at the TV, mouth half full of bread. 'Know what all this is?' she said. 'I've been thinking about it all night.' Leme raised his eyebrows. 'Well, you know,' she said. '*Some* of the night. It's the old cafézinho, but on an epic scale.'

Cafézinho. The old Brazilian bribe. A little coffee, a quick coffee, bought to grease the wheels. The whole public official service lived on it. To *expedite*, in any other language. You can't even get an ID card without wetting someone's palm. Cafézinho. An outlandish euphemism for systemic corruption. That diminutive ending: cute. They'd both done it, Leme thought. And not long ago. To sort out documents and other admin when they'd moved in together.

Everyone does it. *Everyone.*

report that just yet? Any cunt with any sense would assume the poor little fuck's off the grid for a little fun, sabe?'

Leme thought this was about right.

Missing persons cases were rife, and reported promptly, on the whole, a hysterical mother weeping at a police block in the favela –

Fear of the old bala perdida. Or an unjust stop and search that ended in resisting arrest and a self-defence shooting in the back –

But not with this demographic, not with a playboy.

There was less worry of a random event. If one of these boys disappeared, you could bet that the kid's rich grandfather would be getting a call sharpish, an empty-a-considerable-part-of-your-bank-account call and tell no one.

But there was a body. Leme had seen it and it existed, so where the fuck was it?

They'd met in the padaria as a lay-low move. Leme had phoned Lisboa, told him to meet there. He gave him the lowdown and Lisboa had skedaddled, made some calls, asked a few questions –

Leme sat tight and made a few calls of his own. He was trying to find a way to get hold of Fat João. The only contact he had beyond Lisboa was his old journo friend Silva. But he wasn't answering. Leme sent him a text in no uncertain terms.

'Strikes me the Militar lot are holding the kid somewhere,' Lisboa said. 'Question is why. And it strikes me there are three basic scenarios here, given your little bate papo with Carlos post-corpse bait and switch.' He laughed.

'Not very reassuring, mate,' Leme said.

As Lisboa was making his enquiries, Leme had let his mind drift, let his mind hear her voice, Renata's voice. *That* was reassuring, the sense that no problem could not be overcome. That's what she was telling him: you overcame grief, you can do anything after that. He'd never got over *her* – he never would; he didn't have to – but he'd got over grief.

He knew what she'd be saying about this whole business, about the fortnight of protests, about what it meant –

Leme grunted.

'Point is, querido,' Antonia went on, 'it happens – and *this happened* – because of the general belief that everything – *everything* – is corrupt. And therefore everything *is* corrupt. Even if you don't have to buy a cafézinho, you still do. Why not? It might speed things up. Even though everyone else has done too, so the queue is just as it would be. Too risky not to, though, ne? Lava Jato is simply an understanding of scale.'

On the TV: a vast oil refinery construction project. A name: Odebrecht.

Antonia chewed. She nodded again at the TV. 'Scale, see? Can you imagine the size of that project? Of course not. They thought they'd get away with it purely because how on earth can anyone really get their heads around the scale? The difference between zero and 60 million dollars is vast and fucking easy to see. The difference between 120 and 160 is fuck all. *That's* what these fuckers understood.'

'They might not get away with it.'

'Well, yeah, and that's because we don't know what it is yet that they're getting away with.'

Leme nodded.

He poured them both more coffee. He spritzered the coffees with milk.

When he's with her, nothing else matters.

'Course it's not the companies or the politicos who are suffering, you know, on the ground.'

'Only the poor get arrested,' Leme said.

'Not quite what I mean.'

'No?'

'No. I mean the economy's in the tank, unemployment's up, massive construction projects are frozen, precisely because of this. Petrobras is told to suspend work with its chosen contractors, that fucking cartel, then the country suffers, right or wrong, end of story. Well, at least this exacerbates it all. The recession is more than just that, but you know what I mean.'

'Uh-huh.'

'Hence the backlash. Last week and yesterday.'

When he's with her, nothing else matters.

She smiled. 'Might be the first time the economy has become political, you know, big picture-wise. I mean, the question that your average Joe wants answered is quite simple, really: *where the fuck is all our money?*'

Leme laughed. 'Fair point.'

'What was it Tim Maia used to say?'

Tim Maia. Leme's all-time favourite Brazilian singer. Renata had introduced Leme to his music. That series of four eponymous albums in the early seventies *shone*. He was a hero to a lot of people, old Tim Maia.

Leme said, 'Oh, you know, that his doctor told him to give up drinking, drugs and fast food for two weeks and all he lost was a fortnight.'

Antonia laughed. 'No, not that. About the poor, and the right wing.'

'Huh,' Leme said. He thought about it. He smiled. 'He was bang on. What he said was Brasil is the only country where you have whores cumming, jealous pimps, addicts for drug dealers and poor people voting for the right wing. Something like that.'

Antonia nodded. 'Good old Tim Maia. One day it's going to happen, I'm sure of it. This whole thing will not end well.' She shrugged on her coat. 'Anyway, querido. I'll see you tonight?'

'You will.'

Antonia smiled. Leme smiled. And she was gone and then he was alone.

When he's with her, nothing else matters.

Last night hit him with a sucker gut-punch. He shook his head, took a breath, nodded, game-faced it.

He ran it:

A tip-off from a low life, dedo-duro, a textbook rat, Fat João –

Leme becomes a suspect or at least an accessory –

Old Carlão reminds him of their somewhat chequered past, owes who, who did what and blah blah blah –

Old Carlão threatens to put him in the frame –

Why?

And who was the kid?

If he is in the frame, be nice to know who he's supposed to ironed out, Leme thought.

He playbooked it:

One thing at a time: first talk to Lisboa –

Then find Fat João.

Leme was not a happy rabbit.

And he was confused. 'So you're telling me,' he said to L 'what you're *telling* me, is that there's no report or record of any from yesterday other than a few arrests for agitation, a cou weed pulls, and, what, one or two *traffic* casualties?'

Lisboa made a face. 'I'm telling you what they're telling m of.'

They were sitting in a padaria round the corner from the Civil building that they worked out of at the bottom of the hill. It was mid-morning, second breakfast-time –

Half a lager and a plate of cheese pastel, smothered in hot

Lisboa called it the happy ulcer. He said, 'Look, this is from our boys only. If you're saying the Military lot carted off body…'

Leme nodded.

'…well if you're saying that, then I'm not sure our boys necessarily know. *That's* what I'm saying.'

'And there's been no reports of any missing persons?'

'Nope. Nada. Not a sausage.' Lisboa laughed at that. 'So you know, it's likely a little early for that.'

Leme raised an eyebrow. Thought: true.

'I mean,' Lisboa went on, 'you said the kid is, what, ear ties? A playboy? Ah, it's not even twenty-four hours. Who's

A plague on both your houses.

That sort of thing: anger at the lack of debate. Fear at the lack of nuance. One thing she'd often talked about was the inherent weakness of a political system that requires citizens to vote. She believed, and believed that she was – that *they* were – lucky enough not to have experienced it in their lifetime, which was, what, five, six years ago now. Christ, how quickly things have normalised.

Her point: you have to vote, you have to vote for some*one*. And in a system that preyed on fear and division, relied on corruption and sleight of hand to maintain a political majority, that some*one* will one day sooner or later be the populist demagogue type; will, in fact, very closely resemble the promises and government of the military dictatorship. And it's hard not to vote that way when you have nothing, when you're invisible and erased, disenfranchised and under-represented –

And there are an awful lot of people like that in Brazil.

A lot more of them than us, Leme thought now. Difficult to know quite what *us* is anymore. He knew that Renata would be worried about the way things were going right now.

Let alone if she knew what had happened to him only the day before.

'OK, so, three options, if you ask me,' Lisboa said. Leme opened his mouth to speak. Lisboa raised his palm. 'Settle down, Mario, I'm telling you what I think whether you've asked me to or not.'

Leme smiled. 'Então vai,' he said. 'Pode falar.' Go ahead, be my guest: tell me.

'Number one. The body is in the Militar deep freeze up in Lapa or somewhere, and they're doing an autopsy, etc. They haven't ID'd the poor sod and they're not sure what's going on exactly, but they don't like the look of it.'

'Crime scene,' Leme said. 'There isn't one.'

'Maybe not, but they had to get the lad out of there before the rally turned. Short cut, but maybe, *just about* like, doable.'

Leme grunted.

'Number two. The body isn't in the fridge, they had something to do with it, for whatever fucking reason, it's not like they need one, really, and our dead rich boy is wrapped up in a hula hoop of burning tyres in a favela.'

Leme nodded. 'And the only other cunt to know about it is me.'

'Hence,' Lisboa said, 'Carlos's little reminder of your history, and his threat: stay out of it. That's all.'

'It makes sense. If I don't know who it is, then why push it? But then why did our friend Fat João tip me off?'

'Which leads me to scenario number three,' Lisboa said. 'Which is a combination of one and two, stiff-wise: either the lad's in the deep freeze or a well. Point is someone wanted you to find it. Right?'

Leme nodded. 'It seems that way.'

'And this someone knew that the Militars were very close behind.'

Leme said nothing.

'Which puts you in the frame. They iron out the playboy and you swing for it. Or you don't, and they have one in the bank in case things get complicated.'

'So, what, I'm an insurance scheme?'

Lisboa grinned. 'It might be the most practical use you've ever been.'

'You know,' Leme said, 'your three scenarios are kind of all the same scenario.'

Lisboa laughed.

'It's really a question of how soon I'm fucked.'

'*That's* the scenario, son,' Lisboa said. 'And Carlos is either straight up with his threat or it's a bluff and they'll be coming for you when you're not expecting it.'

'Great,' Leme said. 'What a fucking start to the week, eh?'

Lisboa laughed. He signalled for another round of beers. 'They can't do anything while they're keeping the information – and the fucking evidence, let's not forget – of the dead young man to themselves. While the kid isn't even missing, *officially*, you've got nothing to worry about.'

'So the answer is?'

'Find out who's the fucking kid. And don't hang about doing it.'

Leme smiled. His phone beeped. Silva. A text with an address and a time.

They nailed their beers. They slapped hands, embraced.

'You keep your ears pinned and your eyes skinned,' Leme said. 'I'm off to meet Silva.'

Lisboa roared. 'Batman and fucking Robin.'

Leme watched him leave. His heart swelled. Lisboa would protect him – always had. Family.

And Silva might just know what lay behind all this.

After all, if Leme was sure of one thing, it's that *something* did.

The address in the text from Silva:

A bar. Of course it was.

And when Leme arrived:

Silva tucking into bife a cavalo com fritas. Of course he was. *Cowboy Beef.* Huge plate, two steaks, smack bang in the middle, topped by fried eggs, a cholesterol island surrounded by a sea of chips. Proper lunch. Silva slurping at a bucket of red. Lips purple and swollen. Suit: shoddy. Tie: egg-stained, though who's to know when this happened. It was probably clean a few years ago. But there's been a lot of bife a cavalo since then.

Leme smiled. It'd been a while. He *liked* Silva.

Silva looked up as Leme approached his table, quickly looked back down at his plate. Between mouthfuls he said, 'E aí, seu gayzão. Beleza?'

Leme shook his head, a sort of half-reluctant, half-smile.

Alright, you big homo? How's tricks?

Charming.

Leme sat. The waiter approached. Leme waved him away.

'That's rude, mate,' Silva said. 'You're not going to leave me to chow down all alone, surely?'

Leme laughed. 'Good to see you, Francisco.'

Silva raised his eyebrows. 'I doubt that. You only ever seem to want to see me when you're in trouble.'

'Ah, don't be like that, querido,' Leme said. 'I didn't think social calls were really your thing.'

Silva grunted. He applied himself to his rapidly diminishing plate of food. He waved at the waitress and ordered another red wine, one for Leme too.

'Shape up, man,' he said. 'Think of it as a cafézinho. Paying for my time.'

Very apt, Leme thought. He said, 'This one's on me, mate.'

'Don't be cheeky.'

They knocked glasses and drank. It was a typical Silva haunt: an old-school joint on Rua dos Pinheiros, up towards the turnoff to Vila Madalena. At that end it was all still pretty basic: you had your corner bars and their grumpy regulars, their plastic awnings and rickety tables and chairs, doing burgers and shoe-leather steak, cheap cachaça and beers in frozen bottles, the odd, starkly lit buffet restaurant with its piles of day-old feijoada and gleaming veg. Further down: trendy taco chains and concept micro-breweries, a high-end French restaurant, a couple of live music venues where São Paulo hipsters covered Pink Floyd and moneyed men and women drank R$20 glasses of Guinness. The street as symbol: it roughly divided posh Jardins and hippie Vila Madalena. In between, there was something of a mash-up. You were making a point drinking there. Or, you used to be. Leme was well out of touch, on that score –

And thank fuck for that, he thought.

'You well?' Leme asked.

'Let's talk about why you're here, shall we?'

Leme allowed himself a smile. 'OK,' he said.

Silva finished his meal. He coughed and lit a cigarette. He plucked a toothpick from the dispenser on the table and forked at his mouth. It looked painful.

'I'm all ears, mate,' he said.

'I'll get straight to the point,' Leme said. He decided not to fuck about. He and Silva went *waaay* back, a lot of history, a lot of incriminating work they'd done together, and they trusted each other, so it seemed a waste of both of theirs to not get *straight* to the point. Question was how to frame it.

'The rally yesterday,' Leme said. 'I've heard that the body of a wealthy young man was found not far away. But it's not been made official. So I've got two questions for you.'

Silva nodded. 'Vamos lá,' he said. Go on then, let's hear it.

His interest was piqued. Leme could tell by his body language: he didn't look like he was about to fall asleep.

'OK, so,' Leme said, 'firstly, is there anything at all you know that might connect a playboy type with this political clusterfuck? And by that I mean, obviously, anything that might not be strictly legal. Make sense?' Silva nodded. 'Two... actually, you know what,' Leme said, 'let's just stick to the first question for now.'

'OK,' Silva said. 'First up, I'm guessing you're asking me as you reckon there's a fair chance that I might be balls deep into something like this myself?'

Leme smiled. 'Ah, vai, come on. I figured you know more than I do, that's all.'

'Flattery will get you everywhere, my son,' Silva said. 'And yes, of course I know more than you do.'

'So let's hear it, então.'

Silva nodded, sat up. 'Key thing, obviously, is Lava Jato and the way it's going. I'm sure you know it's got political. I'm sure you know what's happened this year has led to this state of affairs. And I'm sure you know that at first it was a straightforward corruption and money-laundering deal.'

'More or less, sabe? I read the papers.'

'Good for you. It's a lost art.' Silva lit another cigarette. 'Point is that it started like all serious criminal enterprises start: money. Illegal, dirty money. And the need to shift it, right? You ever heard the phrase follow the fucking money?'

'Yeah, matter of fact your young colleague introduced me to it.'

'Ellie?'

'Ellie.'

Ellie. Eleanor Boe. Leme's gringa friend. She'd started out as a messy bird with a job writing arts listings in a local bilingual rag. She was now full on with the investigative journalism scene, a part of Silva's mob. Quite handy, by all accounts. He hadn't seen her in a little while. He'd saved her life, not long ago, she'd tell anyone that'd listen.

More or less, *sabe*, was the truth of it.

'We'll come back to her,' Silva said. 'So look, if you're going to shift and clean dirty money, you need some dirty fuckers to do it for you, villains, right? At least at first. That's how it starts. The doleiros – the bagmen – doing the pick-ups and drop-offs are all at the criminal end of the social spectrum. But then things changed.'

'OK.'

'Yeah, suddenly there was more money than anyone knew what to do with. A fucking car wash and a few mules with shrink-wrapped packages of cash strapped to them just ain't going to cut it, *entendeu*?'

'So.'

'So. They need lawyer types and finance types to set up offshore businesses and companies to get the money out and about in order to get it back in.'

'Which means –'

'Which means that whereas a year or so ago, we – well, your mob – were dealing with low-lifes, now you're having to have a pop at the establishment. My guess is that your dead playboy was one of these. How old you say he was?'

'I didn't.'

'Any idea?'

'Early twenties, apparently.'

Silva weighed this. 'Fair enough. Most likely a fairly low-level middle-management type at a private finance company or law firm.'

'And he's doing what, exactly?'

'Well, fuck knows, I've no idea who the kid is, *was*, but my guess is, if he's carked it and no one's saying anything, he was one of these new doleiros, these new bagmen.'

'Sort of virtual bagman?'

'Yeah, why not? Some online, some wire, some cash. So I've heard.'

'Oh yeah?'

'You mentioned Ellie. She's just got back from London, couple of days ago, following something up.'

'London? That's quite an investment for a páo duro like you.' Pão duro: hard bread, a skinflint.

Silva glared – ironic. 'Holiday, fucksticks. And she funded it. As you say, I'm not swinging for a shot in the fucking dark. And it's just a hunch. A hedge fund, that's all, with some São Paulo connection. Could be anything. She's back now. You can fucking ask her yourself.'

Leme smiled. 'Bagman and Robin,' he said.

'You what?'

'Nothing.'

'So what's the second question? I ain't got all day.'

Leme grinned. 'How do I find Fat João?'

Silva laughed – loud. 'Urgent, is it?'

Leme nodded.

'I'll give him a tinkle right now,' Silva said, keying in a number on his phone.

'Good lad,' Leme said. 'Let me buy you lunch.'

Silva winked and waved for another drink. 'Hello mate,' he said into the phone. He stood up and moved away from the table. 'I need a little word with you.'

Leme smiled. Good old Silva.

Article by Eleanor Boe

OLHA! Online magazine, 21 March 2016

São Paulo: the capital of the world? A tale of two cities...

I'm afraid not, readers. That title goes to London. São Paulo is the capital of South America, *Latin* America, I'll give it that, but I've just come back from a visit to the Motherland, and, well, London takes the cake. Forgive my shameless click-baiting.

São Paulo makes London look like a village. I've said that before. I've *written* that before. The two cities have a surprising amount in common. There is gentrification and social cleansing; there is a political elite deaf to the plight of the disenfranchised; there is the recent, tragic collapse of a social housing project; there are acid attacks; there is the dichotomy of a thriving construction industry, and yet a deepening housing crisis, luxury buildings inhabited by ghosts. And like São Paulo you feel energised, politicised, important.

Back in my old home, I realised a few things about my new home. One thing about living in São Paulo is how quickly you get used to the normalisation of crime, the threat of crime. Everyone knows someone who has suffered some terrible experience. Driving in the city illustrates this: the winding up of your car windows when you stop; the jumping of red lights after a certain time of night; the constant checking that your doors are locked. It became clear to me that preparing for crime, or its prevention, is the same thing as living with its threat; one way or another, it very quickly becomes a mundane part of your daily life.

São Paulo exists in a state of heightened paranoia that lends itself to massive gun ownership, distrust of the police and armies of private security. Drive around any relatively wealthy area and you'll find high walls ringed with barbed wire, doormen, security teams and CCTV everywhere. That this is normal terrifies me. And it's now completely normal.

In London, I listened to a lot of Brazilian music, especially the Cazuza song, *O Tempo Não Para* – time doesn't stop. Cazuza died young due to complications with AIDS. He remains the poet of the disaffected. His work is discursive and profane, preaching inclusivity and tolerance. It is a staunch representative of a growing alternative movement that rejects the nepotism and vulgar capitalism of the country's elite. The political protests of the last two weeks recalled one of his songs, 'Brasil', and a specific line:

Brasil, mostra tua cara, quero ver quem paga para a gente fiche assim.

Brazil, show your face, I want to know who pays for us to end up like this.

His lyrics were prescient in the early years of democracy in the post-dictatorship period, and now they reflect a deepening dissatisfaction with the political system. Many Brazilians have had enough of the endemic corruption, the widening inequality: the general passivity in the face of societal injustice. There's a recurring slogan: *O gigante acordou*. The giant awoke. In Portuguese the verb 'acordar' means to wake up, and, as in English, there is the connotation of stirring yourself to action. One couplet was a refrain on my visit home:

Transformam o país inteiro num puteiro
Pois assim se ganha mais dinheiro

They turn a whole country into a whorehouse
Because that way it makes more money

Later that day, same place:
São Paulo, 21 March 2016

In São Paulo we thrive in the mess, enjoy the confusion – it's alive!

Marcos, 44, restaurateur

Brasil: love it or leave it. *This was the nationalist slogan of the Brazilian military dictatorship. The regime was repressive and there was media censorship and torture, but it was popular, too! Don't forget we saw the Brazilian Miracle, a period of considerable economic growth. You forgive an awful lot when you're making money. Brazil feels like a young democracy. The legal obligation to vote is… I don't know. Let's just say the legacy of the dictatorship is felt keenly. But for the young people like me, in the sixties and seventies, we saw those Tropicália guys in exile – Gilberto Gil, Caetano Veloso, Chico Buarque – and it gave us hope. They seemed to be thriving, and we thought we could too.*

Clayton, 66, retired

Junior

Junior stood outside the door of the flat where Gabriel had told him to meet, not half an hour after he'd received the text. An address, a time and an instruction:

don't knock

He'd watched Gabriel leave the building and turn left. Junior had waited a moment, turned right, then scampered around the block, doubled back, in effect, knowing exactly where Gabriel would end up. Junior knew the neighbourhood, he'd grown up there, and he knew there was only one place nearby where Gabriel might find a taxi:

A small, informal cab rank on a quiet street outside a stand-up corner bar that catered to manual labourers and anyone else who dared chance their arm at getting served –

Which weren't many.

Junior was quicker than Gabriel. He could see him dawdling on his phone, heels clicking, moving with a confident economy that surprised Junior, given that this area wasn't exactly his comfort zone.

Junior went straight for him. Gabriel, startled, dropped his phone, scrambled for it, kicked it forwards, tripped –

Junior grabbed him by the lapel.

'Vamos, cara,' he said. Let's go.

Junior dragged Gabriel down the tiny alley that led off to the side of the bar. No one paid them any heed. Or chose not to. Either way. The alley ran between the backs of two rows of improvised houses and was a common place to have a quiet word, or make a drop, or simply take a short cut between the two main roads that flanked this residential pocket.

'OK, let's make this quick,' Junior said. 'What exactly do you know?'

Gabriel was hyperventilating, no longer a privileged young man and now just another bleat in trouble. Junior examined him. He was fairly pathetic, Gabriel, at this exact moment, fairly desperate, pretty wretched; he was well out of his depth. And it was then, watching this rich prick blub, that Junior understood why he, Junior, was doing this: he didn't want the fucker to get away with it, simple as that. Junior wanted to *know* that he wouldn't. This power Junior had, for a moment – and he recognised that it *was* power – this power, over a young man whose whole being was based on power, on being *in* power, this power was intoxicating.

'Relax, man, breathe,' Junior said. 'I'm not going to hurt you.'

Gabriel nodded. He swallowed, took a breath, exhaled, settled –

'OK, come on, we haven't got all fucking day, entendeu?'

'I don't know anything,' Gabriel said. 'I've no idea why your boss chose me. I've no idea what he wants. I'm just going to do what he said. I swear, that's it.'

Junior pulled Gabriel's face close to his own. He could smell his beer-soured tongue. He could hear the phlegm-rattle of a smoker, the nasal-dust of a gak-hound.

'Tell me the truth.'

Gabriel tried to pull back, squirm free, raised a hand –

Junior gripped his wrist and pushed him back against the fence that ran behind.

'I'm telling you the truth, please, you have to believe me.'

Junior pressed his forehead against Gabriel's. 'I don't have time to fuck about,' he spat. 'You want me to turn you over and let you rot? You playboy fuckhead prick. You ain't going to last long here, son, believe me. Talk.'

Gabriel breathed. 'I'm serious, there's nothing I can tell you. What was I supposed to do? I'm being blackmailed and I don't know why. You saw yourself! Come on, please.'

Junior took a step back. He studied the lad's face –

He didn't look a liar. He looked like a dozy cunt in well over his pretty little head, like a scared little boy.

'OK,' Junior said, letting him go. 'Go straight down this alley. In about a hundred metres you'll come out onto a main road. I'll watch you. Get a taxi there and go wherever it is you're going. And you call me when you call my boss, certo? You've got my number.'

Gabriel nodded.

'Good, now jog on.'

Gabriel didn't need a second invitation: he was down and out of the alley like a cockroach across a kitchen floor.

Junior took stock.

All he could think at this point was that he needed to know the ID of the dead kid. And this was the only jeitinho, the only way that he could think of to maybe get a jumpstart, maybe get a sense of what the fuck was going on and why Big Carlos was keeping him sweet. This was the only thing he had to hold on to.

So here he was, a few hours later, and Gabriel had news –

He waited for the door to open.

And when it did, right on time, right on the fucking nose it was, he got a helluva shock, a serious jolt –

Jesus fucking Christ

He should have known –

Idiot.

Junior clocked the plastic sheet on the floor.

He clocked the chair in the middle of it.

He clocked the figure slumped in the chair –

This was a relief. The chair was not meant for him.

There were dark stains, puddles, pooling at the feet of the figure slumped in the chair. There was a slow, steady drip, like ink spilled from a school desk, Junior thought. There was no one else in the room, that he could see –

The door closed behind him and he turned –

A sharp explosion at the front of his head, a crack-crunch in his nose, pain spreading behind his eyes, an instant light, a flash of incomprehensible pain, he felt his features form an expression of shock and confusion –

Then blackness. He felt himself fall, quickly, into nothingness.

Then:

A wet rush of cold, a light slap, and he opened his eyes.

'Glad you could join us, young man,' Carlos said. 'And right on time. Good lad.' Carlos nodded at the Heavy Mob, gestured at Junior with his chin. 'Get him up.'

They pulled Junior to his feet and gave him a cloth to wipe his face.

'Sorry about that,' one of the Heavy Mob said. 'Needs must and whatnot.'

Carlos laughed. 'That was just a little warning, lad. You had to take one for the team. The bruising will come in *very* useful in our report, entendeu?'

Junior widened his eyes. He wiped his face. Carlos handed him a beer. Junior looked at it without understanding quite what it was, why he was being given a *beer*, what, the chair, the figure, Gabriel's text, who, what, I don't –

Junior's head rolled. Junior's head *lolled*. Junior's head flopped –

Junior, at this moment, was thinking *very slowly*. Time, he realised was passing, but passing in a way that it hadn't ever really passed before. It flowed, slowly, time did, flowed like a river weighed down with sludge.

Junior shook his head, loosened, and then tightened, his neck.

Time wasn't there, but it wasn't *not* there either.

Junior's eyes were glazed, empty –

For that moment, he was all in his head, Junior.

There was movement from the chair. Junior saw it, in a blur, as if underwater. Carlos noticed Junior's eyes drift to the slumping figure.

'Don't worry about him.'

The room slid into focus.

A wooden floor covered in a plastic sheet.

A fireplace.

A long, curved balcony to the right, beyond a closed glass door behind which Driver smoked –

Nothing else. Whitewashed walls. Furniture cleared, if there ever was any. Junior made out dark shapes in a doorway at the end of the room that led to a corridor, so perhaps piled up there, he thought, making space for, for this –

Whatever *this* was.

Junior coughed, caught thick coppery blood at the back of his throat –

'Who is it?' he asked.

'You what?'

Junior rasped, hawked phlegm. He looked down at the plastic sheet, then back up at Carlos, enquiringly.

'Knock yourself out,' Carlos said.

Junior spat. 'Who is it?' he said again, louder, clearer this time.

'I told you not to worry about him. Come.'

Carlos gestured for him to come closer to the chair. He nodded at the slumping, groaning figure, the murmuring, bleeding figure. Through dazed eyes, Junior had a gander. The poor cunt had been knocked about a fair bit, taken a hell of a leathering, it seemed to Junior through his tired, anxious eyes.

'Recognise him?' Carlos asked.

Junior shook his head, his groggy head. 'I don't know him.'

'For the best,' said Carlos. 'I tell you what though, son, you're not going to forget him, so have a good look at that face.'

Junior did as he was told. The face, the bloodied swollen face, swam into focus. Its mouth was taped shut. Its left eye was closed. In its right eye, Junior saw fear and anguish, and, as he looked deeper into this bloodshot and blackened eye, Junior saw resignation, Junior saw *tiredness* –

Junior saw relief.

'Like I say, you're going to remember this one.'

Carlos nodded at one of the Heavy Mob. He approached Junior and handed him a weighty object wrapped in an old cloth, still oily from use on some shitheap car or other.

Revolver. Junior opened the cloth. An old-looking street weapon: *not* standard Militar issue. Junior turned it over in his hands.

'Who's is this?'

Carlos grinned. 'Don't worry, lad, we'll find out, we'll find him. Sharpish, too, I'd say, entendeu?'

The scene, quickly and definitively, sharpened, shunted into focus.

Carlos handed Junior a pillow. 'Through this, we don't want to frighten the neighbours. Three, got it? This is going to look like a PCC interrogation and execution, so don't be too precise.' Carlos nodded at the Heavy Mob. 'These two will carpetbag him and take him home, leave him in bed.'

Junior did nothing. PCC, First Capital Command, a gangland interrogation and execution. Huh. There had been little happening with the gang and the Militars for a while, everyone knew that. Since 2012, and the snide eye-for-an-eye that had been going on, there'd been an uneasy sort of peace. Fact is, ROTA, the Military Police top boys, crossed a line a few years before when they undertook the in-custody snuff job of a lad who was resolutely not on the turn. And the parking lot incident, too. Six villains offed with automatics, self-defence the claim, but there were no bullet marks on any Militar SUVs, let alone any injuries. Rumour was the lads they picked were low-level workers, sorting out a delivery. It was, Junior had heard, very much a show killing, a disruption, a power-grab, a your-boys'-families-will-suffer type of move, no strategic value. So what was this? There were whispers the PCC were planning to end their twenty-year truce with the Rio mob, Comando Vermelho, Red Command. That would be a bloody move. Prison bloodshed, first off, most likely –

Riot, riot.

This was something like a calling card then, perhaps, a pre-empt, get the game up and running, blow the whistle and kick the fuck off.

'You didn't think we wouldn't find out, Junior?' Carlos said. He paced the room. 'I'm going to put it down to a well-intentioned, but misguided, act of diligence, certo?'

Junior said nothing. He weighed the revolver, weighed the pillow. He watched as the slumping, bleeding, murmuring figure, breathed heavily, wheezed, as he slumped, his blood trickling, dripping in time with these heavy breaths, these final, heavy breaths –

'People don't forget, Junior,' Carlos continued, a new steel in his voice. 'Your first outing with us, back in spring, what, four years ago now, you remember that?'

Junior nodded.

'Well, then. This is the same thing. Work, sabe? This is work and it's an order.'

Carlos turned to the Heavy Mob. They both unclipped their holsters, rested their hands on their guns. Driver came in from the balcony. He closed the door. He shuttered the blinds.

Carlos slapped Junior on the back. 'I'll be in the car park downstairs. We'll go for a bite. On me. You'll have earned a top-notch steak dinner, son. And a chat about your future.'

Carlos turned and took two steps to the door. He turned back. 'You're a very lucky young man, Junior.'

Junior nodded.

He heard the door close behind Carlão.

He gripped the gun, felt its warmth, slid off the safety catch.

The figure on the chair roused himself at this, squirmed, tried to talk through the brown tape over his mouth, then tried to shout, then tried to scream, then tried to squeal –

Junior took a step towards him, this poor, squirming man, a man he didn't know, a man who was a pawn in some miserable game, a man who had committed crimes, perhaps killed, who had contributed to chaos and misery in this miserable game, a squirming, cowardly snake, a nasty fucker, a man who Junior now saw as work, OK, work, it doesn't matter, it doesn't matter, this is a consequence, a consequence of a bad choice, a well-intentioned but fundamentally bad choice, a real stinker, and so this, and if not him then anyone and this way, now, this way, it's over and you're in, and steady, but not too steady –

And Junior smothered the muffled squealing, smothered the bleeding face, smothered it, *it*, as that's what it was, it –

Three shots, not too precise.

Roberta

Roberta didn't cry for long.

Not her style. She'd taken a deep breath, thought about the person she'd like to be, how she'd *like* to behave in this moment, in this uncertainty, in this not-quite crisis.

So she'd done what she often did in moments of confusion:

Made a list.

Well, she made several lists, lists that detailed what she knew and what she didn't know, what she could do and what she couldn't do, what was verifiable and what was not, and who she might contact – and why. And *how*, of course.

And it all felt so dramatic.

And she didn't like that one bit, she wasn't that person – she was unflappable! She hated any feeling of helplessness or powerlessness or confusion, and so she always assumed control, she eliminated confusion on her terms, assumed that others – her friends, her family, her lovers – were all as independent-minded as she, all as far from that sickening, cloying, clinging dependency in their relationships with her as she with them, all as –

But, when it came down to it, he wasn't at work, had taken *holiday*, for crying out loud, and she didn't know where the fuck he was. He had told *other people* he wasn't around on this day, people he barely knew, he had told other people and not her.

Other people and not her.

That was the gist of the email she sent to Lis, who she'd seen at the rally, and who knew she'd argued with him, and knew she'd stormed off, knew the context of the day, or some of it. That was the *gist* of the email, though it was couched in rather more relaxed terms, rather more the *can you believe it, amiga! What a cheek!* sort of terms –

Within half an hour of sending the email, Lis was sitting across from her. And this made Roberta think.

First thing Lis said when she arrived:

'Let's go and get a proper fucking drink.'

They went to Bar do Juarez on Juscelino Kubitschek in Itaim, a local haunt of some of Antonio's friends. They sat on the upper balcony and ordered draught beers, glasses of choppe. Mid-afternoon and the traffic was chock-a-block on the main road. It was basically stationary on the side street they looked down on, the lights were on the blink, the taxistas and the motoboys swore at each other and the world in general. Roberta took all this in despite how she was feeling –

Funny how the world never stops.

'Right,' Lis said. 'You drink and calm yourself, menina. I'm going to make some calls.'

'Just keep it casual, please,' Roberta said.

Lis gave her a look. 'Querida, I know you, I got this. This was me, though, I'd out the fucker on social, entendeu, then we'd know what was going on.'

Roberta made a face. She did as she was told.

Lis called anyone she knew who knew him or who was connected to him, on the premise that she had a surprise lined up for Roberta and needed to get hold of *him* to help her set this little surprise up –

But, então, couldn't ask *her* for his number, sabe? Don't want to ruin nothing, you understand? Could you get him to give her a call or something?

Clever girl.

It got the response they wanted –

But not the response they wanted.

Funny how the world never stops.

Nobody could get hold of him, anyone who had his number got voicemail, he wasn't at work, he wasn't at home, he wasn't at his parents' place, he wasn't at his parents' place out of town –

After about an hour of this and five beers –

'There's something fucked up going on here, querida,' Lis said.

'Remember my English friend Ellie, journalist? You've met a bunch of times. I used to work with her at the magazine?'

'Sim, of course, I remember her, she's cool. Why?'

Lis made a face. 'She might have some ideas. You know what she's been doing last few years, ne?'

Roberta nodded. The booze suddenly took a hold. She shook.

'It doesn't mean anything, menina,' Lis said. 'Just not a bad idea, get another head on this, sabe?'

Roberta took a deep breath and saw the sense in mapping this out to, and with, someone else. 'Call her,' she said.

'It makes sense.' She picked up her phone and dialled, put it to her ear. 'Either this is your boyfriend dicking you about or it's not. And if it's not, well – ' She raised her palm. 'Sweetheart! How is my English princess?'

And half an hour after that, Ellie was with them.

They told Ellie everything that had happened.

Ellie took it all in. Roberta noted her expression, which was serious, sympathetic, concerned, but not panicked, and with just the hint of something in her eyes, something Roberta thought looked a little like excitement –

Bit snide.

'So,' Ellie said, eventually, 'if you can't contact him, he's not at work, you've heard nothing from anyone else, it's pretty likely, it seems to me, that you're not going to, sabe? He'll either turn up and explain, or he won't. I reckon it's down to us to figure out where he is and why, ne?'

She paused. Roberta felt a heat creeping up her neck, felt her stomach tighten and contract, felt the hunger she'd been obliterating with beer and cigarettes come back, sharply, she felt, suddenly, lightheaded, weak.

'I think,' Ellie said, 'I know just the person we can talk to.'

Lis smiled. Roberta felt her take her hand, felt her own, damp and clammy in her friend's grip.

'I was hoping you'd say that, querida,' Lis said.

Mario

Leme watched Silva leave. He had a few hours before he was set to meet Fat João.

His phone beeped:

hello stranger

He laughed –

She was right on cue.

Leme returned Ellie's message quickly.

They arranged to meet the following day. He was looking forward to it. He hadn't seen her for almost a year, he thought. They'd kept in touch; he'd kept himself apprised of what she was getting up to, work-wise. The Olha Online stuff was entertaining; he liked her mix of serious and silly, a bit high-low. She was good at it, and for a gringa she had a real feel for the pulse of São Paulo, seemed to know instinctively what mattered to Paulistanos –

And how the different city tribes would react.

She'd matured, he thought, too. It felt patronising to voice that thought, but it was true. She was only a kid when he first met her, a kid who was a long, long way from home. When he met her, investigating the disappearance of her best friend, her only real friend, she was just a careless gringa, just that, a gringa –

So yeah, she'd matured. She'd *lived.*

And she'd handled the situations she'd found herself in extremely well, given the circs. And her presence had been helpful, effective; she was a worker, she got her head down and got on with it, and Leme understood why Silva had taken her under his wing.

So yeah, he was looking forward to seeing her. He'd tell Antonia in the evening. She wasn't Ellie's biggest fan, but that was really only because Ellie knew what she'd got up to in the Cracolândia land beef a couple of years back. Ellie knew and didn't do anything, didn't write anything, didn't suggest any follow-up at all. So Antonia felt like she had one over on her, which, he supposed, was exactly the case.

And Antonia's way of dealing with people who had one over on her:

Not to like them –

And make that fact very clear.

This was not something that they had in common –

Leme was scared of anyone who had one over on him. Largely as anyone who did was usually pretty fucking scary.

While it was not his style, he did respect and even envied a little Antonia's approach, her philosophy, if you could call it that, if that wasn't too *grand*.

The ability to not worry about what others thought of you.

Leme reckoned that was a quality he had never quite mastered. Renata had encouraged it in him, and Antonia too. He wasn't convinced it was a bad thing that he hadn't got the hang of it.

But it did mean he had to watch his nature, his instincts, around the likes of old Carlão.

They might well have something over each other, but Big Carlos was a lot scarier than Leme –

Old Carlos, Leme's former friend, had a lot more nasty surprises at his disposal.

Finding Fat João's place of residence was a fair bit harder than Leme expected.

The address Silva gave him was *waaay* out past Lapa, textbook bandit country –

It was, Silva had said, one of a stretch of semi-shacks in a grid almost slap bang on the Marginal. But, Leme was finding out, you couldn't simply make a right off the main road: you had to go beyond and then double back and the grid was fluid and the houses packed tight and the roads single-track and in bits and there were deposits where mudslides had hardened so it wasn't even possible to negotiate some of the corners –

And there was hardly anyone about. This was not reassuring. This was a place it would be very easy to get lost in –

And very easy to *stay* lost in.

Leme was not in the best of spirits. He was tense. He was sweating in the heat. He was aware that the longer he took, the more likely he'd be stuck in an almighty traffic jam on his way home.

A woman, dressed in little more than rags, pushed a shopping trolley slowly past his car. In it: piles of moody Adidas tracksuits.

Classy. Leme wound down his window.

'E aí,' he said. 'You know a little fucker called Fat João?'

The woman grinned. She revealed a dark expanse for a mouth. The few teeth she had were brown-yellow and mismatched, oddly shaped. When she smiled, her face looked like the beginnings of a construction project, all soil and rock and brick strewn about all over the shop, no evidence at all of any rhythm or planning. She rolled her dark, fat tongue. She spat. She licked her cracked, muddy lips with her blackened tongue. She was still smiling.

'Então?' Leme said.

'Over there.' She pointed down the road. 'The horrible-looking one, see it? Filthy yellow door, the real shithole of a house,' she said, laughing. 'Lucky you!'

Leme thanked her. He watched her wheel her trolley down the road in the other direction. He smiled to himself. She was a character.

He swung out of the car and crossed the road. He stopped by the filthy yellow door, which was in fact filthy, and had once, long ago, been yellow.

He looked up and down the tiny cramped street –

Dogs slept.

Cars rusted.

Rubbish bags heaved and sweated.

Washing dried.

A heavy odour sat just above the row of tiny cramped houses –

An odour of decay, of stale food, of rank water –

The river, you could almost feel it, slopped and sludged, throbbed and pulsed its way past, just beyond the wall of traffic, the constant lines of belching cars and trucks.

This was proper no-man's-land. The very fringe of the city –

And exactly where a dirty little grass like Fat João would end up.

Leme knocked.

Nothing.

Leme knocked harder.

The door gave slightly, creaked and opened.

Leme, again, checked the road, up and down.

Nothing.

He pushed into the tiny, cramped shithole of a house –

The smell was intense. A very different smell.

The living room was empty.

A wooden crate was covered in dirty plates and dirty cutlery.

A smaller, wooden box for a chair.

No carpet over the concrete floor.

No windows.

Like a cell, Leme thought. But without the facilities.

Leme edged to the bedroom. The smell thickened.

It was then, he realised, that he knew –

Fat João in his bed, dead, lying in his bed but wrapped in a carpet, wrapped like that so that his cremation would be straightforward, but left like that as there would be no cremation. The body, his body, had been left to be found by someone, an old PCC calling card –

His face: a pulp. A real mess. A battered, beaten, oozing piece of rotten fruit. Somebody had gone to town alright. Old Fat João had never stood a chance. Leme doubted he'd been given one at all.

Something didn't add up though. The place, while undoubtedly a shithole, was not disturbed. There were no signs of a struggle, no signs of a break-in.

Leme weighed it:

The execution – the torture and execution – and he was sure it was both these things – had taken place somewhere else.

They'd brought Fat João home

First thought:

Who the fuck is trying to stitch me up this time?

Here we fucking go again, old son.

Article by Eleanor Boe

OLHA! Online magazine, 12 March 2016

What is the PCC and why should we even care?

Here's a story that answers these questions.

The PCC gang runs São Paulo crime. The men that run the PCC run it from prison. These men want to watch the 2006 World Cup on large, flat, wide-screen TV sets. The PCC is like a corporation – none of the flip-flop / assault-rifle shtick of the Rio gangs. They are *very* organised. And they generally get what they want.

So the PCC leaders ask for large, flat, wide-screen TV sets. They pitch for more frequent conjugal visits. These requests are nixed. In response, the PCC leaders tell the authorities that they will 'cause some chaos'.

For three days, São Paulo experiences some righteous, PCC-brand chaos. Gangbangers attack the police. They hijack buses. They evacuate them. They set them on fire and leave them burning on major highways. There are rumours of raids on public buildings, that schools and hospitals are next. Over a hundred and fifty people are killed – police, gangsters and the inevitable unfortunate bystanders. The stray bullets: the *bala perdidas*. The city goes into lockdown. The authorities throw in the towel. The PCC get their TVs and, I believe, their conjugal visits.

I have friends at the British school who were there when this kicked off. I speak to the headmaster. The chief of police's son studied there, he told me, and his father dropped him off the morning after the weekend's violence. The officers who had been shot were receiving danger money. Trauma and whatnot, apparently, so the chief of police is supposed to have said. Thing is, hearing this, a number of officers have shot at their own police stations. The bullet holes can be used as proof they've been attacked. They too, the chief of police said, are claiming danger money.

São Paulo is a city of great contrasts. That weekend in 2006, according to those I've spoken to, the gap between the have-nots and the elite seemed to close a little. The peculiarity of the crime, the brazenness of the requests and response, and the behaviour of the police seem distinctly Brazilian to me.

PART TWO: **AWAYDAYS**

The week before, 12 March 2016

We flirt, but we don't flirt. There's a difference between São Paulo and London. People say I'm flirting when I'm not. I'm quite reserved, but they say that's the point. Something about the look in my eyes, poking fun. I'm just chatting, laughing, enjoying myself with the playful banter. It's normal. When I flirt, I think I make it fairly obvious! English colleagues don't get it. When you came in to talk to me, they were sure we were flirting. It's the Brazilian way of chatting, which we have, that physical to and fro, the gestures and eye contact, the smiling. Affectionate and always keen to make the other person laugh, to communicate that warmth we feel for our friends. That's all it is. And I love it. And that's something São Paulo is the best at in the world. Not that I've ever dated a Brazilian. Too jealous, too insistent on doing everything together, too much cheating. In São Paulo there are more beautiful women than in London; but in London there are more handsome men.

Gabriela, 28, receptionist

London: *we will be arriving at London Heathrow in one hour.*

Back to Blighty! Ellie thought, half-dreaming, half-laughing. She yawned. She massaged her neck. She ran her dry tongue round her cracked, dry mouth. She shifted in her seat, bending her knees and rubbing at her lower back. She lifted her eye mask and looked around –

Premium Economy. What style. The Prodigal Daughter. The returning hero –

Ghengis Khan across the fucking Alps she was.

Shame there was no one to see it, really. It didn't matter which bit of the plane you were in when you came through Arrivals to a barrage of Ealing's finest mini-cab drivers, dressed like chauffeurs. No one *there*, no one in *Arrivals*, knew about your extra legroom, your ample buttock space, enough for *both* to really settle in, your early dinner service, your tiny, basically non-existent queue for the British Airways snacking tray, the fact – the key, incontrovertible fact! – that there were only two of you in your row, *even though you had a window seat.* You only ever had to disturb *one person* if you fancied a piss. This was, many would agree, the height of civilisation, pure *class.*

Pure Premium Economy Class.

She thought that maybe she'd had about an hour's sleep, had drifted off – well, nodded off, with a jolt, *finally* – at the same time as she'd given up on a predictable romantic comedy, turned off the entertainment system and realised that she'd run out of peanuts from the British Airways snacking tray. She liked to fly long haul. Who wouldn't? Free booze, free food, free films. The British Airways snacking tray behind the stewards' curtain was a thing of beauty to an Englishwoman coming home after a few years living abroad without any of her cultural reference points, her *staples.* The brackish clarity of a Walkers Salt 'n' Vinegar crisp. The elevenses snap and crunch of a KitKat. The reassuring heft of a Mars bar. The punch in the teeth of your European can of Coke, somehow more unpleasant – and all the better for it – than the Brazilian equivalent. The warm miniature of London Pride ale.

She looked out the window and down towards where she assumed the city must be. The stewards were delivering breakfast. The plane was waking up, shafts of yellow through partially opened blinds. Stiff-backed men and women shuffled in queues for the toilets. (But not in Premium Economy. The queue in Premium Economy was basically non-existent.) Children whimpered, confused. Teenagers slept on. There were others, like Ellie, who had barely slept at all, and they gulped at water, trying to create some distance from the last half-bottle of red wine they'd drunk not an hour before.

The light was sharp, otherworldly in its brightness. The horizon stretched out, piercing blue, translucent, lazy in the effortless way it rolled on beyond the clouds, beyond the light, beyond. Ellie thought she could make out a faint green, but she didn't think they could be over England yet. There was still a good hour or more until they landed. There'd likely be all that holding-pattern palaver. London: the gateway to Europe. Was that a phrase?

'Tea or coffee?' the steward asked.

'Oh, tea,' Ellie said.

'Breakfast?'

Ellie nodded. 'Cooked, thanks.'

The woman sitting next to Ellie turned to her.

'You're English,' she said.

'Very.'

'Ha.' The woman smiled. 'Well, your Portuguese is impressive then.'

'Merci,' Ellie said.

'You're funny.'

'Only first thing in the morning.'

'Or last thing at night, ne?'

Ellie smiled. They sat in silence for a few moments. Ellie sensed that now was the time to duck out of this conversation, if she wanted to.

'*Your* Portuguese however – ' she said.

'You *are* funny.' The woman offered her hand to shake. 'I'm Giovanna.'

Ellie smiled. 'I'm Ellie.'

They shook hands.

'What are you doing in London, Giovanna?' Ellie asked.

Giovanna smiled. 'Visiting family. Work. You know. A holiday, I suppose.'

'Here for long?'

'Couple of weeks.' She smiled again. She took a sip of her coffee. 'And you?'

'Same thing, basically.' Ellie laughed.

'What do you do in São Paulo?'

'I'm a writer. Well, a journalist.'

'There's a difference.'

'There is.'

'What's the difference?'

'It's a bit like the difference between Economy and Premium Economy.'

Giovanna smiled. 'Financially?'

'Not at all.'

'What do you write about? Sorry, *journal* about.'

'Very good.' Ellie laughed. She turned slightly towards Giovanna, in her ample seat, her vast writerly seat. 'I do a few bits and bobs, you know, online, sometimes print stuff.'

'Anything I might know?'

'Ah, the question any writer – sorry, any journalist – loves to hear.'

Giovanna made a face.

'Sorry,' Ellie smiled. 'I, oh thanks – '

The steward handed them their meals. They considered them and they set to work. They peeled back their plastic covers at almost exactly the same time, and, in this moment of triumph, steam rose, ominously, *wafted* from their meals, briefly filling the space between them, like in a sauna.

It felt, to Ellie, quite intimate.

She inspected the goods. Volcanic scrambled egg, a sort of blood-yellow tinge to it, rubbery, it would surely bounce if you dropped it; a piece of thick bacon that curled in on itself in disgust, its slimy fat dripping grease, its meat somehow dry from over cooking; a tomato, oozing; a solitary, firm potato –

A sausage.

'You know,' she mused, 'there is a certain type of English person who, no matter how they feel or where they are, will always, always, without fail, order the cooked breakfast if it is an option.'

Giovanna laughed. 'I think there's the exact same type of tourist.'

They worked diligently and uncomplainingly at manoeuvring their food around in the plastic tray with their sets of plastic cutlery.

'This is the main difference between Premium and Business,' Giovanna said.

'The food?'

'The cutlery. You get a proper knife and fork, an actual glass of wine.'

'With breakfast?'

'Ha. I'm sure you can ask.'

They laboured on. The sausage work, Ellie noted, was especially Sisyphean.

I *am* funny, she thought.

'You were about to tell me what it is you write?' Giovanna said.

Ellie smiled through yet another mouthful of sausage. The hum-rattle of the aircraft was a constant once more. Her ears cleared, popped.

'I suppose you could call it political journalism, now,' she said. 'I write a sort of column for Olha Online. Reflections on politics, that sort of thing, but not very serious, or at least not always.'

'Interesting.'

'And it's written in English,' she added, quickly. 'I think the idea was to try and reach a quote unquote *international audience.*' Ellie made the quote signs, then immediately hated herself for doing so. 'Or, you know, more likely,' she said, 'reach a few expats who have yet to learn any Portuguese.'

'And that's why you came to São Paulo?'

'Not exactly.'

Giovanna raised her eyebrows in that dry, amused, mock-shocked Paulistana manner that was not so much an invitation to continue as an instruction.

'I was working for *Time Out* São Paulo at first.'

'I know it.'

Ellie smiled. 'But I wanted to do investigative stuff, you know?' She paused, made a face. 'I had *ambition*, entendeu?'

'And you've achieved your goals. Muito bem. Brava, querida.'

'Mais ou menos, ne?' More or less.

Of course she wasn't going to tell this stranger what brought her into contact with the kinds of people who could help shape a career in this kind of journalism. Even if this stranger was making her feel remarkably relaxed, forthcoming. No, she wasn't going to tell her about what had happened with her best friend Ana, with the politician Jorge Mendes, with snide Alex, and sweet Fernando, with the redevelopment of Cracolândia, Leandro, and her first forays into politics, into corruption, into storytelling as whistle-blowing, she wasn't going to tell this stranger about how this had all come about through her friendship – and professional relationship too, come on, Ellie, don't do yourself down *that* much, with Leme, and, oh yeah, fuck, *that's* who this stranger reminds you of –

Antonia: Leme's missus. Identikit type:

Muito droll, drolly bird –

Ha. Clever girl, Ellie.

They continued to work on their breakfasts.

'What is it that you do?' Ellie asked.

'I'm a lawyer.'

Bingo. *Very* Antonia.

'And that's why you're over?'

'Partly.' Giovanna gave a thin smile. 'And my daughter studies in London, at King's. Work, family, holiday, all that. At my age,' she said, 'you have to combine these things, sabe?'

Ellie wasn't exactly sure what she meant by *at my age*. Resigned – or lapsed – feminist and whatnot, she thought.

'You said you were doing some work here too. A story?'

Ellie nodded. 'More of a hunch.'

That arched eyebrow thing again.

'Lava Jato, you know,' said Ellie, knowing that it was something of a catch-all now, the phrase, what with everything it entailed.

'Uh-huh. Like the international angle? Follow the money, that kind of thing?'

Ellie laughed. 'I've written that phrase before. But yeah, something like that.'

'The world's financial playground now, London, so they say.'

'And I've heard that phrase before too.'

'It's the Wild West, totally unregulated, much of it, apparently. Only thing that matters is cash. What a city.'

'Europe, eh?'

'The old world.' Giovanna smiled.

Their breakfasts were, by now, basically done with, the debris drowning in congealing grease. The steward collected their trays, refilled their tea.

'Well, good luck with it,' Giovanna said. 'I'm going to use the heavy fuel we've just consumed to help me commit to a quick nap before we land.'

'I like your style.'

Giovanna slipped on her eye mask.

Ellie looked out the window. The light refracted, dispersed, through cloud. The air looked thin, fragile, out there.

Not long now. *Home*, quite soon.

She'd be with her mum in not too long. She hadn't seen her for almost four years. She'd done exactly what her mum had said she would – *stay away*.

And this hunch –

Gawd knows what the week would bring.

São Paulo: the toilets of a mercilessly swank bar in Itaim –

Business time.

'Mate, trust me, it's a piece of piss and it's – hang on. Here.'

Antonio took the silver coke straw his friend and slightly older, *slightly* senior colleague Rafael handed him.

'Classy,' he said.

He hoovered his line. It tasted good. The back of his throat was briefly numbed. The whiskey fire was doused. The coke snapped into his brain. He felt his eyes widen, for a moment, in agreement with what he'd done, applauding him with a smile, then narrow again, more focused.

He grinned.

'That's some decent chop,' he said.

'Ah, you get what you pay for, entendeu?'

Rafael flicked the lock of the toilet cubicle and shouldered the door. He nodded at the attendant, who fingered the fifty Rafael had palmed him when they went in.

'Textbook,' Rafael said.

Antonio looked at his phone. A little after nine on Monday, 12 March 2016. Pretty late – or early – to be getting on the bugle, but fuck it, why not? No messages or calls from Roberta. Likely for the best, for now. He would see her tomorrow. Last thing she needs to know is he's out and about on a Monday. She's never been one for the drunken late-night cuddle, he thought. Though fair play, really, not a great deal of romance in being pawed and slobbered over by a half-continent, ethanol-breathing, coke-chattering dragon. Antonio used to tell her that he'd love it if she came round to his, drunk and horny, clambering all over him.

It had been a lie; he knew that now, after the one time she'd tried it –

Turns out when you go to bed early, when you want an early night, you go to bed early because you want an early night.

They sat back down at their table. It overlooked the dance floor. A waitress hovered. Rafael made a circle with his finger around the drinks on the table indicating another round. The waitress smiled. Rafael smiled. 'Get one for yourself, too,' he said.

'Maybe later?' she said. 'If you'll both join me?'

She left.

'Christ,' Antonio said. 'It's like walking into a cliché in here.'

Rafael grinned. 'Ah, you get what you pay for.'

'She's too expensive for you, mate.'

They looked around. The music was loud. They peered over the edge of the VIP area, watched as young women danced self-consciously in groups, their eyes over their shoulders, their purses held casually in one hand, like ping pong bats, protection, Antonio thought, as young men circled, talking only to each other –

It wasn't exactly a sociable scene.

Rafael worked his jaw. Antonio suspected that it wasn't his first line. It rarely ever was Rafael's first line. The lights flashed low, the music changed gear, there were cheers from the boys near the dance floor, demonstrably recognising the new tune, half-hearted enthusiasm from the girls.

At least, Antonio thought, doing drugs in here felt like you were doing drugs for *something* and not simply doing drugs to do drugs, sitting in a friend's apartment until the sun rose and calculating to the minute the sleep you might get in if you left in a cab *right now* before showering and heading to work. And then instead getting a patchy half-hour on a sofa, hopeful the shower made up for the lack of sleep. The elusive pursuit of drug-taking, and especially the mirthless, relentless, joyless pursuit of taking cocaine –

They had a mate, Octavio, who would sit at the kitchen table, plate in front of him, hammering out, then distributing, line after line, endlessly *working* his way through the diminishing pile, really putting in a shift, like, well, like a production line, Antonio supposed.

Ha.

It wasn't always like that, of course, he reflected.

Though, to be fair, he was always delighted on the nights when he *hadn't* taken it. It was such a relief! That next morning, fresh, productive, applying himself in new and interesting ways.

Fear of *not* missing out, Roberta had joked.

But he was enjoying it now, and the waitress was back with their whiskeys and he felt that little tug he sometimes did to misbehave –

'So, it's a piece of piss, right?' Rafael was saying. 'Honestly there is nothing to it, and if you're in, if you *help*, the dividends are heavy. It's not a percentage cut of the transactions, nothing like that, it's a salary; the weeks you work you're paid. They *employ* you, so that way the activity goes on regardless, there's no risk, no red flag fees or changing amounts, no odd giveaways like divisible movement through multiple accounts, and some weeks you make more even than the money you're moving. Some weeks nothing like it, but, you know, that goes without saying, ne?'

'OK. So what about where we *are* employed, what do they make of it all?'

Rafael made a face. 'Mate.'

'What?'

'It's freelance, they don't give a fuck.'

'But you're using contacts you've made through the firm, it's our clients. That not a bit fucking shady? What's the phrase,' he said, '*conflict of interest?*'

'Nah, it's all good. It's sideline.' He paused, looked around. 'Look, fact is, it's part of the same process – our clients are glad of the dinheiro, glad of the business, and that feeds back into us, sabe?'

'You really think that's true?'

'It's the universal language of love, amigo: cash. And all's fair in love and whatnot.' He smiled, gestured, palms out. 'Mate, trust me, I know what I'm doing.'

Antonio nodded. He was sure of that, at least. Rafael always knew what he was *doing*; he just didn't always realise what he'd done.

'Come on, let's do another line of chang and see when that

waitress gets off.' He laughed. 'Or *how* that waitress gets off, know what I mean?'

Rafael was out of his seat and headed to the gents. Antonio followed. The attendant smiled and shook his head in mock despair.

'You two,' he said.

Rafael shot Antonio a look. Antonio placed a fifty on the tip tray. The attendant doffed an imaginary cap. 'Much obliged, gentleman,' he said, cackling.

'He's making decent bank, that fella,' Rafael muttered, as he closed the cubicle door and locked it. 'It's a fucking *Monday*.'

He opened the silver cigarette case he carried with him, what he called his handbag, or his gak bag, or sometimes, simply, his bag bag. Inside was a vial. He opened it and shook out a fair wallop of powder into the inside of the lid. Using the razor blade he stored in a tiny sheath in his handbag, he chopped and divided the mound into two snaking lines. He took the silver coke straw and offered it to Antonio.

'Much obliged, gentleman.'

Rafael disintegrated into a giggling fit.

'Mate, hold it steady,' Antonio said, laughing.

They both had their lines. They both washed their faces. They both left the toilets grinning, alert. They were both shaping up nicely.

'I guess I just want to know how you got in on it,' Antonio said. 'And how you've got the, I don't know, the authority or whatever, to recruit me, sabe?'

'Fuck me, Tônico, it's not a fucking cult. *Recruit*, Jesus.'

He laughed. They drank deeply at their whiskeys. 'I've got a serious thirst on,' Rafael said. 'Beers, ne?'

Antonio nodded. 'Então?'

'Look, this is not a job interview, entendeu? I just thought you'd be interested.'

'I am.'

'Good.' Rafael glanced this way and that. His eyes darted. He chewed on his cheek, his bottom lip. He was about one bump away from a gurn. 'So, the contact is a client we have, who is a part of Odebrecht, OK?'

Antonio nodded.

'He's got his own portfolio that we manage through the fund, but he wanted to do something different. He spoke to Senhor Matheus, who asked me to set it up.'

'Matheus? So it's sanctioned then.'

'Yeah, *mais ou menos.*' More or less. OK. Rafael's eyes followed two young women's legs. 'It's sanctioned by him, but off the record. He set me up with a separate account, which is what I'm using. You'll get one too. That's the point, there's more work than I think they realised.'

'OK.'

Antonio turned it over. Senhor Matheus was Rafael's line manager and senior partner of the fund, a board member. It was likely some sort of tax loophole, this off-the-books shit.

'You get an account to handle. Just a number, no names. Trades and payments go through that. And *you* get paid into another account, which is yours, *entendeu?* Mate, it's fucking golden. I do like two, three trades a week? Takes an hour, tops.'

Antonio was nodding. 'Set it up.'

They slapped hands. Rafael was grinning like a cunt. Antonio felt himself do the same. 'Pocket money, pal, that's all.'

'A fucking paper round.'

'It is almost literally that.'

'Come on, let's go and find someone to talk to.'

They swaggered through the VIP area, two lairy cunts in lairy shirts, drinks in their hands like weapons, a lazy economy to their steps, in time, they were, to the music, in fact they moved almost *around* the rhythm. Their sleeves were rolled up and their arms were muscular and tanned. Their feet: sockless. Their ankles glimpsed from above their expensive shoes, also tanned. They circuited; they turned a slow circle. They jawed their gum for extra swagger, extra nonchalance. They looked away from each other, over heads and shoulders. They spoke without making eye contact, heads nodding in opposite directions. This, they both believed, made their friendship appear greater and more intimate than it actually was, and this, in turn, made them more attractive to women. While they both believed these things to be true, they had never discussed them, never even noted these things in conversation.

It was this that ran through Antonio's head as they plotted their next moves. Plotted without any actual discussion, of course. It all took, Antonio guessed, about two minutes.

'Line?'

'Thought you'd never ask.'

'You're as dry as bone, young man,' Rafael laughed.

They went to the bathroom, and then twice through their little routine. There wasn't a great deal of point, it seemed, to keep turning circuits of the fairly deserted VIP area.

'That waitress,' Rafael said. 'Let's get her and a friend to come back to mine.'

Antonio weighed this. He knew that Roberta would not be pleased if she knew he was even entertaining the idea. But he also knew that he was entertaining the idea only for Rafael's sake. He *knew* that. It didn't hurt, not to misbehave. Fear of not missing out ran deep.

'You're having a laugh, mate,' Antonio said, knowing that this was part of the process, the transaction.

'In what way?'

'She ain't coming with us, and I ain't coming with you, entendeu?'

'Don't be soppy. Roberta's not going to know.'

'That's right, she's not, as there won't be anything *to* know.'

'Selfish. That's what it is, you're being selfish. I'm asking for a favour, entendeu? You're supposed to be a mate.' He paused, smiling. 'Mano, you really do not see anything beyond your own needs, ne?'

Mano. Brother. Antonio noted, once again, how often his middle-class friends were so quick to adopt the language and attitudes of gangsters, of the street, of, well, *poor* people. Why is that? Is everyone so uncomfortable in their own skin, or is it just his boys? *His boys.* A case in point, ne? And does this posturing work the other way round, class-wise? Probably not, he reflected. Privilege is the thing you're disabusing, pretending you don't have it.

After all, he thought, I'd rather have hustle than a trust fund; better a pimp than a prince.

Rafael flicked the lock and shouldered the door.

Monday slides into Tuesday.

Monday night *bleeds.*

The next morning –

Antonio sat at his desk. *His head throbbed.* He couldn't really call it the morning after, as the night hadn't really ever finished. *His head pounded.* There was the shower he took at Rafael's. *His head ached.* There was the walk to the office, in the clear light of morning, the clear, promising light of morning, the kind of light that seemed to offer something, seemed to offer at least to clear his throbbing, aching head –

But it didn't last long.

The computer yawned into life and numbers flashed and slid into view. They pounded his eyes, his head, these numbers. Thank fuck, it wasn't a busy morning. Not for the first time, Antonio was grateful for the hours of the finance world, the hedge fund shuffle:

Early start, boozy lunch, slow and easy afternoon, fast and furious night –

It's a lot easier to function at seven or eight in the morning than it is at eleven if you've been hammering at the gak all night. Two espressos and a fried egg sandwich would see him through until ten. Keep your fuzzy, throbbing, pounding head down and don't panic –

Easy to say when the slightest noise sets you off.

Easy to say when you shrink and prepare to take cover or flight whenever a colleague, let alone a stranger, walks towards you.

Antonio had some serious edge on this morning.

And then there were those messages from Roberta, affectionate, playful, but fucking spot on too –

Hey fuckhead. Late night? ;)
I imagine it was Rafael's fault, ne, querido?!
Enjoy work! It'll be fun contributing further to a horrendous
mechanism of greed and power with your little old self-
loathing, baby xx

Serious edge on, he had. It was hounding him, *pulverising* him, it was coursing through him, really giving him a good hiding.

He stared at his screen.

His mind whirred, his mind buzzed, his mind *crunched* –

This hangover was really taking the piss.

His tongue grew fatter, drier, raspier –

He could feel his fat tongue fill like a sponge, then dry out like water evaporating in hot sand whenever he gulped at his bottle of Evian.

His head was piercing.

Bloody espresso.

And then Rafael hove into view, loomed right over him, all teeth and flashing eyes, a right hard-on he's got, really pleased with himself, really *thrilled*, he looked.

Terrific.

'Oi, oi,' he said, grinning. 'You alright, mate?'

'No.'

Rafael smirked. 'Settle down. It's only a hangover.'

'Yeah, well.'

'Come on, it was a good night. Ended well, at least.' Rafael looked around. Then leaned in close. 'That thing we talked about. It's on. Meet me downstairs in the bar, nine thirty, we'll sort it, certo?'

'Yeah, sure.'

'Yeah?'

'Certeza, cara.'

'Beleza.' Nice one. 'We'll have a sharpener while we're there. Just a drop, you know, take the edge off.'

'Sounds good.'

'Toast our bright futures and whatnot.'

'If you say so.'

'I fucking do. Now shape up, lad, and I'll see you in about an hour.'

Antonio nodded. What stamina. It's got to catch up with you at some point, hasn't it? Rafael wasn't much older, but he *was* older, he'd been around, been doing this longer. It's *got* to catch up with you.

And *he* can't have got any sleep, Antonio thought.

Antonio would never know if the waitress did have him in mind when she'd decided to stay. But he'd made it pretty clear he wasn't interested, just in case. And the thing was, he *wasn't* interested. He really wasn't. He hadn't been interested in anyone else at all since he'd met Roberta. To the extent that it was kind of a surprise. He kind of almost tested himself once in a while. And the same result: he didn't give a fuck about anyone else.

And it was a relief. Yeah, a fucking relief.

What a feeling.

Course, staying up all night at Rafael's with two birds didn't exactly look good.

Neither did calling them birds.

If there was a way he could show that last night was about that urge to stay up, to talk shit, to hang out and feel something, to feel that joy in misbehaving a bit, in chasing *fun,* but also nothing to do with cheating, it'd be fine, it'd be clear and it'd make sense.

But he wasn't sure he could.

Best not to then. Something he was learning in this relationship: What matters and what doesn't.

And sure as eggs are eggs, as sure as fucking mustard, he wouldn't get very far explaining it with this throbbing, piercing, pounding head. His head was a fucking carousel –

He'd sit tight, keep his head down, then meet Rafael and do this thing, do this thing he'd promised he'd do, he wasn't the sort to welch sober on promises made when drunk.

And it *did* seem like a good idea, after all.

Rafael was already in the bar, tucked into a dark quiet corner out of sight of the door when Antonio got down there.

He was nursing a beer and his laptop glowed in the gloom.

Rafael looked up. 'Look what the cat dragged in.' He clicked his fingers. 'Two,' he said to the old geezer that ran the place. The old geezer raised an eyebrow and muttered something about it being alright for some.

Antonio sat.

The old geezer, muttering something about a champion's breakfast, handed them their beers.

Rafael raised his glass. 'To world peace,' he said, cackling. That post- or mid-bender energy crackling away, tangible excitement.

'Yeah, cara. I suspect we can help with that.'

'Mate, you are a right laugh first thing, eh?'

Antonio drank deeply. The beer was restorative, tasted *good*.

Rafael spun the computer round so he could see it.

'Right,' he said. He pointed at the screen. 'Here. That's the account you're dealing with, certo? There, that's the trade.' He flipped the window. 'And here, that's your account, that's where you're paid. Details here.'

He pushed a piece of paper across the table.

'So what's the trade exactly?'

Rafael clicked and pointed. 'This goes here. Simple as that.'

'That doesn't look like a trade. Looks like a transfer, something like that.'

'It's a one-way trade, sabe?'

'You what?'

'You're buying into a fund. *That's* the trade.'

'OK.'

'On behalf of the client. Simple.'

Antonio nodded. He knew the principle. They did it sometimes for their regular clients. A sort of straightforward investment-type situation. Difference was in this trade, in this investment, there were only numbers. Nothing else to identify what he was doing. It wasn't clear at all what the investment was *in*.

What *was* clear was the amount, which was big, real fuck-you money.

'OK?'

Antonio drank more. His head started to clear, just enough to remember what they'd talked about last night, that Senhor Matheus was involved, that Rafael was, essentially, showing him the ropes.

This was a good idea. Pocket money, a paper round, a cakewalk –

'OK,' he said.

'Então, cara, vamos lá.' Let's do it.

Antonio nodded. 'Vamos, sim, cara.'

Rafael pushed the laptop to him. Antonio finished his beer.

Antonio examined the screen.

He clicked –

Job done. You're in, he thought.

'Nice one,' Rafael said. 'You're in like gin, filho. You're not going to regret this, nem fodendo.'

Antonio laughed.

You're not going to regret this, no fucking way, not even if you're fucking, not even if you are having sex, *while you're regretting it.*

An apt little phrase, that one, he thought. Nem fodendo.

Good old São Paulo slang, right on the money –

He laughed, raised his glass, smiled –

Right on the fucking money:

Now *that* was an apt little phrase.

London Calling. Ellie laughed. Heathrow corridors and the song's already playing.

Except –

Except it was her ringtone. Of course it was. It seemed funny, doing that, a couple of nights ago in São Paulo. Not so funny now, of course. A few giggles, a few eye rolls as she fumbled for her phone.

She should have chosen the other one:

London calling, Speak the slang now, Boys say –

Mum.

Of course it was.

'Mum, I –'

'Oh, good you've landed. Excellent. When can you talk, do you think? I expect you've got customs and duty-free and passport and bags and everything else, haven't you? I probably shouldn't have. I probably should just. Oh, yes, please, just the coffee, thank you. No milk. No. You still there, love? Can you? No, no, that's it. No milk. I –'

'Mum. Mum. *Jesus.* Mum.'

'You're still there? Hello? Ellie?'

'Yes, Mum.'

'Oh, you *are* still there. Great, I was going to ring off.'

'Hang up.'

'What?'

'You were going to hang up.'

'Why, you're still there, aren't you?'

'Mum, I –'

'Oh, wait, I need to go, I'll call you back, OK?'

'OK.'

Welcome home.

As uncanny and welcome too, in its way, but infinitely less heartening than the British Airways snacking tray, was the Piccadilly line.

Ellie was on it for *hours.* She was on it for hours, it felt to her, and yet she had only reached Russell Square, where she got off. Zone 1, that was all. Along the Piccadilly line, sitting with her legs wrapped awkwardly around her case to stop it rolling off, trying to read, not trying to read, trying to be entranced by London and its new yet familiar mystery, its *surroundings*, trying to drink it all in, what with the first few hours of the journey on the Piccadilly line actually outside, then trying *not* to drink it in, as, frankly, it's the suburban London nightmare part of London.

She got off the tube and navigated the lifts, schlepped her case past the Brunswick centre, with all its brutal charm really *on show* in the sunlight, and then up Lambs Conduit Street with its extremely pricey clothes shops – Christ, is it actually *allowed* for clothes to cost that much? – and on to Theobalds Road and her digs above a faux-Italian café chain where her friend from school, Lizzie, now lived.

Lizzie. The one friend she'd kept in touch with. Skype calls and texting, so that it seemed faintly ridiculous that they, in fact, hadn't seen each other in years –

'Ellie!'

'Lizzie!'

They hugged. For some time, they hugged.

Lizzie pulled away. 'I have to go to work, like, right now.' She led Ellie down a short, thin corridor. 'This is you. Keys on the bed. I'll be back at sixish if you fancy a drink or something?'

'Nice place.'

'Yeah, thanks. It does me.' She smiled.

'How did you…?'

'Long story.'

'You mean it's your mum's.'

'Something like that. Look I really have to go. You'll be OK?'

'I'll be fine. You crack on. *Definitely* up for a drink later.'

'Great. Make yourself at home. I'm so glad you're here!'

They hugged again, a quicker hug.

'Go, go,' Ellie said.

'What are you going to do today?'

'I said *go*.'

Lizzie made a face.

'I don't know,' Ellie said. 'Take a shower. That's the first thing. Then I'm going to meet that contact, you know, guy I told you about.' Lizzie frowned. '*Work* thing, remember? Then I'm going to spend the evening with you.'

She squeezed Lizzie's hand and winked.

Lizzie smiled. 'See you *very* soon.'

And then Ellie was alone again, and she lay down on the bed in the spare room, which was, for a few days at least, hers. Her mind whizzed with possibilities of what she might do, but the pull of tiredness was overwhelmingly strong, and in moments she sank into sleep.

Ellie dozed, she thought back, she dreamt.

Ellie had always wanted to become a journalist and her degree choice was supposed to set her up for it.

The girls she grew up with were drifting off to colleges of their own, preparing to become lawyers and doctors, though secretly terrified they'd end up as clerks and medical secretaries.

'It's like feminism never happened,' Lizzie said once as they sneaked cigarettes at lunch. 'All those promises that we can have it all. The problem is that if we can *all* have it all, then some of us are not going to have anything, as there won't be anything left. In the current career climate, it makes sense to become a housewife.'

Current career climate. That was a phrase their advisor had used so often and so solemnly that it had taken on political significance, like Global Warming or Teenage Pregnancy. The worst: *Sexually Active*. 'We used to have domestic science and tips on the best forms of contraception,' Lizzie continued. 'Now it's all about marketable personal statements and the right college fit. It feels like if we get this wrong, we'll never recover.'

It didn't stop the frenzied end to their school days, though, with its alco-pop binges and hurried attempts to leave for college without the burden of virginity. And it didn't stop the listless summer in limbo that all school leavers throughout history surely go through, with their promises to keep in touch and resolutions not to change: as if they were fully formed at eighteen and owed it to themselves to be faithful to that adolescent image. Ellie though *was* keen to change, as she didn't want to have to do the same thing again.

She was her friend, her *best* friend. Her *first* friend. Lizzie. Lizzie was the first person to recognise what Ellie could be, who Ellie actually was. That thing she said, 'We've got so much potential, you and I.' That had killed Ellie, lit her up, showed her what it was like to meet a kindred spirit. 'We are muy simpatica,' Lizzie told her just days after they first met. *Muy simpatica!* That was how Ellie wanted to talk.

The days with Lizzie passed in a haze of banter and cigarettes and questionable decisions regarding boys and drugs. And she truly felt she was as clever and funny and vital as Lizzie. Most of the time. On darker days, when she was alone at home struggling over her homework, she felt very different. She realised that what she wanted wasn't to be *with* Lizzie, to be her friend, to be her *best* friend even, but to actually *be* Lizzie. She wanted Lizzie's life. She was clever enough, even then, to give the condition its proper Latin name: invidia.

From *invidere*: to look at something and to want to possess it.

She stirred. She stretched. She smiled. She was glad to be back, glad to see her friend. It was time to get to work.

An hour later and Ellie was in a moderately swank restaurant in the City sitting opposite a well-heeled, well-dressed young man.

'Who are you again?' he asked.

Ellie smiled. 'You know perfectly well. Friend of a friend. A *contact*.'

'Umm.'

Well, he was youngish. Likely late-thirties, she'd guess, but gym-ready with it, a sort of pre-emptive strike. She could imagine him doing something like fencing or equestrianism, no, *polo*. Stomach crunches, that sort of thing. A cruellness to him, there was, a competitiveness that'd suit those activities.

There was something, she'd been thinking that day, about well-dressed men: they're either doing something very right, or they're dressing up to hide the fact that they're doing something quite wrong.

English men were funny creatures, never quite sure how to realise their potential, looks-wise, blindly following fashions with no regard for body shape. Brazilians: they understood body shape. They understood – well, some of them understood, *rich* Brazilians understood – that skin-tight jeans on a round-bellied, wide-hipped, pear-shaped man do not go. And should not go, ever. A surprisingly large number of English men did not, Ellie noted on the walk from Theobalds Road to the City, know how to buy jeans.

'No, of course, I understand *that*,' the man was saying. 'But I don't really know *who* you are, as in, *what* you are. You know?'

Ellie smiled. She was prepared for a bit of evasiveness –

She hadn't been a hundred per cent truthful in terms of why she had arranged this meeting and what she was hoping to get out of it. And that, of course, meant that Christopher, the young, well-dressed man now sitting opposite her in this moderately swank restaurant in the City of London, didn't know what *he* was hoping to get out of it, didn't know, exactly, what he was doing there.

'Christopher – '

Christopher smiled. 'Chris, please,' he said.

'Chris. We have a mutual friend, a mutual colleague, I suppose, as you know.'

Christopher nodded. 'Yeah, of course, Zack, Zack the Yank.' He grinned. 'He told me about you.'

'I'm sure he did,' Ellie said. 'He's quite something, right?'

Christopher examined her. He twirled, delicately, the stem of his wine glass. It was a decent dollop of a red, Ellie thought. She'd give him that.

'How is it that you know him *exactly*?'

'I suppose you could call it the São Paulo expat scene.'

'OK.'

'He works with a friend of a friend of a friend and everyone ends up, well ends up knowing each other, you know what I mean?'

That smile again. 'Yeah, I rather think I do.'

'Barbecues and whatnot. Tennis. There's an English Club where they serve tea, play bowls. I first met him at a thing there. And you worked with him in the States, I think he said.'

The connection, Ellie knew very well, was fairly tenuous between herself, Zack the Yank and this smooth, posh City gentleman. She didn't want to dwell on this aspect; she needed to get him interested in her and sharpish.

'Bowls?' he said. He raised his eyebrows. 'OK.'

'And,' Ellie said, hurriedly, 'he told me I should look you up as a favour to *him* because what I'm doing, in my work, there's a sort of overlap, and he seemed to think there might be some benefit in it for you.'

She grinned.

'So, what is it that you do then?'

'I'm a writer.'

'OK.'

'Political commentator sort of thing.'

'And this is a favour to him *how* exactly?'

Ellie breathed lightly, took a sip of her wine. She leaned forward. 'He thinks it'll help you out, though I've no idea how on earth I might help *you*.' She paused. 'Anyway, that, apparently,' she said, 'is a good thing for him. Doing you a favour, I mean.'

Christopher made a face, a sort of six-of-one-half-a-dozen-of-the-other type of face. A certain amount of male jostling going on in that face, Ellie thought, some calculation in that *expression*.

'OK.'

'So here we are,' Ellie said. 'And just so we're clear on something else, this isn't a set-up, it's not a *date*, yeah?'

That smile again. 'OK.'

'So I suppose you must be wondering how it is I can help you.'

'I'm wondering why I'm here. Not quite the same thing.'

Ellie nodded. 'Fact is,' she said, 'I can't really help you.'

'OK.'

'That is unless you're interested in cleaning dirty money from a political- and construction-based kickback scheme in Brazil?'

Christopher nodded slowly. He raised a finger. 'Do you think we could have another two glasses of the same thing?' he asked the waiter. He looked at Ellie. 'Assume that's OK?'

'Might as well make it a bottle,' she said.

'Sir?' The waiter looked at him.

'Yeah, bottle, thanks.'

Christopher said, 'I *am* interested, yes, but not in cleaning any money, of course. However, I am *interested* in who is or who might be.'

'I'm guessing this is unlikely to be an altruistic interest?'

'It's not. In our game, it's always useful to have something on the competition.'

Ellie nodded.

'So why don't you tell me what you know.'

'OK,' Ellie said.

The waiter brought the bottle. Christopher waved away the offer of a sniff and a taste. 'You can pour,' he said.

It turned out Ellie didn't know very much, after all.

'Look, I'll level with you,' she said. 'I want to know how it is dirty Brazilian money can be dealt with in London. I don't understand how it works, how it's possible. You tell me that – i.e. if it *is* possible – and I'll give you the name of a hedge fund I know for a fact is doing it.'

'Financialisation.'

'You what?'

'Financialisation, it's a term, relatively new. A cultural thing.'

'Cultural?'

Christopher leaned forward. He was purring. 'It's a term that means that finance has become an end in itself,' he said. 'The generation of finance, of more wealth, is what companies are now interested in. Services are no longer important. A company's raison d'être is the generation of wealth, not to provide decent services.'

'OK.'

'I'll give you an example. Let's say you buy something, like a train ticket from a third-party seller. You'll pay a booking fee, right? Something like a quid fifty. Now, you'd think that that charge is a cost in order for this third-party seller to exist as a company to provide a service, wouldn't you?'

'That would make sense, yes.'

'You ever heard that phrase follow the money?'

Ellie laughed. 'I certainly have.'

'Well that little booking fee doesn't simply feed back into the company. Instead it goes on a tortuous journey. It flows up and through a whole host of companies each one owned by the next. It'll take a little detour through somewhere like Jersey, a tax haven, perhaps, off to Luxembourg, then the US, to an investment firm, through all the shareholders, then, eventually more than likely it'll end up in the Cayman Islands, in some anonymous corporate entity, feeding everyone along the way. It's a sort of invisible superstructure, to use a phrase I've read somewhere.'

'So what does that mean for the original company?'

Christopher smiled. 'It means, ultimately, that this company might well be providing a useful and beneficial service, a profitable service, even, but that's not the point, as money is being siphoned off upwards and offshore at every stop on this journey. This is the priority. The services are absolutely *not* a priority.'

'And this is legal.'

Christopher grinned. 'Legal is a funny word.'

'So no?'

'There are various definitions.'

'Bloody hell. And this is sanctioned by the government then?'

'They're the worst of the lot.'

'I suppose that's not a huge surprise,' Ellie said. 'You said it's cultural.'

'Yes, I did. What I mean is that this is how we do business, government included.'

'Example?'

'There's something called the private finance initiative, PFI, OK?'

Ellie nodded.

'In practice, and in simple terms, this means when the government wants to build schools or housing or hospitals or anything else like that, instead of doing so directly, they borrow the money in the City to finance the projects, the construction.'

'And this money follows similar journeys?'

'More or less, yes.'

'And the government pays them back when?'

Christopher sipped at his wine. 'A long, long time later, with interest and incentives.'

'Like?'

'I don't know, tax breaks, things like that.'

'So the taxpayer gets fucked?'

'The taxpayer always gets fucked.'

'Jesus.'

'Quite right.'

They sat in silence for a moment. Ellie let this marinate. 'And what happens to all this new wealth then? Where does it *go*?'

'It lines pockets all over the world. Misallocation costs, it's called. It's worth hundreds of billions of pounds. Privately run, taxpayer-funded public services.'

'That's outrageous.'

'The City is run by cunts.'

'And you work in it.'

'I am, also, something of a cunt.'

Ellie smiled, despite herself. 'So, what's all this got to do with the dirty Brazilian cash I'm talking about?'

Christopher grinned. He was enjoying himself. 'It comes into the system,' he began, 'in an investment, or a trade, and then it goes on a similar journey. The point is, the structure is in place so it is very possible for exactly this: an injection of dodgy money will disappear up and through the chain and end up in an offshore account, or more likely many offshore accounts or offshore corporate entities. The provenance of the investment or trade is no longer especially of interest to anyone. They call it a competitive economy. Means London is in the pink. But as corporation tax is lowered to entice more foreign business, the taxpayer loses out on services, key services. They reckon it's something like a sixteen billion deficit now.'

Christopher sat back. 'I mean that's roughly how it works.'

Ellie chewed this over. 'You know what,' she said, 'it's not so different from Brazil. In fact, in my mind, it's almost exactly the same.'

Christopher raised his eyebrows. 'OK,' he said.

Ellie continued. 'Basically the government hands out construction contracts with kickbacks included, yeah? So it's a bit more blatant than borrowing from the City and everything you've just described, and different people are getting rich off it, different *types*, but it's the same overall effect.'

'The taxpayer's fucked.'

'Exactly.'

'Well we're just as bad as them, I suppose,' Christopher said. 'Now you better give me the name of this fund.'

Ellie opened her purse. She pushed a business card across the table. On it:

Capital SP

'Thanks.' Christopher fingered the card. 'And you'll obviously see to it I'm not quoted in the article I assume you're writing? Not that I've really told you anything, of course.'

'I never reveal my sources.'

'Jolly good,' Christopher said.

Some hours later, and Ellie was getting drunk.

On reflection, Ellie was *drunk*.

She and Lizzie were sitting in The Duke, drinking. Ellie had been at it on and off all afternoon, and she'd forgotten about the English and their brutal pace, pounding pints and large glasses, rounds collected before the last is actually finished, the joylessness of those final gulps to make room for the next –

Fun, though, she had to concede.

'So wait, hang about,' Lizzie was saying, 'you've been in mortal danger, *just the once*. Is that what you're saying? Just the bloody once?'

'You know how it is, querida. Brazil's the Wild West.'

'Not funny.'

'No, I mean, there's a lawlessness, totally. I do what I want. I'm an outlaw.'

'*Not* funny.'

Ellie smiled. She took Lizzie's hand. 'It's perfectly safe, sweetheart. But why let, you know, what's the phrase? Why let the truth get in the way of a good story. Know what I mean?'

Lizzie shook her head, smiling. 'You've really developed your London accent out there, haven't you?'

'Totally. I had to. No one's interested in anyone from *Bournemouth*.' She looked around the pub. 'Nice place this. Proper boozer.' She laughed.

'You're drunk.'

'It's the pace,' she said. 'Brutal.'

'Have you eaten *anything* today?'

'Lunch. Those chips.' She pointed at the remains of a bowl of chips and sweet chilli sauce, mayonnaise. 'Proper boozer, bringing over free chips like that. Old-school.'

Lizzie laughed. 'Yeah, well, keeps you drinking, doesn't it?'

'And stops you eating.'

The pub was busy but not rammed. This was rare in central London, so Lizzie told her. And it *was* a cracking boozer. Art deco façade, quiet little dark booths in the back, loads of wood everywhere, dark wood, *proper* wood, not too many cunts, braying –

Ellie liked it very much indeed. She took a hefty swig from her large glass of wine. She examined the glass. She smiled, shook her head.

'Christ, that barely touched the sides,' she said.

'So what about this posh bloke you met today then?' Lizzie asked.

'Friend of a friend of a friend, blah blah blah. Might help with a story, a hunch, anyway. Let's see.'

'Did it work?'

Ellie's eyes twinkled. 'Did it fuck.'

'Your expression, darling, seems to suggest otherwise.'

'Let's just say I know who to talk to when I get back to São Paulo.'

Lizzie's eyes narrowed. 'Lucky them.'

'I'll drink to that.'

They continued to make slow progress on their large glasses.

'What about your mum?'

'What about her?'

'When are you going to see her?'

Ellie thought for a moment. 'Tomorrow,' she said. And then, more firmly: 'Yes, tomorrow. I'll go tomorrow.'

São Paulo, the morning after the morning after –

Or should that simply be the morning after? Fine line, Antonio thought, when all lines are blurred. And snorted. His stomach twisted in some disgust.

He was, he would admit, thrilled that he had managed to put some distance between himself and the shenanigans of Monday evening. Rafael, he had decided, was to be avoided at all costs that early in the week. In a few hours' time he would be at Roberta's flat, where she would cook him dinner. He missed her, simply. He knew he couldn't see her the morning after – the *same* day, effectively – when his spirits were crashing and his comedown toxic and all he really wanted was a hug and a wank. Nope, that would not have been sensible; she did not deserve that.

'Go out as much as you like, porra,' she once told him, 'just steer clear of me until it's well out of your system.'

He wasn't sure if she was being *completely* serious. But, fair play, and the message had got through. The real message:

Grow the fuck up.

He wasn't sure it was simply a question of *growing up* exactly. He'd heard older colleagues banging on about this. How they were as game as they had been when they were twenty, just realised that with age, it was simply not possible to sustain it. Their only responsibilities, they seemed to be saying, were to their bodies; the only thing they were respecting was the extra recovery time they had to factor in to a bender.

Or it might have just been mouth: all talk. You couldn't tell with that mob. Bluster was all part of the game, after all. The Hedge Fund shuffle.

Perhaps, then, the message was about *change*, actual change, which might not be the same thing as growing up. And part of the message, implicit in Roberta's words and in her tone, in her expectations, was this: *deserve me.*

Fair play, it was. And he did want to deserve her.

The message didn't matter if he knew what he wanted, of course.

Work was easy and the hours passed quietly, without incident. He ate a simple lunch of rice and beans and salad, prepared by his maid, alone in the sunshine. He let the sun warm his cheeks, and, as he sat on a bench in the courtyard at the centre of the office complex, he looked up into the blue sky, closed his eyes and smiled.

The sun was still hot when he left the office, avoiding the attentions of anyone who might try and entice him for a quick drink, and he decided to walk a little before setting off to Roberta's apartment in Paraíso. Walking was something they had in common, something they both liked to do, which was rare in São Paulo.

'Aren't we European?' Roberta would say. 'Look at us, using the sidewalk, saving the environment, browsing. What is it they call that?'

In English, Antonio replied. 'Browsing? Oh, window-shopping, ne?'

'Window-shopping. I love that. What are you up to? Me? Oh, I'm window-shopping. I'm shopping for windows. Just a little window-shopping.'

There were a number of reasons not to walk in São Paulo, but Antonio was unconvinced by most of them. The principal reason – that it was dangerous – was simply not an issue, considering where he spent most of his time. In fact, you were far more likely to be threatened sitting in your car in traffic in the nicer parts of the city than you were to have a problem on foot. In Rio, OK, but in São Paulo, street mugging wasn't that common. The villains were far more inventive than that.

Another reason his friends always pulled was the lack of pavement, of *sidewalk*. This was more nonsense, Antonio told them. That, he said, time and again, was about distance, not convenience. No fucker's going to walk along the Marginal; if you need to take the Marginal, it is too fucking far to walk. São Paulo, despite appearances, despite its vastness, its concrete desert, was a city of neighbourhoods like any other; the key to happiness within it, Antonio reckoned, was making sure you spent most of your time in one or two closely linked neighbourhoods.

And now Antonio walked through one of the very nicest, Jardim Paulistano, close by in fact to where he went to school.

Born and bred São Paulo, Antonio was. Proper Paulistano. Proper in that it was his birthright to claim this, and he did so, and proper as a true Paulistano knew his place in the city, respected it, and respected the rules and traditions that governed that place, that position in the city, that *role*. He knew what he was about. The city did that for you rather well –

São Paulo defined you.

The city's motto:

I lead I will not be led.

As the song goes: *quem e seu dono? Ninguem, São Paulo.*

Who is your owner? No one, São Paulo:

No one's the boss of you.

Pretty easy to find a bit of purpose, a bit of direction, when you're basically told who you are and what you should be doing with your life.

Antonio walked through the pockets of residential streets between Faria Lima and Avenida Brasil, a rectangular maze of low-rise, expansive housing, curving, narrow roads, dead ends, private lanes and cute cul-de-sacs, genteel-looking shops and restaurants, expensive cars and private security booths on every corner.

Women exercised. Women dressed up. Women nattered. Faces were *wealthy*. There was a lot of money in the faces around here, he thought, remembering chucking-out time at school, with all those expensive faces nattering. They'd ploughed a lot of money into their brows this lot, their unfurrowed brows.

On Gabriel Monteiro da Silva the houses were slightly set back from the road. There were trees. They were placed, these trees, strategically. The road led *somewhere*. It had that possibility, Gabriel Monteiro da Silva. The schools were *loaded*.

Despite the traffic, it always felt an unhurried and civilised place –

Cars queued. Women tottered. Nannies shepherded. Kids ambled. Kids chattered. Teenagers smoked. Teenagers gabbed. Teenagers flirted.

These teenagers sat outside Primo Basilico, a pizza restaurant that doubled up in the afternoons as a clubhouse for rich kids –

Been there, Antonio thought.

He certainly had been there. The sixth form at the British school would all pile down after lessons, sit and drink coffee, the occasional beer, and smoke. They loved to smoke, back then. One after another, passing them round and round, and lighting them up one after another: chain smoking was exactly right.

Most of Antonio's classmates had been going there since they were three years old, their cousins and siblings paving the way. Before that uncles and sometimes even parents.

Jobs for the boys –

They were families of the elite. This meant politicians' children – including the family of one infamous former mayor of São Paulo after whom the phrase *roba mais faz*, steals but get things done, was coined. Acceptable to be a crook if the rubbish is being collected on time and the buses are running. It meant the children of media figures, of lawyers, of the city's rule-makers: the head of the Polícia Civil had sent his two sons there. It meant the children of famous people, most notably, of course, Sir Michael Jagger.

It meant a sort of mafia.

But it didn't only mean this.

Antonio arrived at the school aged fourteen on a scholarship. This was not well known. His parents were white collar, middle class, absolutely: his mother worked as an administrator in a private university; his father was a minor bureaucrat in the lower echelons of city hall.

'I'm a cog in the labyrinthine system of legal admin,' he'd say. 'It's overwhelming to all but those who can afford to use a despachante. I'm needed. I'm performing a vital service.'

That was how he'd speak, like he was a kind of paperwork Batman.

Antonio wasn't convinced. Whatever good his father was doing still left him in shabby suits and driving – driving himself – around in a Volkswagen estate.

His parents worked hard, and he knew it, but their earnestness was suffocating. Antonio was an only child and he bore the slow decline of expectations that his family experienced; when he was twelve years old, he remembered waking up and realising that *this is it*, this is *really* it.

Not long after this, he'd got up in the night and overhead his parents talking in the living room of their tasteful, modest apartment in Pinheiros. An apartment that was fifteen minutes' walk from Gabriel Monteiro da Silva, from where Antonio was now.

'But don't you see,' his mother was saying, 'he can sense it, he can *feel* this stasis, this entropy.'

'Where did you learn words like that?' his father said.

His mother ignored him. 'This is not about you and me, it's not about where *we* are, entendeu? What he can sense, what he can feel is that we know we can't offer him any more than we already have. Like, there is nothing else. We need him to know there can be.'

'And sending him to a posh school run by exactly the sort of people I work against is some sort of answer, porra?'

'Horizons. It'll broaden his horizons. He'll... meet people, sabe?'

'People that can offer more than us, ne?'

Antonio knew, despite the silence, the gesture his mother made at this moment:

I'm not discussing it. I know this is exactly what we always promised we wouldn't do.

'And how is this supposed to happen, querida?' his father said. 'We're supposed to just, what, turn up there with him? Demand they let him in?'

'I've spoken to a few people at the university.'

'Same people that taught you about entropy, eh, menina?'

'Actually, you know what? Yeah, porra. People I talk to, sabe?'

'Uh-huh.'

'There's a way. A scholarship. And we can do it without Tônico even knowing, so if it doesn't work out –'

'How?'

'Transcripts from the last couple of years at school. And we plead a case. We tell them why it's important to us and what help we'd need.'

'Important to us?'

'Sim.'

'Help.'

'Porra, you know exactly what it all means.'

'Uh-huh. And I suppose we have to prove why we need this help while we're grovelling about what this means to us?'

Antonio knew the answer to that, even at twelve years old.

Main thing was though –

He was excited. He'd get in. He was as smart as a tack; it'd be a cakewalk. He'd heard that most of the posh lot were thick as fuck. Inflated opinions of themselves, so he'd heard, so he'd seen in his brief experience with them at the odd birthday party.

They *oozed* entitlement.

It was this: they couldn't actually believe that someone worse off than them – socially, financially, opportunity-wise – could possibly be better than them in any way. They couldn't fathom it. It was an alien concept.

Antonio knew this, and yet, even at twelve, he was excited.

Roberta was good on it all. 'You know what we live in? What age?' she said to him once on one of their early walks through the city. 'The age of entitlement.'

'The age of enlightenment?'

'You heard.' She smiled. 'The age of instant enlightenment, perhaps.'

He laughed. 'Oh, very good.'

'I'm serious. All this social media malarkey, all this rampant consumerism, everyone lives in their heads these days. No one gives a monkey's about anyone else, sabe?'

He grinned. 'Oh yeah?'

'Porra, tou falando sério!'

Antonio knew she was being serious.

Roberta continued. 'Everyone's like head down, block out every single sensation other than what they're feeding into their gobs and feeding into their brains off their phones, entendeu?'

'Uh-huh.'

'It's a classless phenomenon too, you know. Look at the queues at the coffee stands at the bus stops, certo? It's the same thing as in fucking Starbucks. Head cowed over phone, thumb flicking, other hand shovelling in coffee and pão de queijo.'

'That's how you distinguish class, querida? Starbucks?'

Roberta made a face. 'Mate, you know it's about the price, not the quality.'

'The great sociologist.'

'No, but think about it: the basic goal of globalisation is that everything is the same, everywhere. So, it follows: everyone, sabe?'

'So the mobile phone and readily available coffee is what's dissolving class boundaries, then?' He laughed. 'Try telling that to all your friends on the march on Sunday.'

Roberta grinned. She took his arm. 'I guess I just mean that doing something like this – you know, *walking* – is pretty valuable to me.' She kissed him. 'It means a lot. It's not something many people appreciate. You know?'

He did know.

He decided to wander up to the school, have a little look, at least from a distance.

He stopped just past the Pão de Açúcar supermarket where the road cut Gabriel in two. The school was on the other side of the road; he could see its great green doors, its security measures softened by the neutral colour. Where he stood was a small, old-school padaria. They'd occasionally eat lunch there in the sixth form. Cheap burgers. Mixto quente. Bottled beer. Labourers and manual workers and dustmen sat at the counter. Dirty and sweaty, lined faces, they drank shots. Antonio never understood why no one complained about him and his friends being there. The labourers and manual workers and dustmen seemed unbothered by the flash, lairy rich boys wearing loafers and no socks. This always surprised Antonio; he assumed a default antagonism. His mates didn't care, either. There was some truth, he thought now, in the idea that the rich and poor get on fine; it's the middle classes that have all the hang-ups.

He went in.

He ordered a Serra Malte beer – a middle-class signifier, Roberta joked on their second date – and sat outside at a table that had a view of the school. It was a little after five o'clock, so there weren't many kids or parents milling about. He could hear cheers, chanting; the gymnasium stretched out almost to the road. Basketball. Or volleyball. He didn't especially care for either, gave up sport when he could. School sport. He still played tennis at Clube Harmonia, the most exclusive and pleasant of all the extremely expensive São Paulo sporting establishments. His parents could never afford the fees, but one of his closest school pal's granddad's membership number was 002, which meant some serious privilege. They swung it for him, on the house.

Cheers.

His beer arrived and he poured a dose into the tiny glass, made sure the bottle was secure in its little – fuck, what's the word? He chuckled. Roberta called it a camisinha, a little condom. Well, it was a form of protection, keeping it cold.

The beer was cold and delicious.

Serra Malte was, unmistakeably, a quality lager. Your thinking man's lager. A notch up from Original, which was the default choice of lager for your São Paulo thinking man, but Serra Malte had the edge: it was harder to find; it was *rarer*.

He smiled to himself as he ran through this little routine. This was what he and his friends would do, routines. He smiled as he thought of them, of evenings and lunchtimes passed in this way, riffing.

They were funny, his friends.

Friends. You're stuck with them, really. That old Paulistano shrug, apologetic raise of the eyebrows and the simple admission:

What are you going to do? He's a mate.

Take Rafael, he thought. They went *waaay* back. Rafael was a few years above in school, but his cousin was a mate of Antonio's, so once they started going out, started drinking, they all mobbed up and those few years stopped mattering. And they became friends, and that meant you had your mate's interests at heart: you had their back. It was childish, perhaps, but it was true. His father told him, when he was around seventeen, that women could never really *be* friends, there was always something getting in the way. And by that, Antonio supposed, he meant men, competing for men, that there was always that danger, that your friend might nick your man, so women could never really be friends, and, of course, lads would never do that to each other was the implication.

'Que isso?' Roberta said, when he told her. 'That is a quite disgusting view of the world.'

'I know, that's why I told you.'

'I mean, que porra essa?' What the fuck?

'I did say I realised that it was, that it's curious to me that he could even believe it. That's why I told you.'

'The man's a monster.'

'Look –'

'I mean. It's not. I can't. I – entendeu?'

He did understand.

He also knew that it was total nonsense. He poured himself more beer. God, it wasn't half crisp, this thinking man's lager.

The traffic on Gabriel thickened. The heat seemed to balloon above the road. Clouds were gathering. Angry-looking clouds mobbed up, gathered above. Cars were itchy. Cars revved and nudged. There was impatience in the air. You did not want to get stuck on the Marginal in a storm. And these cars looked Marginal-bound. Their disposition was prickly. Their body language was entirely unwelcoming.

Antonio reckoned he didn't have long before the storm. It was

PLAYBOY

that time of year. Clockwork. He could shelter the twenty minutes or so in the bar, then walk up to Roberta's in the fresh air, in the new air, in the gift of cleared air.

He had a little time yet. He drained his glass and ordered another bottle of lager. He knew he'd be a touch buzzed after his second lager, but he was relaxed and it was part of a bigger buzz, the excitement, the anticipation, of the evening ahead with Roberta.

She was funny about his friends. She liked them, he thought, some of them, but she also thought they were pretty trivial. She tended to value those that brought something, who added something to society, who did something *worthwhile*. Of course, this was based entirely on her own definition of what that was. Antonio and his school friends had, almost to a man, left school and attended an expensive, private and not especially well-respected academic institution: TAAP. This institution was, in Roberta's words, a sort of finishing school for rich kids who would go on to work in their family's companies, or in finance, or not at all.

'I mean,' she'd said more than once, 'what is the point of these people? It's a bubble they live in, a fucking echo chamber, entendeu?'

Antonio would shrug. He'd say that there is nothing wrong with living within certain parameters, certain boundaries. 'It only looks narrow if you ignore the fact of their families, their desires to be a part of a very specific, and loving, community.'

He was keenly aware of the uncharacteristic earnestness of this statement. And it was deliberate. It didn't work though.

'Ah, vai, meu,' she said. 'You're using family to justify their weekends at the club drinking beer, sabe? The fact that their parents and nephews and uncles are all there too does not make it some noble exercise, entendeu?'

In some ways, it was difficult to argue with. Well, perhaps it was difficult to argue with *her*. There was certainly no chance of any softening in her position. This was frustrating. Antonio didn't think she'd ever really understood how important these friends were to him. He was a scholarship boy; he was both insider and outsider.

When his mother and father had let him down, in his eyes, it was his friends who were there: they were the ones providing him with a life and with opportunities to live it. For him, there was never any question that he would follow them to the same university and the same kind of job. If nothing else, money, and having some of it for a change, was extremely welcome. He had always relied on the generosity of his friends' parents for invitations to restaurants, private clubs, holidays – he had got used to a particular lifestyle, and working for a hedge fund was a conscious decision made to allow him to pursue it.

His second lager was, it felt, even colder, even crisper than his first. He sank back into the plastic chair and watched the school gates, though no one came in or out. For a moment, the clouds broke and the sun beat down. The sun throbbed. The sun ached. It didn't last. The clouds closed up shop. The clouds darkened.

Antonio poured himself another glass and prepared to find a table inside.

The lager, for a second, seemed to rear up in him, together with a welling of resentment –

She needed to be a little more open, a little more understanding, ta ligado? I mean, apart from anything else, the brazen hypocrisy of attacking their wealth, he thought: textbook champagne lefty, textbook rich hippie sort. Very nice, it is, to study for a worthy PhD at USP, intern at an NGO, and live alone in a cushy gaff in town, ne? Very *activist*, know what I mean? Very fucking Robin Hood.

He laughed at himself. She'd like the Robin Hood bit.

The lager, the cold, crisp, middle-class lager that he drank down, settled him once again and he moved inside as the first spots of rain arrived. On Gabriel, cars sighed. Cars settled in. They would not be moving when the rain really hit. Around the corner from the school, these flash floods could leave the cars floating. After one such storm, he and his friend Fabio went to collect Fabio's car. It was not where Fabio had left it. They found it, a few minutes later, on the other side of the square, nestled perfectly in a fairly tight parking spot.

The thing is, he thought, there was no contradiction, no problem in working his job and sharing the same interests as Roberta *outside* of this job.

And he thought that nas fim das contas, at the end of the day, she agreed.

There were, she said, two ways to address their backgrounds –

Do what she did; do what he did.

That was exactly what they were doing; what they did was absolutely fine.

He found a corner table. He studied the bar. It had changed very little: the same yellowing walls, the same red plastic tables, the same napkin dispensers on these tables, the same tiny TV up in the corner, the same grumpy owner behind the counter, surrounded by the glass of the cigarette display. The clientele was basically the same. The same wearied but good-humoured men stoically working their way through their drinks, working on plates of cheap meat and cheap cheese, working on bowls of tart, bitter olives. There were, Antonio realised, three teachers from the school drinking lager and eating sandwiches and talking loudly in English about the weather. He turned slightly away from them. He laughed. Today, he reflected, an English person talking about the weather was totally reasonable.

The rain battered the street outside, gave the street a real hammering. It came down in missiles. The street was being beaten into submission by this rain, this São Paulo rain. The street, Antonio saw, was giving up. The water level, in only five minutes, had risen above the pavement. Rubbish was collecting in pockets, like branches snagged in the eddies and rapids of a river. Soon, the mud and the dirt, the spent cans of drink, the empty packets of crisps, the garbage, would all flow down the road. On this street, that was fine; it cleared quickly. This was not the case elsewhere. Elsewhere there would be mudslides and lost cars; cars may, in extreme cases, float off and into the river from the Marginal –

'Oi, cara, oi, playboy – '

A ratty little fucker was in front of Antonio's table, his hand out –

'Posso falar alguma coisa? Pode?'

Can I say something? he was saying. Can I talk to you?

Antonio shook his head. Antonio raised a palm. 'Não tem cara, desculpe, viu?'

Antonio wagged his finger. I've nothing, sorry, he was saying, shaking his head and wagging his finger, grimacing as if he were really keen to help, but sorry, mate, I've got nothing –

The lad was not, however, perturbed. He was scrawny, weaselly, with bad hair and few teeth. His clothes shone. He glistened. His wet head dripped.

'No, you don't understand,' he was saying now, 'Rafael, ne? No, Rafael?'

'Do I know Rafael?' Antonio's face creased in confusion and annoyance. 'Que isso, cara?' What are you going on about?

The clientele began to notice. The owner began to notice. There were one or two whistles. One or two shouts of *vai embora, seu caralho*, get out, you little fuck, go and ply your rent-boy trade elsewhere, bicho, that lad's too good-looking for you, son, little bitch looks like the devil sucking on a mango, and then laughter –

The guy was panicking now. 'Rafael, ne? Here. Take this.'

Antonio shrugged. 'Meu, me deixe em paz, eh, cara?'

Come on, mate, leave it out.

'Here,' the guy placed a piece of paper on the table. 'Rafael,' he said again. 'For you. Take it.'

'Que isso? Você ta viagando, cara.' You're having a laugh, mate.

'Pra você,' he said. It's for you. He made a face.

What the fuck is this? Antonio thought. 'Que porra essa?' he said.

The guy nodded. He looked down at the paper. Nodded again. He scuttled away, into the rain, to bar-wide whistles and jeers, some applause.

Antonio raised his eyebrows, shook his head: what the fuck was that all about?

He smiled at the bar. He swooned. He played it for laughs. He gave a mock bow. The gallery laughed, whistled. He feigned camp delight. Who me? Why, thank you. He fluttered eyelids. The bar roared. The English table faked interest.

In a moment, everyone was back to their drinks.

Antonio looked at the piece of paper, folded, with **Rafael** written across it.

He unfolded it. There was a time: **4pm**.

There was a place: **South side of the park, Praça Alexandre de Gusmão**.

There was a date: **20 March**.

What the fuck *is* this? Antonio mulled it over. The lads at the bar were joking, weren't they, about the rent-boy business? If that rodent was trade, God help us all, Antonio thought. But the park in Praça Alexandre de Gusmão was a hotspot for cottaging and discreet fuck jobs: the place was crawling with underage strange offering services in the shrubbery after dark. So he'd been told.

But Rafael? It must be something else. The lad was as hetero as a bull. Though, you know, could be bluster, overcompensation. Nah, it couldn't be. I mean, I'm very much a whatever-floats-your-boat kind of a fella, Antonio thought, but this would be very surprising indeed.

It had to be something else. Muito odd this, he thought.

He finished his beer. He pulled his phone to check the time. It had been on silent. He had two missed calls: Rafael. And two text messages: Rafael.

Muito odd.

The text messages:

Where the fuck did you get to? I've spoken to Matheus and arranged for us both to take a few days off next week. Holiday, certo? You know what I mean.

Keep to yourself – sério. Abraço

Muito odd, all this. Coincidence? Of course, but still –

He needed a pow-wow with old Rafael. He'd get in early doors and have a word. Deliver this love letter, perhaps.

He smiled. Whatever. It was time to go.

The rain had eased. The roads shone. The roads *glistened*. The smell hung –

Petrichor. Roberta had taught him that word. Of course she had –

Roberta.

He *grinned*.

The train from London Waterloo to Bournemouth had not changed. Neither had the fact that Ellie generally sat on it hungover.

She was humming. Really hum-*dinging*, she was. She was necking water and sipping coffee and picking at a particularly unpleasant ham and egg brioche drenched in a sort of Benedict sauce that was exactly the wrong temperature and was kind of congealing, but the egg was doing something right, at least, she thought.

She sat in First Class. Style Queen.

She was disappointed, however, that South West trains no longer offered any complimentary food and drink. She was quite ready to get stuck into a gin and tonic by the time they reached Southampton Parkway. The British Airways snacking tray this was not. She made do with a dehydrated coffee buzz, rode it hard; it put her in mind of teenage experiments with dodgy bags of speed, where you had to will yourself into a wired state. This was better, but what with the obscene pricing of branded coffee these days, not a great deal cheaper.

Southampton Water was always a shock. The train drifted through the industrial outskirts of the city before suddenly finding itself crossing a fairly significant drop of estuary, as if by accident. If you slumped low enough in your seat it was impossible to see anything *but* water, and there was an odd sense, as the train slowed down, that the tracks had simply run out, that the train had ploughed on into the water under its own momentum and would, at any moment, sink.

Ellie's phone rang.

'Hi, Mum.'

'Where are you, darling?'

'Just about to come into the New Forest.'

'OK, perfect. I'll pick you up as planned, OK?'

Ellie shook her head, gave a rueful smile. 'That's the plan.'

'Thank you, darling,' her mum said, pointedly, but not without humour.

'Thank *you*, Mum.'

Ellie hung up. She looked out at the New Forest. She relaxed, as she always had. It was a soothing experience. There was a wildness to the place, but also a calm, an order. The heather, the bracken, the yellow-green hue stretched out, becoming, in parts, a marshy, boggy playground for the ponies that wandered wild. She'd never seen one actually run, she thought. The way they seemed to gather, move in groups of four and five, picking their way through clusters of trees, feeding on patches of grass: there was something reassuring about it. She felt, as she often did at this point in the journey, while watching them interact, as if she were narrating an animated children's film with talking ponies. It was a pretty good idea.

The coffee buzz softened; the gentle hum of the train's air conditioning eased, in tune with the environment. She spotted two groups of walkers, flashes of red and yellow waterproof clothing and expensive North Face hiking boots; bare legs and backpacks, maps and aluminium walking sticks: it could be her mum.

It was good to come home. It had been four years, just under. She hadn't seen her mum in four years. This was not as remarkable as it perhaps should have been. Time passed. And while it passed in the same way that it always had, being abroad somehow distorted it: you're learning, you're growing at a different rate when you're living abroad. The simplest admin task requires skills and knowledge you don't even know you have until you try to undertake it. Time speeds by; your ageing feels accelerated.

And, of course, what with technology and blah blah blah, it no longer felt like you were cut off; her relationship with her mother had rarely been better over these last few years, she thought now, smiling.

As the train approached Bournemouth, she remembered the last time that she had seen her mum, sitting on the rocks in Poole harbour, where the wooden groynes used to be, watching two pink, naked toddlers splashing about below them, their mother reading hungrily, the kids laughing and squealing. Here was another mother and her daughter, the same duty of care, the same desire, the same love –

'You can come back any time you want. I'll always be –'

'Mum, *please*.'

Ellie remembered her mother turning to her and cradling her head in her hands. 'I'll miss you is all.'

'You don't have to do this, Mum.'

'I'll never stop being your mum, Ellie.'

Ellie remembered now her steadfastness, her need for independence.

'I'm doing this on my own, Mum.'

She remembered how her mum smiled and wrapped her arms around her. She remembered how she had squirmed a little, then had let her. She remembered the children eating ice-cream cones on the sand, smearing it over their faces and bodies. She remembered their mother hopping from one to the other with a tissue that was quickly disintegrating, the paperback abandoned.

And now, as she stepped off the train, she remembered the overwhelming feeling of family, of having a mother, of being loved and looked after by *your* mother, of knowing that however awful you can be, she will love you, that however irritating she can be, you will know why, the feeling of safety, of comfort, this overwhelming feeling of *home* –

And at the end of the platform she was waiting for Ellie, her purse clutched to her, her hair recently cut, her make up fresh and understated, her body tense with anticipation, yet aiming, clearly, for some sort of nonchalance, for some sense of distance, and Ellie too, but it dissolved immediately, it melted, it dripped out of them, and they held each other and sobbed.

And that's when Ellie realised –

She'd go back to São Paulo as planned, she'd finish this story on the Lava Jato, she'd attend the march on Sunday, she'd tie things up, complete everything she'd worked so hard for, everything she had *risked* –

Then she'd come home.
Home, where she belonged.
She would come home –
In a few days, she'd have done everything she'd set out to do.
Home.

On the night before Ellie was due to fly back, she looked over the notes she'd made, the transcripts of interviews she'd conducted, both in São Paulo and over the last two days with Paulistanos in London, the quotes about the city she'd gathered. She was preparing a longer piece, a piece based on real people, on real Paulistanos, and she felt that when she returned to England, when she returned home, she'd get the distance she needed to really write about the city. *Paulistano.* It was a punchy title.

Ellie began to see how best to understand the city. It's about voices, words and living as a Brazilian – experiencing *saudades, alegría, jeitinho.*

One thing that struck her about the interviews: preoccupations change, but despite years passing between them, they all reference exactly the same problems that Brazil faced now, in 2016, problems of division, problems that many of her friends felt would only get worse as the Lava Jato got deeper; there was a belief that this investigation, this Lava Jato would bring down core democratic parties, figures, structures –

And the next logical step was a populist, neo-dictatorship.

Was this possible? Ellie didn't know, but many of these quotes spoke for themselves.

I've been involved with USP for many years, as a law student in the 1990s to doing research at post-doctoral level and teaching film studies at the Film, Radio and Television Department since 2008. Both the city of São Paulo and USP have been gradually changing in the past two decades, and it would be fair to say that the city is now much kinder to its students and recent graduates than it was twenty years ago. I feel a much greater, tangible enthusiasm in the younger generation for all things Brazilian, from politics to culture and arts. USP has contributed to this renewed enthusiasm by continuing to develop indigenous and original research. We're a more international institution, each year attracting more students and visiting researchers from abroad and setting up international cooperation agreements all over the world. And as with other public universities in Brazil it does not charge tuition fees, remaining at least in principle true to its modern democratic origins in the 1930s, when it played a significant role in turning São Paulo into Brazil's most important city.

This was Ciça, a university professor of nearly forty. They had spoken four years before. Four years! Look at the optimism! She really should contact her again, Ellie thought.

Finance was, of course, never far from anyone's agenda.

That fucking credit card system! Man, that is the worst thing that exists in Brazil, and in São Paulo it's worse than anywhere else because of this material culture. It's a way of devaluing money. No one knows the true value anymore, what they should get in their lives for what they have. They say that you can stagger payment over twelve months without paying interest, but of course the interest is already included. Of course it fucking is! Look at the size of the discount you get when you pay in cash. Look: you buy a pair of shoes and divide payment over a year, but by the time you actually own the shoes, you need another pair! And then you do the same thing again. For a nation with so many uneducated people, this financial system is not an opportunity. It's irresponsible. They're lying to us.

She looked at her own notes, from 2013:

Today São Paulo is one of the most expensive cities in the world. In 2025 it will be the sixth richest city on the planet. It is currently home to twenty-one dollar billionaires, ranking it in sixth place behind Moscow, New York, London, Hong Kong and Istanbul. Seven of these billionaires became so only in 2011. A Big Mac in São Paulo is the fourth most expensive in the world. The most profitable Louis Vuitton store in the world is in São Paulo. The GDP of São Paulo in 2011 was larger than the combined GDPs of Argentina, Chile, Uruguay, Bolivia and Paraguay. São Paulo has the highest Ferrari sales in the world. It is little wonder then that Paulistanos are obsessed with status and wealth. How did this happen and why?

Two colleagues, Marcos and Tulio, business partners in London in a Brazilian restaurant in Hackney Ellie had visited only last night. They talked about football, of course. Look at the contradiction: unity and disunity. And look at the analogy: tragedy, family, philosophy.

In 1994 there was a big moment in my life when I watched Palmeiras against São Paulo in the semi-final of the Paulista championship. It was the day of Senna's funeral. He was a Corinthians fan, but in the moments before this huge match, the two sets of supporters of Corinthians' fiercest rivals started chanting his name. 'Senna, Senna, Senna!' It showed me how we could all come together. It was a tragedy, but it meant something to the city to express our unity, our love. That is São Paulo.

Supporting Palmeiras is a lifestyle. We're passionate, educated, there's an Italian fan base too, so it feels close to home. Point is, we've got a different philosophy to the fans of Corinthians and São Paulo. They're more interested in conflict. We're about unity, manners, family, friends. That's something you don't see in London. Not as much, anyway.

She'd spoken to Ruth, another restaurateur now based in London, but one who had worked the airlines.

*As a flight attendant you can see the difference between Paulistanos
and other Brazilians. Leaving São Paulo for another state is like
going to another country – there's less freedom, less tolerance, fewer
chances for a woman to be independent and live a life separate
from marriage and raising children. In some places, the women
would get on the plane as if they'd just left the beauty parlour! Hair
straightened, nails long and painted, heels high; for them it was an
event to travel. Paulistanos are more sophisticated. They know what
they're doing. You look at them and you can't tell if they're high-flying
executives or lowly employees. Both types are at home. I'd work the
thirty-eight minute flight from São Paulo to Rio, and the hicks from
smaller states would order everything they possibly could to get their
money's worth. Beer, Campari, coffee, vodka, wine! Paulistanos don't
do that. I prefer the Brazilians in São Paulo. I go home wearing
Converse and my mother's like, 'Uh-huh?' sucking her teeth and
raising her eyebrows. A thirty-two year old isn't supposed to wear
trainers. I'm supposed to be dressed in pearls and sensible pencil skirts.*

Ellie was fascinated to hear from those Paulistanos who had left.
There was something about their pride in the city that had altered,
yet its core remained. They were quick to judge, and quick to defend;
quick to point out frescura, if someone is being a little combative, or
unnecessarily rude, snobbish even: *frescura*, or being *fresca* or *fres-
cinha*. Like everything in São Paulo, there was a class element to it
as well: the perception being that someone who is *fresca* thinks they
are better than you.

And there was bitterness too. Adriana, an educational administrator now living in London, had worked at one of those swank,
wealthy international schools in São Paulo, one of those schools that
churned out playboys and patrocínias. Ellie had met a fair few of
them, dated one or two.

*Working at an international school was tough. The school was full
of rich kids, and, though they were charming, they represented the*

*city's prejudice. They lived in a bubble. There was a hierarchy at
the school, and the Brazilian administrative staff were firmly at the
bottom. What upset me was that I was treated as inferior, in my
own country. My own city. It was a shock, you know? I felt more
of a foreigner than ever before. And the teachers that did come
from abroad would never have the same quality of life at home
that they have in São Paulo! The free rent, high salary and all the
administrative help they need. I'd look at them and think: 'I know
where you're coming from and I know where you're going. You're the
same as me.'*

This was a starting point, perhaps, these interviews, these feelings,
these ideas.

It was all about the discourses of power, the structures of power,
and that's what Ellie wanted to interrogate.

When she returned to São Paulo, she was about to see it in all its
ugly glory – power. Who had it, who deserved it, where it went when
it disappeared.

She opened a new document, tapped out PAULISTANO at the
top and started to write:

Order and Progress, it states on the Brazilian flag.

'Love as a principle and order as the basis; progress as the goal.'

*Arguably, for modern-day São Paulo, the followers of Antonio
Comte who deposed the monarchy and secured independence for
Brazil in the nineteenth century focused on the wrong words.
Undoubtedly there is a principle of love in Brazil, and São Paulo
represents nothing if not progress as an ultimate goal; but order?*

*'I lead, I will not be led.' Economically, the city is the beating
heart of Brazil. If it stops, the country dies. More and more, this is
true in all areas of society and the rallying cry is deeply Brazilian
with its double-consciousness, its affection and passion, and sense of
longing, nostalgia, of saudades, captured in a banner I saw more
than once at recent political protests:*

'*São Paulo, I'm not proud of you, but I love you.*'

When this was all done, when she had the story she was looking for, it would be time to come home.

Sunday, 20 March. The March in March –

This weekend they were picking sides. Attendance meant you were parking your flag. Today, they were coming down firmly on the left, with Dilma, and therefore making a statement to the conservative elite that the Workers' Party was not finished.

Happy, peaceful thoughts.

Antonio was wide awake. It was six in the morning, and he'd been fairly awake, his sleep patchy at best, he now thought, since about half four. He was, it was safe to say, on edge.

Roberta slept on soundly, oblivious, next to him. *The sleep of those without secrets.* She gurgled occasionally, every now and then gave a surprisingly loud snort, or honk, not quite the full snore, not *quite*, that might have made him nudge her or adjust her position, but enough to remind him that he was keeping something from her, *what* it was, in fact, that he was keeping from her. *The sleep of those without shame.*

It had, so far, been a wonderful weekend, had been a pretty fucking wonderful few days ever since their dinner, the evening after the morning after the morning after. The evening of the day he'd been given that strange note addressed to Rafael. *The sleep of those without doubts.* The evening *before* Rafael had fronted up about what this holiday malarkey actually meant.

'Mate, just allow it,' he said. 'It's a precaution, that's all.'

'Precaution for what?'

'We might need some time away from the office, that's all, for this off-the-books job, entendeu? Here. In São Paulo. We ain't going anywhere.'

'So it's just daytime then? Working hours, like?'

Rafael grinned – mean. 'If you're worried about your bird, don't. You'll be back home in time for your tea.'

'Don't be a cunt.'

Rafael smiled – genuine. 'Settle down, I'm just fucking about, mate, relaxa, sabe?' He breathed out. 'We might not even need to take the time off. But we *might* need a day or two. It's important. And it's well worth it, dollar-wise. It's easier this way, trust, cara. Simpler to pre-empt it than fuck off from our desks without telling anyone exactly why. And if we *don't* use it, it'll be there for you down the line, you know, pending, and Bob's your mother's brother and you and Miss Prissy can fuck off shopping to Miami for a few days. Or Guatemala, you know, dig a fucking well.' He winked. 'Whatever takes her fancy, entendeu?'

Bob's your mother's brother. He said that in English. Antonio couldn't help but laugh. The lad's been watching some dodgy films, he thought.

Fact is, he was reassured; he *was* thinking about Roberta. If he had to take a day or two off in São Paulo, it was doable. It was work, after all, even if it was off the record. And while that worried him a touch, while he wasn't entirely sure what he was getting himself into, Rafael's superior, Senhor Matheus, had green-lit it, and off the record was how the system often worked.

None of this, of course, helped much with the nagging guilt he felt for not sharing any of it with Roberta. He looked at her now. *The sleep of those without suspicion.* And as the date on Rafael's misplaced invitation arrived, and the hours and minutes crept towards the time printed on this invitation, Antonio felt overwhelmed by what it all might mean, felt numb, paralysed, and this paralysis extended out towards Roberta. The knowledge that he would be difficult with her today, reticent, irritable, thanks to this paralysis, *compounded* the anxiety he felt as it brought that nagging guilt crashingly into focus.

Roberta sighed, muttered something in her sleep. He eased his arm out from under her neck. She hugged her softest pillow to her and sighed again. Antonio lay back and placed his hands beneath his head, watching as the light gathered pace outside and the wood in her tasteful, elegant, but ineffective slatted blinds brightened.

Why hadn't he said anything to Rafael about the note?

It was, essentially, the same basic reason he hadn't said anything to Roberta –

Fear.

Fear of embarrassing Rafael.

Fear of embarrassing himself.

Fear that he would discover – from either or both of them, intentionally or not – that he was doing something really quite stupid indeed.

Fear, he realised, that was rooted in uncertainty, in the not-knowing, and talking about any of this would reveal this lack of knowledge quite sharply, reveal this lack of certainty, which, in turn, would trigger another kind of knowledge: that at best he was being an ingénue, at worst, really quite stupid indeed.

Roberta stirred and he looked at her.

She was, he had to admit, outrageously sexy. Objectively speaking, to *objectify* her, as she would say, she was seriously fucking hot. Mischievous eyes, a tangle of brown hair, loads of legs –

And the sex. Well quite, the *sex*. Antonio smiled to himself. Let me put it this way, he thought, before Roberta, he'd only ever used the phrase *make love* ironically.

It is easy to say to someone that you have never felt this way before, Antonio thought. And, to an extent, that's the case in every relationship, you haven't ever felt this way before as you've never felt this way about this particular person before –

But it was true. He had never felt this way before.

He understood, now, what those words meant.

Roberta stretched. Her eyes closed, she smiled, turned to him, wriggled into him, buried her head in his chest, her hands found his neck, she said, simply –

'Amor.'

He kissed her. 'I'll make you some tea.'

'Wait, just two minutes.' She held him. 'Please.'

He kissed her again –

The tea *could* wait.

Eight hours later and Antonio was all alone in a fuck-off big crowd, spinning out from a good slap of strong weed and cursing the fact that he couldn't hide his agitation and simply enjoy the day with Roberta, that he couldn't help being a snide little fucker and that *she* couldn't give him a fucking break considering what he was going through.

Which was stupid, he knew. But still. Silly cow, she should have known that *something* wasn't right. Fucking Rafael. What a fucking joke, eh? he thought. The lad's having a laugh, stitching me up like this. Because that's what this is, Antonio thought, a stitch-up. He didn't know how, he didn't even know what he'd done even, but he did know that what Rafael was doing was very likely connected to the very thing they were protesting about, in theory, that day:

The greased-hand and lined-pocket chain-of-corruption agenda that Dilma was hammering, that Dilma was claiming did not take place on her watch, or even in her party before her watch, the funnelling-off of funds out of the country.

Yeah, right.

There were fucking millions of people on Avenida Paulista, and Roberta had skedaddled with some purpose, some real urgency. There was no way, at this point in the rally, that he was going to find her. And, to make it considerably worse, he had her mobile phone in his pocket. It had seemed like a good idea at the time. Left-wing get-together or not, there'd still be some cruel little prick lifting purses, rifling through bags. It's hard to pickpocket a pair of good, fashionable, slim-cut jeans: a benefit of this narrow-legged new world we all now lived in.

Yeah, right.

His head *swam*.

The pre-march joint also seemed like a good idea at the time. Get into the whole hippie vibe. Say things like vibe. Christ, you didn't need to even have your own: there was a great cloud of it bursting and sagging just above.

He tried to focus. Colours everywhere. Shouting. Smiles.

This was defiance.

Defiance of the people that ran the city.

For a moment, a righteous energy surged through him –

It didn't last.

God he was a prick. Why couldn't he have just agreed with her rant?

All she'd said was that there was no debate, that impeachment *claimed* to be a debate, but that it was, in fact, the opposite. Almost those exact words, he thought.

'It is *closing down* the debate,' she said. 'Polarising the country, dividing families, friends, colleagues. Dividing *us*, sometimes. It is us and them now, entendeu? That simple, that basic. Two sides, us and them and no grey, no nuance, just black and white and it is terribly sad and that is not democracy, not what politics is, should be, we no longer deserve the democracy we'd earned.'

He could see the drugs drive this rant on.

'Dilma had been a part of achieving it, right, I know that, but now, who knows, ne? And she's either a snake in the grass or a terribly wronged woman in a society that is more misogynistic, conservative, backward-looking than ever. Who the fuck knows, sabe? I do not. That's all I can tell you.'

And she looked angry. Not hurt, not sad, not confused, not even bitter. Angry.

And this, for some reason, pissed him off.

'Settle down,' was all he could bring himself to say.

What a cunt.

No wonder she bolted. She was absolutely furious. Fair enough, really.

But now what?

Christ he was stoned. How did these hippies do it? It's exhausting, terrifying. This weed was *killer*. Imagine LSD or DMT! It's a fucking full-time job, being a hippie. He was definitely a 'bit of a sharpener and let's dance to some fucking Motown' kind of a man. Stoners were, in the end, fucking useless. Lazy. Everyone knew that. They never actually *did* anything.

The crowd heaved. The crowd swayed. The crowd throbbed.

He could make no sense of any of it.

Slogans. Banners. Music. Groups. Workers. Maids. Students. Activists. Anarchists. Face paint. Klaxons. Flags. Megaphones. Balaclavas. Pipes. Whistles. Handclaps. Cheers. Singing. Placards. Jokes. Cartoons. Thumbs-up. V-signs. Masks. Balloons. Red. Red. Red. Red. Red. Rainbows. Faces. Arms. Legs. Backsides. Shoulders. People. People. People.

He had to get off Avenida Paulista. There were too many people. It was suffocating.

And Lula was expected on stage in not too long and the hypocrisy of cheering that backward, gyppo hick was making Antonio angry, especially after it was now pretty fucking clear that Dilma had made him her chief of staff so he couldn't be prosecuted and sent to jail, as being left wing doesn't mean you can't also be a thieving gyppo cunt after all, and why didn't I think of that when Roberta was getting all arsy, and if the fucker's going down then I don't see why I need to be here any longer –

But not being there any longer was a tall order.

People fucking everywhere. There was a considerable body of them, a growing, slithering body, between Antonio and the other side of Avenida Paulista.

And he was stoned, he reminded himself.

Logistics, at this point, were not his friend.

He saw the pokey little shopping centre across the road from the museum, Conjunto Nacional. He should use that as a beacon, a lighthouse. He could then duck off the strip, pass the park, and hotfoot it up Alameda Santos towards Roberta's place and hope to fuck she'd decided to do the same.

Roberta. What a wally, he was. Is it so hard to simply love the one you love? To bury all the inconsequential shit of the last week or so – and it *was* inconsequential – and simply *put her first?*

Well, he thought in a fug, spaced out, his brain literally taking up more space, we live and learn. And she says I'm good at that: learning.

Yeah, he thought, his brain, his dispersed brain, his new, hippie brain catching up with his movements, his *plans*, I'll go to Roberta's and wait for her there. I'm off. Ciao, fuckers.

Crowd-surfing was out, he thought. He plotted a line from where he was at the end of Rua Augusta to the shopping mall. It would, under normal circumstances, even factoring in traffic light changes, take fewer than five minutes. He got his elbows ready, he got his regretful face on, he put his head down and he bustled –

It took longer than five minutes. There was dancing in the way. He bought a beer from a vendor to try and rid himself of some of his edge. Then another, from another vendor, as it had worked.

At Conjunto Nacional, he stopped for a moment, drank it in. He looked up and down Paulista. He smiled, despite himself. He could turn this story into something funny. Roberta would get it. They would laugh. There was one thing he knew about them: they were quick to get over themselves, quick to realise when they'd been ridiculous, quick to laugh at their ridiculousness, each other's and their own. He remembered the first time they'd travelled together and she'd forgotten to put her toiletries in a plastic bag and was pulled by security. He went over to check everything was alright and she snapped at him, and he took offence and flounced off saying, 'I was *just* trying to be supportive.'

They laughed very quickly about that.

It would be OK. It simply would. *They* would.

The road either side of the shopping mall was jammed. Ram-jammed. The shop fronts that opened out onto Avenida Paulista had been quickly shut up, their grills pulled down. The main entrance was still just about accessible. He took a deep breath and heaved, hefted his way through the crowd, into the mall, where it was clear and cool, really cool, and he didn't think, in fact, he'd ever been this thankful to be on the inside of a shopping mall before, let alone one that was as low-rent as Conjunto Nacional, and he could get through to the other side, and the lager had really *softened up* his head, really *eased* him into a much better mood, so he'd cross the mall, he resolved, then nip down the side of the park and take Alameda Santos up to Paraíso, where –

The park. Fuck. Praça Alexandre de Gusmão.

He looked at his watch. Not long until four. In his dope-fudged brain, with the dope-edged roundabout mood swings of anger and regret, frustration and excitement, he'd forgotten all about one of the key reasons he was anxious in the first place.

Well, this might be interesting, he thought. He smiled. He was a touch unmoored by the beer-weed combo. Yet, he thought, he had nailed the ratio, got it just right, you know, bang on, even if he did say so himself.

Jesus, imagine old Rafael having his cock sucked behind a tree! Now *that* would be a valuable bit of information. He laughed at his own insincerity. Not my style, he thought, knowing that was true. But it wouldn't hurt to know, would it? And, after all, it was on his way to Roberta's, wasn't it?

He left the shopping centre and snaked across the road. The backstreets were quiet. The backstreets were blowing political rally debris. The backstreets were empty, cleaned out by some cataclysmic event.

Antonio drank it in.

South side, the note had said. He should hang about, hang back a tad, scope the square, all corners like. Which side was fucking south anyway?

He stumbled over a loose paving stone. He chuckled.

He thought: Rafael, homo –

Nah. The lad's got something going. Some of the birds he's been with are scandalous. Not that that means anything though. Yeah, he's got something going.

Let's go and have a gander.

At the top end of the square was an underground car park. There was always someone manning the entrance, but only once you'd gone down a level from the street. Antonio figured he'd walk in to the park by this entrance, hang back there. If he saw Rafael he could tell him something like Roberta was in there fetching her vehicle, something like that.

The park was dead. Not a soul about the place. The rally noise filled it. It echoed – eerie. Antonio wasn't sure what he was doing there exactly. But he'd come this far; might as well put one little mystery to bed.

On the far side of the square, right down on Alameda Santos, he could make out a few lads horsing around.

He decided to head that way.

He got half a dozen or so yards into the park.

In front of him –

A figure, scurrying.

This figure scurried straight at him.

This scurrying figure: the snide rent-boy postman.

Antonio, frozen, eyes wide:

Fuck.

'You,' he said, as the scurrying figure hurried past. 'You –'

The figure turned. The figure scurried on. The figure spoke. 'You!' he said. 'You need to go. You need to go. I've seen you now, I've seen you.'

Antonio, frozen, watched the man rushing away. Antonio turned back.

Beyond –

Two men dressed in black, arms extended.

Beyond them –

A young man in a pink shirt, sharp trousers, shiny –

Rafael.

Antonio, frozen, watched as the two men dressed in black extended their arms and, noiselessly, shot Rafael in the chest.

I've seen you.

Antonio, frozen, watched Rafael crumple.

Antonio, frozen, watched the two men dressed in black drag the body into the bushes and disappear. He heard a shout. He heard the roar of a motorcycle.

I've seen you.

Antonio, frozen, dumbstruck –

He heard the scurrying figure call out: 'Go, caralho, go, you need to go, to disappear, bicho. Vai embora!'

Antonio headed back out of the park and did a left.

I've seen you.

As he did, he found first his phone then Roberta's, turned them off, pulled the Sim cards, destroyed these under his feet and chucked the phones back into the bushes in the park, at the opposite corner to, at the opposite corner to –

At the opposite corner to where Rafael had crumpled.

I've seen you.

To where Rafael had been shot in the chest, and lay –

I've seen you.

To where Rafael lay crumpled, dead.

I've seen you.

Antonio kept moving. He pulled his wallet. He found an ATM. He boosted all the cash he could. He bent and snapped his bankcard. He pocketed the cash. He emptied his wallet. It did not take long. It was fashionable among the playboys and fuckheads to keep a money clip and a single bankcard in a slim wallet.

Antonio noted the convenience of this fashion.

Antonio noted this note.

I've seen you.

Antonio: brain scrambled.

He hotfooted.

He moved *fast*.

I've seen you.

He kept moving –

I've seen you.

Where to?

I've seen you.

Where to? Where to?

PART THREE: **FORTUNE'S ALWAYS HIDING**

Interrogation room, Polícia Civil HQ
São Paulo, 22 March, lark-time

'I don't suppose you've ever sat on that side of the table, have you, son?'

Leme shook his head. Leme smiled. He rolled his neck. He stretched his arms. He went eye to eye with his questioner. He *glared* him down.

'I'm choosing to sit here, don't forget,' Leme said. 'I'm doing your job for you, mate. If it weren't for me, you wouldn't even know there'd been a crime. That poor cunt's body would be on the slow rot, a worm-frenzy. So leave it out, entendeu?'

Leme's questioner raised an eyebrow. He angled his head left, then right.

'Fair point well made,' he said. 'Still, you *are* on that side of the table, aren't you? So be nice, certo?'

Leme nodded. Fact is he liked old Lutfalla. They'd never quite crossed paths professionally, but he was alright. Decent rep, known to be a worker, nothing too shady in his locker, family man, sense of humour, put his hand in his pocket when the need arose. Leme could have had a lot worse sitting across from him –

Luck of the morning-shift draw.

Well, late-night shift really. Leme was likely the last task old Lut had to get done before home and bed and a day or two off, play with the kids, shout at the wife, wank in the shower, that sort of thing.

Lutfalla yawned.

'You tired?' Leme asked.

'Exhausted, mate. Last thing I fucking need, *this*,' he said.

'It wasn't exactly top of my list of things to do either, mate.'

'Let's start there then.'

'You what?'

'Some people are saying that this is you turning yourself in, right? That's what some people are saying.'

'I guess it's not a million miles off, is it?'

Lutfalla smiled. 'You confessing to something?'

'Don't be a cunt.'

'I said be nice.'

Leme shrugged. 'Protective custody, you know, for now.'

'What does that mean?'

'It means that someone's stitching me up.'

'Oh yeah?'

'Two days, two bodies. And I'm at both scenes, corpses good as new.'

'*Two* bodies?'

Leme said nothing.

'You said two bodies.'

'I figure we work out the first one, it's easy to work out the second.'

'We know who the second one is, mate.'

Leme nodded. Leme grimaced. 'I mean work out *why*, entendeu?'

'Right.'

'You didn't know there was another stiff?'

'No. I did not. Enlighten me.'

'Sunday. By the rally. A youngish, playboy type. In the park off Paulista.'

'Alexandre de Gusmão, you mean? The square? OK, that's likely a botched homo whack-job.'

'I don't think so.'

'No?'

'The Militar boys showed up just when I discovered the poor lad.'

'Right.'

'And the tip-off came from our second corpse, our good friend – our *former* good friend – Senhor Fat João.'

Lutfalla said nothing. He rubbed his eyes. He rubbed his hair. With both hands, he rubbed his cheeks, his stubble.

Leme sat tight.

'What do you expect me to do here, Mario?' Lutfalla said. 'You call in the stiff, but you refuse to say what you're doing there at the end of the fucking world finding the little rat fuck. That's why you're here, certo? You know that. Então? You best not be messing me about, sabe?'

'Like I said, the little rat fuck led me to the first body. So I went to see what he might know that might shed a little luz on the matter.'

'As far as anyone here is concerned, there is no other body.'

'Donkeys in the fucking shade, ne?'

Lutfalla smiled. 'And that's your problem. Your reason for being at our dead friend's gaff is a reason that's news to us.'

'Thanks, Sherlock.'

Lutfalla made a face. 'Tell you what,' he said. 'I'm going to log this as all good, give you the all-clear, the whole slap-bang investigative-work trip that paid out a tasty dividend. But I'll also log that it's on hold, decent-result-at-half-time situation. I don't know what's going on, but I ain't going to stop you trying to find out. This is done, for now. You've got a day, maybe a couple, tops. OK?'

Leme grinned. 'Nice one. You're a good lad.'

It wasn't rocket science what Leme had to do next –

And double-quick. Set up a meet with Fat Silva to find out why the slovenly fuck had sent him to Fat João's palatial pad on the day that life, and all its opportunities, were cruelly taken from him. Actually, there was no need to set up a meet and old Silva never liked a surprise. Leme knew where he would be: home or breakfast. Leme knew that Lutfalla would give him a bit of breathing space. Leme knew that Superintendent Lagnado would be enough hours behind play to give him a chance. The fact is he needed the same information he needed twenty-four hours ago.

The name of dead guy numero uno –

Leme jumped the stairs two at a time. Less chance of running into anyone on the stairs. The elevator *heaved*. He arrowed across the open-plan space. He pushed into the tin-can office he shared with Lisboa.

'Well, well,' Lisboa said. 'If it isn't Harrison Ford in the fucking *Fugitive*.'

Lisboa gunned the engine. The engine sputtered. The engine growled. He aimed his rust bucket up and through Jardins. They bounced through the slick-swank shopping pocket of Oscar Freire. Leme noted Diesel, Louis Vuitton, Levi's, Gucci. They hopped the grid system, diagonally, rode traffic-light luck. They said nothing. They angled across by going *around*. Crow flies and whatnot it was no more than two clicks to Silva's. They skipped the school bus jams – *just*. Fifteen minutes of honking and cranking, crunching and kerb-bothering, they parked. Silva's building looked *tired*.

Leme watched as Lisboa shambled over to the condo entrance. Lisboa spoke into the intercom. A moment later, the porteiro, a youthful pup of a doorman, came out. Lisboa spoke to the young pup. Lisboa's message was communicated, Leme thought. Lisboa stomped back across the road: *pissed*. He ducked his head into Leme's window.

'Out, you, I know where he is.'

Silva looked *tired*. He was taking on a full Brazilian: eggs, bread, cold cuts, yoghurt, sweet breads, fruit, sausage, flask of coffee, vase of orange juice, cigarette burning in an ashtray just east of his bursting plate, his plate spilling food, *glutting* food –

'I wondered when you two would show up,' he said.

'Here.' Leme passed him a napkin. 'You've got egg on your face, son.'

Silva knew the expression. 'It appears that way, doesn't it?'

Crime pops up all over the shop. About six months after Leme and Renata first got together they were invited to spend the weekend at the country house of friends of Renata's. They were looking forward to it. The condominium where the house had been built was not far out of São Paulo, an hour, hour and a half, but the air was always fresher, the space greener. There was a swimming pool. There would be barbecued meals. There would be plenty of booze. A handful of

Renata's close friends were going. Leme was most excited by this last aspect. He was going to get involved, going to become a part of her life. They'd reached that point; they spent their weekends together, regardless. In fact, that point was the point: it'd happened naturally, seamlessly.

Leme had three days off and eased into the Friday. Renata was working in her legal aid office in Paraisópolis. She had to work late, in the end. She always had to work late. Working late cost her her life, to a point, in the end. But not this weekend. She was late getting home, she was late getting packed, she was late getting showered, she was late getting dressed, she was late having a quick – just a quick – supper, a bite really, just to be sure, you know, she was doing the driving after all –

So they were late on the road. And a Friday, a Friday evening at that. Traffic was *heavy*. An hour, hour and a half, was more like three, three and a quarter. The condominium was quiet, on the outside, dark, when they arrived not long before midnight, hopeful that the evening would be in full flow, and they'd catch the end of dinner and something of the weekend spirit, late-night booze-fuelled Friday fun, and all that ruckus. Leme was *psyched*. He was well up for it. He was about to establish to everyone else what he and Renata already knew: that this was the real deal.

They arrived at the security gates, showed ID, bit of back and forth with the security detail, and ghosted through.

It was one of those condos where the architecture made no sense. Each house a testament to its owner's folly. Like a sort of Disneyland for flash, garish gaffs. Flash, garish, *second* gaffs of course. Most of these flash gaffs were lit up, obviously full for the weekend, kids playing, adults playing, driveways rammed with flash cars, sounds of food cooking outside and splish-splashing in pools. Renata crept along the grid of roads, looking for the turn to her friends' place, windows down, air cool, air expectant. They found the turn. This road was quiet, dark. The houses were empty. This was common, certainly possible, not everyone fled the city every weekend. They crept further, slowed right down. When Renata recognised the house, she stopped the car. 'We're here,' she said. 'I'm sure this is it.' Leme scanned the street. No one around, lights off, house, it seemed, deserted. 'Stay here,' he said. Leme skirted the grounds. A sprinkler in the back garden sprayed water left right left right left right. This was triggering the security light. It flashed on off on off on off. The windows, most of them, were ajar. There was a buzz of electricity. There was silence. There were, he thought, whimpers, sobs.

Leme nudged the front door and it swung open. He called out. Shouts, swearing, who the fuck are you, you said you weren't coming back, we haven't moved, take what you want, don't touch the women. Leme turned on the lights. He identified himself. He told them to stay calm. He asked what was going on, what had happened. He said: one of you, just one of you, tell me. And stay down, stay down on the floor, stay down with your hands behind your head until I say so, just for now, just in case, don't panic, I'm one of you. A man told him what had happened. He told him in a tone of disbelief. He couldn't fathom what had happened. He couldn't fathom that it was over, almost over, and yet far from over. He couldn't fathom it, it made no sense to him, he couldn't *process* any of it. Leme nodded. Wait here, he told them. He went upstairs. He checked from room to room. Women, in each room, whimpered and sobbed, their hands behind their heads, whimpered and sobbed face down on the floor. They were all OK. Leme brought them downstairs. He instructed the guy whose house it was to call security. To call security, now. He instructed the man to tell security there had been a breach. He went to the fridge and handed out beers. He found a bottle of whiskey on the kitchen counter, some glasses. He poured shots. There was some hysteria, but then there was a calm, a relief. Then euphoria, a softening. What doesn't kill you, etc. We made it, we fucking made it. Fuck them! We made it. I love you. He went to fetch Renata. She was confused, scared. When he told her what had happened, she broke down sobbing.

They'd been making dinner when three men in balaclavas carrying guns walked through the front door, and two more men also in balaclavas, also carrying guns, came in through the back door. With guns to their heads, the men were forced to lie face down on the floor, downstairs. The women were taken upstairs. Renata sobbed. The women were taken upstairs and two of the men stayed with them while the other three men stripped the house, and all the people in it, of valuables. They told the men to stay where they were, that any move to help their women would be punished, that the throats of their women would be cut, after they'd been raped. The men sobbed. The men yelled. The men could do nothing. There were guns trained on their heads. The women were OK. It was a threat. The threat was enough. The robbery went off without incident.

Leme went next door. The same scene. He went to the house next to that. The same scene. Five houses had been turned over. Five sets of occupants terrified and stripped.

They never caught the gang that did it.

Silva said, 'I know about Fat João. I'm sorry. I *didn't* know. Why would I? And even if I did, why would I do that, eh? To you? We're mates.' Leme nodded. Leme was fairly certain all along that Silva hadn't grassed. 'Anyway, you're in luck,' Silva said. 'My young protégée is coming along in a minute and might have something for you.' Lisboa shot Leme a look. The look said: don't be too quick to forgive, this might not add up.

Leme never told Renata what that night had done for him, long-term, not really. It had made it clearer than ever that she would be his wife, that he would be her husband. The idea of it, the two of them split like that, appalled him.

The *idea* of it.

Later, it made him think about how crime, about how the ordinary horror of crime, crime in São Paulo, was democratic. You could, like Renata, in her legal aid office in the favela, work in a place where criminals lived and operated with impunity, work with people directly touched by these criminals, touched in their daily lives by the rules and routines of these criminals, and you could live happily alongside them, work alongside them, *for* them, and you could live by these rules and routines. Or you could get deeply unlucky, like Renata had, and you could die by these rules and routines, die at the hand of a stray bullet.

Or you could just go away for the weekend and stay with your friends, your rich middle-class friends, and something terrible could happen. Or not. It was democratic.

Of course, Leme found out later that Renata's death, killed by this stray bullet in a firefight between police and thieves, while an accident, wasn't simply an accident.

Even that felt democratic, in its way, to him now.

Ellie jumped from the back seat of a cab. 'Ah,' she said, 'the three amigos. The three wise men.' She paused. She pointed at Silva's plate, raised her eyebrows, laughed. 'The three little pigs.' Lisboa glared at Silva. 'We're not the three anything, sweetheart,' he said. Silva raised his palms. 'I know how it looks.' Lisboa nodded. Silva said, 'Ellie here has something. Can we just suspend the hostilities until she's told us what it is? Favor?' Leme nodded.

'Right,' Ellie said. 'So this is what I *have*, as Francisco puts it.' The three wise men kept their counsel, kept schtum. Ellie went on. 'I got back Sunday morning. I headed to the rally. Yesterday, that's Monday, I get a call from my friend, Lis, we used to work together, she went travelling, she's back, whatever. Anyway, so her friend Roberta's in a right two and eight, you know, a state? Her boyfriend's missing. Well, they had a row at the rally, she stormed off and she hasn't seen him since. It hadn't even been twenty-four hours, sure, but he had her phone and he's not answering and not replying to emails and Lis had been calling round, subtle, you know, and no one had heard or seen hide nor hair and whatnot. So the poor girl's on the hysterical edge of concerned, entendeu? Lis called me as she knows about my, you know, my *connections*, the three little pigs, as it were –' She made a face at Lisboa. 'So here I am. I thought you could help. That's why I got in touch, *Leme*. Nice of you to follow up properly.' Leme ignored this. 'And Francisco, when I told him last night, seemed to think I might be able to help *you*, which, I'll be honest, was something of a surprise.'

'What's the lad's name?' Lisboa asked.

'Antonio. Antonio Neves.'

'Where does he work?'

'He's a finance guy. Sleek little hedge-fund operation called Capital SP.'

'We better pay them a visit,' Lisboa said.

'Not sure how much point there is in that,' Ellie said.

Lisboa raised a hard eyebrow – oh, yeah, fucking educate me, gringa, it said.

'Roberta was there yesterday. They told her this Antonio had taken a few days of holiday. All legit. Cleared with the fucking line manager and blah blah blah. First she'd heard of it. Didn't help with her strop, that bit of info.'

'No, I don't suppose it would,' said Leme.

Silva gestured at Ellie. 'Now tell them the other thing.'

Ellie grinned. 'So later on yesterday, Lis *and* Roberta both get emails calls texts whatever, totally separate, no obvious connection, about some rumours of someone who's missing. Some lad in that posh playboy circuit had been asking around, apparently.'

'Asking about what exactly?' Lisboa said.

'This is the odd bit: asking if anyone knew of anyone missing, entendeu? Like he was just sort of curious.'

'And please tell me neither of your friends mentioned this Antonio?'

'They're not stupid.'

Lisboa coughed. Ellie glared. Leme gestured: go on, please.

A bala perdida, a stray bullet, is not as random, not as unlucky, not as *rare* as you might think. Adilson, a friend from Leme's condo, one of a group of middle-aged tennis players who liked to drink courtside after their bad-tempered doubles, was shot in the chest. When he got out of hospital Leme saw him sitting by the pool in customary fashion, Speedos and lager. A little quieter, a little recalcitrant even, but basically the same. There was a group of friends and well-wishers surrounding him and he knocked them aside to embrace Leme.

'Feel this,' he said. 'It's still there. Can you feel it? The bullet.'

It was hard and lumpy like a growth. If you pushed firmly, you could trace the edges, Leme thought. It was like someone had forced a bottle cap under his skin.

'They weren't able to take it out,' he said, 'without causing further problems.'

He laughed. He raised his can of lager.

'What doesn't kill you, eh?'

He was hit by a bala perdida. Nine a.m., and Adilson had been walking to work in Itaim, a respectable and desirable area of offices and residences, quiet streets and fashionable restaurants. Shots were fired; a robbery. He felt his legs give way and warmth in his chest. His head spun and there was a sharp and nagging pain in his back. When he looked up, he saw his dead father talking to God. That's the last thing he remembered before coming round in hospital. He was fine now, the bullet worn like a badge of honour, a greying lump of skin that didn't tan like the rest of him. Thing was, there were rumours that it wasn't a stray bullet at all. Story was that the woman he was fucking, her son didn't like it. This lad was a coke fiend, Leme had heard. The delusional sort. The scratching-around-in-the-dark and cooking-up-plans sort of fiend. He didn't like old Adilson. And he had the sort of wedge that could arrange a stray-bullet whack-job. That's the story going round now. Democratic.

'You know what's next, right?'

'Gabriel Carvalho. Here's his address and his work details.' Ellie pushed a piece of paper across the table. 'It doesn't sound to me that this lad's got a great deal up here.' She tapped her forehead.

'Definitely one of your mob then,' Lisboa muttered.

Leme sat tight. He gave Lisboa a pointed look: we're fucking off out of it.

'What can I do now then?' Ellie asked.

'She's got a great story, which might –'

'She does nothing, Francisco,' Leme said. 'Fuck all, zip, certo? This is very useful and we're grateful, but you tell your friends to sit tight, hold tight and do nothing. Give me their contact details.' He handed her his notebook and pen. 'And tell them I'll be in touch. Apart from that, nada. Ta ligado?'

Ellie nodded. Her eyes darted.

The normalisation of crime was something else that made it demo-cratic in its reach. If democracy is about creating opportunities, then crime in São Paulo did that in unexpected ways. Opportunities in how you respond to it. Crime creates scenarios, Leme thought, the idea of which is appalling, unimaginable –

And yet. A democracy of opportunity. Leme was put on a kid-napping case a year or so ago. The daughter of a media magnate. A serious name. *Serious* cash behind this serious name. Key point: Leme wasn't put on the case until *after* it had been resolved. Oppor-tunities, democracy.

The media magnate, the media *baron*, got the call on a Monday. The call was detailed on three fronts: 1) that the location of where the kidnappers held his daughter was known by no one outside the core senior leadership group of the kidnapping gang 2) that this senior leadership group would accept not a cent less than the total amount of money they believed to be a fair trade for the baron's lovely daughter 3) that any contact with the police would result in the baron's dutiful daughter being relieved, bit by bit, of a series of fairly significant parts of her body. So far: standard. Leme rolls in with a firm jaw and a swagger expecting to marshal the rich ingénue legacy-makers into a dignified submission, and what does he find when he knocks on their door? The lovely, dutiful daughter, safe and sound, bubble gum popping away and clearly quite enjoying a week or two off school.

The magnate had balls, Leme later decided, of pure titanium. After the call, the magnate hung up, saying nothing, agreeing to nothing, asking for nothing. He then set in motion a number of instructions for his accountant. First, he sold his primary residence. Second, he sold his secondary residence. Third, he sold his other place. Fourth, he sold his boat. Fifth, he emptied his bank accounts of any cash. Sixth, he moved any residual savings in his Brazilian accounts into a number of his offshore interests. Seventh, he signed over all the stock and shares he owned in the conglomerate of media companies in which he had controlling stakes. This last one was the most complicated of the transactions, which was why he left it until last. He really didn't want to have to go through all that. It was a titanium ball-ache. But he did have to do it. The senior leadership group of the kidnapping gang demanded it. Indirectly. Imagine: you hold the daughter of an extremely rich man, you are blackmailing him for a fortune; what is the one, foolproof way this blackmail, this threat, cannot possibly work? If the incredibly rich man is not, in fact, incredibly rich, if, it turns out, he has nothing. Word got to the senior leadership team that the magnate was ridding himself of property, cash and assets, and the proceeds of any sales distributed among business contacts, family. They panicked. It was the untangling of the knot of media company interests, the symbol of it, really, that pushed them too far. The magnate showed that he was not prepared to pay a ransom to such an extent that he was, genuinely, leaving himself destitute and with no possibility of a future. The magnate at no point communicated with the senior leadership team; they could see it happening with their own eyes. They knew his portfolio; they watched his wealth plummet. They were left, after seven days, with a young woman who couldn't be, and wouldn't be, paid for. Fair play, they thought, and let her go. Execute her, and things get sticky. Word is, Leme heard, they were in awe of the size of the magnate's titanium balls.

And the punchline: all the assets, all the property, all the controlling stakes were his again after another week. It was all paperwork; nothing actually changed hands. Leme had asked how he did this. 'I've got a lot of cousins. Sales generate wealth. If anything, I *made* money.' Which gave Leme another idea, of course. Democracy. Normalisation creates democratic opportunities. Leme was one hundred per cent that the magnate didn't set the whole thing up, that was clear.

But what was also clear: his example meant someone else certainly would.

As Silva sloped off looking forlorn, Lisboa boosted the car, kicked the engine into gear. Leme hung back. 'I'll call you later,' he said to Ellie. 'We need to have a word.' She nodded. He smiled. 'Stay lucky,' he said.

It was still early. Second breakfast-time. They swerved out of Paraíso and headed to this Gabriel lad's home address in Jardins. The address *reeked* cash. The address said: old school, old money. Gabriel, Leme would not be surprised, lived with his parents. This would help swing the right kind of conversation. In Leme's experience, rich kids liked to keep their parents out of any police enquiries. And then later they called their parents' lawyers.

'You're quiet,' Leme said.

Lisboa grunted. Leme left it. He knew Lisboa was going out on something of a limb. It wasn't the first time. Lisboa was family. Better than family. Leme *knew* he could rely on him. At this point, he reasoned, he wasn't actually in the frame for either murder. At this point, he was just out of shot. It wouldn't take too much though to line up the photo and snap. At this point, Lisboa was assisting with an investigation sanctioned by Lutfalla's interview. That was the only way to put it, at this point.

'I don't trust Silva,' Lisboa said. 'He always seems to know a bit too much.'

'Prides himself on it.'

'Pride comes before one, as we well know. Let's hope it's him and not you that comes a cropper, copper.'

'It's not like that.'

Lisboa sighed. 'The man's only ever going to put himself first, entendeu? I don't like his style.'

Leme left it at that.

Not long after the kidnapping incident, Leme was pulled into another one-way-or-another type of dilemma. One lunchtime at the swank British school in Jardins, the security guards told the employees no one is allowed out, no trips to the supermarket or whatnot, everything cancelled. You're all staying in, protective custody, yeah?

Turned out the local bank had been robbed about half an hour earlier and the two villains were hiding out somewhere in the neighbourhood. This was a posh neighbourhood, spacious houses, foreign cars and private security booths on most corners. In the immediate, emergency-call aftermath, the ground-force police only managed to catch one of the thieves. Not long later, the other was shot dead by a student's bodyguard. This bodyguard was waiting around outside the school and noticed someone suspicious, pursued him, realised who it was and killed him. Shot him in the chest and head. A very professional job.

No one cared.

Most Paulistanos shrugged it off, clicked their teeth and said:

'Ah, menos um, ne?' Oh well, that's one less, right?

Normalisation. Democracy. The security guard was, Leme had heard, fighting off multiple offers of work. The democracy of opportunity.

Leme left it at that as there wasn't much else to do, at this point. The case, Fat João's murder, if it could even be considered a case, would only unfold if they unfolded it. The case reeked. The case had 'police beak offed by the criminal fraternity' written all over it. Or, 'police beak offed by his own runner'. Leme didn't run snitches, but if that's how the big boys wanted the cookie to crush, then it didn't take Einstein to join the dots. The key was to ID the dead playboy. But they knew that already. The new information was this lad Antonio. Leme hoped, for Ellie's sake, for the sake of her mate, that it wasn't him. But if it wasn't him, then where the fuck was he? That was question number two on this morning's agenda. Question number three was precisely what old Carlos was up to. Fat João was wrapped up in a rug. This was an old-style PCC gang calling card. The idea was cute: swallowed up by a part of your own home, meaning you've sold out the cunts who protect you. The rug, literally, pulled out from under your feet. It also made the cremation that bit easier. In Rio, they piled tyres over your head until you were coiled up to your chin and then they burnt you alive. This was a tad more civilised. The PCC fancied themselves as a classier outfit than their coastal competition. Of course, it wasn't unknown for our friendly Militars to mock up a PCC execution if it suited. What Big Carlos was currently up to was therefore very interesting indeed. Wherever this Antonio lad was hiding, and whoever dealt the cards on poor old Fat João – young Antonio was looking like hot property. Everyone, Leme figured, would be extremely keen to find him. And if he *was* the dead playboy, then the fact he's now known missing by his missus and her best mate *and* Ellie, who was not exactly famous for keeping things to herself, meant that there would be some heavier questions coming Leme's way about why he was found at the scene. Leme did not have long. And if Lutfalla had reported with any truth their conversation earlier that morning, then Leme did not have long at all. How long before Carlos let slip Leme's place in the dead playboy scenario? Carlos was keeping that card close to his chest, or up his fucking sleeve. This was, Leme thought, a thin-ice, heavy-skate situation. They needed to crack on. Time was very fucking far from being on his side. Time was three nothing up against Leme and playing keep ball. Time was *toying* with Leme. They had to, as the saying went, keep riding the bike; if you stop pedalling, the bike stops.

And if the bike stops, you're fucked.

Lisboa jammed the brakes and jammed the car into a messy double-park. He jerked his chin right. 'Here.'

The point about the two investigations – the kidnapping, the sanctioned security guard whack-job – was that by the time Leme was put on them, by the time the Polícia Civil had begun any kind of official investigation at all, there was nothing left to investigate, já era, the city had already made up its mind, had already passed judgement, had already acted as judge, jury, and, in the second case, executioner. Leme didn't have to *do* anything. São Paulo sat in the saddle and the wheels turned.

Leme popped the glove box. He fished. He found his moody security company executive ID badge. He pulled a metallic case of fake business cards. He pulled a fake company letterhead. He would go easy on the lad; give him a chance. 'Stay here,' he told Lisboa. 'But get out, show your teeth, as it were.'

'Yes, sir.' Lisboa saluted ironically.

Leme marched. The garden path was *looong*. Leme buzzed maid-quarters. The maid trotted down. The maid kept good house.

'Pois não?' the maid asked. Can I help you?

Leme played charm school. His eyes dazzled. He flashed teeth. He flashed all of his moody credentials. 'I need to speak to the young man of the household,' he said.

The maid smiled, made nice, nothing more. 'He's asleep.'

Leme grinned. 'Wake him up.'

The maid crossed her arms. She raised her eyebrows. She grinned back. 'May I ask to what the young man of the household owes the pleasure of this visit?'

'You can ask.'

'So?'

Leme smiled – thin, this time. He didn't have time to fuck about. If charm school wasn't going to work, he'd have to play old school. He glanced left then right.

He leaned in.

'Look, love, fact is I'm a detective in the Polícia Civil and I need a word with young Gabriel, and I will have one, at least one word. Two choices: you go and wake him up and tell him the neighbourhood security firm have a few questions that might help with a public nuisance order, that *he* might be able to *help*, and you show him this card, or I go round the front door and tell Mr and Mrs upstairs you weren't prepared to let an officer of the law into the house for a friendly chat. Alright?'

The maid nodded. The maid took the card Leme held in the air.

'Wait here,' she said.

Leme wondered what it is he even *did* do, sometimes. The whole city had a code, a system, an understanding. It wasn't so much the Wild West, as a lot of people made out, more a sort of self-policing social contract: São Paulo was like one big favela –

Run by the bad-apple one per cent.

Leme's own building had a clever little routine. When you drove into the garage, you identified yourself at the bulletproof-glass booth in which three or four of the seguranças sat. But car-jacking in Morumbi happened.

A pair of thieves stops you at a traffic light, one hops in the back with a gun trained on your head. When you approach your building, they crouch down low and tell you they'll kill you if you do anything suspicious. So you wave nonchalantly at the glass booth and ghost inside. Then, the thieves go from flat to flat stripping them of valuables, load up and leave in the car in which they arrived.

It's a clever scam, Leme thought, if a little high-risk. In his building they had a system. If you do happen to drive in with a couple of malandros tucked away in the back, you park in a special bay which the security guys have designated as a signal to them you're in trouble. Once parked there, all hell breaks loose. Leme didn't think it had ever happened.

Point is, it might. And if it did, and Leme was put on the case, he wouldn't have to do anything. Everything that needed doing had already been done.

Leme looked this Gabriel lad up and down. Slick pair of pyjamas he was wearing. Really Hugh Hefnering up the place. 'I'll keep this simple,' Leme said. 'You cooperate, all good, as they say. You don't, you see that big fella down there?' He pointed at Lisboa. 'Well, he'll give you a slap until you do, entendeu?'

Gabriel nodded.

'Right then,' Leme said. 'So I've heard from a decent source, decent sources, in fact, that you've been asking around your friends, and their friends, and *their* friends if anyone knows of anyone missing in action, sabe? You follow? That sound familiar, lad?'

Gabriel looked shifty. 'What do you mean?'

'I mean you've been making some enquiries, is the phrase. I want to know why. And who for.'

Gabriel looked muito shifty. The pyjamas *shone*. 'I really don't know what you're talking about. I'd love to help but –'

Leme raised a finger. He then pointed with this finger at Lisboa.

'I'm telling the truth. Listen, I swear –'

Leme nodded at Lisboa. Made a face: don't mug me off, pal.

'Really, I promise.' Gabriel raised his palms.

'You're telling me you *haven't* been asking around.'

'I haven't been making any enquiries, Senhor, I swear.'

'Easy. Not quite the same thing.'

Gabriel shook. Gabriel breathed. He made a 'calm down' gesture with his hands. He said, 'Why don't you give me your card, and I'll get in touch if I hear anything at all that might relate to whatever it is you're talking about.' He paused. Gathered himself. 'I could make some enquiries for you, entendeu? That work?'

Leme looked this Gabriel up and down, looked this rich prick Gabriel up and down again. Leme smiled. Leme crackled.

'Nice jammies, son,' he said.

Leme slammed the door. Lisboa pulled away. Minor tyre squeal. Rubber and exhaust.

'Well?' he said.

Leme said, 'Kid's terrified. Playing the big man, doing us a favour, that kind of chat. Whatever he's up to though, he's going to tell his line manager, sharpish, know what I mean?'

Lisboa nodded. 'As the saying goes,' he said, 'if you're going to sup with the devil, you better make sure you use a long old spoon.'

Leme snorted. 'That a saying, is it? We best get after young Antonio.' He tapped Antonio's work address into his phone. 'The chances of him being at the office are slim to none,' he said, 'as the saying goes, of course, and none's just fucked off out of it.'

Lisboa grunted. Lisboa drove. 'We have to start somewhere, mate,' Lisboa said.

What Leme *did* do was live with Antonia. He grieved, still, of course he did, grieved for Renata. Living with someone new was in no way a comment on his grief. Grief doesn't leave; absence remains. His life with Antonia was a treat. Living with someone, it turned out, is a lot of fun when you like that person, when you get on, when you love that person. Antonia was *funny*. And Leme was funny! He hadn't ever thought he was funny. But they seemed to spend a fair bit of time in stitches, hooting with laughter. Laughing at each other, making each other laugh. They talked, regularly, about themselves, about their relationship. 'It's not tiresome talking about our relationship with you, sabe?' Antonia said. 'I must say, it's something of a surprise. The words alone make me shudder, and not in a good way.' They talked about the future and what that future might look like. For Leme, love, this time, was different: it felt like nothing he'd ever experienced, infinite possibilities unfolding in front of him. This love, he realised, was awe-inspiring. Renata would always be a part of his life. It was she who encouraged Leme to be happy, showed him that he could be. This, Leme now understood, is what love is. We let each other go and we understand. Love, like São Paulo, has no past. Only *now*. And *now* being now, now brought with it certain other conversations, other feelings, feelings that Leme hadn't known existed, feelings that Antonia shared, which was something else of a surprise to her, feelings to express. Quite a surprise, it was, when she said, yes, yes I do want to have a baby with you. I do want that very much, yes, yes I do. They had stopped worrying about contraception long ago; Leme realised that the main reason for this was that he didn't mind if she got pregnant. Obviously, that didn't feel like the most enthusiastic starting point, but the fact was it didn't panic him, and that grew quickly into something much more. Their Catholic approach to contraception then took an even further back seat. It felt very good indeed when he came hard inside her.

Leme's phone yapped. Text from Ellie:
Capital SP: dodgy lava jato doleiro work. More in an email soon… Ex
Good girl.

Leme and Lisboa crowded the reception desk at Capital SP. They *squeezed*. They felt bad for the receptionist, crowded behind her desk, squeezed and jostled by these strange men. Needs must. They made big.

The receptionist did not hang around with these big men and their Polícia Civil badges. She said, 'There are two men on holiday according to my calendar. Antonio Neves and Rafael Marquez.'

Rafael Marquez. A new name. Leme and Lisboa shared a look. Right then.

Lisboa nodded. 'And you don't know when they're back?'

'Thursday, it says here, but I remember that when Senhor Matheus authorised the holiday request, he said they might be back Wednesday, or even today.'

'But they're not?'

'They're not. Not yet, at least.'

'And they booked this time off together?'

'Rafael submitted the request for both of them, yes. His boss, Senhor Matheus authorised it, like I said.'

Lisboa looked at Leme. *Rafael submitted the request for both of them.* Lisboa looked at the receptionist. She shrank. Her desk dwarfed her. *Time off together.* He said, 'I think we need a word with this Senhor Matheus.'

The receptionist nodded. She picked up her phone. She spoke in hushed tones. She spoke fast. She replaced the phone.

'You can go up,' she said. 'Third floor. He'll meet you out of the elevator.'

Leme hadn't told Antonia anything. Not this time. He did not want to know what she would think of it all. He knew, of course, what she would think of it all. She had previous with Carlos. He wondered how far this Lava Jato beef really stretched. How many respectable companies, firms, businesses were implicated, perhaps even without knowing they were. Antonia was a lawyer. She had a certain amount of form herself, of course. Her company had been involved in some fairly questionable dealings. Leme knew this. It was how it was. That intersection of private-owned and state-run, or state-owned and private-run was murky. Bureaucracy and administration, legal nit-picking was a clusterfuck. But not understanding what was strictly legal and what was strictly not, was no defence. Or, more pertinently, understanding that other people didn't understand what was strictly legal and what was all-out dodgy, was not a defence. What was tolerated was not the same as what was right. And as much as Leme didn't want Antonia to know about what he was up to, about the pickle he was well and truly in, he didn't want to know if she had some role to play in this unfolding head-scratcher of a corruption situation. Leme loved Antonia. He had not spoken to her since telling her he would not make it home on the evening after discovering Fat João. This was not usual, but it was also not unusual. Leme missed Antonia.

Leme and Lisboa stood shoulder to shoulder in the glass lift. They had a three-sixty view of the really quite impressive facilities. Lisboa tapped the glass. 'There's two goldfish in a bowl,' he said. 'One says to the other, "You wanna hang out later?" The other one thinks about it and says, "Yeah, probably."'

Leme smiled. 'You know what they say about people and glass houses.'

Lisboa elbowed Leme, quite hard, in the ribs. 'Don't be soppy, eh.'

Leme was born in Paraíso and grew up first there and then in Morumbi near Paraisópolis. That old joke: France has Paris, we have Paraisópolis. His first school was the only school in the area for kids that age. Morumbi had once been a farm. Construction happened at quite a lick. Leme grew with it. The school was public. It was just your basic school. Morumbi, then, was not so sharply divided. Paraisópolis was a fraction of the size. There were none of the swank condos that now lined the roads. The first, Portal do Morumbi, was founded by residents the same year Leme was born. The second one that rose up and spread itself out in a fat, proprietary, *imperialist* gesture was Portal da Cidade, where Leme now lived. When he was eight years old, his best friends were Rodrigo, Zé Duda, and Pão de Queijo, cheese-bread, his nickname earned by his hatred for cheese-bread, his disgust for it, the smell especially. Whenever anyone had any cheese-bread, they threw it at Pão de Queijo.

Rodrigo was mixed race, Zé Duda and Pão de Queijo were both black. Leme was neither, in first generation terms. But Leme's mother was from the favela and she made sure he saw the world in the same terms as she did. It meant being understanding; it also meant being uncompromising, tough in how you move through the world. Leme's dad had never allowed Leme to forget how close he had come to a favela half-life. 'I rescued your mother,' he'd always told Leme, 'gave her a life she wouldn't have had, you wouldn't have had.' It was never exactly clear to Leme what his mother had been rescued *from*. Leme's memories of his mother were abstract now: a figure at home, tending home, tending to Leme and his father. Leme never got to ask her about *her*. It never occurred to him. And then when it did, when he was old enough, it was too late. When Leme was very young, she'd take him at weekends to the public swimming pool on the outskirts of the favela Paraisópolis. He'd splash around half-naked with dozens of other children, baking in the midday sun, throwing footballs at each other, laughing and shrieking with delight. She'd watch as they'd form small groups with friends, race each other underwater, chase each other through the shallows, diving into the deep end. She'd sit under an umbrella in a swimsuit that would never get wet, chatting with other mums about school and work, anxiously checking every few moments that Leme was within his depth, that his head still bobbed in the clear, blue water. At first, Leme remembered that he'd struggle to make friends and he'd spend more time sitting with his mum and the other women, basking in the sun and half-listening to their adult jokes and concerns. Then, as he got a little older, he spent more time with his friends; he spent his weekends without her. He remembered her saying: 'Watching you grow up, young man, fills me with both pride and fear. And the great fear, Mario: not making the most of what God gives you. Do that, keep faith, work hard, put your family first and you'll be alright, be rewarded in the next life, the one our *Padre* guarantees every Sunday.' Leme remembered that. He wasn't sure his father rescued her from anything.

They were funny, Leme's little friends. Aged nine, Leme changed schools. A better school. It was where, later, he met Lisboa. It was not a posh school, not British, American, *international*. But it was a better school. Leme lost touch with his friends. But he didn't move, he still lived in the same neighbourhood, still lived his life in the same places like any other kid, and then like any other teenager. When he was thirteen years old he was walking home, not too late, dark, but not too dark, still plenty of people kicking about. Morumbi had turned by then into the cheek-by-jowl, poverty-wealth scenario that dominated it today. But that didn't stop Leme walking home, walking the streets he had always walked, walking his neighbourhood. As he reached the corner of his street, his street, in his neighbourhood, his street, where he lived, where he had always lived, four boys surrounded him. They were boys, his age, but they were bigger, they looked tougher, they had edge. They wanted what Leme had in his pockets. It wasn't much, but that wasn't the point. Leme felt the threat of weapons without the visible threat of weapons. This edge these kids had was sharp. Leme swallowed. He felt lightheaded, faint. Some energy seemed to leach from him. He breathed. He swallowed. He felt hands rifle pockets. And then: 'Mario? Não! Mario!' And Leme, even in the faint panic of being boxed in, of being worked over, of being scared, recognised the ringleader. 'Pão de Queijo! Seu caralho.' Leme played it very cool. He faked nonchalance. The mugging was off. They swapped a few old jokes. They asked after one or two of the old gang. It was nice, Leme reflected, when he did get home. Pão de Queijo, he thought, laughing, shaking his head. When he got older he told the story a few times. He told it with humour, a sort of 'you'll never fucking guess what Morumbi used to be like' kind of humour. Older still, he thought about how depressing a story it was. He never saw Pão de Queijo again.

The office was *long*.

It oozed dark wood and leather. It *sang* privilege. The office was a butler with white gloves *bowing*. It welcomed you, this office, made you feel perfectly at home.

'Let's have a drink, shall we?'

Leme and Lisboa looked at each other. Their expressions said: why the fuck not?

There was a globe in the middle of this long, oozing office. One of those old ones, wooden-topped, elegant, absolutely not for children, not a toy, no Senhor, nem fodendo, no fucking way –

Senhor Matheus popped the lid. He took out a crystal decanter and three fat glasses. He poured three fat measures. He hesitated. 'Chorinho?' he said. A teardrop, a drop more? That same expression: why the fuck not? Senhor Matheus poured all of them a chorinho. He handed them their drinks. The fat glasses sat nicely in the palms of their hands.

'Single malt,' Matheus said. 'Lagavulin, sixteen years.'

'Thought so,' Lisboa said, fairly seriously.

Leme said nothing.

They sat for a moment enjoying their sixteen-year-old Lagavulins. Good time to drink whisky this, Leme thought, a sort of early elevenses. Better than a second breakfast. Then Matheus suggested that they talk freely and off the record. And again, Leme and Lisboa, that expression: why the fuck not? They weren't, after all, expecting that.

'It appears,' Matheus continued, 'that you want to know something about two of my employees. I also want to know something about them.'

'We'd like to know where they are,' Lisboa said.

'I'd also like to know where they are.'

'Holiday, no?'

Matheus leaned back in his extremely leather chair. 'They are supposed to be on something like a holiday, yes.'

'But they're not.'

'I don't know *where* they are.'

This, to Lisboa, did not seem a hugely helpful statement. Leme lifted a palm. 'Why don't you tell us about this not-quite holiday they may or may not be on.'

Matheus nodded. 'They're both doing some off-the-books work for us here. For me. Rafael has been doing this work for me, for us, for, I don't know, around two months. He told me last week that he needed some help, and he suggested Antonio.'

'Off-the-books work.'

'I know,' Matheus said, 'that you won't have any interest in the nature of this work. And if you did have any interest in the nature of this work, which I know you don't, you wouldn't be here talking to me. Off the books,' he put down his fat glass, his fat, empty glass, 'does not mean off limits, does not mean illegal, entendeu?'

Lisboa nodded. He offered his glass. Matheus filled it.

Leme checked his phone. Email from Ellie. Subject: **Capital SP**. He read fast. Leme nudged Lisboa. Lisboa took Leme's phone. He scanned lines.

'Is there something I can help you with there?' Matheus said.

Lisboa looked at Leme. Lisboa raised an eyebrow. Leme nodded.

Lisboa said, 'You done much business this last two months or so for your Petrobras or Odebrecht clients?'

'There's such a thing as client confidentiality, you know.'

Lisboa looked at Leme. Lisboa looked back at Matheus. 'I thought that was an oath your doctor had to take. I'm pretty sure we could get a warrant, or whatever it is we'd need.'

'As I said before, I know you're not really interested in the work we're doing here.'

'Perhaps not, but I suspect some of these clients of yours might be interested in where some of their money is going.'

Matheus smiled, shifted in his seat. He grimaced, played cuckold, the wronged man. 'Which is why I want to find my employees as much as you do.'

'So what's the point of this conversation?' Lisboa said.

'I haven't heard from them. Well, I haven't heard from Rafael, he's my contact, since Sunday morning.'

'Right.'

'And I should have done. They're supposed to be doing this work for me, for *us*, and checking in as they're doing it. They've been doing neither of these things, as far as I – as far as we – can see, certo?'

'And you want to report them missing then?'

Matheus smiled. 'They're on holiday.'

Leme nodded. He glanced at Lisboa. He flicked his fingers to say, right, embora, let's fuck off. Two of this Matheus's employees –

Two. Leme had what he needed.

It was something, one of your former best mates trying to mug you. Yep, it was definitely something. Talk about your mugging off! Bit snide, even if, at the end of the day, it was accidental. It was Leme's first direct experience of crime. And the thing was, he didn't feel anything but an understanding. Not an understanding in the sense of some liberal, enlightened position that blamed all crime on the poor, desperate circumstances in which the poor, desperate criminal grew up, he didn't have a *sociological* understanding, no, nem fodendo, not at all. He simply understood that it had happened and why. And the key to why was that it *had* happened. That was what Leme learnt in his first direct experience with crime.

Ellie's email went like this: I had word from a contact in UK. He confirmed money coming into London from Capital SP, but indirectly. And business has been much more brisk the last few months. Money goes from public work contracts to Petrobras, to the cartel of construction companies that Petrobras has an exclusive deal with to carry out these public works (incl. Odebrecht, Camargo Correa, Andrade Gutierrez, Mendes Jr, UTC), then to the public officials and politicians who make them happen. The kickback percentage, at each stage, plus commission, is then funnelled off into Panama, which has the laundering structure to set up thousands of shell companies and legitimate but essentially fake firms all over places like the British Virgin Islands. Key figure is a law firm called Fonseca, apparently. All the legal work goes through them. Money then trickles off in increments to all these offshore launderettes (very English word there for you) and then after this into financial hubs in multiple forms – accounts, funds, businesses – like London for pick-up or further travel. Capital SP is doing some straightforward laundering of client money hidden in existing legit trades. But paying well over the odds for stock, investments, etc., other stuff I don't understand. And helping themselves to a fair bit, so my contact reckons. That's what I have. I won't say a word to this chick Roberta, don't fret, querido.

Leme thought: rich people are savages the world over. And they're the ones that want protecting. Barbarians. What they want: dirty cash, clean hands.

Part of understanding crime was understanding how you react to it, Leme learned. Two years after the not-mugging, Leme was with some friends, messing about near their homes. One of his friend's older brothers pitched up. A favela kid, a young black kid with a shank, had just jumped their youngest brother, and this tooled-up little cunt had jacked the youngest brother's watch, a watch that had been given to him by their grandmother, a watch that had once belonged to their late grandfather. Well out of order. Leme's friend's older brother told Leme and his friends that he knew where the fucker was and that he needed them to come with. 'And bring that bat, porra,' he instructed another of the group, pointing at the baseball bat they were using to smack old cans into the wasteland that bordered the favela. Leme remembered how they'd begun by smacking cans of fizzy pop into this wasteland, and then moved on to empty beer bottles, and then rotting fruit. All three had made a very different, very satisfying sound when hit cleanly off the bat. It was a solid bat. It was a bat for a job. And so, it was a gang of scrawny, spotty, teenage no-marks that stood in front of the pathetic, terrified, little favela kid, the black kid carrying the blade, this favela kid who'd swiped the watch. Leme remembered being nervous about the solidity of this bat, the tangible existence of it, and nervous about how it might be employed to satisfy the solid rage that Leme's friend and his brother were feeling. What Leme hadn't reckoned with was his friend's brother's imagination. The bat was a very tangible, very *real* threat. And only that: a threat. What Leme's friend's brother did to the poor, pathetic little black kid cowering from the threat of this bat, was make him eat the watch. This kid, this thief, this *mugger* ate their watch. He put the watch, piece by piece, into his mouth, and he chewed, he crunched and he swallowed down the small bits of metal and wire and spring. He coughed and he retched, but he swallowed, he *ate*.

The desire for a revenge that might match the rage of the two brothers, might come close to illustrating how unhappy they were, how out of order it all was: that was what won out. The watch, the family heirloom that they were so upset to lose, was put, in the end, to good use.

This was Leme's second direct experience of crime, and the first of its consequences.

Next stop: a meeting with Ellie and this friend of hers, Roberta –

They had to start somewhere. Antonio had to be somewhere.

Lisboa silent, stoic, steaming: left arm tanning out the window. Sunglasses mirrored. Necking coffee and digging into a bag of Pão de Queijo –

Lisboa offered. Leme didn't eat it, wagged a finger, clicked his tongue. I'm alright, mate, thanks. Suit yourself.

The heat was tremendous. They turned right off Brigadeiro, the main drag on their route. The whole Avenida seemed to chunt and shunt, ripple and shimmer, cough and belch. They arrowed in on Brasil and did a left onto Veneza, one of the side streets in the grid of Jardim Europa, not far from the slightly swankier Jardim Paulistano.

Lisboa grunted. He tapped the rear-view mirror. 'Been about ten minutes. Two of them, I think. Look like couriers.'

Leme angled the mirror. There was a motorcycle two cars behind. Black leather get-up. For a courier, he was dawdling. Those fuckers died, one a day in São Paulo on average, so keen were they to rip it up to their destinations. A mug's game. But this lad was not in a huge rush, it seemed.

'Sure there's another?'

Lisboa nodded. 'Yep. Hang about.'

Lisboa, out of the blue, floored it. They raced to the end of Veneza, did a left, then an immediate right, cornering tight, rubber *burned*. He slowed. This was a short, quiet road with a roundabout, fed from four sides, halfway down it, which came out onto Oliveira Días, just off São Gabriel. The roundabout was at the centre of a square grid of streets. In other words, if they were being followed, and the tail was a good one, they shouldn't have lost the tail.

Lisboa trod water.

Two motorcycles came at them as they crossed the roundabout, one from either side.

They growled. They ripped like chainsaws.

They skidded to a stop either side of the car. They pulled weapons.

The riders yelled hands out, out where I can see them.

Leme and Lisboa did as they were told.

The riders kept their visors down.

Leme and Lisboa looked dead ahead. Their hands were on the dash. Full sun. Their hands *roasted*.

The road was empty. Leme saw a third motorbike at the end of it, square on, blocking any potential traffic.

There was a faint blue-red flash, sharp and sudden, but brief in the late-morning sunlight, like the flash of the optician's torch in your light-flooded eyes, hard to see. But if you did see it, it registered. Leme saw it. Rider all in black. Not kosher.

Huh.

Not a coincidence.

The riders pulled guns.

The riders extended their arms.

The riders pointed with their guns.

The windows were open. The heat was still. The air was still –

The silence bristled.

The guns snuck, a touch, through the open windows and into the car.

The guns were suspended there, just inside the car, inches from Leme's head, inches from Lisboa's head, suspended there, just for a moment.

Leme and Lisboa held tight. Their palms sweated. Their palms slipped.

Hold tight.

The riders held tight. The riders held their poses.

Then:

The poses broke.

The riders tapped with the guns on the roof of the car. They holstered the guns. The rider on Leme's side leaned slightly in.

He said: 'Entendeu?'

He wheeled away. He made a gun shape with his hand. He pulled the trigger.

All three bikes skedaddled.

Leme and Lisboa breathed. Lisboa said, 'I think we know what that means.'

Leme nodded. It was a traditional warning, the tap on the roof, a sign of things to come if other things weren't squared, straightened.

Leme tapped the dash, twice. Let's go.

It's how you react to it, crime.

The city took care of itself. The neighbourhood took care of itself. One day, when Leme was fifteen, he went round to Lisboa's house after school. Lisboa's dad was a cop, a detective in the Polícia Civil, and was why, in the end, the two of them ended up on the force. He was a good lad, a fair man, and he understood the good in *doing*, in effecting change, in being a *force for good*. Lisboa had a younger cousin, a girl of twelve. That day, she was expected at the house too, her parents were busy and she needed minding for a few hours. She was late. Not too late, but late enough. Lisboa's dad came home quick, nonetheless. Moments later the cousin came through the door crying and shaking. A young lad had followed her there. He had followed her before, but he was just a kid, he'd never done anything, but this time he had tried to touch her.

He tried to what?

What did he do?

He tried –

When?

Now.

Where?

Lisboa's dad grabbed the cousin and was out the door in seconds.

Leme and Lisboa trailed him. Lisboa's dad found the kid round the corner. The cousin said yes, that's him. Leme and Lisboa watched.

Lisboa's dad picked the kid up, picked the small, terrified, confused kid up, picked him up by his neck, a hand tight round his neck –

And put him up against the wall.

Lisboa's dad put this scrawny weasel, this sex-pest, pervert kid, put him hard, put him hard up against the wall.

He said something to the kid.

Whatever he said, the cousin never had any problems again.

That threat, Leme thought, *solid*.

Ellie's eyes twinkled. Ellie's eyes danced. It might, Leme thought, be a touch indelicate, given the circs. Her mate Roberta was *grey*. It does that to you, worry. It gets at you, keeps at you. It leaves you greyed out, deathly pallor, all that. It's a cunt, worry, a relentless cunt.

Ellie, meanwhile, was enjoying being back in the game, it appeared, thrilled to be in the mix. She was conducting the whole show.

'Tell them,' she said to Roberta, 'tell them about Gabriel.'

Roberta told them what they already knew.

She spoke quietly, with a sniffle, a sort of shock. It had still only been a day and a half since she'd seen him, she said, since she'd heard from him, she knew that, knew it wasn't very long, knew couples had fought and blanked each other for far longer, but it worried her, and no one knew where he was, she'd had her friend Lis asking, carefully, for her, and now this business with Gabriel, some lad everyone knew, you know, on the scene, not exactly friends, but not exactly *not* friends, she said, just wondering, he was, if anyone wasn't about, it didn't feel good, let alone this business with the holiday –

Lisboa interrupted. 'Have you spoken to Antonio's parents?' He looked bored, restless, not digging the investigative thrill like young Ellie. Itching, it looked to Leme, to get on, to get about it.

'No.'

'Why not?'

'I didn't want to worry them.'

'OK, but *you're* worried.'

She nodded. 'My friend Lis knows they haven't heard from him. But it's totally normal. It's the time-off thing that I can't handle. Why would he do that? He wouldn't do that.'

'She hasn't slept,' Ellie said. 'Look at her.'

'You're sure he wouldn't?'

'I don't –'

'Oh come on, give her a break.'

'You're absolutely sure he's not been keeping something from you?'

'Mario, tell him –'

'I –' She shook her head. 'I can't believe –'

'Do you know Rafael Marquez?'

'Yes. Not very well.'

'Can you be nice? Mario, please.'

Lisboa ignored Ellie. 'And you know him through Antonio, I guess?'

Roberta nodded. She gripped her coffee cup tight. 'They were at school together, he's older, I think college too, they work together.'

'So they're mates?'

'Isn't that pretty fucking obvious? Porra, meu.'

'Antonio's got a lot of mates.'

'You say that like it's not a good thing.'

Roberta smiled – rueful. 'I don't think it *is* a good thing.'

'Is this relevant?'

Leme looked at Ellie. She mouthed sorry with exaggerated, ironic deference. Same as ever with this one. Older, but cheekier with it. Bit of experience, and it's pride before one and all that. Leme, with a look, pleaded patience.

'Why is it not a good thing?'

Roberta steeled herself a touch. She straightened her back. She drew deep. 'Antonio has always felt in debt to his friends.'

'Literally?'

'No, not literally, I mean his background is a little different, he's not a playboy by birth, entendeu? He's a scholarship boy. He's a clever fucker, but he chooses a life that isn't challenging.'

'You mean working where he does?'

Roberta nodded. 'Not my place to judge.'

'And yet.'

'Yeah.'

'So you don't like his friends.'

'It's not just that. It's his loyalty to them.'

'Mates come first.'

'That's a bit fucking sexist!'

'Ellie, be quiet,' Leme said.

'It's simplistic,' Roberta said. 'It's more than that. Point is, he'd do anything for them. If he made a promise, whatever it is, he'd honour it.'

Leme shot Lisboa a look: let's wrap this up. Leme glared at Ellie: keep schtum.

Lisboa nodded. 'I understand. Here's what we know: Rafael Marquez is also off the grid. He booked the two of them the holiday from work. They were supposed to do some off-the-books job for their boss.'

Leme's phone flashed, ringing. Antonia. He silenced it. He turned it over, face down. He hadn't spoken to her today. He should.

Roberta reddened. Her anger surged. 'The fucker! I –'

Lisboa raised a palm. 'Wait, just a moment. Is there anywhere that you know of that Antonio may have gone? Somewhere, I don't know, secret, somewhere he went, I don't know, to go fishing or meditate or whatever.'

Leme smiled – quiet. Lisboa nailed the tone.

Roberta shook her head.

'And this Rafael, do you have any –'

'None at all.' She pursed her lips. Her brain whirred. Her brain sang.

Lisboa, nodding: 'Right, this is what we need you to do.' He looked at Ellie. 'You too. Listen very carefully, love.' He focused again on Roberta. 'I want you to go and see one of Antonio's closest friends, preferably one who is also close to Rafael. I want you to tell them that two Polícia Civil detectives came to see you.'

'Wait, hang on. What the fuck?'

Lisboa glared at Ellie. He touched Roberta's hand. 'We want to find him too, and not because he's done anything wrong. You tell this friend that we're looking for him and Rafael. You tell the friend that it was confusing, but you hadn't seen Antonio since Sunday, you'd had a row, tell him, basically, the truth. Don't focus on how worried you are. And don't mention our names.' Lisboa looked pointedly at Ellie. 'Point is, in moments it'll get back to this Gabriel. We just don't want you to be the one feeding the information, certo?'

Roberta nodded. Leme stood. 'Stay stylish,' he said. 'Everything's going to be alright.' He looked at Ellie. 'And you, behave, entendeu? We'll talk about that email.'

Ellie waved them off, blew them both an ironic kiss, swooned.

Leme eyes *rolled*.

Those were the stories they told themselves, about how the city worked, about justice. About what was just and was unjust. About what exactly justice was. About how exactly justice *worked*. If it ever really did. These were the questions they asked themselves. And there were many answers. When they asked each other what those answers were, that was when there were problems. It was easier not to ask.

Leme looked at his phone. A message from Antonia: **It's happened. I love you.** Leme shook. Leme surged inside. It's happened. I love you. Leme knew what that meant. It meant everything.

Leme held tight. Leme rode track. 'What now then?' he asked Lisboa.

Lisboa weighed this question. 'Lunch, fuck it.'

That look again, they both had it: why the fuck not?

They were, it turned out, ravenous. Worry was a persistent fucker. If worry didn't let up on poor Roberta, if worry hadn't left her alone *for a moment,* it was funny how Leme's appetite had gone largely unscathed. Worry had been a little slack with Leme, bit workshy, to be fair. Leme smiled.

He was feeling pretty fucking euphoric. He had to compartmentalise. Stick it in a happy place. He had to take each game as it comes. You can only beat what's put in front of you. And what was in front of him at this point? That was the task at hand. Figure that out. Meantime, late-lunch chow-down. Stick it in a happy place.

'You're quiet,' Lisboa said.

Lisboa drooled juice from his hefty steak. Lisboa sucked salt from his fries. Lisboa heaved lager. He seemed to be both mopping up and refilling at the same time. A perfect storm. Appetites in sync, appetites *feeding* off each other.

It was quite special.

'I am.'

'Focus on getting some food down you, lad.'

'I'm not struggling.'

Lisboa jabbed the air with his knife. 'Eat now or forever rest in peace, entendeu?'

Leme smiled. 'I do know what you mean.'

'That's what we do, us funny people, we riff, sabe?'

Leme forked fries.

'It's the back and forth, we thrive on it.'

Leme raised his eyebrows.

'It's the camaraderie, the team spirit. Call and response, ta ligado?'

Leme gulped lager.

'It's the joy of working with someone you know, the simple pleasures involved in the art of conversation. Solving problems *together.* And it is an art.'

Leme wiped his chin. 'Leave it out, Ricardo.'

Lisboa snorted. Lisboa guffawed. Lisboa wolfed chow. 'You're let off until I'm done with this steak.'

Leme ate circumspectly. They were at an outdoor table at a neigh-bourhood restaurant in Itaim. Leme needed to talk to Antonia. Compartmentalisation only worked so much. *It's happened. I love you.* Leme needed to get on the blower.

He dabbed at his mouth with a napkin. He shook a toothpick from the plastic dispenser. He killed the end of his beer. He stood up.

'Just got to make a call,' he told Lisboa. 'Antonia, entendeu?'

Lisboa nodded. He swallowed. He grunted. 'On you go, mate,' he said.

Leme pulled his phone as he left the table. He stepped onto the street and turned right. He wandered twenty or so paces down the road, where it was quieter, and stopped outside a residential build-ing. Light breeze, shade. Trees swayed. Leaves breathed in the wind. No restaurant chat and clatter. Nice spot to share in some beauti-ful news. He flicked to calls made and hit her name. He turned a circle as he waited for the connection. Come on. Nothing. He examined his phone: 'calling Mobile.' No dial tone, no ring tone. Calling Mobile. Come the fuck on. He hit hang up. He redialled. He turned another circle. The buzz from nearby bars was low. The odd clank of a condo gate opening and closing. The odd honk of a car horn, the shout of an angry driver – distant. His phone: nothing. Fucking phones. Fucking phone reception. Either way. Again: no sound, just stamped across the screen: calling Mobile. He smiled. It'll work, there's no rush, be patient. The exact words she would speak, her patience with his impatience. Then: voicemail. Odd, phone off. Could be in a meeting. Or it could be reception his end. Try again. Same delay. He examined the screen. Again: calling Mobile. He put the phone back to his ear –

'Hang up.'

A voice behind him. Leme felt something in his back.

'Hang up. Turn around slowly. Hands where I can see them. Easy, there are people about. Phone wallet cash and anything else, certo?'

Leme did what he was told. He was fairly sure he was not being mugged.

He faced his assailant. He was dressed in motorcycle leather, trousers and boots. He wore a black cotton long-sleeve T-shirt. He sweated, lightly. He had that lazy, post-exercise economy and confidence in his movements. He did not look like he was going to be messed about. He knew what he was doing.

'I know you,' Leme said.

The man nodded. 'You do.'

'What do you want? My partner's just over there.' Leme nodded back towards the restaurant. 'And you're not going to use that here, after all.' Leme nodded at the gun half-concealed in the man's sleeve. 'What's your name again, young man?'

'Junior.'

'One of Carlos's boys. Paraisópolis driver, four years or so ago, ne? And we met again on Sunday, I believe.'

'Isso mesmo.' Exactly that.

'Old Carlos want to see me, does he?'

Junior shook his head.

'Come on, son, spit it out.'

'You're looking for a playboy lad called Antonio. I know where he is. I know the name of the body we found you poking around at. I know why Fat João was put out of his misery. And I want to help.'

'And I'm going to trust you, am I?'

Junior gestured with the half-concealed weapon.

Leme nodded towards the restaurant again. 'And my partner?'

'Best you come alone.'

'So you don't fancy a Militar promotion after all, then.'

'Something like that. Get in the car. Driver's side.'

Junior pointed a few yards down the road. Leme did what he was told.

'Key's in the ignition.'

'Where we going? Not fucking Lapa again, I hope.'

Junior shook his head. 'Just drive for now,' he said. 'I'll tell you my story and then I'll tell you where we're going.'

Leme gunned the engine. It growled. It roared. It settled, *purred*.
Leme raised an eyebrow, appreciatively. 'Nice wheels,' he said.

Junior nodded.

'Então,' Leme said. 'Let's have it then.'

Junior gave it to him, his story. Leme had to admit –

It was a good one.

Crime: it was how you react to it. Leme listened to Junior's story.

Junior left the apartment in Lapa. Fat João was well dead, pronto
corpse-stiffness. Must have been something to do with his bad diet,
the body freezing up that rapid. Big Carlos was downstairs in the
condo garage. Junior took the elevator. They sat high in the back seat.
Militar SUV, like a tank. Driver popped the engine then popped the
siren. They blue-red-flashed it, a high-tailed wail out of there. Driver
swerved left right left right, pavement-riding, traffic-bullying, horn-
honking: the works. They roared down the Marginal, in and out
of the safety lane, up and over the central reservation. Emergency
service. Junior told Leme the emergency was getting old Carlos to a
steak dinner.

They piled off the Marginal and into Morumbi. Headed for a
high-end joint on Giovanni Gronchi. Leme knew it. Leme made a
face: it's all *right*. Driver waited in the SUV. Junior and Carlos settled
into a booth. Muito romantic, Leme said. Junior glared. Carlos said,
food first then we'll talk. Carlos ordered for both of them. A fat por-
terhouse, a baked potato, a portion of fries, a salad, you know, pay
lip service to the old greens, the old cholesterol levels, corn drenched
in butter, a bottle of red –

Two beers each as a warm-up.

Junior was *hungry*. It happens, Leme said. Believe me. Carlos was
methodical in his approach, scientific. He first ate his steak, all of it,
without touching anything else, then his baked potato, same format,
then his fries, then his salad, and then his corn, with his hands,
butter all over his fat chin. He drank a full glass of red wine between
each component. Leme shook his head. The man's a monster. No

argument, Junior said. Carlos mopped up, ordered a second bottle and got to it. Why do you think our rat cunt friend there had to go? Carlos asked. Junior didn't know. Well, he knew, Fat João was a rat cunt, but he didn't *know*. He made a mistake, Carlos said. One that might cause us problems. Junior waited. Junior's belly heaved. It throbbed. It was very present, Junior's belly. That lad on Sunday, Carlos said. The dead playboy. It's connected. Junior told him that he thought it might be. Yeah, Carlos said. Fat João helped set that up. Junior nodded. But not before he fucked up. Junior waited. He had a message to pass on to this playboy, Carlos said, only he followed the wrong fucker out of the office. He delivered it to the wrong playboy. Junior nodded. We only found that out after the event, entendeu? How? Junior asked. The lad was a rat cunt, how do you think? Fair enough. Now then, Carlos said, your little stunt earlier might have worked out for the best. What little stunt? Leme asked. Junior told Leme about Gabriel. Leme didn't let on that he knew about this Gabriel. You're lottery-level lucky, my son, Leme said. I'm surprised Carlos didn't do you straight off the bat. Carlos poured them more wine. So, you've let the side down, in principle, but your show of allegiance to the flag and your bit of quick thinking means I'm going to give you something. Junior waited. Carlos smiled. The toothy gash of his grin was purple and dark. The name of the dead playboy. It might be a poisoned chalice, so to speak. Junior nodded. He knew. This was a see-no-evil hear-no-evil sort of a deal. Rafael Marquez, Carlos told him. That piece of gold is your way into our team, young man. Junior nodded. Poisoned chalice, Leme said. Right.

'I've got two questions,' Leme said. Junior nodded. 'One: why did this Rafael have to go? Two: did you do Fat João yourself?' Junior nodded. 'First answer: money and lies. Part of a clean-up. The kid was skimming – heavy. This doleiro business is classless now. It's money, money, money – everyone is in on it. That's enough, as you know.' 'This what Carlos told you?' Junior nodded. 'Second answer,' he said. 'I was there, that's all that matters.' Leme nodded. 'Church.'

It's how you react to crime. On a normal day in November in 2011, Leme's wife Renata went to her office as she did every day. She was a lawyer who worked in the favela Paraisópolis, legal aid, not quite pro bono but not far off. Like every other day, Renata worked hard. This day, she was helping a man with a land dispute. His wife was heavily pregnant. He wanted to build an extension to his rough, brick-and-wood favela house. This man lived next to a bar and a tyre shop and the owners of these businesses were not happy with these plans. In fact, they were blocking them, not legally, but literally blocking this poor man's plans, filling the space with their own crap where he intended to extend. Instead of a single extra room to house his growing family, there was a pile of tyres four deep and ten tall, surrounded by crates of empty beer bottles. Renata had spent all day talking to these owners. Back and forth, negotiating a compromise, showing them how they would be helping her client, and how they would be helping each other, and finally how they would be helping themselves. By mid-afternoon the two business owners had their lackeys shifting tyres and crates. By the end of the afternoon, Renata's client arrived home from work to see the cleared space and then he was buying drinks for the two men, and all three of them toasting the right decision for each other, for themselves, for the community. And then, in the early evening, just as Renata was preparing to head home, before it got dark, her client arrived at her office to pay his respects, to thank her and to bless her. He stayed for a long time. Too long. She left in a hurry. She fumbled her keys. Fireworks crackled and spat at the top end of the favela, meaning: danger. There had been more frequent invasions of the favela by the Military Police. They were warming up for Operação Saturação, an all-out assault to end the war on drugs. It would claim lives. Renata dropped her keys. Men in flip-flops carrying automatic weapons snaked around the backstreets. Renata's office was located on a corner where five dirt roads met. It was a community hub. A por kilo restaurant, another bar, another tyre shop, a greengrocer, a butcher, her legal aid office. It was the closest thing in the favela to a high street. The men drinking in the makeshift, hole-in-the-wall bar moved slowly inside, pushed tables in front. The grill came down quickly at the restaurant. The shops slammed doors, locked windows. They all knew what was coming. Renata scrabbled for her keys. She needed to get back into her office. The flash and single siren wail. Motorcycles skidded. SUV doors flung open. Renata was paralysed, unsure what to do, dithered right then left. She aimed back for the office; it was closer than her car. Then: machine-gun fire from all sides. Policemen and thieves. A kid with dreadlocks and gold teeth spraying lead.

It's called a bala perdida, a stray bullet.

It's how you react to crime.

Junior continued his story.

Driver dropped Carlos home then delivered Junior to his. The car ride was relaxed. Junior asked the one question: what about this Rafael's body? Carlos just shook his head. Who? He smiled – mean. Junior got it. Knowing the kid's name meant he was involved. They were after full deniability. Fuck knows where the kid's going to turn up. I can think of a few places, Leme said. Junior shook his head. Carlos told Junior that it was done, they had insurance, there were whispers that a Polícia Civil lemon was in place for the stitch-up. Rumours, Leme said. Junior smiled. Yeah, well. At home, Junior got on the phone, sharpish. He called Gabriel. He got the name Rafael Marquez. He told Gabriel nothing. He got another name: Antonio Neves. Colleagues. Friends. Finance guy at Capital SP. Junior instructed Gabriel not to tell Carlos this second name. Gabriel pleaded no can do. Junior was persuasive. You can be persuasive, son, Leme said. You've really come on, entendeu? Junior glared. Junior got on his bike over to Gabriel's. The parents let him in. Junior played the race card: the quota-filling intern at Gabriel's office. Gabriel: shit-scared. Junior bled Gabriel for information. It was forthcoming. Junior got on his bike to where young Antonio was hiding out.

'And that's where we're going,' Leme said. 'Good work, detective.'

Junior smiled – snide. 'You're the lemon, right. You need to help me. I'm not senior enough to pull this off.'

'Too junior, mate.'

'Very funny. You can help me resolve this.'

Leme nodded. He could.

Leme wondered about his phone wallet cash. There would be missed calls. Certainly from Lisboa. Antonia may have seen that he'd called. She may not have. She'd certainly know that there was no word exactly. Junior pulled his own phone and tap-tapped into it. He held his gun and kept one eye on Leme. 'You can put that thing away, mate.' Leme nodded at the gun. 'I ain't going anywhere.'

Leme didn't exactly react to that crime. It was hardly one he could comprehend. That it happened. How it had. How it. How. There were no referents, no precedents, no ways that he could contextualise it, no attempts to situate it in the city, in the city's self-governance, in the city's understanding of justice, in the city as judge, in the city as, in the city –

For a year, Leme sat in the favela, in his car, watching, looking at the scene, looking at where it happened, sat in his car, every morning for a year, looking, watching, sitting, where it happened, every day, for one year –

Why?

He didn't know. It was a compulsion, a need, it was, it –

'You remember when we first met then?'

Junior grunted. Junior nodded.

'Quite a night,' Leme said.

'For you maybe.'

'Rookie.'

'Just drive, porra.'

'Just like you that night.'

Junior shrugged. 'It was what it was, porra.'

Yeah, Leme remembered.

Leme used to be friends with old Carlos. Pretty tight, they were. Always had a laugh and old Carlão had his back, you know, a mate, a good lad. And a year or so after Renata, Carlos got some information. About a young drug dealer with dreadlocks and gold teeth. And it felt like something. It felt like an opportunity.

Junior was Driver that night. Heavy Mob, Big Carlos and Leme. They snaked through the favela in unmarked SUVs, lights down. During Operação Saturação there was a heavy presence of Militars. They kept an empty shack high up in the labyrinth. It was pretty much a lookout point. Not many other houses about. Well, relatively. It was still dense as fuck, but some of the buildings were decrepit, some abandoned. This was right in the fucking jungle. From the middle, uppermost point of Paraisópolis, you were three miles from the main road in every direction. This is what many people will never understand: the favela is alive; it *crawls*. It has its own life, cut off. When you're in it, you're *in* it. From high up in the air, during the day, in the blanket of sun, the heat so intense the heat itself seems to sweat, it looks like a great sprawling rubbish dump, or an anthill, seething with ants, *throbbing* with ants. Or a pile of rotting food, slowly devoured by maggots. After dark, lights flickered, electricity buzzed, the air cooled, the laughter from the counter-top bars was fresh, the smell of cheap pork and black beans hung, kids played until late, flip-flops smacking out clear like bells, the whole place eased into night.

They headed in and up. Two vehicles. These were tiny, poorly lit streets, with shop-front bars, mosquitoes buzzing around naked bulbs, crates of empty beer bottles stacked up in the street. Stoic, ageing drinkers, backs bent by unforgiving manual labour, legs cracked with rickets, sat at rusting tables, not talking. Hills dropped up and down; the houses listed at peculiar angles, lines of washing strung between them. Each house unique; each house the same. The same exposed cheap brick and rustled corrugated iron, the same painted-on house number, childlike, daubed as in a school project, the same family noises slipped through the holes in the walls for windows, the same thick smells like clouds. Here, you had to be up in the middle of the night to feel it. The houses that bent over Leme in the tight street, extensions hanging low, seemed to sway with the wind. There was a low, constant crackle in the wires strung criss-crossed above them, straining to carry the current around the Paraisópolis warren.

Leme had never been this far in, this far up.

In the Militar safe house, a young man, a kid, a black kid with dreadlocks and gold teeth, a young black kid sat tied to a chair, dripping blood.

Junior outside in the car; the rest of them got to work.

It didn't take long. The bucket of water and the plastic bag. Suffocate, drown, rinse, repeat. Carlos got the confession. Then it was open season. Boots, chair legs, half-bricks. Leme was there. Leme was involved. It was menos um, one less, no doubt, but it was one less villain who happened to have, who happened to have, who more than likely, who –

It was some sort of justice.

Leme was there. Junior was there.

That's all that matters.

Traffic was tight. They dallied. Junior relaxed, gun holstered. Leme fatalistic.

'I'm impressed with your calm, son.'

Junior smirked. 'Done some growing up.'

'Broke your cherry, did you? Old Fat João, I mean? I imagine that does leave you rather more relaxed.'

Junior, smiling, shook his head.

'What was with the whole PCC-imitation execution then?'

'Who's to say it wasn't the PCC?'

'Don't be a cunt, lad.'

Junior considered this. 'You probably know as much as I do.'

'I doubt that.'

'There's whispers that the PCC truce with Comando Vermelho is coming to an end. Seems there's money to be made from Lava Jato. This business is like fucking sand: it gets everywhere.'

Leme nodded. 'And Fat João has links with Rio.'

'Close enough. It can go either way, entendeu?'

'More insurance.'

'E isso aí.' Right on the money.

'Old Carlos is really stacking the deck, ne?'

Junior smiled. 'Just drive, porra.'

Lights changed. Leme crunched into first gear. They were on Nove de Julho, Paulista-bound. Late-afternoon traffic-level not too shabby. Buses and school vans. Motorbikes in and out of lanes, patience thin. From Avenida Paulista, could be any number of destinations. Leme's dinheiro was on a dirty little room in a half-built condo.

'I reckon Carlos stacking the deck is about saving face or saving his own skin.'

'Você que sabe.' You're the boss.

'He's a dirty bastard. Up to his ears in filth, dodgy schemes and whatnot.'

Junior said nothing.

'Someone's had a word. He's doing a favour.'

Junior tightened. They rode bus rhythm: stop, start, weave left, weave right.

'It's a thought, ne?'

Traffic hum. Traffic song. Traffic lullaby. Leme eased the gas. Leme rode the gas half time. Leme hit the Paulista traffic-light optimal speed right on the nose. Eased the gas and drifted through, no stopping, no pause, clean as a Portuguese whistle. Textbook light timing. Junior looked sleepy. He had the look of a nap-ready milk-drunk toddler, eyes lolling.

Leme drifted. Antonia. *It's happened. I love you.* Leme dreamed. Antonia. *It's happened. I love you.* Leme leaned back, sank – happy. Antonia. *It's happened. I love you.* This was her. This was them. This was theirs. Antonia. *It's happened. I love you.*

Leme remembered. Leme looked back.

It was easy, it turned out, to fall in love again, to love again.

They moved in together around the same time as the Cracolândia land deal beef, and the crisis that entailed. They got over that without any real drama. They understood each other. They knew that neither of them had done anything to threaten the two of them as a couple; that seemed like the most important thing. They worked together, in fact; they became a team. They had overcome adversity. Not long afterwards, they went away for a weekend. Monte Verde. A mock Alpine-style resort. They booked a cabin. There was a hot tub and a bar. They piled the car high with red wine and French cheese. They were going to feast on fondue. Antonia drove. Two and a half hours out of São Paulo and up up up. Windows down. Cool air. Green. No mobile phone service. Dirt tracks leading to rivers and streams. Gates opening to farm roads and crop fields. Hedges. The sun no longer beat down, it no longer burned. It *shone*. It glistened. Antonia smiled. Her face shone. Her hair shone. Her hair glistened. Leme laughed. Leme dozed. They played rock and roll on the stereo. They sang Stones. Their song: Loving Cup.

Their cabin overlooked a valley. Their cabin was on a hillside. There were complimentary bubbles in the mini-bar. Leme popped the cork. They drank from deep wine glasses. Bucket-sized. Pure class, Antonia said. They stripped for the hot tub. They made love. They made a naked dash for it. There were no other guests about, and it was private, after all, their hot tub. They knocked back their bubbles and toasted each other and they drank and they laughed and they made love again, quietly, with a degree of circumspection, in amongst the bubbles, their heads light, their smiles full, their love full, their love ballooning, their love bursting, their love –

Monte Verde had a single road, Leme remembered. They ate raclette in their warm jumpers. They sat at an outside table under heaters. The restaurant was full of couples sitting in their warm jumpers, playing at being in Europe, in Switzerland, eating raclette. The reality was that the temperature, as Antonia joked, was about as cold as a São Paulo shopping mall. There was a lot of expensive gear, waterproofs and scarves, warm jumpers and fur-lined boots, swaddling the city getaway crowd. They went quickly back to their cabin, their red wine and their hot tub. They placed manicured logs in their luxury wood-burning stove. They caught and crackled. Flames licked the glass. They eyed a thick, shag pile rug. They smiled at each other.

It was quite a weekend. They walked wooded trails. They ate melted cheese in their warm jumpers. They wandered chocolate shops. They pottered. They browsed knick-knacks and curios. They drank beer at lunch from huge mugs. They made love on their shag pile rug in front of their wood-burning stove. They made love in their hot tub.

Sunday morning, they headed home, the first time they had returned to their home together. Leme drove. Antonia dozed, her head on his shoulder. She murmured. He stroked her hair when he could. They played no rock and roll; it was peaceful. Leme felt content. Leme felt excited.

It had been easy, it turned out, to fall in love again, to love again. Whatever anyone says, he thought now, his eye on Junior, perhaps it really is simply about the right person. All that business about timing and whatnot, and it's not you it's me, and I'm really focusing on work, and I'm not ready, it's too soon, I'm not over her, when in fact meeting Antonia and loving Antonia were something separate and something singular. Antonia. *It's happened. I love you.* He wondered now, his eye on Junior, what Renata would make of all this. He smiled. Antonia. *It's happened. I love you.* Everything was different now.

Leme was *goood.*

Junior got into a rhythm of his own.

Monosyllabic imperatives. Right. Left here. Left. Next right. Left at the lights. He held his phone in front of him, pointedly, like a weapon. He examined its screen with serious intent. He held his weapon loosely, like a notebook. They'd done a right off Paulista and down Rua Augusta. The neon bristled. The student bars heaved and cackled. The motels did a brisk trade with women who came in and out of neon-fronted strip bars with happy-looking Johns. There were queues of boho types outside the theatres. An angry bouncer relieved a tourist of his cash. Men and women devoured enormous deli sandwiches in padarias. Business as usual.

'We there yet?' Leme asked.

Junior gave him the sidelong fisheye. He was a bit moody. Nervous, Leme thought. Not really a surprise considering the lad was about to screw over his boss, a boss who did not take kindly to being screwed over, who, in fact, was known to ruin the lives, even *end* the lives, of any cunt that dared to even think about screwing him over. Yeah, Leme thought, twitchy, edgy. The man's early poise and quiet swagger had done one; Junior was shitting it.

'Don't worry, porra,' Leme said. 'I've got this. Stroll in the woods, mate.'

Junior grunted. 'Another five minutes, porra. Shape up.'

Leme nodded. Here we go. Here we fucking go.

At the end of Rua Augusta, once you've got past the skin clubs and motel-brothels, past the cheap bars and artsy performance spaces, past the hip nightclubs and twenty-four-hour bakeries, and past Parque Augusta, with its desperate junkies and crack-addicted, toothless whores engaged in their terrible transactions, once you've crossed beneath Viaduto Júlio de Mesquita Filho, you arrive at a quiet square, benches and low-hanging trees, circled by Rua Avanhandava, which is home to a few old-school Italian canteens, most famously, Famiglia Mancini, run by families that don't ask too many questions. These restaurants are frequented by the detectives and more senior members of the Civil Police based at the 4th Distrito Policial Consolação station that flanks Parque Augusta. So when Junior indicated that Leme was to ghost round the back and creep quietly past the Mancini Pizzeria, the Madreperola seafood place, the swank Walter Mancini restaurant, and then the eponymous family canteen, Leme felt pretty secure. Just past the eponymous family canteen was a cheap hotel, not much more than a doss house, and slightly behind it, an auto repair shop. A narrow entrance closed off by a garage door ran between. Junior tapped at his phone and the door opened. They went through, and down to a tiny underground car park, clearly not used by the hotel. There was space for, perhaps at most, if cleverly arranged, two other vehicles. The detritus was oily: rusting parts, rags and half-empty paint buckets. Leme made it for the auto repair storage facility. It was tucked almost under the Museo Judaico de São Paulo. Nove de Julho rumbled overhead. Belly-of-the-beast type of scene, Leme thought: right in the gut of the city.

Leme killed the engine, killed the lights. It was murky down there. Damp. It was not welcoming. It seemed like a strange sort of a safe house.

'Where's the kid?' Leme asked.

Junior gestured with his chin at a doorway in the corner. 'There's an office.'

Leme nodded. 'You thought about what you're going to do next?'

Junior shook his head.

'Best course is probably do nothing.'

Junior grunted.

'No need for anyone to find out how this came to pass, entendeu?'

'Uh-huh.'

'So,' Leme said, 'you going to get the kid or what?'

Junior opened his door. He waved his revolver to show Leme he was to do the same. Leme did as he was told. Junior flicked a wall switch, and a naked bulb buzzed, sputtered, lit. Leme's eyes adjusted. He'd stopped the car in the middle of the concrete space, driven right into it. Behind, the ramp bent sharply to street level. In front of the car: the oily detritus, and to the left, the doorway, no door. No light came from the space on the other side of this doorway. It was, definitively, your basic shithole. To the right there was a broken-looking chair, a filthy blanket. Leaning against the chair: a battered acoustic guitar, strings torn from it, snapped and hanging loose, its neck twisted, its body warped and scratched, the victim of some outrage. A couple of ropes lay coiled like whips. Next to these: a small pile of empty, rusting tins, beans and frankfurter, tops opened up and levered to the side, food forked straight from it, cold. Dirty.

Junior held out a hand. 'Keys.'

Leme tossed them over. Junior caught them, pocketed them – deft.

'Então?' Leme nodded at the doorway.

'Wait here.'

'I'll take a number and have a seat,' Leme said.

They were not far from Cracolândia. There had been further attempts to clean it up a little, but they were largely half-hearted. Leme remembered poor old Leandro, from Antonia's law firm, plucked from the favela on an affirmative action internship and used as a go-between, poor old Leandro who found himself accidentally treading on Militar cash-dope turf down there in the streets of very hell, his throat cut in his own home for the privilege. Leme had last worked the Centro in 2014. There had been a spate of brutal killings, six seemingly random attacks, a couple of homeless men, a prostitute, a working mother travelling to her job, a professional beggar, a man out jogging mistaken for a drug dealer: only the prostitute survived, though she remained in a critical condition for months afterwards. She had no insurance, of course, and no job security. Four were killed with an axe. Three of the bodies had been decapitated. The man out jogging was stabbed and burned. They caught the killer easily enough: a witness noted the number plate of a car apparently fleeing a crime and called it in. They traced the number plate to its owner, Jhonathan Lopes de Santana. Leme was part of the team that arrested him. He was, it appeared to Leme, indifferent to what he had done. He had targeted the homeless, beggars, drug dealers and addicts as it was 'less serious' than killing taxpayers. He told the police he would have continued to kill. He had the number thirty-six tattooed on his leg: his intended victim total. He had etched a drawing of an axe into his arm, using needle and knife. There was nothing in his background to suggest he was a threat to society. His motivation, he told police, he didn't really know, but it was likely because he watched a lot of war videos. He was inspired, he said, by the ISIS beheading films. Leme remembered his eyes. They were blank, but puzzled, like he didn't know why he had done what he had done, but he did know he *had* done what he had done, and that was OK. It had happened before, the homeless and the destitute, the worthless and the scourges of decent society murdered by a single killer or a gang. It was not vigilante justice; more like an experiment. It was how you react to crime. Leme didn't know how to react to this young man, this monster. How to react to such a thing, how to fathom that his lack of contrition was more like a simple acceptance of what he'd done? The story was well-known; it was all over the national media, some international outlets. If friends or acquaintances ever asked Leme about it, he told them he'd had nothing to do with the case.

Leme waited. A light came on in the dark space behind the empty doorway. He heard quiet, scratching noises, as if furniture were being moved around, or the place was being straightened, tidied up a little, a quick geral. The room couldn't be much bigger than a cell, he thought. Then: a much louder noise –

The garage door jerked and crunched open, a low hum as it rose and slid into place. A black car with blacked-out windows pulled in.

Here we go.

The woman, who had been on her way to work, had got up early. She lived with her daughter in Brás in a simple house and was walking up to the Centro to her job as an administrative assistant in the law faculty of the University of São Paulo. She had left early that morning as she wanted to get a head start at work so that she could then leave early to cook a birthday dinner for her daughter, who turned thirty that day. It was five thirty in the morning when she was killed. She was dressed in nondescript clothes; her daughter later told police that she always walked to work in clothes like those so as not to attract attention, and changed into her office outfit when she arrived. Lopes de Santana told police he thought she was a prostitute on her way home. It was the clothes, he said, they were baggy, comfortable, thrown on, casual, but the woman wearing them alert and confident. She was the kindest, most warm-hearted woman you would ever meet, her daughter said to the press. It was a wrong-place wrong-time situation, the police told the daughter. The woman's name was Maria; she was fifty-nine years old. Lopes de Santana shrugged. She was a whore, he thought.

The back and passenger doors opened. Leme felt a surge of fear, a light-headed rush like he might faint. He had felt this before, many times, and he controlled it. Junior appeared in the doorway, his weapon raised. The Heavy Mob climbed out from the back seat, either side. Then, on the near side, closer to where Leme stood, one of them yanked Ellie out by the arm. She looked dazed, said nothing. After this, a pair of sturdy, meaty, leather-booted legs swung out from the front seat, and Carlos heaved himself out after them.

'Oi, oi,' he said.

Leme looked at Junior. Junior shrugged. 'Ah, it is what it is, porra, entendeu?'

Leme shook his head. 'Vagabundo,' he muttered. 'Seu caralho.'

Leme had known Ellie for more than four years. He remembered the way she had spoken, in paragraphs, opinions formed, considered and communicated, a mixture of insight and understanding, self-deprecation about how messy she could be. That joke: thank God, she'd said to a new lover, my last boyfriend's cock was so big I had cystitis pretty much constantly. Leme remembered that. He remembered her voice. He looked at her now, quiet, confused, scared, and he thought of her voice, he thought of her voice to give her strength, to give *himself* strength. The strength she showed when her friend Ana, her best friend, her only friend really, went missing. I met Ana in São

Paulo, the first words she said to him. I wasn't prepared; I know that now. For her or the city. The city leapt up at me the moment I arrived.

Leme looked at her now. Was she prepared for this? Confused, mute, in danger. She was brave, Ellie.

Look where that had got her.

'Carlão,' Leme said. 'This is out of order, mate.'

Leme remembered Ellie, her first impressions of the city she wasn't prepared for. From the air, São Paulo goes on forever, she said, a dense building site, dust and pollution hovering above skyscrapers, flashing lights distant in the cloud, bridges that cross the stinking river. Futuristic and apocalyptic, Leme remembered that idea, had liked it, the image: helicopters dropping off businessmen on the roofs of their workplace, their heads encased in helmets, their briefcases handcuffed to their hands. That is the fantasy. She'd looked at him then, made a face. The reality arrived as the plane touched down. The heat rose from the gutters. Sticky with sweat, I struggled to collect my baggage, she told him, Paulistanos talking loudly to each other and into mobile phones in a perverse-European language, mellifluous and harsh. Foreigners shouldered away, baking in the artificial light. I noticed the manner, the entitlement of the men. The expectancy of the women. In the well-dressed, at least. And then the shuffling resignation of the darker faces. The oversized vests and shorts. I wondered where I would fit in. Pink-cheeked and pale, creeping patches under my arms. There were a couple of sharp glances, head to thigh. My skirt was too short for an airport.

Leme looked at her now. Look how far you've come, querida.

'Settle down, Mario,' Carlos said. 'This is just a straightener, entendeu? Your little friend here is a curious cat, that's all. And we all know what happens to them.'

Leme shook his head, smiled – rueful. She was, he thought.

Her voice flashed through Leme. Hold tight, he thought. I started off in one of those flat-services, he heard her saying. The magazine had set it up but told me that I probably wouldn't be able to afford it for too long. That wasn't too encouraging. I moved out from top-floor quality to a fifth storey with dodgy plumbing and permanent stains. My balcony attracted smoke from the passing trucks. When I first moved in there, I tried to sit out in the evenings and read, sip at a glass of wine, but I'd be quickly forced inside by the fumes. And the noise. The noise! The noise: a constant low thunder pierced by car horns and angry shouts from the drivers. On my first night, sweating in the heat, I'd opened the bedroom window and lay awake until dawn, writhing around under the sheets. I thought, as I stood under the electric shower, terrified the water would react with the open wires, my head fuzzy from lack of sleep: does no one go to bed in this city?

Look where it has got you, Leme thought. *Look.*

Her voice echoed. On my first day at the office, a group of my colleagues invited me out for a drink. We went to a local bar, Vaca Veia, which they told me translated roughly as old cow. I wasn't sure what to make of that. They drip-fed me Caipirinha until the bar became a carousel of grinning, flushed faces, wild, gesticulating arms and noisy laughter. There was a confident man outside the ladies toilets: he handed me a shot. I staggered back to the flat-service and passed out in my clothes, waking a couple of hours later to throw up in the pristine toilet. My mouth tasted of scorched limes and after-shave, my skin raw from stubble. That first night, with its seductive mix of abandon and professional intent, had offered adventure. The cloying looks of my colleagues the next day, the sweaty paranoia of my hangover, did not.

This voice flashed, echoed, this voice, this girl, this woman, this woman who had done so much for Leme, with him, and he looked at her now, and his eyes said: *Hold fast, querida.* Hold tight.

Leme looked at Carlos. He nodded at Junior. 'Your boy deserves a promotion.'

Carlos smiled. 'He's a stone killer, this lad.'

Leme watched as the Heavy Mob moved either side of him. 'Well, he's a good actor. Played that bad-guy-on-the-turn very well indeed. Bravo, *Junior*.'

Carlos laughed. 'Sometimes it takes making a little mistake to understand which side your bread is buttered, sabe? Young Junior here catches on quick.'

'As the saying goes,' Leme said, 'love or fight, ne?'

'What a wordsmith.'

'Uh-huh.'

Leme and Carlos looked at each other. Carlos had a firm grip on Ellie's arm. She was standing, but she was slumped, head lolling, Carlos's grip helping her to stay upright. Carlos clocked Leme's concern. He smiled.

'You worried about your little gringa cunt, are you?' he said. 'Mate, she's a floozy doozy, primeiro classe. Told me all about the botched illegal scrape job she had to have last year. One night stand with a Big Man down at Love Story, you know what I mean? The fucker wasn't having any of it. Poor slag had to figure it out all alone. Damaged goods, mate. I don't know why you bother.'

'That's not true.'

'Don't shoot the messenger, son.'

Leme saw the Heavy Mob edge round a touch further, their weapons drawn but held in front, pointed at the ground. Junior leaned against the door frame, cool as fuck. Leme faced the two cars, wall behind him, chair and guitar to his left. Carlos levered Ellie round and propped her up on the bonnet of Junior's vehicle.

'What have you done to her?' Leme asked.

'She's fine.'

'She doesn't look it.'

'Trust me.'

'Ha.'

Leme examined Ellie. She looked drunk, a little high, perhaps. Some sort of pill, he thought, a tranquiliser or some shit like that.

'Why is she here anyway?'

Carlos turned to Ellie and spoke into her ear. 'She's been a nosy cow, that's why, haven't you, querida?' He looked back at Leme. 'She was sniffing around Capital SP, I believe you know it. Productive meeting? We had someone keeping an eye on the place. She was causing something of a ruckus in reception. They were very pleased we could help escort her off the premises.'

'Right.'

Ellie coughed, seemed to shake herself awake. Carlos handed her a bottle of water. 'Here you go, love. Drink up.' He made a face at Leme. 'Told you. She'll be right as rain in no time.'

Ellie drank deeply. She seemed to come out of the daze for a moment. She saw Leme. Her eyes widened. Her chest swelled. Leme felt it too. That look again: hold fast.

'So,' Carlos said. 'We find ourselves in something of a pickle, do we not?'

Leme grunted.

Carlos continued. 'Fact is old Fat João fucked it all up by involving this lad Antonio. He's what takes it out of the realm of a fairly simple clean-up of a couple of wide-boy doleiros who got greedy, sabe?'

Leme nodded. 'So you had Fat João point me to the body so I might be put in the frame. Like you told me before, insurance, porra.'

Carlos smiled – nasty. 'They've got me over a fucking barrel and you know full well why.'

Leme nodded. 'The Gold Teeth beef, I suspect.'

Carlos grimaced. 'Let's just say that some of my activities over the years have been remarked upon.'

'And now you have to take care of a few bits and pieces for the big boys.'

'Yeah, you can call it that. It's quite a racket though. This Lava Jato nonsense is scaring a lot of people, and there is a lot of money to be made helping these pussies cover their tracks.'

'So you're performing a public service.'

'For those who can afford it.'

Leme smiled. 'And Fat João?'

'Do you really give a fuck?'

'I found the poor cunt.'

Carlos nodded. 'Handy that. We can play it out however we like. End of the day, no cunt cares, and we can close the book on it.'

'And this lad Antonio? Where's he then?'

'We don't know.'

'You don't know.'

'He'll come home when he's hungry.'

'And when he does?'

'He's implicated, to an extent. That Capital SP mob are well dodgy. And they've got some important clients. We'll come to an agreement.'

Leme's stare hardened. 'What kind of an agreement?'

'I think there's been quite enough unpleasantness. I suspect he'll be happy to keep his trap shut, with what we know.'

Leme weighed it. Capital SP was connected. Leme was in the frame for Rafael and Fat João: if need be. Leme knew all about Gold Teeth. Leme also knew all about Carlos's excursions into the Cracolândia drug-trafficking game and his subsequent real-estate investments. Two options, as Leme saw it: one, Leme takes a fall as there will be fallout from Rafael, if not Fat João, and there will be a fall to take. Two, well, Leme knew the other option, the safer option, for them, and they could make it work.

'It'd be a balancing-out, porra,' Carlos said, watching Leme's mind work.

Ellie though. Ellie was there. Ellie.

Leme had told her a couple of years ago that she should go home. He told her that you couldn't do the work she wanted to do and stay sane. Look at Silva, he said, the man's a mess, lost all sense of what life is about, can't even think about it, can't even think about what might have been as it's long gone, it's only the story, the next story, and it's no life. Ellie waved Leme away. Ah vai, she said, don't be such a drama queen. Leme laughed. But he looked her straight and said, one day, querida, you're going to come up against something that's too big for you. You should go home before that happens. Her bravado was cute, Leme remembered that. Look where it had got her.

Carlos eyed Leme. Carlos nodded at Ellie. 'We've also got an arrangement. She's going home.'

'Yeah?'

'One of you has to. She'll be on a plane in a day or two. I've had a word with our Federal friends. Her visa's compromised, entendeu? Suits everyone. Trust me.'

Leme nodded. 'On that point, OK.'

Carlos gestured at Junior. He lifted his gun and trained it on Leme. Carlos gestured at the Heavy Mob. They went into the back of the vehicle they'd arrived in and pulled out a rolled plastic sheet. They unrolled it. They pulled a fat rug. Carlos raised his eyebrows at that. Made a face: oh the irony.

Leme nodded.

Leme thought of Antonia. Her face. Her arms. Her arms carrying their child. Antonia dancing a lullaby, cradling their child in her arms.

Ellie looked at Leme. She couldn't speak. In her eyes: understanding. In her eyes: tears. She tried to speak. She couldn't speak. He felt her eyes, the meaning in her look. Strength. She gave him strength.

He tightened. He shaped up. He rolled his neck.

Leme closed his eyes. A tear fell, slid down his cheek. Carlos said something to one of his boys, one of the Heavy Mob. Leme opened his eyes. Junior stood still. Junior did not smile. Leme nodded. Junior looked away. Leme looked at Ellie. He urged her to understand. Ellie like a rabbit stuck on a metro track, train bearing down, confused. Leme nodded. He mouthed the words: *Antonia. Tell her to change nothing.* He spoke the words. Carlos shook his head: pipe down, mate.

Carlos gestured at Junior. Junior took Ellie's arm. Junior stiff-armed Ellie into the passenger seat of his vehicle. He buckled her in. Leme watched Ellie frantic. She shook her head. She sobbed fat tears. She tried to scream. She couldn't scream. Junior jumped in. Junior slammed doors. Junior fed her water. The engine growled. The engine purred. A hard reverse screech and Junior did one.

Leme closed his eyes. He saw Antonia's face. Renata's face. Antonia's face. Their words echoed. He was loved, he is loved.
    Leme breathed –
    Lights out.

Postscript

President Dilma Rousseff was formally impeached on 17 April 2016. She was charged with criminal administrative misconduct and disregard for the Federal budget.

The Lava Jato investigation paralysed government: coalitions cannot be built without bribes. Prosecutors suspended Petrobras contracts with all major suppliers, key construction and shipping firms in Brazil. The country faced a devastating recession.

Faith in the political system was eroded. In 2016 a series of huge protests against corruption were staged in over 200 cities in every state in the country. In São Paulo, the largest demonstration in the history of the city took place, with over 2.5 million in attendance.

The protests, it became clear, were not just about the government, but the whole, rotten political structure of the country.

In October 2018, the far-right, populist Jair Bolsonaro campaigned to be elected president. He promised to unite the country, purge the corrupt leftists and fight crime with a ruthless and brutal no-mercy, no-leniency policy. He is renowned for his misogyny and his racist, homophobic views. Weeks before the election took place, Bolsonaro was attacked and stabbed while speaking at a rally.

He survived and won the election in a landslide.

Glossary

Abraço(s)	Hug(s)
Acho que eu vou embora	I think I'll head off
Alegría	Joy
Amarelou	In this instance, 'Coward'
Amigo/Amiga	Friend
Amorzinha	Sweetheart
Até mais	See you later
Bala perdida	Stray bullet
Batendo papo	Chatting, banter, literally, 'hitting chins'
Beleza	Beautiful
Bem	Well, as in 'all well?' Also, as intensifier, 'well hot!'
Boca/Boca de fuma	Place in a favela where drugs are sold
Cafézinho	Euphemism for bribe, literally, small or quick coffee
Caipirinha	Cachaça and lime-based cocktail
Cão de guarda	Guard dog
Cara	Dude
Caralho	Derogatory term, generally 'motherfucker' or 'dick'
Claro	Of course
Certo	OK

Chega!	Enough!
Chorinho	Idiom, meaning a drop more, or a top-up when drinking, literally, a little tear or teardrop
Coitado/Coitada	Poor thing!
Comando Vermelho	Red Command, a gang based in Rio de Janeiro
Dedo-duro	Grass/snitch
Dinheiro	Money
Doleiro	A bagman, money launderer
E aí	Hey
E isso aí	That's exactly right
Embora	In this instance, 'let's go'
Então…	So…
Entendeu?	Know what I mean/understood/you get me? Etc
Favela	Slum
Faz o que?	What are you going to do?
Filho da puta	Son of a bitch
Foi legal	It was cool
Frescura	Literally, 'to get fresh', in this instance, act superior
Garoto/garota	Boy/girl
Geral	In this instance, a quick tidy up, clean up
Graças a Deus	Thank God
Gringa	Foreign woman
Hoje	Today

Isso mesmo	Exactly right
Já era	Already happened, or, it's over
Jeitinho	A shortcut, often used in terms of bribery/cheating
Jeito	Style/method/way
Luz	Light
Mais ou menos	More or less
Malandro	A young punk, or petty criminal
Mano	Slang, 'brother', similar to 'dude'
Mata saudades	To catch up after time apart, literally to kill longing
Menina	Girl
Menos um	In this instance, when a criminal dies, a shrug, 'one less'
Meu	In this instance, 'mate'
Militar	A member of the Military Police
Muito bem	Very good, or Very well
Nada	Nothing
Não e/Ne?	Isn't it/Innit?
Não tem problema nenhuma	No problem at all
Não tem	I don't have it
Nas fim das contas	Idiom, At the end of the day
Nem fodendo!	No way am I doing that!
Noia	Crack addict/paranoid drug user
Nossa!	Wow!
Obrigado/Obrigada	Thank you

Ótimo	Excellent
Padaria	Bakery, simple restaurant/bar
Papo furado	Bullshit/nonsense
Pão de Queijo	Cheese-bread
Pão duro	Stingy, tight-arse, literally, hard bread
Pão na chapa	French bread fried in butter
Pastel	A deep fried pastry
Pegou?	In this instance, '[drugs] kicked in?'
Polícia Civil	Civil Police, which undertakes criminal investigation
Polícia Militar	Military Police, which polices the city
Polícial	Police Officer
Pois é	In this instance, 'you're telling me'
Pois não?	Can I help you?
Porra	Literally, 'semen', but used as a catch-all swear word
Porteiro	Doorman
Pouquinho	Small amount
PCC	First Capital Command, Primeiro Comando da Capital, São Paulo based gang
Primeiro classe	First class
Puta	Whore
Puta que pariu!	Expletive, similar to, 'Fuck me!'
Que porra essa?	What the fuck is this?
Que coisa!	Amazing!
Quem fala?	When answering the phone, 'Who's that?'

Querido/Querida	Term of affection, similar to 'my dear/sweetheart'
Relaxa!	Relax!
Rodizio	System that allows certain cars in the city at rush hour
Roba mais faz	He steals but he gets things done, coined after a corrupt politician, a former mayor of São Paulo
Sabe?	You know?
Saudades	Longing, when you miss someone/something
Segurança	Security guard
Sem graça	Literally 'without grace', meaning gauche/clumsy/tacky
Sério	Seriously
Ta boa?	You OK?
Ta ligado?	Know what I mean/understood/you get me?
Ta vendo?	Do you see/understand?
Ta entendendo?	Know what I mean?
Taxista	Taxi driver
Tou falando sério	I'm serious
Tudo bem?	How are you?
Vai com Deus	God be with you
Vai se foder!	Go fuck yourself!
Vai tomar banho!	Literally, 'go take a shower!', a play on 'up yours!'
Vai tomar no cú!	Up yours!

Vagabundo	Derogatory term, similar to 'arsehole' or 'wanker' or 'dick' or 'douchebag', with an emphasis on betrayal, literally, a vagrant
Vamos	Let's go
Vamos jantar	Let's have dinner
Vamos ver	Let's see, We'll see
Você	You
Você que sabe	Up to you, You're the boss
Você ta viagando!	Idiom, that's ridiculous!, literally, you're travelling (in the mayonnaise)

Acknowledgments

The K Blundell Trust, Piers Russell-Cobb, Martin Fletcher, Will Francis, Joe Harper, Angeline Rothermundt, Kid Ethic, Nicci Praça, Rosie Stevens, Lucy Caldwell – for her insight, and her time – and Martha Lecauchois, for our time.

GRONINGEN

• Leeuwarden

• Groningen

FRIESLAND

• Assen

DRENTHE

• Emmen

elystad

• Zwolle

LAND

OVERIJSSEL

Apeldoorn •

Enschede •

GELDERLAND

• Arnhem

Nijmegen •

• Eindhoven

LIMBURG

• Maastricht

Friesland
Pages 294–305

Groningen
Pages 280–293

Drenthe
Pages 306–315

Flevoland
Pages 326–333

Gelderland
Pages 334–349

Overijssel
Pages 316–325

Limburg
Pages 370–385

0 kilometres 20

0 miles 20

D0319083

EYEWITNESS TRAVEL

THE
NETHERLANDS

Main Contributor **Gerard M L Harmans**

DK

DK | Penguin Random House

Produced by Van Reemst Uitgeverij/Unieboek bv

Main Contributor Gerard M L Harmans

Design Studio Putto, De Rijp

Art Editor Dick Polman

Editorial (Dutch original) *de Redactie*, boekverzorgers, Amsterdam

Photographers
Max Alexander, Anwb Audiovisuele Dienst
(Thijs Tuurenhout), George Burggraaff, Jurjen Drenth,
Rubert Horrox, Kim Sayer, Herman Scholten

Illustrators
Hilbert Bolland, Jan Egas, Gieb van Enckevort,
Nick Gibbard, Mark Jurriëns, Maltings Partnership,
Derrick Stone, Khoobie Verwer, Martin Woodward

Cartography
Jane Hanson, Armand Haye, Lovell Johns Limited
(Oxford, UK), Phil Rose, Jennifer Skelley, Peter de Vries

Picture Researcher Harry Bunk
Production Sarah Dodd

English-language adaptation produced by
International Book Productions Inc.,
25a Morrow Ave, Toronto, Ontario M6R 2H9, Canada

Managing Editor Barbara Hopkinson
Editor Judy Phillips
DTP Designers Dietmar Kokemohr, Sean Gaherty

Printed and bound in China

First Published in Great Britain in 2003
by Dorling Kindersley Limited
80 Strand, London WC2R 0RL

17 18 19 20 10 9 8 7 6 5 4 3 2 1

Reprinted with revisions 2005, 2008, 2011, 2014, 2017

Copyright © 2003, 2017 Dorling Kindersley Limited, London
A Penguin Random House Company

Front cover main image: Schermerhorn, North Holland, Netherlands

◀ Tulip fields with a windmill in the background

CONTENTS

How to Use
this Guide **6**

Zeeland's coat of arms

Introducing the Netherlands

Discovering the
Netherlands **10**

Putting the Netherlands
on the Map **18**

A Portrait of the
Netherlands **20**

The Netherlands
Through the Year **36**

The History of
the Netherlands **42**

Girl with a Pearl Earring (1665)
by Johannes Vermeer *(see p227)*

The 15th-century Koppelpoort in Amersfoort

Thialf fans *(see p304)*

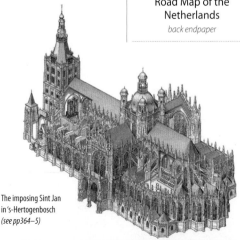
The imposing Sint Jan
in 's-Hertogenbosch
(see pp364–5)

HOW TO USE THIS GUIDE

This guide helps you get the most from your stay in the Netherlands. The first section, *Introducing the Netherlands*, places the country on the map and puts it in its historical and cultural context. Chapters on the provinces and the capital, Amsterdam, describe the most important sights and places of interest. Features cover topics

from architecture to tulip growing. They are accompanied by detailed and helpful illustrations. *Travellers' Needs* gives specifics on where to stay and where to eat and drink, while the *Survival Guide* contains practical information on everything from the public transport system to personal safety.

Amsterdam

Amsterdam is divided into five tourist areas. The corresponding chapters all begin with a list of numbered sights and places of interest, which are plotted on the Area Map. The information for each sight follows this numerical order, making sights easy to locate within the chapter.

Sights at a Glance groups the sights by category: historical buildings and monuments, streets, squares and gardens, museums and churches.

All pages about Amsterdam are marked in red.

1 Area Map
This map is numbered to show the most important attractions. They are also given in the Street Finder section on pages 154–63.

A locator map places the district in the context of the rest of the city.

A recommended route covers the most interesting streets in the area.

2 Street-by-Street Map
This map gives a detailed summary of the heart of the five main tourist areas of the city.

Stars indicate sights that should not be missed.

3 Detailed Information
All main attractions are described individually, including their addresses, opening hours and other practical information. Keys to the symbols used are on the back flap of this book.

GELDERLAND

1 Introduction
The scenery, history and character of each province are outlined here, showing how the area has changed through the centuries, and what it has to offer today's visitor.

The Netherlands Area by Area

The Netherlands is divided into 12 provinces. Each of these provinces, together with Amsterdam and the Wadden Islands, are dealt with in separate chapters. The most interesting towns, villages and places are shown on the Regional Map.

Exploring Friesland

2 Regional Map
This map shows the main roads and the main tourist attractions of an area, and also gives useful information about driving and rail travel.

Colour tabs are used to colour-code each province a different shade for easy reference.

3 Detailed Information
Major sights and attractions are described in detail in the order in which they are numbered on the Regional Map. Within each entry is detailed information on buildings, parks, museums and other sights.

Story boxes explore specific topics.

Visitors' Checklist gives practical information to help you plan your visit.

Oosterschelde Stormvloedkering

4 The Top Sights
These sights are described on two or more pages. Cutaway illustrations and floor plans show the most important buildings, museums and other sights.

INTRODUCING THE NETHERLANDS

DISCOVERING THE NETHERLANDS

The following itineraries have been designed to include as many of the country's highlights as possible, while keeping long-distance travel manageable. First come three two-day tours of the Netherlands' most important cities: Amsterdam, The Hague and Utrecht. Visitors can combine these into a single six-day tour by catching a train to the next city. Next come four, seven-day tours. The first of these covers the principal cities in the south, while the second ventures further north to the more rural province of Friesland and the islands that lie just offshore. The third suggested itinerary is a circular tour beginning and ending in Amsterdam, which takes in the quiet towns on the eastern side of the country. The fourth tour is a linear cycle route threading through the towns and countryside along the River IJssel; this last itinerary can also be followed by car. Pick, combine and follow your favourite tours, or simply dip in and out and be inspired.

A Week in the South

- See beautiful paintings displayed at Haarlem's **Frans Hals Museum**.

- Learn about the ancient culture of the Egyptians at **Rijksmuseum van Oudheden** in Leiden.

- Admire the wonderful blooms of the **Keukenhof** gardens near **Leiden**.

- Visit the handsome old houses of the **Delfshaven**, Rotterdam's earliest harbour.

- See the superb stained-glass windows in Gouda's **St Janskerk**.

- Don't miss the spectacular sight of 19 vintage windmills at **Kinderdijk**.

Keukenhof Gardens, Lisse
Colourful blossoms at the Keukenhof flower gardens, located near the small town of Lisse in South Holland

◀ *View of Delft* (1660) – a masterpiece by Johannes Vermeer

A Week in the North and the Islands

- Explore the culture of the Zuiderzee at the **Zuiderzeemuseum** in Enkhuizen.

- Drive along the 32-km **Afsluitdijk**, built between 1927 and 1933, and enjoy the spectacular views.

- Relax in one of the country's prettiest villages – tiny **Hindeloopen**.

- Cycle the quiet byways of the island of **Vlieland**.

- Visit the **Groninger Museum**, the finest art gallery in Groningen.

A Circular Tour from Amsterdam

- Learn about the strong seafaring traditions of the Dutch at the pretty little village of **Urk**.

- Don't miss the **Schokland Museum**, which showcases the remains of the former Zuiderzee island.

- Take a boat ride among the peaty canals of beautiful **Giethoorn**.

- Saunter the streets of the well-preserved historic town of **Elburg**.

- See the **Mondriaanhuis**, where Dutch painter Piet Mondriaan was born.

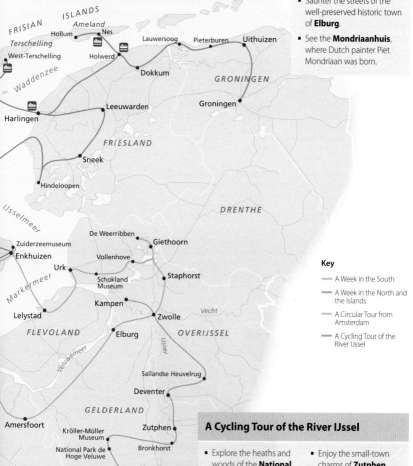

Key

— A Week in the South

— A Week in the North and the Islands

— A Circular Tour from Amsterdam

— A Cycling Tour of the River IJssel

A Cycling Tour of the River IJssel

- Explore the heaths and woods of the **National Park de Hoge Veluwe** by bicycle.

- See the splendid collection of Dutch art at the **Kröller-Müller Museum** near Arnhem.

- Enjoy the small-town charms of **Zutphen** and the medieval library at **St Walburgskerk**.

- Wander the streets of **Zwolle**, one of the country's most beguiling cities.

Two Days in Amsterdam

Known as home to Anne Frank and Van Gogh, Amsterdam is brimming with sights and beautiful canals to explore.

- **Arriving** Schiphol Airport is a 20-minute train journey from the city centre. Amsterdam also has good train connections with the rest of Europe.

Brightly lit houses overlook the canal in the Jordaan, Amsterdam

Day 1
Morning Begin the tour in Dam Square, a bustling open space at the heart of the city, and visit the **National Monument** (*p90*), an evocative war memorial erected in 1956. Then, pop into the **Nieuwe Kerk** (*p90*), one of Amsterdam's most beautiful Gothic buildings. Stop next at the imposing **Koninklijk Paleis** (*pp92–3*), built in the 17th century as the Stadhuis (Town Hall) when the city was at its richest. Afterwards, detour south to the **Begijnhof** (*p91*), a set of pretty medieval almshouses grouped around a small green.

Afternoon Take a stroll along the Singel, the first of the four canals that make up the **Grachtengordel** (*p99*), or "girdle of canals". With a string of hump-backed bridges spanning olive-green canals, this is Amsterdam at its most beautiful. Pop into the **Museum van Loon** (*p119*) for an insight into the life and times of the Dutch merchant elite, and then head for **Westerkerk** (*p114*), with its soaring spire and cavernous interior. From there, slip along the street to the city's most popular attraction, the **Anne Frank Huis** (*pp112–13*).

Day 2
Morning Dedicate this day to exploring some of the city's best museums. Expect to spend at least a couple of hours at the **Rijksmuseum** (*pp126–9*), Amsterdam's principal art museum, which

features a fabulous collection of Dutch paintings, most notably the wonderful Rembrandts. Then, proceed to the superb **Van Gogh Museum** (*pp130–31*), devoted to the greatest of all Dutch painters. After all this art, take a break at a local café or go for a stroll amid the greenery of the neighbouring **Vondelpark** (*p124*).

Afternoon After lunch, visit the city's third major museum, the **Stedelijk Museum** (*pp132–3*), whose excellent collection of contemporary art is housed in a lavishly refurbished gallery. Or, if museum fatigue is setting in, venture out of the tourist zone to explore the maze-like streets of the **Jordaan** (*pp110–111*), or rest your legs on a **canal boat trip** (*p117*).

A sculpture in the Begijnhof, a tranquil space away from the bustle of the city

Two Days in The Hague

An important political centre since the 13th century, The Hague is a fascinating city with aristocratic charm.

- **Arriving** The Hague has good train connections with the rest of the Netherlands. The nearest airport is Rotterdam, 21 km (13 miles) away, while Schiphol airport is 48 km (30 miles) away.

Day 1
Morning Stroll the streets of **The Hague** (*pp222–3*), pausing on Lange Vijverberg for a panoramic view of the **Binnenhof** (*p224*), a long and elegant series of high-gabled buildings that now house the Dutch parliament. Venture into the Binnenhof and take a guided tour of the **Ridderzaal** (*p224*), the Hall of the Knights, which dates back to the 13th century. Continue onto the **Mauritshuis** (*pp226–7*), an out-standing art gallery with a wonderful collection of Dutch paintings, including several exquisite paintings by Johannes Vermeer.

Afternoon Visit the **Museum Bredius** (*p224*) to enjoy a connoisseur's collection of Dutch art. Wander along the tree-lined Lange Voorhout, which is framed by handsome old mansions, one of which, the **Escher in Het Paleis** (*p225*), exhibits the startling compositions of the graphic artist Maurits Escher. Then, head north towards the unusual **Panorama Mesdag** (*p228*), where a massive circular canvas depicts the beach at Scheveningen as it was in the late 19th century.

Day 2
Morning Spend the morning at the **Gemeentemuseum Den Haag** (*p228*), whose vast permanent collection includes a wonderful display of Delft pottery and an extravagant collection of modern Dutch artists, with special reference to the austere Piet Mondriaan. Be sure to pop next door to the **Fotomuseum** (*p228*), which has built up an international reputation for its temporary exhibitions of photography.

Afternoon If the weather is good, take the tram or cycle through the woods to **Scheveningen** (*p229*), a popular seaside resort where the main attraction is a sandy beach that stretches out as far as the eye can see. You can also take your chances at the casino, enjoy high tea at the **Kurhaus** (*p229*), stroll along the pier and, finally, admire the outdoor sculptures of the **Museum Beelden aan Zee** (*p229*).

Intricately designed gardens of the Palais Het Loo

Imposing ceiling of the Gothic Domkerk in Utrecht

Two Days in Utrecht

Home to many superb museums, Utrecht is a lively city with magnificent canalside houses.

- **Arriving** Served by Schiphol airport, Utrecht also has good road and train connections. Apeldoorn is just 40 minutes by train and there are departures every 20–30 minutes. There are regular buses from Apeldoorn train station to the Paleis Het Loo.

Day 1
Morning Begin your tour of **Utrecht** (*pp204–5*) at the **Domtoren** (*p206*). At 112 m (368 ft), this is the highest bell tower in the country and a symbol of the city. The panoramic view from the tower is worth the climb. Next, drop by the **Domkerk** (*p206*) with its fine Gothic stonework. Continue west to the **Nationaal Museum Speelklok** (*p207*) to explore its fascinating and most unusual collection of mechanical musical instruments, from fairground organs to musical boxes.

Afternoon Continue your tour by walking along the prettiest stretch of the **Oude Gracht** (*p204*) near the Stadhuis, where

bars, cafés and restaurants occupy the old cellars and street level is one storey up. Follow the Oude Gracht south to the **Museum Catharijneconvent** (*p206*), which displays an excellent collection of medieval art and religious sculpture. Pushing on, walk to the **Centraal Museum** (*p206*), noted for its fine art dating from the 16th century onwards.

Day 2
Morning Don't miss the remarkable **Rietveld Schröderhuis** (*p208*), one of the most influential pieces of modern architecture in Europe, designed by Gerrit Rietveld, a leading member of the De Stijl movement. Allow at least an hour to explore the house. In particular, look out for the retractable, shape-changing windows in the dining room.

Afternoon Take the train from Utrecht to **Apeldoorn** (*p340*), a modest country town, on the outskirts of which is the **Paleis Het Loo** (*pp338–9*), a lavish palace built in the 17th century and occupied by the Dutch royals until the 1970s. Admire the palace's magnificent dining hall, gawp at the extravagant bedroom of William III, enjoy the paintings in the picture gallery, and wander through the lovely formal gardens to finish the tour.

A Week in the South

- **Arriving** Start in Haarlem, easily accessed from Amsterdam's Schiphol airport.

- **Transport** Most of this itinerary can be completed using local trains and buses, but a car will give added flexibility. The Kinderdijk windmills are only accessible by car or bicycle.

A row of windmills at Kinderdijk in Dordrecht

Day 1: Haarlem
Explore the centre of **Haarlem** (*pp186–7*), one of the country's prettiest towns, with a cluster of old and distinguished buildings framing the expansive Grote Markt. Be sure to visit the **Grote Kerk** (*p188*), a huge and imposing structure with a magnificent nave. Afterwards, admire the potpourri collections displayed at the **Teylers Museum** (*p189*) and then head over to the town's key attraction – the outstanding **Frans Hals Museum** (*pp190–91*), which features the paintings of Golden Age artist Frans Hals.

Day 2: Leiden and Keukenhof
Start the day by strolling through the lovely old streets of **Leiden** (*pp218–19*), where a maze of cobbled lanes conceals a string of excellent attractions. These include the **Rijksmuseum van Oudheden** (*p221*), which houses an outstanding ancient Egyptian collection, ranging from mummies to temples. Look out also for the sterling Gothic architecture of **St Pieterskerk** (*p221*), the handsome **Korenbeursgrug** (*p219*) and Leiden's much praised botanical gardens, the **Hortus Botanicus** (*p220*). In the afternoon, catch the bus or drive out of Leiden to the nearby **Keukenhof** (*p217*), the largest flower garden in the world, famed for its tulips.

Day 3: The Hague
Pick a day from the city itinerary on *p12*.

Day 4: Delft
Delft (*pp230–33*) is a charming little town with an especially fine Grote Markt (main square), with the Stadhuis at one end and the splendid **Nieuwe Kerk** (*p232*) at the other. Explore the town's network of narrow lanes and visit both the **Oude Kerk** (*p232*) and the **Stedelijk Museum Het Prinsenhof** (*p232*), where a hired assassin murdered the heroic William of Orange – the bullet holes can still be seen in the wall.

Day 5: Rotterdam
Enjoy the big city feel of **Rotterdam** (*pp234–41*), a pulsating metropolis of lively bars, great restaurants and a bustling street life. Take a detour to see the modernist architecture of the famous cube houses or **Kubus-Paalwoningen** (*p235*), stroll along the old city harbour of **Delfshaven** (*p236*) and take a trip up the **Euromast** (*p236*) for the panoramic view. Finish the day at the outstanding **Museum Boijmans Van Beuningen** (*pp238–9*), which houses an internationally famous collection of Dutch art.

Day 6: Gouda
Enjoy the small town atmosphere of **Gouda** (*pp242–3*) with its cobbled streets, slender canals and handsome main square, the Grote Markt, where you can admire the magnificent **Stadhuis** (*p243*). Try to visit on a Thursday morning in the summertime to enjoy the town's famous cheese market

with its fancily dressed porters. Be sure to drop by **St Janskerk** (*p242*), a distinguished Gothic structure with a breathtakingly beautiful set of stained-glass windows dating from the late 16th century.

Day 7: Dordrecht
Spend the morning exploring **Dordrecht** (*p244*), an ancient port that nudges up against one of the busiest waterways in the world. Highlights here include the ornate and rather fanciful **Grote Kerk** (*p244*) and the **Huis Simon van Gijn** (*p244*), with its period rooms and magnificent Brussels tapestries. Venturing out of Dordecht, cycle or drive over to the **Kinderdijk** (*p245*), where no fewer than 19 vintage windmills line up along a canal, looking proudly out over the surrounding polders.

Colourful buildings in the pretty town of Haarlem

A Week in the North and the Islands

- **Arriving** Head from Amsterdam to Alkmaar.
- **Transport** Hoorn, Enkhuizen, Leeuwarden, Harlingen and Groningen are easy to reach by train, and there are regular daily ferries from Harlingen to Vlieland, Holwerd to Ameland, and from Harlingen and Vlieland to Terschelling. However, to complete this itinerary, hiring a car is essential.

Day 1: Alkmaar

Heading north out of Amsterdam, stop at **Alkmaar** (*p185*), whose charming old centre is encircled by olive-green canals. On Friday mornings, the main square comes alive with the town's famous cheese market. Afterwards, be sure to visit **Hoorn** (*p182*), an old Zuiderzee seaport with a fine ensemble of old buildings, as well as the **Westfries Museum** (*p182*). Moving along the coast, you soon reach **Enkhuizen** (*p182*), another handsome former seaport and the home of the outstanding **Zuiderzeemuseum** (*pp180–81*).

Day 2: Friesland

Drive north from Enkhuizen to cross the Waddenzee via the **Afsluitdijk** (*p168*), thus reaching the province of **Friesland** (*pp295–305*) at a point near the exquisitely pretty waterside hamlet of **Hindeloopen** (*p302*). Proceed northeast from here to reach **Sneek** (*p303*), a relaxing little village famous for its sailing clubs, and **Leeuwarden** (*p300*), a good-looking town well worth an afternoon's wanderings. Admire the wonderful ceramic collection at **Het Princessehof** (*p300*), and allow some time for the **Fries Museum** (*p300*) with its displays on all things Frisian.

Day 3: Harlingen to Vlieland

Begin the day amid the maritime atmosphere of **Harlingen** (*p301*), an ancient seaport where vintage sailing boats crowd the harbour. Then, catch the ferry over to **Vlieland** (*p277*), the smallest of the Waddenzee islands, whose sand dunes stretch out along its northern shore. Take a hike or a bike ride along one of the many trails, or hunker down in the island's one and only village, **Oost-Vlieland** (*p277*), where there is an interesting museum, the **Tromp's Huys** (*p277*).

Day 4: Terschelling

Take the ferry from Harlingen or Vlieland to **Terschelling** (*p278*). The first port of call will be **West-Terschelling** (*p278*), a lovely little village that houses the **Museum 't Behouden Huys** (*p278*). Wander through the village, a popular summer resort, and then cycle out across the island, either to the dunes and beaches of the north coast or to the woods and mud flats of the south.

Day 5: Ameland

Catch the ferry from Holwerd to **Ameland** (*p278*) and arrive in the village of **Nes** (*p278*). Here, choose between the mud flats, marshland and bird reserves of the south coast and the sand dunes of the north, but be sure to visit tiny **Hollum** (*p279*), a picturesque hamlet of old seafarers' cottages and thatched farmhouses fanning out from a delightful country church.

Day 6: Dokkum to Pieterburen

Head to **Dokkum** (*p300*), an ancient town where the Christian missionary St Boniface met a grisly end. Explore the town centre with its pretty canals and

Transporting cheeses at Alkmaar cheese market, North Holland

old houses, and then push on to **Lauwersoog** (*p290*), a tiny village deep in the countryside, and **Uithuizen** (*p291*), where you can sign up for a guided walk across the mud flats (an activity known as *wadlopen* in Dutch). Also visit Pieterburen for its Seal Sanctuary, the **Zeehondencrèche** (*p291*).

Day 7: Groningen

Don't miss out on **Groningen** (*pp284–9*), a bustling city flush with excellent restaurants and a busy nightlife. Spend the morning exploring the city centre; highlights include the imposing **Martinikerk** (*p286*) and the delightful **Prinsenhof Gardens** (*p287*). The big attraction, however, is the **Groninger Museum** (*pp288–9*), where a wide-ranging art collection is housed in a splendid modern building designed by Alessandro Mendini and opened in 1994.

Spritsail barges in Sneek, Friesland

A Circular Tour from Amsterdam

- **Duration** Seven days – if travelling by bike, consider building in extra rest stops and extending to 10 days.
- **Arriving** This tour starts and ends in Amsterdam.
- **Transport** The towns in this itinerary are readily accessible by train, but local buses do not run regularly, so visitors will need a car to travel to the villages. For the energetic visitor, this tour can be done by bike.

Day 1: Marken to Volendam

See the famous stilt houses of **Marken** (p178), a tiny village perched on an island in the Markermeer. Learn more of the island's heritage at the **Marker Museum** (p178), which occupies six old island houses. Continue up the coast to **Volendam** (p178), where a dyke still protects the village.

Day 2: Edam and Enkhuizen

Edam (p178) is extremely pretty, its cluster of ancient houses huddled around a network of narrow canals and swing bridges. Allow an hour to explore Edam and then move on to **Enkhuizen** (p182), a handsome old seaport with a splendid harbour in the lee of a mighty, defensive tower, the **Drommedaris** (p182). Finish the day at Enkhuizen's excellent **Zuiderzeemuseum** (p180).

Day 3: Urk

Cross the Markerwaarddijk from Enkhuizen to reach the outskirts of **Lelystad** (p331), a modern town whose main pull is the replica 17th-century sailing ship on the **Bataviawerf** (p331). Pushing on, it's a short haul to **Urk** (p330), an intriguing little place and one-time island fishing village now attached to the mainland. Grab a plate of seafood before continuing on to the delightful **Schokland Museum** (p330). Just like Urk, Schokland was once an island and the remains of the old fishing village are fascinating.

Day 4: Vollenhove and Giethoorn

Traversing the polder landscape, visitors soon reach minuscule **Vollenhove** (p321), once an important seaport. Allow an hour to explore the village, and then push on east to **Giethoorn** (p322), one of the country's most unusual villages, with a string of old thatched farmhouses dotting a network of peaty canals. Take a boat ride here; spare some time to explore the unspoiled wetlands of **De Weerribben** (p321) conservation area.

Day 5: Staphorst to Zwolle

Take a detour south from Giethoorn to **Staphorst** (p324), an old-fashioned village whose elongated main street is flanked by thatched farmhouses. Visit on Sunday morning when the locals head off to church in traditional costume (note: taking photos is considered impolite). Continue to **Zwolle** (p320), a distinguished city whose star-shaped fortifications encase a centre of narrow lanes, elegant squares and attractive old buildings. Visit the **Grote Kerk** (p320) for its splendid interior, the **Stedelijk Museum** (p320) for its Golden Age period rooms, and the **Paleis aan de Blijmarkt** (p320) for its exhibitions of contemporary art. Last but not least, stroll along the harbour, where vintage canal boats are polished and scrubbed to delightful effect.

Day 6: Elburg

Discover the gentle charms of **Elburg** (p340), a former Zuiderzee seaport that now sits beside the

Boat travelling along the waterways of Giethoorn, Overijssel

Veluwemeer, the narrow waterway separating the mainland from reclaimed polder lands. See the medieval town gates, pop into the St Nicolaaskerk and drop by the **Gemeenteemuseum Elburg** (p340), where pride of place goes to a fine collection of silverware, once the property of the local guild of sailors.

Day 7: Amersfoort

Head southwest along the Veluwemeer waterway towards **Amersfoort** (p210), a medium-sized town whose ancient centre is still encircled by canals. Visit the key attractions: the splendid Koppelpoort, one of three surviving medieval gates; the soaring Onze Lieve Vrouwetoren (the Tower of the Church of Our Lady); and the **Mondriaanhuis** (p210), a museum in the former home of artist Pier Mondriaan. Allow an hour or so to cover the 50 km (31 miles) back from Amersfoort to Amsterdam.

The medieval gate of Koppelpoort in Amersfoort

For practical information on travelling around the Netherlands, see pp432–49

A Cycling Tour of the River IJssel

- **Duration** Seven days.
- **Arriving** Arnhem, at the start of this itinerary, is easy to reach by train, bus and car, as is Kampen at the end of the itinerary.
- **Transport** To complete this itinerary, hire a bike in Arnhem or take one with you on the train or by car.

Cycling trail in the National Park de Hoge Veluwe, Gelderland

Day 1: Arnhem

Begin the tour with a stroll through the centre of **Arnhem** *(p344)*, a lively city that suffered terribly during the Battle of Arnhem in 1944. It now hosts a vibrant restaurant and nightclub scene. Pause to admire the imposing edifice of the **Eusebiuskerk** *(p344)*, restored after wartime damage – as were the neighbouring Stadhuis and **Duivelshuis** *(p344)*, both of which are fine examples of Dutch Renaissance architecture. Then, go down to the Rijnkade, where there is a walking and cycling path along the bank of the River Rhine.

Day 2: National Park de Hoge Veluwe

Pedal out to the **National Park de Hoge Veluwe** *(p343)*, a chunk of mixed woodland, heath, marshland and sand dunes that stretches north of Arnhem. Explore the park's maze of cycling trails, and be sure to visit the **Museonder** *(p343)*, a subterranean museum that offers a picture of what the natural world looks like below ground level – from how roots grow to the animals that burrow there. Afterwards, head for the park's crowning highlight – the **Kröller-Müller Museum** *(p342)*, with its world-famous art collection and open-air sculpture garden, Beeldentuin. Return to Arnhem for the night.

Day 3: Bronkhorst to Zutphen

Head out of Arnhem to **Bronkhorst** *(p345)*, a tiny but immensely pretty little place with a cluster of immaculate cottages. Then, continue to **Zutphen** *(p345)*, a beguiling country town with a huddle of ancient buildings and the remnants of medieval walls. Look out for the **Drogenapstoren** *(p345)*, a fortified tower dating from the 15th century, and drop by **St Walburgskerk** *(p345)*, a splendid Gothic church with a medieval library, where the books are still chained to the desks.

Day 4: Deventer

Cycle onwards and relax in **Deventer** *(p324)*, a small and historic town that nudges up against the River IJssel. Watch the heavily laden barges ploughing up and down the river, and then wander along the main square, the Brink, as it curves past the town's intriguing **Historisch Museum** *(p324)*, which occupies the old

The Deventer skyline across the River IJssel

and very ornate weigh house, the Waag. Don't leave town without trying the local speciality, Kruidkoek, a tangy spice cake.

Day 5: Sallandse Heuvelrug

From Deventer, travel northeast to the partly wooded, sandy heathlands of the **Sallandse Heuvelrug** *(p324)*, now protected as a national park. At the Bezoekscentrum (Visitor Centre), visitors can get their bearings and pick up maps of the park and its myriad cycling routes. While wandering through the park, look out for the black grouse – this is its last remaining breeding ground in the whole of the Netherlands.

Day 6: Zwolle

Cycle to Zwolle *(see p16 for details on Zwolle)*.

Day 7: Kampen

Approach **Kampen** *(p320)* from the east across the River IJssel to appreciate the town's fine riverside setting and soaring spires. Once in town, make a beeline for the unusual **Ikonenmuseum** *(p321)*, with its substantial collection of Russian and Greek icons, and get the low-down on the town's long history at the intriguing **Stedelijk Museum** *(p321)*. Finish the day by wandering through the town centre, admiring its handsome old buildings, most memorably the Oude Raadhuis and the three remaining town gates, which date back to the 14th century.

Putting the Netherlands on the Map

The Netherlands is situated in Western Europe, bordering Belgium to the south and Germany to the east. To its north and west is the North Sea. The country is popularly known as Holland, although the provinces of North and South Holland form only part of the Netherlands in reality. Since the completion of the Deltawerken (Delta Works), the coastline now reaches some 800 km (500 miles) in length. The country's major waterways and excellent road and rail systems make it an important gateway to the rest of Europe, and to Germany in particular. Approximately one-sixth of its total area is covered with water. The Netherlands has a population of just over 17 million.

Western Europe

NORWAY
SWEDEN
DENMARK
North Sea
REP. OF IRELAND
UNITED KINGDOM
NETHERLANDS
○ Amsterdam
GERMANY
BELGIUM
CZECH REPUBLIC
Atlantic Ocean
FRANCE
SWITZ.
AUSTRIA
ITALY
SPAIN

Key

- ☐ Greater Amsterdam
- ▦ Land below sea level
- ━━ Motorway
- ━━ Major road
- ── Railway
- ━━ National border

Waddenzee

Den Helder
A31
A7
NOORD HOLLAND
IJsselmeer
N9
N242 Enkhuizen
Hoorn N302
A6
Alkmaar
Markermeer
Leylstad
Newcastle
See inset map below
Almere
Haarlem **AMSTERDAM**
Schiphol ✈
Amersfoort
Leiden
ZUID HOLLAND
Utrecht
Den Haag A44
UTRECHT
A12 Gouda
Delft Lek
Lek
✈ Rotterdam
A27
Hull, Harwich
Hoek van Holland
Rotterdam
A15
Waal
Barendrecht
Dordrecht
A29 A16
's Hertogenbosch
Hull
Zierikzee
NOORD BRABAN
A17 A59
Breda A27
ZEELAND
Tilburg
Middelburg A58
Bergen op Zoom A58
A58
Ramsgate
Eindhoven ✈
Zeebrugge
A12 A1
Turnhout
A67
Oostende
N49
A21
Brugge
Antwerpen
A14
✈ Antwerpen
A13
Nieuwpoort
A1
Albert Kanaal
A10
Mechelen *Demer*
A17
Gent
B E L G I U M
A2 Hasselt
Kortrijk
A14
A10
✈ Brussels
Leuven
Sint-Truiden
Ieper A25
Bruxelles
A3
Oudenaarde

A PORTRAIT OF
THE NETHERLANDS

From the Frisian Islands in the north to Zeeland in the south, the Netherlands is a place of contrasts, with fine sandy beaches, picturesque villages and vibrant towns with multilingual and outward-looking people. The mighty River Rhine bisects the country, bringing trade and prosperity from far and wide.

The landscape of what is now the Netherlands has changed considerably over the past 2,000 years. Since Roman times, large tracts of land have been swallowed up by the sea in areas such as Zeeland and the former Zuiderzee. Old maps show that during the Middle Ages almost half of today's provinces of North Holland and South Holland were under water. Since then, large parts of this land have been reclaimed. The constant battle with the sea reached its height with the Delta Works. This massive hydraulic engineering achievement *(see pp250–51)* was designed to protect the southwestern part of the country against flooding. The project was started after the disastrous floods of 1953, in which more than 1,800 people died.

The Netherlands covers an area of 41,547 sq km (16,040 sq miles), about one-tenth the size of California. With just over 17 million inhabitants, this means a population density of around 380 per sq km (1,000 per sq mile), making it the third-most densely populated country in Europe after Monaco and Malta. However, this is not something that is readily noticeable to visitors outside the main cities, as the flat landscape seems anything but crowded.

Dutch people are friendly, outgoing and direct. They care about social issues and the environment and almost everyone speaks English, many fluently. They live in a country that is neat and tidy, where there is excellent public transport and where visitors find it easy to get around.

The pier, the focus of social life on the beach at Scheveningen

◀ Flowers in the Keukenhof garden near Lisse, the largest flower garden in the world

Holland's dunes, a natural barrier against the sea and an important water catchment area

Introducing the Netherlands

Although the Netherlands is the country's official name, most of the rest of the world calls it Holland. This book uses both names. However, Holland actually comprises only two of the 13 Dutch provinces. North and South Holland contain the country's three main cities of Amsterdam, Rotterdam and Den Haag (The Hague), which together with the cities of Dordrecht, Utrecht, Leiden and Haarlem form a horseshoe-shaped conurbation known as the Randstad, literally, "rim city" *(see pp170–71)*.

When people ask, "What is the capital of the Netherlands?", the smiling Dutch

Shoppers at the Albert Cuypmarkt in Amsterdam

tend to reply: "Our capital is Amsterdam, and the government sits in The Hague." Amsterdam is the most cosmopolitan of these three cities, as well as the country's centre for cultural life. Rotterdam, home to the Europoort, one of the world's largest ports, is the Netherlands' industrial centre. The Hague is the seat of government and quarters many prestigious institutions, including the International Court of Justice. With its neighbouring seaside resort of Scheveningen, The Hague is where most of the foreign embassies and consulates are situated.

Holland can be roughly divided into the Protestant north and Catholic south, separated by the great rivers flowing into the North Sea: the Rhine, the Waal and the Maas (Meuse). The people in the north of the country tend to be more sober and matter-of-fact, whereas those of the south tend to be much more flamboyant in their lifestyles.

Society and Politics

Social life in the Netherlands was for many years based on the idea of *verzuiling*, wherein different sections of society rested their beliefs on four pillars *(zuilen)*: Protestantism, Catholicism, liberalism and socialism. At one time, these groups had almost no contact with one another. Catholics would always vote for the *Katholieke Volkspartij*, join Catholic trade unions, base their social lives on Catholic societies and send their children to Catholic schools. The Protestant "pillar", on the other hand, was formed of two main factions: the Dutch Reformed Church and the Calvinist Church. Both had their own political parties, their own trade unions and their own schools and societies. As for socialism and liberalism, the division was less explicit, though the gap between the world of the "workers" and that of the "entrepreneurs" was huge.

A major step towards unity came in 1980, when the three largest religion-based political parties united in the CDA, a Christian Democratic alliance that went on to dominate government coalitions for the next 20 years. The gap between the other parties closed in 1994, when the Labour Party

The picturesque Dordrecht marina

A hollow post mill in the polder landscape

(PvdA) and the small D66 formed a coalition with the conservative Liberal Party (VVD). This resulted in a tripartite "purple" cabinet, which appeared so successful that the coalition was continued in 1998.

The Dutch elections of May 2002 surprised everybody as the country moved to the right of the political spectrum. The assassination, nine days before, of the popular, flamboyant and openly gay Pim Fortuyn had shocked the entire country. With his unyielding views on Muslims and immigration, and his criticism of the establishment, Fortuyn

The de Geul river at Epen in Zuid Limburg

Football fans sporting orange costumes

Language and Culture

Dutch, a Germanic language, is used by more than 20 million people in Holland, Flanders and parts of the former Dutch colonies. Afrikaans, a language of South Africa closely related to Dutch, is a separate language, as is Frisian, which is spoken by more than 400,000 people in the province of Friesland. Dutch has many dialects, each of which has numerous regional differences. However, these differences are gradually disappearing because of the far-reaching influences of radio and television.

Culturally, Holland has plenty to offer. The country's colourful history is reflected in its many old buildings and large number of valuable museum collections. Exhibits range from those with local themes to world-famous art such as the collections in Amsterdam's Rijksmuseum (see pp126–7) and the Mauritshuis in The Hague (see pp226–7). In addition to the major museums of the cities, contemporary art can be seen in galleries all over the country, and in the profusion of works displayed in the streets and at numerous local markets. As for the performing arts, more variety is available today than ever before. Holland boasts a number of renowned orchestras and is an established name in ballet. Stage and theatre have recently marked a shift from experimental to more conventional performances.

Dutch beer, fresh from the tap

was the antithesis of the Dutch tradition of consensual politics. Despite the loss of their charismatic leader, LPF became the second-largest party in the Lower House; only the Christian Democrats (CDA) did better. The coalition parties of the former government lost 43 seats between them, making this the biggest shake-up in Dutch politics since World War II.

Since 2010, the Dutch political climate has changed completely. Dissatisfied with the coalition between PvdA, CDA and conservative Christen Unie, the Dutch voted en masse for VVD and Geert Wilder's Party for Freedom (PVV). However, in 2012, the VVD, CDA and PVV government resigned when the PVV refused to sanction the austerity measures. New elections were held, resulting in a VVD-PvdA government.

The Dutch Way of Life

The German poet Heinrich Heine (1797–1856) described Holland as a place where "everything happens 50 years later than anywhere else". But today, anyone who reflects on the tolerant Dutch attitude towards drugs, the country's relaxed laws regarding euthanasia and the popular opposition to the deployment of nuclear weapons will come away with a different picture. In fact, the Netherlands was the first country to legalize gay marriages, regulate prostitution, officially sanction euthanasia and tolerate the over-the-counter sale of

A herring stall in Amsterdam

marijuana. Even the attitude of the Dutch towards their monarchy is modern – they are regarded with an affection more commonly extended to family members than to rulers.

Since the depredations of World War II, much has changed in the way the Dutch live their lives. Thrift and moderation, the two traditional virtues of Calvinism, are no longer writ large in society. A measure of flamboyance is slowly but surely making its way into the Dutch lifestyle. Today the Dutch eat out enthusiastically and often. Restaurant and cooking columns are now featured in newspapers and magazines, and there are also many cookery programmes aired on television.

A Dutch production of *The Three Musketeers*

Dutch drinking habits have also changed. On fine-weather days, people throng the pavement cafés to end the working day with a beer or a glass of wine. They also drink a great deal more wine with meals than once was the case. The renowned Dutch gin, *jenever (see p420)*, is still popular, though younger people prefer cocktails. As in a lot of countries, there are concerns about youngsters and binge-drinking.

In their spare time, Dutch people head outdoors, often on bicycles, which are enormously popular. Love of the environment is a strong Dutch charac-teristic. There are hundreds of organized rambling and cycling tours, funfairs and theme parks, as well as a wide assortment of festivals and other events held throughout the year *(see pp36–9)*. And wherever you are, you will always find a flea market – with items ranging from flowers to antiques for sale – not far away.

The new-found *joie de vivre* of the Dutch reflects the general trend evident in Western European coun-tries. This is the result of a new leisure culture, one which is more "sensory". Less time is devoted to reading and contempla-tion, while food, drink, sport and the arts all take on increasingly prominent roles. Politically, socially and culturally, the Dutch are embracing the 21st century with confidence.

De Waalkade, the promenade in Nijmegen

Holding Back the Water

Recent floods in the Netherlands' river valleys, particularly the one which occurred in 1995, when 200,000 people needed to be evacuated from the area, have shown what a threat water continues to pose to the Netherlands. The only way the sea can be held back is by dams, but in order to contain rivers at high tide, the country is adopting a new approach, that of "controlled flooding".

Flooded farm in Gelderland (1995)

Since the 11th century more and more land has been reclaimed from the sea. Countless dykes were built over the centuries using elementary tools, such as spades and "burries", a kind of stretcher. The illustration shows a breached dyke being filled.

At the Hook of Holland the sea is not held back by dunes, as it is along the entire coast of North Holland and South Holland, but by a dyke.

The lowest point in Holland is the Zuidplaspolder at Gouda, 6.74 m (22 ft) below sea level.

At Krimpen the IJssel discharges into the Nieuwe Maas.

The Krimpenerwaard between the IJssel and the Lek, consists of high-quality hayfields and pasture.

The River Lek

A large part of the Netherlands (blue on the map) is below sea level. These areas have been called "laag-Nederland", or the "low Netherlands", and have only come into being over the past 10,000 years.

Cross-section of the Netherlands

This cross-section of the Netherlands follows a straight line from the Hook of Holland to Achterhoek (*see Locator Map*) and shows clearly how low much of the land is. Only some 65 km (40 miles) inland, at Neder-Betuwe, does the ground rise above sea level. The lowest point in the Netherlands is the Zuidplaspolder, which is more than 6.74 m (22 ft) below sea level. Comparatively elevated areas like the Betuwe have nothing to fear from the sea, but this does not mean that they are not at risk of flooding: the Waal River, which runs more or less parallel to this cross-section, may flood at unusually high tides or after a heavy rainfall.

Key

 Above sea level

Below sea level

Floods in the river valleys in 1993 and 1995
led to the implementation of large-scale dyke
reinforcement projects, known as the "delta plan
for the large rivers". Old flood channels were
also repaired as a matter of priority to allow
more water to drain off.

The Story of Hans Brinker

The tale of the little boy who held his
finger in a leak in a dyke to hold back
the sea is not a figure from Dutch
folklore but probably originated in the
book *Hans Brinker, or, The Silver Skates*,
by American writer Mary Mapes
Dodge (1831–1905). It tells the story
of a poverty-stricken boy who helps
his ailing father. Hans and the doctor
in the book (Boerhaave) are historical
figures. The story was published in
over 100 editions in Dodge's lifetime.

Statue of Hans Brinker in Spaarndam

Neder-Betuwe is probably
Holland's most important
fruit-growing region.

Over-Betuwe is an area of
fruit orchards, horticulture
and cattle farming.

**The Pannerdens
Canal** currently
connects the Upper
and Lower Rhineland.

Montferland is an important
region of lateral moraines.
These moraines were
formed by
the actions
of glaciers.

67.1 m (220 ft)
above sea level

Merwede
Canal

Sea level

6.74 m (22 ft) below sea level

Locator Map

Cross-section of a Modern River Dyke

Blocks of boulder clay protect the dyke from the wash of the river. The water seeps through the
water-resistant clay layer slowly, draining off quickly only once it reaches the sand layer. This way the
body of the dyke stays dry and hard.

Water table   Winter dyke   Concrete blocks   Water meadows   Summer dyke

Farmhouses and Windmills

In the mainly flat landscape of the Netherlands, farmhouses always stand in the shelter of trees. Windmills, on the other hand, needing as much wind as they can get, usually stand in very exposed areas. Both are highly valued because they are so picturesque, and it is easy to forget that they actually belong in the category of functional architecture. How a windmill works is explained on page 183.

In the farmhouses of North Holland, the barn, threshing-floor and house are all under one pyramidal roof.

This Drenthe farmhouse is a modern version of what has been known since the Middle Ages as a *los hoes* (detached house).

The inner yard of the Zuid Limburg farmhouse once teemed with animal life.

Main house

Cattle shed

The Zuid Limburg Farmhouses

The traditional farmhouses of Zuid Limburg have a distinctive inner yard, enclosed by the house and farm buildings. In the inner yard, ducks, chickens and pigs once roamed, rummaging in the dunghill. The picture may have been lively but was not particularly hygienic.

The gateway is large enough to let in a horse and wagon.

The walls are made of marl and covered in plaster.

The krukhuis is a hall-type house, distinguished by the main house being at right angles to the barn.

The hallenhuis has a low-hanging roof held up by uprights kept in position by cross-beams. The side walls are half-timbered.

The kop-hals-romp farmhouse is found mainly in Friesland. In this type of farmhouse, the long, oblong barn is separated from the mainhouse by a small, intermediate building.

Langgevel (long-gable) farmhouses are common on the sandy ground of Peel and Kempen. In this type of farmhouse, the living accommodation and farm buildings are arranged in a row.

Paltrok Mills

Paltrok, or smock, mills were developed for use as sawmills around 1600. They were so called because of their resemblance to the *paltrok*, a smock that was commonly worn at the time. These windmills were mounted on a circular track, allowing them to rotate in their entirety. Generally, smock mills were used to saw *wagenschot* – entire oak trunks that had been split in two.

Sail

Wheels allow the windmill to rotate on its axis.

Ridge post

Underneath the porch is a crane for lifting the tree trunks from the water.

The mill house is divided into two wings.

Saw floor

Under the cap the wind shaft propels the heavy brake wheel.

Belt or berg mills have an extra-high body because of surrounding buildings or trees. A mound (*berg*) made at the base of the mill provides access to the sails.

Toren mills (tower mills) have a brick cylindrical body and a cap that can be rotated from inside. Only four survive in Holland today. The oldest one can be seen at Achterhoek near Zeddam.

Stander (post) mills are the oldest type of mill in Holland. The entire wooden body rotates on a central wooden post. Most post mills were used to grind corn.

Wipmolen are a later version of the stander mills and were designed to pump water. The smaller body rotates on a fixed, pyramidal base.

Stellingmolen, like the belt mill, have an extra-tall body. This type was used to produce dye, oil or paper. An encircling platform halfway up the body enables the mill to be rotated and the sails to be reefed on the wings.

The tjasker was used to drain small areas of water. It consisted of a sloping axle with sails at one end and an Archimedes' screw at the other.

The Dutch Masters

The proliferation of painting in the Netherlands during the 17th century – the country's Golden Age – corresponded with the great demand for paintings among newly rich townspeople. The lack of major royal and ecclesiastic patrons meant that there was no official school of painting, which left artists free to specialize in particular fields, such as historical subjects, portraits, landscapes and still life, as well as genre painting.

Willem Heda (1594–1680) was one of the masters of still life. The painter's simple compositions reflect his signature use of sober colours.

Frans Hals (c.1580–1666) left an oeuvre of some 200 portraits and more than 50 genre paintings. He painted not only regents and wealthy townsmen but also peasants, soldiers, fishermen, publicans and drunkards. No sketches for his paintings are known, and it is assumed that he painted *alla prima*, that is, straight onto the canvas without sketches. *The Fool*, shown above, dates from around 1623.

Rembrandt van Rijn

Rembrandt van Rijn is regarded by many as the greatest Dutch painter of all time. He was born in Leiden in 1606, but lived in Amsterdam from 1632 until his death in 1669. Rembrandt was a master in the use of light and shadow. *The Jewish Bride* (painted around 1665) is regarded as one of the best portraits of his later period.

Jacob van Ruisdael (1628–82) was an unrivalled landscape painter. In his *View of Haarlem* depicted here, the low horizon is dwarfed by an imposing sky with clouds.

The silversmith Adam van Vianen (1569–1627) was famous for his ornamental style, which was known as *kwabstijl*, or "flabby style", and distinguished by flowing ornamentation and the use of various fantasy elements. This gilded silver jug is an example of his style. Much of the silver work from this time has been lost because pieces have been melted down in order to trade in the metal for cash.

Jan Steen (1625–79) was a prolific painter with a variety of works, 800 of which survive today. They include everything from altar pieces through landscape paintings to works with mythological themes. However, Steen is known primarily for his genre painting, which gives a detailed, humorous picture of 17th-century society. *The Family Scene*, shown above, is a typical "Jan Steen household" – one in disarray. Tavern scenes were another of the artist's favourite subjects.

Gerard van Honthorst (1590–1656) was greatly influenced by the works of Caravaggio. As well as historical scenes and portraits, he painted genre pieces such as *The Merry Fiddler* (above). His famous nocturnal scenes lit by candle-light led to his being nicknamed "Gherardo delle Notte" in Italy.

Johannes Vermeer (1632–75) spent his entire life in Delft. Only 40 of his works are known today, but even this modest oeuvre plays a prominent role in the history of painting. His balanced compositions appear very modern. Long before the Impressionists, Vermeer succeeded in conveying light through colour. The street depicted in *View of Houses in Delft* (c.1658), left, has become known as "Vermeer's street".

Pottery and Tiles

When in 1620 exports of porcelain from China to Europe fell because of the troubles in China, Dutch potters seized the opportunity and started to produce their own wares, imitating the Chinese style on a large scale. The quality of the Dutch blue-white pottery was excellent. The city of Delft became one of the prime centres for the production of this china, which reached its height between 1660 and 1725. During the Art Nouveau and Art Deco periods, Dutch potters regained their international renown. The best known of them was TAC Colenbrander.

Tulip vase

De Porceleyne Fles is the only Delftware shop which has managed to survive throughout the centuries. The business was bought in 1876 and revived by Joost Thooft, whose initials can still be seen on the workshop's mark. The exquisite painting on the porcelain continues to be done by hand, although the rest of the manufacturing process no longer involves the craft's traditional methods.

Stylized flowers reflect the Italian majolica tradition.

Delftware

Although tin-glazed earthenware was also made in other parts of the Netherlands, "Delft" came to describe almost all earthenware made in the Netherlands during this period. Any piece made after 1650 will always have a workshop mark. Later, the glazer's initials, as well as a code denoting the year and a serial number, were added.

Artist's initials

Year code – DB stands for 1982

Workshop's mark

Serial number

Underside of a vase

This set of four tiles features a pattern of pomegranates, grapes, rosettes and lilies.

The first Dutch porcelain was made in 1759 in the North Holland town of Weesp. At the time, it was second in quality only to Meissen porcelain. However, production was halted after 10 years because of financial difficulties. In 1774, a new factory was opened in Loosdrecht, which was moved to Ouder-Amstel in 1784. This large vase from 1808 is a typical example of the Amstel china that was produced there.

Delft design is used here to decorate a plane tail. The artist Hugo Kaagman decorated the tails of four British Airways' aircraft with blue Delft designs.

Tiles

Majolica wall tiles – decorated earthenware on a tin-glazed background – were made for the first time in the Netherlands during the 16th century, with production reaching its peak in the 17th century. Until 1625, polychrome decoration predominated, after which the majority of tiles were painted in blue on white. Major centres were Makkum – where in the 17th century the Tichelaar family firm, which operates to this day, was established – as well as Harlingen, Delft, Gouda, Amsterdam, Utrecht and Haarlem. The tiles depicted here are from Haarlem. *(See also p419.)*

TAC Colenbrander

One of the biggest names in Art Nouveau pottery is TAC Colenbrander (1841–1930). Originally an architect, he became known for his fanciful floral-based designs for the Rozenburg earthenware and porcelain factory in The Hague, where he was chief designer from 1884 to 1889. As celebrated as his designs were, the ceramics had limited commercial success. One reason for this was their expense, a reflection of the labour-intensive production. In 1912–13, Colenbrander worked for the Zuid-Holland pottery in Gouda. In addition to pottery, he designed wallpaper and carpets, and worked as a graphic and interior designer.

The lily often features as a corner motif on Dutch tiles.

The Art Nouveau plate by WP Hartgring was made in 1904, the same year as this master potter won a gold medal at the world exhibition at the St Louis World's Fair. Hartring worked for 20 years at the Rozenburg factory in The Hague and for 10 years at the Zuid-Holland pottery. His works reflect the Japanese style.

"Day and Night" set by Colenbrander, 1885

The Netherlands in Bloom

The Dutch love affair with flowers began rather unromantically in homes during the 17th century, when flowers were used to keep bad smells at bay. The aesthetic aspect soon developed, and today the Netherlands is one of the world's most important flower-growing countries. It has an unrivalled distribution system, keeping Holland ahead of competition from countries such as Israel, Spain, Colombia, Kenya, Zimbabwe and Zambia. The Netherlands has a 92 per cent share of the world market for flowers.

Fields of flowers are not confined to the west of the country. These rose fields are outside Lottum in the north of the southern province of Limburg, where every year a special rose competition is held.

Tulips were introduced to Holland from Turkey in the 17th century. They became the subject of an unparalleled speculative bubble which has become known as "tulip mania". Today the tulip is considered a quintessentially Dutch product, with innumerable varieties.

The annual flower competition *(bloemen corso)* in the bulb-growing region is a grand event *(see p36)*.

Cut Flowers From Dutch Nurseries

As consumers have become increasingly demanding, the number of flower species and varieties is constantly on the rise. Consumer tastes vary from place to place: in France, gladioli are very popular, whereas in Great Britain, it is lilies and carnations. In Asia, tulips are in great demand. A small sample of the flowers grown commercially in the Netherlands is shown here.

The chrysanthemum *(Chrysanthemum)* originated in China.

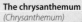

The iris *(Iris)* flower and bulb are in demand.

The sandy soil in the high areas behind the dunes of Holland is known as "geest soil" and is very well suited for cultivating bulbs.

Not all daffodil bulbs can survive the winter.

Crocus bulbs should be planted in September.

Hyacinth bulbs range in colour from violet red to white.

Tulip bulbs are highly resistant to disease and pests.

Iris bulbs should be dug up after flowering.

Flower Sellers

Flower sellers are part and parcel of the Netherlands' street scene. They can also be found indoors, in places such as stations or shopping centres. In most countries, cut flowers are considered expensive and a luxury. In the Netherlands, however, they are practically a daily shopping item and quite cheap. The Netherlands is indeed the land of flowers *par excellence*.

Dahlias (*Dahlia*) come in 20,000 varieties.

The lilac (*Syringa*) is often bought for its fragrance.

The carnation (*Dianthus*) is loved as a spray.

The rose (*Rosa*) is known as "the queen of flowers".

THE NETHERLANDS THROUGH THE YEAR

The Netherlands has much to offer in the way of holidays, festivals and other events. The choice of cultural events is greatest in summer – several cities host theatre festivals in June. Some festivals, such as Leiden's 3-Oktoberfeesten, have deep historical roots, whereas others, such as the multicultural Zomercarnaval in Rotterdam, are much more modern. Many of the events are held to honour navigation and fishing, such as Flag Day (Vlaggetjesdag), held each May in Scheveningen. Music, too, plays a prominent role. The world-renowned North Sea Jazz festival brings the genre's greats to Rotterdam.

Spring

In March, daffodils and crocuses burst into bloom in the country's towns and villages. From mid-April onwards, when the tulips are in flower, the bulb fields along the Dutch coast are a spectacular sight to see.

March

Meezing Matthäus *(Easter)*, Amsterdam and elsewhere. Concert-goers are welcome to sing along during many performances of Bach's *St Matthew's Passion*.
Keukenhof *(end Mar to mid-May)*, near Lisse. These 32 ha (79 acres) of landscape gardens demonstrate the best of all the flowers Holland has to offer. This open-air exhibition was started in 1949, and has become internationally renowned.

April

First of April Celebrations, Brielle. Dressed in 16th-century-style clothing, the inhabitants

Blossoming fruit tree in the Betuwe

of Brielle (Den Briel) recreate the 1572 recovery of the city from the Spaniards.
Foto Biënnale *(Apr to Jul)*, Amsterdam and other cities. Biannual international photography exhibition takes place in even-numbered years.
Bloemen Corso (Flower Competition) *(late Apr)*, Bollenstreek. Floats with floral sculptures travel a 40-km (25-mile) route through Haarlem, Hillegom, Lisse and Noordwijk.
Koningsdag (King's Day) *(27 Apr)*. The birthday of King Willem-Alexander sees festivities throughout the land; the biggest event is held in Amsterdam.

May

Landelijke Fietsmaand (National Cycling Month) *(all month)*. Cycling activities throughout the country.
Nationale Moldendag (National Windmill Day) *(second Sat in May)*. Some 600 of the 1,000 windmills

in the country are opened up to the public.
Vlaggetjesdag (Flag Day) *(May)*, Scheveningen. The arrival of the first herring catch of the season is celebrated with demonstrations of traditional fishing-related crafts, music and a race.
Aspergerie Primeur (Ascension Day), Venlo. In a festive atmosphere on a re-created old-time village green, visitors can tuck into deliciously cooked asparagus.
Keidagen *(around Ascension Day)*, Lochem. Five days of

A young street musician on King's Day in Amsterdam

Flag Day, the start of the new herring fishing season

music, funfairs, street fairs and performances by international artists.
Sloepenrace (Boat Regatta). A regatta from Harlingen to Terschelling.
Jazz in Duketown (around Whitsun), 's-Hertogenbosch. Four days of open-air high-quality jazz and blues bands at various venues in town. The beer flows freely.

The increasingly popular boat race to Terschelling

Summer

Summer in the Netherlands is a time of major cultural events. These include the Holland Festival in Amsterdam, the Theater a/d Werf in Utrecht, the Parade (Amsterdam, Utrecht, The Hague, Rotterdam), and the Haagse Zomer in The Hague. And if theatre is not your favourite pastime, there are plenty of other activities to keep you entertained.

June

Holland Festival (3 weeks of Jun), venues throughout Amsterdam and major cities. A varied programme of concerts, plays, opera and ballet.
Aaltjesdag (Eel Day) (second Sat in Jun), Harderwijk. Major fishing celebration in this former harbour on the Zuider Zee.
Oerol Festival (mid-Jun), Terschelling. This alternative cultural festival lasts for ten days, with clowns, street theatre, acrobats, pop concerts and music from around the world.
Poetry International (mid-Jun), Rotterdam. Prestigious poetry festival featuring an international programme, in Rotterdam's Doelen district.
Pasar Malam Besar (second half of Jun), The Hague. This festival of Indonesian music and dance, shadow puppets, cooking demonstrations and colourful eastern market takes place at Malieveld in The Hague.
Nationale Vlootdagen (Navy days) (end Jun/early Jul), Den

Herring-eating by hand

Helder. A chance to see frigates, submarines, torpedo boats and mine hunters belonging to the Netherlands Navy, with spectacular shows put on by the Netherlands Marines.

July

Oud Limburgs Schuttersfeest (Marksman's Festival) (first Sun in Jul). The annual tournament by the marksmen of Limburg is a colourful folk event held in the hometown of the previous year's winner.
North Sea Jazz (mid-Jul), Rotterdam. A three-day spectacle widely acknowledged as the world's largest jazz festival, featuring performances by the biggest names in jazz.
Tilburgse kermis (Tilburg Fair) (end Jul). One of the biggest and most exuberant fairs in Holland, with a special gay Pink Monday.

Zomercarnaval (Summer Carnival) (last Sat in Jul), Rotterdam. A lively Caribbean carnival with exotic music, plenty to eat and drink and a swirling procession.

August

Gay Pride (first weekend in Aug), Amsterdam. One of the very best Prides in the world; the highlight is the Canal Parade.
Mosselfeesten (Mussel Festivals) (third Sat in Aug), Yerseke; (last weekend in Aug), Philippine. Harvest festival presenting the new crops of Zeeland.
Preuvenemint (last weekend in Aug), Maastricht. Flamboyant festival of food and drink at the historical Vrijthof.
Uitmarkt (last weekend in Aug), Amsterdam. Festive opening of the theatre season with performances and information booths. There is also a book fair, where literary publishers are represented.

North Sea Jazz, one of the world's major jazz events

The Nijmegen Fair, a popular tradition dating back centuries

Autumn

As the cold weather starts slowly but surely to set in, indoor events become more prominent. In autumn, the theatres are full in the evenings, and museums are routinely busy. However, open-air events are still held, the golden light of dusk and magnificent clouds adding to the atmosphere.

September

Monumentendag (Monument Day) *(second Sat in Sep)*. Private historic buildings open to the public.

Fruitcorso *(second weekend in Sep)*, Tiel. Spectacular parade of floats with gigantic fruit sculptures.

An elaborate fruit sculpture at the Tiel Fruitcorso

Vliegerfeest (Kite Festival) *(mid-Sep)*, Scheveningen. For two days, hundreds of strange creations hover over the beach.

Jordaanfestival *(second and third weeks in Sep)*, Amsterdam. Fairs, street parties, talent contests and live music are held in the southern part of the picturesque former working-class district of Jordaan.

Prinsjesdag *(third Tue in Sep)*, The Hague. Accompanied by high-ranking government officials and with a guard of honour, the king rides in his golden carriage from Noordeinde Palace to the Binnenhof (Parliament Building), where he makes his Royal Speech in the Ridderzaal (Hall of the Knights) in order to open the Dutch Parliament.

Nijmeegse kermis (Nijmegen fair) *(end Sep/early Oct)*. Held every year since the 13th century, the fair stretches ribbon-like through the centre of the city. On Mondays and Tuesdays are the "piekdagen", when children can visit the attractions for the entrance fee of 50 cents.

October

3-Oktoberfeesten, Leiden. A large public festival to commemorate the relief of Leiden from its siege on

3 October 1574. Permanent fixtures in the festivities are the distribution of herring and white bread to the townspeople, as well as the procession and funfair.

Eurospoor *(mid-to late Oct)*, Utrecht. Europe's biggest model train show takes place in the Jaarbeurs.

Soldiers accompanying the King before he makes his Royal Speech in the Ridderzaal

November

Sint-Maarten *(11 Nov)*, Western and Northern Netherlands. In the early evening, children equipped with lanterns walk from door to door, singing songs, for which they are given sweets.

Intocht van Sinterklaas (arrival of St Nicholas)

(second or third week in Nov). St Nicholas is celebrated in every town and village in Holland. He arrives by ship near St Nicholaaskerk *(see p95)* and then rides on his grey horse through town. Until 5 December, children traditionally sing Nicholas carols in the evenings, and every morning find sweets in their shoes.

The distribution of white bread in celebration of the relief of Leiden

Winter

December aside, there are not as many events in the winter calendar as there are for the rest of the year – perhaps to the relief of those who need January to recover

from the celebrations of St Nicholas, Christmas and the New Year.

December

Sinterklaasavond (St Nicholas's Day) *(5 Dec)*. St Nicholas ends with St Nicholas's Eve on 5 December. Both young and old are brought gifts, more often than not in person by (a hired) Santa Claus. Friends give poems caricaturing each other.
Cirque d'Hiver *(between Christmas and New Year's Eve)*, Roermond. Four days of world-class circus acts in the Oranjerie theatre hotel, in the historic town centre.
New Year's Eve *(31 Dec)*. The Dutch spend the last evening of the old year in festive surroundings at home or with friends. Fritters and apple turnovers are eaten and, in many houses, the champagne corks pop at midnight. Afterwards, people walk the streets to see in the New Year with organized and individual firework displays.

January

Nieuwjaarsduik (New Year's Dip) *(1 Jan)*, Scheveningen. Every year, at noon on New Year's Day, a starting-gun is fired on the pier in

The latest boats on display at the annual Hiswa

Scheveningen, and hundreds of people in swimsuits run down the beach to take a dip in the ice-cold water.
Leidse Jazzweek *(mid-Jan)*, Leiden. Throughout the week, jazz of all styles is played in the halls and cafés of the old town.

February

Hiswa *(Feb or Mar)*, Amsterdam. Boat show in the RAI *(see p141)*, featuring all types of crafts, from dinghies to yachts.
Carnival *(Feb or Mar)*. Officially three, but in practice five, days before Lent, the Catholic south celebrates wildly. There are processions with colourful floats, and costumed people sing and dance in the cafés and in the streets.

The arrival of St Nicholas, attracting a great deal of attention

The Climate in the Netherlands

The Netherlands has a maritime climate, characterized by cool summers and mild winters. In summer, the average maximum temperature is around 20°C (68°F), while in winter the average minimum temperature is around 0°C (32°F). It is slightly warmer south of the country's big rivers than north of them, and there are slightly more hours of sunshine on the coast than inland. Because of the temperature difference between the land and the sea, there is a constant westerly sea breeze on the coast in summer.

WEST FRISIAN
ISLANDS

Leeuwarden •

FRIESLAND

NORTH
HOLLAND

• Lelystad

Haarlem •

FLEVOLAND

Amsterdam •

The Hague •

• Utrecht

SOUTH
HOLLAND

UTRECHT

• Rotterdam

Nijmegen

's-Hertogenbosch •

ZEELAND

NORTH BRABANT

• Middelburg

• Eindhoven

DEN HELDER

°C/°F						
			19/66	18/64		
		14/57	14/57	13/55		
		9/48				9/48
	7/45					5/41
5/41	2/36					
1/34						
48 hrs	111 hrs	227 hrs	212 hrs	145 hrs	50 hrs
76 mm	45 mm	32 mm	67 mm	76 mm	79 mm
month **Jan**	**Mar**	**May**	**Jul**	**Sep**	**Nov**

DE BILT

°C/°F						
			21/70	19/66		
		17/63				
		12/54		10/50	9/48	
	9/48	7/45				
5/41	1/34					3/37
−1/30						
54 hrs	118 hrs	214 hrs	191 hrs	143 hrs	53 hrs
76 mm	44 mm	43 mm	82 mm	73 mm	55 mm
month **Jan**	**Mar**	**May**	**Jul**	**Sep**	**Nov**

Average maximum temperature

Average minimum temperature

Average hours of sunshine per month

Average rainfall per month

BEEK

°C/°F						
			22/72	19/66		
		18/64				
		13/55		10/50	9/48	
	10/50	8/46				
4/39	2/36					4/39
−1/30						
44 hrs	109 hrs	202 hrs	181 hrs	145 hrs	53 hrs
68 mm	45 mm	62 mm	89 mm	81 mm	62 mm
month **Jan**	**Mar**	**May**	**Jul**	**Sep**	**Nov**

Maas-
tricht
•

GRONINGEN

• Groningen

Assen •

DRENTHE

• Zwolle

OVERIJSSEL

Enschede

Apeldoorn

GELDERLAND

Arnhem

IMBURG

EELDE

°C/°F

	21/70	**18**/64	
16/61			
	12/54	**9**/48	**8**/46
8/46	**6**/43		
4/39			**3**/37
0/32			
−1/30			

46 hrs	104 hrs	214 hrs	183 hrs	142 hrs	50 hrs
72 mm	46 mm	53 mm	95 mm	72 mm	66 mm
month **Jan**	**Mar**	**May**	**Jul**	**Sep**	**Nov**

Spring

Summer

Autumn

Winter

THE HISTORY OF THE NETHERLANDS

In 12 BC, the Romans conquered southern Holland, and in AD 50 they declared the Rhine the northern border of their empire. The region north of this was conquered by the Frisians. At the end of the 4th century, the Romans withdrew from the Low Countries, which were taken over by the Frisians, Franks and Saxons. In the 8th century, the Franks ruled the region alone. Christianity was introduced by the missionary Willibrord in 695, and was completed under Charlemagne.

After the disintegration of the Frankish Empire, the Netherlands fell under German rule. Actual power was exercized by the vassals, of whom the Bishop of Utrecht was the most powerful – until the Concordat of Worms in 1122, when the German king lost the right to appoint bishops. During the 12th century, the Count of Holland was the most important figure in the region.

In the 14th and 15th centuries, the dispute between the two factions – the Hooks and the Cods – marked the end of the feudal age. At the end of the 16th century, the Northern Netherlands liberated itself from the Habsburg Duke Philip II, and enjoyed a period of unprecedented economic and cultural flowering. By the mid-17th century, it had become the greatest trading nation in the world, a status gradually relinquished during the 18th century.

The different independent regions making up the republic were joined together under Napoleon, with William I becoming king in 1815. However, unification with Belgium proved unsuccessful and was officially ended in 1839, although it had already ended *de facto* in 1830.

In the 20th century, Holland maintained neutrality during World War I, but suffered greatly during World War II. Invaded by the Nazis in May 1940, the country was not liberated entirely until May 1945. It subsequently developed into one of the most prosperous states within the European Union. Today, the country remains a constitutional monarchy, with the royal family enjoying great popularity among the Dutch.

Map of the world from 1564 by the cartographer Ortelius of Antwerp

◀ *The IJ at Amsterdam, Viewed from the Mussel Quay*, painted by Ludolf Backhuysen (1631–1708)

Rulers of the Netherlands

In the Middle Ages, the Netherlands were run by local feudal dukes, as well as by the counts of Holland and the bishops of Utrecht. They were all officially vassals of the German king. In the 15th century, the region came under the rule of the House of Burgundy through marriage alliances, after which it was incorporated into the Habsburg Empire. In 1581, the Northern Netherlands freed itself from the Habsburgs. Since then – with some interruptions – the House of Orange has ruled over parts of what are today called Holland, initially as stadholders, but from 1815 as monarchs.

1417–1433 Jacoba of Bavaria

c. 685–719 Radboud, King of the Frisians

1152–1190 Frederik Barbarossa (German king)

1342–1364 Jan IV van Arkel, Bishop of Utrecht

814–840 Louis the Pious

885–889 Gerulf, Count of Holland

1312–1355 Jan III (Duke of Brabant and Limburg)

1404–1417 Willem VI, Count of Holland

1203–1222 Willem I, Count of Holland

| 700 | 800 | 900 | 1000 | 1100 | 1200 | 1300 | 1400 |

BUR

| 700 | 800 | 900 | 1000 | 1100 | 1200 | 1300 | 1400 |

936–973 Otto I (German king)

1371–1402 Willem I, Duke of Gelre and Gulik

918–976 Balderik, Bishop of Utrecht

1345–1354 Margaretha of Bavaria

1433–1467 Philip the Good (House of Burgundy)

1069–1090 Egbert II, Count of Friesland, last of the Brunonen

1271–1326 Reinald I, Count of Gelre

1091–1121 Floris II, Count of Holland

1267–1294 Jan I, Duke of Brabant (from 1288 also Duke of Limburg)

1234–1256 Willem II (Count of Holland)

1128–1139 Andries van Kuik (Bishop of Utrecht)

1256–1296 Floris V (Count of Holland)

768–814 Charlemagne

1585–1625
Maurits

1559–1567 and 1572–1584
William of Orange, "The Silent"
(stadholder of Holland, Zeeland
and Utrecht, under Philip II
until 1581)

1806–1810 Louis
Napoleon (French
viceroy, king of Holland)

2013
Willem-Alexander
(king)

1567–1573 Ferdinand,
Duke of Alva (viceroy
under Philip II)

1815–1840
William I (king)

1625–1647
Frederick-Hendrik

1467–1477
Charles the Bold

1647–1650
William II

1477–1482 Maria
of Burgundy

1672–1702
William III

1482–1506 Philip the
Handsome (House
of Habsburg)

1687–1711
Johan Willem
Friso, stadholder
of Friesland
(1696), Prince
of Orange (1702)

1890–1898 Emma
(regent)

1898–1948
Wilhelmina

1500	1600	1700	1800	1900	2000
DY	HABSBURG	HUIS VAN ORANJE			
1500	1600	1700	1800	1900	2000

1849–1890
William III

1840–1849
William II

1795–1806
Batavian Republic

1890–1948
Wilhelmina

1559–1567 Margaretha of Parma
(governor under Philip II)

1751–1795
William V

1948–1980
Juliana

1506–1555
Charles V

1555–1581
Philip II

1747–1751
William IV

1980–2013 Beatrix

Holland and its Monarchy

The Dutch royal family is extremely popular. The
former queen, Beatrix, was the fourth queen in a
row. The present king, Willem-Alexander, is the
country's first king since 1890.

Prehistoric and Roman Times

About 13,000 years ago, the Low Countries emerged from under the ice of the last Ice Age. Temperatures gradually rose, turning the tundra into areas of forest and marshes, inhabited by nomadic hunters. In the Early Stone Age (4500–2000 BC), farming communities were established here and there. The megalith builders were the best known of these settled inhabitants. Around 600 BC, Germanic and Celtic tribes settled in the Low Countries. They were here when the Romans conquered the southern part of the region, in the 1st century BC. In AD 50, the Romans finally declared the Rhine as the Roman Empire's northern frontier, establishing Roman settlements in Utrecht and Maastricht.

The Low Countries (AD 50)

- Germanic peoples
- Roman territory
- Coastline in 3000 BC

Megaliths
Between 3400 and 3200 BC, the inhabitants of the Drenthe plateau built some 100 megaliths. Of these, 54 have survived into the present *(see pp310–11)*. These impressive tombs were once concealed beneath a mound of sand.

Urns
These urns date from 1150–800 BC.

The dark rings in this picture are of the ditches that originally surrounded the urn-mounds. The rings are interrupted at their southeastern edge, possibly to represent the symbolic entrance to the tomb.

55,000 BC Small groups of Neanderthal people inhabit the surroundings of Hijken and Hoogersmilde. A few hand axes and two campsites have been found

4500 BC Farmers settle on the loess land of Zuid Limburg. They have been referred to as "Bandkeramikers", or the Linear Pottery Culture, after their striped pottery

1900 BC Start of the Bronze Age the Low Countri

10,000 BC	7500 BC	5000 BC	2500 BC	2000 BC

11,000 BC Reindeer hunters of the Hamburg Culture inhabit Drenthe

3400–3200 BC Farmers of the Beaker Folk build megaliths at Drenthe, Overijssel and Groningen

Wheel from 2700 BC

The Simpelveld Sarcophagus
In the 1930s, a Roman burial urn was excavated at Simpelveld near Limburg. The interior of the urn is decorated with reliefs depicting the exterior and the furnishings of a Roman house.

Where to See Prehistoric and Roman Holland

In addition to the megaliths of Drenthe and the Someren urnfield, prehistoric graves have been discovered at Almere, Hilversum, Vaassen, Lunteren, Goirle and Rolde, and at Toterfout/Halfmijl in Brabant, where 16 burial mounds have been restored to their original condition, complete with trenches and rings of stakes. The urnfield on the Bosoverheide, a couple of kilometres west of the Weert, was, around 800 BC, one of the largest burial grounds in northwestern Europe. Roman finds can be seen in places like Oudheden in Leiden (see p221) and the Valkhof museum in Nijmegen (see p347). The Archeon archaeological theme park in Alphen a/d Rijn (see p426) is highly informative and entertaining, for adults and children alike.

The Urnfield

In 1991, an urnfield dating from 600 BC was discovered at Someren near Brabant. It had been ploughed under by farmers during the Middle Ages. The dead were cremated in southern Holland from 1500 BC, and in northern Holland from 1000 BC. The burial mounds of Someren were arranged closely together, and each contained its own urn.

Glass Flasks
These Roman flasks from the 2nd century AD were excavated at Heerlen.

Roman Mask
This mask was found near Nijmegen, which was once the camp of a Roman legion.

Farmer with Plough
The plough was used in the Iron Age.

Bronze Age sacrificial dagger

750–400 BC First Iron Age in the Low Countries

450 BC Start of the Second Iron Age, or La Tène Age

55–10 BC Batavians settle in the river area, the Cananefates in the coastal area and the Frisians in the north

Roman temple in Elst

1500 BC	1000 BC	750 BC	500 BC	250 BC	AD 1

1300 BC The Exloo necklace is made from tin beads from England, Baltic amber and Egyptian pottery beads

300–100 BC The Germans expand southwards across the Rhine, clashing with Celtic tribes

57 BC Caesar conquers the Belgae, who inhabit present-day Belgium

AD 69–70 Batavian Uprising, followed by the re-establishment of Roman rule

Frisians, Franks and Saxons

When the Romans withdrew at the end of the 4th century, the Low Countries, like the rest of Europe, experienced a great migration of peoples. By around 500, the Frisians had spread their territory southwards to the great rivers, while the Saxons lived east of the IJssel and the Franks had settled in the area south of the great rivers. Approximately two centuries later, the Franks took over the whole region as far as the Lauwerszee. With the spread of Christianity under Charlemagne, the entire area of the Netherlands became Christian. After Charlemagne's death, the region belonged first to the Middle Kingdom of Lothair, and then, from 925, to the German Empire.

The Low Countries (AD 700)

- Frisians
- Franks
- Saxons

Widukind
In 785, Charlemagne defeated the Saxons led by Widukind. This event led to the east of Holland finally being incorporated into Charlemagne's empire.

The Life of St Boniface

Two episodes in the life of the Anglo-Saxon missionary Boniface are illustrated here: on the left, he is shown baptizing a convert; on the right, his martyrdom is depicted. In 716 and 719, Boniface went on missionary expeditions to Friesland. He was subsequently made bishop and later archbishop. In 753, he embarked on a further missionary expedition to Friesland, which resulted in his death the following year.

The staff is one of Boniface's constant possessions. He was reputed to have used it to make a spring well up.

Early Medieval Pottery
For the Frisians, pottery was an important barter good, along with cattle and dye.

A convert
being baptized

Fibula from Dorestad

Relief showing a Roman galley

295 Constantius Chlorus defeats the Franks at the battle of the Rhine delta, but allows them to remain in the Betuwe, where they are used to defend the frontiers

600–700 Dorestad becomes an important trading settlement

AD 200	400	500	550	600	650

350–400 Romans leave the Low Countries

500 The territory of the Frisians stretches from the Zwin in Zeeland Flanders to the mouth of the Weser in Germany

Frankish denarii

Radboud, King of the Frisians

The Frisian king Radboud was forced to capitulate to the Frankish ruler Pippin II. He later regained the land he had lost, and with his army marched on Cologne. In 734, the Frisians under Count Bubo were again defeated at the de Boorne River, allowing Charles Martel to extend Frankish domain up to the Lauwerszee.

Boniface uses his Bible to protect himself from the sword.

Pagan ceremonial axe

Dorestad

Situated at the confluence of the Lek and the Kromme Rijn (by present-day Wijk bij Duurstede, *see p211*), Dorestad was the most important trading settlement in northern Holland during the Early Middle Ages. It was the centre of Frisian trade in the 7th century and afterwards under the Merovingians and Carolingians. In the 9th century, Dorestad was repeatedly plundered by marauding Vikings, who sailed up the rivers in their longboats in search of booty. The settlement's decline, however, was due to the damming of the Rhine against flooding rather than because of the Viking raids. There is no reference in historical records to Dorestad after 863. During the 10th century, Dorestad's functions were taken over by Tiel, Deventer and Utrecht. In Wijk, the Museum Dorestad (tel. 0343-571448) gives an excellent idea of what life must have been like here during the Early Middle Ages through its various displays of archaeological finds from that period, as well as its informative diorama, complete with models of port houses.

Viking Sword

This sword, dubbed "Adalfriid's sword", was found in the Waal.

689 Pippin II defeats the Frisian king Radboud at Dorestad and gains the river region and Utrecht

768–814 Rule of Charlemagne. Holland is divided into *pagi* (cantons), each of which is ruled by a count

925 Holland is taken over by the German Empire

1007 Last Viking invasion of the Low Countries

700   750   800   900   1000

695 Willibrord becomes bishop of Frisia and establishes his see in Utrecht

754 Boniface is killed at Dokkum by pagan looters

834–837 Dorestad plundered at various times by Vikings

Viking longboat

The Emergence of Towns

In the 13th century, towns started to acquire considerable economic power. At that time, the Low Countries were nominally under the rule of the German king, but in practice local nobles ran things themselves. In the north, the counts of Holland were the most powerful. In the mid-14th century, their territory fell into the hands of the House of Bavaria. Disunity between Margaretha of Bavaria and her son William marked the beginning of the dispute between the Hooks and the Cods, which split towns as well as noble families for one and a half centuries.

The Low Countries (1300)
German Empire
France

The Fulling Industry
During the 15th century, the cloth industry flourished in Leiden and 's-Hertogenbosch. This painting by IC Swanenburgh shows the fullers and dyers at work. In the background to the right, inspectors are checking the quality of the cloth.

Minting Coins
Minting rights lay not only with the sovereign. Local rulers, both church and secular, were entitled to mint coins.

Pilgrims who had visited Santiago de Compostela, well established as a place of pilgrimage by the 11th century, wore the scallop shell of the apostle St James on their hats.

The sheriff, with his distinctive chain of bells, was the representative of the sovereign. Here he is on the way to pronounce a death sentence, which is shown by the red pole, the 'rod of justice' carried by an executioner.

The coat of arms of 's-Hertogenbosch

c.1050 The first dykes are built

1185 's-Hertogenbosch is granted its town charter

1247 William II of Holland is appointed king of Germany by the pro-Papal party

| 1000 | 1050 | 1100 | 1150 | 1200 | 1250 |

1076–1122 Investiture dispute between the German king and the Pope on the right to appoint bishops

1165 Frederick Barbarossa places Friesland under the joint rule of the Bishop of Utrecht and the Count of Holland

Cruel Punishment
In the Middle Ages, barbaric punishments were often meted out. This cask on the wall of the Waag in Deventer was once used to immerse counterfeiters in boiling oil.

Grain brought by farmers to the towns was inspected by officials. Produce in the meat and fish markets was also inspected daily. An excise tax was charged on the basis of the inspection.

A Medieval Town

Demands of trade and industry meant that towns were given all kinds of privileges from the 13th century onwards. Often important allies for the counts of Holland against local feudal lords, Dutch towns were more powerful than in other countries during this period because of the lack of a powerful central authority.

Where to See the Late Medieval Netherlands

Famous monuments from this period are the Oude Kerk in Amsterdam (14th century, *see pp84–5*) and the Begijnhof, which has the city's oldest house (1420, *see p91*); the Cathedral Tower (1382) and the Catharijneconvent (15th century) in Utrecht *(see p206)*; the Onze-Lieve-Vrouwebasiliek (11th–12th centuries) and the St-Servaasbasiliek (11th–15th centuries) in Maastricht *(see p381)*; the 13th-century Ridderzaal and the 14th-century Gevangenpoort in The Hague *(see p224)*; the Pieterskerk (15th century) and the town walls of the 12th-century castle in Leiden *(see p221)*; the Lange Jan (14th century, *see p253*) and the restored abbey (11th–15th centuries) in Middelburg *(see p254)*; the centre of Deventer around the Brink and Bergkerk, including the oldest stone house in Holland *(see p324)*; and the Martinitoren in Groningen (1469, *see p286*).

Silver Chalice
As guilds prospered, they attached increasing importance to appearances. This chalice is decorated with a picture of St George defending a maiden against the dragon.

The Guild of St George (1533)
This painting by Cornelis Antonisz shows marksmen at a meal. Originally, each guild was responsible for protecting a part of the city walls; later, special guilds were set up.

1296 Floris V is assassinated by the nobles	*Willem Beukelsz* **c.1380** Willem Beukelsz. invents the herring-gutter	**1421** The Biesbosch is built as a result of the St Elizabeth Day flood	**1477** Marriage of Maria of Burgundy and Habsburg Maximilian I brings together Holland and Zeeland under the House of Habsburg	**1550** Charles V introduces the death penalty for all forms of heresy
1300	**1350**	**1400**	**1450**	**1500**	**1550**
1306 Amsterdam gains city status	**1345** Dispute between the Hooks and the Cods begins. At first a disagreement over the successor to William IV, it develops into a struggle between the feudal barons and the cities	**1428** Philip the Good of Burgundy forces Jacoba of Bavaria to withdraw from Holland, Zeeland and Hainaut	**1517** Luther publishes the 95 theses	

Luther

The Dutch Trading Empire

The early 17th century marked a period of expansion worldwide for northern Holland. Within a few decades, the Levant, the Gulf of Guinea, the Caribbean, North and South America, the East Indies, Persia, Arabia, Japan, India and China were all on the Dutch trading routes. The republic's merchant fleet became the world's largest. The powerful Dutch East India Company (VOC), established in 1602, dominated trade with Asia, with a monopoly on all profits from trade east of the Cape of Good Hope, while the Dutch West India Company, established in 1621, concentrated on the New World and the slave trade.

Dealers on the Stock Exchange
With its market traders and exchange, Amsterdam was the undisputed trading centre of Europe.

Purchase of Manhattan
Pieter Minnewit bought Manhattan Island in 1625 from the Delaware Indians for 60 guilders, 10 guns and a brass cauldron.

The Dutch on Desjima
The Dutch trading office on the island of Desjima was in 1854 the main conduit between Japan and the world.

1625 The Dutch found New Amsterdam, later to become New York

1667 Abraham Crijnssen conquers Suriname

1627 Prince Maurits conquers Recife

1652 Jan van de Riebeeck founds Cape Town

Key

•••• **1595–7** De Houtman and Keyzer

- - - - **1596–7** Barents and Heemskerck

•••• **1616** Le Maire and Schouten

-- -- **1642–3** Tasman

VOC Plaque
The Dutch East India Company (VOC) obtained sole rights to trade for the republic in Asia. It had the authority to make treaties with other powers and even to declare war.

The Silver Fleet
In 1628, Piet Hein captured the Silver Fleet of Spain off the north coast of Cuba.

Surviving the Winter in Novaya Zemlya (1596–7)
During an attempt to find a northern route to the Indies, an expedition led by W Barents and J van Heemskerck ended up on the coast of Novaya Zemlya. The group survived in the Behouden Huys, a hut built from pieces of ships.

The 80 Years War

In the second half of the 16th century, Holland officially belonged to the Spanish branch of the House of Habsburg. In 1567, Philip II sent troops to put down Protestant unrest in Flanders and halt the Protestant Reformation sweeping through northern Europe; this led to a revolt against Spanish rule in northern Holland and resulted in years of civil war and religious strife. The 80 Years War ended in 1648 with the Peace of Münster.

Statesman Johan van Oldenbarnevelt and the Count of Nassau, Prince Maurits, were the main Dutch figures in the conflict with Holland's Spanish rulers during the 17th century.

1596–1597 The winter camp in Novaya Zemlya

1641 The Dutch establish themselves on Desjima

1624 The Dutch establish themselves on Formosa

1658 The Dutch establish themselves in Ceylon

1619 JP Coen founds Batavia

1606 Willem Jansz discovers Australia

1642 Abel Tasman discovers Tasmania

Johan van Oldenbarnevelt

Prince Maurits

The Great Voyages

While Willem Barents was exploring the Arctic seas, de Houtman and Keyzer set off on the "first voyages" to Java. In 1606, Willem Jansz discovered the north coast of Australia, and in 1616, Jacob le Maire and Willem Schouten were the first to sail around Cape Horn. Abel Tasman discovered Tasmania and New Zealand in 1642–3.

Three-Master Ship
These top-of-the-line 17th-century Dutch merchant ships required only a small crew.

The Golden Age

For the north of Holland the 17th century was a time of unprecedented flowering in trade, art *(see pp30–31)* and science. While elsewhere in Europe economies were in stagnation, the republic's merchant fleet brought great prosperity, particularly to the towns of Amsterdam and Utrecht. The Amsterdam Exchange (Amsterdamse Wisselbank), which was founded in 1609, ensured that Amsterdam became the financial centre of the world. Trade was protected by a powerful navy, which enjoyed significant victories under Michiel de Ruyter.

The Low Countries (1650)

■ Republic
▨ Spanish possessions
░ Germany

Johan de Witt
At the time known as the first stadholder-free period (1650–72), the political scene in the republic was dominated by the provincial governor Johan de Witt. This brilliant, impeccable statesman was murdered along with his brother Cornelis by Orange supporters in 1672.

Tapestries and exquisite gilded leather hangings decorated the living rooms.

View of the Weigh House in Haarlem
In the 17th century, Holland became Europe's main commodities market, with strategic logistic and financial advantages. Products from the Baltic Sea, southern Europe, the Levant and Asia were loaded into the holds of merchant ships which came from all over the world.

Oriental carpets were too valuable to put on the floor and so were draped over a table or bench.

Colourful clothes came into fashion in the second half of the 17th century and became a widespread object of study for portrait painters.

1559 Philip II names Margaretha of Parma the governor of the Netherlands

1572 The "Beggars of the Sea" take over Den Briel

1574 The relief of Leiden

Spanish stew-kettle recovered after the relief of Leiden

1584 Assassination of William of Orange

1585 Fall of Antwerp

1602 Dutch East India Company founded

1550	1565	1580	1595	1610

Caricature painting of the Pope as a pontiff and devil

1566 Iconoclastic Riots

1567 Duke of Alva arrives in Holland

1581 Northern Holland declares independence from Spain

1588 The States General proclaim the Republic of the Seven United Netherlands

The Enlightenment

The Enlightenment, or the "Age of Reason", has its roots in the 16th century. In Holland, this emerged in the work of the natural scientists Swammerdam and Van Leeuwenhoek, and the thinker Spinoza. The jurist Hugo de Groot was the first to formulate a rational – as opposed to a theological – basis for what he called "natural law", that is, a universal law applicable to all humans everywhere, which was one of the great themes tackled by thinkers of the Enlightenment.

Antonie van Leeuwenhoek

Where to See the Netherlands' Golden Age

Good examples of 17th-century architecture are the Trippenhuis in Amsterdam (see p80), the Lakenhal in Leiden (see p220) and the Mauritshuis in The Hague (see pp226–7). Vlissingen has the Arsenaal (see p255); Haarlem, the Grote Markt (see p186). Outstanding merchant houses can be seen in the major trading towns of the time, such as Delft (see pp230–33) and Utrecht (for example, the Oudegracht, see p204).

Wan-Li China Porcelain, also known as egg-shell porcelain, served as a model for blue Delft pottery.

Michiel de Ruyter
The admiral of the Dutch fleet during the Second and Third English-Dutch Naval Wars was a great tactician held in high esteem by his sailors. His nickname "Bestevaer" meant "Grandfather".

The Muider Circle
The artists and scholars who met at the home of the poet PC Hooft at Muiderslot Castle are now known as the members of the "Muiderkring" (Muider Circle).

Interior of a Patrician Home

This painting by Pieter de Hooch, Portrait of a Family Making Music *(1663), shows the wealth of a patrician residence in the second half of the 17th century. Around 1660, portrait painting shifted in style from sobriety to opulence, a reflection of the flourishing economy.*

Prince of Poets
Joost van den Vondel (1587–1679), depicted here by HG Pot as a shepherd, is widely regarded as the greatest Dutch poet and playwright of the 17th century.

17th-Century Microscope
Antonie van Leeuwenhoek made numerous important discoveries with his home-made microscope.

1642 Rembrandt completes *The Night Watch*

1650–1672 First stadholder-free period starts when the states fail to name a successor after the death of William II

1672–1702 Rule of stadholder William III

1698 Tsar Peter the Great visits Amsterdam and Zaandam

1625 | 1640 | 1655 | 1670 | 1685 | 1700

1625 Frederick-Henry becomes stadholder of Holland, Zeeland, Utrecht, Gelderland and Overijssel

1648 The Peace of Münster marks the end of the 80 Years War

1665–1667 The Second English-Dutch Naval War. Michiel Adriaansz. de Ruyter scores legendary victories (Four Days' Battle, The Battle of Chatham)

1689 William III becomes king of England

Calvinism

From the end of the 1500s, Calvinism took hold in the Netherlands as Protestant opposition to Spanish Catholic rule. Amsterdam, which had sided with Spain, switched loyalties in 1578 to become the fiercely Protestant capital of an infant Dutch Republic. Reformed Church doctrine was to have a profound influence on Dutch history. Strict living and industriousness became ingrained in the character of Calvinists as well as of Catholics and agnostics and was instrumental in the country's prosperity during the Golden Age.

Gold and paintings decorated all churches.

The iconoclasts use combined efforts to topple a huge religious image from the wall.

The Statenbijbel was the translation of the Bible officially recognized by the Synod of Dordrecht (1618–19). The language used in it helped to standardize Dutch. The New Translation (Nieuwe Vertaling) did not appear until 1957.

The Iconoclastic Riots

Underground Calvinist preachers goaded troublemakers into the Iconoclastic Riots of 1566, when the decorations of Catholic churches were destroyed with great violence. Invaluable works of religious art were lost in this way. The interiors of Dutch churches were no longer given the Baroque ornamentation that characterizes churches in the rest of Europe. After all, according to the Ten Commandments in the Bible, "Thou shalt not make graven images" and "Thou shalt not worship nor serve them".

Traces of the damage caused by the iconoclasts can still be seen today in some places, such as this retable in Utrecht.

Pieter Saenredam (1597–1665) painted unrivalled pictures of the plain Calvinist churches – this one is *Interior of the Sint-Odolphuskerk in Assendelft*.

Where to See Calvinist Netherlands

Strict Calvinism can be found in the Netherlands "Bible belt", which stretches from Zeeland and southeastern South Holland via the Veluwe to the cape of Overijssel and Drenthe. The strict Sunday worship, black clothes and head coverings when attending church, as well as abstinence from modern developments (such as television and vaccinations), are gradually disappearing. However, when visiting such areas, do remember that photography and driving are still not looked upon kindly in Reformed Church villages. These communities are closed, with strong social controls. Calvinist villages worth visiting are Goedereede (*see p245*), in South Holland, and Staphorst (*see p324*), in Overijssel, as well as the former Zuiderzee island of Urk (*see p330*), where older people continue to wear traditional dress.

Priceless stained-glass windows are systematically smashed to pieces.

The leaders of the Iconoclastic Riots came from all classes of the population. In addition to fervent Calvinists, there were also paid helpers and all kinds of hangers-on who used the opportunity to do some plundering.

Early to Church by A. Allebé

Ons' Lieve Heer op Solder

Clandestine Churches

When, in 1597, the Union of Utrecht proclaimed mandatory Calvinist services throughout the Netherlands and Zeeland, a blind eye – in return for payment – was turned to other confessions. Catholics, Remonstrants and Mennonites held their services in secret churches, which were unrecognizable as such from the outside. They were generally held in town houses, although later they were held in secret churches that were built for the purpose, particularly in Amsterdam, with De Zon and De Rode Hoed. The St Gertrudiskapel (1645) in Utrecht and Ons' Lieve Heer op Solder (1663, now the Amstelkring Museum) in Amsterdam are the finest surviving early examples of these institutions.

From Republic to Kingdom

After the death of the powerful stadholder William III, the republic no longer played an important role within Europe. Britain took over as the principal maritime and trading power. At the end of the 18th century, a long dispute began between the House of Orange and democratically minded patriots, which was resolved in favour of the latter with the founding of the Batavian Republic (1795). After the Napoleonic era, the House of Orange returned to power, this time not as stadholder but as monarch. In 1839, the borders of the present-day Netherlands were finally established.

The Low Countries in 1800

■ Batavian Republic

□ French territory

The British ensign flying on the English warship the *Warrior*, the boat which brought William I back to the Netherlands.

William I Landing at Scheveningen

In 1813, almost 20 years after the House of Orange had been ousted by the patriots, Prince William returned to the Netherlands. He landed on the shore at Scheveningen, the same place where his father had departed for England. Two days later, he was inaugurated as sovereign. In 1815, he also claimed possession of present-day Belgium and pronounced himself king of the Netherlands.

Goejanverwellesluis
In 1785, the patriots took power, and the stadholder William V and his wife Wilhelmina of Prussia fled from The Hague. Wilhelmina attempted to return in 1787 but was stopped at Goejanverwellesluis. It was at this point that the Prussian king decided to send troops to restore the power of the stadholder.

The prince is lowered from the ship in a rowboat, but a farmer's wagon from the beach picks him up to take him ashore through the surf.

1702–1747 Second stadholder-free period

1747 William IV "the Frisian" becomes hereditary stadholder of all provinces

1756–1763 The great powers of Europe become embroiled in the Seven Years War. The republic remains neutral

1791 Abolition of the Dutch West India Company

| 1700 | 1720 | 1740 | 1760 | 1780 |

1713 The Peace of Utrecht marks the end of the republic as a great power

The city hall of Utrecht, where the Peace of Utrecht was signed

1786 The patriots take hold of power in various towns. The rule of stadholder William V is restored in 1787 with the help of Prussia

1795–1806 The Batavian Republic

The Siege of Bergen op Zoom
During the War of Austrian Succession, the French occupied the Southern Netherlands, which had been a possession of Austria. In order to strengthen their hand at the peace negotiations vis-à-vis the republic, in 1747 they also annexed Zeeland Flanders and the fortified town of Bergen.

The Schools Controversy
The 19th-century schools controversy between liberals and denominational supporters was over the inequality between independent education and public education. Under HJAM Schaepman and Abraham Kuyper, Catholics and Protestants joined forces and in 1889 laid the foundations for government subsidies for independent education.

Dr Schaepman   Dr Kuyper

The church of the fishing village of Scheveningen is visible in the background.

Child Labour
The Industrial Revolution led to social deprivation in the towns. In 1875, Van Houten's child law was passed, prohibiting children under age 12 from working as paid labourers.

The people of The Hague were overjoyed at the return of the prince. Celebrations were held throughout the town. The times during which the House of Orange had been regarded as a "clique of tyrants" were definitely over.

Domela Nieuwenhuis

1806 Louis Napoleon, brother of Napoleon I, becomes king of Holland

1830 The Belgian Revolution. Nine years later, the Netherlands and Belgium separate

1848 Revision of the constitution and introduction of parliamentary system

1885 Van Gogh paints *The Potato Eaters*

1888 First socialist, Domela Nieuwenhuis, elected to Parliament

1800	1820	1840	1860	1880	1900

1798 Abolition of the Dutch East India Company

1815 The Northern and Southern Netherlands are united under William I

1839 Haarlem–Amsterdam railway opens

Steam train

1870 Abolition of the death penalty

1863 Abolition of slavery

1886 Parliamentary inquiry reveals dire conditions in factories

Colonialism

Dutch colonial history started in the 17th century when trading settlements were established in Asia, Africa and America. Many colonies were lost during the course of time, but the Dutch Indies (Indonesia), Suriname and the Dutch Antilles remained under Dutch rule until far into the 20th century. In the Indonesian archipelago, Dutch power was for a long time limited to Java and the Moluccas. It was only in 1870 that a start was made on subjugating the remaining islands. Indonesia gained independence in 1949 and Suriname in 1975. The Antilles, Aruba and the Netherlands are now equal parts of the Kingdom of the Netherlands.

Tortured Slave
Rebellion was cruelly punished.

Jan Pieterszoon Coen
Appointed governor-general in 1618, Jan Pieterszoon Coen devastated the Javanese settlement of Jakarta in 1619, founding in its place the new administrative centre of Batavia. He bolstered the position of the Dutch East India Company on the spice islands (the Moluccas) and is considered one of the founding fathers of Dutch colonialism.

Selling female slaves half-naked at auctions was condemned by Holland.

Slave Market in Suriname

In total, over 300,000 slaves were shipped to the Dutch colony of Suriname to work the plantations. The slave trade was abolished in 1819, though slavery itself was not abolished until 1863, making Holland the last Western European power to do so.

Session of the Landraad
This *landraad*, or joint court, is presided over by the assistant resident. The *landraad* was the civil and criminal common-law court for native Indonesians and all non-European foreigners in the Dutch Indies. The court could, with government approval, inflict the death penalty.

Batavia During the 17th Century
This painting by Andries Beeckman shows the fish market with the "Kasteel" in the background, from which the Dutch ruled over the strategic Sunda Strait.

Multatuli
The writer Multatuli, in his novel from 1860, *Max Havelaar*, condemned colonial rule in the Dutch Indies. In the book's final chapter, the author directly addresses King William III, in whose name the people of the Indies were being exploited.

The Establishment of Cape Town
In 1652, Jan van Riebeeck set up a supply station for ships of the Dutch East India Company en route to the Indies. The settlement soon grew into a Dutch colony, which was settled by immigrants from the republic, and to a lesser extent from France (Huguenots) and Germany. Those who moved farther inland were later to become the Boers ("farmers") or Afrikaaners. In 1806, the Cape Colony was taken over by the British Empire.

Kris from Java
Many travellers to the Indies brought back characteristic items to Holland. The Javanese kris was a favourite souvenir.

The auctioneer sits taking notes at the table. The slaves whom he is selling were delivered by special traders. Until 1734, slaves were auctioned exclusively by the Dutch West India Company, which had the monopoly on the slave trade.

Colonial Wares
From the end of the 19th century, a number of Dutch grocers offered for sale "colonial wares" such as coffee, tea, rice, sugar and various exotic eastern herbs and spices, including the much-prized peppercorns, cloves, nutmeg, mace and cinnamon.

The Modern Netherlands

Neutrality during World War I meant that the Netherlands survived the first decades of the 20th century relatively unscathed. However, the economic crisis of the 1930s and particularly World War II left deep wounds. In 1957, as the country was rebuilding, it became one of the six founding members of the European Economic Community (EEC). The Dutch welfare state flourished in the 1960s and 1970s, and Amsterdam's tradition of tolerance made it a haven for the hippy culture. In a survey carried out by the United Nations in 2015, the Netherlands ranked fifth in the list of best countries to live in.

The Netherlands Today

1917 The magazine *De Stijl* is set up by figures from the movement of the same name, such as Theo van Doesburg, Piet Mondriaan and JJP Oud

1930–1940 During the economic crisis of the 1930s, hundreds of thousands of Dutch are unemployed

1949 Holland recognizes the independence of its former colony Indonesia

1953 On 1 February, storms cause severe flooding in Zeeland and South Holland, drowning more than 1,800 people

1910	1920	1930	1940	1950	1960

TIMELINE

1910	1920	1930	1940	1950	1960

1918 German kaiser Wilhelm II flees to Holland, where he is given asylum

1926 Road tax introduced. Approximately 10,000 lorries and 30,000 cars are on the roads of Holland

1948 Willem Drees Sr becomes prime minister of four successive Catholic socialist Drees cabinets and lays the foundations of the Dutch welfare state

1934 KLM's plane "Uiver", a DC-2, wins the handicap section in the London–Melbourne air race

1962 The release of Jan Vrijman's film *De werkelijkheid van Karel Appel* brings the postwar Dutch painter to the attention of the general public. Karel Appel (b. 1921) caused a sensation with his statement: "I'll just mess something up"

1940 On 10 May, Nazi troops enter Holland. Rotterdam capitulates on 14 May. Despite this, the city is bombed

1985 A government decision to deploy 48 NATO cruise missiles on Dutch territory causes a storm of opposition. The Komité Kruisraketten Nee (anti-cruise coalition) submits a petition of 3.5 million signatures to Prime Minister Lubbers in October

2000 The Dutch team at the Sydney Olympics wins a record 25 medals, including 12 golds

1995 Paul Crutzen is awarded the Nobel Prize for Chemistry for his ground-breaking investigations of the ozone layer

2002 On 2 February Crown Prince Wilem-Alexander marries Argentinian Máxima Zorreguieta in Amsterdam's Beurs van Berlage

1975 Holland recognizes the independence of its former colony Suriname

2010 Geert Wilders' PVV gains the most seats in the elections

1970	1980	1990	2000	2010	2020
1970	1980	1990	2000	2010	2020

1980 The KVP, ARP and CHU combine to form the CDA, the large Christian Democratic Party

1992 Under Dutch presidency, the European partners sign the draft Maastricht Treaty in 1991. In 1992, the treaty, under which the European Community becomes the European Union, is ratified

2004 On 2 November, controversial filmmaker Theo Van Gogh is murdered by a radical Islamist, spurring a national debate on immigration

2013 Willem-Alexander becomes king of the Netherlands

2002 Right-wing politician Pym Fortuyn is assassinated on 6 May

2001 The Netherlands is the first country to legalize same-sex marriages

1980 The coronation of Queen Beatrix on 30 April is accompanied by heavy battles between police and anti-monarchy demonstrators and squatters

1971 Ajax wins the First Division European Cup at Wembley Stadium in London with star player Johan Cruijff. The club continues as champion in 1972 and 1973

AMSTERDAM

Amsterdam's Best: Canals and Waterways

From the grace and elegance of the waterside mansions along the Grachtengordel (Canal Ring) to the rows of converted warehouses on Brouwersgracht and the charming houses on Reguliersgracht, the city's canals and waterways embody the very spirit of Amsterdam. They are spanned by many beautiful bridges, including the famous Magere Brug *(see pp118–19)*, a traditionally styled lift bridge. You can also relax at a canalside café or bar and watch an array of boats float by.

Brouwersgracht
The banks of this charming canal are lined with houseboats, cosy cafés and warehouses.

Bloemgracht
There is a great variety of architecture along this lovely, tree-lined canal in the Jordaan, including a row of houses with step gables.

CANAL RING

Prinsengracht
The best way to see all the beautiful buildings along Amsterdam's longest 17th-century canal is by bicycle.

MUSEUM QUARTER

Leidsegracht
Relax at a pavement café along the exclusive Leidsegracht.

Keizersgracht
A view of this canal can be had from any of its bridges. If frozen in winter, this canal is used for ice skating by many Amsterdammers, both young and old.

◀ Façades of buildings along the Damrak canal

Singel
The *Poezenboot*, a boat for stray cats, is just one of the many sights to be found along the Singel, whose distinctive, curved shape established the horseshoe contours of the Canal Ring.

Entrepotdok
The warehouses on the Entrepotdok *(see p138)* were redeveloped in the 1980s. The quayside is now lined in summer with lively café terraces that overlook an array of houseboats and pleasure craft.

NIEUWE
ZIJDE

OUDE
ZIJDE

Herengracht
Known as "the twin brothers", these matching neck-gabled houses at Nos. 409–411 are two of the prettiest houses on the city's grandest canal.

0 metres	500
0 yards	500

Reguliersgracht
Many crooked, brick buildings line this pretty canal, which was cut in 1664. The statue of a stork, located at No. 92, is symbolic of parental responsibility and commemorates a 1571 bylaw protecting this bird.

Amstel
This river is still a busy thoroughfare, with barges and, above all, many sightseeing boats.

The Golden Age of Amsterdam

The 17th century was truly a Golden Age for Amsterdam. The population soared; three great canals, bordered by splendid houses, were built in a triple ring round the city; and scores of painters and architects were at work. Fortunes were made and lost, and this early capitalism produced many paupers, who were cared for by charitable institutions – a radical idea for the time. In 1648, an uneasy peace was formalized with Catholic Spain, causing tension between Amsterdam's Calvinist burgomasters and the less religious House of Orange, which was dominant elsewhere in the country.

Spice Trade
In this old print, a VOC spice trader arrives in Bantam.

Livestock and grain trading

Self-Portrait as the Apostle Paul (1661)
Rembrandt *(see p80)* was one of many artists working in Amsterdam in the mid-17th century.

The new Stadhuis (now the Koninklijk Paleis) was being constructed behind wooden scaffolding.

Nieuwe Kerk, 1395 *(see p90)*

The Love Letter (1666)
Genre painting *(see p127)*, such as this calm domestic interior by Jan Vermeer, became popular as society grew more sophisticated. Jan Steen, Honthorst and Terborch were other famous genre painters.

Dam Square in 1656

Money poured into Amsterdam at this time of civic expansion. Holland was active overseas, colonizing Indonesia, and the spice trade brought enormous wealth. The Dutch East India Company (VOC), the principal trade organization in Holland, prospered – gold seemed almost as common as water. Dutch painter Jan Lingelbach (c.1624–74) depicted the city's Dam square as a busy, thriving and cosmopolitan market, brimming with traders and wealthy merchants.

Delft Tiles
Delicate flower paintings were popular themes on 17th-century Delft tiles *(see pp32–3)*, used as decoration in wealthy households.

Flora's Bandwagon (1636)
Many allegories were painted during "tulip mania". This satirical oil by HG Pot symbolizes the idiocy of investors who paid for rare bulbs with their weight in gold, forcing prices up until the market collapsed.

Commodities weighed at the Waag

Ships sailing up the Damrak

Spices
A load of spices was worth a fortune in the 17th century. The VOC traded in a great variety of these costly spices, primarily pepper, nutmeg, cloves, mace and cinnamon. As early as 1611 the VOC was the largest importer of spices.

Cargo unloaded by cranes

Turkish traders

Pepper, nutmeg, cloves, mace, cinnamon

VOC
In the Scheepvaart Museum *(see pp136–7)*, an entire room is dedicated to the Dutch East India Company.

Giving the Bread
This painting by Willem van Valckert shows the city's needy receiving alms. A rudimentary welfare system was introduced in the 1640s.

Where to See 17th-century Amsterdam

Many public buildings, such as churches and palaces, sprang up as Amsterdam grew more wealthy. The Westerkerk *(see p114)* was designed by Hendrick de Keyser in 1620; the Lutherse Kerk *(see p94)* by Adriaan Dortsman in 1671. Elias Bouman built the Portugees-Israëlitische Synagoge *(see p82)* in 1675 for members of the city's immigrant Sephardic Jewish community.

Apollo (c.1648) Artus Quellien's statue is in the South Gallery of the Koninklijk Paleis *(see pp92–3)*. Construction of the palace, a masterwork by Jacob van Campen, began in 1648.

Museum het Rembrandthuis (1606) Jacob van Campen added the pediment in 1633 *(see p80)*.

Amsterdam's Best: Museums

For a fairly small city, Amsterdam has a surprisingly large number of museums and galleries. The quality and variety of the collections are impressive, covering everything from bibles and beer to shipbuilding and space travel. Many are housed in buildings of historical or architectural interest. The Rijksmuseum, with its Gothic façade, is a city landmark, and Rembrandt's work is exhibited in his original home.

Anne Frank Huis
Anne Frank's photo is exhibited in the house where she hid during World War II.

Amsterdam Museum
A wealth of historical information is on display here. Once an orphanage for boys, it is depicted in *Governesses at the Burgher Orphanage* (1683) by Adriaen Backer *(see pp96–7)*.

Rijksmuseum
An extensive collection of paintings by Dutch masters can be seen in the country's largest national museum. Jan van Huysum's *Still Life with Fruit and Flowers*, dating from about 1730, is a fine example *(see pp126–9)*.

CANAL RING

MUSEUM QUARTER

Stedelijk Museum
Gerrit Rietveld's simple Steltman chair (1963) is one of many exhibits at this modern art museum *(see pp132–3)*.

Van Gogh Museum
Van Gogh's *Self-portrait with Straw Hat* (1870) hangs in this large, stark building, built in 1973 to house the bulk of his work. A chic glass entrance hall was added in 2015 *(see pp130–31)*.

Koninklijk Paleis
The royal palace on the Dam, a former town hall designed in 1648 by Jacob van Campen, is still regularly used today by the queen on official occasions *(see pp92–3).*

NEMO Science Museum
This amazing building, designed in the form of a ship, overhangs the water by 30 m (99 ft) and houses an educational centre for science and technology *(see pp140–41).*

Scheepvaart Museum
This maritime museum is decorated with reliefs relating to the city's maritime history. Moored alongside is a replica of the East Indiaman, *Amsterdam*, which is open to the public *(see pp136–7).*

NIEUWE ZIJDE

OUDE ZIJDE

0 metres	500
0 yards	500

Joods Historisch Museum
Four adjoining synagogues are linked to form this museum *(see p81).*

Verzetsmuseum
Located in the Plantage, this museum documents and commemorates the activities of Dutch Resistance workers in World War II *(see p145).*

Amsterdam's Best: Cafés

Amsterdam is a city of cafés and bars, about 1,500 in all. Each area has something to offer, from friendly and relaxed brown cafés – a traditional Dutch local pub characterized by dark wooden panelling and furniture, low ceilings, dim lighting and smoke-stained ceilings – to lively and crowded designer bars. Each café and bar has some special attraction: a large range of beers, live music, canalside terraces, art exhibitions, board games and pool tables or simply a brand of *gezelligheid*, the unique Dutch concept of "cosiness".

De Drie Fleschjes
In one of the oldest pubs (1650) of Amsterdam, you can choose from a wide variety of gins.

Café Chris
This brown café, allegedly the oldest café in the Jordaan, is patronized by regular customers (artists and students).

CANAL RING

Walem
This designer eatery, one of Amsterdam's oldest cafés, has a sunny canal terrace and is popular with the international crowd.

MUSEUM QUARTER

Groot Melkhuis
Originally a farm dating back to 1874, this modern café is very popular, especially on warm summer days.

Hoppe
The dark wooden interior and tang of cigar smoke in the air are the essence of this classic brown café, situated on the lively Spui.

Karpershoek
This lively café (the oldest café in Amsterdam) is close to the Centraal Station and is frequented by travellers looking for a cup of coffee.

Kapitein Zeppos
This café, frequented by trendy Amsterdammers, often hosts live concerts on Sunday afternoons.

NIEUWE ZIJDE

OUDE ZIJDE

| 0 metres | 500 |
| 0 yards | 500 |

De Jaren
Popular with students, this trendy two-storey café has a superb view of the Amstel and a wide selection of newspapers.

Grand Café Soccerworld
In the café of the arena you can admire the football shirts of the famous Ajax team.

| 0 kilometres | 3 |
| 0 miles | 3 |

OUDE ZIJDE

The eastern half of Amsterdam became known as the Oude Zijde (Old Side). Originally it occupied a narrow strip on the east bank of the Amstel river, running between Damrak and the Oudezijds Voorburgwal. At its heart was built the Oude Kerk, the oldest church in the city. In the early 15th century the Oude Zijde began an eastward expansion that continued into the 1600s. This growth was fuelled by an influx

of Jewish refugees from Portugal. The oldest of the four synagogues, now containing the Joods Historisch Museum, dates from this period. These were central to Jewish life in the city for centuries. During the Golden Age *(see pp54–5)*, the Oude Zijde was an important commercial centre. Boats could sail up the Geldersekade to Nieuwmarkt, where goods were weighed at the Waag before being sold at the market.

Sights at a Glance

Historic Buildings and Monuments
- ❷ Waag
- ❺ Agnietenkapel
- ❻ Oudemanhuispoort
- ❼ De Waalse Kerk
- ❽ Trippenhuis
- ⓰ Pintohuis
- ⓱ Montelbaanstoren
- ⓲ Scheepvaarthuis
- ⓳ Schreierstoren

Opera Houses
- ⓫ Stadhuis-Muziektheater

Museums
- ❹ Hash Marihuana Hemp Museum
- ❿ Museum het Rembrandthuis
- ⓮ Joods Historisch Museum

Churches and Synagogues
- ❾ Zuiderkerk
- ⓭ Mozes en Aäronkerk

- ⓯ Portugees-Israëlitische Synagoge
- ㉑ *Oude Kerk pp84–5*

Streets and Markets
- ❶ Red Light District
- ❸ Nieuwmarkt
- ⓬ Waterlooplein
- ⓴ Zeedijk

See also Street Finder maps 2 & 5

0 metres   250
0 yards   250

◀ The impressive Oude Kerk, Amsterdam's oldest building

For map symbols *see back flap*

Street-by-Street: University District

The University of Amsterdam, founded in 1877, is predominantly located in the peaceful, southwestern part of the Oude Zijde. The university's roots lie in the former Athenaeum Illustre, which was founded in 1632 in the Agnietenkapel. Beyond Damstraat, the bustling Red Light District meets the Nieuwmarkt, where the 15th-century Waag evokes a medieval air. South of the Nieuwmarkt, Museum Het Rembrandthuis gives a fascinating insight into the life of the city's most famous artist.

❶ ★ **Red Light District**
The sex industry brings billions of euros to Amsterdam every year.

❹ **Hash Marihuana Hemp Museum**
This museum showcases marijuana through the ages.

❼ **De Waalse Kerk**
Built in the early 1400s, this church was frequently visited by Vincent van Gogh. Services are still conducted here today.

❺ **Agnietenkapel**
Like many buildings in this area, the chapel belongs to the University of Amsterdam.

House (1610), unusually facing three canals

❻ **Oudemanhuispoort**
The spectacles carved on the gateway into this 18th-century almshouse for elderly men symbolize old age.

Lift bridge over Groenburgwal

For hotels and restaurants in this area see pp396–7 and pp406–9

⑧ Trippenhuis
Although it appears to be a single 17th-century mansion, this building is in fact two houses, the middle windows being false to preserve the symmetry.

③ Nieuwmarkt
Despite redevelopment southeast of this once-important market square, the Nieuwmarkt itself is still bordered by many fine 17th- and 18th-century gabled houses.

NIEUW-MARKT

NIEUWE ZUIDE
OUDE ZIJDE
CANAL RING

Locator Map
See Street Finder maps 1, 2 & 5

BURGWAL

VENIERS

RAAMGRACHT

GROENBURGWAL

ZWANENBURGWAL

WATERLOO-PLEIN

② ★ Waag
Amsterdam's only remaining medieval gatehouse now houses a café-restaurant.

⑨ Zuiderkerk
This prominent city landmark is now used as a wedding and conference venue.

Key
— Recommended route

0 metres   50
0 yards   50

⑩ ★ Museum het Rembrandthuis
Hundreds of Rembrandt's etchings are on display in the artist's former home.

❶ Red Light District

Map 5 A1. 🚊 4, 9, 16.

Barely clad prostitutes bathed in a red neon glow and touting for business at their windows is one of the defining images of modern Amsterdam. The city's Red Light District, referred to locally as de Walletjes (the little walls), is concentrated on the Oude Kerk *(see pp84–5)*, although it extends as far as Warmoesstraat to the west, the Zeedijk to the north, the Kloveniersburgwal to the east and then along the line of Damstraat to the south.

Prostitution in Amsterdam dates back to the city's emergence as a port in the 13th century. By 1478, prostitution had become so widespread that attempts were made to contain it. Prostitutes straying outside their designated area were marched back to the sound of pipe and drum.

A century later, following the Alteration, the Calvinists *(see pp56–7)* tried to outlaw prostitution altogether. Their attempts were half-hearted, and by the mid-17th century prostitution was openly tolerated. In 1850, Amsterdam had a population of 200,000, and more than 200 brothels.

Entrance to one of the clubs in the Red Light District

Today, the whole area is crisscrossed by a network of narrow lanes, dominated by garish sex shops, seedy clubs and unsavoury characters. At night, the little alleys assume a somewhat sinister aspect, and it is unwise to wander away from the main streets. But by day, hordes of visitors generate a festive buzz, and amid the sleaze there are interesting cafés, bars, restaurants and beautiful canalside houses to be discovered. The city council is trying to make the area more culturally attractive by cutting down on window-prostitutes, closing the seediest clubs and encouraging non-sex-industry businesses.

❷ Waag

Nieuwmarkt 4. **Map** 2 E5. 🚊 4, 9, 16. Ⓜ Nieuwmarkt. **Closed** Upper Rooms: closed to the public.

The multi-turreted Waag is the city's oldest surviving gatehouse. Built in 1488, it was then, and often still is, called St Antoniespoort. Public executions were held here, and condemned prisoners awaited their fate in the "little gallows room". In 1617, the building became the public weigh house *(waaggebouw)*. Peasants had their produce weighed here and paid tax accordingly. Various guilds used the upper rooms of each tower. From 1619 the Guild of Surgeons had a meeting room and anatomy theatre here. They added the central octagonal tower in 1691. Rembrandt's *Anatomy Lesson of Dr Nicholaes Tulp*, now in the Mauritshuis *(see pp226–7)*, and *The Anatomy Lesson of Dr Jan Deijman*, in the Amsterdam Museum *(see pp96–7)*, were commissioned by guild members and then hung here.

The weigh house closed in the early 19th century and the Waag has since served as a fire station and two city museums. It is now home to the restaurant In de Waag.

The 15th-century Waag dominating the Nieuwmarkt, with an antique market on the right

Part of the commemorative photo display in Nieuwmarkt metro station

❸ Nieuwmarkt

Map 2 E5. 🚋 4, 9, 16. Ⓜ Nieuwmarkt.
Antiques market: **Open** May–Sep: 9am–
5pm Sun. 🍎 Organic farmers' market:
Open 9am–5pm Sat.

An open, paved square, the
Nieuwmarkt is flanked to the west
by the Red Light District. With the
top end of the Geldersekade, it
forms Amsterdam's Chinatown.
The Waag dominates the square,
and construction of this gateway
led to the site's development in
the 15th century as a market-
place. When the city expanded
in the 17th century *(see pp68–9)*,
the square took on its present
dimensions and was called the
Nieuwmarkt. It retains an array of
17th- and 18th-century gabled
houses. True to tradition, an
antiques market is held on
Sundays during the summer.

The old Jewish Quarter
leads off the square down
St Antoniesbreestraat. In the
1970s, many houses here were
demolished to make way for
the metro, sparking off clashes
between protesters and police.
The action of conservationists
persuaded the council to adopt
a policy of renovating rather
than redeveloping old buildings.
Photographs of their protests
decorate the metro station.

❹ Hash Marihuana Hemp Museum

Oudezijds Achterburgwal 148.
Map 2 D5. **Tel** 020-6248926. 🚋 4, 9,
14, 16. Ⓜ Nieuwmarkt. **Open** 10am–
10pm. **Closed** 27 Apr. 🚲 📷

This museum, which has a
branch in Barcelona, charts the
history of hemp (marijuana).
Exhibits refer back 8,000 years to
early Asiatic civilizations, which
used the plant for medicines
and clothing. It was first used in
the Netherlands, according to a
herbal manual of 1554, as a cure
for earache.

Until the late 19th century,
however, hemp was the main
source of fibre for rope, and
was therefore important in the
Dutch shipping industry. Other
exhibits relate to the psychoac-
tive properties of this plant. They
include an intriguing array
of pipes and bongs (smoking
devices), along with displays that
explain smuggling methods.
The museum also has a small
cultivation area where plants
are grown under artificial light.
Police sometimes raid and take
away exhibits, so there may be
occasional gaps in displays.

❺ Agnietenkapel

Oudezijds Voorburgwal 231. **Map** 2 D5.
🚋 4, 9, 14, 16. **Closed** to the public.

The Agnietenkapel was part
of the convent of St Agnes
until 1578 when it was closed
after the Alteration. In 1632,
the Athenaeum Illustre, the
precursor of the University
of Amsterdam, took over the
building and by the mid-
17th century it was a centre
of scientific learning. It also
housed the municipal library
until the 1830s. The
Agnietenkapel itself dates from
1470, and is one of the few
Gothic chapels to have survived
the Alteration. During
restoration from 1919 to 1921,
elements of the Amsterdam
School architecture were
introduced *(see pp146–7)*.
Despite these changes
and long periods
of secular use,
the building
still has the
feel of a
Franciscan
chapel. The large
auditorium on the
first floor is the oldest
in the city. It has a
lovely ceiling, painted with
Renaissance motifs and a
portrait of Minerva, the Roman
goddess of wisdom and the
arts. The walls are hung with
forty portraits of European
humanist scholars, including
one of Erasmus (1466–1536).
The Agnietenkapel once
housed the University of
Amsterdam Museum; now the
museum's collection can be
seen in Oude Turfmarkt 129
(next to the Allard Pierson
Museum). A conference centre
has taken its place.

Entrance to Agnietenkapel, now a
university conference centre

❻ Oudemanhuis-poort

Between Oudezijds Achterburgwal
and Kloveniersburgwal. **Map** 2 D5.
🚋 4, 9, 14, 16. Book market:
Open 10am–5pm Mon–Sat.

The Oudemanhuispoort was
once the entrance to old people's
almshouses (Oudemannenhuis),
built in 1754. Today the building
is part of the University of
Amsterdam.The pediment
over the gateway in
the Oudezijds
Achterburgwal
features a pair
of spectacles,
a symbol
of old age.

Crest of Amsterdam,
Oudemanhuispoort

Trading inside this
covered walkway dates
from 1757 and today
there is a market for second-hand
books. Although the building is
closed to the public, visitors may
enter the 18th-century courtyard
via the arcade.

❼ De Waalse Kerk

Walenpleintje 157–159. **Map** 2 D5.
Tel 020-6232074. 🚋 4, 9, 14, 16.
Ⓜ Nieuwmarkt. **Open** for service
and events only. 🕆 11am Sun.

The origin of this church dates
back to 1409, when it started as
a convent for laymen monks and
was known as Paulusbroederkerk
(Brother Paul Monastery). After
1550 it was handed over to
the Huguenots – Protestant
refugees from France – and
was renamed Église Wallone.
Services and regular lectures are
still conducted here in French.
   The building boasts splendid
acoustics and an impressive
organ built by Christiaan Müller,
one of the finest remaining in the
world. The church is often used
for concerts and various events.

❽ Trippenhuis

Kloveniersburgwal 29. **Map** 2 E5.
🚋 4, 9, 14, 16. Ⓜ Nieuwmarkt.
Closed to the public.

Justus Vingboons designed
this ornate Classical mansion,
completed in 1662. It appears
to be one house: it is in fact two.
The façade, outlined by eight
Corinthian columns, features
false middle windows. The
house was designed for arms
merchants Lodewijk and
Hendrick Trip; the chimneys
look like cannons. The city's art
collection was housed here in
1817–85, when it moved to the
Rijksmuseum (see pp126–9).
Trippenhuis now houses the
Dutch Academy. Opposite at
No. 26 is the Kleine Trippenhuis
(1698). Only 2.5 m (7 ft) wide,
it has detailed cornicing,
including two carved sphinxes.

❾ Zuiderkerk

Zuiderkerkhof 72. **Map** 2 E5. **Tel** 020-
5527987. 🚋 9, 14. Ⓜ Nieuwmarkt.
Ⓦ zuiderkerk.amsterdam.nl

Designed by Hendrick de Keyser
in 1603 in the Renaissance style,
the Zuiderkerk was the first
Calvinist church to open in
Amsterdam after the Alteration.
The spire has columns, decorative clocks and an onion dome.

The spire of the Zuiderkerk, a prominent city landmark

The Zuiderkerk ceased to
function as a church in 1929.
It was restored in 1988 and is
now a commercial venue for
events and private dinners.
The surrounding community
housing includes the "Pentagon"
by Theo Bosch.

❿ Museum het Rembrandthuis

Jodenbreestraat 4–6. **Map** 2 E5.
Tel 020-5200400. 🚋 9, 14.
Ⓜ Nieuwmarkt. **Open** 10am–6pm
daily. **Closed** 1 Jan, 27 Apr, 25 Dec.
🏛️🏛️🏛️🏛️🏛️ Ⓦ rembrandthuis.nl

Rembrandt worked and taught
in this house from 1639 until
1660. He lived in the ground-floor
rooms with his wife, Saskia, who
died here in 1642, leaving the
artist with their only surviving
child, a baby son, Titus.
   Many of Rembrandt's most
famous paintings were created
in the first-floor studio. Lessons
were conducted in the attic. A
fine collection of Rembrandt's
etchings and drawings includes
various self-portraits. There are
also landscapes, nude studies,
religious and crowd scenes, and
sketches of the artist with his
wife. The house has undergone
historically accurate restoration
and a further wing has been
opened to the public.

Self-portrait by Rembrandt with his wife,
Saskia (1636)

⓫ Stadhuis–Muziektheater

Waterlooplein 22. **Map** 5 B2. 🚋 4, 9, 14. Ⓜ Waterlooplein. Stadhuis: **Tel** 020-6241111. **Open** 8:30am–4pm Mon–Fri (free concerts Sep–May: 12:30pm Tue). Muziektheater: **Tel** 020-6255455. *See Entertainment pp150–51.* ⚿ ☑ ⓦ **hetmuziektheater.nl**

Few buildings in Amsterdam caused as much controversy as the new Stadhuis (city hall) and Muziektheater (opera house). Nicknamed the "Stopera" by protesters, the plan required the destruction of dozens of medieval houses, which were virtually all that remained of the original Jewish quarter, and the temporary relocation of a popular market. This led to running battles between squatters and the police.

The building, completed in 1988, is a huge confection of red brick, marble and glass. A mural illustrating the Normaal Amsterdams Peil is shown on the arcade linking the two parts of the complex. The complex has the largest auditorium in the country, and it is also home to the Netherlands' national opera and ballet companies.

⓬ Waterlooplein

Map 5 B2. 🚋 9, 14. Ⓜ Waterlooplein. Market: **Open** 9am–5pm Mon–Fri, 8:30am–5pm Sat.

The Waterlooplein dates from 1882, when two canals were filled in to create a market square. The site was originally known as Vlooyenburg, an artificial island built in the 17th century to house Jewish settlers. The original market disappeared during World War II when most of the Jewish residents of Amsterdam were transported east by the Nazis. After the war, a popular flea market grew up in its place, and today the northern end of the square still hosts a lively mix of stalls.

⓭ Mozes en Aäronkerk

Waterlooplein 205. **Map** 5 B2. **Tel** 020-6221305. 🚋 9, 14. Ⓜ Waterlooplein. **Closed** to the public except for exhibitions.

Designed by Flemish architect T Suys the Elder in 1841, Mozes en Aäronkerk was built on the site of a hidden Catholic church. The later church took its name from the Old Testament figures depicted on the gable stones of the original building. These are now set into the rear wall.

The church was restored in 1990, its twin wooden towers painted to look like sandstone. It is now used for exhibitions, public meetings and concerts.

The central hall in the Grote Synagoge, which opened in 1671

⓮ Joods Historisch Museum

Jonas Daniel Meijerplein 2–4. **Map** 5 B2. **Tel** 020-5310310. 🚋 9, 14. 🚇 Muziektheater. Ⓜ Waterlooplein. **Open** 11am–5pm daily. **Closed** 27 Apr, Jewish New Year, Yom Kippur. ⚿ ⚿ ☑ ⚿ on request, incl. for the visually handicapped. ⚿ ⚿ ⓦ **jhm.nl**

This complex of four synagogues, built by Ashkenazi Jews in the 17th and 18th centuries, opened as a museum in 1987. The synagogues were central to Jewish life here, until the devastation of World War II left them empty. Restored in the 1980s, they are connected by internal walkways. Displays of art and religious artifacts depict Jewish culture and the history of Judaism in the Netherlands.

Highlights include the Grote Synagoge, its hall lined with galleries; and the Holy Ark (1791) from Enkhuizen *(see p182)*, which dominates the Nieuwe Synagoge and holds two 18th-century silver Torah shields and three velvet mantles. Also not to be missed is the 1734 Haggadah containing the Passover order of service.

The buildings were renovated in 2006, when a basement print room was created, and one of the synagogues turned into a children's museum.

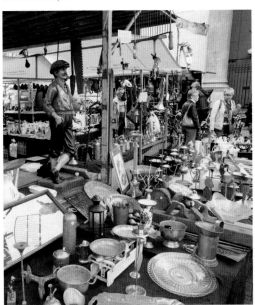

Eclectic goods on offer at the Waterlooplein market

⓯ Portugees-Israëlitische Synagoge

Mr Visserplein 3. **Map** 5 B2. **Tel** 020-6245351. 🚊 9, 14. Ⓜ Waterlooplein. **Open** Apr–Oct: 10am–4pm Sun–Fri; Nov–Mar: 10am–4pm Sun–Thu, 10am–2pm Fri. **Closed** Jewish hols, 27 Apr. 📷 💿 call 020-5310380 to book ♿ 🏠 🌐 **portugesesynagoge.nl**

Elias Bouman's design for the Portugees-Israëlitische Synagoge is said to be inspired by the Temple of Solomon in Jerusalem. Built for the wealthy Portuguese Sephardic community of Amsterdam and inaugurated in 1675, the huge brick building has a rectangular ground plan with the Holy Ark in the southeast corner facing towards Jerusalem, and the *tebah* (the podium from which the service is led) at the opposite end.

The wooden, barrel-vaulted ceiling is supported by four Ionic columns. The interior of the synagogue, with its pews made of mahogany, is illuminated by more than 1,000 candles and 72 windows.

Italianate façade of the Pintohuis, now a centre for culture and literature

⓰ Pintohuis

Sint Antoniesbreestraat 69. **Map** 2 E5. **Tel** 020-6243184. 🚊 9, 14. Ⓜ Nieuwmarkt. **Open** 11:30am–6:30pm Mon–Fri, 1:30–5pm Sat. **Closed** Sun.

Isaac de Pinto, a wealthy Portuguese merchant, bought the Pintohuis in 1651 for the then enormous sum of 30,000 guilders.

He had it remodelled over the next decades to a design by Elias Bouman, and it is one of the few private residences in Amsterdam to follow an Italianate style. The exterior design was reworked from 1675 to 1680. Six imposing pilasters break up the severe, cream façade into five recessed sections, and the cornice is topped by a blind balustrade concealing the roof. Inside, the painted ceiling is decorated with birds and cherubs.

In the 1970s, the house was scheduled for demolition because it stood in the way of a newly planned main road. Concerted protest saved the building and, until 2012, it housed a branch of the Amsterdam Public Library.

⓱ Montelbaanstoren

Oude Waal/Oudeschans 2. **Map** 5 B1. 🚊 9, 14. Ⓜ Nieuwmarkt. **Closed** to the public.

The lower portion of the Montelbaanstoren was built in 1512 and formed part of Amsterdam's medieval fortifications. It lay just beyond the city wall, protecting the city's wharves on the newly built St Antoniesdijk (now the Oudeschans) from the neighbouring Gelderlanders.

The octagonal structure and open-work timber steeple were both added by Hendrick de Keyser in 1606. His decorative addition bears a close resemblance to the spire of the Oude Kerk, designed by Joost Bilhamer, which was built 40 years earlier (see pp84–5). In 1611, the tower began to list, prompting Amsterdammers to attach ropes to the top and pull it right again.

Sailors from the Dutch East India Company would gather at the Montelbaanstoren before being ferried in small boats down the IJ to the massive East Indies-bound sailing ships, anchored further out in deep water to the north.

The building appears in a number of etchings by Rembrandt, and is still a popular subject for artists. It used to house the offices of the Amsterdam water authority but is currently unoccupied.

One of many stone carvings on the Scheepvaarthuis façade

⓲ Scheepvaarthuis

Prins Hendrikkade 108. **Map** 2 E4. 🚊 1, 2, 4, 5, 9, 13, 16, 17. Ⓜ Centraal Station. **Open** Sun. 💿 call 020-6868595 to book 🌐 **hetschip.nl**

Built as an office complex in 1916, the Scheepvaarthuis (shipping house) is regarded as the first true example of Amsterdam School architecture (see pp146–7). It was designed by Piet Kramer (1881–1961), Johan van der May (1878–1949) and Michel de Klerk (1884–1923) for a group of shipping companies which no longer wanted to conduct business on the quay.

The imposing triangular building has a prow-like front and is crowned by a statue of Neptune, his wife and four female figures representing

The medieval Montelbaanstoren, with its decorative timber steeple

the four points of the compass. No expense was spared on the construction and internal decoration of the building, and local dock workers came to regard the building as a symbol of capitalism. The doors, stairs, window frames and interior walls are festooned with nautical images, such as sea horses, dolphins and anchors. Beautiful stained-glass skylights are also decorated with images of sailing ships, maps and compasses.

The Scheepvaarthuis is now a luxury hotel, the Grand Hôtel Amrâth, which offers guided tours for groups.

⓳ Schreierstoren

Prins Hendrikkade 94–95. **Map** 2 E4. 🚃 1, 2, 4, 5, 9, 11, 13, 16, 17. Ⓜ Centraal Station. **Closed** to the public.

The Schreierstoren (weepers' tower) was a defensive structure forming part of the medieval city walls, dating from 1480. It was one of the few fortifications not to be demolished as the city expanded beyond its medieval boundaries in the 17th century. The distinctive building now houses a basement café that offers tastings of genuine sailors' gin.

Popular legend states that the tower derived its name from the weeping (*schreien* in the original Dutch) of women who came here to wave their men off to sea. It is more likely, however, that the title has a less romantic origin and comes from the tower's position on a sharp (*screye* or *scherpe*), 90-degree bend in the old town walls. The earliest of four wall plaques, dated 1569, adds considerably to the confusion by depicting a weeping woman alongside the inscription *scrayer hovck*, which means "sharp corner".

In 1609, Henry Hudson set sail from here in an attempt to discover a new and faster trading route to the East Indies. Instead, he unintentionally "discovered" the river in North America, which still bears his name. A bronze plaque, laid in 1927, commemorates Hudson's voyage.

The Schreierstoren, part of the original city fortifications

⓴ Zeedijk

Map 2 E4. 🚃 1, 2, 4, 5, 9, 13, 16, 17. Ⓜ Nieuwmarkt, Centraal Station.

Along with the Nieuwendijk and the Haarlemmerdijk, the Zeedijk (sea dyke) formed part of Amsterdam's original fortifications. Built in the early 1300s, some 30 years after Amsterdam had been granted its city charter, these defences took the form of a canal moat with piled-earth ramparts reinforced by wooden palisades. As the city grew in prosperity and its boundaries expanded, canals were filled in and the dykes became obsolete. The paths that ran alongside them became the streets and alleys which bear their names today.

One of the two remaining wooden-fronted houses in the city is at No. 1. It was built in the mid-1500s as a hostel for sailors and is much restored. Opposite is St Olofskapel, built in 1445 and named after the first Christian king of Norway and Denmark. By the 1600s, the Zeedijk had become a slum. The area is on the edge of the city's Red Light District, and in the 1960s and 1970s it became notorious as a centre for drug-dealing and street crime. However, following an extensive clean-up campaign in the 1980s, the Zeedijk is much improved. Architect Fred Greves has built a Chinese Buddhist temple, Fo Kuang Shan.

Plaques on the gables of some of the street's cafés reveal their former use – the red boot at No. 17 indicates that it was once a cobbler's.

The Zeedijk, today a lively street with plenty of restaurants, bars and small shops

㉑ Oude Kerk

The origins of the Oude Kerk date from the early 13th century, when a wooden church was built on a sand bank. The present Gothic structure is 14th century and has grown from a single-aisled church into a basilica. As it expanded, the building became a gathering place for traders and a refuge for the poor. Paintings and statuary were destroyed after the Alteration in 1578, but the gilded ceiling and stained-glass windows remain. The Great Organ was added in 1724, and there are two other fine organs in this lovely church, also home to the tomb of Rembrandt's wife, Saskia.

The Oude Kerk Today
The old church, surrounded by shops, cafés and houses, remains a calm and peaceful haven at the heart of the frenetic Red Light District.

★ **Great Organ** (1724)
Vater-Müller's oak-encased organ has eight bellows and 4,000 pipes. The 54 pipes of the magnificent organ front are gilded.

| 1330 Church consecrated to St Nicholas | 1462 First side chapel demolished to build south transept | | 1658 Carillon installed | | 1955–99 Restoration of church | 1979 Church reopens to public |
| 1412 North transept completed | | 1552 Lady Chapel added | | 1724 Great Organ installed | 1951 Church closes | 2014 Renewal of entrance and exit |

1300	1400	1500	1600	1700	1800	1900	2000	2100

	1500 Side chapels added		1578 Calvinists triumph in the Alteration			1912–14 Partial restoration of north-west corner	2011–12 Floor is restored
1340 Church enlarged	1566 Spire added to 13th-century tower		*Stained-glass coats of arms in Lady Chapel*			
1300 Small stone church built						

★ **Gilded Ceiling**
The delicate 15th-century vault paintings have a gilded background. They were hidden with layers of blue paint in 1755 and not revealed until 1955.

VISITORS' CHECKLIST

Practical Information
Oudekerksplein. **Map** 2 D4.
Tel 020-6258284.
w oudekerk.nl
Church: **Open** 11am–5pm Mon–Sat, 1–5pm Sun. 11am Sun.
Tower: **Open** Apr–Sep: 1–5pm Thu–Sat; Oct–Mar: phone 020-6892565 to arrange a visit.

Transport
4, 9, 16.

★ **Lady Chapel**
(1552)
The Death of the Virgin Mary by Dirk Crabeth is one of three restored stained-glass windows in the Lady Chapel.

Brocaded Pillars
Decorative pillars originally formed niches holding a series of statues of the Apostles, all destroyed by the iconoclasts in 1578.

KEY

① **Tomb of Admiral Abraham van der Hulst (1619–66)**

② **Christening chapel**

③ **The spire** of the bell tower was built by Joost Bilhamer in 1565. François Hemony added the 47-bell carillon in 1658.

④ **Tomb of Saskia, wife of Rembrandt** *(see p80)*

⑤ **Tomb of Admiral Jacob van Heemskerk (1567–1607)**

⑥ **17th- and 18th-century houses**

⑦ **Former sacristy**

The Red Door
The inscription on the lintel above the door into the former sacristy warns those about to enter: "Marry in haste, repent at leisure".

NIEUWE ZIJDE

The western side of medieval Amsterdam was known as the Nieuwe Zijde (New Side). Together with the Oude Zijde it formed the heart of the early maritime settlement. Nieuwendijk, today a busy shopping street, was originally one of the earliest sea defences. As Amsterdam grew, it expanded eastwards, leaving large sections of the Nieuwe Zijde, to the west, neglected and in decline. With its many wooden houses, the city was prone to fires and in 1452 much of the area was burned down. During rebuilding, a broad moat, the Singel, was cut, along which warehouses, rich merchants' homes and fine quays sprang up. The interesting Amsterdam Museum, which is now housed in a splendid former orphanage, has scores of maps and paintings charting the growth of the city from these times to the present day. One room is devoted to the Miracle of Amsterdam, which made the city a place of pilgrimage, and brought commerce to the Nieuwe Zijde. Nearby lies Kalverstraat, Amsterdam's main shopping street, and also the secluded Begijnhof. This pretty courtyard is mostly fringed by narrow 17th-century houses, but it also contains the city's oldest surviving wooden house.

Sights at a Glance

Historic Buildings, Monuments and Bridges

2 Koninklijk Paleis pp92–3
4 Nationaal Monument
9 Torensluis
10 Magna Plaza
12 Centraal Station
15 Beurs van Berlage

Churches

1 Nieuwe Kerk
11 Lutherse Kerk
13 St Nicolaaskerk

Museums

3 Madame Tussauds Scenerama
6 Amsterdam Museum pp96–7
8 Allard Pierson Museum
14 Museum Ons' Lieve Heer op Solder

Streets and Squares

5 Nes
7 Begijnhof

See also Street Finder maps 1, 2 & 5

| 0 metres | | 250 |
| 0 yards | | 250 |

◀ Visitors at the Amsterdam Museum on Kalverstraat

For map symbols see back flap

Street-by-Street: Nieuwe Zijde

Although much of the medieval Nieuwe Zijde has disappeared, the area is still rich in buildings that relate to the city's past. The Dam, dominated by the Koninklijk Paleis and Nieuwe Kerk, provides examples of architecture from the 15th to the 20th centuries. Around Kalverstraat, narrow streets and alleys follow the course of some of the earliest dykes and footpaths. Here, most of the traditional gabled houses have been turned into bustling shops and cafés. The lively Rokin, and nearby Damrak, are destined to become the "red carpet" entry to the city, once the new Noord-Zuidlijn metro is completed.

❻ ★ Amsterdam Museum
Wall plaques and maps showing the walled medieval city are on display in this converted orphanage that dates from the 16th century.

Kalverstraat
This busy tourist shopping area took its name from the livestock market which was regularly held here during the 15th century.

❼ ★ Begijnhof
Two churches and one of the few remaining wooden houses in the city nestle in this secluded, tree-filled courtyard.

ST. LUCIËNSTEEG

ROKIN

SPUI

Key

━ Recommended route

❶ ★ Nieuwe Kerk
The carved and gilded ceiling above the choir was one of the few sections to survive the great fire of 1645.

CANAL RING

NIEUWE ZUIDE

OUIDE ZIJDE

Locator Map
See Street Finder maps 1 & 2

LEISSTRAAT

D A M

D A M R A K

St Nicolaas wall statue, depicting Amsterdam's patron saint, is thought to date from the 15th century.

SINTER CLAES

VERSTRAAT

ROKIN

NES

❹ Nationaal Monument
Two heraldic stone lions represent the Netherlands on this imposing memorial to the Dutch who lost their lives in World War II.

❸ Madame Tussauds Scenerama
As well as waxworks and animated scenes, there is a fine view of the city from here.

0 metres 50
0 yards 50

❺ Nes
This street, one of Amsterdam's oldest, has been a centre for theatre for over 150 years

❷ ★ Koninklijk Paleis
Built as the town hall, the building's Classical façade and fine sculptures were intended to glorify the city and its government.

❶ Nieuwe Kerk

Dam. **Map** 1 C4. **Tel** 020-6386909.
🚊 1, 2, 4, 5, 9, 13, 14, 16, 17.
Open during exhibitions only *(phone to check)*. **Closed** 27 Apr. 🖼 ♿ 🖵
🆆 nieuwekerk.nl

Dating from the late 14th century, Amsterdam's second parish church was built as the population outgrew the Oude Kerk *(see pp84–5)*. During its turbulent history, the church has been destroyed several times by fire, rebuilt and then stripped of its finery after the Alteration. It reached its present size in the 1650s.

The pulpit, not the altar, is the focal point of the interior, reflecting the Protestant belief that the sermon is central to worship. Unusually flamboyant for a Dutch Protestant church, it was finished in 1664 and took Albert Vinckenbrink 15 years to carve. Above the transept crossing, grimacing gilded cherubs struggle to support the corners of the wooden barrel vault. Magnificent three-tiered brass candelabra were hung from the ceilings of the nave and transepts during restoration work following the fire of 1645. The colourful arched window in the south transept was designed by Otto Mengelberg in 1898. It depicts Queen Wilhelmina surrounded by courtiers at her coronation. In the apse is Rombout Verhulst's memorial to Admiral De Ruyter (1607–76), who died at sea in battle against the French.

Stained-glass window at the Nieuwe Kerk in Amsterdam

❷ Koninklijk Paleis

See pp92–3.

Scene after Vermeer, in Madame Tussauds Scenerama

❸ Madame Tussauds Scenerama

Gebouw Peek & Cloppenburg, Dam 20. **Map** 2 D5. **Tel** 020-5221010.
🚊 4, 9, 14, 16. **Open** 10am–6:30pm daily (to 8:30pm Jul & Aug).
Closed 27 Apr. 🖼 📷 ♿
🆆 madametussauds.com

Madame Tussauds offers an audiovisual tour of Amsterdam's history, as well as projected future developments. Some of the displays, such as the animated 5-m (16-ft) figure of "Amsterdam Man", are bizarre, but the wax models of 17th-century people give an insight into life in the city's Golden Age. Current celebrities and pop stars also feature among the exhibits.

❹ Nationaal Monument

Dam. **Map** 2 D5. 🚊 4, 9, 14, 16.

Sculpted by John Raedecker and designed by architect JJP Oud, the imposing 22-m (70-ft) obelisk in the Dam commemorates Dutch World War II casualties. It was unveiled in 1956 and is fronted by two lions, heraldic symbols of the Netherlands. Embedded in the wall behind are urns containing earth from all the Dutch provinces as well as from the former Dutch colonies of Indonesia, the Antilles and Suriname.

❺ Nes

Map 2 D5. 🚊 4, 9, 14, 16.

This quiet, narrow street is home to several theatres and good restaurants. In 1614, Amsterdam's first pawnshop opened at Nes No. 57. A wall plaque marks the site, and pawned goods continue to clutter the shop window. At night, Nes can prove to be dangerous for the unguarded visitor.

❻ Amsterdam Museum

See pp96–7.

⑦ Begijnhof

Spui (but public entrance at Gedempte Begijnensloot). **Map** 1 C5. 🚊 1, 2, 5, 9, 14, 16. **Open** 9am–5pm daily.

The Begijnhof was originally built in 1346 as a sanctuary for the Begijntjes, a lay Catholic sisterhood who lived like nuns, although they took no monastic vows. In return for lodgings, these women undertook to educate the poor and look after the sick. Nothing survives of the earliest dwellings, but the Begijnhof, cut off from traffic

noise, retains a sanctified atmosphere. Among the houses that overlook its well-kept green is the city's oldest surviving house at No. 34. On the adjoining wall there is a fascinating collection of wall plaques taken from the houses. In keeping with the Begijntjes' religious outlook, the plaques have a biblical theme.

The southern fringe of the square is dominated by the Engelse Kerk (English Church), dating from the 15th

Plaque on the Engelse Kerk

century. Directly west stands the Begijnhof Chapel, a clandestine church in which the Begijntjes and other Catholics worshipped in secret until religious tolerance was restored in 1795. Stained-glass windows and paintings depict scenes of the Miracle of Amsterdam. Public tours are not allowed. Also, visitors are requested to be quiet and not visit the Begijnhof in large groups.

Begijnhof Houses
These are still occupied by single women.

Biblical plaques cover the wall behind No. 34.

The Begijnhof Chapel, a clandestine church (Nos. 29–30), was completed in 1680. It contains many reminders of Amsterdam's Catholic past.

No. 19 has a plaque depicting the exodus of the Jews from Egypt.

Spui entrance

Main entrance from Gedempte Begijnensloot

Houten House
No. 34 is Amsterdam's oldest house, dating from around 1420. It is one of the city's two wooden-fronted houses; timber houses were banned in 1521 after a series of catastrophic fires. Most of the Begijnhof houses were built after the 16th century.

Engelse Kerk
This church was built around 1419 for the Begijntjes. It was confiscated after the Alteration and rented to a group of English and Scottish Presbyterians in 1607. The Pilgrim Fathers may have worshipped here.

❷ Koninklijk Paleis

Formerly the town hall, the Koninklijk Paleis (Royal Palace) is still regularly used by the Dutch royal family on official occasions. Construction of the sandstone building began in 1648, at the end of the 80 Years War *(see p53)*. The Neo-Classical design of Jacob van Campen (1595–1657) reflected Amsterdam's new-found self-confidence after the victory against the Spanish. When not in use by members of the Royal House, the Paleis is open to the public.

★ Burgerzaal
The Burgerzaal (citizens' hall) has an inlaid marble floor depicting the two hemispheres (western and eastern).

★ Sculptures
The palace is decorated with a large number of sculptures of mainly allegorical figures.

Chamber of the Commissioners of Petty Affairs

Courtyard

South gallery

Sculptures

Chamber of the Thesaurie Ordinaris

Mayor's office

Mayor's chamber

View of the Dam and the Vierschaar

Court of Justice

High Court of Justice (Vierschaar)

Entrance

Key to Floorplan

☐ Ground floor

☐ First floor

Alderman's hall

Courtyard

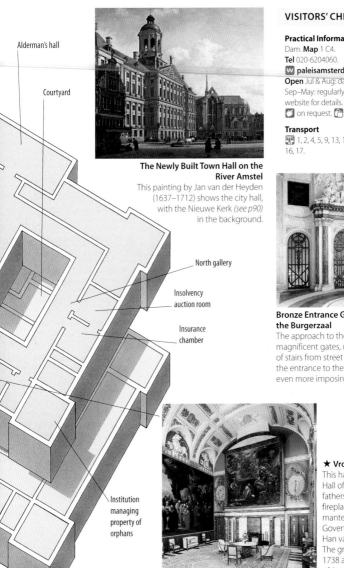

The Newly Built Town Hall on the River Amstel
This painting by Jan van der Heyden (1637–1712) shows the city hall, with the Nieuwe Kerk *(see p90)* in the background.

North gallery

Insolvency auction room

Insurance chamber

Institution managing property of orphans

VISITORS' CHECKLIST

Practical Information
Dam. **Map** 1 C4.
Tel 020-6204060.
Ⓦ paleisamsterdam.nl
Open Jul & Aug: daily;
Sep–May: regularly, check
website for details.
on request.

Transport
1, 2, 4, 5, 9, 13, 14,
16, 17.

Bronze Entrance Gates to the Burgerzaal
The approach to these magnificent gates, up a flight of stairs from street level, made the entrance to the Burgerzaal even more imposing.

★ **Vroedschapszaal**
This hall, the Council Hall of the city fathers, has two fine fireplaces with mantelpieces by Govert Flinck and Han van Bronckhorst. The grisailles from 1738 are the work of Jacob de Wit.

1648 Construction begins under Jacob van Campen

1720 Interior decoration completed

1810 Complete refurbishment of the palace, with galleries divided up into rooms with wood partitions; the rooms are furnished in Empire style

2013 Willem-Alexander becomes King of the Netherlands and gives a speech from the palace balcony with Princess Beatrix

1600	1700	1800	1900	2000

1655 Ceremonial inauguration of the building

1665 Building completed

1808 Louis Napoleon converts the town hall into a palace

1960 Thorough restoration work throughout the 20th century undoes the building work of Louis Napoleon

2002 Crown Prince Willem-Alexander kisses his bride, Maxima, on the palace balcony

❽ Allard Pierson Museum

Oude Turfmarkt 127. **Map** 5 A2.
Tel 020-5252556. 🚋 4, 9, 14, 16.
Open 10am–5pm Tue–Fri,
1–5pm Sat, Sun & public hols.
Closed 1 Jan, Easter Sun, 27 Apr,
Whitsun, 25 Dec. 🅿 ♿ 📷
🇼 allardpiersonmuseum.nl

Amsterdam's only specialist
archaeological collection is
named after Allard Pierson
(1831–96), a humanist and
scholar. The collection was
moved into this handsome
Neo-Classical building in 1976.
The museum contains Cypriot,
Greek, Egyptian, Roman, Etruscan
and Coptic artifacts.

❾ Torensluis

Singel, between Torensteeg and
Oude Leliestraat. **Map** 1 C4.
🚋 1, 2, 5, 13, 14, 17.

The Torensluis is one of the
widest bridges in the city. Built
on the site of a 17th-century
sluice gate, it took its name
from a tower that stood here
until demolished in 1829.
Its outline is marked in the
pavement. A lock-up jail was
built in its foundations.

In summer, café tables on
the bridge offer pleasant views
down the Singel.

Allard Pierson Museum's Neo-Classical façade
of Bremer and Bentheimer stone

❿ Magna Plaza

Nieuwezijds Voorburgwal 182.
Map 1 C4. **Tel** 020-6269199. 🚋 1,
2, 5, 13, 14, 17. **Open** noon–7pm
Sun, 11am–7pm Mon, 10am–7pm
Tue–Sat. **Closed** 27 Apr, 25 Dec,
1 Jan. See Shopping: p148. ♿
🇼 magnaplaza.nl

A post office building has been
sited here since 1748. The
present building was completed
in 1899; CP Peters, the architect,
was ridiculed for the extra-
vagance of its Neo-Gothic
design. Redeveloped but well
preserved, in 1990 it opened
as the city's first shopping mall.

⓫ Ronde LuthERse Kerk

Kattengat 2. **Map** 2 D3. **Tel** 020-
6212223. 🚋 1, 2, 5, 13, 17.

This church, also known as
Nieuwe Lutherse Kerk, was
designed by Adriaan Dortsman
(1625–82) and opened in 1671.

It is the first Dutch Reformed
church to feature a circular ground
plan and two upper galleries,
giving the whole congregation
a clear view of the pulpit.

In 1882 a fire destroyed
everything but the exterior walls.
When the interior and entrance
were rebuilt in 1883, they were
made more square and more
ornate. A vaulted copper dome
replaced the earlier ribbed version. Falling attendance led to
the closure of the church in 1935.
The building is now used by
Renaissance Amsterdam Hotel
as a business centre. Concerts
are sometimes held here.

⓬ Centraal Station

Stationsplein. **Map** 2 E3. **Tel** 0900-
9292. 🚋 1, 2, 4, 5, 9, 13, 16, 17.
Ⓜ Centraal Station. **Open** daily. ♿

When the Centraal Station
opened in 1889, it replaced the
old harbour as the symbolic focal
point of the city and curtained
Amsterdam off from the sea. The
Neo-Gothic red-brick railway
terminus was designed by PJH
Cuypers and AL van Gendt. Three
artificial islands were created,
8,600 wooden piles supporting
the structure. The twin towers
and central section have architectural echoes of a triumphal
arch. The façade's decorations

An outdoor café on the Torensluis bridge overlooking the Singel canal

For hotels and restaurants in this area see pp396–7 and pp406–9

show allegories of maritime trade, a tribute to the city's past. Although currently undergoing renovation to accommodate the new Noord-Zuidlijn metro route, the station still handles 250,000 train travellers daily.

Splendid Neo-Renaissance façade of the Sint-Nicolaaskerk

⓭ Sint-Nicolaaskerk

Prins Hendrikkade 73. **Map** 2 E4.
Tel 020-6248749. 🚊 1, 2, 4, 5, 9, 13, 16, 17. Ⓜ Centraal Station.
Open noon–3pm Mon & Sat, 11am–4pm Tue–Fri. ✝ 12:30pm Mon–Sat, 10:30am & 1pm (Spanish) Sun. 🌐 nicolaasparochie.nl

Sint Nicolaas was the patron saint of seafarers, and so was an important icon in Amsterdam. Many Dutch churches are named after him, and the Netherlands' principal day for the giving of presents, 5 December, is known as Sinterklaasavond *(see p39)*.

Completed in 1887, Sint-Nicolaaskerk was designed by AC Bleys (1842–1912). It replaced some clandestine Catholic churches set up in the city when Amsterdam was officially Protestant.

The exterior is forbidding, its twin towers dominating the skyline. The monumental interior has squared pillars and coffered ceiling arches.

Ons' Lieve Heer op Solder, which dates back to the 17th century

⓮ Museum Ons' Lieve Heer op Solder

Oudezijds Voorburgwal 40. **Map** 2 E4.
Tel 020-6246604. 🚊 4, 9, 16.
Open 10am–5pm Mon–Sat, 1–5pm Sun & public hols. **Closed** 1 Jan, 27 Apr. 🅿 📷 🏠

Tucked away on the edge of the Red Light District is a restored 17th-century canal house, with two smaller houses to the rear. The combined upper storeys conceal a secret Catholic church, known as Ons' Lieve Heer op Solder (Our Dear Lord in the Attic), built in 1663. Following the Alteration, when Amsterdam officially

became Protestant, many such hidden churches were built in the city.

The lower floors of the building became a museum in 1888 and today contain elegantly refurbished and decorated rooms, as well as an impressive collection of church silver, religious artifacts and paintings.

Work was completed in 2015 which links the church to the house opposite, now functioning as an entrance building and providing much-needed space for more exhibitions, a shop and a café.

⓯ Beurs van Berlage

Damrak 243. **Map** 2 D4. **Tel** (box office) 020-5304141. 🚊 4, 9, 16. **Open** only during exhibitions. **Closed** 1 Jan. 🅿 📷 ♿ 🏠 🌐 beursvanberlage.nl

The clean, functional appearance of Hendrik Berlage's 1903 stock exchange marked a departure from late 19th-century revivalist architecture. Many of its design features were adopted by the Amsterdam School. An impressive frieze shows the evolution of man from Adam to stockbroker. The building now serves as a venue for exhibitions, concerts and shows.

Decorative brickwork on the façade of the Beurs van Berlage

⊙ Amsterdam Museum

The convent of St Lucien was turned into a civic orphanage two years after the Alteration of 1578. The original red-brick convent has been enlarged over the years; new wings were added in the 17th century by Hendrick de Keyser and Jacob van Campen. The present building is largely as it was in the 18th century. Since 1975 the complex has housed the city's historical museum, charting Amsterdam's development.

Lecture room

★ The Anatomy Lesson of Dr Jan Deijman (1656)
In this painting, Rembrandt depicts the dissection of Black John, a criminal sentenced to death.

Second floor

Library

Orphans' Relief (1581)
The crooked relief above the gateway to Kalverstraat is a copy of Joost Bilhamer's original (on display in the main entrance hall). Its inscription asks people to contribute to the upkeep of the orphans.

Kalverstraat main entrance (to the Begijnhof)

Goliath (c.1650)
This massive statue is one of a trio of biblical figures dominating the museum's café.

Museum Guide

The permanent exhibits are housed around the inner courtyards. The main exhibition is Amsterdam DNA, which provides a fascinating overview into the city's history. Signposting allows the visitor to explore a specific period, such as the exciting 100 Years in Schipol exhibit, which details the history of the city's largest airport .

Key to Floorplan

- Civic Guard Gallery
- Regents' Room
- Origins of Amsterdam
- 14th- and 15th-century history
- 16th-century history
- 17th- and 18th-century history
- 19th-century history
- Modern age
- Temporary exhibition space
- Non-exhibition space

★ **The Flower Market and Town Hall**
Gerrit Berckheijde (1638–98) painted
this scene (1673) showing the site of
Amsterdam's original flower market on
the Nieuwezijds Voorburgwal, which was
filled in at the end of the 19th century. In
the background is the Koninklijk Paleis.

VISITORS' CHECKLIST

Practical Information
Kalverstraat 92, NZ Voorburgwal
357, St-Luciënsteeg 27
Map 1 C5.
Tel 020-5231822.
w ahm.nl
Open 10am–5pm daily.
Closed 1 Jan, 27 Apr, 25 Dec.

Transport
1, 2, 4, 5, 9, 13, 14,
16, 17.

Keys to the Town of Amsterdam (1810)
These two silver keys were presented to
Napoleon upon his entry into Amsterdam.

First floor

★ **Civic Guard
Gallery**
This painting
(1557) shows
17 soldiers of the
Civic Guard who
belonged to *Rot F*
(F squad).

Ground floor

17th-century red
brick façade

Entrance in girls'
courtyard

Entrance on
Nieuwzijds
Voorburgwal

St Luciënsteeg
entrance

Hunting Day (1926)
Johan Braakensiek's illustration shows
the lively carnival atmosphere
in Zeedijk during the celebrations
for this day, which took place every
Thursday throughout August.

CANAL RING

In the early 1600s, construction of the *Grachtengordel* (canal ring) began and the marshy area beyond these fashionable canals, later called the Jordaan, was laid out for workers whose industries were prohibited in the centre. Immigrants fleeing religious persecution also settled here. Historically a poor area, it now has a bohemian air. As the major canals were extended, the merchant classes bought land along the Herengracht, Keizersgracht and Prinsengracht to escape the city's squalor. In the 1660s, the richest built houses on a stretch known today as the Golden Bend. The canal ring was also extended east to the Amstel. Houses here, like the Van Loon, convey a sense of life in the Golden Age. In 2010, the canal ring was declared a UNESCO World Heritage Site.

Sights at a Glance

Historic Buildings and Monuments
4 Huis met de Hoofden
6 Haarlemmerpoort
10 American Hotel
15 Stadsarchief Amsterdam
18 Magere Brug
21 Munttoren

Museums
1 *Anne Frank Huis see pp112–13*
2 Homomonument
13 Bijbels Museum
17 Museum Willet-Holthuysen
19 Museum Van Loon

Churches
3 Westerkerk
5 Noorderkerk
12 De Krijtberg

Markets
5 Noordermarkt
14 Looier Kunst en Antiekcentrum

Theatres
11 Stadsschouwburg
20 Tuschinski Theater

Canals and Squares
7 Brouwersgracht
8 Western Islands
9 Leidseplein
16 Rembrandtplein

See also Street Finder maps 1, 2, 4 & 5

◀ Row of houses along the banks of one of the city's canals

For map symbols *see back flap*

A Guide to Canal House Architecture

Amsterdam has been called a city of "well-mannered" architecture because its charms lie in intimate details rather than in grand effects. From the 15th century on, planning laws, plot sizes and the instability of the topsoil dictated that façades were largely uniform in size and built of lightweight brick or sandstone, with large windows to reduce the weight. Canal house owners stamped their own individuality on the buildings, mainly through the use of decorative gables and cornices, ornate doorcases and varying window shapes.

Broken pediment and vase

"Broken handle" window surrounds

Pediment carvings symbolize the arts and sciences.

Bartolotti House (1617)
The contrasting brick and stone, flamboyant step gable, with its marble obelisk and scrolls, is typical of the Dutch Renaissance style of Hendrick de Keyser *(see p114)*.

Felix Meritis Building (1778)
The Corinthian columns and triangular pediment are influenced by Classical architecture. This marks the building by Jacob Otten Husly as Dutch Classical in style.

Ground Plans
Taxes were levied according to width of façade, so canal houses were often long and narrow, with an *achterhuis* (back annexe) used for offices and storage.

Cornices

Decorative top mouldings, called cornices, became popular from 1690 onwards when the fashion for gables declined. By the 19th century, they had become unadorned.

Louis XV-style with rococo balustrade (1739)

19th-century cornice with mansard roof

19th-century dentil (tooth-shaped) cornice

Gables

The term "gable" refers to the front apex of a roof. It disguised the steepness of the roof under which goods were stored. In time, gables became decorated with scrolls, crests, and even with coats of arms.

No. 34 Begijnhof (c.1420) is one of the few remaining timber houses.

Warehouse-style spout gable

Simple triangular gable

The style of gable on No. 213 Leliegracht (c.1620) was used for warehouses.

Dutch Renaissance style

Step gables like the one on No. 2 Brouwersgracht were in vogue between 1600–1665.

Golden Bend

The stretch of the Herengracht between Leidenstraat and Vijzelstraat was first called the Golden Bend in the 17th century, because of the great wealth of the ship-builders, merchants and politicians who originally lived here. The majority of the buildings along this stretch are faced with imported sandstone, which was more expensive than brick. An excellent example is house No. 412, which was designed by Philips Vingboons in 1664. He was also responsible for the design of the Witte Huis at Herengracht No. 168 as well as Bijbels Museum at Herengracht 366. Building continued into the 18th century, with the Louis XIV style predominating. The house at No. 475, with its ornate window decoration, is typical of this trend. Built in 1730, it is often called the jewel of canal houses. Two sculpted female figures over the front door adorn its monumental sandstone façade.

Ground plan and façade of the building at Herengracht 168

Leaning Façades
Canal houses were often built with a deliberate tilt, allowing goods to be winched up to the attic without crashing against the windows. A law dating from 1565 restricted this lean to 1:25, to limit the risk of buildings collapsing into the streets.

Dutch *Hofjes*
Almshouses (*hofjes*) were built throughout the Netherlands by rich benefactors in the 17th and 18th centuries. By providing accommodation for the elderly and infirm, the *hofjes* marked the beginning of the Dutch welfare system.

Sign of a sailors' hostel

Symbol of a dairy producer

Noah's Ark – a refuge for the poor

Wall Plaques

Carved and painted stones were used to identify houses before street numbering was introduced in the 19th century. Many reflect the owner's occupation.

Shell motif

Dolphin ornament

No. 419 Singel has a neck gable, a common feature from 1640 to around 1840.

No. 119 Oudezijds Voorburgwal has an ornate 17th-century neck gable.

Unadorned bell gable

No. 57 Leliegracht has a plain bell gable, popular from the late 17th century.

Stonework with cornucopia decoration

No. 298 Oudezijds Voorburgwal has a bell gable dating from the 18th century.

Dam Square to Herengracht 487

The walk along Amsterdam's finest canals begins in Dam square *(see p68)*. Following the grey dots on the map, leave the square past the Koninklijk Paleis *(see pp92–3)*, cross Nieuwezijds Voorburgwal and Spuistraat down Paleisstraat, and turn left along the left bank of Singel, marked by purple dots. Further directions are incorporated into the route below.

Locator Map

Singel

No. 239 Singel
AL Van Gendt designed this massive stone office block for trader Julius Carle Bunge. Known as the Bungehuis, it was completed in 1934.

The double-fronted 17th-century canal house at No. 265 Singel has been rebuilt several times since it was first constructed.

The step gable at No. 279 Sir dates from the 19th century – most along this canal were bu between 1600–1665.

The three neck gables on Nos. 353–7 Keizersgracht date from the early 18th century.

Huidenstraat

No. 345a Keizersgracht is a narrow house sharing a cornice with its neighbour.

The Sower at Arles (1888)
In March 1878, Vincent van Gogh *(see pp130–31)* visited his uncle, who ran a bookshop and art dealership at No. 453 Keizersgracht.

In 1708, No. 333 Keizersgracht was rebuilt for tax collector Jacob de Wilde. It has been converted into apartments.

The unusual office block at No. 313 Keizersgracht was built in 1914 by CN van Goor.

No. 319 Keizersgracht was built by the architect Philips Vingboons (1608–78) in 1639. It has a rare, highly decorated façade covered with scrolls, vases and garlands.

Peter the Great (1716) The Russian tsar sailed up Keizersgracht to No. 317, the home of his friend Christoffel Brants. Legend says the tsar got drunk and kept the mayor waiting while at a civic reception.

Leidsegracht This canal marked the end of Daniel Stalpaert's city expansion plan of 1664. It has a mixture of fine 17th- and 18th-century canal houses.

The Louis XIV-style house at No. 323 Keizersgracht was built in 1728. It has a raised cornice embellished with two hoisting beams, one functional and the other to provide symmetry.

No. 475 Herengracht Art patron Jan Gildemester bought this house in 1792. Attributed to Jacob Otten Husly, it has a stuccoed entrance hall.

Jan Corver Burgomaster of Amsterdam 19 times, Corver built No. 479 Herengracht in 1665.

Turn over to continue walk at top of page 106

Herengracht 489 to the Amstel

The second half of the walk takes you along Herengracht, winding past grand, wide-fronted mansions. It then follows Reguliersgracht and Prinsengracht down to the Amstel. Many of the fine houses have been converted into banks, offices and exclusive apartment blocks.

Locator Map

Herengracht

The house at No. 491 Herengracht was built in 1671. The façade, rebuilt in the 18th century, is decorated with scrolls, vases and coats of arms.

No. 493 Herengracht
This 17th-century house was given a Louis XV-style façade in 1767 by Anthony van Hemert.

The Kattenkabinet at No. 497 Herengracht was created by financie B Meijer in 1984. It is devoted to exhibits featuring the cat in art.

Directions to Reguliersgracht

At Thorbeckeplein, take the bridge to the right, which marks the beginning of Reguliersgracht. Follow the left bank.

Reguliersgracht

Amstelveld in the 17th Century
This etching shows the construction of a wooden church at Amstelveld, with sheep grazing in front of it.

Restaurant Nel
The Amstelkerk (Amstel Church) now houses a restaurant and offices, while the square is a popular playground for children from the surrounding area.

Directions to Prinsengracht

Turn left by the church, take the left bank of Prinsengracht and walk to the Amstel river.

Prinsengracht

Tsar Peter *(see p105)* stayed at No. 527 Herengracht, home of the Russian ambassador, after a night of drunken revelry at No. 317 Keizersgracht in 1716.

Herengracht (1790) A delicate watercolour by J Prins shows the "gentlemen's canal" from Koningsplein.

The asymmetrical building at Nos. 533–7 Herengracht was built in 1910 on the site of four former houses. From 1968 to 1988 it was the Registry of Births, Marriages and Deaths.

The façades of Nos. 37 and 39 Reguliersgracht lean towards the water, showing the danger caused by subsidence when building on marshland.

Keizersgracht

Reguliersgracht Bridge Seven arched stone bridges cross the canal, which was originally designed to be a street.

Nos. 1059 and 1061 Prinsengracht have tiny basement entrances, rare amid the splendour of the Canal Ring, where the height of the steps was considered an indication of wealth.

The sober spout-gabled building at No. 1075 Prinsengracht was built as a warehouse in 1690.

My Domestic Companions Society portraitist Thérèse van Duyl Schwartze painted this picture in 1916. She owned Nos. 1087, 1089 and 1091 Prinsengracht, a handsome row of houses where she lived with her extended family.

Nos. 289–293 Singel
These houses stand on an alley once called Schoorsteenvegersteeg (chimney sweeps' lane), home to immigrant chimney sweeps.

Yab Yum Brothel
This famous former brothel with its opulent interior was located at No. 295 Singel.

No. 365 Keizersgracht
The doorway was taken from an almshouse on Oudezijds Voorburgwal in the 19th century.

Jacob de Wit
The artist bought Nos. 383 and 385 Keizersgracht, living in No. 385 until his death in 1754.

34–6 Leidsestraat
...uses the country's first ...ercrombie and Fitch ...thing shop.

Gerrit Rietveld
Rietveld designed the glass cupola on Abercrombie and Fitch, and a line of plain, inexpensive furniture for the store.

De Vergulde Ster
(gilded star), at No. 387 Keizersgracht, was built in 1668 by the municipal stone-masons' yard. It has an elongated neck gable (see pp100–101) and narrow windows.

Directions to Herengracht
Turn left on to Leidsestraat, and walk to Koningsplein, then take the left bank of the Herengracht eastwards towards Thorbeckeplein.

Herengracht

Keizersgracht
This photograph of the "emperor's canal" is taken at dusk, from the corner of Leidsegracht. The Westerkerk (*see p114*) is in the distance.

Behind the 18th-century façade at No. 319 Singel is a second-hand bookshop, which is well worth browsing through.

Directions To Keizersgracht

At Raamsteeg, cross the bridge, take the Oude Spiegelstraat, cross Herengracht and walk along Wolvenstraat to the left bank of Keizersgracht.

Keizersgracht

No. 399 Keizersgracht
dates from 1665, but the façade was rebuilt in the 18th century. Its *achterhuis (see p100)* has been perfectly preserved.

No. 409 Keizersgracht
Built in 1671 on a triangular piece of land, this house contains a highly decorated wooden ceiling.

The wall plaque on No. 401 Keizersgracht shows a bird's-eye view of the port of Marseilles.

The plain, spout-gabled building *(see pp100–101)* at No. 403 Keizersgracht was originally a warehouse – a rarity in this predominantly residential area.

No. 469 Herengracht
The modern office block by KL Sijmons replaced the original 18th-century houses in 1971.

Jan Six II
The façade of No. 495 Herengracht was rebuilt and a balcony added by Jean Coulon in 1739 for burgomaster and art expert Jan Six.

Riots in 1696
No. 507 Herengracht was the home of mayor Jacob Boreel. His house was looted in retaliation for the burial tax he introduced into the city.

Vijzelstraat

Three houses boasting typical neck gables, at Nos. 17, 19 and 21 Reguliersgracht, are now much sought after as prestigious addresses.

The Nieuwe Amsterdammer
A weekly magazine aimed at Amsterdam's Bolshevik intelligentsia was published at No. 19 Reguliersgracht from 1914 to 1920.

The spout-gabled *(see pp100–101)* 16th-century warehouses at Nos. 11 and 13 Reguliersgracht are called the Sun and the Moon.

Café Marcella, at No. 1047a Prinsengracht, is a typical local bar which has seating outside in summer.

Houseboats on Prinsengracht
All registered houseboats have postal addresses and are connected to the electricity mains.

Utrechtsestraat

Herengracht (c.1670)
GA Berckheijde's etching shows one side of the canal bare of trees. Elms were later planted, binding the topsoil, to strengthen the buildings' foundations.

o. 543 Herengracht was built in 43 under the supervision of owner out Bollard. It has a double-onted façade with an ornate lustrade and decorated balcony.

The small houses at the corner of Herengracht and Thorbeckeplein contrast with the grand neighbouring buildings.

Isaac Gosschalk
The architect designed Nos. 57, 59 and 63 Reguliersgracht in 1879. They have ornate stone, brick and woodwork façades.

Reguliers Monastery
This engraving by J Wagenaar (1760) shows the monastery that once stood on the canal.

The Amstel
Turn left and follow the broad sweep of the Amstel river, up past the Magere Brug, on up Rokin and back to the Dam, where the walk began.

Street-by-Street: Around the Jordaan

West of the *Grachtengordel*, the Jordaan still retains a network of narrow, characterful streets and delightful canals. Among the 17th-century workers' houses are dozens of quirky shops, which are well worth a browse, selling anything from designer clothes to old sinks, and lively brown cafés and bars, which spill onto the pavements in summer. A stroll along the *Grachtengordel* provides a glimpse into some of the city's grandest canal houses, including the Bartolotti House.

Egelantiersgracht is a charming tree-lined Jordaan canal over-looked by an interesting mixture of old and new architecture. Its numerous bridges provide pretty views.

EGELANTIERSGRACHT

The quiet **Bloemgracht canal** was once a centre for makers of paint and dye.

BLOEMGRACHT

PRINSENGRACHT

❸ ★ **Westerkerk**
Hendrick de Keyser's church is the site of Rembrandt's unmarked grave and was the setting for the wedding of Queen Beatrix and Prince Claus in 1966.

❶ ★ **Anne Frank Huis**
For two years, the Frank family and four others lived in a small upstairs apartment that was hidden behind a moveable bookcase *(see pp112–13).*

❹ Huis met de Hoofden
The name "House with the Heads" refers to the six Classical busts at the entrance, depicting Apollo, Ceres, Mars, Minerva, Bacchus and Diana.

Locator Map
See Street Finder map 1

PRINSENGRACHT

KEIZERSGRACHT

The Eerste Hollandsche Levensverzekeringsbank building, with its fine façade, is a rare example of Dutch Art Nouveau, designed by Gerrit van Arkel in 1905.

KEIZERSGRACHT

LELIEGRACHT

Key

— Recommended route

| 0 metres | 75 |
| 0 yards | 75 |

❷ ★ Homomonument
The pink triangle used to "brand" homosexual men during World War II influenced the design of this memorial to oppressed gay men and women everywhere. It was unveiled in September 1987.

❶ Anne Frank Huis

On 6 July 1942, to avoid their Nazi persecutors, the Jewish Frank family moved from Merwedeplein to the rear annexe of the house at Prinsengracht 263. Anne; her mother, Edith; her father, Otto; and her older sister, Margot, lived here, along with the Van Pels family and dentist Fritz Pfeffer. It was here that Anne wrote her famous diary. On 4 August 1944, the annexe was raided by the Gestapo. All those hiding there were arrested and taken to Nazi concentration camps.

The Secret Entrance
Behind the hinged bookcase was a small suite of rooms where the eight hideaways lived.

Anne in May 1942
This photograph was taken in 1942, when Anne started writing in the now-famous diary that she had been given on 12 June 1942, her 13th birthday. Less than one month later, the Frank family went into hiding.

KEY

① Bathroom
② Anne's bedroom
③ Frank family bedroom
④ Van Pels family's room
⑤ Attic
⑥ The annexe
⑦ Façade of Prinsengracht 263
⑧ Main building housing offices

View of the Annexe
The rear annexe of the house adjoined the main building, which housed the offices of Otto Frank's herb and spice business. The museum website offers a virtual 3-D tour of the annexe.

Anne and Fritz Pfeffer's Bedroom
Anne and Fritz slept on the first floor of the annexe. On Anne's bedroom walls were photos of film stars, which she collected. Anne wrote most of her diary at the table here.

The Helpers
The people in hiding were wholly dependent on their helpers, all of whom were close colleagues of Anne's father, Otto Frank. From left to right: Miep Gies, Johannes Kleiman, Otto Frank, Victor Kugler and Bep Voskuijl.

Museum Guide

The rear annexe is accessible via the reconstructed offices of Otto Frank. The building beside Anne Frank Huis holds various exhibitions. It also houses a café, shop and information desk.

The Diary of Anne Frank

Otto Frank returned to Amsterdam in 1945 to discover that his entire family had perished: his wife, Edith, in Auschwitz and his daughters, Anne and Margot, in Bergen-Belsen. Miep Gies, one of the family's helpers while they were in hiding, had kept Anne's diary. First published in 1947, it has since been translated into 55 languages, with some 20 million copies sold. For many, Anne symbolizes the six million Jews murdered by the Nazis in World War II. The diary is a moving portrait of a little girl growing up in times of oppression.

School children visiting the Homomonument

❷ Homomonument

Westermarkt (between Westerkerk and Keizersgracht). **Map** 1 B4. 🚊 13, 14, 17. 🚊 Prinsengracht & Keizersgracht. **W** **homomonument.nl**

This monument to the homosexual men and women who lost their lives during World War II provides a quiet place of contemplation amid the bustle of the Westermarkt. The pink triangular badge that gay men were forced to wear in Nazi concentration camps later became a symbol of gay pride, and provided the inspiration for Karin Daan's 1987 design. The monument consists of three large pink granite triangles, one of which bears an engraving from a poem by Dutch writer Jacob Israël de Haan (1881–1924).

On Remembrance Day (4 May), hundreds of gay men and women from all over the Netherlands join delegates from the city council, police, the military and social organisations to lay wreaths and flowers.

❸ Westerkerk

Prinsengracht 281. **Map** 1 B4. **Tel** 020-6247766. 🚊 13, 14, 17. Church: **Open** 10am–3pm Mon–Fri, 11am–3pm Sat. Tower: 🎫 🔲 Apr–Sep: hourly 10am–6pm Mon–Sat (to 8pm Jul & Aug); Oct–Nov: hourly 11am–4pm Mon–Sat. Phone 020-6247766 to book. **Closed** Dec–Mar.

Built as part of the development of the Canal Ring, this church has the tallest tower in the city at 85 m (279 ft), and the largest nave of any Dutch Protestant church. It was designed by Hendrick de Keyser, who died in 1621, a year after work began. Rembrandt was buried here but his grave has never been found. The organ shutters (1686) were painted by Gerard de Lairesse, with lively scenes showing King David and the Queen of Sheba. The tower carries the crown bestowed on Amsterdam in 1489 by Maximilian, the Hapsburg emperor. The stunning views justify the climb.

❹ Huis met de Hoofden

Keizersgracht 123. **Map** 1 C4. 🚊 13, 14, 17. **Closed** to the public.

Built in 1622, the Huis met de Hoofden (house with the heads) is one of the largest double houses of the period. It has a fine step gable and takes its name from the six heads placed on pilasters along the façade. Legend has it that they commemorate a housemaid who, when alone in the house, surprised six burglars and cut off their heads. The sculptures are in fact portrayals of six Classical deities (from left to right): Apollo, Ceres, Mars, Minerva, Bacchus and Diana. The design of the building is sometimes attributed

The Westerkerk in the 18th century, a view by Jan Ekels

For hotels and restaurants in this area see pp396–7 and pp406–9

to Pieter de Keyser (1595–1676), son of Hendrick de Keyser. Huis met de Hoofden, which has housed a business school, a conservatoire and the Bureau Monumenten en Archeologie, has been bought by JR Ritman, owner of the Bibliotheca Philosophica Hermetica.

❺ Noorderkerk and Noordermarkt

Noordermarkt 44–48. **Map** 1 C3. **Tel** 020-6266436. 🚊 3, 10, 13, 14, 17. Church: **Open** 10:30am–12:30pm Mon, 11am–1pm Sat. ✝ 10am & 7pm Sun. General market: **Open** 9am–1pm Mon; Boerenmarkt: **Open** 9am–5pm Sat.

Built for poor settlers in the Jordaan, the North Church was the first in Amsterdam to be constructed in the shape of a Greek cross. Its layout around a central pulpit allowed the congregation seated in the encircling pews to see and hear well.

The church, designed by Hendrick de Keyser, was completed in 1623, in time to hold its inaugural service at Easter. It is still well attended by a Calvinist congregation. By the entrance is a sculpture of three bound figures, inscribed: "Unity is Strength". It commemorates the Jordaan Riot of 1934. On the south façade, a plaque recalls the 1941 February Strike, protesting the Nazis' deportation of Jews.

Since 1627, the square that surrounds the Noorderkerk has been a market site. At that time, it sold pots and pans and *vodden* (old clothes), a tradition that continues today with a flea market. Since the 18th century, the area has been a centre for bed shops. Bedding, curtains and fabrics are still sold on Monday morning along the Westerstraat; you can buy anything from net curtain material to buttons, as well as vinyl records, vintage clothing and other second-hand items. At 9am on Saturdays, the hugely popular *boerenmarkt* takes over, selling health foods, ethnic crafts and candles.

Stone plaque on the *hofje* founded in 1616 by the merchant Anslo

❻ Haarlemmerpoort

Haarlemmerplein 50. **Map** 1 B1. 🚊 3. **Closed** to the public.

Originally a defended gateway into Amsterdam, the Haarlemmerpoort marked the beginning of the busy route to Haarlem. The present gateway, dating from 1840, was built for King William II's triumphal entry into the city and named Willemspoort. However, as the third gateway to be built on or close to this site, it is still called the Haarlemmerpoort by Amsterdammers.

Designed by Cornelis Alewijn (1788–1839), the Neo-Classical gatehouse was used as tax offices in the 19th century and was made into flats in 1986. Traffic no longer goes through the gate, since a bridge has been built over the adjoining Westerkanaal.

In 2016, it was decided to turn the ground floor of the building into a restaurant and café, despite huge protests by the locals.

The "house with the writing hand" (c.1630) in Claes Claeszhofje

❼ Brouwersgracht

Map 1 B2. 🚊 3.

Brouwersgracht (brewers' canal) was named after the breweries established here in the 17th and 18th centuries. Leather, spices, coffee and sugar were also processed and stored here. Today, most of the warehouses, with their spout gables and shutters, are residences that look out on moored houseboats.

❽ Western Islands

Map 1 C1. 🚊 3.

This district comprises three islands built on the IJ in the early 1600s to quarter warehouses and shipyards. Some of these are still in use and many period houses have survived.

Merchant and developer Jan Bicker bought Bickerseiland in 1631. Today, the island is a mix of colourful apartment blocks and a jumble of houseboats.

Realeneiland has the pretty waterside street of Zandhoek. A row of pretty 17th-century houses built by the island's founder, Jacobsz Reaal, overlooks the moored sailboats.

Prinseneiland is dominated by characterful warehouses, many now apartments.

Dutch Hofjes

Before the Alteration, the Catholic Church often provided subsidized housing for the poor and elderly, particularly women. During the 17th and 18th centuries, rich merchants and Protestant organizations took on this charitable role and built hundreds of almshouse complexes, which were planned around courtyards and known as *hofjes*. Behind their street façades lie pretty houses and serene gardens. Visitors are admitted to some but asked to respect the residents' privacy. Many *hofjes* are found in the Jordaan and some still serve their original purpose.

Star-lit façade of De Melkweg
near Leidseplein

❾ Leidseplein

Map 4 E2. 🚋 1, 2, 5, 7, 10.

Amsterdam's liveliest square, Leidseplein is also a busy tram intersection and centre of night-time transport.

The square developed in the 17th century as a wagon park on the outskirts of the city – farmers and peasants would leave their carts here before entering the centre. It takes its name from the Leidsepoort, the massive city gate demolished in 1862, which marked the beginning of the route out to Leiden.

During the day, the square is buzzing with fire-eaters, buskers and other street performers playing to café audiences. It is also popular with pickpockets. At night, it is the focal point for the city's youth, who hang out in the many bars, cafés, restaurants, nightclubs and cinemas in and around the square.

❿ American Hotel

Leidsekade 97. **Map** 4 E2. **Tel** 020-5563000. 🚋 1, 2, 5, 7, 10. ✐ 🖥

Leidseplein was fast becoming a fashionable entertainment area when the American Hotel was built overlooking it in 1882. The hotel got its name because its architect, W Steinigeweg, studied hotel design in the United States, and adorned his Neo-Gothic creation with a bronze eagle, wooden figures of native Indians and murals of American landscapes. Within 20 years it was deemed *passé* and the hotel was demolished.

The present building is by Willem Kromhout (1864–1940) and was completed in 1902. His design marked a radical departure, interpreting the Art Nouveau style in an angular Dutch fashion. The building's turreted exterior and elaborate brickwork anticipated the progressive Amsterdam School (*see pp146–7*).

The Art Deco-style Café Americain is one of the most elegant in Amsterdam. It retains its period furnishings and stained-glass windows. The rest of the hotel was redecorated in the 1980s. Samples of the original furnishings are in the Rijksmuseum (*see pp126–9*).

⓫ Stadsschouwburg

Leidseplein 26. **Map** 4 E2. **Tel** 020-6242311. 🚋 1, 2, 5, 6, 7, 10. Box office: **Open** 10am–6pm Mon–Sat. *See Entertainment p151.* 🎭 ✉ ♿
w stadsschouwburgamsterdam.nl

This Neo-Renaissance building is the most recent of the city's three successive municipal theatres, its predecessors having burned down. The theatre was designed by Jan Springer and AL van Gendt, who was responsible for the Concertgebouw (*see p124*) and for part of the Centraal Station (*see p94*). The planned ornamentation of the theatre's red-brick exterior was never carried out because of budget cuts. This, combined with a hostile public reaction to his theatre, forced a disillusioned Springer into virtual retirement. Public disgust was due, however, to the management's policy of restricting use of the front door to patrons who had bought expensive tickets.

The former home of the Dutch national ballet and opera companies, the theatre today stages plays by local drama groups such as the resident Toneelgroep, as well as international companies, including many English-language productions. The foyer houses a popular restaurant.

The American Hotel seen from Singelgracht

⓬ De Krijtberg

Singel 448. **Map** 4 F1. **Tel** 020-6231923.
🚋 1, 2, 5. **Open** noon–1:15pm & 5–
6:15pm Mon & Fri, noon–6:15pm Tue–
Sat, 9am–6:30pm Sun. ✝ 12:30pm,
5:45pm Mon–Fri, 12:30pm, 5:15pm
Sat, 9:30am, 11am, 12:30pm, 5:15pm
Sun. ♿ 🖥 krijtberg.nl

An impressive Neo-Gothic
church, the Krijtberg (or chalk
hill) replaced a clandestine
Jesuit chapel in 1884. It is
officially known as Franciscus
Xaveriuskerk, after St Francis
Xavier, one of the founding
Jesuit monks.

Designed by Alfred Tepe,
the church was built on the site
of three houses; the presbytery
beside the church is on the site
of two other houses, one of
which had belonged to a chalk
merchant – hence the church's
nickname. The back of the
church is wider than the front,
extending into the space once
occupied by the original gardens.
The narrowness of the façade
is redeemed by its two magnificent, soaring, steepled towers.

The ornate interior of the
building contains some good
examples of Neo-Gothic design.
The stained-glass windows, walls
painted in bright colours and
liberal use of gold are in striking
contrast to the city's austere
Protestant churches. A statue of
St Francis Xavier stands in front
and to the left of the high altar;
one of St Ignatius, founder of the
Jesuits, stands to the right.

Near the pulpit is an 18th-
century wooden statue of

the Immaculate
Conception, which
shows Mary trampling
the serpent. It used
to be housed in the
original hidden chapel.

⓭ Bijbels Museum

Herengracht 366–368.
Map 4 E1. **Tel** 020-
6242436. 🚋 1, 2, 5.
🚆 Herengracht/Leidsegracht.
Open 10am–5pm Tue–Sun & public
hols. **Closed** 1 Jan, 27 Apr. 📷 ♿
🖥 bijbelsmuseum.nl

Reverend Leendert Schouten
founded the Bible Museum in
1860, when he put his private
artifact collection on public
display. In 1975, the museum
moved to its present site,
two 17th-century houses
designed by Philips Vingboons.
Highlights are a copy of the
Book of Isaiah from the Dead
Sea Scrolls and the Delft
Bible (1477).

⓮ Looier Kunst en Antiekcentrum

Elandsgracht 109. **Map** 4 D1.
Tel 020-6249038. 🚋 7, 10, 13, 14, 17.
Open 11am–6pm daily (to 5pm
Sat & Sun). **Closed** public hols. 📷 ♿
🖥 antiekcentrumamsterdam.nl

The Looier antiques centre is
a vast network of rooms in a
block of houses near the canal.
Its 100 stalls sell everything
from glassware to dolls.

Grand façade of the Stadsarchief

⓯ Stadsarchief Amsterdam

Vijzelstraat 32. **Map** 4 F2. **Tel** 020-
5720202. 🚋 16, 24. **Open** 10am–
5pm Tue–Fri, noon–5pm Sat &
Sun. **Closed** Mon & public hols.
♿ (with permission).
🖥 stadsarchief.amsterdam.nl

The Stadsarchief, the city's
municipal archives, moved
from its former location
in Amsteldijk to this
monumental building.
Designed by KPC de Bazel,
one of the principal representatives of the Amsterdam
School of Architecture, the
edifice was completed in 1926
for the Netherlands Trading
Company. In spite of much
renovation work at the end of
World War II and in the 1970s,
the building retains many
attractive original features,
such as colourful floor
mosaics (designed by de
Bazel himself). There is a
permanent display of treasures
from the archives in the
monumental vaults.

On the Canals

Though Amsterdam's canals were built for moving
goods, today they provide a marvellous means of
viewing the city's sights and its everyday life. There
are many operators in the city offering canal tours
with foreign-language commentaries; boats depart
from an embarkation point, mainly from opposite
Centraal Station, along Prins Hendrikkade, the
Damrak and along the Rokin. Another canal-
sightseeing option is the popular canalbus which
runs along three routes, with 14 stops near the
major museums, shopping areas and other
attractions. If you feel energetic, try a canal bike,
which is really a two- or four-seater pedal-boat that
can be picked up and left at any of the canal-bike
moorings in the city centre.

⑯ Rembrandtplein

Map 5 A2. 🚋 4, 9, 14.

Formerly called the Botermarkt, after the butter market held here until the mid-19th century, this square acquired its present name when the statue of Rembrandt was erected in 1876.

Soon afterwards, Rembrandtplein developed into a centre for nightlife with the opening of various hotels and cafés. The Mast (renamed the Mille Colonnes Hotel) dates from 1889, and the Schiller Karena hotel and the Café Schiller both opened in 1892. De Kroon, which epitomizes a typical grand café, dates from 1898. The popularity of Rembrandtplein has endured, and the café terraces are packed during summer with people enjoying a pleasant drink and watching the world go by.

⑰ Museum Willet-Holthuysen

Herengracht 605. **Map** 5 A2. **Tel** 020-5231822. 🚋 4, 9, 14. **Open** 10am–5pm Mon–Fri, 11am–5pm Sat & Sun. **Closed** 1 Jan, 27 Apr, 25 Dec. 📷 ♿ 📷 🆆 willetholthuysen.nl

Named after the building's last residents, the museum now housed here allows visitors a glimpse into the lives of the merchant class who lived in luxury along the Grachtengordel (Canal Ring). The house was built in 1685 and became the property of coal magnate Pieter Holthuysen (1788–1858) in 1855. It passed to his daughter

Two of the many outdoor cafés on Rembrandtplein

Louisa and her art-connoisseur husband, Abraham Willet – both fervent collectors of paintings, glass, silver and ceramics. When Louisa died childless in 1895, the house and its many treasures were left to the city. Room by room, the house is gradually being restored to appear as it did during the time when Abraham and Louisa lived here.

The Blue Room, hung with heavy blue damask and boasting a chimney piece by Jacob de Wit, was the exclusive preserve of the men of the house.

The wallpaper in the dining room today is a careful copy of the 18th-century silk original. The elaborate 275-piece Meissen dinner service provided up to 24 places.

The 18th-century kitchen has been restored using items salvaged from similar houses, including the sink and pump.

On the second floor is a full-length portrait of Willet.

Interior of Willet-Holthuysen museum, on the Herengracht canal

⑱ Magere Brug

Amstel. **Map** 5 B3. 🚋 4.

Of Amsterdam's 1,400 or so bridges, Magere Brug (skinny bridge) is the best-known. The original drawbridge was built in about 1670. According to legend, it was named after two sisters called Mager, who lived either side of the Amstel. It is more likely that the name comes from its narrow *(mager)* design.

Magere Brug, a traditional double-leaf Dutch drawbridge

The present drawbridge was put up in 1969 and, though wider than the original, it still conforms to the traditional double-leaf style. Constructed from African azobe wood, it was intended to last 50 years. The bridge is opened a few times every day. It has been featured in many films, most notable being the James Bond film – *Diamonds are Forever*.

⓳ Museum Van Loon

Keizersgracht 672. **Map** 5 A3. **Tel** 020-6245255. 🚋 16. **Open** 11am–5pm Wed–Mon. **Closed** public hols. 🖼 🗂
W museumvanloon.nl

The Van Loons were one of Amsterdam's most prestigious families in the 17th century. They did not move into this house on the Keizersgracht, however, until 1884. Designed by Adriaan Dortsman, No. 672 is one of a pair of symmetrical houses built in 1672 for Flemish merchant Jeremias van Raey. In 1752, Dr Abraham van Hagen and his wife, Catharina Elisabeth Trip, moved in.

In 1973, after many years of restoration, it opened as a museum, retaining the house's original character. Its collection of Van Loon family portraits stretches back to the early 1600s. The period rooms have fine pieces of furniture, porcelain and sculpture. Outside, the 18th-century coach house has been restored and houses the Van Loon carriages and servants' livery.

⓴ Tuschinski Theater

Reguliersbreestraat 26–28. **Map** 5 A2. **Tel** 0900-1458. 🚋 4, 9, 14. Box office: **Open** 11:30am–10pm. 🖼 🗂 🗂

Abraham Tuschinski's cinema and variety theatre caused a sensation when it opened in 1921. Until then, Amsterdam's cinemas had been sombre places; this was an exotic blend of Art Deco and Amsterdam School architecture (*see pp146–7*). Built in a slum area known as Devil's Corner, it was designed by Heyman Louis de Jong and decorated by Chris Bartels, Jaap Gidding and Pieter de Besten. In its heyday, Marlene Dietrich and Judy Garland performed here.

Now a six-screen cinema, the building has been meticulously restored, inside and out. The best way to appreciate its opulence is to see a film. For a few extra euros, you can take a seat in one of the exotic boxes that make up the back row of the huge semicircular auditorium.

The medieval Munttoren at the base of Muntplein

㉑ Munttoren

Muntplein. **Map** 4 F1. 🚋 4, 9, 14, 16. Munttoren: **Closed** to public. Gift shop: **Open** 10am–6pm Mon–Sat.

The polygonal base of the Munttoren (mint tower) formed part of the gate in Amsterdam's medieval wall. Fire destroyed the gate in 1618, but the base survived. In 1619, Hendrick de Keyser added the clock tower; François Hemony, the set of bells in 1699. During the 1673 French occupation, the city mint was housed here.

How the Magere Brug Works

The arched wooden portal provides a pivot for the balance.

Mechanical chain-drive

The balance is made up of two counter-weighted beams.

Steel cables

Each deck has a span of about 5 m (16 ft).

MUSEUM QUARTER

Until the late 1800s, the Museum Quarter was little more than an area of farms and small-holdings. At this time, the city council designated it an area of art and culture and plans were conceived for constructing Amsterdam's great cultural monuments: the Rijksmuseum, the Stedelijk Museum and the Concertgebouw. The Van Gogh Museum followed in 1973, its striking extension being added in 1999. The

Museumplein has two memorials to the victims of World War II. The *plein* is still used today as a site for political demonstrations. To the north and south are late 19th- and early 20th-century houses, where the streets are named after artists and intellectuals, such as the 17th-century Dutch poet Roemer Visscher. To the west, the Vondelpark offers a pleasant, fresh-air break from all the museums.

Sights at a Glance

Museums and Workshops
❶ *Rijksmuseum pp126–9*
❷ Coster Diamonds
❸ *Van Gogh Museum pp130–31*
❹ *Stedelijk Museum pp132–3*
❾ Vondelparkpaviljoen

Concert Halls
❺ Concertgebouw

Historic Buildings
❼ Hollandsche Manege
❽ Vondelkerk

Parks
❻ Vondelpark

See also Street Finder
map 3 & 4

0 metres 250
0 yards 250

VONDELPARK

◀ Rembrandt's famous painting, *The Night Watch*, at the Rijksmuseum

For map symbols *see back flap*

Street-by-Street: Museum Quarter

The green expanse of Museumplein was once bisected by a busy main road known locally as the "shortest motorway in Europe". But dramatic renovation between 1996 and 1999 has transformed it into a stately park, fringed by Amsterdam's major cultural centres. The district is one of the wealthiest in the city, with wide streets lined with grand houses. After the heady delights of the museums, it is possible to window-shop at the many upmarket boutiques along the exclusive PC Hooftstraat and Van Baerlestraat, or watch the diamond polishers at work in Coster Diamonds.

❸ ★ Van Gogh Museum
The new wing of the museum, an elegant oval shape, was designed by Kisho Kurokawa and opened in 1999. It is dedicated to temporary exhibitions of 19th-century art.

Van Baerlestraat
contains exclusive clothing shops *(see p148)*.

❹ ★ Stedelijk Museum
Housing the civic collection of modern art, this museum also stages controversial contemporary art exhibitions. A sculpture garden is behind the building.

❺ Concertgebouw
Designed by AL van Gendt, the building has a Classical façade and a concert hall with near-perfect acoustics.

❷ Coster Diamonds
Diamonds have been cut, polished and sold at Coster since 1840. The firm now occupies three splendid adjoining villas, built on Museumplein in 1896.

Locator Map
See Street Finder map 4

CANAL RING

MUSEUM QUARTER

Lines of light along the ground

HOBBEMASTRAAT

Pond/ ice rink

❶ ★ Rijksmuseum
The heavily ornamented Neo-Gothic Rijksmuseum holds the magnificent Dutch national art collection of some 5,000 paintings, 30,000 pieces of applied art and 17,000 historical artifacts.

MUSEUMPLEIN

JOHANNES VERMEERSTRAAT

The Ravensbrück monument commemorates women victims of the Holocaust.

The Rijksmuseum is surrounded by gardens that contain statuary. This weathered bronze of Mercury, designed by Ferdinand Leenhoff (1841–1914), is found in the southeast garden.

Key

— Recommended route

0 metres	50
0 yards	50

❶ Rijksmuseum

See pp126–9.

❷ Coster Diamonds

Paulus Potterstraat 2–8. **Map** 4 E3.
Tel 020-3055555. 🚋 2, 5. **Open**
9am–5pm daily. **Closed** 1 Jan, 25 Dec.
🗖 💻 🌐 costerdiamonds.com

One of Amsterdam's oldest diamond factories, Coster was founded in 1840. Twelve years later, Queen Victoria's consort, Prince Albert, honoured the company by giving them the task of repolishing the enormous *Koh-i-Noor* (mountain of light) diamond. This blue-white stone is one of the treasures of the British crown jewels and weighs in at 108.8 carats. A replica of the coronation crown, which incorporates a copy of the fabulous stone, is found in Coster's spacious entrance hall.

More than 1,000 people visit the factory each day to witness the processes of grading, cutting and polishing the stones. The goldsmiths and diamond-cutters work together in the factory to produce customized items of jewellery, in a range of styles, which are available over the counter. In the Diamond Museum, the history of the diamond is traced, from its creation deep in the earth to the dazzling stones that are a girl's best friend.

Glistening diamonds at Coster Diamonds

❸ Van Gogh Museum

See pp130–31.

❹ Stedelijk Museum

See pp132–3.

Façade of the award-winning Concertgebouw (1881) by AL van Gendt

❺ Concertgebouw

Concertgebouwplein 2–6. **Map** 4 D4.
Tel 0900-6718345. 🚋 2, 3, 5, 12, 16.
Box office: **Open** 1–7pm Mon–Fri,
10am–7pm Sat & Sun. 🅿 🚻 ♿ by
arrangement. 🗖 5pm Mon, 12:15pm
Sun. 🌐 concertgebouw.nl

Following an open architectural competition held in 1881, AL van Gendt (1835–1901) was chosen to design a vast new concert hall for Amsterdam. The resulting Neo-Renaissance building boasts an elaborate pediment and colonnaded façade, and houses two concert halls. Despite van Gendt's lack of musical knowledge, he managed to produce near-perfect acoustics in the Grote Zaal (main concert hall), which is renowned the world over.

The inaugural concert at the Concertgebouw was held on 11 April 1888, complete with an orchestra of 120 musicians and a choir of 600. A resident orchestra was established at the hall seven months later.

The building has been renovated several times over the years, most recently in 1983, when some serious subsidence threatened the building's entire foundation. To remedy this, the whole superstructure had to be lifted up off the ground while the original supporting piles, which rested on sand 13 m (43 ft) underground, were removed and replaced by concrete piles sunk into the ground to a depth of 18 m (59 ft). A glass extension and new entrance were added by Pi de Bruijn in 1988. The original entrance was relocated round to the side of

the building. Though primarily designed to hold concerts, the Concertgebouw also hosts business meetings, exhibitions, conferences, political meetings and occasional boxing matches.

Bandstand in Vondelpark, popular among locals

❻ Vondelpark

Stadhouderskade. **Map** 4 E2.
🚋 1, 2, 3, 5,12. Park: **Open** 24hrs daily.
Open-air theatre: **Open** Jun–last week
Aug: Wed–Sun.

In 1864, a group consisting of prominent Amsterdammers formed a committee with the aim of founding a public park, and they raised enough money to buy 8 ha (20 acres) of land. JD and LP Zocher, a father-and-son team of landscape architects, were then commissioned to design the park in typical English landscape style. They used vistas, pathways and ponds to create the illusion of a large natural area, which was opened to the public on 15 June 1865, as the Nieuwe Park. The park's present name was adopted in 1867, when a statue of Dutch poet Joost van den

Vondel (1587–1679) was erected on the grounds. The committee soon began to raise money to enlarge the park, and by June 1877 it had reached its current dimensions of 47 ha (116 acres). The park now supports around 100 plant species and 127 types of tree. Squirrels, hedgehogs, ducks and garden birds mix with a huge colony of greedy, bright green parakeets, which gather in front of the pavilion every morning to be fed. Herds of cows, sheep, goats and even a lone llama graze in the pastures.

Vondelpark welcomes about 8 million visitors a year, and is popular with the locals for dog-walking, jogging, or just for the view. Free concerts are given at the *openluchttheater* (open-air theatre) or at the bandstand during summer.

Façade of the Hollandse Manege, the Dutch riding school

❼ Hollandsche Manege

Vondelstraat 140. **Map** 3 C2. **Tel** 020-6180942. 🚋 1. **Open** 9am–11pm Mon–Fri, 9:30am–6pm Sat & Sun. 🖥

The Dutch riding school was originally situated on the Leidsegracht, but in 1882 a new building was opened, designed by AL van Gendt and based on the Spanish Riding School in Vienna. The riding school was threatened with demolition in the 1980s, but was saved after a public outcry. Reopened in 1986 by Prince Bernhard, it has been restored to its former glory. The Neo-Classical indoor arena boasts gilded mirrors and moulded horses' heads on its elaborate plasterwork walls. Some of the wrought-iron stalls remain and sound is muffled by sawdust. At the top of the staircase, one door leads to a balcony overlooking the arena, another to the café.

❽ Vondelkerk

Vondelstraat 120. **Map** 3 C2. 🚋 1, 3, 12. **Closed** to the public.

The Vondelkerk was the largest church designed by PJH Cuypers, architect of the Centraal Station. Work began in 1872, but funds ran out by the following year. Money gathered from public donations and lotteries allowed the building to be completed by 1880. When fire broke out in November 1904, firefighters saved the nave by forcing the burning tower to fall away into Vondelpark. A new tower was added later by the architect's son, JT Cuypers. The church was deconsecrated in 1979 and converted into offices in 1985.

❾ Vondelpark-paviljoen

Vondelpark 3. **Map** 4 D2. **Closed** to the public, renovations underway.

Vondelpark's pavilion was designed by the architects PJ Hamer (1812–87) and his son W Hamer (1843–1913), and opened on 4 May 1881 as a café and restaurant. After World War II, it reopened as a cultural centre. In 1991, the pavilion was renovated once more. The complete Art Deco interior of the Cinema Parisien, Amsterdam's first cinema, built in 1910, was moved into one of the rooms. At one point, it housed an important national film museum, EYE, which screened more than 1,000 films a year. The museum, however, which also features a lovely film poster collection, has been shifted to a new building on Badhuisweg. The Vondelpark-paviljoen underwent extensive renovations in recent years and now functions as a TV and radio media centre, complete with a café and restaurant. The surrounding garden has been beautifully re-landscaped.

Built in 1880, the striking Vondelkerk now houses a number of offices

❶ Rijksmuseum

The Rijksmuseum, an Amsterdam landmark, possesses an unrivalled collection of Dutch art, begun in the early 19th century. The huge museum opened in 1885 to bitter criticism from Amsterdam's Protestant community for its Neo-Gothic style. Also worth a visit are the surrounding gardens, which were redesigned to match the museum's renovation, completed in 2013.

Second floor

Winter Landscape with Skaters (1618)
Painter Hendrick Avercamp specialized in intricate icy winter scenes.

★ The Kitchen Maid (1658)
The light falling through the window and the stillness of this scene are typical of Jan Vermeer.

First floor

The Gothic façade
of PJH Cuypers' building is red brick with elaborate decoration, including coloured tiles.

Gallery Guide

The basement of the museum houses its Special Collections and Asian Pavilion. The ground floor features works from the 18th and 19th centuries, the first floor has works from the Golden Age, while the second floor features works from the 20th century.

Key to Floorplan

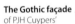

- ▢ Special collections
- ▢ Medieval and Renaissance art
- ▢ Golden Age
- ▢ 18th-century art
- ▢ 19th-century art
- ▢ 20th-century art
- ▢ Asian Pavilion
- ▢ Non-exhibition space

★ St Elizabeth's Day Flood (1500)
An unknown artist painted this altarpiece, showing a disastrous flood in 1421. The dykes protecting Dordrecht were breached, and 22 villages were swept away by the flood water.

VISITORS' CHECKLIST

Practical Information
Museumstraat 1. **Map** 4 E3.
Tel 020-6747000.
🆆 rijksmuseum.nl
Open 9am–5pm daily. 🖼 🖼
♿ 🅿 🎧 📷

Transport
🚊 2, 3, 5, 7, 10, 16.
🚌 Stadhouderskade.

★ **The Night Watch** (1642)
The showpiece of Dutch 17th-century art, this vast canvas was commissioned as a group portrait of an Amsterdam militia company.

Gallery of
Honour

St Catherine (c.1465)
This sculpture by the Master of Koudewater shows the saint stamping on Emperor Maxentius, who allegedly killed her with his sword.

Ground
floor

Cuypers
Library

Entrance

Basement

Auditorium

Jan Steen's *Woman at her Toilet* was painted in about 1660

Genre Painting

For the contemporaries of Jan Steen (1625–79), this cosy everyday scene was full of symbols that are obscure to the modern viewer. The dog on the pillow may represent fidelity, and the red stockings the woman's sexuality; she is probably a prostitute. Such genre paintings were often raunchy, but nearly always had a moral twist – domestic scenes by artists such as ter Borch and Honthorst were symbolic of brothels, while other works illustrated proverbs. Symbols like candles or skulls indicated mortality.

Exploring the Rijksmuseum

The Rijksmuseum is almost too vast to be seen in a single visit. It is famous for owning probably the best collection of Dutch art in the world, from early religious works to the masterpieces of the Golden Age. However, the applied art and sculpture sections, and the Asiatic artifacts, are equally wonderful. In total, 8,000 pieces of art are on display in 80 wings. The selected pieces demonstrate the enormous prosperity of Holland's Golden Age in the 17th century. Rembrandt's *The Night Watch* is one of the masterpieces on display.

Feeding the Hungry from a series of panels by the Master of Alkmaar

Dutch History

The turbulent history of the Netherlands is encapsulated in this section. In the opening room is the medieval altar painting of *St Elizabeth's Day Flood (see p126)*. The central room has 17th-century ship models, artifacts salvaged from shipwrecks and paintings of factories and townscapes from the days of the Dutch Empire. Later displays recall battles in naval history; exhibits from the 18th century deal with the impact of revolutionary France on Amsterdam, ending in 1815 after the Napoleonic Wars.

Early Painting and Foreign Schools

Alongside a small collection of Flemish and Italian art, including portraits by Piero di Cosimo (1462–1521), are the first specifically "Dutch" paintings.

These works are mostly religious, such as *The Seven Works of Charity* (1504) by the Master of Alkmaar, Jan van Scorel's quasi-Mannerist *Mary Magdalene* (1528) and Lucas van Leyden's triptych, *Adoration of the Golden Calf* (1530). As the 16th century progressed, religious themes were superseded by pastoral subjects; by 1552, paintings like Pieter Aertsen's *The Egg Dance* were full of realism, by then the keystone of much Dutch art.

17th-century Painting

By the Alteration in 1578, Dutch art had moved away completely from religious to secular themes. Artists turned to realistic portraiture, landscapes, still lifes, seascapes, domestic interiors, including genre work *(see p127)*, and animal portraits. Rembrandt *(see p80)* is the most famous of many artists who

lived and worked around Amsterdam at this time. Examples of his work hanging in the Rijksmuseum include *Portrait of Titus in a Monk's Habit* (1660), *Self-Portrait as the Apostle Paul* (1661), *The Jewish Bride (see pp30–31)*, as well as *The Night Watch (see p127)*. Look out too for the work of his many pupils, who included, among others, Nicolaes Maes and Ferdinand Bol.

Don't miss Jan Vermeer's (1632–75) serenely light-filled interiors including *The Kitchen Maid (see p126)* and *The Woman Reading a Letter* (1662). Of several portraits by Frans Hals *(see pp190–91)*, the best known are *The Wedding Portrait* and *The Merry Drinker* (1630). *The Windmill at Wijk* by Jacob van Ruisdael (1628–82) is a great landscape by an artist at the very height of his power. Other artists whose works contribute to this unforgettable collection include Pieter Saenredam *(see p57)*, Jan van de Capelle, Jan Steen *(see p127)* and Gerard Terborch.

18th- and 19th-century Painting

In many ways, 18th-century Dutch painting merely continued the themes and quality of 17th-century work.

The Wedding Portrait (c.1622) by Frans Hals

This is particularly true of portraiture and still lifes, with the evocative *Still Life with Flowers and Fruit* by Jan van Huysum (1682–1749) standing out. A trend developed later for elegant "conversation pieces" by artists such as Adriaan van der Werff (1659–1722) and Cornelis Troost (1696–1750). Most had satirical undertones, like *The Art Gallery of Jan Gildemeester Jansz* (1794) by Adriaan de Lelie (1755–1820), showing an 18th-century salon whose walls are crowded with 17th-century masterpieces.

Still Life with Flowers and Fruit (c.1730) by artist Jan van Huysum (1682–1740), one of many still lifes exhibited in the Rijksmuseum

Hague School and the Impressionists

The so-called Hague School was made up of a group of Dutch artists who came together around 1870 in The Hague. Their landscape work, which earned them the alternative title the "Grey School" for their overcast skies, captures the atmospheric quality of subdued Dutch sunlight. One of the prizes of the Rijksmuseum's 19th-century collection is *Morning Ride on the Beach* (1876) by Anton Mauve (1838–88), painted in soft pearly colours. Alongside hangs the beautiful polder landscape *View near the Geestbrug* by Hendrik Weissenbruch (1824–1903). In contrast, the Dutch Impressionists, closely linked to the French Impressionists, preferred active subjects such as *The Bridge over the Singel at Paleisstraat, Amsterdam* (1890) by George Hendrik Breitner (1857–1923).

Sculpture and Applied Arts

Beginning with religious medieval sculpture, this section moves on to the splendour of Renaissance furniture and decoration. Highlights that capture the wealth of the Golden Age include the exquisite collections of glassware and Delftware *(see pp32–3)*, and diamond jewellery. A late 17th-century, 12-leaf Chinese screen incorporates European figures on one side, a phoenix on the other; and two dolls' houses

are modelled on contemporary town houses. Some outstanding 18th-century Meissen porcelain and Art Nouveau glass complete the collection.

Prints and Drawings

The Rijksmuseum owns about a million prints and drawings. Although the emphasis is on Dutch works (most of Rembrandt's etchings as well as rare works by Hercules Seghers (c.1589–1637) are here), there are prints by major European artists, including Dürer, Tiepolo, Goya, Watteau and Toulouse-Lautrec, as well as a set of coloured Japanese woodcuts. Small exhibitions are held on the ground floor of the museum, but particular prints can be viewed with special permission from the Study Collection in the basement.

Late 7th-century Cambodian Head of Buddha

Asiatic Art

Rewards of the Dutch imperial trading past are on show in this department, which has a separate entrance at the rear of the museum. Some of the earliest artifacts are the most unusual: tiny bronze Tang dynasty figurines from 7th-century China and gritty, granite rock carvings from Java (c.8th century). Later exhibits include a lovely – and extremely explicit – Hindu statue entitled *Heavenly Beauty*, luscious Chinese parchment paintings of tigers, inlaid Korean boxes and Vietnamese dishes painted with curly-tailed fish. This is a veritable hoard of delights and, above all, a monument to the sophistication and skill of craftsmen and artists in early Eastern cultures.

❸ Van Gogh Museum

The Van Gogh Museum is based on a design by De Stijl architect Gerrit Rietveld *(see pp208–9)* and opened in 1973. A new wing, designed by Kisho Kurokawa, was added in 1999. When Van Gogh died in 1890, he was on the verge of being acclaimed. His younger brother Theo, an art dealer, amassed a collection of 200 of his paintings and 500 drawings. These, combined with around 850 letters by Van Gogh to Theo, and selected works by his friends and contemporaries, form the core of the museum's outstanding collection.

★ **Vincent's Bedroom in Arles** (1888)
One of Van Gogh's best-known works, this was painted to celebrate his achievement of domestic stability at the Yellow House in Arles. He was so delighted with the colourful painting that he did it twice.

★ **Sunflowers** (1889)
The vivid yellows and greens in this version of Van Gogh's *Sunflowers* have been enriched by broad streaks of bright mauve and red.

Third floor

Stairs

Second floor
(study collection)

First floor

19th-century art

Entrance

Ground floor

Key to Floorplan

- ▢ Works by Van Gogh
- ▢ Study collection and Print room
- ▢ Other 19th-century paintings
- ▢ Temporary exhibitions

Museum Guide

Paintings from Van Gogh's Dutch period and from his time in Paris and Provence are on the first floor. The study collection, occasional exhibits of Van Gogh's drawings and other temporary exhibitions are on the second floor. Works by other 19th-century artists are on the third floor and the ground floor, where there is also a bookshop and café. The new wing houses temporary exhibitions.

An Artist's Life

Vincent van Gogh (1853–90), born in Zundert, began painting in 1880. He worked in the Netherlands for five years before moving to Paris, later settling in Arles. After a fierce argument with Gauguin, he cut off part of his own ear; his mental instability forced him into a psychiatric hospital in Saint-Rémy. He sought help in Auvers, where he shot himself, dying two days later.

Van Gogh in 1871

VISITORS' CHECKLIST

Practical Information
Paulus Potterstraat 7. **Map** 4 E3.
Tel 020-5705200.
🆆 vangoghmuseum.com
Open 10am–5pm daily,
10am–10pm Fri. **Closed** 1 Jan.

Transport
🚃 2, 3, 5, 12, 16.

First floor

Lift

Stairs

Lift

Stairs

Ground floor:
Temporary exhibitions
of 19th-century art

Escalator to
new wing

Lift to new wing

Basement

Lift

Stairs

Main
entrance

Entrance via
escalator

Lift to Rietveld wing

Pool

Pietà
(after Delacroix) (1889)
Van Gogh painted this
work while in the
hospital at Saint-Rémy.
The figure of Christ
is thought to be a
self-portrait.

★ **Wheatfield and Crows** (1890)
The menacing crows and
violence of the sky in one of
his last paintings show the
depth of Van Gogh's
mental anguish.

❹ Stedelijk Museum

The Stedelijk Museum was built to house a personal collection bequeathed to the city in 1890 by art connoisseur Sophia de Bruyn. In 1938, the museum became the national museum of modern art, displaying works by artists such as Picasso, Matisse, Mondriaan, Cézanne and Monet. The building's new wing (nicknamed "the bath tub") is an art piece in itself. The museum also organizes workshops, events and themed guided tours.

Portrait of the Artist with Seven Fingers (1912)
Marc Chagall's self-portrait is heavily autobiographical; the seven fingers of the title allude to the seven days of Creation and the artist's Jewish origins. Paris and Rome, the cities Chagall lived in, are inscribed in Hebrew above his head.

Solidaridad con America Latina (1970)
The Stedelijk's collection of rare posters comprises some 17,000 works, including this graphic image by the Cuban human rights campaigner Asela Perez.

The Museum Building

The Neo-Renaissance building was designed by AW Weissman (1858–1923) in 1895. The façade is adorned with turrets and gables and with niches containing statues of artists and architects. It makes a striking contrast with the spectacular new wing by Benthem Crouwel that houses a restaurant on the ground floor which is also open for dinner.

Hendrick de Keyser *(1565–1621)*

Jacob Cornelisz van Oostzaanen *(1470–1533)*

Pieter Aertsen *(1509–75)*

Joost Jansz Bilhamer *(1541–90)*

De Stijl Movement

The Dutch artistic movement known as De Stijl (The Style) produced startlingly simple designs which have become icons of 20th-century abstract art. These include Gerrit Rietveld's famous *Red Blue Chair* and Piet Mondriaan's *Composition in Red, Black, Blue, Yellow and Grey* (1920). The movement was formed in 1917 by a group of artists who espoused clarity in their work, which embraced the mediums of painting, architecture, sculpture, poetry and furniture design. Many De Stijl artists, like Theo van Doesburg, split from the founding group in the 1920s; their legacy can be seen in the work of the Bauhaus and Modernist schools which followed (see pp208–9).

Gerrit Rietveld's *Red Blue Chair* (1918)

Composition in Red, Black, Blue, Yellow and Grey by Mondriaan

For hotels and restaurants in this area see pp396–7 and pp406–9

Dancing Woman (1911)
Ernst Ludwig Kirchner (1880–1938) was inspired by the primitive art of African and Asian cultures, and by the natural qualities of the materials he worked with.

Man and Animals (1949)
Karel Appel (b. 1921) was a member of the short-lived experimental Cobra movement *(see p193)*. The human figure, dog fish and mythical creature are painted in the naive style of a child.

Elaborate bell tower

Jan van der Heyden
(1637–1712)

Thomas de Keyser
(1596–1667)

Jacob van Campen
(1595–1657)

Untitled (1965)
Jasper Johns (b. 1930) believed viewers should draw their own conclusions from his work. This huge canvas, with its bold rainbow (red, blue and yellow streaks and slabs), invites the viewer to think about the symbolism of colour.

VISITORS' CHECKLIST

Practical Information
Museumplein 10.
Map 4 D3. **Tel** 020-5732911.
🌐 stedelijk.nl
Open 10am–6pm daily,
10am–10pm Thu.
📷 ♿ ♿ ✏ 🛍

Transport
🚊 2, 3, 5, 12, 16.

★ Kazimir Malevich (1878–1935)

The Russian visual artist Kazimir Malevich can be counted, along with Piet Mondriaan, as one of the founders of abstract art. As well as paintings, Malevich created posters, sculptures, furniture, interior decoration and costumes.

After studying Futurism and Cubism in Moscow, he formulated a new art form called Suprematism, an abstract movement known for its experimentation with colour. Suprematism's central element is the theory of unlimited pre-eminence of free invention in the artistic process. Up until his 20s, Malevich painted abstract geometric forms. The square was his "supreme element". The Stedelijk Museum owns the largest part of the paintings and sketches from Malevich's Suprematist period. One of the most important works, *Suprematisme 1920–1927*, was defaced by a visitor to the museum in 1997.

In 1999, a conflict arose between the Malevich estate and the Stedelijk Museum over the ownership of the dozens of Suprematist works from the Stedelijk's collection.

Self-portrait by Malevich

OUTSIDE THE CENTRE

Great architecture and good town planning are not confined to central Amsterdam. Parts of the Nieuw Zuid (New South) bear testament to the imagination of the innovative Amsterdam School architects (see pp146–7). Many fine buildings can be found in De Dageraad Housing complex and the streets around the Olympic Quarter. The area known as the Plantage (plantation) was once green parkland beyond the city wall, where 17th-century Amsterdammers spent their leisure time. From about 1848, it became one of Amsterdam's first suburbs. The tree-lined streets around Artis and Hortus Botanicus are still popular places to live. From the Werf 't Kromhout, once a thriving shipyard, there is a fine view of De Gooyer Windmill, one of the few in Amsterdam to survive. The national maritime collection is kept at Scheepvaart Museum, a former naval storehouse. NEMO, an educational science centre, is nearby. Fine parks are just a short tram ride from the city centre and offer a host of leisure activities.

Sights at a Glance

Historic Buildings and Structures
2 Entrepotdok
3 Java-eiland and KNSM-eiland
4 Muiderpoort
5 De Gooyer Windmill
7 Koninklijk Theater Carré
8 Amstelsluizen
11 Frankendael
14 Heineken Experience
15 Huizenblok de Dageraad
17 De Hallen

Markets
18 De Pijp/Albert Cuypmarkt

Museums and Zoos
1 Scheepvaart Museum pp136–7
6 Werfmuseum 't Kromhout
9 NEMO Science Museum pp140–41
10 ARTIS-Amsterdam Royal Zoo pp142–3
12 Tropenmuseum
13 Hermitage Amsterdam
16 Verzetsmuseum

Key
Central Amsterdam
Motorway
Main road
Minor road
Railway

0 kilometres 1
0 miles 1

Outside the Centre

◀ Replica of the *Amsterdam*, an East Indiaman, moored alongside the Scheepvaartmuseum **For map symbols** see back flap

❶ Scheepvaart Museum

Once the arsenal of the Dutch Navy, this vast Dutch Classical building was designed by Daniël Stalpaert in 1655. Constructed around a massive courtyard, it was supported by thousands of piles driven into the bed of the Oosterdok. The navy occupied the building until the 20th century, and in 1973 it became the Netherlands Maritime Museum. After a major renovation it reopened in 2011; the courtyard, now covered by a vast glass roof, forms the heart of the new exhibition space.

★ **Golden Age**
Seven characters welcome you to this exhibition covering the golden era of Dutch exploration and trade in the 16th and 17th centuries.

First floor

Ajax
This figurehead is from a ship built in 1832. It portrays Ajax, a hero of the Trojan War, who killed himself in despair when Achilles' armour was given to Odysseus.

Classical sandstone façade

Museum Guide

This museum's exhibits reveal Dutch maritime history. On a Virtual Sea Trip or aboard the East Indiaman Amsterdam *you can relive the past; other exhibits tell the stories of whaling, the Golden Age and the port of Amsterdam. Objects on Stage showcases the museum's superb collection of nautical paintings, navigation instruments and antique globes.*

Glass Canopy
The compass rose and navigational lines on old sea maps were the inspiration for architect Laurent Ney's criss-crossing steel armature supporting the glass roof.

Main entrance

Second floor

Ground floor

Auditorium

Full-size replica of a Dutch East Indiaman

Steps down to wooden walkway

Wooden walkway

★ Objects on Stage
This 18th-century clockwork model shows the movements of all the planets known at the time.

VISITORS' CHECKLIST

Practical Information
Kattenburgerplein 1. **Map** 6 D1
Tel 020-5232222.
🔲 hetscheepvaartmuseum.nl
Open 9am–5pm daily.

Transport
🚌 22, 32. 🚢 Oosterdok,
Kattenburgergracht.

Key to Floorplan

- Golden Age
- Paintings
- Port of Amsterdam
- Objects on Stage
- Tale of the Whale
- Temporary space
- Toddlers' Museum
- Virtual Sea Trip
- Non-exhibition space

The Amsterdam
Experience life aboard ship on the replica of the *Amsterdam*, one of the ships that carried and defended the rich cargoes of the Dutch East India Company.

★ Virtual Sea Trip
This exhibit takes visitors on a virtual voyage, aided by artifacts from the museum such as this portrait of one of the most famous admirals in Dutch naval history, Michiel de Ruyter (1607–76).

❷ Entrepotdok

Map 6 D2. 🚃 9, 14, 32. 🚋 22, 43.

The redevelopment of the old VOC warehouses at Entrepotdok has revitalized this dockland area. During the mid-19th century, it was the greatest warehouse area in Europe, being a customs-free zone for goods in transit. The quayside buildings are now a lively complex of homes, offices and eating places. Some of the original façades of the warehouses have been preserved, unlike the interiors, which have been opened up to provide an attractive inner courtyard. Café tables are often set out alongside the canal. On the other side, brightly coloured houseboats are moored.

❸ Java-eiland and KNSM-eiland

Map 6 D2. Java-eiland and KNSM-eiland 🚋 41, 42. 🚃 10.

Situated side by side in the eastern docklands of the city are the islands of Java-eiland, which is long and narrow, and the broader KNSM-eiland. Java-eiland, designed by Sjoerd Soeters during the 1990s, demonstrates a wide variety of architectural styles. By combining these styles with a number of canals across the island, the architect succeeded in creating a very credible

The 18th-century De Gooyer windmill, with its renovated balcony

Amsterdam canal atmosphere. This is enhanced by the many shops and small cafés. KNSM-eiland is slightly broader, giving architect Jo Coenen the space to create a central avenue flanked on either side by tower blocks.

❹ Muiderpoort

Alexanderplein. **Map** 6 E3. 🚋 7, 9, 10, 14. **Closed** to the public.

Formerly a city gate, the Muiderpoort was designed by Cornelis Rauws (1732–72) in about 1770. The central archway

of this Classical structure is topped with a dome and clock tower. Napoleon entered the city through this gate in 1811 and, according to legend, forced the citizens to feed and house his ragged troops.

❺ De Gooyer Windmill

Funenkade 5. **Map** 6 F2. 🚃 10, 14. **Closed** to the public.

Of the six remaining windmills within the city's boundaries, De Gooyer, also known as the Funenmolen, is the most central. Dominating the view down the Nieuwevaart, the mill, built around 1725, was the first corn mill in the Netherlands to use streamlined sails.

It first stood to the west of its present site, but the Oranje Nassau barracks, built in 1814, acted as a windbreak, and the mill was then moved piece by piece to the Funenkade. The octagonal wooden structure was rebuilt on the stone foot of an earlier water-pumping mill, demolished in 1812.

By 1925, De Gooyer was in a very poor state of repair and was bought by the city council, which fully restored it. Since then, the lower part of the mill, with its neat thatched roof and tiny windows, has been a private home, though its massive sails still creak into

Spout-gable façades of former warehouses along Entrepotdok

For hotels and restaurants in this area see pp396–7 and pp406–9

KNSM-eiland: a thriving modern city district

action sometimes. Next to the mill is the IJ brewery, with its own tasting room (www. brouwerijhetij.nl).

❻ Werfmuseum 't Kromhout

Hoogte Kadijk 147. **Map** 6 E2. **Tel** 020-6276777. 🚊 9, 10, 14. 🚌 22, 43. 🚤 Oosterdok or Artis. **Open** 10am–3pm Tue and by appointment. **Closed** public hols. 🎫 ♿ 📷 🅦 machinekamer.nl

The Werfmuseum 't Kromhout is one of the oldest working shipyards in Amsterdam and is also a museum. Ships were being built here as early as 1757. In the second half of the 19th century, production changed from sailing ships to steamships. As ocean-going ships got bigger, the yard, due to its relatively small size, turned to building lighter craft for inland waterways. It is now used only for restoration and repair work.

In 1967, the Prince Bernhard Fund bought the site, saving it from demolition. The Amsterdam Monuments Fund later became involved to safeguard the shipyard's future as a historical site and helped turn it into a museum.

The museum is largely dedicated to the history of marine engineering, concentrating on work carried out at the shipyard, with steam engines, maritime photographs and ephemera. Another point of interest is the shipyard's forge featuring a variety of interesting tools and equipment. Some impressive historical ships are moored at the quayside. The museum's eastern hall is sometimes used for receptions and dinners.

The Werfmuseum 't Kromhout museum, located not far from the inner city

❼ Koninklijk Theater Carré

Amstel 115–125. **Map** 5 B3. **Tel** 0900-2525255. 🚊 4, 7, 9, 10. Ⓜ Weesperplein. Box office: **Open** noon–6pm daily. *See Entertainment p151.* 🎭 📷 11am Sat (phone in advance). 🎫 ♿ 🅦 **theatercarre.nl**

During the 19th century, the annual visit of the Carré Circus was a popular event. In 1868, Oscar Carré built wooden premises for the circus on the banks of the Amstel river. The city council considered the structure a fire hazard, so Carré persuaded them to accept a permanent building modelled on his other circus in Cologne. Built in 1887, the new structure included both a circus ring and a stage. The Classical façade is richly decorated with sculpted heads of dancers, jesters and clowns.

Pillar decoration on Theater Carré

The Christmas circus is still one of the annual highlights at the theatre, but for much of the year the stage is taken over by concerts and blockbuster musicals.

❽ Amstelsluizen

Map 5 B3. 🚊 4, 7, 9, 10, 14. Ⓜ Weesperplein.

The Amstelsluizen, a row of sturdy wooden sluice gates spanning the Amstel river, form part of a complex system of sluices and pumping stations that ensure Amsterdam's canals do not stagnate. Four times a week in summer and twice a week in winter, the sluices are closed while fresh water from large lakes north of the city is allowed to flow into Amsterdam's canals. Sluices to the west of the city are left open, allowing the old water to flow, or be pumped, into the sea.

The Amstelsluizen date from 1673, and were operated manually until 1994, when they were mechanized.

❾ NEMO Science Museum

NEMO Science Museum, an educational centre for science and technology, is housed in a striking modern building by the Italian architect Renzo Piano. Designed as a reflection of the IJtunnel, it overhangs the water by 30 m (99 ft): the view from the roof is breathtaking. There are five floors of constantly changing things to do and discover, including interactive exhibitions, theatre shows, films, workshops and demonstrations.

World of Shapes
Discover mathematics in the world around you.

★ **The Search for Life**
Discover how life began on our world, and explore the possibilities of alien life forms.

Bubble-blowing
Can you fit inside a giant bubble? Experiment with giant rings and vats of soapy water.

KEY

① **The motorway** approach to the tunnel under the IJ is beneath the building.

② **Machine Park** focuses on technology.

③ **In the Laboratory** you can use real scientific equipment to do experiments.

④ **Bridge to the Centraal Station**

★ **Chain Reaction**
This entertaining show demonstrates cause and effect and action and reaction, with plenty of audience participation.

Nemo: the Philosophy

The word "nemo" is Latin for "no one" and refers to a world between fantasy and reality. At NEMO visitors can become a scientist or technician for a day. The name has been used by a number of important writers over the centuries to describe events and people who find themselves on the thin line between reality and fantasy. For example, Nemo turns up in the Latin translation of Homer's *Odyssey*, when the protagonist Ulysses adopts the name to deceive the Cyclops. And Jules Verne, in his 1870 novel *20,000 Leagues Under the Sea*, enlists Nemo as the mystical captain of the underwater *Nautilus*, which journeys in the shadowy world between reality and fantasy. He crops up again in 1905, when American cartoonist Winsor McCay creates *Little Nemo*, a young boy whose dreamland adventures once again suggest a mingling of fact and fiction.

VISITORS' CHECKLIST

Practical Information
Oosterdok 2. **Map** 5 C1.
Tel 020-5313233
(groups 020-5313118).
W nemosciencemuseum.nl
Open 10am–5:30pm Tue–Sun;
during school holidays: 10am–
5:30pm daily. **Closed** 1 Jan,
27 Apr, 25 Dec. 🅿 ♿ 💻 ⚟

Transport
🚋 1, 2, 4, 5, 9, 13, 14, 16, 17, 26.
🚌 22, 42. Ⓜ Centraal Station.

★ **View from the Roof**
The building's roof offers a stunning vista of the port and city. In summer, it becomes a popular leisure area. Visitors can also experience the energy generated from wind, water and the sun at Energetica on the rooftop.

Phenomena
Both ordinary and extraordinary natural and scientific phenomena can be experienced in this interactive exhibition.

Museum Guide

Level 1 (first floor) gives a glimpse into how science works. On Levels 2, 3 and 4 you can unravel everyday technology and learn about the cosmos. The rooftop is home to Energetica, an open-air exhibition where visitors can explore various forms of energy.

⑩ Artis Royal Zoo

Amsterdam's royal zoo is in Plantage, an elegant Amsterdam neighbourhood of broad tree-lined streets with elegant painted sandstone houses. Some 750 different animal species live in Artis Zoo. Visitors can see the historic nature of the zoo as soon as they pass through the entrance gates, which have been decorated since 1854 with two "golden" eagles. The Artis complex includes a planetarium, where you can learn about the heavens and stars, and the fine Neo-Classical aquarium, containing a wide variety of marine life, from tropical fish and sharks to huge moray eels.

Tiger Python
The female specimen in Artis has borne young simply by cloning herself.

★ Planetarium
The planetarium explores the relationship between humans and the stars. The night sky is re-created on the dome, and interactive exhibitions show the positions of the planets. Model spacecraft are on display in the hall around the auditorium. The interesting slide show is specially designed for youngsters.

KEY

① **The playground**, situated next to the Two Cheetahs restaurant, is popular with children.

② **The northern side** of the zoo is currently used as a car park, but in the near future will be added to the zoo, with parking underground.

0 metres 100
0 yards 100

Macaws
These birds are a highly endangered species which Artis helps preserve. The zoo is renowned for its breeding programmes.

For hotels and restaurants in this area see pp396–7 and pp406–9

★ **African Savannah**
In the "African Savannah",
the animals roam in more
natural surroundings. The
zebras, gnus and gazelles
feel at home here.

VISITORS' CHECKLIST

Practical Information
Plantage Kerklaan 38–40.
Tel 0900-2784796.
W artis.nl
Open summer: 9am–6pm daily
(open until sunset on Sat); winter:
9am–5pm daily.

Transport
9, 10, 14.

Gorillas
Gorilla Binti's son
Bwana was born as
part of the zoo's
breeding programme.

★ **Aquarium**
This fine Neo-Classical building from 1882
is home to thousands of marine animals, and
also contains fish from Amsterdam's canals.

Sea Lions
Feeding time for the
sea lions is a popular
daily attraction
at the zoo.

⓫ Frankendael

Middenweg 72. **Map** 6 F5. 🚃 9.
🚌 41, 65, 101, 136, 152, 157.
Gardens: **Open** dawn–dusk.
📧 W **huizefranendael.nl**

During the early part of the 18th century, many of Amsterdam's wealthier citizens built country retreats south of Plantage Middenlaan on reclaimed land called the Watergraafsmeer. The elegant Louis XIV-style Frankendael is the last survivor. The house is closed to the public; the best views of the ornamented façade are from Middenweg. This is also the best place to view the fountain made in 1714 by Ignatius van Logteren (1685–1732), a sculptor who, along with his son, played a central role in the development of Amsterdam's Louis XIV style.

The rear gardens have been restored and are open to the public. Behind the house is a small formal garden, and beyond lies a landscaped, English-style garden. There are also allotment gardens. The coach house is now home to café-restaurant Merkelbach.

The ornamental façade of Frankendael House

Ignatius van Logteren's fountain in the grounds of the Frankendael

⓬ Tropenmuseum

Linnaeusstraat 2. **Map** 6 E3. Tropenmuseum: **Tel** 0800-4280. **Open** 10am–5pm daily, 10am–3pm 24 Dec, 31 Dec. **Closed** 1 Jan, 27 Apr, 5 May, 25 Dec. W **tropenmuseum.nl** Tropenmuseum Junior: **Tel** 0800-4280. **Open** for special programmes in Dutch language only *(phone or see website).* **Closed** as Tropenmuseum. 🚃 9, 14. 🎨 🚻 ♿ 📷 📧 W **tropenmuseumjunior.nl**

Built to house the Dutch Colonial Institute, this vast complex was finished in 1926 by architects MA and J Nieuwkerken. The exterior is decorated with symbols of imperialism, such as stone friezes of peasants planting rice. Upon completion of the building's renovation in 1978, the Royal Tropical Institute opened a museum, with a huge central hall and three levels of galleries. The institute's aims are to study and to help improve the lives of the indigenous populations of the tropics. The displays focus on development issues regarding daily life, education and colonization.

The impressive mask collection includes feathered fertility masks from Zaire and carved wooden masks from Central America. Surinamese

Balinese tiger protector mask and model at the Tropenmuseum

artist Gerrit Schouten's 1819 diorama made of papier-mâché and painted wood depicts life in Suriname.

⓭ Hermitage Amsterdam

Amstel 51. **Map** 5 B2. **Tel** 020-530 8755. 🚃 4, 9, 14. Ⓜ Waterlooplein. 🚌 Muziektheater. **Open** 10am– 5pm daily. 🎫 Free for under 11s. **Closed** 1 Jan, 27 Apr, 25 Dec. ♿ 📷 📧 📺 W **hermitage.nl**

In the early 1990s the State Hermitage Museum in St Petersburg, Russia, chose Amsterdam as the ideal city in which to open a satellite museum displaying temporary exhibitions drawn from the Hermitage's rich collection. It is housed in the former Amstelhof – a shelter for poor elderly women – and opened in 2004 with a spectacular exhibition of fine Greek gold jewellery from the 6th to the 2nd century BC. The museum, which has an auditorium and a children's wing, also has a fine restaurant, Neva, which is open to non-visitors.

⑭ Heineken Experience

Stadhouderskade 78. **Map** 4 F3. **Tel** 020-523 9222. 🚋 7, 10, 16. **Open** 10:30am–7:30pm Mon–Thu, 10:30am–9pm Fri–Sun (Jul & Aug: 10:30am–9pm daily). **Closed** 1 Jan, 25 Dec. ♿ 🅿 Under 18s with parents only. 🌐 heinekenexperience.com

This historic 1867 building once housed the Heineken brewery. Now it offers an exhibition of how beer is made, culminating in a tasting room where you can have a drink.

Visitors inside the Heineken Experience museum

⑮ Huizenblok De Dageraad

Pieter Lodewijk Takstraat. 🚋 4, 12, 25. **Closed** to the public.

One of the best examples of Amsterdam School architecture (*see pp146–7*), De Dageraad (the Dawn) housing project was developed for poorer families following the Housing Act of 1901, by which the city council condemned slums and rethought housing policy. Architect HP Berlage drew up plans for the suburbs, aiming to integrate rich and poor by juxtaposing their housing. After Berlage's death, Piet Kramer and Michel de Klerk adopted his ideas. From 1918–23, they designed this complex for the De Dageraad housing association.

⑯ Verzetsmuseum

Plantage Kerklaan 61. **Map** 6 D2. **Tel** 020-6202535. 🚋 9, 14. **Open** 10am–5pm Tue–Fri, 11am–5pm Sat–Mon. **Closed** 1 Jan, 27 Apr, 25 Dec. ♿ 🅿 📷 💻 🚫 🌐 verzetsmuseum.org

Previously based in a former synagogue in Nieuw Zuid (New South), now at a site in the Plantage, the Resistance Museum holds a fascinating collection of memorabilia recording the activities of Dutch Resistance workers in World War II. It was set up by former members of the Resistance and focuses on the courage of the 25,000 people actively involved in the movement. False documents, weaponry, film clips, photographs and equipment are on display.

By 1945 there were 300,000 people in hiding in the Netherlands, including Jews and anti-Nazi Dutch. Events organized by the Resistance, like the February Strike against the deportation of the Jews, are brought to life by exhibits showing where the refugees hid and how food for them was smuggled in.

⑰ De Hallen

Hannie Dankbaar Passage 33. 🚋 7, 17. **Open** 7am–1pm Mon–Thu & Sun, 7am–3pm Fri & Sat. 📷 🌐 dehallen-amsterdam.nl

A huge, unused tram depot has been transformed into an upscale cultural and commercial centre consisting of a range of designer shops, restaurants, bars and international food market, as well as a cinema complex and a hotel. Visitors can also take guided tours of De Hallen and its neighbourhood that offer a glimpse into the architecture of the area.

⑱ De Pijp/Albert Cuypmarkt

Albert Cuypstraat. **Map** 5 A5. 🚋 4, 16. **Open** 9:30am–5pm Mon–Sat.

The Albert Cuypmarkt, part of the De Pijp area, began trading in 1904 and is still going strong, with over 325 stalls selling flowers, clothing, poultry, fish and other items. De Pijp, once a poor working-class sector, has turned into one of the city's liveliest and most popular areas. The neighbourhood has gentrified and now features designer bars, restaurants and trendy shops, while Sarphatipark is a haven of tranquility amid the hustle and bustle.

Imposing corner block of De Dageraad public housing

The Amsterdam School

The industrial revolution at the end of the 19th century led to a boom in the growth of towns. New districts grew around Amsterdam to accommodate the growing number of factory workers. The architects of these districts, who sought new elements for decorating building façades, became known collectively as the Amsterdam School. Their designs were characterized by exotic rooflines, ornamental brickwork, cornices, window frames and corner formations which gave the façades "movement".

Curves and serpentines on façades are typical features of the Amsterdam School.

The Scheepvaarthuis was erected on the spot where in 1595 Cornelis Houtman set off on his first voyage to the East Indies.

The Betondorp (Concrete Village), officially known as Tuindorp Watergraafsmeer, was the first place where experimental concrete-work was used. It also features many brick buildings in the Amsterdam School style. Dutch football legend Johan Cruiff was born here.

HP Berlage (1856–1934)

Berlage studied at the technical college of Zurich from 1875 to 1878, where he came into contact with architects such as Semper and Viollet-le-Duc. Inspired by their ideas, he developed his own style, which incorporated traditional Dutch materials. It later evolved into the Amsterdam School style of architecture. Berlage designed not only buildings but also interiors, furniture and graphics. In 1896, he was appointed to design the Beurs, the new stock exchange in Amsterdam (see p95). Completed in 1903, it is an austere building whose structure is clearly visible. Berlage was also active as a town planner. His design of Amsterdam-Zuid ("Plan Zuid") consists of monumental residential blocks. At its centre stands JF Staal's *Wolkenkrabber* (skyscraper).

Detail of a set of windows on the Zaanstraat

OUTSIDE THE CENTRE | **147**

Het Schip, built by Michel de Klerk, is a former post office which now provides a home for the Museum voor de Volkshuisvesting (museum of public housing).

Interiors and exteriors are characterized by an excess of expressionist glass ornamentation and details.

An astonishing variety of decoration could be achieved with this kind of brickwork.

Sculptures

Amsterdam School lettering

The Architecture of the Amsterdam School

Michel de Klerk (1884–1923)

From 1911 to 1923, the members of the Amsterdam School built a large number of office and residential complexes. One of the greatest examples of this is the Scheepvaarthuis (1913–16 and 1926–8), which is today the Grand Hotel Amrâth Amsterdam, which also organizes tours for non-residents. It is the first building to be completed entirely in the Amsterdam School style. It was designed by the Van Gendt brothers and JM van der Meij. Michel de Klerk, who later designed Het Schip, was also involved in the project.

Street furniture was among the repertoire of the Amsterdam School architects. In the Spaarndammerbuurt in particular, many examples can still be seen, including fire alarms, cable boxes and post boxes.

SHOPPING IN AMSTERDAM

Amsterdam has a huge range of shops and markets. Most of the large clothing and department stores are to be found in the Nieuwe Zijde, especially along Kalverstraat, but there are many other shopping areas to discover. The narrow streets crossing the Canal Ring, such as Herenstraat and Hartenstraat, contain a diverse array of specialist shops selling everything from ethnic fabrics and beads to unusual games and handmade dolls. The best luxury fashion is to be found on PC Hooftstraat and Van Baerlestraat. However, if you are looking for a bargain, take time to explore the street markets and numerous second-hand shops.

The northern end of the Waterlooplein, home to the famous flea market

Opening Hours

Shops are usually open from 9am to 6pm Tuesday to Saturday, from 1pm to 6pm Mondays. Many are open Sundays. In the city centre most shops now close at 7pm (9pm on Thursdays) and are open on Sundays.

How to Pay

Cash is the most popular method of payment. If you intend to use a credit card, ask first if it is accepted. Cards are becoming more widely accepted, but department stores may require purchases to be paid for at a special till, and smaller shops may accept them only for non-sale items and goods costing more than 45 euros. Some tourist shops take foreign currency but usually offer a poor rate of exchange.

Vat Exemption

Most Dutch goods are subject to value added tax (BTW) of 21 per cent for clothes and other goods, and 6 per cent for books. Non-EU residents may be entitled to a refund. Shops that stock the relevant customs forms post a "Tax free for tourists" sign.

Sales

Sales occur mainly in January and July, but smaller shops and boutiques may offer discounts at any time. *Uitverkoop* describes anything from a closing-down sale to a clearance sale; *korting* merely indicates that discounts are offered. Towards the end of a sale, further discounts are often calculated at the till. Beware of clothes rails marked, for example, *VA 40* or *Vanaf 40*, as this sign means "from 40", not exactly 40 euros.

Department Stores and Malls

Amsterdam's best-known department store is **De Bijenkorf**. It has a huge perfumery and stocks a wide range of clothing. Among the less expensive stores, **Hema** is popular for household goods, children's clothes and underwear, while **Blokker** sells more basic household and electrical items. Both have branches dotted around the city. The only shopping malls in central Amsterdam are the Kalvertoren (Kalverstraat, near Singel) and **Magna Plaza** *(see p94)*, containing upmarket boutiques and shops.

Kitchen gadgets for sale at a shop in Amsterdam

Markets

Amsterdammers' love of street trading is best illustrated on Koningsdag *(see p36)*, when the city centre becomes the world's biggest flea

Trendy clothing store in "De Negen Straatjes" (The Nine Streets) neighbourhood

market as locals sell off their unwanted junk.

Each district in Amsterdam has its own market. The best-known is the Albert Cuypmarkt *(see p145)*. There are also many specialist markets. Visitors and residents alike are drawn to the array of seasonal flowers at the Bloemenmarkt. Another market popular with tourists is Waterlooplein flea market *(see p81)*, where bargains can be found among the bric-à-brac; new and second-hand clothes are also for sale.

Browsers will be fascinated by the dozens of stalls at the **Looier Kunst en Antiekcentrum** *(see p117)*, selling anything from antique dolls to egg cups. On Wednesdays and Saturdays on Nieuwezijds Voorburgwal there is a stamp and coin market. Gourmets should head for the **Noordermarkt** *(see p115)*, for the Saturday organic food market, also known as the

Jenever of Amsterdam

Boerenmarkt. The best prices, however, are to be found about 25 km (16 miles) northwest of Amsterdam at the weekend **Beverwijkse Bazaar**, one of Europe's largest indoor flea markets. Next door you will find Oriental merchandise.

Specialist Shops

Specialist shops are dotted throughout the city. The unusual **Condomerie Het Gulden Vlies**, located in a former squat, sells condoms from all over the world. **Christmas Palace** sells festive adornments year round, and **Party House** has a vast collection of paper decorations. **Capsicum Natuurstoffen** has a huge selection of silks and linens, while **Coppenhagen 1001 Kralen** offers over 1,000 types of beads. It is also worth exploring **Joe's Vliegerwinkel** for kites, **Simon Levelt** for tea and coffee and **De Kaaskamer** for cheese.

Books and Newspapers

English-language books are easily available, particularly at **The American Book Center**, **Waterstones** and **The New English Bookshop**. They can also be picked up cheaply at second-hand shops, such as **The Book Exchange**. Comics collectors should not miss **Lambiek**. *Het Financieel Dagblad* has a daily business update in English and a weekly English-language edition. For the latest news on events, parties and exhibitions, visit the city's official tourist website www.iamsterdam.com.

Organic foods displayed at the Saturday food market, Noordermarkt

DIRECTORY

Department Stores and Malls

De Bijenkorf
Dam 1. **Map** 2 D5.
Tel 0900-0919.

Blokker
Kalverstraat 41. **Map** 4 F1.
Tel 020-6244456.
Ceintuurbaan 109.
Map 4 F4.
Tel 020-6727746.

Hema
Kalvertoren, Kalverstraat.
Map 4 F1.
Tel 020-4228988.
Nieuwendijk 174–176.
Map 2 D4.
Tel 020-6234176.

Magna Plaza
Nieuwezijds
Voorburgwal 182.
Map 2 D4.
Tel 020-6269199.

Markets

De Beverwijkse Bazaar
Montageweg 35,
Beverwijk.
Tel 0251-262666.

Boerenmarkt
Noordermarkt. **Open** summer: 9am–4pm Sat; winter: 9am–3pm Sat.

Looier Kunst en Antiekcentrum
Elandsgracht 109.
Map 4 D1.
🚊 7, 10, 17.
Open 11am–5pm Sat–Thu.

Noordermarkt
Noordermarkt.
Map 1 C3.
🚊 3, 10, 13, 14, 17.

Specialist Shops

Capsicum Natuurstoffen
Oude Hoogstraat 1.
Map 2 D5.
Tel 020-6231016.

Christmas Palace
Singel 508.
Map 4 F1.
Tel 020-4210155.

Condomerie Het Gulden Vlies
Warmoesstraat 141.
Map 2 D5.
Tel 020-6274174.

Coppenhagen 1001 Kralen
Rozengracht 54.
Map 1 B4.
Tel 020-6243681.

Joe's Vliegerwinkel
Nieuwe Hoogstraat 19.
Map 2 E5.
Tel 020-6250139.

De Kaaskamer
Runstraat 7.
Map 4 E1.
Tel 020-6233483.

Party House
Rozengracht 92.
Map 1 B4.
Tel 020-6247851.

Simon Levelt
Prinsengracht 180.
Map 1 B4.
Tel 020-6240823.

Books and Newspapers

The American Book Center
Spui 12. **Map** 4 F1.
Tel 020-6255537.

The Book Exchange
Kloveniersburgwal 58.
Map 2 D5.
Tel 020-6266266.

The New English Bookshop
Kalverstraat 223.
Map 4 F1.
Tel 020-6249789.

Lambiek
Kerkstraat 132. **Map** 4 E1.
Tel 020-6267543.

Waterstones
Kalverstraat 152.
Map 4 F1.
Tel 020-6383821.

ENTERTAINMENT IN AMSTERDAM

Amsterdam offers a diverse array of world-class entertainment. A wide variety of performances are staged in hundreds of venues throughout the city, ranging from the century-old Concertgebouw *(see p124)* to the sleek modern Muziekgebouw on the IJ river. There is a huge choice of plays and films throughout the year, and plenty of free performances are given by a multitude of street performers and live bands in late-night bars and cafés. The city's hottest annual events include the Holland Festival and the Uitmarkt *(see p37)*. Club-goers are in their element in the canal city, which offers club nights to meet most tastes in music and skilled DJs, such as Tiësto, who are renowned around the globe.

The colonnaded façade of the Concertgebouw theatre

Information

Amsterdam's various tourist offices are a good starting point for what's going on in the city. They can usually provide copies of free listings magazines, including the *AUB/Uitburo* and the monthly *Uitkrant*, the definitive source of entertainment information. The latter is also found in many bars and cafés. The city's English website www.iamsterdam.com has up-to-date entertainment listings.

The **AUB/Uitburo** has a last-minute window (open noon–7:30pm daily) selling tickets for same-day shows.

Classical Music, Opera and Dance

Amsterdam is the country's touchstone for classical music and opera, and the principal venues host some of the world's finest events. The open-air theatre in the **Vondelpark** *(see pp124–5)* stages free concerts, and in summer, the Grachtenfestival features mainly classical music on floating canal stages.

The city's musical centrepiece is the **Concertgebouw** *(see p124)*, renowned for its acoustics and home to the celebrated Royal Concertgebouw Orchestra. International orchestras and soloists perform here regularly, and it hosts the Robeco Summer Concerts, a showcase of young talent. The **Beurs van Berlage** *(see p95)*, originally the city's stock exchange, is now a concert venue.

The Netherlands Opera stages performances in the 1,600-seat **Muziektheater** *(see p81)*, whose classical and modern repertoire is without parallel. The iconic **Muziekgebouw** is the place to go for anything from chamber music to the avant-garde.

The Netherlands is home to two world-class ballet companies. The Dutch National Ballet, based in the Muziektheater, puts on classical ballet but also daring works by contemporary Dutch choreographers, while the Nederlands Dans Theater (NDT) specializes in works by its Czech artistic director, Jiri Kylian. Modern companies to look out for include Introdans, which combines jazz with flamenco and other ethnic dance, and Conny Jansen Danst, which combines theatrical elements with strong physical power. **De Meervaart** is a venue that stages modern dance, concerts and theatre.

Jazz, Pop and World Music

The Dutch are avid jazz fans, and big names such as Wayne Shorter, Branford Marsalis and Nicholas Payton show up regularly on local stages. The foremost jazz club is the **Bimhuis**, housed in a purpose-built hall of the Muziekgebouw. The Concertgebouw also hosts regular jazz concerts. Keep an eye out for local talent such as saxophonists Hans and Candy Dulfer. Good jazz cafés can be found along Zeedijk and around Leidseplein, namely **Jazzcafé Alto** and **Bourbon Street**.

Bourbon Street, one of Amsterdam's popular jazz cafés

Disco in the Heineken Music Hall

For most Amsterdammers, rock and pop are synonymous with two venues. **Paradiso**, which has hosted the Rolling Stones, Prince, David Bowie and other international music stars, is housed in a converted church just off Leidseplein, while **Melkweg** occupies a former dairy nearby. Both offer a varied and entertaining diet of rock, pop, dance, rap and world music.

Mega-concerts are booked into the 50,000-seat **Amsterdam ArenA**, and headline acts sometimes play at the more intimate **Heineken Music Hall**.

As a multicultural society, the Netherlands is a natural breeding ground for world music. Traditions from West Africa and the West Indies, Indonesia, Suriname and Turkey come together in this fascinating melting pot. **Akhnaton** is a cultural centre with a potent cocktail of Caribbean, African and Arabic music. **De Badcuyp**, in the lively Pijp district, plays with salsa, tango, African music and other dance options. In bars such as **Café Nol** and **De Twee Zwaantjes** you can enjoy traditional Dutch folk music *smartlappen* and mingle with the locals.

Theatre and Cabaret

The heart of the country's lively theatre scene is in Amsterdam. The premier venue is the **Stadsschouwburg** *(see p116)*, home to the Amsterdam Theatre Group and led by the imaginative director Ivo van

Hove. The annual highlight for opera, theatre and dance is the Holland Festival, held from late May to June. It overlaps with the International Theatre School Festival, whose experimental drama pops up at **De Brakke Grond** and **Frascati**.

The chief musical theatre is the **Koninklijk Theater Carré** *(see p139)*. It stages box-office hits such as *Les Misérables* and *Miss Saigon*. **De Kleine Komedie**, a magnificent 17th-century building on the Amstel river, is a favourite venue for cabaret groups. Stand-up comedy has gained in popularity, led by the hilarious English-language routines of **Boom Chicago**.

Experimental theatre can be found at a range of venues including **Westergasfabriek**, a converted former gas works in a lovely park setting. The company De Dogtroep stages offbeat street theatre, while Theatergroup Hollandia has won great acclaim with its

performances in large halls and aircraft hangars. The musical dramas of Orkater appear mainly at the Stadsschouwburg and the **Bellevue Theater**. Summer outdoor theater can be seen in the Vondelpark *(see pp124–5)* and the Amsterdamse Bos *(see p193)*, a sprawling woodland park on the edge of town.

The Art Deco Tuschinski Theatre, a luxurious cinema experience

Cinema

Film fanatics are well looked after, with more than 40 cinemas in town. Foreign language films are shown in the original language with subtitles. The leading Dutch filmmaker is Amsterdam-born Paul Verhoeven (of *Basic Instinct* fame). He returned to his homeland to shoot *Black Book*, the highest-grossing Dutch film ever.

Cinema programmes change every Thursday, so check the website www.filmladder.nl. *De Filmkrant* is a free monthly film magazine with complete listings.

Musicians providing entertainment in the Vondelpark

The most stunning cinema in town is the **Tuschinski**, an Art Deco masterpiece with a luxurious foyer and stained-glass windows (see p119). Some cinemas such as the mainstream **Pathé de Munt**, **City Theater** and the arthouse **Kriterion** show children's films at weekends. The **Uitkijk** is a cosy, 158-seat venue dating from 1913 that shows mainly classics.

The bright lights of Amsterdam ArenA, a premier sporting venue

Clubs and Discos

Amsterdam's nightclubs are famous for their variety and high energy. The scene throbs hardest in and around Leidseplein, Rembrandtplein and Reguliersdwarsstraat. Most clubs open at 11pm and are at their busiest from around 1am; closing time is 4am during the week and 5am on Friday and Saturday.

Jimmy Woo is famous for its tough door policy. Inside, it's Hong-Kong hip, with lots of black leather and a great sound system. **Escape** draws a young, trendy crowd to its huge split-level complex on Rembrandtplein, and another large, popular venue is **AIR**. On the opposite side of the square, **Rain** spins Latin and World beats.

The leading non-house club in town is **Sugar Factory**, with its diverse menu of soul, funk and jazz-dance. The other discos around Leidseplein are basically extended bars with small dance floors, catering to tourists. At **Odeon** near Spui Square, you can party your way up from the basement restaurant to the

dance palace on the third floor. Located in the former building of Dutch newspaper *De Volkskrant*, **Volkshotel** is home to a restaurant and one of the city's leading nightclubs, which attracts creative hipsters and students. The college crowd also gravitates to the dancehall of **Hotel Arena**, located in a former orphanage.

Clubbing is also at the heart of Amsterdam's gay scene. Crowds are often mixed and most gay clubs will rarely turn away women or straight men. Reguliersdwarsstraat is home to a number of gay bars, such as **NYX**, a slick bar with three levels and a balcony for viewing the dance scene below. Other popular gay bars, such as **Amstel 54** and **Queers Café**, are located on the nearby Amstel.

Prik is a hugely popular bar that turns into a small club at night. Young women like **Vive La Vie**, while **Saarein II** is a friendly, relaxed bar tucked away in a small street in the Jordaan. Details of other venues

are available from the Pink Point kiosk next to the Westerkerk (www.pinkpoint.org).

Spectator Sports

The Dutch are a sport-mad nation, and nothing makes their pulses race faster than football. Three teams enjoy international standing: Ajax Amsterdam, Feyenoord Rotterdam and PSV

Two footballers clashing at an Ajax game

Eindhoven (see p368). They sometimes face off at the spectacular Amsterdam ArenA.

For something different, try watching a game of korfball, invented by Amsterdam teacher Nico Boekhuysen over 100 years ago. It mixes elements of basketball, netball and volleyball, and is the only unisex sport played professionally. Each team has four men and four women. Top-level matches are played on the indoor courts of the Olympic Stadium, built for the Games held in 1928.

Dancers at one of Amsterdam's many clubs

DIRECTORY

Entertainment Information

AUB Ticketshop
Leidseplein 26.
Map 4 E2.
Tel 020-7959950.
W amsterdam
suitburo.nl

Classic Music, Opera and Dance

Beurs van Berlage
Damrak 243.
Map 2 D4.
Tel 020-5304141.
W beursvanberlage.nl

Concertgebouw
Concertgebouwplein 2–6.
Map 4 D4.
Tel 0900 6718345.
W concertgebouw.nl

De Meervaart
Meer en Vaart 300.
Tel 020-4107700.
W meervaart.nl

Muziekgebouw Aan 't IJ
Piet Heinkade 1.
Map 2 F3.
Tel 020-7882000.
W muziekgebouw.nl

Het Muziektheater
Amstel 3.
Map 5 B2.
Tel 020-6255455.
W muziektheater.nl

Vondelpark
Stadhouderskade.
Map 4 E2.
Tel 020-7882000.
W vondelpark.nl

Jazz, Pop and World Music

Akhnaton
Nieuwezijds Kolk 25.
Map 2 D4.
Tel 020-624 3396.
W akhnaton.nl

Amsterdam ArenA
ArenA Boulevard 1,
Zuidoost.
Tel 020-3111333.
W amsterdamarena.nl

De Badcuyp
Sweelinckstraat 10.
Map 5 A5.
Tel 020-6759669.
W badcuyp.nl

Bimhuis
Muziekgebouw aan 't IJ
Piet Heinkade 3.
Map 2 F3.
Tel 020-7882188.
W bimhuis.nl

Bourbon Street
Leidsekruisstraat 6–8.
Map 4 E2.
Tel 020-6233440.
W bourbonstreet.nl

Café Nol
Westerstraat 109.
Map 1 B3.
Tel 020-6245380.

Heineken Music Hall
Arena Boulevard 590.
Tel 0900 687 4242 55.
W heineken-music-hall.nl

Jazzcafé Alto
Korte Leidsedwarsstraat 115.
Map 4 E2.
Tel 020-6263249.
W jazz-cafe-alto.nl

Melkweg
Lijnbaansgracht 234a.
Map 4 E2.
Tel 020-5318181.
W melkweg.nl

Paradiso
Weteringschans 6–8.
Map 4 E2.
Tel 020-6264521.
W paradiso.nl

De Twee Zwaantjes
Prinsengracht 114.
Map 1 C3.
Tel 020-6752729.

Theatre and Cabaret

Bellevue Theater
Leidsekade 90.
Map 4 D2.
Tel 020-5305301.
W theaterbellevue.nl

Boom Chicago
Rozentheater
Rozengracht 117.
Tel 0900 BOOM CHICAGO.
Map 1 A5.
W boomchicago.nl

De Brakke Grond
Vlaams Cultureel
Centrum, Nes 45.
Map 2 D5.
Tel 020-6266866.
W brakkegrond.nl

Frascati
Nes 63.
Map 2 D5.
Tel 020-6266866.
W frascati.nl

De Kleine Komedie
Amstel 56–58.
Map 5 B3.
Tel 020-6240534.
W dekleinekomedie.nl

Koninklijk Theater Carré
Amstel 115–125.
Map 5 B3.
Tel 0900 252 5255.
W theatercarre.nl

Westergasfabriek
Haarlemmerweg 8–10.
Map 1 A1.
Tel 020-5860710.
W westergasfabriek.com

Cinema

City Theater
Kleine Gartmanplantsoen 15–19.
Map 5 C3.
Tel 0900 1458.

Kriterion
Roetersstraat 170.
Map 5 C3.
Tel 020-6231708.

Pathé de Munt
Vijzelstraat 15.
Map 4 F1.
Tel 0900 1458.

Tuschinski
Reguliersbreestraat 24–36. **Map** 5 A2.
Tel 0900 1458.

Uitkijk
Prinsengracht 452.
Map 4 E2.
Tel 020-6237460.

Clubs and Discos

AIR
Amstelstraat 16. **Map** 5 A2.
Tel 020-8200670.
W air.nl

Amstel 54
Amstel 54. **Map** 5 A2.
Tel 06-29557092.

Escape
Rembrandtplein 11.
Map 5 A2.
Tel 020-6221111.
W escape.nl

Hotel Arena
's-Gravesandestraat 51.
Map 6 D4.
Tel 020-8502400.
W hotelarena.nl

Jimmy Woo
Korte Leidsedwarsstraat 18. **Map** 4 E2.
Tel 020-6263150.
W jimmywoo.com

NYX
Reguliersdwarsstraat 42.
Map 4 F1. W clubnyx.nl

Odeon
Singel 460. **Map** 4 F1.
Tel 020-5218555.
W odeon.amsterdam.nl

Prik
Spuistraat 109. **Map** 1 C5.
Tel 020-3200002.
W prikamsterdam.nl

Queers Café
Amstel 60. **Map** 5 A2.
Tel 06-51421222.

Rain
Rembrandtplein 44.
Map 5 A2. **Tel** 020-6267078.
W rain-amsterdam.com

Saarein II
Elandstraat 119.
Map 1 B5.
Tel 020-6234901.
W saarein.nl

Sugar Factory
Lijnbaansgracht 238.
Map 4 E2.
Tel 020-6270008.
W sugarfactory.nl

Vive La Vie
Amstelstraat 7. **Map** 5 A2.
Tel 020-6240114.
W vivelavie.net

Volkshotel
Wibautstraat 150.
Map 5 C1.
Tel 020-2612100.
W volkshotel.nl

Spectator Sports

Ajax Amsterdam Football team
W english.ajax.nl

Olympic Stadium
Oud Zuid.
Tel 020-3054400.
W olympischstadion.nl

STREET FINDER

The page grid superimposed on the *Area by Area* map below shows which parts of Amsterdam are covered in this *Street Finder*. Map references given for all sights, hotels, restaurants, shopping and entertainment venues described in this guide refer to the maps in this section (the *road map* is to be found on the book's inside back cover). An index of street names and places of interest marked on the maps is on pages 162–3. The key below indicates the maps' scale and other features marked on them, including transport terminals, emergency services and information centres. All major sights are clearly marked.

0 metres 500
0 yards 500

Key to Street Finder

- Major sight
- Place of interest
- Other building
- **M** Metro station
- Train station
- Coach station
- Tram stop
- Bus stop
- Tour boat boarding point
- Canalbus boarding point
- Museum boat boarding point
- *i* Tourist information office
- Hospital with casualty unit
- Police station
- Church
- Synagogue
- **C** Mosque
- Railway line
- Pedestrianized street

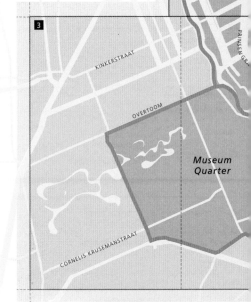

Scale of Map Pages 1–6

0 metres 250
0 yards 250
1:11,250

Fresh fruit for sale in the Noordermarkt *(see p115)*

House with an elevated neck gable
(see p101) on the Geldersekade

Magere Brug, the city's most
famous bridge *(see p118)*

Street Finder Index

Each place name is followed by its arrondissement number and then by its Street Finder reference

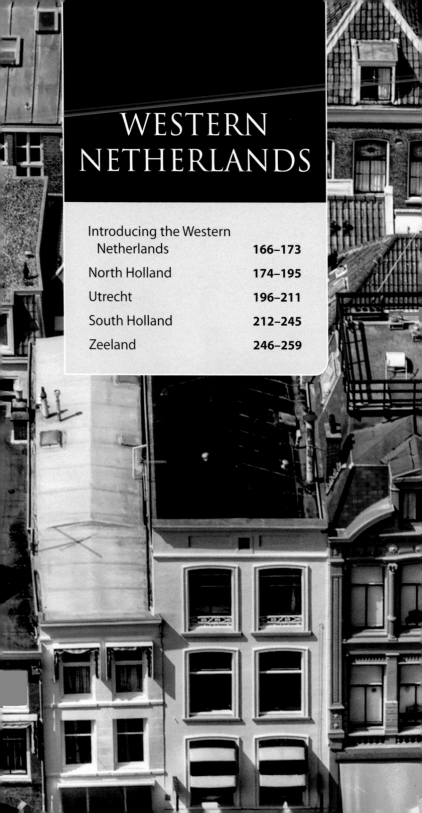

WESTERN NETHERLANDS

Western Netherlands at a Glance

The landscape of the Western Netherlands is strongly influenced by the old ports and commercial towns, which claim a prosperous past. During the 20th century, the most important ones grew together to form the Randstad *(see pp170–71)*. But you can still find plenty of quiet outside the cities – in Europe's biggest coastal dune area, boasting its distinct flora and fauna; along the Vecht, with its pretty country houses; and along rivers such as the Vlist and the Linge. Main watersports areas are Zeeland, on the IJsselmeer and the lakes in the peat region.

The Gothic Sint Bavo Church in Haarlem *(see p188)*, known colloquially as the Grote Kerk, was built between 1400 and 1550. This gigantic building dominates the Grote Markt. Sint Bavo has one of the finest organs in Europe, built by Christiaan Müller.

The Mauritshuis at The Hague *(see pp226–7)* was built by Pieter Post in 1644 as instructed by Johan Maurits van Nassau, in the style of North Netherlands Neo-Classicism. Since 1821 it has been the home of the royal painting collection. This compact collection includes a number of first-rate works by old masters, including Rembrandt, Jan Steen and Johannes Vermeer.

The Hag

Brielle

Goedereede   Hellevo

Westenschouwen

Zierikzee

Middelburg   Goes

Vlissingen

ZEELAND
(See pp246–59)

Terneuzen   Hulst

Sluis

Construction of the Oosterschelde Stormvloedkering (storm surge barrier) *(see pp250–51)* was prompted by the disastrous floods of 1953. To combat the water while preserving the unique mud-flat bed of the Oosterschelde, a half-open multiple buttress dam with 62 sliding gates was built.

◄ Colourful rooftops of Utrecht city, as seen from the Dom tower

Den Helder

Wieringerwerf

Callantsoog

Enkhuizen

Hoorn

Alkmaar

NORTH HOLLAND
(See pp174–95)

Zaanstad

Purmerend

The Zuiderzeemuseum in Enkhuizen *(see pp180–81)* is dedicated to the history of the fishing ports of the Zuiderzee. Access to the North Sea was closed off in 1932 by the Afsluitdijk (barrier dam). Enkhuizen is enjoying renewed prosperity with the opening of the museum and the conversion of the fishing port to a marina.

aarlem

AMSTERDAM
(See pp64–163)

Aalsmeer

Amstelveen

Hilversum

eiden

Alphen aan den Rijn

Amersfoort

UTRECHT
(See pp196–211)

Utrecht

Woerden

Veenendaal

Rhenen

OUTH OLLAND
e pp212–45)

Gouda

otterdam

Ridderkerk

Dordecht

Gouda *(see p243)* is one of the many commercial towns in the Western Netherlands that also has its prime position on the waterways to thank for its period of prosperity. The spirit of liberalism prevalent in Gouda during the 16th and 17th centuries protected the magnificent St Janskerk from the Iconoclasm, meaning that the Gouda stained glass is still here to be enjoyed today.

0 kilometres   20

0 miles   10

The Rietveld Schröderhuis in Utrecht *(see pp208–9)* is a famous example of "nieuwe bouwen" (new building). It was Rietveld's first complete architectural work and reveals his background as a furniture maker. At the time it was considered to be radically modern. Visitors nowadays are struck by the modesty and human proportions of the house.

Reclaimed Land

The Netherlands is continually increasing in size. Various methods of reclaiming land have been employed as far back as the 11th century. One fairly simple method was to build a dyke around a marshy area. Later, deep lakes were drained with the help of windmills. The far-reaching IJsselmeer polders – fertile farmlands – were created after the Zuiderzee was closed off using ingenious reclamation methods. Even now, huge efforts are being made to extend areas of reclaimed land – hence the new Amsterdam residential area of IJburg, which has sprung up from the IJmeer.

To create a polder, a ditch was first dredged. The dredgings were used to build up the dyke.

Gradual Drainage

To overcome the height difference between the polder and the ring canal, which is sometimes large, the water is continually raised metre by metre by three windmills placed in a row, known as a *driegang* or row of three.

Because a polder lies some metres below sea level, the ground water level is always very high and has to be continually drained.

Lower windmill

Middle windmill

Lower reservoir

Polder canal

Land Reclamation

About 3,000 years ago, houses were built on mounds so that they would not be flooded when the water rose. As far back as the 4th to 8th centuries, dykes were built around the houses and land. Land reclamation was carried out on a large scale from the 11th century, when the population increased sharply. In the 17th and 18th centuries, deeper lakes were drained with the help of rows of windmills. The steam engine meant a new phase of land reclamation: it was now finally possible to control the Haarlemmermeer. It is thought that, in Leeghwater's time, at least 160 windmills were necessary for this. In 1891, the engineer C Lely put forward a plan to close off the treacherous Zuiderzee. This only actually happened in 1932, when the Afsluitdijk (barrier dam) was completed. Construction of the IJsselmeer polders then got underway.

Many dyke houses are facing a threat to their continued existence because of the raising of the river dykes.

The Markermeer in the IJsselmeer has become congested with mud and silt. Vereniging Natuurmonumenten is creating islands using mud from the lake, thus cleaning up the water and developing a viable habitat for flora and fauna. It will be open for visitors from 2020.

The old port of Schokland *(see p330)* now lies firmly on the mainland

This view is of the oldest polder in North Holland (anonymous, c.1600). The West Friesland Omringdijk, which runs around Het Grootslag, is 126 km (78 miles) long and was completed as far back as 1250. North Holland ceased to exist to the north of the dyke.

Upper windmill

Archimedes' screw

Middle reservoir

The ring dyke stems the water from the ring canal.

Seepage channel

At low tide the ring canal can drain the water pumped out of the polder.

In the 16th century, Jan Adriaansz. Leeghwater invented a system that used windmills to drain a lake after a ring canal had been constructed around it. This meant that it became relatively easy to pump dry deeper and larger lakes, giving rise to the first pieces of reclaimed land.

Conquering the Sea

God created the earth – except Holland, for the Dutch did that. This statement by the French poet Voltaire comes close to the truth. This is because since the 14th century, the surface area of the Netherlands has increased by approximately 10 per cent, thanks to land reclamation. Land continues to be extended today, with the construction, for example, of IJburg, a new area of Amsterdam, which was built on an island in the IJmeer.

1860 Land could be drained only by using windmills. Limited areas were reclaimed.

1900 Thanks to the steam engine, increasingly lower-lying polders, such as the Zuidplaspolder, at -6.74 m (-22 ft), could be drained.

2000 The new Amsterdam district of IJburg is built in the IJmeer using the most modern methods available.

The Randstad

It appears that the term Randstad (literally, "rim city") was introduced by Albert Plesman, managing director of Dutch airline KLM, which was established in 1919. Apparently he pointed out to the passengers on one of his airplanes the horseshoe-shaped band of towns formed by Utrecht, Amsterdam, Haarlem, Leiden, The Hague, Rotterdam and Dordrecht. The relatively undeveloped area in the middle was quickly named the Groene Hart ("green heart").

By 2025 the population in the Randstad is set to grow by 700,000.

Groene Hart

The Groene Hart is a man-made landscape formed from an association with water that has lasted for centuries. It is characterized by elongated pieces of reclaimed land, peat lakes and river landscape with marshes and pools. The most important agrarian activity is dairy-cattle breeding; the cheese produced here is world-famous. Environmental organizations are dedicated to developing and protecting natural resources and historical landscapes. In De Venen, which surrounds the Nieuwkoopse and Vinkeveense lakes, a project is underway to combine extensive arable farming, natural development of the environment, and recreation facilities. It is hoped that this type of project will provide a balance to urbanization.

Hiking and cycling paths have been erected throughout the Groene Hart. They pass dairy farms, windmills and old villages. Visit the local VVV (tourist board) for more information on recreational paths.

Congestion is a major problem. During rush hour periods, the Randstad is clogged by traffic jams. The government is trying to reduce congestion on the roads by improving public transport and introducing other measures, such as road pricing. Up until now, this has not met with much success. The number of cars in the Randstad is constantly increasing. *Transferiums*, or park-and-rides, are meant to free up the town centres, which often still have old infrastructure and are not geared to a lot of traffic.

Car-pooling is another way of reducing the number of cars. Over 750,000 people have car-pooled in the last few years.

IJburg is a new district, built on the IJmeer to the east of Amsterdam. Another plan for municipal expansion into the water is Nieuw Holland, a long, narrow piece of land in front of the coast between Scheveningen and Hoek van Holland.

Schiphol was, in the last decade, the fastest-growing airport in Europe. It benefits from a central location – close to many of Holland's major cities – and good rail and road connections. Expansion of the airport was halted by the objections of residents and environmental groups, but after considering other locations, such as an artificial island in the North Sea, Schiphol will indeed expand into adjacent areas.

Growth of the Randstad

As far back as the end of the 15th century, the Western Netherlands was one of the most urbanized regions of Europe. It was only during the 20th century that the borders between the towns became blurred and what is now known as the Randstad emerged. At present 6.5 million people live here.

Randstad around 1900

Randstad around 1950

Randstad around 2000

In contrast, the Groene Hart has only 600,000 inhabitants. Earnings in the Randstad account for half of the gross national product. The main product is provision of services, with Amsterdam as the financial centre, The Hague as the administrative centre, Hilversum as the focus of the audiovisual media and Rotterdam-Rijnmond and Schiphol as an important port and airport respectively.

Dunes

The Dutch coast is famous for its dunes. These natural sea walls, with a vegetation of their own, were used in earlier times as common ground for cattle grazing (the *oerol, see p278*) in the absence of sufficient grassland. They now play an important role in the purification of water. The dunes are also a particularly popular recreational area – many of the protected dune areas are open to ramblers and cyclists.

A catamaran on the beach

Marram grass is a sturdy plant whose root system holds new dunes together. It plays an important role in the formation and protection of Holland's dunes.

The sea supplies the sand from which the dunes are built.

On the beach, the dry, white sand drifts and piles up.

A sea inlet is forme the sea breaks thro row of dunes.

Water collection is done by way of the dunes, which retain the fresh water that falls inside them in the form of precipitation. Drinking water has been collected since the 19th century from the dunes of North and South Holland (such as at Meyendel, near Wassenaar, pictured above), helping to eliminate diseases like cholera from densely populated cities.

Nature Reserves

The dunes are being used less and less as areas for water collection, meaning that the groundwater level is rising again and the damp dunes can once again be established. Protected against such environmentally damaging influences as industry and land development, they are becoming important nature reserves where there is a great deal for hikers and cyclists to enjoy. Vegetation includes gorse, spindle trees, creeping willow and hawthorn. Resident and migratory birds, such as curlews, tawny pipits and sometimes ospreys, inhabit the dunes. During World War II, anti-tank trenches with steep banks were built in the Midden-Heeren dunes (in Nationaal Park Zuid-Kennemerland). Today, even the rare kingfisher feels at home there.

The Dutch coast seriously damaged by storms

Rabbits may look cute, but they have been known to seriously undermine the dunes with their intricate network of burrows.

The first row of dunes, golden in colour because of the overgrowth, has higher summits.

The dune valleys have their own particular vegetation.

Origins

Dunes are created by a process which can be seen time and time again during a stormy day on the country's long, flat beaches. The sand carried by the sea dries on the surface of the beach and is then dragged by the wind like a white shroud over the beach. Held back by any obstacles in its way, the sand starts to accumulate. If the obstacle is a plant, a dune begins to form. Plants involved in forming dunes are called pioneer plants. They must be able to tolerate being buried by the sand and also be able to grow back through the sand. Sand couch grass *(Elymus farctus)* is renowned for being one such plant. After the initial dune formation, marram grass often begins to stabilize the new dune with its enormous root system. Dunes along the coast of the Netherlands can become as high as 10 m (33 ft). The dunes here – new dunes – were formed after 1200. When the sea breaks through dunes which have collapsed or have been cut through, it creates a sea inlet, or channel, around which an entire vegetation system develops, attracting all types of birds.

Sea holly and bee

Common sea buckthorn

The sea inlet surface is home to many types of bird.

The dune overgrowth becomes richer as it moves inland, as limestone is replaced by humus.

The Beachcomber gazes out to sea near the North Holland Camperduin, at the start of the Hondsbossche sea wall. The wall was constructed in the 19th century when the sea broke through the dunes. The lessons learned from this were used when building North Holland's Noorder- kwartier (north district).

Bulb fields are evidence that the bulbs thrive in the sandy dune soil. The blooms' vivid colours are a pretty contrast to the yellowish-grey colour of the dunes.

NORTH HOLLAND

Although North Holland's landscape is mainly flat, it is by no means featureless. Low-lying polders, with windmills and grazing cows, give way to market gardens and colourful bulb fields. Around Amsterdam the land is more built-up, with lively towns and picturesque villages almost cheek by jowl.

North Holland has always been one of the most important areas of the Netherlands economically, due to its industry, fishing and commerce. The Zuiderzee ports played a major part in the voyages of the Dutch East India Company *(see p52)*, and their merchants became wealthy from the trade in exotic imports. They built splendid houses and filled them with expensive furniture and fine art, much of which has found its way into the province's leading museums.

This part of the country has learned to live with and profit from water. The province is bordered by it on three sides, with the unpredictable North Sea to the west and the vast IJsselmeer (formerly the Zuiderzee) to the east. The flat land in between is bisected by two major canals; one connects Zaandam to Den Helder in the north, while the other, the important North Sea Canal, gives Amsterdam's busy port access to the North Sea at IJmuiden. Land reclamation, at which the Dutch excel, has been going on since the 14th century, and many historical island communities are now surrounded by dry land.

Tourism is a major industry in North Holland, with Schiphol, the country's major airport, at its heart. The North Sea coast has a string of delightful resorts and sea-front hotels among the dunes, while in the communities on the IJsselmeer such as Edam, famous for its cheese, and picturesque Volendam, you can still find villagers wearing traditional costume and the famous Dutch wooden clogs.

Enkhuizen, a fine historical fishing town on the IJsselmeer

◀ IJsselmeer Dam in the northern Netherlands

Exploring North Holland

The landscape of North Holland is varied and contains many old buildings and fine museums. The province can be easily explored on day trips from Amsterdam but areas such as West Friesland and Het Gooi, a woodland east of Amsterdam, are worth a longer visit. You can also alternate sightseeing with more relaxing activities such as walking in the beautiful nature reserve de Kennemerduinen (Kennemer dunes) near Zandvoort, sailing on the IJsselmeer or sunbathing on one of the many beaches. Round trips through towns or on rivers are also good ways of exploring the province.

The working windmills on the Zaanse Schans

Getting Around

During rush hour, roads around the large towns in the southern part of the province are fairly congested. Parking is also difficult to find in most of the larger towns and as bus and train connections in the area are good, it's often better to leave the car behind. The northern part of North Holland is also easily reached by public transport or by car on the A7 and A9 motorways. The natural landscape of North Holland lends itself to countless footpaths and cycle routes, each with different characteristics. Bicycles can be hired from most of the region's train stations.

Sights at a Glance

1. Marken
2. Monnickendam
3. Volendam
4. Edam
5. Jisp
6. Zaanse Schans
7. De Beemster
8. *Zuiderzee Museum pp180–81*
9. Enkhuizen
10. Hoorn
11. Broek-in-Waterland
12. Medemblik
13. Den Helder
15. Alkmaar
16. Haarlem
17. Egmond
18. Heemskerk

19. Velsen/IJmuiden
20. Zandvoort
21. Cruquius
22. Ouderkerk aan de Amstel
23. Aalsmeer
24. Amstelveen
25. Muiden
26. Naarden
27. 's-Graveland
28. Hilversum
29. Naardermeer
30. Laren

Tour

14. West Friesland

For map symbols *see back flap*

Juliana

Callantsoo

Schoor

ALKMA.
EGMOND 17
Heiloo

Uitgee

HEEMSKERK 18

VELSEN/ 19
IJMUIDEN

Santpoort

Bloemendaal

HAARLEM 16 Zwane

ZANDVOORT 20

CRUQUIUS 21

Hoofddorp

De Koepoort in Enkhuizen, built in 1649

12 MEDEMBLIK

IJsselmeer

WEST FRIESLAND

8 ZUIDERZEE MUSEUM

9 ENKHUIZEN

Andijk

Wervershoof

Hoogkarspel

14

Wognum

10 HOORN

Schellinkhout

Heerhugowaard

Avenhorn

NOORD-HOLLAND

7

DE BEEMSTER

Oosthuizen

Markermeer

enbeemster

Purmerend

4 EDAM

5 JISP

3 VOLENDAM

ANSE SCHANS

MONNICKENDAM **2**

1 MARKEN

Zaanstad

11 BROEK-IN-WATERLAND

Traditional farm in the "De Beemster" region

AMSTERDAM

oevedorp

Diemen

25 MUIDEN

AMSTELVEEN

24

22

NAARDERMEER **29**

26 NAARDEN

Huizen

OUDERKERK
AAN DE AMSTEL

Bussum

Blaricum

LSMEER

30 LAREN

's-GRAVELAND **27**

28 HILVERSUM

N Helder

Den Oever

reezand

Wieringerwerf

Middenmeer

agen

Abbekerk

oord-charwoude

0 kilometres   10

0 miles   10

Key

— Motorway

— Main road

--- Minor road

— Scenic route

--- Main railway

— Minor railway

— Regional border

❶ Marken

Road map C3. ⚅ 2,000. ⛴ 🚌 from Volendam. **W** vvv-waterland.nl

For almost eight centuries, Marken was a fishing community that saw little change. The construction of a causeway link to the mainland in 1957 put an end to its isolation. The island, however, has kept its original atmosphere, retaining its wooden houses built on mounds and piles to guard against flooding. Het Paard Lighthouse is a famous landmark. **Marker Museum**, located in six historic houses, gives a flavour of past and present life in Marken. There is also a cheese factory and clog-making workshop.

🏛 Marker Museum
Kerkbuurt 44–47. **Tel** 0299-601904.
Open Apr–Oct: 10am–5pm daily. 🅿
♿ **W** markermuseum.nl

❷ Monnickendam

Road map C3. ⚅ 10,000. 🚌
ℹ Zuideinde 2 (0299-820046).
🛍 Sat. **W** vvv-waterland.nl

This old town on the Gouwzee, founded by monks, has buildings dating back to the 17th and 18th centuries, including the *stadhuis*, or town hall, and the Waag, or weigh house. The **Museum de Speeltoren** explains the town's history. It is located in the Stadhuis

Traditional dress, today worn as costume at Volendam's fishery

clock tower, with its 15th-century carillon: every hour, clockwork horsemen parade outside.

🏛 Waterlandsmuseum de Speeltoren
Noordeinde 4. **Tel** 0299-652203.
Open Apr–Oct: 11am–5pm Tue–Sat; Nov–Mar: 11am–5pm Sat & Sun. 🅿
W despeeltoren.nl

❸ Volendam

Road map C3. ⚅ 21,000. 🚌
ℹ Zeestraat 37 (0299-363747).
🛍 Sat. **W** vvv-volendam.nl

This old fishing village on the IJsselmeer is world-famous, attracting a huge number of tourists. The village is built along a dyke; at its small harbour, you can still buy all sorts of fish. Traditional costume is one of

this town's biggest attractions: the women wear tight bodices, lace caps and brightly striped skirts; the men, loose trousers and jackets. You too can dress up and have your photo taken. On the other side of the dyke is a different Volendam: an ancient, atmospheric maze of narrow streets, wooden houses and little canals.

❹ Edam

Road map C3. ⚅ 7,200. 🚌
ℹ Damplein 1 (0299-315125).
🛍 Wed; cheese market: Jul–Aug: 10:30am–12:30pm Wed.
W vvv-edam.nl

Edam is known worldwide for the rounds of cheeses covered with red wax it exports. (Yellow wax is used if for local consumption.) Visit the cheese market on Wednesday mornings in July and August to see how they are sold. Founded in the 12th century, the town has many historical buildings, including the brightly painted **Waag** (weigh house). The 17th-century stained-glass windows in the **Grote Kerk** are considered some of the finest in Holland.

The **Edams Museum** is located in a 16th-century merchant's house. Here you can see 17th-century portraits of famous Edammers, such as Trijntje Kever, who was supposedly 2.8 m (9 ft) tall.

🏛 Edams Museum
Damplein 8. **Tel** 0299-372644.
Open Apr–Oct: Tue–Sun. **Closed** 27 Apr. 🅿 **W** edamsmuseum.nl

Distinctive 17th-century wooden houses at Marken

Typical Dutch windmill on the Zaanse Schans

❺ Jisp

Road map B3. 760. ℹ 0299-472718. W **laagholland.com**

The old whaling village of Jisp, on one of the many former Zuiderzee islands, has a 17th-century feel. The *stadhuis* (town hall) and *dorpskerk* (village church) are worth a visit. The village lies in the middle of the **Jisperveld**, a nature reserve which is home to many different birds, such as lapwings, black-tailed godwits, redshanks, ruffs and spoonbills. This is a lovely spot to cycle, row, fish or, in the summer, visit on an excursion. The tourist office, VVV, has information about the various excursions offered.

❻ Zaanse Schans

Road map C3. Schansend 7, Zaandam. 50. Tel 075-6810000. **Open** 9am–5pm daily, some buildings closed weekdays in winter. W **zaanseschans.nl**

The Zaanse Schans is the tourist heart of the Zaan region. This open-air museum, created in 1960, has typical Zaan houses, windmills and buildings. When it's windy, you will be able to see the windmills working. The products (oil, paint, mustard) are for sale. All the houses are built from timber, as stone houses would sink at once into the soft peat earth. Also, at the time they were built, wood was readily available from local sawmills.

A visit to Zaanse Schans will also reveal **Albert Heijn's** first shop from 1887, a baking museum and cheese factory. The **Zaans Museum** showcases the history of the region. Pleasure boats offer trips on the Zaan.

🏛 Zaans Museum
Schansend 7, Zaandam. **Tel** 075-6810000. **Open** 10am–5pm daily. **Closed** 1 Jan, 25 Dec. W **zaansmuseum.nl**

Environs
At the **Molenmuseum** (windmill museum) at Koog on the Zaan, you will learn everything you need to know about the windmills of the Zaan region. It is located in an 18th-century wooden house.

Haaldersbroek, opposite the Zaanse Schans, was once a boating village with narrow locks, brick paths and typical Zaan houses and farmhouses. Here, you'll feel as though you've gone back in time.

🏛 Molenmuseum
Museumlaan 18, Koog a/d Zaan. **Tel** 075-6288968. **Open** Tue–Sun. **Closed** 1 Jan, Easter Sun, Whitsun. W **zaanschemolen.nl**

❼ De Beemster

Road map B3. VVV Middenbeemster (0299-621826). W **beemsterinfo.nl**

The Beemster was once a lake that was drained in 1612 by **Jan Adriaansz Leeghwater** *(see p167)*. This unusual region has hardly changed since the 17th century, and in 1999 it was named a World Heritage Site by UNESCO. You can see historic objects and period rooms in the **Museum Betje Wolff**.

🏛 Museum Betje Wolff
Middenweg 178, Middenbeemster. **Tel** 0299-681968. **Open** May–Sep: 11am–5pm Tue–Fri, 2pm onwards Sat–Sun; Oct–Apr: 2–5pm Sun. **Closed** 1 Jan, 27 Apr, 25 Dec.

Czaar-Peterhuisje (Tsar Peter's House)

In 1697, the Russian Peter the Great visited the shipyards of Zaandam in order to learn how the local people built ships. He lodged with Gerrit Kist, a tradesman whom he had employed in St Petersburg. The tsar paid another visit to the town in 1717. The first mention of "Tsar Peter's house" in an official document was in 1780. This led to the tiny wooden house being supplied with a stone casing and foundations for protection. Every year, this humble house attracts a great number of tourists. (Krimp 23, Zaandam, tel. 075-6810000. Open 10am–5pm Tue–Sun; closed 1 Jan, 25 Dec.)

Peter the Great, who stayed in Zaandam twice

❽ Zuiderzeemuseum

Enkhuizen was one of the towns whose economy was based on fishing and which was devastated when its access to the North Sea was blocked in 1932 by the construction of a barrier dam, the Afsluitdijk *(see p168)*. Enkhuizen is today enjoying renewed prosperity with the opening of the Zuiderzeemuseum complex and the restructuring of the fishing port into a marina. The museum consists of an open-air section in the form of a museum-park, and an indoor area with a large number of exhibition spaces for permanent displays and temporary presentations.

★ **Houses from Urk**
Houses from the former island of Urk *(see p330)* have been rebuilt here. Actors portray life at the beginning of the 20th century.

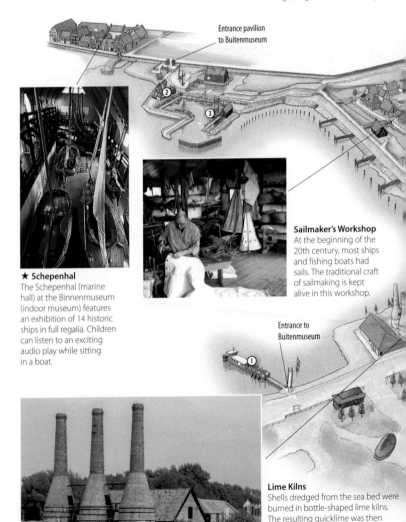

Entrance pavilion to Buitenmuseum

Sailmaker's Workshop
At the beginning of the 20th century, most ships and fishing boats had sails. The traditional craft of sailmaking is kept alive in this workshop.

★ **Schepenhal**
The Schepenhal (marine hall) at the Binnenmuseum (indoor museum) features an exhibition of 14 historic ships in full regalia. Children can listen to an exciting audio play while sitting in a boat.

Entrance to Buitenmuseum

Lime Kilns
Shells dredged from the sea bed were burned in bottle-shaped lime kilns. The resulting quicklime was then used as an ingredient in mortar for brickwork. These ovens come from Akersloot in North Holland.

★ **Contemporary Delft Blue** Hugo Kaagman's paintings juxtapose traditional Delft motifs with present-day designs in refreshing combinations: windmills, tulips and fisherfolk sit beside portraits of popular singers.

VISITORS' CHECKLIST

Practical Information
Wierdijk 12–22, Enkhuizen.
Tel 0228-351111.
🆆 **zuiderzeemuseum.nl**
Indoor and open-air museums
Open Apr–Oct: 10am–5pm daily;
indoor museum also open Nov–
Mar: 10am–5pm daily.
Closed 25 Dec. 🚊 Enkhuizen.
🚤 from the station. ♿ 🖥
✏ 🎒

The Church
The builders of this late-19th-century church, from the island of Wieringen, hid the organ in a cupboard to avoid the tax levied on church organs at that time.

KEY

① **Ferries** take visitors from the station and entrance pavilion to the Buitenmuseum (open-air museum).

② **Monnickendam smoke-houses**

③ **Reconstruction of Marken harbour**

④ **Costume Chest** allows visitors to dress up in traditional outfits.

⑤ **Shipbuilding and repairs**

⑥ **A working windmill** shows how polder drainage works (see pp168–9).

⑦ **The houses in this area** come from Zoutkamp, a fishing village on what was once the Lauwerszee.

⑧ **Houses from the Zuiderzee island of Urk**

Boats moored at Hoorn harbour

❾ Enkhuizen

Road Map C2. 🚹 18,100. 🚌 🚉
🛈 Tussen Twee Havens 1 (0228-313164). 🛒 Wed.
🅦 enkhuizen.nl

Enkhuizen is still a major port. Its many fine buildings are evidence of the wealth of the Golden Age. The most famous building is the **Drommedaris**, dating back to 1540, used to keep watch over the old port. The city walls also date back to the 16th century. Enkhuizen has two splendid churches, the **Westerkerk** and the **Zuiderkerk**. Summer boat trips to Medemblik, Stavoren and Urk are especially pleasant.

❿ Hoorn

Road Map C3. 🚹 68,000. 🚌 🚉
🛈 Schuitjeskade 1 (0229-855761). 🛒 Sat; Jun–Aug: Wed. 🅦 hoorn.nl

Hoorn's rich past, as the capital of the ancient province of West Friesland and one of the great seafaring towns of the Golden Age *(see pp54–5)*, has produced many beautiful buildings. The Late Gothic **Oosterkerk** has a marvellous Renaissance façade,

just like the St Jans Gashuis. Hoorn's historic past is set out in the **Westfries Museum**. A glimpse of the more recent past and a nostalgic trip down memory lane can be experienced at the **Museum van de Twintigste Eeuw** (Museum of the 20th Century).

🏛 **Westfries Museum**
Rode Steen 1. **Tel** 0229-280022.
Open 11am–5pm Tue–Fri (Apr–Oct: also Mon), 1–5pm Sat & Sun.
Closed 1 Jan, 27 Apr, 3rd Mon in Aug, 25 Dec. 🅦 wfm.nl

🏛 **Museum van de Twintigste Eeuw**
Krententuin 24. **Tel** 0229-214001.
Open 10am–5pm Mon–Fri, from noon Sat–Sun & holidays. **Closed** 1 Jan, 27 Apr, 25 Dec. 🅦 museumhoorn.nl

⓫ Broek in Waterland

Road Map C3. 🚹 2,350. 🚌 🛈 0229-820046. 🅦 waterland.nl

Broek in Waterland's status in the 17th century – as a retreat for sea captains of the East India Company – can still be seen everywhere in the village's crooked streets. The ornate clapboard villas are colour-coded: the captains lived in the pastel-tinted houses and non-seafarers in the ones painted grey. Along the **Havenrak**, the road winding along the lake, fine examples of *kralentuinen*, mosaics made from blue glass beads brought back by merchants from the East Indies, can be seen in several

of the gardens. To explore the village and surroundings from a different perspective, canoes and electric motorboats can be rented from **Kano & Electroboot Waterland** (Drs. J. van Disweg 4, 020-4033209, www.fluisterbootvaren.nl).

⓬ Medemblik

Road Map C2. 🚹 8,000. 🚌
🛈 072-5114284. 🛒 Mon.
🅦 medemblik.nl

Many pretty 17th-century houses can still be found in Medemblik. Also worth a look is **Kasteel Radboud**, built in 1288, and its museum. On the town's outskirts, an old pumping station is home to **Het Nederlands Stoommachinemuseum**, a hands-on collection of steam-driven industrial machinery.

🏛 **Het Nederlands Stoommachinemuseum**
Oosterdijk 4. **Tel** 0227-544732.
Open end Feb–early Nov: Tue–Sun.
🅦 stoommachinemuseum.nl

The 13th-century Kasteel Radboud in Medemblik

⓭ Den Helder

Road Map B2. 🚹 57,000. 🚌
🚉 🛈 Willemsoord 52A (0223-616100). 🛒 Jul & Aug: Tue.
🅦 topvanholland.nl

This town, the base for the Dutch Royal Navy, has a **Marinemuseum** that displays marine history from 1488. At the North Sea Aquarium at Fort Kijkduin, a glass tunnel weaves among the fish.

🏛 **Marinemuseum**
Hoofdgracht 3. **Tel** 0223-657534.
Open May–Oct: daily; Nov–Apr: Tue–Sun. **Closed** 1 Jan, 27 Apr, 25–26 Dec.
🅦 marinemuseum.nl

Riverside setting of Broek in Waterland

Windmills

Since the 13th century, windmills have been an inseparable part of the landscape of Holland. They have been used for a variety of purposes, including milling corn, extracting oil and sawing wood. One of their most important uses was to pump away excess water from the polders *(see pp168–9)*. Windmills consist of a fixed tower and a cap which carries the sails. The cap can be turned so that the sails face the wind. The sails can be very dangerous when they are turning – hence the Dutch saying, *"Een klap van de molenwiek hebben"* ("To be struck by a windmill"), that is, to have a screw loose. The Netherlands had thousands of windmills in earlier times, but since the arrival of modern machines, their number has dropped to just over 1,000. Many of these windmills are still working and are open for visits. *(See also pp28–9.)*

Watermill in the Schermer polder

Modern wind turbines are common in Holland. They supply electricity without the pollution caused by burning oil or coal.

Polder mills for draining became common during the 17th century. Standing in groups, they were each responsible for part of the pumping, through the use of an Archimedes' screw.

Lattice and canvas sail

Drive shaft

Archimedes' screw

Upper reservoir

The cogs are turned by the sails. A rotating spindle makes a cog move, causing the water pump to start working.

Rolled-up canvas

The upper section could be turned on its axis in the wind.

Main spindle

Grain was ground by two millstones.

Wooden sails

The sails were covered with canvas to catch more wind.

Flour was poured into bags through chutes.

Flour Mills

Flour mills were covered with reeds and looked like enormous pepper mills. The millstones were linked to the sails by the spindle and gearwheels and milled wheat, barley and oats.

⑭ West Friesland

During Holland's Golden Age, West Friesland played a major part in the Dutch economy as an important centre for trade and shipping. Nowadays the main inland activity is farming. Watersports bring in the most money on the IJsselmeer coast. If you take the route in spring, you will travel alongside blooming bulb fields and orchards. There is a pleasant bustle along the IJsselmeer in the summer, and part of the route is great for cycling.

Tips for Drivers

Length: 80 km (50 miles)
Places to stop: Cafés and restaurants in any of the villages and towns along the way.
Roads: The roads in West Friesland are good. Along the IJsselmeer you will travel over a narrow, winding dyke where you will certainly encounter many cyclists and walkers.

⑤ **Twisk**
This widespread village has pretty farmhouses, many of which can often be reached only by little bridges.

④ **'t Regthuys, Abbekerk**
This museum has collections of West Friesland clothing, curiosities and – most important for the children – toys.

③ **Stoommachinemuseum (Steam Engine Museum)**
The old steam pumping station "Vier Noorder Koggen" near Medemblik has a unique collection of steam-operated machinery.

0 kilometres 5
0 miles 5

① **Schellinkhout**
This attractive village just a stone's throw from Hoorn has been inhabited since prehistoric times. It once had an old sandy cove of the Zuiderzee.

Key

- ▬ Suggested route
- ▬ Other road
- ▬ Railway line
- - - - Tourist railway
- ☆ Good viewing point
- 🏛 Windmill

② **West Friesland Omringdijk**
In the 13th century, a ring dyke to protect against flooding was built around West Friesland. Through land reclamation, a large proportion of the dyke now lies inland. Two *wiels*, or pools, by the IJsselmeer are reminders of when water broke through the dyke.

Porters carrying cheese on sledges at Alkmaar's traditional cheese market

⑮ Alkmaar

Road map B3. 🔟 94,000. 🚌
🚆 ℹ️ Waagplein 2 (072-5114284).
🏪 Weekly market Sat; cheese
market Fri morning, Apr–Sep.
🌐 vvvhartvannoordholland.nl

This old town has at least 400
monuments, and the street
layout has barely changed over
the centuries. Along the canals,
old merchants' houses and small
courtyards can still be seen. The
Stedelijk Museum depicts the
history of the town through
paintings, videos and models. It
also has a collection of paintings
from the Bergen School of the
1920s and 1930s.

Alkmaar is famous for its
traditional **kaasmarkt** (cheese
market), which is held every
Friday morning from early April to
early September. The large yellow
wheels of cheese arrive by barge.
They are tossed from the barges
by four groups of seven porters
from the 400-year-old cheese
porters' guild. The porters are
dressed in white and divided into
guild groups by the colour of
their hats. The cheese is loaded
onto sledges, which the porters
run with to the **waaggebouw**
(public weigh house), where the
cheese is weighed. Once tasting
has taken place, the cheese is
auctioned off by a system called
handjeklap, with sellers clapping
each other on the hands. The
Kaasmuseum (cheese museum)
at the *waaggebouw* shows both
modern and traditional methods
of dairy farming. A little north

of the cheese market is the
**Nationaal Biermuseum De
Boom**. Housed in an impressive
17th-century building, formerly
the biggest brewery in the town,
the museum explores a
millennium of beer drinking in
the Netherlands. The museum
illustrates, for example, how in
the Middle Ages Alkmaar
lacked a supply of safe
drinking water, so
brewers would
ship barrels of
clean water from
the surrounding
dunes and
streams, and then
make it into beer. The
collection of equipment shows
the beer-making process over
the last 100 years, from copper
vats, kettles, barrels and bottles
to examples of the modern
laboratory technology that

The Renaissance façade of the
weigh house

breweries now use. There is
also a reconstruction of an old
café interior. Under the same
roof is a lovely waterside café
and "tasting house" where 86
different beers, many of them
Dutch, can be sampled.

South of the *kaasmarkt*, on
the corner where Mient meets
Verdronkenoord, is the **vismarkt**
or fish market, which dates
back to the 1500s and was
still in use until 1998. The low,
colonnaded stalls are covered
to protect traders and their
wares from the elements,
and contain brick and stone
benches where catches of fish
were displayed to customers.
The current buildings date
back to the mid-18th century.
Further along Verdronkenoord
is the Sint Laurenskerk or
Grote Kerk. This 15th-century
church has one of the most
important organs in Europe,
built in 1639–46, and is
noteworthy for its painting
on the ceiling depicting
the *Last Judgment*
by Jacob Cornelisz.
van Oostzanen.
The scene was
painted on nine
wooden panels
in 1518–1519.
In 1885, due to
water damage,
the panels were
taken to the Rijksmuseum,
only to return during the
German occupation.

🏛️ **Stedelijk Museum**
Canadaplein 1. **Tel** 072-5489789.
Open 10am–5pm Tue–Sun
(to 7pm on Fri). **Closed** 1 Jan,
27 Apr, 25 Dec. 🅿️ ♿
🌐 stedelijkmuseumalkmaar.nl

🏛️ **Waaggebouw and
Kaasmuseum**
Waagplein 2. **Tel** 072-5114284.
Open Mar & Oct: Mon–Sat, Apr–
Sep: daily; Nov–Feb: Sat. 🅿️ ♿

🏛️ **Nationaal Biermuseum
De Boom**
Houttil 1. **Tel** 072-5113801.
Open Mon–Sat. **Closed** public hols.
♿ 🌐 biermuseum.nl

🏛️ **Grote Kerk**
Koorstraat 2. **Tel** 072-5140707.
Open Apr–May: 10am–4pm Thu–Sat;
Jun–Sep: 10am–4pm Tue–Sun; during
exhibitions. 🌐 grotekerk-alkmaar.nl

The Biermuseum, where a variety of beers
can be sampled

For hotels and restaurants in this region see p397 and pp409–10

⑯ Street-by-Street: Haarlem

Haarlem is the commercial capital of North Holland province and the eighth largest city in the Netherlands. It is the centre of the Dutch printing, pharmaceutical and bulb-growing industries, but there is little sign of this in the delightful pedestrianized streets of the historic heart of the city. Most of the sights of interest are within easy walking distance of the Grote Markt, a lively square packed with ancient buildings, cafés and restaurants. Old bookshops, antique dealers and traditional food shops are all to be discovered in nearby streets.

Statue of Laurens Coster
According to local legend, Haarlem-born Laurens Jansz Coster (1370–1440) invented printing in 1423, 16 years before Gutenberg. The 19th-century statue in the Grote Markt celebrates the claim.

The Hoofdwacht
is a 17th-century former guard house.

Stadhuis
Lieven de Key's allegorical figure of *Justice* (1622) stands above the main entrance. She carries a sword and the scales of justice.

★ **Vleeshal** (1603)
The old meat market is part of the Frans Hals Museum
(see pp190–91).

Grote Markt
The tree-lined market square is bordered with busy pavement restaurants and cafés. It has been the meeting point for the townspeople for centuries.

★ Grote Kerk
The huge church *(see p188)* is dominated by a decorative organ (1735) with soaring pipes, which drew many famous composers to Haarlem.

VISITORS' CHECKLIST

Practical Information
Road Map B3. 🚗 151,000.
🌐 haarlem.nl
ℹ️ Verwulft 11 (0900-6161600).
🏪 Mon & Sat. 🎷 Haarlem Jazz
Festival: end Aug; Bloemen
Corso: end Apr.

Transport
🚇 Stationsplein.

★ Teylers Museum
Physical and astronomical instruments, like this brass electrostatic generator by Pieter van Marum (1784), form part of the collection in this museum of science, technology and art *(see p189)*.

Shops and houses cling to the walls of the Grote Kerk.

JANSSTRAAT

LANGE BEGIJNESTRAAT

KLOKHUIS-PLEIN

WIJDEAPPELAARSTEEG

NAUWEAPPELAARSTEEG

BAKENESSERGRACHT

DONKERE SPAARNE

RIVER SPAARNE

Gravestenenbrug
This lift bridge crosses the river Spaarne. Located on the south bank is the embarkation point for boat trips along the river and canals.

Key

— Recommended route

0 metres   50
0 yards   50

Exploring Haarlem

Haarlem became a city in 1245, and had grown into a thriving clothmaking centre by the 15th century. But the city was sacked in the Spanish siege of 1572–3, and a series of fires wreaked further destruction in 1576. The town's fortunes changed in the 17th century, when industrial expansion ushered in a period of prosperity lasting throughout the Golden Age. The centre was largely rebuilt by Lieven de Key (1560–1627) and still retains much of its character. The Grote Kerk continues to overlook the city's *hofjes* (almshouses), and the brick-paved lanes around the Grote Markt are little changed.

Grote Markt, Haarlem (c.1668) by Berckheijde, showing the Grote Kerk

⬛ Frans Hals Museum
See pp90–91.

⬛ Grote Kerk
Grote Markt 22. **Tel** 023-5532040.
Open 10am–4pm Mon–Sat (Apr–Oct till 5pm). **Closed** Easter, Whitsun, 27 Apr, 5 May, 25 Dec–2 Jan. 🅿 ⬛ 📷
W bavo.nl

The enormous Gothic edifice of Sint Bavo's great church, or Grote Kerk, was a favourite subject of the 17th-century Haarlem School artists Pieter Saenredam (1597–1665) and Gerrit Berckheijde (1639–98). Built between 1400 and 1550, the church and its ornate bell tower dominate the market square. Clinging on to the exterior of the south wall is a jumble of 17th-century shops and houses. The rents raised from these ramshackle, untidy buildings contributed to the maintenance of the church.

Today, the entrance to the Grote Kerk is through one of the surviving shops, a tiny antechamber that leads straight into the enormous nave. The church has a high, delicately patterned, vaulted cedarwood ceiling, white

upper walls and 28 supporting columns painted in greens, reds and golds. The intricate choir screen, like the magnificent brass lectern in the shape of a preening eagle, was made by master metal worker Jan Fyerens in about 1510. The choirstalls (1575) are painted with coats of arms, and the armrests and misericords are carved with caricatures of animals and human heads. Not far away is the simple stone slab covering the grave of Haarlem's most famous artist, Frans Hals.

The Grote Kerk boasts one of Europe's finest and most flamboyant organs, built in 1735 by Christiaan Müller. In 1738 Handel tried the organ and pronounced it excellent. It also found favour with the infant prodigy Mozart, who shouted for joy when he gave a recital on it in 1766. The organ is still often used for concerts, recordings and teaching.

⬛ Stadhuis
Grote Markt 2. **Tel** 023-5115115.
Open by appt only. ⬛

Haarlem's Stadhuis (town hall) has grown rather haphazardly since 1250 and is an odd mixture of architectural styles. The oldest part of the building is the beamed medieval banqueting hall of the counts of Holland, originally known as the Gravenzaal. Much of this was destroyed in two great fires in 1347 and 1351, but the 15th-century panel portraits of the counts of Holland can still be seen.

The wing of the town hall bordering the Grote Markt was designed by Lieven de Key in 1622. It is typical of Dutch Renaissance architecture, combining elaborate gables, ornate painted detail and Classical features, such as pediments over the windows.

In a niche above the main entrance is a plump allegorical figure of Justice, bearing a sword in one hand and scales in the other as she smiles benignly upon the pavement cafés in the market below. To the left, in Koningstraat, an archway leads to the university buildings behind the Stadhuis, where there is a 13th-century cloister and library.

⬛ De Hallen
Grote Markt 16. **Tel** 023-5115775.
Open Tue–Sun. **Closed** 1 Jan, 25 Dec.
📷 **W** dehallen.nl

The Verweyhal (museum of modern art) and the Vleeshal (exhibition space), both in the Grote Markt, are part of the Frans Hals Museum *(see pp190–91)*. The Verweyhal accommodates exhibitions of Dutch Expressionism, the Cobra School *(see p193)*, Impressionism and contemporary works. It is named after the painter Kees Verwey, whose Impressionist still lifes are an important feature of the collection. The heavily ornamented Vleeshal (meat market), just to the west of the church, houses temporary exhibitions of modern

Detail on Vleeshal façade by Lieven de Key

The west gate of the Amsterdamse Poort (1355)

art. It was built in 1602 by the city surveyor, Lieven de Key, and has a steep step gable which disguises the roof line. The extravagantly over-decorated miniature gables above each dormer window bristle with pinnacles. A giant painted ox's head on the façade signifies an earlier function of the building.

🏛 Amsterdamse Poort

Amsterdamsevaart. **Closed** to public.

The imposing medieval gateway that once helped protect Haarlem lies close to the west bank of the river Spaarne. The Amsterdamse Poort was one of a complex of 12 gates guarding strategic transport routes in and out of Haarlem. The gate was built in 1355, though much of the elaborate brickwork and tiled gables date from the late 15th century.

The city defences were severely tested in 1573, when the Spanish, led by Frederick of Toledo, besieged Haarlem for seven months during the Dutch Revolt. The city fathers agreed to surrender the town on terms that included a general amnesty for all its citizens. The Spanish appeared to accept the terms, but once the city gates were opened, they marched in and treacherously slaughtered nearly 2,000 people – almost the entire population of the city.

🏛 Teylers Museum

Spaarne 16. **Tel** 023-5160960. **Open** 10am–5pm Tue–Sat, noon–5pm Sun & holidays. **Closed** 1 Jan, 5 & 25 Dec. 🅿 ♿ 📷 📱 **W** teylersmuseum.nl

This was the first major public museum to be founded in the Netherlands. It was established in 1778 by the silk merchant Pieter Teyler van der Hulst to encourage the study of science and art. The museum's eccentric collection of fossils, drawings and scientific paraphernalia is displayed in Neo-Classical splendour in a series of 18th-century rooms. The two-storey Oval Hall was added in 1779 and contains bizarre glass cabinets full of minerals and cases of intimidating medical instruments. A significant collection of sketches by Dutch and Italian masters, including Rembrandt and Michelangelo, is shown a few at a time.

Tiles depicting various modes of transport, Haarlem Station

🏛 Museum Haarlem

Groot Heiligland 47. **Tel** 023-5422427. **Open** daily. **Closed** 1 Jan, Easter, 27 Apr, Whitsun, 25 Dec. 🅿 ♿ **W** museumhaarlem.nl

Located in one of Haarlem's prettiest streets, Museum Haarlem features an interesting display of artifacts that focuses on the history of the city and its environs. The museum is housed in the St Elisabeth's Gasthuis, a hospital founded in 1597. After extensive restoration, this almshouse was opened as Haarlem's principal historical museum. The present building dates back to 1610. A stone plaque carved above what used to be the main doorway in 1612 depicts an invalid being carried off to hospital. Changing exhibitions connect the past with the present, making it a perfect starting point for exploring the city. Walking tours are also available.

🚉 Haarlem Station

Stationsplein.

The first railway line in the Netherlands opened in 1839 and ran between Haarlem and Amsterdam. The original station, built in 1842, was refurbished in Art Nouveau style between 1905 and 1908. It is a grandiose brick building with an arched façade and rectangular towers. The interior is decorated with brightly coloured tiles depicting various modes of transport. Other highlights are the woodwork of the ticket offices and the highly decorative wrought ironwork, particularly on the staircases.

Gabled houses from the 17th and 18th centuries along the river Spaarne in Haarlem

Frans Hals Museum

Celebrated as the first "modern" artist, Frans Hals (c.1582–1666) introduced a new realism into painting. Although his contemporaries strove for perfect likenesses, Hals knew how to capture his models' characters by using an impressionistic technique. Even at the age of 80, he still painted impressive portraits, such as *De regentessen van het Oude Mannenhuis in Haarlem* (Regentesses of the Old Men's Home in Haarlem) (1664). The Oude Mannenhuis (old men's home) became the Frans Hals Museum in 1913. It also has on show many paintings by other artists from the Dutch Golden Age, as well as 16th- and 17th- century artifacts.

★ **Banket van de Officieren van de St-Jorisdoelen (Banquet of the Officers of the Civic Guard of St George)**
(1616) The features of each of the archers and the luxury of their banquet room are beautifully portrayed in this group portrait by Frans Hals.

Key to Floorplan

- Works by Frans Hals
- Renaissance Gallery
- Old Masters
- Frans Hals' workshop
- The Hals Phenomenon
- Non-exhibition space

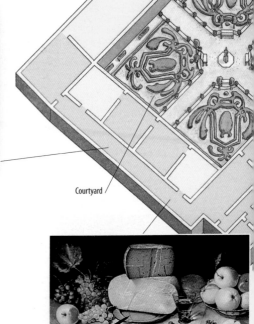

Militia paintings by Hals

Courtyard

Moeder en Kind (Mother and Child)
After the Reformation *(see pp56–7)*, artists such as Pieter de Grebber (1600–53) painted secular versions of religious themes. This work of a mother feeding her child (1622) is reminiscent of Mary with Jesus.

★ **Stilleven (Still Life)** (1613)
Floris Claeszoon van Dyck (1574–1651) was famous for his minute attention to detail and texture.

★ **Mercurius** (1611) Hendrick Goltzius (1558–1617) is particularly well known for his studies of classical nudes. One of a three-part set, this canvas was donated to the museum by a rich Haarlem mayor.

VISITORS' CHECKLIST

Practical Information
Groot Heiligland 62, Haarlem
Tel 023-5115775.
Ⓦ franshalsmuseum.nl
Open 11am–5pm Tue–Sat, noon–5pm Sun & public hols.
Closed 1 Jan, 25 Dec.

St Luke Painting the Virgin and Child (1532), Maerten Jacobsz van Heemskerck. St Luke was the patron saint of artists' professional associations, the Guilds of St Luke. This was painted for the Haarlem Guild.

The Grote Markt in Haarlem, (1696), Gerrit Adriaensz Berckheijde. The Grote Kerk or St Bavokerk, seen here from the west, is built in the Gothic style and is Haarlem's largest church.

Main entrance

Delft Plate (1662) The Grote Markt and Grote Kerk in Haarlem (see p186) are depicted on this earthenware plate by M Eems.

Museum Guide

The best direction to take through the museum is counter-clockwise, as exhibitions of the works of Frans Hals, other portraits, still lifes and pieces of genre paintings are displayed in roughly chronological order. In the Verweyhal and the Vleeshal (see p188) temporary exhibitions are held of modern and contemporary art.

Egmond lighthouse, a welcoming beacon for ships at sea

⓱ Egmond

Road Map B3. 🏠 11,600. 🚌 **i**
Voorstraat 141, Egmond aan Zee (072-5061473). 🅿 Thu. **w** vvvegmond.nl

Egmond is divided into three parts: Egmond aan de Hoef, Egmond-Binnen and the seaside resort of Egmond aan Zee. The counts of Egmond once lived in Egmond aan de Hoef. Only the foundations remain of the **kasteel** (castle), which is open to visitors.

Egmond abbey, in Egmond-Binnen, is the oldest abbey in Holland and Zeeland. This 10th-century structure was destroyed, however, by Sonoy, chief of the Beggars of the Sea *(see p245)*. It was not until 1934 that a new abbey was built; Benedictine monks still live here today. The small **Abdijmuseum** (abbey museum) and **candle factory** can be visited (tel. 072-5062786, www.abdijvanegmond.nl).

⓲ Heemskerk

Road Map B3. 🏠 36,200. 🚌
Tel 020-7026000. 🅿 Fri.
w vvvijmuidenaanzee.nl

An obelisk honouring Dutch artist Maarten van Heemskerck stands in the cemetery of the 17th-century **Hervormde Kerk** (Reformed church). **Slot Assumburg** (Assumburg castle), dating from the 15th century, was built on the site of a 13th-century fortified house. **Slot Marquette** is just as old but acquired its present form only two centuries ago. **Fort Veldhuis** is part of the **Stelling van Amsterdam**, a 135-km (84-mile) defensive line that encircles Amsterdam. It is now a small war museum, dedicated to the sacrifices made by pilots during World War II.

Ⅲ Fort Veldhuis
Genieweg 1. **Tel** 0251-230670.
Open May–Oct: Sun. 🚗 ♿

⓳ Velsen/IJmuiden

Road Map B3. 🏠 67,600. 🚊 🚌 ⛴
i Marktplein 33 (020-7026000).
🅿 Thu.

Holland's largest fishing port is IJmuiden – as visitors can guess from the penetrating smell of fish and the wonderful restaurants in the port. The **Noordersluis** (north lock), which forms part of the North Sea canal lock system, is one of the biggest locks in the world. While coming across you will pass by the Hoogovens (blast-furnaces), where you can take a round trip on a steam train.

The area around Velsen was inhabited in Roman times; archaeological finds are exhibited in the **Ruïne van Brederode**, a 13th-century fortress. You will also feel you are going back in time in the Romanesque **Engelmundus-kerk**. **Buitenplaats Beeckestijn** is one of the many houses built on the coast in the 17th and 18th centuries by rich Amsterdammers. Its gardens, as well as the period rooms on the ground floor, are open to the public.

🏚 Ruïne van Brederode
Velserenderlaan 2, Santpoort. **Tel** 023-5378763. **Open** Mar–Oct: Wed, Fri–Sun ♿ **w** heerlijkheidbrederode.nl

🏚 Buitenplaats Beeckestijn
Rijksweg 136. **Tel** 0255-522877. House: **Open** Thu–Sun. ♿ Garden: **Open** daily. **w** buitenplaatsbeeckestein.nl

⓴ Zandvoort

Road Map B3. 🏠 15,500. 🚊 🚌
i Bakkerstraat 2b (023-5717947).
🅿 Wed. **w** vvvzandvoort.nl

Once a fishing village, Zandvoort is now a modern seaside resort where in the summer half the population of Amsterdam relaxes on the beach or saunters down the busy main street. The village centre still has old fishermen's houses. Zandvoort is famous for its motor racing circuit, where Formula 1 races were once held. It has since been restored and is now attempting to achieve its former status. To escape the crowds, ramble through the **Amsterdamse Waterleidingduinen**.

Circuit Park Zandvoort
Burg. van Alphenstraat 108. **Tel** 023-5740740. **Open** daily. 🚗 during meets. **w** cpz.nl

㉑ Stoomgemaal De Cruquius

Road Map B3. Cruquiusdijk 27. 🚌
Tel 023-5285704. **Open** Mar–Oct: daily; Nov–Feb: Wed, Sat & Sun. 🚗 ♿ **w** museumdecruquius.nl

The Stoomgemaal (steam-driven pumping station) at De Cruquius is one of the three steam-driven pumping stations used to drain the

Slot Assumburg in Heemskerk, a youth hostel since 1933

The Cruquius steam pump at Museum De Cruquius

Haarlemmermeer. It has not been in use since 1933 and is now a museum. The original steam engine is in the machine hall, which has eight pumps moved by beams. An exhibition gives a comprehensive overview of water management in the Netherlands.

㉒ Ouderkerk aan de Amstel

Road Map C3. ⛰ 8,200. 🚌 Amstelveen.

This pretty village at the junction of the Amstel and the Bullewijk rivers has been a favourite with Amsterdammers since the Middle Ages. They had no church of their own until 1330, and worshippers had to travel to the 11th-century Ouderkerk that gave the village its name. The Old Church was

destroyed in a tremendous storm in 1674, and a fine 18th-century church now stands on its site. Today Ouderkerk aan de Amstel is popular with cyclists who come to enjoy its waterfront cafés and restaurants.

㉓ Aalsmeer

Road Map B3. ⛰ 22,900. 🚌 🚆 Tue.

Aalsmeer is famous as the centre for floriculture in the Netherlands (*see pp34–5*). It also holds the biggest **bloemenveiling** (flower auction) in the world; you can take part in the auction from a special gallery.

Many greenhouses are to be seen around Aalsmeer. One important activity here is the development of new varieties and colours of flower. Many modern heroes have a "new" flower named after them.

🚆 **Bloemenveiling Flora Holland**
Legmeerdijk 313. **Tel** 0297-397000.
Open 7–11am Mon–Wed & Fri,
7–9am Thu. 🅿 ⓦ **floraholland.nl**

㉔ Amstelveen

Road Map B3. ⛰ 78,800. 🚌 🚆 Fri.

Amstelveen is home to many interesting modern art museums,

such as **Museum van der Togt**, with its unique collection of glass objects. The **Electrische Museumtramlijn** (Electric Tramline Museum, tel. 020-6737538) keeps the past alive. On Sundays from April to October you can take a return trip from Amsterdam to Amstelveen on a historic tram. The **Amsterdamse Bos** (Amsterdam forest) is lovely for rambling, picnicking or playing sport. The **Bosmuseum** is dedicated to the origins of the forest.

The **Cobra Museum voor Moderne Kunst** (Cobra Museum of Modern Art) concentrates on the work of the Cobra group, established in 1948 by Danish, Belgian and Dutch artists. During its brief existence, Cobra abandoned dreary postwar art and introduced modern art definitively to the Netherlands.

Electric tram, Electrische Museumtramlijn

🏛 **Museum Van der Togt**
Dorpsstraat 50. **Tel** 020-6415754.
Open Wed–Sun. **Closed** 1 Jan,
27 Apr, 25 Dec. 🅿 ⓦ **jvdtogt.nl**

🏛 **Cobra Museum voor Moderne Kunst**
Sandbergplein 1–3. **Tel** 020-5475050.
Open Tue–Sun. **Closed** 1 Jan, 27 Apr,
25 Dec. 🅿 ♿ ⓦ **cobra-museum.nl**

Women, Children, Animals (1951) by Karel Appel in the Cobra Museum

The Muiderslot, built in 1280, a site of many legends

㉕ Muiden

Road Map C3. 6,700.

In the Middle Ages, the pretty town of Muiden was an outpost for Utrecht but later became part of the defence system of the **Stelling van Amsterdam** *(see p192)*, together with fort island **Pampus**. The town is mainly known for its castle, the **Muiderslot**, which is more than 700 years old and was built by Floris V. After his death it was demolished and rebuilt. The most famous inhabitant was the 17th-century poet PC Hooft, who formed the *Muiderkring* (Muiden circle), a circle of friends occupied with literature and music. Most of the castle rooms are furnished in 17th- and 18th-century style. The garden and orchard also retain their former glory. Visitors can take the ferry to Pampus.

Muiderslot
Herengracht 1. **Tel** 0294-256262.
Open Apr–Oct: daily; Nov–Mar:
Sat & Sun. **muiderslot.nl**

Pampus
from Herengracht 33 (Apr–Oct:
Tue–Sun) **Tel** 0294-262326.
pampus.nl

㉖ Naarden

Road Map C3. 17,000.
Sat.

The fortified town of Naarden lies behind a double ring of canals and walls. The original town is thought to have been founded in the 10th century,

then later destroyed and rebuilt around 1350. In the 15th and 16th centuries, it was occupied in turn by the Spanish and the French. The first thing you notice on arrival is the tower of the 14th-century **Grote Kerk**. The church's wooden vaulted ceiling has been beautifully decorated with pictures from the Old and New Testament. Around 400 years ago, Czech priest Comenius fled to the Netherlands, and now lies buried in the 15th-century **Waalse kapel** (Walloon chapel). The Spaanse Huis (Spanish house), which was converted into the Waag (weigh house), is now home to the **Comeniusmuseum**, which explores the life and ideas of the Czech scholar Jan Amos Comenius (1592–1670), who is buried here. The **Nederlands Vestingmuseum** (fortress museum) is in one of the six bastions of the fortress and has an exhibition of the Hollandse Waterlinie, a strip of land

flooded as a defence line in Holland, and of Naarden's eventful past. Costumed gunners regularly demonstrate the ancient artillery. There is a nice walk around the town along the footpaths on the walls.

Comeniusmuseum
Kloosterstraat 33. **Tel** 035- 6943045.
Open Tue–Sun. **Closed** 1 Jan, 27 Apr,
25 Dec, 31 Dec.
comeniusmuseum.nl

Nederlands Vestingmuseum
Westwalstraat 6. **Tel** 035-6945459.
Open 10:30am–5pm Tue–Fri, from
noon Sat & Sun. **Closed** 1 Jan,
27 Apr, 25 Dec.
vestingmuseum.nl

㉗ 's-Graveland

Road Map C3. 9,200.

's-Graveland is a special place in Het Gooi *(see p176)*. In the 17th century, nine country estates were built here for rich Amsterdammers. Just across from these lie the modest houses that belonged to the labourers. Businesses now use the country houses, as the upkeep is too expensive for individuals. Five parks are owned by the Vereniging Natuurmonumenten and are open to visitors. You can learn more at the **Bezoekerscentrum** (visitors' centre).

Bezoekerscentrum Gooi-en Vechtstreek
Noordereinde 54b. **Tel** 035-6563080.
Open Tue–Sun.
natuurmonumenten.nl

Star formation of the fortress of Naarden

Hilversum town hall, finished in yellow brick

❷⑧ Hilversum

Road Map C3. 🛈 Kerkbrink 6. **Tel** 035-5446971. 🚆 84,500. 🚌 🚇 🚍 Wed & Sat. 🅦 vvvhilversum.nl

This dynamic centre in Het Gooi is known as the media centre of the Netherlands, because of the large number of broadcasting companies that have been established here.

Hilversum boasts a busy shopping centre and attractive residential areas with a lot of greenery. Here and there you will see houses and buildings designed by architect Willem Dudok (1884–1974), a representative of the Nieuwe Bouwen. One of his most famous creations is the 1931 **Raadhuis** (town hall), with its towers and beautiful interior (tours are given on Sundays). Its basement holds an exhibition on Dudok and temporary architectural exhibitions. The **Museum Hilversum** combines the Goois Museum and the Dudok Centrum, illuminates the past of Het Gooi and features an archaeological collection. The Neo-Gothic **Sint-Vituskerk**, designed by PJH Cuypers *(see p94)*, with its 98-m (322-ft) tower, dates from 1892 and is worth a visit.

🏛 Museum Hilversum
Kerkbrink 6. **Tel** 035-5339601. **Open** daily. **Closed** 1 Jan, 27 Apr, 25 Dec. 🅦 museumhilversum.nl

❷⑨ Naardermeer

Road Map C3. 🛈 Meerkade 2, Naarden (035-6990000). 🏁 ♿ 🅦 natuurmonumenten.nl

The Naardermeer is an area of lakes and marshland renowned for its breeding colonies of cormorants and purple herons. Several other birds, such as the marsh harrier, the bittern, the reed warbler and the spoonbill, can also be observed here. Unusual orchids, rare mosses and fungi grow here. The Naardermeer is the oldest protected nature reserve in the Netherlands. Its creation was the start of the Vereniging Natuurmonumenten (Nature Reserve Association). The association has set out several walking tours around the area, which are accessible to everyone. From April to November there are guided boat tours on the lakes. Book via 035-6559955 or online. No dogs allowed.

❸⓿ Laren

Road Map C3. 🚆 11,100. 🚌 🚍 Fri.

Alongside pretty villas and country houses, Laren has many converted old farmhouses, a reminder of the time when it was a farming village. In the 19th and early 20th centuries, Laren and its surroundings were the inspiration for many landscape and interior painters, such as Mauve, Israëls and the American W Singer. The **Singer Museum** has been set up in his old house. Here you can see his work and that of other 19th- and 20th-century artists. There is also a sculpture garden. **Sint-Jansbasiliek** (1925) towers above the Brink and its charming restaurants.

🏛 Singer Museum
Oude Drift 1. **Tel** 035-5393939. **Open** Tue–Sun. **Closed** 1 Jan, 27 Apr, 25 Dec. 🏁 ♿ 🅦 singerlaren.nl

---

The Erfgooiers

During the Middle Ages, the farmers of Het Gooi *(see p176)* joined together in a group to regulate the use of the heathland and meadows. From 1404, their rights were held in plough share notes. Members of the group were known as *erfgooiers*, men living in Het Gooi who were descendants of these medieval farmers. The right of use was later converted into common property. The *erfgooiers* had to constantly fight for their rights. From the 19th century onwards, the government strived to disband the group. In 1932, the heathland was sold, as were the meadows after 1965. The Association of *Erfgooiers* was disbanded in 1971.

De Erfgooiers (1907) by F Hart Nibbrig

UTRECHT

The province of Utrecht, with the lively university city of the same name at its heart, has a vast range of attractions for visitors, including farmhouses, mansions, museums and castles, all set in a varied and attractive wooded landscape, and with a fascinating history dating back to Roman times.

The city of Utrecht has its origins in AD 47, when the Romans built a camp by a ford *(trecht)* at the river Rhine, which followed a different course in those days. In 695, Bishop Willibrord established himself here to promote the spread of Christianity. From the 11th century, the church authorities enjoyed not only spiritual but also secular power in this region, which has seen much conflict: over the centuries the counts of Holland, the dukes of Burgundy, the Spaniards, the French and the Germans have all tried to make their mark here.

The region's proximity to Amsterdam has meant that it has been able to share in the capital's prosperity as wealthy merchants and landowners built their mansions and estates along the river Vecht *(see p202).*

In more recent times, the University of Utrecht has been a great source of economic and artistic development, and the city is home to a modern manufacturing industry and major Dutch corporations.

Visitors will enjoy the pretty country-side – ideal for car or cycle touring – the country houses and historic buildings, the street markets and a great variety of attractions ranging from old steam locomotives to barrel-organs and Australian Aboriginal art. But in this eco-conscious country, with its awareness of the need for conservation, it may be the outdoors, with its sparkling lakes and possibilities for leisurely country walks, that will appeal the most.

De Haar castle in Haarzuilens, a Neo-Gothic construction (1892) built by Pierre Cuypers

◀ Koppelpoort, one of Amersfoort's 15th-century gates

Exploring Utrecht Province

The city of Utrecht is the central point of the province and is therefore the ideal base for sightseeing in the surrounding area. The Vinkeveense Plassen (Vinkeveense Lakes) are popular for watersports, and nature lovers will appreciate the woodland area of the Utrecht Heuvelrug. There are castles in Amerongen and Wijk bij Duurstede and numerous imposing country houses along the Vecht. Windmills and working farms can be spotted here and there in the countryside. Many defence points, such as in Woerden, serve as reminders of the turbulent past of this province, which has been at stake during fierce battles more than once.

The Vinkeveense Plassen, formed by peat excavations

The *heksenwaag* (witches' scales) in Oudewater

Getting Around

Larger towns have railway stations; smaller ones can be reached easily by bus. Utrecht, the capital of the province, is the biggest railway junction in the Netherlands and so train connections from this town are excellent. There is also a regional bus station. Utrecht has a highly developed road network and is served by important main roads such as the A2 (north–south) and the A12 (east–west), but there is also a large number of minor roads, tourist routes and cycle paths in the area.

Rhenen, with its characteristic Cuneratoren

Key

▬▬ Motorway
▬▬ Main road
▭▭ Minor road
▬▬ Scenic route
▬▬ Main railway
▬▬ Minor railway
▬▬ National border

For map symbols *see back flap*

Paleis Soestdijk, its park designed by landscape gardener Zocher

Historical centre of Amersfoort, largely still preserved

The Windmill at Wijk by Jacob van Ruisdael *(see p128)*

Sights at a Glance

1. Vinkeveense Plassen
2. Loenen
3. Slot Zuylen
4. Woerden
5. Oudewater
6. Nieuwe Hollandse Waterlinie
7. Country Estates along the Vecht
8. Baarn/Soest
9. Soestdijk
10. Lage Vuursche
11. Bunschoten-Spakenburg
12. *Utrecht pp204–9*
13. Amersfoort
14. Doorn
15. Wijk bij Duurstede
16. Amerongen
17. Rhenen

For hotels and restaurants in this region see p397 and p410

❶ Vinkeveense Plassen

Road Map C3. 🚌 🛥️

De Vinkeveense Plassen (Vinkeveense Lakes) came about through human intervention – this site was once marsh. The thick peat layers have been excavated over the centuries. The large towns in the surrounding area needed peat; sales of this fuel meant that the people here started to earn a decent living. The peat was therefore dug up more and more extensively, eventually leading to a large area of lakes.

Today, the Vinkeveense Lakes attract many watersports lovers, cyclists and walkers. When it's not the breeding season, you can take a rowing boat through the nature reserve of **Botshol**, which is home to marsh and grassland birds.

❷ Loenen

Road Map C3. 🚶 8,350. 🚌 🚏 Tue am.

In the 10th century, this place was called Lona, meaning "water" or "mud". Loenen fell under two jurisdictions and has two courts dating from the beginning of the 18th century. Loenen on the Vecht is famous for its rural atmosphere, castles and country estates complete with coach houses,

Stately Slot Zuylen, where Belle van Zuylen lived in the 18th century

summerhouses and boathouses, built over the centuries. It is now a protected village.

Kasteel Loenersloot, built on the bank of the Angstel, is one of Loenen's oldest country estates. The building dates back to the 13th century, though only the round defence tower remains; the rest dates from the 17th and 18th centuries.

🏠 **Kasteel Loenersloot**
Rijksstraatweg 211. 📷 Apr–Oct: Thu & Sat. 🔲 utrechtslandschap.nl/loenersloot

Loenen on the Vecht still boasts an aristocratic appearance

❸ Slot Zuylen

Road Map C4. 🚌 36,120. Castle: Tournooiveld 1, Oud-Zuilen. **Tel** 030-2440255. **Open** Apr–Oct: 11am–5pm Tue–Sun; Nov–Mar: 11am–5pm Sat & Sun. **Closed** 1 Jan, 27 Apr, 25, 26 & 31 Dec. 🦽 📷 🔲 **slotzuylen.nl**

The original U-shaped castle was built around 1520 on the remains of a medieval residential tower. At the beginning of the 16th century, a new castle was built on the foundations of the old house and the gateway was added. Up to the 18th century, extensive rebuilding brought the castle into line with contemporary architectural style.

The author Belle van Zuylen (1740–1805) was one of the castle's most famous inhabitants. She was renowned for her correspondence at home and abroad, which she cleverly used to show her modern attitude. Several rooms are furnished as they were when she resided here.

The serpentine wall that runs alongside the castle is interesting because its unique shape provides so much protection that even in this cool sea climate, subtropical fruits such as peaches and grapes can flourish here.

❹ Woerden

Road Map C4. 🚗 34,800. 🚉 🚌
🚢 Sat am.

Woerden came into being on the dykes along the Rhine and Lange Linschoten. Granted its town charter in 1372, it has been besieged many times but always managed to hold out. Between 1575 and 1576, during the Thirty Years War, the Spaniards tried to conquer Woerden, as did the French in 1672, but neither invader succeeded in capturing the town. Impenetrable **kasteel van Woerden** (Woerden castle), built between 1405 and 1415, was extensively restored around 1990.

In the 18th century, the **Oude Hollandse Waterlinie** (old Holland waterline) – a strip of land flooded as a defence line – was extended, thereby strengthening Woerden.

❺ Oudewater

Road Map C4. 🚗 10,000. 🚌
🛈 Leeuweringerstraat 10 (0348-561628). 🚢 Wed. 🅦 oudewater.net

This little town, thanks to its favourable position on the IJssel and the Linschoten, became a prosperous town early on and, by 1265, had been granted its city charter. The counts of Holland and the bishops of

Nesting storks in Oudewater

Utrecht fought fiercely for Oudewater, which was converted into a border stronghold by Floris V. In 1349, Oudewater was captured by Jan van Arkel, the Bishop of Utrecht. In 1572, Oudewater sided with the Prince of Orange and, as a result, the town was seized in 1575 by the Spanish. They exacted a bloody revenge by burning the town to the ground. Oudewater flourished again during Holland's Golden Age.

The town's most famous attraction is the scales, dating from the 16th century, better known as the **heksenwaag** (witches' scales). Women who were suspected of witchcraft came here to be weighed. If their weight and their outward appearance tallied, they were given a certificate as proof of

their innocence. Oudewater was the only place where "witches" could be legally weighed in public.

🏛 **Heksenwaag**
Leeuweringerstraat 2. **Tel** 0348-563400.
Open Apr–Oct: 11am–5pm Tue–Sun; Jun–Aug: daily; Nov–Mar: 11am–5pm Sat & Sun. 🅿 ♿ ground floor.
🅦 heksenwaag.nl

❻ Nieuwe Hollandse Waterlinie

Road Map C3–C4.
🅦 hollandsewaterlinie.nl

The Nieuwe Hollandse Waterlinie (New Dutch Inundation Line), laid out from 1815 to 1940, is comprised of 68 forts and public works, from Muiden and Naarden in North Holland to Werkendam in North Brabant. Utrecht has 27 installations, more than any other province. The Waterlinie was intended as a defence against invading armies; a wide strip of land would simply be flooded. Utrecht's installations are now being protected, and have been put forward for UNESCO's World Heritage Site register. The original reconnaissance positions and unimpeded lines of fire will hopefully be preserved. The best installations are at Rijnauwen, Groenekan and Tull and 't Waal.

"Bombproof" barracks of the Nieuwe Hollandse Waterlinie (Fort Rijnauwen, Bunnik)

❼ Country Estates along the Vecht

Country estate houses, with their summerhouses, magnificent railings and extensive gardens, can be seen threaded along the Vecht, especially between Maarssen and Loenen. They were built in the 17th and 18th centuries by wealthy Amsterdam inhabitants who wanted to escape the noise and stench of the city in the summer. The estates were status symbols, places where city-dwellers could devote themselves to hobbies such as tree cultivation, hunting and still-life painting.

VISITORS' CHECKLIST

Practical Information
Road Map C4. Vechtstreek-museum: Diependaalsedijk 19, Maarssen. **Tel** 0346-554440.
Open May–Sep: 11am–5pm Wed–Sun; Oct–Apr: 2–5pm Wed–Sun. 🚗 ♿ ground floor.

Goudestein in Maarssen

One of the first country estates in the Vecht, Goudestein was built in 1628 by Joan Huijdecoper. The present building, which dates from 1775, is now used as government offices. The coach house is now a fascinating pharmacy museum.

Nijenrode
A university has now been set up in this castle formerly belonging to the Lords of Nijenrode.

The chimneys were considered to be decorative elements.

The coat of arms of the Huijdecoper family decorates the façade.

The entrance has an impressive flight of stone steps.

The house contains a grand staircase and rooms furnished with decorative drapes. One of the rooms is now used for wedding ceremonies.

Between Breukelen and Loenen the Vecht resembles an architectural museum. The country estates (Vechtvliet is shown here) are surrounded by established parks and ornamental outbuildings.

❽ Baarn/Soest

Roadmap C3. 🚉 🚌 🏛 70,000.
🛈 Van Weedestraat 131, Soest (035-7400074). 🛥 Baarn Tue, Soest Thu.

During the Netherlands' Golden Age, regents and wealthy merchants had splendid summer residences built in Baarn and its environs. This place has retained its leafy, elegant appearance. The **Kasteel Groeneveld** (1710) lies in the middle of a magnificent park. Soest's past is pre-9th century, and the old centre remains largely in its original state. The church dates from 1400. The surrounding area is beautiful and offers a wealth of leisure activities.

🏰 Kasteel Groeneveld
Groeneveld 2. **Tel** 035-5420446.
Castle: **Open** 11am–5pm Tue–Sun.
Closed 1 Jan, 27 Apr, 25 & 31 Dec.
🌳 Park: **Open** sunrise–sunset Tue–Sun. 🅿 🖥 🌐 **kasteelgroeneveld.nl**

❾ Soestdijk

Road Map C3. 🛈 Van Weedestraat 131, Soest (035-7400074). Paleis Soestdijk: Amsterdamsestraatweg 1, Baarn (035-5412841).
Open Check website for details.
🌐 **paleissoestdijk.nl**

Just outside Baarn lies **Paleis Soestdijk**. It was built in 1674 as a place for Viceroy William III to hunt. In 1815, it came into the hands of the crown prince, who later became King William II. The two wings of the palace were added in 1816 and the park was designed by landscape gardener Zocher. The **Naald van Waterloo** (Waterloo needle) stands opposite, erected in honour of William Frederick, Prince of Orange, for his services during the Battle of Waterloo.

❿ Lage Vuursche

Road Map C3. 🏛 250. 🚌 🛈 Van Weedestraat 131, Soest (035-7400074).

The name "Furs" for Lage Vuursche has been around since 1200, though the village itself has existed only since the 17th century. The village, surrounded by woodland, is very popular with ramblers.

Bunschoten-Spakenburg, once home to an important fishing industry

The small octagonal castle **Drakenstein**, which dates back to 1640–43, is the residence of Princess Beatrix, former Queen of the Netherlands.

⓫ Bunschoten-Spakenburg

Road Map C3. 🏛 19,500.
🚌 🛈 Oude Schans 90 (033-2982156). 🛥 Sat.

Over the years, the towns of Bunschoten and Spakenburg have merged into one another. Livestock farming was the traditional livelihood in Bunschoten, and there are still some pretty farms to see here. Bunschoten, granted its town charter in 1383, is older than Spakenburg, which came into being in the 15th century. It was once an important fishing town; its smokehouses, fishermen's houses and shipbuilding yard are reminders of this time. When the Zuiderzee was closed in 1932 because of partial land reclamation, the inhabitants had to look for other work. Some of the women in the town still wear traditional dress. **Museum Spakenburg** brings the fishing activities of the past back to life.

🏛 Museum Spakenburg
Oude Schans 47–63. **Tel** 033-2983319.
Open Apr–Oct: 1:30–5pm Mon, 10am–5pm Tue–Sat; Nov–Mar: 1–4pm Wed–Sat. 🌳 🅿
🌐 **museumspakenburg.nl**

Outdoor cafés in Lage Vuursche offering respite after a walk in the woods

⑫ Street-by-Street: Utrecht

The area to the south of the centre gives one a good idea of how people once lived in Utrecht. Rich citizens lived in the stately houses on the Nieuwegracht, with its typical Utrecht wharves, and built almshouses for their less fortunate neighbours. No doubt because of the great number of museums in this area, it came to be called Museumkwartier (museum district). The old city walls gave way to a magnificent park which was designed by landscape gardener Zocher.

KORTE SMEESTRAAT

OUDEGRACHT

NIEUW STRAAT

VROUW JUTTENSTRAAT

LANGE

AGNI

★ **Oudegracht**
The Oudegracht represented a vital transport route for the economy of Utrecht in the 13th century. When the water level fell, cellars were built along the wharves. These were used as warehouses or workshops. Today, some of them house cafés and restaurants.

Centraal Museum
The rich and varied contents include works by the 16th-century artist Jan van Scorel, as well as the largest collection of Rietveld furniture in the world.

0 metres	100
0 yards	100

Almshouses
The Pallaeskameren (Pallaes rooms) are 12 little almshouses built on the instructions of Maria van Pallaes in 1651. The inhabitants had free accommodation and a certain amount of food and drink annually.

For hotels and restaurants in this region see p397 and p410

Cathedral

BRIGITTENSTRAAT

NIEUWE GRACHT

BRUNTENHOF

SERVAASBOLWERK

GRACHT

VISITORS' CHECKLIST

Practical Information
Road Map C4. 340,000.
visit-utrecht.com
Domplein 9–10 (0900-1288732). Wed, Fri & Sat. Liberation festival: 5 May; Festival Oude Muziek: end Aug; Netherlands Film Festival: end Sep.

Transport
Stationsplein.
Stationsplein.

★ Catharijneconvent
Museum Catharijneconvent (Lange Nieuwstraat 38) is devoted to religious art. It is located in the former St Catherine's convent, dating back to 1468. Part of the convent church dates from 1529.

Nederlands Spoorwegmuseum
(Dutch railway museum) Old carriages and steam locomotives can be seen in the former Maliebaan Station, dating back to the 19th century. The exhibition room features the history of the Dutch railways.

Key

— Recommended route

Sonnenborgh
The 19th-century observatory, now home to an astronomy museum, was established on one of the four bulwarks along the Singel.

Exploring Utrecht

Utrecht, founded by the Romans in AD 47, has been a bishopric and university town for centuries. It has grown into a lively city, thanks to its central position. Utrecht was very prosperous during the 16th and 17th centuries, when many of the magnificent canalside houses were built. These houses are a characteristic feature of the town centre, as are the medieval churches and monasteries. The city centre is compact, so is very suitable for exploring on foot.

The 112-m (367-ft) Domtoren rises above the town

🎠 Domtoren

Domplein. ☎ **Tel** 030-2360010. **Open** 10am–5pm Tue–Sat, noon–5pm Sun–Mon. **Closed** 1 Jan, 27 Apr, 25 & 26 Dec. 🎠 🎠 obligatory. **w** domtoren.nl

The first thing you will see from the distance is the Domtoren (cathedral tower) rising above the town. The Dom (cathedral) has become the symbol of the town. Utrecht came into being on the Domplein (cathedral square), where the Romans had a settlement in the 1st century AD. In 695, Bishop Willibrord established himself here. In 1040, Bishop Bernold ordered a "cross of churches" to be built, which meant four churches with the later Domkerk in the centre. Work began on building the Domkerk in 1254 and in 1321 on the tower. The Gothic tower was finally finished in 1382.

Collegiate churches usually have two towers, but the Domkerk has only one. The nave of the church was connected to the tower by an arch, allowing the bishop to move safely to and from the church. In 1674, the nave was destroyed by a hurricane. The tower has stood on its own since then. The interior of the church, with its stained-glass windows, Neo-Gothic organ (1831) and magnificent chancel, is worth a visit.

🏛 Aboriginal Art Museum

Oudegracht 176. ☎ **Tel** 030-2380100. **Open** 10am–5pm Tue–Fri, 11am–5pm Sat & Sun. **Closed** 1 Jan, 27 Apr, 25 Dec. 🎠 🎠 🎠 🎠 **w** aamu.nl

This museum, the only one of its kind in Europe, is devoted to the many different styles of Aboriginal art, including painting and sculpture. The focus is on traditional art produced in Australian co-operatives.

🏛 Museum Catharijneconvent

Lange Nieuwstraat 38. ☎ **Tel** 030-2313835. **Open** 10am–5pm Tue–Fri, 11am–5pm Sat, Sun & hols. **Closed** 1 Jan, 27 Apr. 🎠 🎠 🎠 🎠 🎠 **w** catharijneconvent.nl

The museum is split between a canalside house and a 15th-century former convent. Its fascinating collection provides a good overview of the troubled history of Christianity in the Netherlands. It includes paintings by, among others, Rembrandt van Rijn, ancient manuscripts and richly decorated books. The museum also houses numerous visiting exhibitions. From the museum you can enter into the Catharijnekerk (1529).

🏛 Centraal Museum

Agnietenstraat 1. ☎ **Tel** 030-2362362. **Open** 11am–5pm Tue–Sun. **Closed** 1 Jan, 27 Apr, 25 Dec. 🎠 🎠 🎠 🎠 **w** centraalmuseum.nl

Centraal Museum, the oldest municipal museum in the Netherlands, has a large and extremely varied collection, the oldest pieces of which date from the Middle Ages. Extensive rebuilding and renovations were carried out in 1999 and 2015, giving rise to an interesting combination of old and new. The museum has the largest collection of Gerrit Rietveld furniture in the world. Works by Utrecht artists such as Van Scorel and Bloemaert, as well as 20th-century artists such as Pyke Koch and Dick Bruna – creator of the children's character Nijntje (Miffy) – are also showcased. Bruna's works are shown in the Brunahuis across the road. The varied exhibitions range from traditional art to fashion and historical costumes, to modern art and applied art and design, to the local history of Utrecht.

The Matchmaker by Gerard van Honthorst in the Centraal Museum

Garden of the beautiful inner
Domkerk quadrangle

🏛 Nederlands Spoorwegmuseum

Maliebaanstation. 🚋 **Tel** 030-2306206. **Open** 10am–5pm Tue–Sun & public hols (also Mon in school hols). **Closed** 1 Jan, 27 Apr. 🅿 ♿ 📷
🖥 🇼 spoorwegmuseum.nl

The superb Dutch Railway Museum is very appropriately situated in a former railway station, in use from 1874 until 1939. Magnificent old locomotives, carriages and trains line the platforms. Children can ride around the museum grounds on a miniature railway. Adults and children alike will enjoy the exhibition inside, which includes old advertising posters and model trains.

🏛 Nationaal Museum Speelklok tot Pierement

Steenweg 6. 🚋 **Tel** 030-2312789. **Open** 10am–5pm Tue–Sun & hols (also Mon in school hols). **Closed** 1 Jan, 27 Apr, 25 Dec. 🅿 ♿ 📷 🖥
🇼 **museumspeelklok.nl**

This museum is inside the 13th-century Buurkerk – Utrecht's oldest church. The museum's collection displays the history of mechanical musical instruments. The showpiece is a rare 15th-century musical clock. You will also see – and hear – *pierementen*, the large organs pushed by organ grinders, music boxes, fairground organs and chiming clocks, as well as many smaller instruments with chiming mechanisms. Many of the instruments are demonstrated on the guided tour.

🏛 Universiteitsmuseum

Lange Nieuwstraat 106. 🚋 **Tel** 030-2538008. **Open** 10am–5pm daily. **Closed** 1 Jan, 27 Apr, 25 Dec. 🅿 ♿ 📷 🖥 🏛
🇼 universiteitsmuseum.nl

The Universiteitsmuseum is in a purpose-built building close to the Centraal Museum. The collection here covers education since the university was established in 1636 and includes weighing and measuring instruments and a "collection of curiosities". Behind the museum is the University of Utrecht's lovely Old Botanical Garden (1723), which is open to the public.

🛒 Markets

The Vredenburg holds a general market on Wednesdays and Saturdays. On Fridays it holds a market for ecologically genuine agricultural produce. On Saturdays, the Janskerkhof hosts a large flower and plant market. On the same day, magnificent bouquets are sold along the Oudegracht, the old canal. The Breedstraat market, also held on Saturdays, is the venue of the cloth market.

Utrecht City Centre

① Nationaal Museum
   Speelklok tot Pierement
② Domtoren and Domkerk
③ Aboriginal Art Museum
④ Museum Catharijneconvent

Key

■ Street-by-street map (pp204–5)

Rietveld Schröderhuis

When designing this house, architect Gerrit Rietveld worked closely with his client, Mrs Schröder, who lived here from 1924 until her death in 1985. The house was to epitomize all that was "modern" and broke with many of the architectural standards of the time. This can be seen in the design of the top floor, which may be divided in different ways by sliding partitions, according to the requirements of the inhabitants. The house was declared a World Heritage Site by UNESCO in 2001.

The Hanging Lamp
Rietveld designed this unusual lamp in around 1922.

★ **Sliding Partitions**
Using sliding partitions, the top floor could be divided into separate rooms for Mrs Schröder's children.

Telephone Seat
The house was to reflect the modern times in which it was designed, and so functional items like the telephone and fuse box were given a prominent location.

De Stijl

This Dutch artistic movement, founded in 1917, aimed to integrate art further into everyday life. Proponents wanted to bring painting and architecture closer together in a new way. The use of colour in the Rietveld Schröderhuis is one expression of this idea. Rietveld was a member of De Stijl from 1919, though he disagreed with certain ideas held by others in the group *(see p132)*.

De Stijl member Theo van Doesburg was mainly interested in straight lines and primary colours. The geometric surfaces of this painting do not depict reality but offer a glimpse of universality.

BOODSCHAPPEN
EERST BELLEN BIJ GEEN GEHOOR SPREEKBUIS

Intercom
The Schröder's intercom sign instructed visitors to "First ring. If no answer use mouthpiece".

Gerrit Rietveld
The architect always used scale models when designing houses, but could also draw excellent floor plans (contrary to what was often said).

The skylight in the roof above the stairs allows additional light to reach the top floor.

The Hanging Lamp

VISITORS' CHECKLIST

Practical Information
Road Map C4. Prins Hendriklaan 50, Utrecht. **Tel** 030-2362310. **Open** for guided tours only. **Closed** 1 Jan, 27 Apr, 25 Dec. 🅿 ✉ 📷 11am–5pm Tue–Sun (book through website). 🅆 **centraalmuseum.nl**

Transport
🚌 8.

★ **Rietveld Furniture**
In 1918, Rietveld designed what we now know as the Red Blue Chair. It was originally finished in clear varnish; only in 1923 did Rietveld paint it in what would become classic De Stijl colours.

★ **Disappearing Corner**
The dining corner has a spectacular feature: when the windows are opened, the corner disappears. Formerly the view from here was panoramic but in 1939, much to Rietveld's consternation, a road was built just next to the house.

⑬ Amersfoort

Road Map C4. 🖼 149,700. 🚌
🚌 *i* Breestraat 1 (0900-
1122364). 🛒 Thu, Fri & Sat.
W vvvamersfoort.nl

The old town centre of
Amersfoort contrasts sharply
with the districts that surround
it, which reflect a contemporary
architectural style. The centre is
defined by small streets with
old houses and gardens. The
Muurhuizen (wall houses) were
built on the site of the old
defence ring. The **Onze Lieve
Vrouwetoren** (Tower of Our
Lady) is difficult to miss. The
contours of this old chapel can
still be seen in the stones of the
pavement. In 1787, the chapel,
which was used to store
gunpowder, was blown up.

The **Amersfoortse kei**
boulder appeared in the town
in 1661, when a nobleman bet
he could drag the stone from
the Leusderheide. Ever since,
Amersfoort has held the annual
Keistadfeest (Keistad festival) in
celebration of the event.

The **Museum Flehite** gives
an overview of the history of
Amersfoort from the Middle Ages.
The town was the birthplace of
abstract painter Mondriaan, the
leading light of the De Stijl and
Neo-Plasticist movements. The
house where he was born is now
home to the **Mondriaanhuis
voor Constructieve en Concrete
Kunst**, a study centre and archive
of the artist's life and work,
including several of his paintings.
On the edge of town, housed in
an eye-catching building named
Eemhuis, is **Kunsthal KAdE**. This

The 15th-century Koppelpoort, one of Amersfoort's three surviving gates

artspace does not have its own
collection but curates exhibitions
on contemporary art and culture,
architecture and design. Attached
to it is an art school and a shop
that sells books on art and other
memorabilia. The library, the
Amersfoot Archives, is a must visit.

Environs

Some 4 km (2 miles) away,
in the village of Leusden, **Kamp
Amersfoort** is a grim reminder of
the area's history. A Dutch army
barracks was transformed in 1941
into a work camp for more than
35,000 people, including Jewish
prisoners and Jehovah's Witnesses.
Many were later transported to
concentration camps. The camp
also held American and Russian
prisoners of war. The site is now
a national monument. Several
commemorative ceremonies
are held each year.

🏛 **Museum Flehite**
Westsingel 50. **Tel** 033-2471100.
Open 11am–5pm Tue–Fri, noon–5pm
Sat & Sun. **Closed** Mon & public hols.
🅿 **W** museumflehite.nl

🏛 **Mondriaanhuis voor
Constructieve en Concrete Kunst**
Kortegracht 11. **Tel** 033-4600170.
Open 11am–5pm Tue–Fri, noon–5pm
Sat & Sun. **Closed** 1 Jan, 27 Apr,
25 Dec. **W** mondriaanhuis.nl

🏛 **Kunsthal KAdE**
Eemplein 77. **Tel** 033-4225030.
Open 11am–5pm Tue–Fri, noon–5pm
Sat–Sun. **Closed** 1 Jan, 27 Apr, 25 Dec.
🅿 ♿ 🏠 **W** kunsthalkade.nl

🏛 **Kamp Amersfoort**
Loes van Overeemlaan 13, Leusden.
Tel 033-4613129. **Open** Tue–Sun.
W kampamersfoort.nl

Onze Lieve Vrouwetoren, a church tower
in Amersfoort

⑭ Doorn

Road Map C4. 🖼 10,000. 🚌
i Langbroekerweg 10 (0343-421020).
🛒 Thu am. **W** vvvheuvelrug.nl

Doorn, originally called Thorheim
(home of Thor, god of thunder),
is a pretty village in wooded
surroundings. The greatest tourist
attraction here is **Huis Doorn**,
where between 1920 and 1941
the German Kaiser, Wilhelm II,
lived with his retinue. (He fled his
country after World War I.) The
kaiser lies buried in a mausoleum
in the castle gardens. The kaiser's
former garage is now a pavilion
commemorating World War I, and
its impact on the Netherlands.

The **Von Gimborn Arboretum**
is a 27-hectare botanical garden
begun in 1924. Part of the
University of Utrecht, it was originally the private garden of Max
von Gimborn, an ink manufacturer
who was a tree expert and plant
collector in his spare time.

Von Gimborn Arboretum, one of the
Netherlands' largest gardens

One of the country's largest gardens, it is home to ten huge sequoia trees and a collection of rhodo-dendrons. Although best visited in spring and summer to see (and smell) the flowers in bloom, the gardens contain plants for all seasons.

🏠 Huis Doorn
Langbroekerweg 10. **Tel** 0343-421020. **Open** 1–5pm Wed–Fri, noon–5pm Sat & Sun. 🎫 mandatory. 🅿 ♿ 📷
W huisdoorn.nl

🌳 Von Gimborn Arboretum
Velperengh 13. **Tel** 0343-412144 **Open** daily. 🅿
W gimbornarboretum.nl

⑮ Wijk bij Duurstede
Road Map C4. 🏠 23,000. 🚌
ℹ Markt 24 (0343-575995). 🛍 Wed.

Dorestad was an important trade centre in Carolingian times. Plundering Vikings and a shift in the river basin of the Rhine led to its decline. In the 13th century, Wijk (near Dorestad) emerged and became the home of the Utrecht bishops around 1450. They brought prosperity and influence to the town until, in 1528, the bishop lost his secular power. The impressive **Kasteel Duurstede** dates from the 13th century, when it was originally built as a donjon, the castle's fortified inner tower, surrounded by a moat. This was extended in 1500, and bishops lived here until 1580. The castle's park was laid out in 1850 by Jan David Zocher.

🏰 Kasteelpark Duurstede
Langs de Wal 7. Castle: **Open** Apr–Oct: Tue–Sun (by appt). Park: **Open** daily.

⑯ Amerongen
Road Map C4. 🏠 7,000. 🚌
ℹ 0343-412015.

Situated on the bank of the lower Rhine, which can be crossed by ferry, Amerongen lies in the ridge of hills known as the Utrechtse Heuvelrug, a national park. The Amerongense Berg marks the highest point in the ridge and has earned the name

Medieval castle tower in Wijk bij Duurstede

"mountain", despite being just 69 m (225 ft) high. The town lay originally on the Via Regia, the "royal route" from Utrecht to Cologne. From the 17th to 19th centuries, tobacco was grown in this area, as is evident by the drying sheds which are still standing. You can have a proper look at an old drying shed in the **Tabaksteelt Museum**. In 1672, the town's castle, **Kasteel Amerongen**, was destroyed by the French. It was rebuilt in the Dutch Classical style.

🏛 Tabaksteelt Museum
Burg. Jhr van den Boschstraat 46. **Tel** 0343-456500. **Open** Tue–Sun pm. ♿ 🅿

🏠 Kasteel Amerongen
Drostestraat 20. **Tel** 0343-563766. **Open** Apr–Oct: 11am–5pm Tue–Sun; Nov–Mar: 11am–5pm Thu–Sun. 🅿 🎫 mandatory.
W kasteelamerongen.nl

⑰ Rhenen
Road Map C4. 🏠 19,000. 🚌 🚌
ℹ Markt 20 (0317-612333). 🛍 Thu.

Rhenen lies on the north bank of the Rhine, at the border between the flat Betuwe and the Utrecht Heuvelrug. This area was inhabited as far back as the Iron Age. Many of the town's historic buildings were destroyed during World War II, but the Late Gothic **Cuneratoren** (Cunera tower), built between 1492 and 1531, escaped the bombs. The **Raadhuis** (town hall) dates from the Middle Ages. May 1940 saw a fierce battle on the 53-m (174-ft) **Grebbeberg**, a long-time strategic point in the surrounding area. The victims lie buried in the military cemetery.

East of the town, on the road to Wageningen, is the **Ouwehands Dierenpark**. This zoo contains all the favourites, like tigers, monkeys and elephants. There is also a large "bear wood", the *berenbos*, 20,000 sq m (66,000 sq ft) of forest-like landscape, where brown bears and wolves wander free. Other attractions include a tropical aquarium and plenty of children's activities, from a huge, jungle-themed adventure playground called RavotAapia, to special weekends dedicated to particular animals, and educational programmes.

🐻 Ouwehands Dierenpark
Grebbeweg 111. **Tel** 0317-650200. **Open** daily. **W** ouwehand.nl

A country house set in one of the large parks surrounding Wijk bij Duurstede

SOUTH HOLLAND

For tourists, South Holland is pure delight. Although densely populated, the province still has plenty of open space and offers a remarkable range of attractions for visitors of all kinds. The landscape is typically Dutch, with large areas of reclaimed land dotted with windmills and grazing cattle.

From Roman times on, South Holland was principally a low-lying swampy delta as the various courses of the river Rhine reached the sea. The influence of the counts of Holland (9th–13th centuries), who took up residence in The Hague, attracted trade with Flanders, Germany and England, and settlements became towns. Leiden's university, the oldest in the country, was founded as long ago as 1565. Peat extraction for fuel created lakes, reclaimed land *(see pp26–7)* was turned into productive farmland, and the Dutch dairy industry flourished. Other products in international demand included beer and textiles and, in more recent times, year-round flowers and the famous Dutch bulbs. Overseeing all this activity is the

port of Rotterdam, one of the largest in the world, and The Hague, home of the Dutch government, the royal family and the International Court of Justice. Delft is famous for its exquisite hand-painted porcelain and china, while Gouda is renowned for its cheese. The North Sea coast has charming resorts, from busy Scheveningen, with its attractive pier, to the smaller seaside towns of Katwijk and Noordwijk, with long sandy beaches. It is an ideal region for family holidays and for children of all ages.

Visitors in spring are in for a treat when they tour the north of the province. Bulb fields erupt in a riot of colour, and the Keukenhof's flower gardens are simply unforgettable.

Servants waiting for the queen next to her Golden Coach on the third Tuesday of September (Prinsjesdag)

◀ Sunrise over the windmills at Kinderdijk

Exploring South Holland

In the north of the province of South Holland are the colourful bulb fields and the Keukenhof, while in a semi-circle to the south lie the old university town of Leiden, bustling The Hague, cosy Delft and the modern port city of Rotterdam. The islands of South Holland bear witness to the country's military history in Hellevoetsluis and Brielle. Ramblers will find all they wish for in the dunes by Wassenaar or in the river countryside at Leerdam, which is best known for its glass-blowing industry. From Gorinchem you can take a passenger ferry to the 14th-century castle of Slot Loevestein, which played a key role in the history of Holland.

The 14th-century Huys Dever, near Lisse

The Panorama Mesdag in The Hague

Greenhouses in the Westland

Getting Around

South Holland has a comprehensive system of roads, and both big cities and small towns can be reached equally quickly. However, during the morning and afternoon rush hours you should watch out for traffic jams. In the centres of the big cities it is best to leave your car in a car park, as finding an on-street parking space can often be a problem. Trains are a fast way of getting from A to B. As a rule you will find a train for your particular destination departing every quarter or half hour. Lisse and the bulbfields, Nieuwpoort and the towns on South Holland's islands can be reached only by local bus. VVV and ANWB tourist information offices provide information on cycling routes.

One of the Keukenhof's spectacular flowering fields

For map symbols see back flap

Sights at a Glance

Tour

0 kilometres 10

0 miles 5

Key

━━ Motorway
━━ Main road
┈┈ Minor road
━━ Scenic route
━━ Main railway
━━ Minor railway
━━ Regional border

The Flemish Gothic Stadhuis in Gouda

For hotels and restaurants in this region see p398 and pp410–11

❶ Bulb Fields

The Bollenstreek, a 30-km (19-mile) stretch between Haarlem and Leiden, is Holland's primary bulb-growing area. From March, the polders are aglow with glorious colours – the crocuses are the first to flower and the season culminates around mid-April with the majestic tulips. The lilies then follow at the end of May. Visitors without cars can obtain information about cycle routes from the tourist information office, the VVV, at Lisse. Bikes can be hired at railway stations in Haarlem and Heemstede-Aerdenhout.

Tips for Drivers

Starting point: Haarlem.
Distance: Approximately 30 km (19 miles).
Stopping-off points: Along with the places discussed below, where various cafés and restaurants are to be found, Noordwijk aan Zee is worth a short detour. This lively coastal town, with its wonderful beach and dunes, makes an ideal place for a stopover.

The dunes of North Holland

0 kilometres | 4
0 miles | 4

③ Keukenhof
Visitors are greeted by the intoxicating aroma and vivid colours of millions of flowering bulbs.

⑤ Sassenheim
To the west of the town lie the ruins of Burcht Teylingen, the 11th-century castle where Jacoba of Bavaria, countess of Holland, died in 1436.

① Cruquiusmuseum
In this former steam-driven pumping station, you can see how the people of Holland managed to keep the water in check (see pp192–3).

② Linnaeushof
This huge park, named after the famous 18th-century botanist, has one of the biggest playgrounds in Europe.

④ Lisse
Lisse's museum showcases the bulb-growing industry; you can also take a boat trip on the lakes.

Key

▬▬ Route
═══ Roads

Map labels: N208, A5, Amsterdam, N201, Haarlem, Zandvoort, N201, N201, Aalsmeer, Amsterdamse Waterleiding-duinen, N206, N208, Hillegom, Haarlemmermeerpolder, A206, Noordwijk aan Zee, North Sea, N208, Ringvaart van de, Aalsmeer, N206, A44, Kager-plassen, A44, Rijnsburg, Leiden/The Hague

⑦ Katwijk
An unusual early 17th-century lighthouse stands to the north of this coastal town, which lies on the estuary of the Oude Rijn.

⑥ Voorhout
Panorama Tulip Land is a panoramic painting of the Bollenstreek. Its dimensions are enormous: 63 m (207 ft) wide and 4 m (13 ft) tall.

A tulip field in the Bollenstreek

owering Bulbs

wers such as gladioli,
es, narcissi, hyacinths, irises,
ocuses and dahlias are mainly
own in the Bollenstreek.
far the most important,
ough, is the tulip, which
ginally came from Turkey
d was cultivated by Carolus
usius in 1593 for the first time
the Netherlands.

addin" tulips

ina Pink" tulips

hiti" narcissi

innow" narcissi

lue Jacket" hyacinths

Colourful flowering bulbs in the shady Keukenhof

❷ Lisse

Map B3. 🚹 20,000. 🚌 50
(from Leiden & Haarlem) & 90 (from
Noordwijk). 🚹 Heereweg 219 (0252-
417900). 🆆 vvvlisse.nl

The best time to see Lisse is
at the end of April, when the
colourful **Bloemen Corso**
(flower parade) takes place *(see
p36)*. A vibrant procession of
floats passes from Noordwijk
to Haarlem, where they are
brightly illuminated at night
and can still be seen the next
day. On the two days before the
parade, you can see close-up
how the floats are decorated
in the *Hobaho* halls in Lisse.

The **Museum De Zwarte Tulp**
(black tulip museum) covers
the history of bulb growing
and illustrates the life cycle of
bulbs. It also touches upon the
"tulipomania" in 1620–37 *(see
pp34–5)*, when investors pushed
up the demand for rare tulip
bulbs to such an extent that
they were worth their weight
in gold.

🌼 **Bloemen Corso**
🆆 bloemencorsobollenstreek.nl

🏛 **Museum De Zwarte Tulp**
Heereweg 219. **Tel** 0252-417900.
Open Mar–Aug: 11am–5pm; Sep–
Feb: 1–5pm. **Closed** public hols. 📷
♿ 💻 🆆 museumdezwartetulp.nl

Environs
Just outside Lisse is **Huys Dever**,
a fortified residential tower which
dates from the second half of the
14th century. The permanent exhibition at the tower illustrates the
lives of the families who lived here.

🏠 **Huys Dever**
Heereweg 349a. **Tel** 0252-411430.
Open 2–5pm Tue–Sun. **Closed**
public hols. 🎫 by arrangement.
🆆 kasteeldever.nl

❸ Keukenhof

Map B3. 🚌 854 (from Leiden Centraal
Station), 858 (from Schiphol airport).
Tel 0252-465555. **Open** late Mar–mid-
May: daily. 📷 8am–6pm. ♿ 📷
🆆 keukenhof.nl

Lying in a wooded park of 32 ha
(79 acres) close to Lisse, the
Keukenhof is one of the most
spectacular public gardens in the
world. It was set up in 1949 as a
showcase for bulb-growers and
currently has around 6 million
bulbs planted in it. Fields are full
of dazzling narcissi, hyacinths and
tulips in bloom from the end of
March to the end of May. You can
also see the white blossom of the
Japanese cherry tree in the park
early in the season and, later,
the bright flowers of the azaleas
and rhododendrons.

❹ Street-by-Street: Leiden

Leiden is a thriving university town which dates from
Roman times. The town developed because of its
position on a branch of the Rhine and is still an
important trade centre. Some excellent museums
chart Leiden's eventful past, including the Golden
Age, when the town was a centre for world trade *(see
pp52–3)*. Rembrandt van Rijn *(see pp30–31)* was born
here in June 1606 – a plaque on the façade of a
Weddesteeg house marks his birthplace. During
term time, the streets of Leiden are busy with
students cycling between lectures or frequenting
the cafés and bookshops.

**★ Rijksmuseum
van Oudheden**
This squat statue of a
kneeling treasury
scribe is just one of
the many impressive
Egyptian artifacts on
display in this fascinating
museum of antiquities.

★ Hortus Botanicus
The botanical gardens belonging to the
University of Leiden *(see p220)* were started
in 1590 "for the teaching of every body who
studies in the medicinal sciences".

| 0 metres | 50 |
| 0 yards | 50 |

Façades
Aristocrats, professors
and textile families all
contributed to the face
of the Leiden canals.

Dutch Classicism can be
seen in the university
buildings on Rapenburg.

Het Gravensteen
Part of the law faculty is now
accommodated in this former
count's prison, built between
the 13th and 17th centuries.

LANGEBRUG

PAPENGRACHT

SCHOOLSTEEG

GERECHT

HOUTSTRAAT

RAPENBURG

KLOKSTEEG

NONNENSTEEG

Hoogstraat
The Hoogstraat, where two canals meet, is popular for its floating terraces and basement restaurants.

Korenbeursbrug
The stone corn-exchange bridge over the Nieuwe Rijn was given a roof in 1825 in Neo-Classical style so that the corn traders would be protected from the rain.

The Stadhuis
(1596) by Lieven de Key.

Around the Pieterskerkhof
you will find antique shops, cafés and restaurants.

Key

— Recommended route

★ Pieterskerk
This church contains the tombstone marking the oldest intact grave in the Netherlands – that of the 15th-century merchant Floris van Buschuyse and his wife.

Exploring Leiden

Leiden is famous for its university, which is the oldest in the country. It was founded in 1575, one year after the Beggars of the Sea *(see p245)* freed the town from a protracted siege by the Spanish *(see p53)*. As a reward for their endurance, William of Orange offered the people of Leiden the choice between a university and the abolition of taxes. The people made a shrewd choice and the town went on to become a centre of intellectual progress and religious freedom. English Puritan dissidents, victims of persecution in their homeland, were able to settle here in the 17th century before undertaking their journey to the New World.

One of the 35 almshouses in Leiden

🏛 Museum de Lakenhal

Oude Singel 28–32. **Tel** 071-5165360. **Closed** to the public, renovations underway (scheduled to reopen in 2018). 🖼 ♿ 🎧 💻 🖥 **W** lakenhal.nl

In the 17th century, the *lakenhal* (cloth merchants' hall) was the centre of the Leiden textile industry. Arent van 's Gravesande designed the building in 1640 in Dutch Classical style. The municipal museum has been here since 1874. The showpiece of the collection, which was rescued from the Pieterskerk (St Peter's Church) during the religious disputes of 1566 *(see pp56–7)* is *The Last Judgment* (1526–7), a triptych in Renaissance style by Lucas van Leyden. Other Leiden artists, from Rembrandt to Theo van Doesburg, are also featured. The museum has displays of silver, glass, tin and tiles and explores the history of Leiden. Not

to be missed is the large bronze cooking pot said to have been left by the Spaniards during the relief of Leiden in 1574. The spicy casserole it contained is re-created as a stew cooked every year on 3 October to commemorate Dutch victory over the Spanish.

⚜ Hortus Botanicus Leiden

Rapenburg 73. **Tel** 071-5275144. **Open** summer: 10am–6pm daily; winter: 10am–4pm Tue–Sun. **Closed** 3 Oct, 24 Dec–1 Jan. 🎧 ♿ 🖼 partial. **W** hortusleiden.nl

The botanical garden of Leiden was founded in 1590 as part of the university. A number of its trees and shrubs are particularly old, such as a laburnum dating from 1601. In 1593, Carolus Clusius, who introduced the tulip to Holland *(see pp34–5)*, became the first professor of botany at the University of Leiden. The Hortus Botanicus features a reconstruction of his walled garden. Also worth a look are the tropical greenhouses, the rose garden and the Von Siebold Japanese memorial garden.

🏛 Museum Boerhaave

Lange St Agnietenstraat 10. **Tel** 071-5214224. **Closed** to the public, renovations underway. 🎧 🖼 ♿ 🖼 📷 **W** museumboerhaave.nl

Located in the former Caecilia Hospital in the centre of Leiden, this is the Netherlands' National Museum of the History of Science and Medicine. It is named after the great Dutch professor of medicine Herman Boerhaave (1668–1738). The collection reflects the development

Lucas van Leyden's triptych of *The Last Judgment*, in the Museum de Lakenhal

of mathematics, astronomy, physics, chemistry and medicine. Exhibits range from a magnificent 15th-century astrolabe and pendulum clocks by Christiaan Huygens (1629–95) to surgeons' equipment of yesteryear and early electron microscopes.

🏛 Museum Volkenkunde

Steenstraat 1. **Tel** 071-5168800. **Open** 10am–5pm Tue–Sun & public hols. **Closed** 1 Jan, 27 Apr, 3 Oct, 25 Dec. 🎨 ♿ 🖥 📷
W volkenkunde.nl

This excellent ethnological museum, founded in 1837, has collections which feature non-Western cultures, such as ethnographic items brought by the German explorer Philipp von Siebold from Japan in the 19th century. The vast collection focuses on the interaction between various cultures and their links with the Netherlands; hence Indonesia has a considerable amount of floor space. The museum covers practically the whole world, from the Arctic to Oceania.

🏛 Naturalis Biodiversity Center

Darwinweg 2. **Tel** 071-5687600. **Open** 10am–5pm daily. **Closed** 27 Apr, 3 Oct, 25 Dec. 🎨 ♿ 🖥 📷
W naturalis.nl

Opened in 1998, the national natural history museum, attracted a record number of visitors. It provides a truly fascinating insight into the evolution of the earth and its inhabitants with displays of fossils more than a million years old, and lifelike replicas of animals, stones and minerals. The star exhibit is a complete skeleton of a Tyrannosaurus rex, discovered in Montana in 2013. Special exhibitions for children are also held.

🏛 Pieterskerk

Pieterskerkhof 1a. **Tel** 071-5124319. **Open** 11am–6pm daily, except when church is hired out (check website). **Closed** 3 Oct. ♿ **W** pieterskerk.com

This impressive Gothic cruciform church, built mainly in the 15th

The Pilgrim Fathers

In the 17th century, the Netherlands was a refuge for English Puritans. Minister John Robinson (1575–1625) founded a church in Leiden in 1609, where he inspired his congregation with his dream of the New World. The Pilgrim Fathers set out in 1620 from Delfshaven aboard the *Speedwell*, but the ship proved to be unseaworthy. They then crossed the Atlantic from Plymouth, England, on the *Mayflower*, but Robinson stayed behind, too ill to travel. He died in Leiden in 1625.

The *Mayflower* crossing the Atlantic Ocean

Heraldic lion at De Burcht

century, stands in the middle of a shady square that seems to be from a different age. It is worth a visit for its austere interior and the carefully restored Van Hagerbeer organ (1639–43), one of the world's few meantone-tuned organs. The floor of the nave is covered with worn stones, which mark the graves of famous 17th-century intellectuals such as Puritan leader John Robinson, physician Hermanus Boerhaave and Golden Age artist Jan Steen.

🏰 De Burcht

Burgsteeg. **Open** daily.
The Burcht is a 12th-century fortress which features a still-intact circular wall and crenellated battlements. At the foot of the 12-m (39-ft) artificial mound is a wrought-iron gate covered in heraldic symbols.

There is a marvellous view of Leiden's historic centre from the gallery.

🏛 Rijksmuseum van Oudheden

Rapenburg 28. **Tel** 0900-6600600. **Open** 10am–5pm Tue–Sun & public hols. **Closed** 1 Jan, 27 Apr, 3 Oct, 25 Dec. 🎨 ♿ 🖥 📷 **W** rmo.nl

This museum has one of the top seven Egyptian collections in the world, the centrepiece of which is the 2,000-year-old Taffeh Temple. Other civilizations from the Near East and from Classical Antiquity are also represented. The section on archaeology of the Netherlands gives visitors an idea of what the Low Countries were like from prehistoric times to the Middle Ages. Mummies, textiles and shoes, musical instruments and fragments of Roman mosaics and frescoes form just part of the museum's impressive holdings.

A drawbridge across the Oude Rijn in Leiden

❺ Street-by-Street: The Hague

The village of Die Haghe ("the hedge") grew around the Binnenhof (inner courtyard), which has been an important political centre since the 13th century. The princes of Orange, the upper classes and an extensive diplomatic corps gave instructions for palaces and mansion houses to be built, and a stroll across the Voorhout or along the Hofvijver will still evoke its aristocratic charm. The Hague today is represented by the new Spuiwartier (Spui district), with the city hall by Richard Meier and the Lucent Danstheater by Rem Koolhaas. To the west, the dunes and many parks and woods are still reminiscent of the country estate it once was.

★ Escher in Het Paleis
A permanent exhibition of the graphic artist Maurits Cornelis Escher can be visited in the Paleis Lange Voorhout, where Queen Emma and Queen Wilhelmina once lived.

Gevangenpoort
The Dutch lion adorns the façade of the Gevangenpoort (prison gate), originally the main gate of the 14th-century castle of the counts of Holland. From the 1400s, it was used as a prison.

Galerij Prins Willem V
This was the first public art gallery in the Netherlands.

Key
— Recommended route

| 0 metres | 50 |
| 0 yards | 50 |

Jantje, a statue based on a Dutch nursery rhyme, points to the Binnenhof.

Haags Historisch Museum
Featured is the history of The Hague, from the Middle Ages to the present day.

★ **Mauritshuis**
On display here in an exquisite collection are 17th-century old masters, including works by Rembrandt and Vermeer.

The Tweede Kamer
The accommodation for the Tweede Kamer, the Dutch Lower House, was designed by Pi de Bruijn and has been in use since 1992. The building blends tastefully with the older buildings surrounding it. Plenary sessions are held in the Grote Vergaderzaal (great assembly hall) behind the circular extension.

TOURNOOIVELD

LANGE HOUTSTRAAT

KORTE VIJVERBERG

PLEIN

BINNENHOF

HOFPLEIN

LANGE POTEN

"The Hague, you tap it and it sings" wrote Dutch poet Gerrit Achterberg in "Passage". The elegant covered arcade of shops in Neo-Renaissance style on the Hofweg is a famous feature of the town centre.

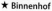

★ **Binnenhof**
This ancient structure comprises the parliament and government buildings and was originally the 13th-century hunting lodge of the counts of Holland.

Exploring The Hague

The Hague has numerous attractions and museums, of which the Mauritshuis *(see pp226–7)* and the Gemeentemuseum (municipal museum) *(see p228)* are the most famous. There are many bookshops, antique shops and cafés on and around the Denneweg, which comes out onto the Lange Voorhout, as well as luxury boutiques on the promenade beginning at Paleis Noordeinde. Behind the Mauritskade lies the stately late-19th-century Willemspark, which is still almost completely intact, with the Panorama Mesdag *(see p228)*. You can admire the peaceful Japanese garden in Park Clingendael *(see p228)*. The old fishing village of Scheveningen has expanded to become a lively seaside resort, but the dunes all around still offer peace and quiet.

Binnenhof met Ridderzaal

Binnenhof. **Tel** 070-7570200.
Open for guided tours only. **Closed** Sun, public hols, 3rd Tue in Sep.
Booking obligatory (via website).
W prodemos.nl

The historic Binnenhof is a series of buildings erected around the hunting lodge of the counts of Holland. In 1247, William II was proclaimed Holy Roman Emperor; he later had the Gothic Ridderzaal (Hall of the Knights) built as a banqueting hall. The Binnenhof has since then been the residence of stadholders, princes and governments. The court of Holland has administered justice since 1511 in the Rolzaal (Roll Court). The northern provinces of the Netherlands broke free from Spanish rule in 1581 with the *Plakkaat van Verlatinge* ("Decree of Abandonment"); they held a huge feast for William of Orange in the Ridderzaal. The Binnenhof was one of the most important European centres of diplomacy in the Golden Age. The magnificently ornate meeting hall dates from this period and is where the Upper House currently sits. The Lower House met in William V's old ballroom until 1992, when it was moved to a new location. Tours of the building begin in the medieval cellars and pass through the Ridderzaal and debating chambers of the Upper or Lower House.

Museum De Gevangenpoort

Buitenhof 33. **Tel** 070-3460861.
Open 10am–5pm Tue–Fri, noon–5pm Sat & Sun. **Closed** 1 Jan, 25 Dec. obligatory; last guided tour 3:45pm. **W gevangenpoort.nl**

The prison-gate museum, in a 14th-century gatehouse, contains an old prison still largely in its original state. Cornelis de Witt was kept here on suspicion of conspiracy against Prince Maurice. In 1672, as he and his brother Johan left the prison, they were murdered by a provoked mob. The museum has a unique collection of horrific torture instruments. It shares an entrance with Galerij Prins Willem V.

Galerij Prins Willem V

Buitenhof 33. **Tel** 070-3023456.
Open noon–5pm Tue–Sun.
Closed 1 Jan, 5 & 25 Dec.
W galerijprinswillemv.nl

Prince William V was an enthusiastic collector of 17th-century art. In 1774, his private collection was put on show for the public in this former inn, which the prince had converted into his office. The treasures in this gallery include paintings by Rembrandt, Jan Steen and Paulus Potter (1625–54).

Porcelain from the Museum Bredius collection

Museum Bredius

Lange Vijverberg 14. **Tel** 070-362 0729. **Open** 11am–5pm Tue–Sun. **Closed** 1 Jan, 25 Dec.
W museumbredius.nl

Art historian and art collector Abraham Bredius was also director of the Mauritshuis *(see pp226–7)* from 1895 to 1922. On his death in 1946 he bequeathed his collection of 17th- and 18th-century art, including paintings by Rembrandt and Jan Steen, to the city of The Hague. The elegant 18th-century mansion on the north side of the Hofvijver which houses the museum also has fine antique furniture and porcelain and beautifully engraved silver.

Landscape by Fading Light by Albert Cuyp (Museum Bredius)

The Classical-style Paleis Noordeinde, where King Willem-Alexander has his offices

🏛 Escher in Het Paleis

Lange Voorhout 74. **Tel** 070-427 7730. �ꢀ 🚋 **Open** 11am–5pm Tue–Sun. **Closed** 1 Jan, 3rd Tue in Sep, 25 Dec. 🅿 🆆 escherinhetpaleis.nl

A large proportion of MC Escher's (1898–1972) work is displayed in the Paleis Lange Voorhout, including well-known works such as *Day and Night*, *Rising and Falling* and *Belvédère*. In addition to graphic works, there are sketches, personal documents and photographs. The museum also features the Escher Experience, a virtual journey through his world.

🏛 Paleis Noordeinde

Noordeinde. **Open** only the Paleistuin *(palace garden)* is open to the public.

In 1640, Stadholder Frederik Hendrik had his mother's house converted into a grand palace built in the Dutch classical style. The property of the Princes of Orange since William V (1748–1806), this is the building where the present King of the Netherlands, Willem-Alexander, has his offices, and also where he leaves from for the state opening of parliament.

🏛 Vredespaleis

Carnegieplein 2. 🚌 22 and 24. 🚋 17. **Tel** 070-3024242. **Open** Tue–Sun (Visitor's Centre). 🅿 Sat–Sun. **Closed** public hols and when court is in session. 🅿 ♿ ✉ 🆆 vredespaleis.nl

In 1899, The Hague hosted the first international peace conference. Contributions from the court's members decorate the interior of the mock-Gothic Vredespaleis (peace palace), designed by the French architect Louis Cordonnier and completed in 1913. The International Court of the United Nations, formed in 1946, is based here.

🏛 Passage

Between the Spuistraat, Hofweg and Buitenhof. 🚌 🚋

A visit to The Hague would not be complete without a stroll along the elegant Passage, the only covered arcade remaining from the 19th century in the Netherlands. Unusual specialist shops can be found here, such as the umbrella and fountain pen shop. The arcade wing that leads to the Hofweg was added in 1928–9.

Den Haag City Centre

① Het Paleis
② Museum De Gevangenpoort
③ Galerij Prins Willem V
④ Museum Bredius
⑤ Ridderzaal
⑥ Passage
⑦ Mauritshuis

Key

⬛ Street-by-street map *(pp222–3)*

For map symbols *see back flap*

Mauritshuis

After he was recalled as captain general of Brazil, Johan Maurits of Nassau commissioned this house. It was completed in 1644 by Pieter Post in the North Dutch Classical style with influences from the Italian Renaissance and has a marvellous view of the Hofvijver. After the death of Maurits in 1679, the house passed into state hands and, in 1822, became the home of the royal painting collection. Though the collection is not large, it contains almost exclusively superior works by old masters. This, combined with the exquisite presentation in elegant period rooms, makes the Mauritshuis one of the finest galleries in the Netherlands.

★ **The Anatomy Lesson of Dr Nicolaes Tulp** (1632)
Rembrandt's painting of doctors examining a corpse reflects the burgeoning contemporary interest in anatomy and science.

Museum Guide

The three floors of this museum are hung with paintings from top to bottom. To feature all aspects of the collection, the exhibits are constantly changing. The masterpieces are always on view, although not always hanging in the same location. Presentation is pleasantly haphazard, but all the paintings are labelled with the artist, title and year. A new exhibition wing has been added to the museum, connected to the historic building by an underground foyer, which also houses a brasserie and a well-stocked shop.

Ground floor

Basement

Vase with Flowers (1618)
Ambrosius Bosschaert captured the beauty of summer flowers but added the flies to remind us of our mortality.

Bordello Scene
(1658) This typical 17th-century genre painting of a brothel scene by Frans van Mieris de Oude (1635–81) has an unmistakable erotic undertone.

Main staircase

VISITORS' CHECKLIST

Practical Information
Plein 29, The Hague.
Tel 070-3023456.
ⓦ mauritshuis.nl
Open 1–6pm Mon, 10am–6pm
Tue–Sun (to 8pm Thu). **Closed**
1 Jan, 25 Dec. 🚾 ♿ 🗂 🖥 📷

Transport
From Den Haag CS: 🚌 22.
🚊 2, 3, 4, 6, 15. From Den
Haag HS: 🚌 18. 🚊 1.

The Goldfinch (1654)
This small, elegant painting
is by Carel Fabritius (1622–54),
a pupil of Rembrandt.

First floor

**The Way You Hear It Is
the Way You Sing It** (1663)
This moralistic genre
painting by Jan Steen *(see
p127)* probably shows
what is meant by a
"huishouden van Jan
Steen" – keeping one's
house like a pigsty.

★ The Louse Hunt (1653)
Gerard ter Borch's painting
depicts a domestic tableau
and reflects the Dutch
preoccupation with order
and cleanliness during the
17th century.

★ Girl with a Pearl Earring (1665)
At the mid-point of his career,
Johannes Vermeer painted this
haunting portrait of a girl wearing a
pearl earring. Stories about the true
origins of the girl abound.

Key to Floorplan
- ▢ Portrait gallery
- ▢ 15th- and early 16th-century works
- ▢ 18th-century Flemish paintings
- ▢ Golden room
- ▢ 17th-century Dutch paintings
- ▢ Non-exhibition space

The Hague's municipal museum, one of HP Berlage's most handsome designs

🏛 Panorama Mesdag

Zeestraat 65. 🚋 22, 24. 🚌 17.
Tel 070-3106665. **Open** 10am–5pm
Mon–Sat, noon–5pm Sun & public
hols. **Closed** 1 Jan, 25 Dec. 🅿
📷 on request. **W** panorama-
mesdag.com

Panorama Mesdag is one of the
best remaining panoramic
paintings of the 19th century. The
circular canvas, with a circum-
ference of 120 m (395 ft), depicts
the old fishing village of
Scheveningen. It is a breathtaking
moment when, after climbing
the creaking stairs leading
up to the panorama, you
suddenly emerge into
daylight, to be surr-
ounded by the
dunes and the sea.
The illusion is strength-
ened by genuine sand
and pieces of wreckage   *Victory Boogie*
laid at the foot of the   *Woogie*
painting. The painting was
done in 1881 by members of the
Haag School, led by HW Mesdag
(1831–1915) and his wife Sientje
(1834–1909). George Hendrik
Breitner (1857–1923) painted the
cavalrymen on the sand.

🏛 Gemeentemuseum Den Haag en Fotomuseum

Stadhouderslaan 41. 🚋 24.
Gemeentemuseum: **Tel** 070-3381111.
Open 11am–5pm Tue–Sun. **Closed**
1 Jan, 25 Dec. Fotomuseum: **Tel** 070-
3381144. **Open** noon–5pm Tue–Sun.
Closed 1 Jan, 25 Dec. 🅿 ♿ 🛗 📷
🏠 **W** gemeentemuseum.nl

The Gemeentemuseum
(municipal museum) was the

last piece of work to be carried
out by HP Berlage, founder of the
Amsterdam School. The museum
was completed in 1935, one year
after his death, and now contains
the largest collection of paintings
by Mondriaan in the world, with
works from all his various periods.
One of the high points of the
collection is *Victory Boogie
Woogie* (1943). Other works
exhibited here include paintings
by JH Weissenbruch and brothers
Maris and Josef Israëls, all of
whom were representatives of
the Haag School, which was
profoundly inspired by
the coastal landscape.
The main feature of
the applied art
section is the antique
Delftware and oriental
porcelain. The "Wonder
kamers" or "Wonder
Rooms" are housed in
the basement which is a
labyrinth of quirky displays, with
teenagers as the target audience.
Part of the Gemeente-museum,
with its entrance next door, is
the **Fotomuseum**, (www.
fotomuseumdenhaag.nl) which
stages temporary exhibitions of

Dutch and international
photography.

Omniversum

President Kennedylaan 5.
🚋 24. 🚌 17. **Tel** 0900-6664837.
Open daily, first show at 11am.
🅿 ♿ 📷 **W** omniversum.nl

The Omniversum (next to the
Gemeentemuseum) is a cross
between a planetarium and a
high-tech cinema. It puts on a
programme of films of space flights,
volcanic eruptions and ocean life.

🌳 Park Clingendael

Entrance from Alkemadelaan or
the Ruychrocklaan. 🚋 18. Park
Clingendael: **Open** sunrise–sunset
daily. Japanese Garden: **Open** end
Apr–mid-Jun & Oct: sunrise–sunset
daily. 📷

This country estate already existed
in the 16th century, when it had a
large, formal French-style garden.
In 1830 it was converted into a
pretty landscaped park. It contains
a Dutch garden, a rose garden,
grazing land for animals, rhodo-
dendron woods and an ancient
beech tree.

Overgrown bunkers in the
wood are a sombre reminder of

The picturesque Japanese Garden in Park Clingendael

For hotels and restaurants in this region see pp397–8 and pp410–11

World War II, when the Netherlands was occupied and the most senior German authorities took up quarters in Huis Clingendael. At the centre of the park lies the famous Japanese Garden, which was laid out in 1903 on the instructions of Baroness Marguérite Mary after a trip to Japan. The tea house and all the stones and ornaments in the garden were brought over from Japan by boat at the time.

🏰 Madurodam

George Maduroplein 1. 🚌 22. 🚊 9.
Tel 070-4162400. **Open** Jan–Mar & Nov–Dec: 11am–5pm; Apr–Aug: 9am–8pm; Sep–Oct: 9am–7pm; 24–31 Dec: 10am–7pm. 🏰 ♿ ♻
W madurodam.nl

Madurodam depicts the Netherlands in miniature – it consists of replicas of historical buildings such as the Binnenhof in The Hague (see p224), canal-side houses in Amsterdam and the Euromast tower in Rotterdam (see p236), built to a scale of 1:25. Other models include Schiphol Airport, windmills, polders, bulb fields and some examples of the country's modern architecture. At night, the streets and buildings are lit up by 50,000 tiny lamps.

Madurodam was opened in 1952 by Queen Juliana. JML Maduro designed the town in memory of his son George, who died at Dachau concentration camp in 1945. Profits go to children's charities.

The model city of Madurodam

❻ Scheveningen

Road Map B4. 🏔 52,000. 🚌 22.
🚊 1. 🚹 Gevers Deynootweg 990-58 (0900-3403505). 🛒 Thu.

This pleasant seaside resort is just 15 minutes by tram from the centre of The Hague. Like so many of the North Sea beach resorts, Scheveningen had its heyday in the 19th century. Nowadays it is a mixture of faded charm and modern garishness, though it remains a popular holiday resort because of its long sandy beach and the **Pier**, which, after years of neglect, has been renovated and reopened in 2015. There are many restaurants serving seafood.

The impressive **Kurhaus**, designed in the Empire style and now a luxurious hotel, was built in 1885, when Scheveningen was still a major spa town. Not far from the

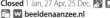

Kurhaus is **Sea Life Scheveningen**, where you can look through transparent tunnels at stingrays, sharks and many other sea creatures.
Muzee Scheveningen is devoted to the history of the village and the spa. Tours of Scheveningen lighthouse can also be booked.

Designed by Wim Quist, **Museum Beelden aan Zee** (seaside sculpture museum) can be found on the boulevard, half-hidden by a sand dune. Contemporary sculptures on the theme of the human figure are shown in the light rooms, on the terraces and in the garden.

Although the seaside resort has all but swallowed up the original fishing village, there is still a harbour and a large fish market. Fishing boat trips can be booked on the southern side of the harbour – a fun outing for the afternoon.

🐠 Sea Life Scheveningen

Strandweg 13. **Tel** 070-3542100.
Open 10am–6pm daily (to 8pm Jul & Aug). **Closed** 25 Dec. 🏰 ♿ 📷
W sealife.nl

🏛 Muzee Scheveningen

Neptunusstraat 92. **Tel** 070-3500830.
Open 10am–5pm Tue–Sat, noon–5pm Sun. **Closed** 1 Jan, 27 Apr, 25 Dec. 🏰 📷 🏰 **W** muzee.nl

🏛 Museum Beelden aan Zee

Harteveltstraat 1. **Tel** 070-3585857.
Open 10am–5pm Tue–Sun.
Closed 1 Jan, 27 Apr, 25 Dec. 🏰 📷
🏰 **W** beeldenaanzee.nl

Thsuki-no-hikari (Light of the Moon) by Igor Mitoraj in the dunes of the Museum Beelden aan Zee

❼ Street-by-Street: Delft

Delft dates back to 1075, its prosperity based on the weaving and brewing industries. In October 1654, however, an enormous explosion at the national arsenal destroyed much of the medieval town. The centre was rebuilt at the end of the 17th century and has remained relatively unchanged since then – houses in Gothic and Renaissance styles still stand along the tree-lined canals. Town life is concentrated on the Markt, which has the town hall at one end and the Nieuwe Kerk at the other. Visitors can dip into the scores of shops selling expensive, hand-painted Delftware or take a tour of local factories, the shops of which are often reasonably priced.

★ **Stedelijk Museum Het Prinsenhof**
William of Orange was killed on this staircase in 1584, the bullet holes still visible.

SCHOOLSTRAAT

ST AGATHAPLEIN

HIPPOLYTUSBUURT

OUDE DELFT

NIEUWSTRAAT

BOTERBRUG

OUDE DELFT

PEPERSTR

★ **Oude Kerk**
The 13th-century Oude Kerk contains the graves of prominent citizens such as that of the inventor of the microscope, Antonie van Leeuwenhoek.

The Oude Delft is lined with canalside houses in Renaissance style.

| 0 metres | 50 |
| 0 yards | 50 |

Sint-Hippolytuskapel
This austere red-brick chapel (1396) was used as an arsenal during the Reformation (see pp56–7).

Key

 — Recommended route

View of Delft (c.1660)
Johannes Vermeer's painting captures Delft on a cloudy summer afternoon. The original tower of the Nieuwe Kerk can be seen in the distance.

VISITORS' CHECKLIST

Practical Information
Road Map B4. 95,000.
delft.nl
Hippolytusbuurt 4. Tue, Thu, Sat. Mooi Weer Spelen (street theatre): mid-Jun; Delft Chamber Music Festival: early Aug.

Transport
Stationsplein.

★ Nieuwe Kerk
The church was built in several phases spread over many years. This statue of William of Orange stands in the middle of his opulent mausoleum.

KERK

MARKT

HOORSTRAAT

VROUW JUTTENLAND

DE VLOUW

VOLDERSGRACHT

OUDE LANGENDIJK

Koornbeurs (1650)
The façade of the old meat hall is decorated with animal heads. After 1871, the building was used as a corn exchange.

Stadhuis (1618)
The Renaissance-style town hall was designed by Hendrick de Keyser. The building is erected around a 13th-century Gothic tower.

Exploring Delft

Attractive Delft is world-famous for its blue-and-white pottery and is renowned in Holland as being the resting place of William of Orange (1533–84), the "father of the Netherlands". William led the resistance against Spanish rule in the 80 Years War *(see p53)* from his Delft headquarters; his victory meant religious freedom and independence for the Dutch. Delft was the Republic's main arsenal in the 17th century; an explosion of gunpowder destroyed a large part of the town in 1654. Artist Johannes Vermeer (1632–75) was born and lived in Delft.

The impressive Renaissance-style pulpit (1548) in the Oude Kerk

⬆ Oude Kerk

Heilige Geestkerkhof 25. **Tel** 015-2123015. **Open** Apr–Oct: 9am–6pm Mon–Sat; Nov–Jan: 11am–4pm Mon–Fri, 10am–5pm Sat; Feb & Mar: 10am–5pm Mon–Sat. 🎧 ♿ 🌐 oudeennieuwekerkdelft.nl

The original 13th-century church on this site has been extended many times. The beautifully carved clock tower, with its eye-catching steeple, dates from the 14th century. The Gothic north transept was added in the early 16th century by architect Anthonis Keldermans. Inside, the most striking feature is the wooden pulpit with canopy. The floor is studded with 17th-century gravestones, many beautifully decorated, including those for Johannes Vermeer and admiral Piet Hein (1577–1629).

⬆ Nieuwe Kerk

Markt 80. **Tel** 015-2123025. **Open** Apr–Oct: 9am–6pm Mon–Sat; Nov–Jan: 11am–4pm Mon–Fri, 10am–5pm Sat; Feb & Mar: 10am–5pm Mon–Sat. 🎧 ♿ 🌐 oudeennieuwekerkdelft.nl

The Nieuwe Kerk was built between 1383 and 1510 but needed large-scale restoration after the fire of 1536 and the massive explosion of 1654 in the arsenal. In 1872, PJH Cuypers *(see p375)* added the 100-m (328-ft) tower to the Gothic façade. Inside, the most noticeable feature is William of Orange's imposing mausoleum, designed in 1614 by Hendrick de Keyser. In the middle stands a statue of William, impressive in his battledress. Not far from him is the lonely figure of his dog, which died a few days after his master. The tombs of the royal family lie in the crypt. The church is being restored, so parts of it may not be accessible.

🏛 Stedelijk Museum Het Prinsenhof

St-Agathaplein 1. **Tel** 015-2602358. **Open** 11am–5pm daily & public hols. **Closed** 1 Jan, 27 Apr, 25 Dec. 🎧 📷 🌐 prinsenhof-delft.nl

This peaceful former convent was the scene of William of Orange's assassination. It now houses Delft's history museum, with pottery, tapestries and portraits of royalty. In 1572, during the uprising against the Spanish, William commandeered the convent as his headquarters. In 1584, a fanatical Catholic, Balthasar Geraerts, shot and killed him on the instructions of Philip II of Spain.

The Nieuwe Kerk overlooking Delft market

Delftware

Delftware *(see pp32–3)* stems from majolica, introduced to the Netherlands in the 16th century by Italian immigrants who had settled around Delft and Haarlem and begun producing wall tiles with Dutch designs, such as birds and flowers. By the next century, however, Dutch traders had started to deal in delicate Chinese porcelain; this eventually led to the collapse of the market for the less refined Dutch earthenware. Towards 1650, though, the Chinese example was adopted in the Netherlands and craftsmen designed plates, vases and bowls with pictures of Dutch landscapes, biblical tableaux and scenes from everyday life. De Porceleyne Fles factory, which dates from 1652, is one of the several Delftware potteries open to the public for tours.

17th-century hand-painted Delft tiles

🏛 Vermeer Centrum Delft

Voldersgracht 21. **Tel** 015-2138588.
Open 10am–5pm daily. **Closed** 25 Dec.
📷 🎨 Fri (Dutch) & Sun (English). 🚻
🖊 🏠 **W** vermeerdelft.nl

The Vermeer Centrum celebrates the work of one of Delft's most enigmatic artists, Johannes Vermeer (1632–75). The space, dedicated entirely to the life of the artist, has a series of beautifully designed displays including a life-size copy of his famous masterpiece, *The Girl with a Pearl Earring (1665–67)*. On the upper floor, visitors can learn about his painting techniques, particularly his use of perspective, colour and light.

❽ Maassluis

Road Map: B4. 🗻 31,600. 🚉
🛈 Heldringstraat 101 (010-5911440).
🗓 Tue, Fri. **W** ervaarmaassluis.nl

The settlement of Maassluis grew up around the locks, which date from 1367; the herring trade brought prosperity to the town. The historic town centre is adorned with 17th-century buildings, such as the **Grote Kerk**, with its famous organ, and the **Stadhuis**, from 1650. The town's fine steam tug still goes out to sea. Many of Dutch writer Maarten 't Hart's novels are set in the Maassluis of his youth.

❾ Schiedam

Road Map: B4. 🗻 75,000. 🚉
🛈 Buitenhavenweg 9 (010-4733000).
🗓 Tue am, Fri. **W** sdam.nl

Schiedam was granted its city charter in 1275 and soon afterwards expanded into a centre for trade and fishing.

It became the centre of the genever (Dutch gin) industry. The production of genever is still important to the town, as evidenced by the **five tallest windmills in the world** and the old warehouses and distilleries. In the bar of the **Jenever Museum** (national genever museum), you can familiarize yourself with the enormous range of Dutch genevers and liqueurs.

The **Stedelijk Museum** (municipal museum), with exhibits of contemporary art and on modern history, is in the former St-Jacobs Gasthuis. Its main attraction is the collection of artwork by the group known as COBRA (consisting of painters from COpenhagen, BRussels and Amsterdam).

🏛 Jenever Museum

Lange Haven 74. **Tel** 010-2469676.
Open noon–5pm Tue–Sun & public hols. **Closed** 1 Jan, 27 Apr, 25 & 26 Dec. 🚻 **W** jenevermuseum.nl

🏛 Stedelijk Museum

Hoogstraat 112. **Tel** 010-2463666.
Open 10am–5pm Tue–Sun.
Closed 1 Jan, 25 Dec. 🚻 📷 🏠
W stedelijkmuseumschiedam.nl

Genever and corn brandy, products of the genever capital of Schiedam

⑩ Street-by-Street: Rotterdam

This route takes you through the area to the south of the town centre, which was devastated by heavy bombing in May 1940. On your way you will see the Witte Huis (White House), one of the few buildings spared by the bombs. Further on you will pass by some unusual modern architecture, such as the cube-shaped apartments, "Het Potlood" ("the pencil"), and the maritime museum, devoted to the history of shipping. In front of this museum is a monument by Ossip Zadkine, which is one of the symbols of Rotterdam. The undeveloped area around Station Blaak was completely built up before the bombing.

★ Schielandhuis
Built between 1662 and 1665, the Schielandhuis is one of the few surviving buildings from the 17th century.

BLAAK

GLASHAVEN

BOOMP

★ De Verwoeste Stad
The statue *De Verwoeste Stad* (The Devastated City) by Ossip Zadkine, located in front of the maritime museum, commemorates the bombing of May 1940. It is considered one of the most famous statues in the country.

De Buffel
The old armoured vessel *De Buffel*, now open for visitors, was for many years a training ship.

Key
— Recommended route

Erasmusbrug
(Erasmus Bridge)
The glittering
Erasmusbrug is now
one of the symbols
of Rotterdam.

VISITORS' CHECKLIST

Practical Information
Road Map B4. 🚊 598,500.
🌐 rotterdam.info
ℹ️ Coolsingel 195–7 (010-7900
185). 🏪 Tue–Sun. 🎬 Film
festival: Jan; ROBIN Rotterdam
Unlimited (carnival): Apr;
Metropolis (pop concerts): Jul;
Zomercarnaval: Jul;
Wereldhavendagen: Sep.

Transport
🚇 Stationsplein.
🚌 Stationsplein.

| 0 metres | 150 |
| 0 yards | 150 |

Station Blaak is an
unusual metro and railway
station, designed by
architect HCH Reijnders.

Het Potlood (the pencil), an
unusually shaped apartment
block near Station Blaak, was
designed by P Blom.

★ Kubus-Paalwoningen
A bizarre creation (1978–84) by
architect P Blom, the cube-
shaped apartments are among
the most striking buildings of
modern Rotterdam.

VERLENGDE WILLEMSBRUG

Willemswerf
Willemswerf is one of
Rotterdam's highest and most
impressive office blocks. The
building, which is completely
white, was completed in
1989 and is a design by
architect WG Quist.

Witte Huis (White House)
This is one of the few buildings
to survive the World War II
bombing raids. For a long time,
the 45-m (148-ft) building was
one of the tallest office blocks
in Europe.

Exploring Rotterdam

Rotterdam is not only a symbol of post-war economic recovery – it has more to offer than endless stretches of thriving docklands and industrial areas. Rotterdam has increasingly become one of the most important cultural centres of the Netherlands. Although the city was a wasteland immediately after World War II, it quickly recovered and now boasts one of the country's largest universities, a park containing a number of interesting museums and a large zoo.

Canalside houses in a peaceful corner of Delfshaven

A gorilla sitting with her young at Diergaarde Blijdorp

🐾 Blijdorp

Blijdorplaan 8. 🚌 40, 44. **Tel** 0900-1857. **Open** 9am–6pm daily. 🅿️ 👶 ♿ 🎫 W **rotterdamzoo.nl**

Rotterdam Zoo, often called *Diergaarde Blijdorp*, is in many ways a unique zoo. Its predecessor, De Rotterdamsche Diergaarde (Rotterdam zoo), was built in 1857 in the town centre. In 1937, the zoo was moved to Blijdorp polder, outside the centre. The architect Van Ravesteyn designed the new zoo and Blijdorp became one of the first zoos to be designed by one architect.

Blijdorp is also one of the few European zoos to have its own research department. It plays an important part in breeding programmes for rare and endangered species, such as the black-footed penguin.

For the last few years, attempts have been made to convert Blijdorp to the type of zoo which tries to present the animals in the most natural habitat possible. Another addition at the zoo is the gorilla island. The huge, extremely popular Oceanium is a theme park showcasing sea creatures, including sharks.

🏛 Delfshaven

Rotterdam City Tourist Information, Coolsingel 195–7 **Tel** 010-7900185 . M

Delfshaven, which is outside the town centre and is mainly famous for being the birthplace of naval hero Piet Hein, looks very different from the rest of Rotterdam. This oasis of both history and culture within the modern city consists of a few streets with historic buildings and a harbour with old sailing boats. The former warehouses are now shops selling antiques, paintings and antiquarian books. There are also museums and restaurants.

It was from Delfshaven that the Dutch Pilgrim Fathers left for America in 1620.

☀️ Euromast

Parkhaven 20. M Dijkzicht. **Tel** 010-4364811. **Open** Apr–Sep: 9:30am–10pm daily; Oct–Mar: 10am–10pm daily. 🎫 🅿️ ♿ W **euromast.nl**

One of the most famous symbols of Rotterdam, Euromast is the tallest building in the town. Before its construction began, in 1960, the mayor at the time, Van Walsum, complained that there was only enough money to build a 50 m (165 ft) tower. This caused an uproar, because the mast was meant to be higher than the Utrecht Domtoren (cathedral tower), which was, at 112 m (367 ft), the highest building in the country. That same evening, the mayor was called by rich Rotterdam port barons wanting to contribute money to the construction of the building. These donations in part enabled the tower to reach 110 m (361 ft). A space tower was later added to the top of the building for the Communicatie-'70 show in 1970, bringing the tower to a total height of 185 m (607 ft).

The Rotterdam Beurstraverse, or "Koopgoot", a bustling shopping mall

For hotels and restaurants in this region see pp397–8 and pp410–11

Peter Struycken's masterpiece of light effects under the Het Nieuwe Instituut

Kunsthal

Westzeedijk 341, Museumpark.
🚊 8, 20. **Tel** 010-4400301. **Open** Tue–Sun. **Closed** Mon, 27 Jan, 30 Apr, 25 Dec. 🅿 📷 ⚡ **w** kunsthal.nl

The Kunsthal, with its austere style, is used for temporary exhibitions, putting up around 25 per year, with "high art" and pop culture going cheek by jowl. It offers a journey through modern art, fashion, photography and design, featuring artists from all around the world.

Designed by the avant-garde architects OMA, the building has ramps instead of stairs.

Kinderkunsthal Villa Zebra

Stieltjesstraat 21. **Tel** 010-2411717.
🚊 20, 23, 25. 🚌 48. Ⓜ D.
Open noon–5pm Wed, Fri–Sun; Tue–Sun summer hols. **Closed** 1 Jan, 27 Apr, 25, 26 & 31 Dec. 📷 🅿 ⚡
w villazebra.nl

This is an arts centre specifically for children, where they can become familiar with art and express themselves via poetry, theatre and visual arts.

Het Nieuwe Instituut

Museumpark 25. **Tel** 010-4401200.
🚊 4, 5. 🚌 32. Ⓜ Eendrachtsplein.
Open 10am–5pm Tue–Sat, 11am–5pm Sun & public hols.
Closed 1 Jan, 27 Apr, 25 Dec. 📷 ⚡ 📷 **w** hetnieuweinstituut.nl

After being bombed in 1940 and then ravaged by fire, the old city centre was a wasteland. Thanks to large-scale rebuilding after the war, Rotterdam now has many fine examples of modern architecture. This includes famous structures such as the *paalwoningen* (cube-shaped apartments), and the spectacular developments along the Kop van Zuid across the Nieuwe Maas. Het Nieuwe Instituut is the result of a merger between the national architectural archives, the Premsela Institute for Design and Fashion and Virtueel Platform (which aims to promote digital culture). The Instituut hosts regular exhibitions examining the influence of new technologies on art and design.

Rotterdam City Centre

① Kunsthal
② Euromast
③ Het Nieuwe Instituut
④ Museum Boijmans Van Beuningen
(see pp238–9)

Key

■ Street-by-street map (pp234–5)

For map symbols see back flap

Museum Boijmans Van Beuningen

The museum is named after two art experts, FJO Boijmans and DG van Beuningen, who presented their own private collections to the town. The museum thus ended up with one of the finest collections in the Netherlands. Although it is particularly renowned for its unique collection of old masters, the museum also represents all aspects of art and design, from medieval works by Jan van Eyck to imaginative exhibitions of contemporary artists' work.

Three Marys at the Tomb
(1425–35) Brothers Jan and Hubert Van Eyck collaborated on this colourful work depicting the tomb of the resurrected Christ. Acquired with the collection of D. G. van Beuningen in 1958.

Ticket desk

Library

Ground floor

Courtya

Exhibition entrance

Nautilus Cup
(c.1590) The god Neptune sits on top of this beautiful piece from the Dutch Renaissance.

Entrance to temporary exhibitions

Entrance to permanent exhibitions

Key to Floorplan

- 15th–17th centuries
- Surrealists
- Print collection
- Applied art and design
- Temporary exhibitions
- Non-exhibition space
- 18th century–1945 and Surrealists

★ **The Pedlar**
(c.1500)
Hieronymous
Bosch's painting
shows mankind
trying to avoid the
hazards of life.

First
floor

Stairs

Auditorium

Restaurant

Basement

VISITORS' CHECKLIST

Practical Information
Museumpark 18–20, Rotterdam.
Tel 010-4419400.
W boijmans.nl
Open 11am–5pm Tue–Sun &
public hols. **Closed** 1 Jan, 27 Apr,
25 Dec.

Transport
Centraal Station. 32.
7. M Eendrachtsplein.

La Petite Danseuse
(1880–81) Impressionist
Edgar Degas made several
studies in bronze of this
young Belgian dancer.

★ **Titus at his Desk**
(1655) Rembrandt portrayed his sickly
son in an introspective mood, bathed
in a tender light that heightens the
pallor of his brooding features. Titus
was to die aged 27.

★ **The Tower of Babel**
(c.1568) Pieter Brueghel took
an Old Testament theme and
painted a ten-storey structure
swarming with people.

Rotterdam, City of Water

One of Rotterdam's biggest and busiest attractions is its port, one of the largest ports in the world. Various operators organize daily tours around the port area, where you will see container ports, shipyards and dry docks. The sheer scale of the port and related industrial areas, which have a turnover of billions of euros, is quite staggering. Europe's largest container port, the Europoort alone stretches for 40 km (25 miles) along the river banks.

Rotterdam
The port sees approximately 30,000 vessels docking each year. Germany's Ruhr district is the main destination for the transported goods.

The Port of Rotterdam

The port of Rotterdam, of which only a fraction is shown by this map, stretches from the town centre to the North Sea coast and is divided into nine areas. These are, from east to west, the Stadhavens, the Vierhavens, Merwehaven, Waalhaven, Eemhaven, Vondelingenplat, Botlek, Europoort and the Maasvlakte. The port is still expanding and will soon run out of available space. Land reclamation from the North Sea is considered the most appropriate solution.

Old Delfshave

Pernis
The biggest refinery in the world, Pernis operates day and night refining crude oil, which is used to make hundreds of products. Lit up at night, it looks like something out of science fiction.

Dry docks

Spido Tour
Various tours around the port of Rotterdam are
available. Those lasting an hour and a half visit
the town centre ports *(see map below)*, whereas the
day-long tours travel as far as the Maasvlakte.

World Port Days
There are many types of ships to be admired
on the World Port Days, which are held in
early September and attract thousands
of visitors.

Euromast

Hotel New York
This hotel has been set up in the
early 20th-century head office of
the former Holland-America Line.
The nearby arrival halls are also of
architectural significance.

Maashaven

Zuiderpark

Maastunnel filtration plant

0 Kilometres	3
0 miles	3

Europoort

A total of 29,122 ocean-going vessels and 110,000
inland vessels put in at Rotterdam Port during 2015.
This makes it the busiest port in Europe. The name
"Europoort" says it all – Rotterdam is Europe's port.
Rotterdam Port is one of the major employers of the
Netherlands, with more than 300,000 people working
for it either directly or indirectly. Total added value of
the port is more than €28 billion, approximately 10 per
cent of the country's gross domestic product.

Bustling Rotterdam port, loading and unloading many millions of
containers every year

Key

--- Road

— Railway

St Janskerk, Gouda

This former Catholic church dating from 1485 was rebuilt in the Gothic style after it was struck by fire in 1552. The church received a number of unusual stained-glass windows from rich Catholic benefactors, such as Philip II of Spain, between 1555 and 1571. After the Reformation *(see pp56–7)*, the church became Protestant, but even the fanatical Iconoclasts did not have the heart to destroy the windows. Prominent Protestants, including Rotterdam aldermen, donated stained-glass windows to the church up to 1604. The stained-glass windows are heavily symbolic of the politics of the time – Bible stories had to be covered after the conflict between the Catholics and Protestants, which led to the Thirty Years War between Spain and the Netherlands.

The Nave
At 123 m (404 ft), this nave is the longest in Holland. The floor is inset with memorial stones.

Judith Beheading Holofernes
This is a detail from a window which depicts Judith beheading Holofernes. Dirck Crabeth, who made the window, shows John the Baptist holding a lamb. Next to him kneels Jan de Ligne, the count of Arenberg, who commissioned the window.

Visitors' entrance

KEY

① **The Adulteress** (1601) Dressed as a Franciscan monk, Jesus appeals to the people in the temple to forgive the adulteress, who is being guarded by Spanish soldiers.

② North aisle

③ Baptism of Jesus

④ The Purification of the Temple

⑤ South aisle

The Relief of Leiden (1603) William of Orange as leader of the resistance of the people of Leiden against the Spanish siege of 1574.

Nieuwpoort town hall, built over the canal in 1696

The Purification of the Temple
William of Orange donated this
window, symbolizing the
Netherlands' longing to drive out
the Spaniards, in 1567. Traders
watch angrily as Jesus drives
moneylenders from the temple.

Baptism of Jesus (1555)
John the Baptist baptizes Jesus in
the Jordan River. The window was
a gift from the Bishop of Utrecht.

⓫ Gouda

Road Map B4. 72,000.
Markt 35 (0182-589110).
Thu am & Sat; phone tourist office
for information on cheese markets.
welcometogouda.com

In 1272, Floris V granted Gouda its
city charter. Thanks to its strategic
position on the Hollandse IJssel
and the Gouwe, the town
developed into a flourishing
centre for beer brewing and
the textile industry in the 15th
century. However, Gouda became
economically and politically
isolated during the Thirty Years
War. The town recovered in the
17th and beginning of the 18th
century due to its trade in cheese,
candles and pipes.

Gouda is still famous today for
its **cheese** and **cheese markets**.
The markets are held on an
enormous three-sided square
around the **Stadhuis**, which
dates from 1450 and is one of
the oldest in the Netherlands.
With its many pinnacles and
turrets, the building gives the
impression of being in the
Flemish Gothic style.

The **Museum Gouda**
(municipal museum) is in the
former **Catharina Gasthuis** (St
Catherine's hospital), which
dates from the 14th century
and later. The museum features
paintings from the Hague
School and unusual 16th-
century altar pieces.

🏛 Stadhuis
Markt 1. **Tel** 0182-589110.
Open timings vary, call to check.
Closed public hols. by appt.

🏛 Museum Gouda
Achter de Kerk 14. **Tel** 0182-
331000. **Open** 11am–5pm Tue–Sun.
Closed 1 Jan, 27 Apr 25 Dec.
museumgouda.nl

⓬ Reeuwijkse Plassen

Road Map B4. 0182-589110.

The Reeuwijk lake district
was formed through peat
excavation. Narrow roads pass
through the rectangular lakes,
which owe their shape to former parcels of land. The small
village of **Sluipwijk** seems
almost to fade away into the
water. The best way to explore
this area is by bicycle or on
foot. In the summer months
you can also take a boat trip
through this typically Dutch
lakeland scenery.

⓭ Nieuwpoort

Road Map B4. 1,600. 90
from Utrecht.

The whole of this magnificent
fortified town, which obtained
its city charter in 1283, has
been declared a listed area. The
17th-century street layout is
practically intact. The city walls,
which are also intact, were
originally built to ward off
attacks from the French but
served mainly to protect the
town against flooding. The town
hall, built over the inundation
lock, dates from 1696, while
the arsenal dates from 1781.
Restoration work was carried
out in 1998.

⓮ Gorinchem

Road Map C4. 🚗 35,000. 🚉
ℹ️ Grote Markt 17 (0183-631525).
🛍️ Mon am. **W** vvvgorinchem.nl

Gorinchem, situated on the Linge and the Waal, was the property of the Lords van Arkel in the 13th century. They were driven out by Count William VI and the town was then absorbed into Holland. Fortifications built at the end of the 16th century are still partially intact and offer marvellous views over the water meadows and the Waal. Of the four town gateways, only the **Dalempoort** remains. The Linge harbour, in the heart of the town, is still mostly authentic, especially the narrow part.

Environs

On the other side of the Waal is the 14th-century **Slot Loevestein**. It has a very eventful history as a toll castle, a defence point along the Hollandse Waterlinie (a strip of land flooded as a defence line, *see p201*) and a state prison in the 17th century. From Gorinchem, the castle can be reached by ferry, changing at Woudrichem.

🏯 Slot Loevestein

Poederoijen. **Tel** 0183-447171.
Open May, Jun & Sep: 11am–5pm Tue–Sun; Jul & Aug: 11am–5pm daily; Oct–Apr: 11am–5pm Sat & Sun. **Closed** 1 Jan, Good Friday, 27 Apr, 25 Dec. 🐾 🔲 🎥 🏠 May, Jun & Sep: Tue–Sun; Jul & Aug: daily; Oct–Apr: weekends. **W** slotloevestein.nl

Glass blower in Leerdam

⓯ Leerdam

Road Map C4. 🚗 20,000. 🚉
ℹ️ Sundsvall 2 (0345-614960).
🛍️ Thu am, Sat pm. **W** vvvleerdam.nl

Leerdam is renowned for its glass industry. Royal Dutch Glass Factory designs by Berlage, Copier and other artists can be admired in the **Nationaal Glasmuseum** (national glass museum), and traditional crystal production can be observed at Royal Leerdam Kristal. **Fort Asperen**, on the Linge, is one of the best-preserved defence points remaining along the Nieuwe Hollandse Waterlinie (*see p201*).

🏛️ Nationaal Glasmuseum

Lingedijk 28. **Tel** 0345-614960.
Open 10am–5pm Tue–Sat, noon–5pm Sun. 🐾 🏠
W nationaalglasmuseum.nl

⓰ Dordrecht

Road Map B4. 🚗 118,600. 🚉 ℹ️
Spuiboulevard 99 (0900-4636888). 🛍️
Tue am, Fri & Sat. **W** vvvdordrecht.nl

The oldest town in Holland, Dordrecht received its city charter in 1220 and was the most important harbour and commercial town of the region until the 1500s. Even after being outstripped by Rotterdam, Dordrecht remained an important inland port. In the old port area, mansions, warehouses and almshouses are reminders of the past. The **Grote Kerk** (13th to 17th century), in the Brabant Gothic style, has an ornate interior. **Huis Simon van Gijn**, in the period rooms of an 18th-century house, has a collection of old prints, clothes and toys. The shady **Hof** (court of justice) (1512) contains the **Statenzaal** (state room), where the States of Holland met for the first time in 1572, thus laying the foundation of the independent Republic of the Netherlands.

🏛️ Grote Kerk

Lange Geldersekade 2. **Tel** 078-614 4660. **Open** Apr–Oct:10:30am–4:30pm Tue–Sat, noon–4pm Sun; Nov & Dec: 2–4pm Tue, Thu & Sat. 🎥 Apr–Oct: 2:15pm Thu & Sat. 🏠
W grotekerk-dordrecht.nl

🏛️ Hof and Statenzaal

Hof 6. **Tel** 078-7705250. **Open** 11am–5pm Tue–Sun. **Closed** 25 Dec, 1 Jan.
W hethofvannederland.nl

A group of windmills at Kinderdijk, for centuries draining water from the Alblasserwaard

⓱ Kinderdijk

Road Map B4. 🚌 90 from Rotterdam Lombardijen station; 18 from Dordrecht Centraal Station. 🛈 Nederwaard 1 (078-6912830). 🚲 🖥 kinderdijk.nl

The famous **19 windmills** which were used to drain the Alblasserwaard in the past are situated where the Noord and the Lek converge. New *boezems* (drainage pools) and windmills, however, were needed time and time again in order to span the height differences as the land settled. The group of windmills is a UNESCO World Heritage Site.

Middelharnis Lane (c.1689) by Meindert Hobbema

⓲ Brielle

Road Map B4. 🏠 16,000. 🚇 metro Rotterdam CS to Spijkenisse, then 103. 🛈 Markt 1 (0181-475475). 🛍 Mon; Jul & Aug: Wed.

The magnificent port of Brielle is a protected town. The 18th-century fortifications are still mostly intact. The town, birthplace of Admiral van Tromp, held a strategic position until the 1872 opening of the *Nieuwe Waterweg* (new waterway). The **Historisch Museum Den Briel** (historic museum of Brielle) depicts this and the famous Beggars of the Sea invasion in 1572 *(see box)*. The tourist information office is inside the museum. The 15th-century **St.-Catharijnekerk**, in Brabant Gothic style, rises from the surrounding monuments.

🏛 **Historisch Museum Den Briel** Markt 1. **Tel** 0181-475475. **Open** 10am–5pm Tue–Sat, 1–5pm Sun. **Closed** Mon, public hols. 🚲 ♿ 🖥 historischmuseumdenbriel.nl

⓳ Hellevoetsluis

Road Map B4. 🏠 40,000. 🚇 metro Rotterdam CS to Spijkenisse, then 101. 🛈 Industriehaven 8 (0181-314479). 🛍 Sat.

At the end of the 16th century, this was the naval port for the States of Holland. Fleets led by van Tromp, de Ruyter and Piet Hein left from Hellevoetsluis for their naval battles in the 1600s. Within the old fortifications, visitors are reminded of the town's naval past by the

Prinsehuis, the 17th-century lodgings of the Admiralty of the Maze, the dry dock and **Fort Haerlem** from the 19th century.

You can learn all about fire and fire-fighting in the local **National Brandweermuseum** (fire service museum). It also houses the tourist information office.

🏛 **Nationaal Brandweermuseum** Industriehaven 8. **Tel** 0181-314479. **Open** Apr–Oct: 10am–4pm (from 11am Sun). ♿ 🖥 🖥 nationaalbrandweermuseum.nl

⓴ Middelharnis

Road Map B4. 🏠 17,900. 🚌 436 from Rotterdam Zuidplein. 🛍 Wed.

During the 16th century, Middelharnis became the regional port, outstripping Goedereede. Until the end

of the 19th century, fishing remained the most important source of income.

The Late Gothic cruciform church (15th century) stands at the heart of the village. Outside the town hall (1639) hang the wooden blocks that women branded as gossips had to carry through the town.

㉑ Goedereede

Road Map A4. 🏠 1,900. 🚇 metro R'dam CS to Spijkenisse, then 111 to Hellevoetsluis, then 104. 🛍 Tue.

Goedereede was an important port in the 14th and 15th centuries. This town, where Pope Adrianus VI was born, began to decline when it began to silt up. The early harbour houses are reminiscent of the livelier days of old.

The Beggars of the Sea

The Beggars of the Sea were a pirate fleet which consisted of minor Dutch and Flemish nobles who had fled at the beginning of the Inquisition and sailed across the North Sea. They plundered other ships and caused trouble in English and German ports. They were forced to leave England, where

Van Lumey

some of their ships were berthed, in spring 1572. Without any clear plan, they entered Den Briel on 1 April under the command of van Lumey, which they then held "for the Prince". Other towns joined the Beggars of the Sea or were forcibly occupied by them. Their pursuits represented the first steps towards Dutch independence from Spain and the creation of Dutch sea power.

ZEELAND

The tiny province of Zeeland, as its name implies, is inextricably linked with water and the sea. For hundreds of years, the power of the North Sea and the flooding deltas of the Maas and Schelde rivers have shaped the landscape, encouraging resilience in the inhabitants and the desire to control the elements.

From earliest times, storms and floods have taken their toll here. In the last century, the devastation of two world wars was followed by the disastrous floods and storm surges of 1953. Although there are a number of fine churches and public buildings dating as far back as the 14th century, in places near the coast there are very few houses more than 50 years old. As a result, determination to keep the waters at bay has spawned massive construction and canal building, with giant dams and land reclamation schemes offering a level of security that has changed the landscape forever.

The storms were not all bad news. Traces of Roman settlements were uncovered, and lakes and inland waterways have become a haven for wildlife and a playground for lovers of watersports. Towns such as Middelburg, Zierikzee and Veere and villages such as Nisse, St Anna-ter-Muiden and Dreischor have lots of old buildings, some of which have been restored to their 17th-century grandeur, with attractive features such as bell towers and frescoes.

The close relationship with water and the sea is well documented in a variety of small museums. The tangible benefits are perhaps twofold: an abundance of seafood for the province's restaurants, and the aforementioned opportunities for watersports. Few regions in Europe offer as much scope for sailing, windsurfing, water skiing and diving as does little Zeeland.

The 15th-century Stadhuis (town hall) dominating the historic town of Veere

◀ Aerial view of the beach at low tide, Domburg

Exploring Zeeland

Touring around Zeeland, you cannot ignore the sea. The journey becomes a small adventure as you encounter bridges, dams and ferry docks. Sometimes you will travel along a straight ribbon of a road, sometimes a windy lane. The ever-present and often turbulent water is never the same colour for long: it can quickly change from a grey-green reflecting the vivid blue sky to the white of wave crests beneath leaden skies. Passing over one of the many dams, you will reach the next island, with its own special character. Tholen, for example, is quiet – almost morose – whereas Walcheren is full of surprises and has a wonderful atmosphere. Travelling through Zeeland is a journey of discovery.

Getting Around

The best way to visit all the islands of Zeeland is by car. The roads here are excellent – the A58 or the N57 will quickly bring you to the centre of the province, where you can choose one of the smaller roads to take you to your destination. The through train will take you from Amsterdam to Middelburg and Vlissingen in just two and a half hours. If you want to explore other islands, you will need to continue on a regional bus – though this can be quite time-consuming. There are many cycle paths and it is great fun cycling over the dykes.

Sights at a Glance

1. *Oosterschelde Stormvloed-*
   kering pp250–51
2. *Middelburg pp252–3*
3. Veere
4. Domburg
5. Vlissingen
6. Westkapelle
7. Zierikzee
8. Haamstede
9. Brouwershaven
10. Bruinisse
11. St Annaland
12. St Maartensdijk
13. Tholen
14. Goes
15. Yerseke
16. Nisse
17. Hulst
18. Terneuzen
19. Sluis
20. Cadzand

Key

━━━ Motorway
━━━ Main road
┄┄┄ Minor road
━━━ Scenic route
──── Minor railway
▬▬▬ National border
▬▬▬ Regional border

Tilting at the ring – a Zeeland sport

Divers at Zeeland's inland lakes

Fishing nets drying at Yerseke

The fertile black clay soil of Zeeland

❶ Oosterschelde Stormvloedkering

Throughout the centuries, the history of the Netherlands has been dominated by its people's struggle against the sea. After the disastrous floods of 1953, which hit Zeeland heavily, the battle to remove the danger of the sea once and for all was undertaken in earnest. Now the Dutch seem to have minimized the threat of flooding by building dykes and dams and closing off tidal inlets, all of which has had a major impact on the landscape.

The Windsock
When the windsock is full, a warning is sounded, and people are advised to avoid driving over the dams and bridges between the islands. Vigilance saves lives.

Storms
Storms are a part of everyday life in Zeeland: storms on the beach or over the flat polders, storms which blow the cobwebs away and storms which make you fear for your life.

The Fateful Night of 1953
On the night of 31 January 1953, an event considered impossible in modern times occurred. A combination of spring tides and storms breached the dykes and washed them away as loose sand. A total of 1,835 people lost their lives.

Deltapark Neeltje Jans

This attraction has been built on an artificial island, Neeltje Jans, on which the piers for the Oosterschelde Stormvloedkering (storm surge barrier) were assembled, then taken by special barges to their positions. Now that task is finished, the island is being used mainly for recreational and informative purposes. At the Deltapark you can find out about the Delta projects and about how the barrier works. You can see the barrier from the inside, and then take a boat trip to view it from the outside. There is an aquarium here, as well as a seal show; you can also experience a simulated hurricane in the "hurricane machine".

Neeltje Jans, educating visitors about the sea

Luctor et Emergo
This Latin motto meaning "I struggle and emerge victorious" is on Zeeland's coat of arms, which depicts the Netherlands lion half in the water. This was wholly appropriate for 1953.

Concrete Piers
The piers were made on the artificial island of Neeltje Jans and then transported by special barges to their destination. This mighty task attracted a great deal of attention.

VISITORS' CHECKLIST

Practical Information
Road Map A4–5. Deltapark Neeltje Jans, Faelweg 5, Vrouwenpolder.
Open Apr–Oct: 10am–5:30pm daily; Nov–Mar: 10am–5pm Wed, Sat & Sun. 🅿️ ♿ 🖥️ 🍴 🎦

Transport
🚌 133.

The Delta Works
The Delta Works have had far-reaching consequences for the landscape and environment. The Zeeland islands, having been joined to the mainland, are no longer isolated.

Half-open Buttress Dam

It took 13 years and €3.6 billion (two-thirds of the cost of the Delta Works) to build the Oosterscheldekering. After much deliberation, the decision was made to keep open the estuary and to preserve the salty estuary habitat. A half-open multiple buttress dam was built, with 62 sliding gates, which are closed on average once a year during heavy storms. This keeps the water salty and has preserved the unique salt marshes and mud flats of the Oosterschelde.

KEY

① **Concrete piers** bear the sea wall.

② **The sliding gates** are closed only when the water is high.

③ **A road** has been built over the dam.

④ **Ground protection** prevents the earth from being washed away.

⑤ **The piers** rest on solid foundations.

The Terps
Man-made mounds, such as these near Borssele, were built in the 11th and 12th centuries to protect farms and villages from the water.

Street-by-Street: Middelburg

Middelburg suffered heavy Nazi bombing in 1940. A lot of what is to be seen in the town today has been rebuilt, including the Stadhuis (town hall) and the abbey. The town is still redolent with the atmosphere of the Golden Age, an era during which the Dutch East India Company thrived in the port area along the quay. Middelburg is a pretty town and there is plenty to be seen on a walk around the centre. Children will be kept busy by Mini Mundi.

★ **St-Jorisdoelen**
This *doelen*, the guardsmen's guild building, was built in 1582 and destroyed in 1940; the façade was rebuilt in 1969.

Zeeuws Archief, the archives of the province, are now housed in a historic monument, the van de Perre House on the Hofplen, which has been given a spectacular new wing.

Key

— Recommended route

0 metres   50
0 yards   50

★ **Stadhuis**
The 15th-century town hall was completely destroyed by fire in 1940 and has been partially rebuilt. A 20th-century extension can be seen on the northern side.

The fish market
already existed in 1559. The passageway, with its Tuscan pillars, dates from 1830.

Mini Mundi
This miniature town, started in 1954, now contains more than 350 buildings, and forms part of the Mini Mundi amusement park.

VISITORS' CHECKLIST

Practical Information
Road Map A5. 🏔 47,500.
🅦 minimundi.nl
🅦 uitinmiddelburg.nl
🛈 Markt 51. **Tel** 0118–674300.
Open Mon–Sat. 🕒 🔥
🚌 Thu, Sat. Stadhuis: Markt.
🚗 from Stadhuis (tickets are available from Markt 51).

Transport
🚌 🚉

★ **Abbey**
Many years of restoration work on the abbey have finally paid off.

Lange Jan
Translated as "Long John", this 91-m (300-ft) high tower belongs to the Nieuwe Kerk in the abbey complex. It has an octagonal plan and dates from the 14th century.

London Quay
The names of the quays reflect the goods that were being exported from and imported to the Netherlands during the Golden Age *(see pp54–5)*.

Zeeuws Museum

Middelburg Abbey dates back to 1100, when it was inhabited by Norbertine monks from the monastery of St Michiel of Antwerp. These very powerful monks were driven away in 1574 by William of Orange, after which the abbey was secularized. The renovated Zeeuws Museum is situated in the wing of the building that was once the monks' quarters. The completely redesigned interior presents the museum's fine collections of china, silver, paintings and its famous tapestries in a completely new light.

VISITORS' CHECKLIST

Practical Information
Zeeuws Museum, Abdij 3–4.
Road Map A5. **Tel** 0118-653000.
Open 11am–5pm Tue–Sun.
Closed 1 Jan, 27 Apr, 25 Dec.
W zeeuwsmuseum.nl

Altar of Nehalennia
The altars found near Domburg in the 17th century were consecrated to the indigenous goddess Nehalennia, who was worshipped by the Romans.

Museum Guide

The Zeeuws Museum is located in one of the oldest wings of the abbey. It is a provincial museum with various different sections, including History, Fashion, Chamber of Wonders and the famous Tapestry Room. There are also temporary exhibitions that cover a wide variety of subjects.

Key to Floorplan

- Art and History
- Chamber of Wonders
- Fashion
- Temporary Exhibitions
- Non-Exhibition Space

Costume Collection
The museum has a collection of jewellery, accessories and costumes, here displayed with video made for the museum by contemporary artists.

❸ Veere

Road Map A5. 🚶 1,500. 🚌
ℹ️ Grote Markt 5 (0118-435858).
🌐 vvvzeeland.nl

Past and present merge in Veere. Modern pleasure boats moor along the quay opposite the Gothic façades of **Het Lammetje** (the lamb) (1539) and **De Struijs** (the ostrich) (1561). These **Schotse Huizen** (Scottish houses) serve as a reminder of the time that the port was important for its trade in precious Scottish wool. Other monuments to Veere's illustrious past are the **Stadhuis** (1474), the **Campveerse Toren**, a tower dating to around 1500, and the **OL-Vrouwekerk** (Church of Our Lady), dating from the 15th–16th centuries. This enormous church, once almost demolished, is now used as a venue for baroque, classical and contemporary music concerts.

❹ Domburg

Road Map A5. 🚶 1,600. 🚌
ℹ️ Schuitvlotstraat 32 (0118-583484).

Domburg was one of the first seaside resorts in the Netherlands. In the 19th century, this little town 5on Walcheren was popular among prominent Europeans, who came here to relax and recuperate in the chic seaside hotels on the dunes. It has now given way to mass tourism.

Environs

An inland lake lies hidden between dunes, woods and the Oostkapelle polder. The pretty nature reserve **De Manteling** is worth visiting, as is **Westhove** castle, which was the Abbot of Middelburg's country house until the 16th century. It now houses a youth hostel. **Terra Maris**, Zeeland's natural landscape museum, is in the castle's former orangery.

🏛️ **Terra Maris**
Duinvlietweg 6. **Tel** 0118-582620.
Open May–Oct: 10am–5pm daily; Nov–Apr: noon–5pm Wed–Fri, noon–4pm Sat & Sun. 📷 🏠
🌐 terramaris.nl

Pleasure boats moored at the marina in Vlissingen

❺ Vlissingen

Road Map A5. 🚶 43,200. 🚌 🚂
ℹ️ Spuistraat 46 (0118-715320). 🛒 Fri.

Vlissingen is a bustling town. The main thrust behind the economy of this, the largest town in Zeeland, are the ports in Vlissingen itself, as well as those of the industrial area Vlissingen-Oost and **scheepswerf De Schelde** (De Schelde shipyard). Vlissingen has always been of great military significance. The wartime activity this attracted meant that the town could not escape the consequences. One of the few remaining buildings from the time of Michiel de Ruyter to have withstood the ravages of the years is the **Arsenaal**, dating from 1649. A second arsenal from 1823 is now the **Amusement Park Het Arsenaal** (see p426), which is especially interesting for children. The reptiles and insects showcased at **Reptielenzoo Iguana**, which is housed in two adjoining 18th-century mansions, offer a different type of attraction.

Exterior façade of the chic Badhôtel in Domburg

🏛️ **Amusement Park Het Arsenaal**
Arsenaalplein 7. **Tel** 0118-415400.
Open check website for opening times. **Closed** 25 Dec. 📷 ♿
🌐 arsenaal.com

🏛️ **Reptielenzoo Iguana**
Bellamypark 35. **Tel** 0118-417219.
Open Jun–Sep: 10am–5:30pm Tue–Sat, 1–5:30pm Sun & Mon; Oct–May: 1–5:30pm daily. **Closed** 1 Jan, 25 Dec.
📷 🌐 iguana.nl

❻ Westkapelle

Road Map A5. 🚶 2,800. 🚌 ℹ️
Zuidstraat 154 (0118-570700). 🛒 Fri.

The most impressive sight in Westkapelle is its sea wall, the history of which is fascinating. In former times, this town lay securely behind the dunes, but these were washed away in the 15th century. This meant that the access route to the island shifted. A dyke was built, which was completed in 1458. The lighthouse, once a church, also dates from this time. The dyke was bombed by the Allies in order to flood Walcheren so it could be liberated. At the **Polderhuis** visitors can learn more about Westkapelle's history, including the wartime years.

🏛️ **Polderhuis Dijk en Oorlogsmuseum**
Zuidstraat 154. **Tel** 0118-570700.
Open Apr–Oct: daily; Nov–Mar: Wed–Sun. **Closed** 1 Jan, 25 & 31 Dec.
📷 📷 🏠

For hotels and restaurants in this region see p398 and pp411–12

The medieval Zuidhavenpoort in Zierikzee

❼ Zierikzee

Road Map A4. 🚹 11,100. 🚌
ℹ️ Nieuwe Haven 7 (0111-410940).
🚢 Thu.

With 568 listed houses, Zierikzee ranks eighth in the list of Dutch historic towns. The impressive city gateways can be seen from afar. The many terraces on the Havenplein offer a marvellous view of the two harbour entrances and ornate mansion houses on Oude Haven (old harbour), and the trickle of the **Gouwe**, the creek that brought trading prosperity to Zierikzee. The Gothic **Gravensteen** (1524–6), once the home of the Count of Holland, now houses a fair-trade shop.

The Zierikzee skyline shows the still unfinished **Dikke Toren** (great tower), construction of which began in 1454. At 130 m (425 ft), it must have been the highest point of the colossal 12th-century **St-Lievenskerk**, which burnt to the ground in 1832.

Strolling through the narrow streets along the new and old harbours, you will chance upon passageways that offer glimpses of old façades, such as of the 14th-century De Haene house, or the former Stadhuis (1550–54), now the **Stadhuismuseum**.

One of the most famous historic events in Holland, the revolt of Zierikzee in 1472

against Charles the Bold, is re-enacted each summer.

🏛 **Stadhuismuseum**
Meelstraat 6. **Tel** 0111-454464. **Open** 11am–5pm Tue–Sat (Jul–Aug: Mon–Sat), 1–5pm Sun. **Closed** 1 Jan, 27 Apr, 25 Dec. 🌐 **stadhuismuseum.nl**

Environs
A museum in Ouwerkerk is devoted to the floods of 1953.

🏛 **Museum Watersnood 1953**
Weg van de Buitenlandse Pers 5. **Tel** 0111-644382. **Open** Apr–Oct: 10am–5pm daily; Nov–Mar: noon–4pm Tue–Sun. 🅿️
🌐 **watersnoodmuseum.nl**

❽ Haamstede

Road Map A4. 🚹 3,800. 🚌 ℹ️
Noordstraat 45a (0111-450524). 🚢 Thu.

Haamstede is a peaceful town built around a church. The

Slot Haamstede, painstakingly restored in the 1960s

nearby **Slot Haamstede**, a castle dating from the 13th century, is surrounded by a park with pleasant walks.

🏰 **Slot Haamstede**
Haamstede, near church.
Open grounds only; castle closed to public.

Environs
Westerschouwen, 5 km (3 miles) southwest of Haamstede, has an impressive landscape and illustrious past. The dunes lie on the western edge, barren with a scattering of gorse in places, in others covered with coniferous forest.

You can climb to the top of **Plompetoren**, the tower of the now-submerged Koudekerke, which rises from the salt marshes. On the edge of the dunes is **Slot Moermond**.

🏛 **Plompe Toren**
Corner of Plompetorenweg & Koudekerkseweg. **Open** 10am–6pm daily.

Isolated Plompe Toren of the now-submerged Koudekerke

❾ Brouwershaven

Road Map A4. 🚹 1,400. 🚌 🚢 Mon.

Quiet Brouwershaven combines a historic centre with a modern port. The Havenkanaal to the marina and the Stadhuis date from 1599. The 14th-century **St-Nicolaaskerk** (Church of St Nicholas) is a monument to past glory. The town prospered again as an outport to Rotterdam until the Nieuwe Waterweg (new waterway) was built in 1870.

🏛 **Brouws Museum**
Haven Zuidzijde 14–15. **Tel** 0111-691342. **Open** 1–5pm Mon–Fri.
🅿️ 🌐 **brouwsmuseum.nl**

Brouwershaven, now a focus for water recreation

❿ Bruinisse

Road Map B4. 3,000. VVV
Zierikzee (0111-410940). Wed.

Bruinisse is now mainly a centre
for watersports. The modern
bungalow park **Aqua Delta** is
situated outside the old village
next to the marina.

Environs
To get an idea of what this
countryside looked like in
earlier times, visit the *ringdorp*
(circle-shaped village)
Dreischor, 10 km (6 miles)
west of Bruinisse. It has a
typical village church and
town hall. On the edge of the
village is **Goemanszorg**, an
agricultural museum devoted
to farming past and present.

Goemanszorg
Molenweg 3, Dreischor. **Tel** 0111-
402303. **Open** Easter–Oct: 11am–5pm
Tue–Sun & public hols.
goemanszorg.nl

⓫ St Annaland

Road Map B5. 3,000. see
St Maartensdijk.

Tholen is the least well- known
island of Zeeland. Here there is
a constantly changing scenery
of poplars and pollard willows,
fields and quiet towns, such as
St Annaland, with its picturesque
harbour on the Krabbenkreek.
Streekmuseum De Meestoof
(regional madder museum) is an
interesting reminder of Zeeland's
industrial past. The cultivation

of the madder plant and
processing of its root into a red
dye was, until the 19th century,
one of the main livelihoods of
the region. It was brought to an
end in 1868 by the invention of
artificial dyes.

Streekmuseum De Meestoof
Bierensstraat 6–8. **Tel** 0166-652901.
Open Apr–Oct: 2–5pm Tue–Sat.
demeestoof.nl

⓬ St Maartensdijk

Road Map B5. 3,300.
Markt 1 (0166-663771).

St Maartensdijk has been the
"capital" of Tholen since 1971.
This town has much to remind
us of its patrons, the powerful
Lords van Borssele. The remains

of the tomb of Floris van
Borssele (who died in 1422) and
his wife are still to be seen in a
burial chapel of the slender
14th- to 15th-century church.
Much of the original carving
and fragments of the old
paintings have been preserved.
The foundations and moat of
the van Borssele castle, which
was demolished in 1820, can
still be found outside the town.
   The most impressive part of
the town itself is the Markt, with
its 16th-century houses and
elegant Stadhuis.

⓭ Tholen

Road Map B5. 6,100.
see St Maartensdijk.

Tholen is a Zeeland town with
a Brabant flavour. Two buildings
dominate the town – the
marvellous Stadhuis (1452),
with its robust battlements,
and the ornate **OL-Vrouwekerk**
(Church of Our Lady), dating
from the 14th to 16th
centuries. The **kapel van
het St-Laurensgasthuis**
(St Laurensgasthuis chapel),
which has been rebuilt into
a residential home, stands
opposite the church. Even
though Tholen became a
fortified town in the 16th
century, it has retained its old
character. Gothic façades are
everywhere to remind us of
its former prosperity.

Pumping station in a rural setting in the neighbourhood of Tholen

⑭ Goes

Road Map A5. 🚹 24,000. 🚌 🚉
ℹ️ Singelstraat 13 (0113-235990).
🛒 Tue, Sat.

Some of the historical towns of Zeeland are charming yet sleepy, but Goes is wide-awake. Every Tuesday there is an old-fashioned market featuring fabrics and groceries which takes place on a square full of Zeeland atmosphere, the Grote Markt. The Raadhuis (town hall), dating from 1463 (rebuilt between 1771 and 1775), stands at the front of the square, representing the magistrates' power with all its bulk and loftiness. The rococo interior with its grisailles and stucco ceiling is particularly attractive. The majestic St-Maria-Magdalenakerk (Church of Mary Magdalen) (15th to 16th century) rises up behind the town hall. The cruciform basilica has been restored.

Imposing heraldic ornament on Goes Raadhuis

⑮ Yerseke

Road Map A5. 🚹 6,100. 🚌 🚉
ℹ️ Kerkplein 1 (0113-571864). 🛒 Fri.

As they say in Zuid-Beveland, *"De een zijn dood de ander zijn brood"* ("One man's meat is another man's poison"). Yerseke came to be situated on the Oosterschelde following the St-Felixstormvloed (St Felix storm flood) of 1530. So began a tradition of oyster farming and mussel fishing that has continued until the present day.

The nature reserve Yerseke Moer, to the west of the village, shows how the island used to look: a desolate patchwork of inlets, hamlets, rough pasture lands, coves, peat moors and water holes. To the east of Yerseke lies the submerged land of

A fishing boat in Yerseke bringing home the catch

Oyster Farming

Oysters apparently have all sorts of beneficial side effects, improved virility being the most well known. Whether this is true or not, this slippery delicacy makes any meal seem festive. Oyster farming began in 1870 when suitable parts of the river bed were no longer available for free fishing and were transferred to private use. Oyster farming flourished along the Oosterschelde, particularly in Yerseke, but the oysters were vulnerable to disease and harsh winters.

Oysters, a tasty delicacy

Concern that oyster farming would be impossible when the Grevelingen was changed from an open estuary to a lake after the completion of the Delta Works *(see pp250–51)* has so far proved unfounded – the oysters already are less prone to disease.

Zuid-Beveland, lost in 1530 along with Reimerswaal, at the time the third-largest Zeeland town.

⑯ Nisse

Road Map A5. 🚹 580. 🚌
ℹ️ see Goes.

Nisse is a typical Beveland village with square, ford and church. The church is worth a visit; though it does not look like much from the outside, inside you will be surprised by unique, 15th-century frescoes depicting the saints, scenes from the life of Mary and the coats of arms of the Lords van Borssele. Carvings on the choir vault and stalls are also from the 15th century.

🔼 **Hervormde kerk**
Key available from church secretary
Tel (0113-649780). **Open** Jul–Aug: 1:30–5pm Sat. 📷 for groups only (call to book). 🌐 **mariakerk-nisse.nl**

Environs
The **Zak van Zuid-Beveland**, south of the railway line to Middelburg, is characteristic for its balance between nature and culture. The landscape is a succession of polders, divided by dykes covered with flowers or sheep grazing.

⑰ Hulst

Road Map B5. 🚹 10,800. 🚌 ℹ️
Steenstraat 37 (0114-315221). 🛒 Mon.

Cross over the Westerschelde and you are simultaneously in Flanders and in the Netherlands. **St-Willibrordus-basiliek** (St Willibrordus basilica) towers above the town from afar. Generations of Keldermans, a Mechelen building family, have worked on this church. One unusual feature in Hulst is the trio of hostels, once safe houses for the monks from the Flemish abbeys Ten Duinen, Baudelo and Cambron.

Nearby is the former village of Hulsterloo, famous from the medieval epic *Reynard the Fox*.

⑱ Terneuzen

Road Map A5. 🏔 24,500. 🚌
ℹ️ Noordstraat 62 (0115-760122).
🛒 Wed, Fri.

Terneuzen has an important port. The mighty sea locks in the **Kanaal van Gent naar Terneuzen** (Gent-Terneuzen canal), built between 1825 and 1827, are also impressive. The town has industrial areas to the north and nature reserves to the west (de Braakman) and the east (Otheense Kreek).

⑲ Sluis

Road Map A5. 🏔 2,100. 🚌 ℹ️
Groote Markt 1 (0117-461700). 🛒 Fri.

The Zeeland-Flanders landscape is scarred by the effects of floods and the dykes built to deal with them. Both polders and inner dykes bear witness to the constant struggle with the sea. The liberation of Zeeland-Flanders in 1944 was also hard-fought, devastating towns and villages such as Sluis. The 14th-century **Stadhuis**, with its belfry, the only one existing in the Netherlands, was restored in its former style after 1945, including the bell tower with the statue, which has the nickname Jantje van Sluis.

Environs
St-Anna-ter-Muiden, 2 km (1.5 miles) to the west of Sluis, is a village beloved by artists. Once prosperous, the town now has just a few houses around the square, with a village pump and the stump of a tower. To the south is the oldest town in Zeeland: **Aardenburg**. The Romans built a fort here in the 2nd century to ward off Saxon pirates. Aardenburg later became one of the most

Gentse Poort, the gateway to the Flemish-tinged town of Hulst

powerful towns in Flanders. This can still be seen from **St-Baafskerk**, a flawless 13th-century example of the Scheldt Gothic style famous for its painted sarcophagi. The **Gemeentelijk Archeologisch Museum Aardenburg** (Aardenburg municipal archaeological museum) deals solely with the Romans.

🏛 **Gemeentelijk Archeologisch Museum Aardenburg**
Marktstraat 18. **Tel** 0117-492888.
Open May–Sep: 10am–5pm Tue–Fri, 1–5pm Sat–Sun. **Closed** Oct–Mar. 🎫
🖥 🔲 **museumaardenburg.nl**

⑳ Cadzand

Road Map A5. 🏔 800.
ℹ️ Boulevard de Wielingen 44d (0117-391298). 🛒 Jul & Aug: Mon pm.

The modern seaside resort Cadzand is particularly popular for its wide stretch of sand. A common pursuit here is to search for fossilized sharks' teeth. Along the dunes are dignified seaside hotels reminiscent of those of Domburg. A little way past Cadzand is the Zwin nature reserve, which extends as far as Knokke in Belgium. The resort of Nieuwvliet lies to the east of Cadzand.

The broad sandy beaches of Cadzand, always popular in summer

NORTHERN AND EASTERN NETHERLANDS

Northern and Eastern Netherlands at a Glance

The Northern and Eastern Netherlands are more sparsely populated than other areas. They encompass the West Frisian Islands (Waddeneilanden) and the provinces of Groningen, Friesland, Drenthe, Overijssel, Flevoland and Gelderland. Agriculture and trade have always played a predominant role here. This part of Holland has many natural and recreation areas, such as the Waddenzee mud flats, Frisian coast, coastal Lauwersmeergebied, Hondsrug, Nationaal Park De Hoge Veluwe, Sallandse Heuvelrug and the Oostvaardersplassen.

WEST FRISIAN ISLANDS
(see pp268–79)

Harlingen

Den Burg

Bolsward

Leeuwarden

FRIES
(see pp.

Snee

He

Lemmer

Emmeloord

Dronten

Lelystad

FLEVOLAND
(see pp326–33)

Almere

Nuns

Zeewolde

Ermelo

Nijkerk

Ede

Tiel

Nij

Zaltbommel

The waddengebied *(see pp272–3)* provides a habitat for many species of birds. It is an important area for both resident and migrating birds. The worms, molluscs and crustaceans are an ideal source of food for ducks, seagulls and wading birds.

De Elfstedentocht *(see pp298–9)*, a long-distance ice-skating race, was held 15 times during the last century. Over 16,000 skaters have skated the Tocht der Tochten, a 200-km (124-mile) stretch.

| 0 metres | 20 |
| 0 yards | 20 |

The Batavia *(see p331)* was owned by the Dutch East India Company. This three-master was 45 m (148 ft) long and had room for 350 men. A replica of the *Batavia* was built between 1985 and 1995 at the Batavia-Werf (Batavia wharf) in Lelystad, which is now working on a replica of Michiel de Ruyter's 17th-century flagship, *De Zeven Provinciën*.

 The picturesque outline of the fortified city of Doesburg, Gelderland

Groninger Museum *(see pp288–9)*, designed by Alessandro Mendini, has a large collection of archaeological pieces and works of art.

Megaliths *(see pp310–11)* were built some 5,000 years ago by the Neolithic Beaker Folk. There are 54 megaliths – almost all of them are to be found in Drenthe.

Giethoorn *(see pp322–3)*, a village in the Kop van Overijssel, consists of farmhouse-style buildings along the canal. The village is surrounded by woods and lakes, which is why it has been called the Green Venice.

Paleis Het Loo (Het Loo Palace)
The building now housing the National Museum *(see pp338–9)* was constructed in 1692 as a hunting palace for the stadtholder William III. The palace's chief architect was Jacob Roman; both the interior and gardens were designed by Daniël Marot.

Environmental Policy

In the 1990s, the Dutch government drew up the Natuurbeleidsplan, a programme designed to make nature reserves accessible to the public. This is of great importance to the northern and eastern Netherlands, with their many lakes, woods and polders. The region's ecosystem has been divided into core areas, development areas and connecting zones in an attempt to give permanence to the natural environment. The connecting zones join the areas together. When the policy is fully implemented, it will aid in the survival of many plant and animal species.

Key

Core area

Natural development area

• • • • • Existing or planned connecting zone

. . . . Existing or planned connecting zone to cross-border nature reserve

0 kilometres   10
0 miles   10

The Waterleidingduinen (water supply dunes) are only partly open to the public.

The osprey was a rare sight in Holland for many years. Thanks to the Natuurbeleidsplan, sightings of this bird of prey have become more frequent in recent years.

Special road signs have been designed to warn motorists of migrating toads during that animal's mating season. Usually shy, toads come out en masse when mating.

WEST FRISIAN ISLANDS
VLIELAND
TEXEL
NORTH HOLLAND
AMSTERDAM
Haarlem
The Hague
SOUTH HOLLAND
UTRECHT
Rotterdam
ZEELAND
's-Hertogenbosch
Middelburg
Antwerp
BELGIUM

Read the Signs!

Most natural areas (or parts of them) in the northern and eastern Netherlands are freely accessible. However, some parts are open only from sunrise (*zonsopkomst*) to sunset (*zonsondergang*), and it is therefore important to read the signs. It goes without saying that you should not make excessive noise, cause damage or leave litter in the area. Further information is available at VVV offices, the ANWB and the Vereniging Natuurmonumenten (tel. 035-6559933).

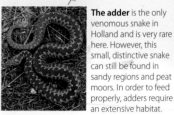

The adder is the only venomous snake in Holland and is very rare here. However, this small, distinctive snake can still be found in sandy regions and peat moors. In order to feed properly, adders require an extensive habitat.

The otter was extinct in Holland for many years, but has recently been reintroduced and is beginning to flourish.

The golden plover, a rare wading bird which has been put under pressure by the reclamation of peat bogs and heathland, is the object of a special plan that will enable it to recover its numbers in the Netherlands.

Connecting zones in Flevoland linking various natural areas are now being set up for, among others, the common frog, the polecat, the European water shrew, the pond bat, the grass snake and the beaver. Specific corridors are being developed for butterflies.

The common hamster and other protected animals cause headaches for developers. The Nature Protection Act prevents building on or the use of areas they inhabit.

Connections between core areas and development areas in some cases consist of "ecoducts". The vegetated passages atop the tunnels are designed to allow wildlife access to either side of the road, thereby linking two areas of great importance for flora and fauna without exposing them to road hazards.

Distinctive Landscapes

The northeast of the Netherlands has a number of distinctive landscape types, such as the unique mud flats, or Waddenzee, where the sand and clay is exposed at low tide; the peat moors in southeast Groningen; the enchanting heathland of Drenthe; the endless polder landscape of Flevoland; the splendid forests of Gelderland (Hoge Veluwe and Posbank) and the magnificent riverscapes and seascapes in the northeast of Overijssel.

The Oostvaardersplassen (lakes), between Lelystad and Almere, make up a unique natural landscape. It is a breeding ground and feeding area for hundreds of species of birds.

Glasswort is a wild plant which grows in mud flats and on silt deposits. It is a prized culinary delicacy.

West Frisian Islands

The Waddenzee *(see pp274–5)* is an area of mud flats which is largely dry at low tide. It attracts many species of birds that come here to forage and to feed. The island of Texel features the peat walls of the Hoge Berg.

Water crowfoot occurs in both flowing and standing water.

Rapeseed plantations are used for land improvements in new polders. The yellow fields seem to stretch endlessly to the horizon.

Bulrushes were once common in the region. The "cigars" grow only by fresh water and are now protected.

Polder Landscape

Forests (het Knarbos), lakes (the Oostvaardersplassen) and coastal lakes (the Veluwemeer) punctuate the flat polder landscape of the "new" province of Flevoland *(see pp326–33)*.

Boletus edulis is a delicious edible mushroom. Picking it, however, is no longer allowed.

Bracken fern grows in sparse woodland on lime and nutrient-poor sand and loamy ground, and on dried peat moors.

Common polypody occurs in juniper brush and in woodlands on poor sandy soil.

Mosses thrive in humid environments such as forest floors. Shady areas with acidic soil are ideal for sphagnum moss.

The cranberry grows in sphagnum moss on peat moors and in fens.

Forests

One of the best-known and largest forest areas in the Netherlands is at Hoge Veluwe in the province of Gelderland *(see pp334–49)*, where a variety of animals, such as wild boar and red deer, are to be found.

Common sundew, an insect-eating plant, grows on heathland and in the fenland of Groningen and Drenthe.

Cross-leaved heath thrives on nutrient-poor, dry, sandy soil and in the troughs of dunes.

Heather occurs mainly in sand and peat bogs, typically poor in nutrients.

Heathland

The northeastern Netherlands abounds with delightful heathland. Some of the most picturesque heathland can be found at Drenthe *(see pp306–15)*; herds of sheep still graze in the region of Ellertsveld.

THE WEST FRISIAN ISLANDS

Perhaps the least known part of the Netherlands despite their natural beauty, the West Frisian Islands form a barrier protecting the north of the country from the turbulent waters of the North Sea. Comprising five main islands and a few sandbanks, they are among Europe's last areas of wilderness.

The West Frisian Islands are the remaining fragments of an ancient sandbank that once stretched from Cap Gris Nez in France to Esbjerg in Denmark, a remnant of the last Ice Age. Since Roman times the sea has been eroding this sandbank, creating the shallow Waddenzee behind and washing away much of the peat soil that lay beyond the dunes. The islands of Griend and Rottumeroog were threatened to such an extent that they were abandoned. Rottumerplatt, too, is uninhabited.

Monks established the first settlements as far back as the 8th century; islanders made a living from farming, fishing and collecting shellfish. On Texel and Terschelling, the two largest islands, churches dating from the 15th century still stand. Later, the islands prospered from links with the Dutch East India Company and, in the 19th century, from whaling. Vlieland and Ameland are quieter islands, good for bird-watching. Schiermonnikoog is the most isolated, with rare plant life.

Nowadays the islands, reached by ferries from the mainland, have much to offer the visitor in search of peace and quiet, with nature rambles over dunes and salt marsh, and seal- and bird-watching, especially in summer. The islands' quaint museums are strong on ecology and conservation. The best way to get around is by bicycle, and visitors will find a wide range of hotels and guesthouses, excellent seafood restaurants, and some of the best sunsets anywhere.

Former captain's house *(commandeurhuisje)* on Ameland

◀ Traditional cargo ships sail down the Waddenzee at dusk

Exploring the West Frisian Islands

The history of the West Frisian Islands (Waddeneilanden) has been shaped by the wind and the sea. It was not until the 17th century that the larger islands were stabilized by dykes. Den Burg on Texel, the largest village on the islands, is a historic fortification with a pleasant old centre. Nearby is Hoge Berg, with its characteristic peat walls; in the west, the distinctive tower of Den Hoorn can be seen. To the north is the unique natural area of De Slufter. The crown of the Frisian Islands, Vlieland, has the prettiest village of the islands. Terschelling, Ameland and Schiermonnikoog are typical Frisian islands, with wide beaches, partly forested dunes, villages and polders or mud flats on the Waddenzee side.

Shrimp fishermen sorting their catch

Bird-watching in the Mookbai, Texel

Sights at a Glance

1 Noorderhaaks
2 Den Burg
3 De Koog
4 De Slufter
5 Den Hoorn
6 Vlieland
7 Griend
8 Terschelling
9 Ameland
10 Schiermonnikoog
11 Rottumerplaat
12 Rottumeroog

TERSCHELLING — Oosterend
8 — Hoorn
West — Midsland

Oost-Vlieland — *Richel*

6 VLIELAND

7 GRIEND

Waddenzee

Harlingen

De Cocksdorp

DE SLUFTER 4

Texel

DE KOOG 3
— Oosterend

DEN BURG 2

— Oudeschild

DEN HOORN 5

1
NOORDER-
HAAKS — Den Helder

The Koegelwieck seacat (West Terschelling)

Getting Around

The West Frisian Islands are reached by ferries from the mainland. **Texel** is served by TESO (tel. 0222-369600). Foot passengers can take a bus to De Koog or De Cocksdorp via Den Burg, or order a taxi-bus when buying their ticket. **Vlieland** is served by Rederij Doeksen (tel. 0900-3635736); cars not permitted. On arrival, a bus takes passengers to Posthuis, where there are taxis. **Terschelling** is served by Rederij Doeksen (0900-3635736); reservations recommended for cars. There is a bus service on the island, and taxis are available on arrival. **Ameland** is served by Rederij Wagenborg (tel. 085-4011008); reservations recommended. There are bus services to all villages. **Schiermonnikoog** is served by Rederij Wagenborg (tel. 085-4011008); foot passengers only. Bus service and taxi-buses connect the dock and village. Bicycles can be hired easily.

De Wadden – the mud flats are ideal for beach walks

ROTTUMERPLAAT **11**

12
ROTTUMEROOG

SCHIERMONNIKOOG
10

Schiermonnikoog

ELAND
9
○Buren
Nes

Waddenzee

Lauwersoog

Holwerd

0 kilometres   10

0 miles   10

Rescued seals being returned to the wild by members of EcoMare, Texel *(see p427)*

Key

▬▬ Motorway

━━ Main road

┄┄ Minor road

━ Scenic route

── Minor railway

The splendid coastline of Vlieland

For hotels and restaurants in this region see pp398–9 and p412

Birds of the Waddenzee

The extensive wetlands of the Waddenzee are an important area for breeding and migratory birds. The North Sea coasts of the islands are sandy, with little animal life; the Waddenzee coasts of the islands, however, consist of fine sand and clay which are rich in minerals and nutrients. The innumerable worms, molluscs and crustaceans that live here are an ideal source of food for a huge variety of ducks, seagulls and wading birds. At the peak of the migratory season (August), the number of birds here runs into millions.

Curlew
This is the largest European wading bird and is easily recognizable by its long, curved beak.

Bird-watching Hide
There are many hides for bird-watchers on the mud flats of the Waddenzee, allowing the birds to be observed without being disturbed.

Bird Catchers

Bird catchers, whose interests in the Netherlands have gone far beyond mere hunting, have become an important pressure group for the protection of birds and the natural environment. Their organization is Vogelbescherming Nederland, based in Zeist.

Beak Shapes

People are often surprised at the many varieties of birds that feed on the mud flats. The different species, however, have managed to avoid competing with one another. The various shapes and lengths of their beaks are suitable for the assorted types of food that can be found in the water and in the sand. Ducks get their food from the surface or dive for it, whereas wading birds get their food from underground – what prey at which depth underground depends on the shape of the beak. Other birds catch fish (spoonbills, cormorants or terns), shellfish (eider ducks) or even other seabirds (the white-tailed eagle), or steal their food from other birds.

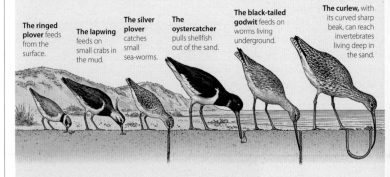

The ringed plover feeds from the surface.

The lapwing feeds on small crabs in the mud.

The silver plover catches small sea-worms.

The oystercatcher pulls shellfish out of the sand.

The black-tailed godwit feeds on worms living underground.

The curlew, with its curved sharp beak, can reach invertebrates living deep in the sand.

Arctic Tern
This extremely rare bird, which breeds in the West Frisian Islands, spends the winter in the Antarctic. This gives it the longest migratory path of all birds.

Sandwich Tern
This bird has its largest breeding colony in Holland on Griend. Its dwindling numbers means it requires careful protection.

Oystercatcher
The oystercatcher is characteristic of the Waddenzee. It forages for cockles and mussels.

Bird Species

The wealth of bird species – including diving birds, petrels, cormorants, spoonbills, ducks, birds of prey, waders, scavengers, seagulls, terns, razorbills and songbirds – that occur in the Waddenzee is a good reason to ensure that the area is carefully protected. For many of the birds, these are the only breeding grounds in the Netherlands, as they are the only wetlands remaining in the Netherlands. Various parts are closed to visitors, and it is important to observe the regulations in order to help preserve the bird population.

Avocet
This magnificent wading bird has an upward-curving bill and black and white plumage.

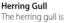

Large numbers of oystercatchers can be seen both in winter and in summer.

Black-Tailed Godwit
This wading bird, with fiery red-brown plumage, is a bird of passage but spends the winters and summers in the Waddenzee.

Ringed Plover
This is an active bird that rarely breeds here but passes through in large numbers.

Eider Duck
The eider duck has breeding colonies on Texel, Vlieland and Terschelling. The male is far more impressive in appearance than the brown-coloured female.

Herring Gull
The herring gull is just one of the many varieties of gull that occur here. At more than half a metre (1.5 ft) long, it is an impressive bird.

Red Knot
This bird of passage stops over sometimes in summer and sometimes in winter. It is a robust bird, one that is always on the move.

The Waddenzee

The Waddenzee is a tidal area whose sand or mud flats *(wadden)* are mainly exposed at low tide and disappear at high tide. Together with the West Frisian Islands, the Waddenzee forms the last extensive wild part of Holland. The entire area has an extremely rich ecosystem because of the large sources of nourishment. It is a feeding and breeding ground for many species of birds. Two species of seal, 30 species of fish, shrimps and crabs live in the Waddenzee or come here to breed.

Cockles *(Cardium edule),* which form the diet for many bird species, are intensively harvested using mechanical methods. The catch is exported.

The VVVs (tourist offices) on the West Frisian Islands offer all kinds of sailing trips around the islands, including romantic luxury cruises on a three-master. Rederij Vooruit (tel. 0515-531485) arranges sailing trips on local boats.

Sea Lavender *(Limonium vulgare),* along with sea purslane and sea aster, grows in the higher parts of the salt marshes. Fields of blue-violet sea lavender flowers make a very pretty sight.

Exposed Sections of the Mud Flats

Much of the Waddenzee mud flats is exposed during low tide. This leaves places like the marina, pictured below, high and dry. Mooring places that are inaccessible at low tide are increasingly being dredged as marinas.

Low tide

High tide

Flora in the Waddenzee

Because of the diversity of the Waddenzee landscape, with its changing environment (salt water and fresh water, lime-rich soil and lime-poor soil, wet land and dry land, clay ground and sandy ground), almost 900 plant species grow here. Many of them grow on the island-side of the old dunes in the dune valleys. Amongst the flowers to be found here are autumn gentian and creeping willow, as well as grasses and weeds such as black bog-rush, fragrant orchid and grass of Parnassus. Lavender is among the plants which grow on the higher ground.

Lavender (*Salicornia europaea*) is one of the first plants to colonize the mud flats and the low-lying parts of the salt marshes. When the land has silted up completely, the salt marsh grass establishes itself.

Cracks in the dried silt provide a good foothold for lavender, as well as for other plants.

Wadlopen (walking the Mud Flats)

walk on the Waddenzee takes you through salt marshes and past the *wantij*, a place below an land where two tidal flows meet. Since the id-1970s, walking on the mud flats has been a popular hobby. There are now a number of major mud-flat walking societies, including Dijkstra's Wadlooptochten (Pieterburen, tel. 0595-528345); ammert Kwant (Ezinge, tel. 050-5792414); ichting Uithuizer Wad (only for Rottumeroog; tel. 511-522271), Stichting Wadloopcentrum Friesland Holwerd, tel. 0519-242100) and Stichting Wadloopcentrum Pieterburen (tel. 0595-528300).

Threats to the Waddenzee

According to the Dutch oil company NAM, there are between 70 and 170 billion cubic metres (2,500 and 6,000 billion cubic feet) of natural gas beneath the Waddenzee. The value of this gas runs into many billions of euros. The Waddenzee Society is completely opposed to any gas drilling in the Waddenzee on several grounds: first, because there is no social need for it and second, because the environmental effects of drilling – in particular, the consequences the falling ground level would have on life in the Waddenzee – have not been properly investigated. For the time being, therefore, drilling on the Waddenzee is banned, pending further environmental impact studies. But the Waddenzee is also threatened by the harvesting of mussels and cockles. Since 1992, the Dutch government has scaled this back, and is considering closing the area to the shellfish industry.

Cockle harvesting

Noorderhaaks, above sea level at high tide for some decades now

❶ Noorderhaaks

Road Map B2. none. Emmalaan 66, Den Burg (0222-314741).

Noorderhaaks, also known as Razende Bol (raging ball), is a fairly bleak sandbank west of Den Helder, 2.5 km (1.5 miles) offshore. The sea currents cause the island to shift eastwards towards Texel, after which another "raging ball" appears at the same point off Den Helder. The Dutch air force occasionally uses the island for target practice, but it is not off-limits for visitors. Rowing and swimming here are risky because of the powerful currents. Adventure-seekers regularly visit Noorderhaaks by boat or by helicopter, unable to resist this piece of total wilderness, where mirages are common.

❷ Den Burg

Road Map B2. 6,000. Emmalaan 66 (0222-314741). Mon am; Jul–Aug: Wed.

Den Burg is the main town of Texel and situated right in its centre. Around 1300, the village was fortified by a circular rampart with a moat, which are now marked by the Burgwal and Parkstraat Streets. A sheep market was once held in April and May at the Groeneplats, Den Burg's main square, with the present-day town hall. Today, a sheep day is held on the first Monday of September. Further on, by the Binnenburg, or inner castle, stands the 15th-century Late Gothic **Hervormde kerk** (Protestant church). The

Kogerstraat runs the length of the Binnenburg. Located here is the **Oudheidkamer**, an antiquities museum set up in a picturesque 16th-century building, which used to be a doss-house. Today it contains period rooms, a display of artifacts and works of art in the attic, and a herb garden.

Along and around the town wall are several interesting shopping streets, such as the Weverstraat. A number of excellent restaurants are to be found on the Warmoesstraat.

Environs
South of Den Burg is a sloping landscape with the 15 m (50 ft) **Hoge Berg** (high mountain), which offers a great view of the island. For a good walk, follow the Skillepaadje from the tomb of the Georgiers (resistance fighters who died fighting the Germans in 1945) to the fishing village of Oudeschild, past the peat walls and sheep pens.

Oudheidkamer
Kogerstraat 1, Den Burg.
Tel 0222-313135. **Open** 1 Apr–31 Oct: 11am–5pm Mon–Fri, 2–4pm Sat.
Closed 1 Jan, Easter, Whitsun, 25, 26 & 31 Dec, public hols.

Beachcomber on Texel, the most populated of the Frisian Islands

❸ De Koog

Road Map B2. 1300. Emmalaan 66, Den Burg (0222–314741). Jul–Aug: Tue.

In 1900, the former fishing settlement of De Koog consisted of a church (built in 1415) and a few houses and farms. The first tourist facility was the Badhotel, later the Hotel Prinses Juliana, with a garden overlooking the sea. Today, De Koog has accommodation for 20,000 visitors in hotels, pensions and camp sites. The centre of De Koog is the Dorpsstraat, which has cafés, snack bars and discos. De Koog's attractions for visitors are the Calluna waterpark and EcoMare, an information centre for the Waddenzee and the North Sea (see p427).

The Nederlands-Hervormde church in Den Burg (1481)

❹ De Slufter

Road Map B2. 🅼 none. 🚌 🚲
Open all year, northern part closed
1 Mar–1 Sep. 🛈 Emmalaan 66, Den
Burg (0222-314741).

The distinctive natural area of
De Slufter, consisting of salt
marshes covering 450 ha
(1,100 acres), is covered with
salt-loving plants such as sea
thrift and sea lavender, and is
an important breeding and
feeding ground for many
different bird species. De Slufter,
and the neighbouring **De Muy**,
where spoonbills breed, are
magnificent rambling areas.

❺ Den Hoorn

Road Map B2. 🅼 450. 🚌 🚲
🛈 Emmalaan 66, Den Burg (0222-
314741). 🛥 Jul–Aug: Thu.

Like Den Burg, Den Hoorn
stands on boulder clay. It has a
distinctive **Hervormde kerk**
(Protestant church) with a
pointed steeple and churchyard dating from 1425. This
exquisitely restored village has
been given protected status.

❻ Vlieland

Road Map C1. 🅼 1,000. 🚌
🛈 Havenweg 10, Oost-Vlieland
(0562-451111).

Vlieland is the smallest of the
Waddenzee Islands. In some
places, less than one kilometre
(half a mile) separates the
Waddenzee and the North Sea.

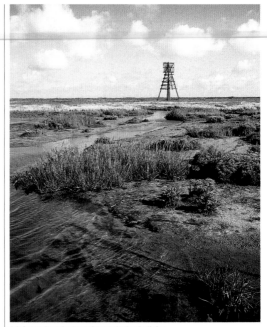

Salt-loving plants thriving at the water's edge, De Slufter

Unlike the other islands, Vlieland
consists only of dunes, covered
with a purple haze of heather,
marram grass and sea buckthorn.
In the east, the woods planted
just after 1900 provide a bit of
variety in the landscape.

In the south is the only village,
Oost-Vlieland, where the boat
from Harlingen docks. Many old
buildings line the main street.
One of them, the **Tromp's Huys**
(1576), used to belong to the
Amsterdam Admiralty. Today it
houses a museum with

19th-century paintings. The
houses are separated by alleys
known as "gloppen". There is no
room for cars here, not even for
those of the islanders.

The best way to explore
Vlieland is by bicycle; the island
can be covered in one day. From
Oost-Vlieland, you can cycle
westwards along tracks through
the dunes or along the Waddenzee shoreline to the **Posthuys**
(post house), where in the 17th
century the overseas mail was
brought from Amsterdam to be
loaded onto ships waiting to sail.
Further westwards is **de Vliehors**,
an area of natural interest which
can be explored if no military
exercises are taking place here.
Beware of getting stuck in the
soft drifting sand. This is also
where the wealthy village of
West-Vlieland once stood. It was
consumed by the waves after it
was abandoned in 1736.

🏛 Tromp's Huys
Dorpsstraat 99, Oost-Vlieland.
Tel 0562-451600. **Open** school hols:
10am–5pm Tue–Fri, 2–5pm Sat, 2–4pm
Sun; outside school hols: 2–5pm Tue–
Thu, 10am–1pm Fri, 2–5pm Sat.
Closed 1 Jan, Easter, Pentecost. 🏛

The village hall in Oost-Vlieland

The Oerol Festival on Terschelling

❼ Griend

Road Map C1. 🏔 none. 🚗 very limited. ℹ️ Vereniging Natuur-monumenten (035-6559933).

Half-way through the boat trip from Harlingen to Terschelling or Vlieland, one will come across Griend. The island was abandoned by its inhabitants after the St Lucia's flood of 1287. For centuries it seemed about to disappear beneath the waves. In 1988, the Natuurmonumenten trust, which has leased Griend since 1916, had a dam built to prevent further erosion. At high tide, the highest part of the island is just 1 m (3 ft) above the water. Access to Griend is forbidden, save for a handful of bird wardens and biology students. This is Holland's largest breeding ground for great tern.

Tombstone from Striep

❽ Terschelling

Road Map C1. 🏔 4,900. 🚢 🚌 ℹ️ Willem Barentszkade 19a, West-Terschelling (0562-443000).

Terschelling is the second-largest of the West Frisian Islands. The north of the island consists of dunes, where in the olden days cattle were let out to graze everywhere ("oerol"). This is where the Oerol Festival, held each year in June, gets its name.

In Formerum, West, and Hoorn, the dunes have been planted with coniferous and deciduous woods. In the south are polders, and beyond the dykes are the salt marshes. There is a nature reserve at either end of the island: the Noordvaarder in the west, and the Boschplaat in the east. If you happen to be sailing over from Harlingen at low tide on a sunny day, you may see seals basking in the sun on the de Richel and Jacobs Ruggen sandbanks.

West is a real mud-flat village, with old houses and a famous lighthouse, the **Brandaris**, dating from 1594. It is closed to visitors, but the same view can be enjoyed from the high dune known as the Seinpaalduin behind the village. **Het Behouden Huys** is a local history museum dedicated to famous islanders such as Willem Barentsz; there is also the educational **Centrum voor Natuur en Landschap**, where you can learn about the ecology of the mud flats.

The two largest villages in the west are Midsland and Hoorn. Midsland is surrounded by small hamlets with intriguing names such as Hee, Horp and Kaart, which date back to when the Frisians settled on the islands. The hamlet with the **kerkhof van Striep** cemetery is where the first church on the island was built, in the 10th century. Its outline is still visible. Further eastwards is Hoorn, with 13th-century Gothic-Romanesque St Janskerk standing on the site of the original church.

🏛 **Museum 't Behouden Huys**
Commandeurstraat 32, West-Terschelling. **Tel** 0562-442389.
Open Apr–Oct: 10am–5pm Tue–Fri, 1–5pm Sat & Sun; Nov–Mar: 1–5pm Wed, Sat & Sun. 🐾

🏛 **Centrum voor Natuur en Landschap**
Burg. Reedekerstraat 11, West-Terschelling. **Tel** 0562-442390.
Open Apr–Oct: 9am–5pm daily; Nov–Mar: 11am–5pm Tue, Sat & Sun. 🐾 ♿

❾ Ameland

Road Map C/D1. 🏔 3,500. 🚢 🚌 ℹ️ Bureweg 2, Nes (0519-546546). 🌐 vvvameland.nl

The dunes in the north of this island are dry, with the exception of **Het Oerd**, a wet valley in the east which is a bird reserve. The region is best explored by bicycle; there is a cycle track to a scenic spot on a 24-m (79-ft) dune. In the mud flats in the south there are four villages. The largest of these is **Nes**, where the boat from Holwerd calls. **Commandeurshuizen** (commodores' houses)

Het Oerd – the edge of the mud flats on Ameland

A horse-drawn lifeboat, the pride of Ameland

in the old centre recall the days when many islanders made their living from whaling.

If you want to see the real Ameland, you must visit **Hollum**. The Zuiderlaan and Oosterlaan are steeped in the atmosphere of past times. At the southern end of the village is the church, surrounded by an oval cemetery with tombstones where the deeply pious inscriptions are overgrown with lichen.

Beyond Hollum lies the **Reddingsmuseum Abraham Fock**, a museum dedicated to life-saving, where the pride of Ameland, a lifeboat launched by horses, is kept operational.

▥ Reddingsmuseum Abraham Fock
Oranjeweg 18, Hollum. **Tel** 0519 542737. **Open** Apr–Nov: 10am–5pm Mon–Fri, 1:30–5pm Sat & Sun. ▨ ♿

⑩ Schiermonnikoog

Road Map D1. ▨ 900. ▦ ▦
▯ Reeweg 5, Schiermonnikoog (0519-531233).

Schiermonnikoog, or Lytje Pole (small land), was a farm belonging to Cistercian monks during the Middle Ages. The village of Schiermonnikoog, which is named after them, has many exquisitely restored houses. The island as a whole is a national park and under the protection of Natuurmonumenten. The beach of Schier is one of the widest in Europe. The eastern side of the island (Het

Balg, Kobbeduinen and the salt marshes) in particular make for wonderful walking areas, with their varied flora (including many orchids) and bird life. No cars at all are allowed on the island.

⑪ Rottumerplaat

Road Map D1. ▨ none.
▯ Waddenkust Noord-Groningen, Uithuizen (0595-434051).

Nature has been left to her own devices with the 900 ha (2,225 acre) uninhabited island of Rottumerplaat. This protected nature reserve is jointly managed by the Ministry of Agriculture, Waterways and Planning, and the Friends of Rottumeroog and Rottumerplaat Society (SVRR). Outsiders are rarely admitted to the island. This has had a good effect on Rottumeroog as well as on Rottumerplaat, which has been expanding quickly. Dunes many

metres in height and an impressive salt marsh are its characteristic features. The island also belongs to the seals and birds.

⑫ Rottumeroog

Road Map D1. ▨ none. ▧ very limited. ▯ Waddenkust Noord-Groningen, Uithuizen (0595-434051).

This most eastern of the West Frisian Islands is due to disappear into the mouth of the Ems soon. Since 1991 it has been left in the hands of nature. Attempts over many years to prevent it from drifting eastwards were unsuccessful. In 1998, the northern dunes collapsed, after which the last traces of human settlement were removed by the state forestry commission. The island is now less than 300 ha (740 acres) in size and shrinks with each storm. Walkers are prohibited in the area.

The uninhabited island of Rottumerplaat, with its high dunes

GRONINGEN

The Netherland's northernmost province is distinguished by its rich cultural history and unusual landscape, where you often see *terps* or small areas of elevated land. To the north and west it is bounded by the shallow Waddenzee, and to the east by the Ems river estuary and the border with Germany.

The *terps* originated centuries ago, when the inhabitants of this region needed to protect themselves from high water levels. The elevated land is sometimes crowned by a solitary Romanesque church, visible for miles across the fens. Elsewhere in the province you will see straight roads and canals, often evidence of reclaimed land. The region grew rich during the Middle Ages from agriculture and peat extraction, and the medieval port of Appingedam, nowadays a little town inland from the port of Delfzijl, was once a member of the powerful Hanseatic League.

Groningen province is also noted for its windmills, castles and moated manor houses and, in the east, for its restored fortified towns, such as picturesque Bourtange, which is right on the border with Germany. Conservation areas abound. Close to Lauwersoog, where you can catch a ferry to Schiermonnikoog, one of the West Frisian Islands *(see p279)*, a vast nature reserve has been established. Nearby Pieterburen has a seal sanctuary.

Groningen, the provincial capital, is proud of its glorious past and boasts a wealth of world-class museums, historic buildings and other attractions. A number of Dutch corporations have their headquarters in this thriving university city, and a further boost to the economy arrived in the 1960s after the discovery in nearby Slochteren of some of the world's largest natural gas deposits.

Hay bales in Westerwolde, near the old fortified town of Bourtange

◄ Fair by the Martinitoren in Groningen, Netherlands

Exploring Groningen

Some of the country's most attractive and historically interesting castles, or *borgs*, are in the Groningen region: the medieval Fraeylemaborg in Slochteren, Menkemaborg in Uithuizen and the charming Verhildersum in Leens. The natural area around the Lauwersmeer is particularly suitable for rambling. Not far from here, in Pieterburen, is a famous refuge for seals. Ter Apel, which is on the province's eastern boundary, is a magnificent medieval monastery. Groningen itself *(see pp284–9)* has much to offer, including the peaceful Prinsenhof, with its beautiful gardens, and the ultra-modern Groninger Museum *(see pp288–9)*, which houses collections that range from archaeology to oriental porcelain to modern art.

Wensum, one of the prettiest villages in Groningen

The Lauwersmeer nature reserve, created through the draining of the Lauwerszee

Getting Around

Groningen can be reached from the south along the A28 motorway; the A7 crosses the province from Friesland in the west to Germany in the east. The best way to see the town of Groningen is on foot. From Groningen there are rail links to Roodeschool in the north, Delfzijl in the northeast and to Nieuweschans in the east. Most of the countryside is accessible by regional *(interlokal)* or local *(buurt)* buses. The Groningen region is well suited to cycling and rambling, especially the area around the Lauwersmeer, the mud-flat region *(waddengebied)* and Westerwolde, in the south.

Sights at a Glance

Recreation possibilities on the Paterswoldse Meer, south of Groningen

The canalside kitchens of Appingedam

Farmhouse in Beerta, east Groningen

Key

━━ Motorway

━━ Main road

┈┈ Minor road

━━ Scenic route

━━ Main railway

─── Minor railway

━━ Regional border

━━ International border

For hotels and restaurants in this region see p399 and pp412–13

❶ Street-by-Street: Groningen

The town of Groningen has for centuries been the cultural and historical capital of the province. Its glory was at its height in the 15th century, when the town was freed from the jurisdiction of the Bishop of Utrecht and was able to extend its influence into the present-day province of Friesland. In 1614, the Groninger Academie was founded, which was the precursor of the Rijksuniversiteit. Thus, in addition to being a centre of trade and government, the town also became an academic centre.

TURFSINGEL

SINT WALBURGSTR.

MARTINIKERKHOF

★ Prinsenhof
In the gardens of the Prinsenhof, where in 1568 the first Bishop of Groningen, and later the stadholder, resided, stands a magnificent sundial from 1730. The garden is laid out as it was in the 18th century.

★ Martinitoren
The 97-m (318-ft) Martinitoren (St Martin tower) dating from 1496 is called The Old Grey by the locals because of the colour of the Bentheim sandstone.

The Martinikerk (St Martin's Church) dates back to the 13th century, though only parts of the original basilica are preserved. The Romanesque church was extensively remodelled in Gothic style in the 1400s.

Stadhuis
The Stadhuis on the Grote Markt is a monumental Neo-Classical building, completed in 1810.

Goudkantoor
This 1635 Renaissance building on the Waagplein was known as the "Goudkantoor" (gold depository) in the 19th century, when it functioned as a treasury. It now houses an inn.

VISITORS' CHECKLIST

Practical Information
Road Map D1. 177,000.
Grote Markt 25 (050-
3139741). Tue–Sat.
Flower fair: Good Friday;
Bevrijdingsfestival (Liberation
festival): 5 May; funfairs: May;
Groningen holiday: 28 Aug.

Transport
Stationsplein.
Stationsplein.

Key
— Recommended route

Ome Loeks' horse, a statue by Jan de
Baat in front of the train station,
illustrates a famous local folksong, "Ome
Loeks' horse is dead". Pikeur "Loeks"
(Lucas) van Hemmen (1876–1955)
wanted to shoo away his horse and so
stabbed it with his pitchfork. The animal
got an infection and later died.

The Poelestraat is
lined with cafés
and restaurants.

0 metres 100
0 yards 100

★ St Geertruidshofje
This inn on Peperstraat, founded in
1405 as a hostel for poor pilgrims, has
two courtyards. The first is bounded
by the convent church, refectory and
warden's chambers; guest rooms
surround the second.

Exploring Groningen

The city of Groningen has a number of interesting buildings and museums, among them the Noordelijk Scheepvaartmuseum (northern maritime museum) which illustrates the history of navigation. The Groninger Museum *(see pp288–9)* possesses an art collection of international stature. A visit to one of the gardens of Groningen will provide peace in the middle of the bustling university city.

The distinctive Gasunie building, known locally as the "monkey cliff"

🏠 Martinikerk and Martinitoren

Martinikerkhof 3. **Tel** 050-3111277.
Open Easter–11 Nov: noon–5pm Sat; Jun–Aug & two Sats in Sep: noon–5pm Tue–Sat. 🎫 1:30pm. Martinitoren Grote Markt. **Tel** 050-3135713. **Open** Apr–Oct: 11am–5pm Mon–Sat; Nov–Mar: noon–4pm Mon–Sat; Jul & Aug: 11am–4pm Sun. **Closed** 1 Jan, 25 Dec. 🐾

The Grote Markt is the old city centre. Many of the buildings standing on the square were badly damaged by air raids near the end of World War II. When it was rebuilt, the market was enlarged on the northern and eastern sides, and new buildings of a modern character were added.

The famous Martinitoren (St Martin tower) was also damaged but still standing, and it was possible to rebuild it. The carillon of d'Olle Grieze ("The Old Grey"), whose bells were cast by the Hemony brothers, has since been enlarged and now has four octaves and 49 bells. The Martinikerk (St Martin's Church), dating from the 13th century, still retains traces of the original building: both the northern and southern façades of the transept and the ornamental brickwork of the windows and window niches of the northern side are recognizably 13th century. During the 15th century, when the city was at the height of its development, the church was extended in Gothic style. The choir, which features sumptuous murals from 1530 illustrating the life of Christ, had been completed before 1425. The central part of the church became a hall-type church. East of the Grote Markt is the Poelestraat, which on fine days comes to life with outdoor cafés and restaurants.

🏛 Gebouw van de Gasunie

Concourslaan 17. **Tel** 050-5219111. **Closed** to the public.
The main office of the Dutch Gasunie (gas board) was designed by the Alberts and Van Huur architects on the principles of "organic" architecture, the inspiration of which lies with natural forms. The "organic" nature of the building can be seen at every turn, even in the specially designed furniture. The locals' nickname for the building is the "apenrots" (monkey cliff).

🏠 St Geertruidshofje

Peperstraat 22. **Tel** 050-3124082.
Groningen has a number of pretty *hofjes*, or courtyards surrounded by almshouses, often belonging to inns. They were once charitable institutions whose aim was to help the poor. The finest of these is the complex of the 13th-century Heilige Geestgasthuis, or Pelstergasthuis (in the Pelsterstraat), and St Geertruidshofje *(see p285)*, whose Pepergasthuis inn was established in 1405. It later became a senior citizens' home. The pump in the courtyard dates from 1829.

The Poelestraat: a favourite haunt for the students of Groningen

For hotels and restaurants in this region see p399 and pp412–13

🏛 Noordelijk Scheepvaartmuseum

Brugstraat 24–26. **Tel** 050-3122202.
Open 10am–5pm Tue–Sat, 1–5pm
Sun & hols. **Closed** public hols. 🖼

This maritime museum,
arranged over two restored
medieval houses, deals with
the history of navigation in the
northern provinces from 1650
to the present. Exhibits are
arranged in chronological
order, from the Utrecht ships,
Hanseatic cogs, West Indies
merchantmen, peat barges
and Baltic merchant ships to
Groningen coasters from the
20th century. A number of
historical workshops, such as a
carpenter's shop and a smithy,
are held in the attic of
the museum. The
museum also has
an excellent
programme of
temporary
exhibitions,
featuring all
things marine.

The magnificent Prinsenhof, formerly the stadholder's residence

Decorative element from the
Provinciehuis of Groningen

🌿 Prinsenhof and Prinsenhoftuin

Martinikerkhof 23. **Tel** 050-3176555.
Open 9am–noon daily.

The Prinsenhof originally
housed the monastic order of
the Broeders des Gemenen
Levens. It later became the
seat of the first Bishop of
Groningen, Johann Knijff, who
had the entire complex
converted into a magnificent
bishop's palace. Until late into
the 18th century, the building
served as the residence of the
stadholder. The Prinsenhoftuin
(Prinsenhof Gardens) is truly an
oasis in the midst of the busy
city. Its highlights include a
herb garden and a rose garden.
There is also a flowerbed that
is arranged into two coats of
arms, one with the letter
W (for William Frederick,
the stadholder of
Friesland), the other
with a letter A (for
Albertine Agnes,
William's wife).
At the side of the
entrance is a fine
sundial (see p284) which dates
back to 1730. The course of
the old city walls of Groningen
is still clearly discernible in
the Prinsenhoftuin.

🏛 Hortus Haren

Kerklaan 34, Haren. **Tel** 050-5370053.
Open 9:30am–5pm daily.
Closed 1 Jan, 25 Dec. 🖼 🅿 🖥 🖼

Immediately south of the
city is the fashionable town
of Haren, where an extensive
park, Hortus Haren, is situated.
The park was set up in 1642
by Henricus Munting. Its 20 ha
(50 acres) include a large hothouse complex comprising
several different greenhouses
dedicated to a wide array of
climatic zones. There is a tropical
rainforest with a great variety of
exotic flowers. A subtropical
hothouse numbers orange trees
among its plants. The various
climatic areas continue with a
desert section. Here, gigantic
cacti are showcased. Another
greenhouse featuring a mon-
soon climate contains unusual
carnivorous plants. In the
tropical culture greenhouse,
you can admire a traditional
Indonesian *sawah* (ricefield).

The Chinese garden ("Het
verborgen rijk van Ming", or "The
hidden Ming Empire") is well
worth a visit. It is a faithful reconstruction of a real garden owned
by a 16th-century high-ranking
Chinese official of the Ming
Dynasty (1368–1644). It features
original Chinese pagodas, which
have been painstakingly restored
by Chinese craftsmen into fine
pavilions and then beautifully
decorated with carvings of lions
and dragons. Het verborgen rijk
van Ming also has a waterfall and
a tea house where visitors can
enjoy Chinese refreshments.

Another interesting theme
garden is the Ogham Gardens,
a Celtic garden whose main
attractions is the Horoscope of
Trees, consisting of an earth-
and-stone circular wall, which
is a replica of the enclosures
the ancient Celts built to live
within. Inside the circle is a
labyrinth representing life; at its
centre is a small garden and the
Well of Wisdom.

In summer, a variety of exhibitions and events are held in the
grounds, attracting locals and
tourists alike.

The fascinating Hortus Haren, with its innumerable attractions

Groninger Museum

Between the central station and the inner city lies the Groninger Museum, standing on an island in the 19th-century Verbindingskanaal. Designed by internationally renowned Italian architect Alessandro Mendini and opened in 1994, the museum showcases archaeology and history, applied arts (including a remarkable collection of Chinese and Japanese porcelain), early art and cutting-edge modern art.

★ **Spiral Staircase**
The spiral staircase, which visitors have to descend to see the exhibits, is the museum's main meeting point and a work of art in itself.

Curtains
The applied arts section, which includes oriental porcelain, is divided by winding curtains.

The museum shop
sells reproductions of the exhibits and books about the artists who are represented in the museum.

KEY

① **The museum café** features furniture by various designers and was set up as an addition to the museum collection.

② **A cycle and pedestrian bridge** connects the museum with the station square. There is also a direct connection with the station and the town centre.

③ **Temporary exhibitions**

④ **The Mendini Pavilion** is easily distinguished by its apparent haphazardness and chaos, and is a good example of deconstructivism.

⑤ **This wing** of the museum was designed by Wolfgang Prix and Helmut Swiczinsky.

⑥ **A large concrete staircase** in the spectacular Mendini Pavilion leads to the upper pavilion, where some of the collection of art is on display.

Rembrandt
This ink drawing of *Saskia in Bed* by Rembrandt
can sometimes be seen in the Mendini Pavilion.

★ De Ploeg
The Groningen art
collective De Ploeg has its
own pavilion. In addition
to works by the group, the
section also displays works
by other Expressionists
from northern Europe. The
picture *Rotating Door of the
Post Office* is by De Ploeg
painter HN Werkman.

Bridge in the Coop
Himmelb(l)au Pavilion

Museum Guide

*Groninger Museum was designed by
Alessandro Mendini (born 1931). He based the
design around the collections of the museum,
which consisted of archaeology, applied arts
and early and modern pictorial arts. The focus
of the building is the 30-m (98-ft)
tower in the middle.*

❷ Grootegast

Road Map D1. 🚶 11,500. 🚌 33, 38, 39, 98, 101, 133. ℹ️ Nienoord 20, Leek (0594-512100). 🛒 Fri.

The little town of Lutjegast, close to Grootegast, is the birthplace of the 17th-century explorer Abel Tasman *(see box)*. The **Abel Tasmankabinet** houses an interesting exhibition about his life. The collection includes old sea charts and books.

🏛️ **Abel Tasmankabinet**
Kompasstraat 1. **Tel** 0594-613576.
Open 1:30–4:30pm Tue–Sat.

❸ Leek

Road Map D2. 🚶 18,000. 🚌 81, 85, 88, 98, 306, 316. ℹ️ Nienoord 20 (0594-512100). 🛒 Thu.

In the small town of Leek stands the castle of Nienoord, built in approximately 1524 by Wigbold van Ewsum. During the 19th century, things at the castle seemed to be taking a turn for the worse.

Landgoed Nienoord

In 1846, the then owner, Ferdinand Folef Kniphausen, nicknamed "the mad squire", burned all the family portraits in a drunken fit. Later, the orangery and part of the upper floor were destroyed by fire. In 1950, the municipality bought the castle. Eight years later, the **Nationaal Rijtuigmuseum**, featuring horse-drawn vehicles, was established here. It contains a unique collection of royal coaches, gigs, mail coaches and hackney carriages.

🏛️ **Nationaal Rijtuigmuseum**
Nienoord 1. **Tel** 0594-512260.
Open Apr–Oct: 11am–5pm, Tue–Sun. **Closed** Mon. 🅿️ ♿

The harbour of the delightful fishing village of Zoutkamp

❹ Zoutkamp

Road Map: D1. 🚶 1,200. 🚌 63, 65, 69, 136, 163, 165. ℹ️ Reitdiepskade 11 (0595-401957).

The small fishing village of Zoutkamp changed its character dramatically after the damming of the Lauwerszee in 1969. By the waterside (Reitdiepskade) there are still a number of fishermen's cottages retaining the erstwhile charm of the village.

❺ Lauwersoog

Road Map D1. 🚶 350. 🚌 50, 63, 163. ℹ️ Reitdiepskade 11, Zoutkamp (0595-401957).

At Lauwersoog, from where the ferry leaves for Schiermonnikoog *(see p279)*, is the Lauwersmeer, a 2,000-ha (4,940-acre) nature reserve. When the Lauwerszee was drained, the land was designated for four purposes: agriculture, recreation, a nature reserve and an army training area.

Environs
Lauwersoog is a good base from which to explore the tuff churches that, in the Middle Ages, were built in villages such as Doezum, Bedum and Zuidwolde. They can be recognized by their grey or green porous stone.

Abel Tasman (1603–59)

Abel Janszoon Tasman was born in Lutjegast in 1603 but lived in Amsterdam from an early age. In 1633, as a navigating officer for the Dutch East India Company *(see pp52–3)*, he travelled to Asia. In 1642, he sailed on the yacht *De Heemskerck* and then with the cargo ship *Zeehaen* in search of the legendary southern continent. Tasman charted some of the coast and later reached New Zealand's South Island. On 13 June 1643, he arrived in Batavia (now Jakarta), which he called home until his death 16 years later. From 1644 to 1648, he sat on the Batavian council of justice; during this time he also joined trading missions to Sumatra (1646) and Siam (1647). Tasman died on 10 October 1659, having bequeathed his money to the poor of Lutjegast.

❻ Pieterburen

Road Map D1. 🏛 500. 🚌 65, 67, 68.
🛈 Waddencentrum, Hoofdstraat 83
(0595-528522).

One of the best-known places in
Groningen is Pieterburen, home
to the **Zeehondencrèche**. This
seal nursery was founded by
Lenie 't Hart and others as a
reception centre for sick and
disabled seals from the nearby
Waddenzee, where some 1,750
seals live. Half of these owe their
lives to care they received here.
The **Waddencentrum**, also
located here, is an exhibition
centre dedicated to the mud
flats of the Waddenzee. It also
provides useful information for
people wishing to walk there.

Recovering seal in one of the ponds at Pieterburen

🦭 **Zeehondencrèche Pieterburen**
Hoofdstraat 94a. **Tel** 0595-526526.
Open 10am–5pm daily.

🏚 **Het Waddencentrum**
Hoofdstraat 83. **Tel** 0595-528522.
Open 9am–6pm daily. 🖵

Environs
In Leens, 10 km (6 miles) to the
southwest of Pieterburen, is
the stunning 14th-century
borg (moated manor house)
Verhildersum, which contains
19th-century furnishings. The
castle is surrounded by a wide
moat. Its gardens include an
arbour and sculptures. The
castle's coach house is regularly

used as a venue for exhibitions,
while the Schathuis (treasury) is
now a lively café and restaurant.

🏛 **Borg Verhildersum**
Wierde 40, Leens. **Tel** 0595-571430.
Open Apr–Oct: 10:30am–5pm
Tue–Sun. 🖼

❼ Uithuizen

Road Map E1. 🏛 5,300. 🚌 41, 61,
62, 641, 662. 🛈 Mennonietenkerk-
straat 13 (0595-434051). 🛒 Sat.

The exceptionally pretty castle
of Menkemaborg in Uithuizen
dates back to the 14th century.
It acquired its present-day form
around 1700. The bedroom

features a ceremonial bed-
stead dating from the early
18th century, when King
William III stayed here. The
kitchen in the cellar has all the
old fittings. The gardens were
laid out during restoration
work in the 18th century. The
Schathuis (treasury), formerly
used to store the food brought
by the townspeople to the
castle, currently houses a café
and restaurant.

🏛 **Menkemaborg**
Menkemaweg 2. 🚌 61. **Tel** 0595-
431970. **Open** Mar–Jun & Sep:
10am–5pm Tue–Sun; Jul–Aug:
10am–5pm daily; Oct–Dec: 10am–
4pm Tue–Sun. **Closed** Jan–Feb. 🖼

Wedding in traditional dress in the gardens of the 14th-century Menkemaborg in Uithuizen

❽ Appingedam

Road Map E1. ⚑ 12,400. 🚌 40, 45, 78, 140, 178. ℹ️ Oude Kerkstraat 1 (0596-620300). 🛒 Sat.

This town, a member of the Hanseatic League in the Middle Ages, was granted its charter in 1327. Standing at a junction of waterways as it once did and with a seaport, it quickly grew into a major international trading city. The medieval layout of the city has remained largely unchanged. The **hanging kitchens**, visible from the Vlinterbrug bridge, were built this way to create more space in the houses. Directly over the water are doors from which people drew water for their household needs.

In the 18th century, the town again prospered, as the **Ebenhaëzerhuis** well illustrates. Appingedam, with over 65 listed buildings, has a preservation order as a town of historical interest.

❾ Slochteren

Road Map E1. ⚑ 2,600. 🚌 78, 178. ℹ️ Noorderweg 1 (0598-422970). 🛒 Thu.

When a natural gas field was discovered here in 1959, Slochteren gained overnight national renown. The "Slochteren Dome" appeared to be the largest in the world when it was first discovered, and the revenue it brought in made Holland rich.

The past of this historic town is closely associated with the lords of the Fraeylemaborg. The Reformed Church in Slochteren consists of the remnants of a 13th-century Romanesque-Gothic cross-naved church. The

Steam pumping station (1878) at the Winschoten polder, now a museum

environs are excellent for walking or cycling, particularly around places like nearby Schildmeer.

❿ Fraeylemaborg

Road Map E1. ℹ️ Noorderweg 1, Slochteren (0598-422970).

Fraeylemaborg is one of the most imposing castles of Groningen. It dates back to the Middle Ages. Three embrasures in the kitchen and the hall above it bear silent witness to the defensive functions the castle once had. In the 17th century, two side wings were added, and in the 18th century it was given its present form with the addition of the monumental main wing. The castle is surrounded by a double moat.

The extensive wooded park just beyond the castle is an interesting combination of the 18th-century Baroque garden style and the 19th-century English landscape gardens.

🏛️ **Fraeylemaborg**
Hoofdweg 30–32, Slochteren.
Tel 0598-421568. **Open** 2 Jan–31 Dec: 10am–5pm Tue–Fri, 1–5pm Sat, Sun & public hols. 🅿️

⓫ Winschoten

Road Map E2. ⚑ 18,500. 🚌 10, 12, 13, 14, 17, 29. ℹ️ Torenstraat 10 (0597-430022). 🛒 Sat.

This little town in Oost-Groningen is known primarily for its three mills: Berg, a corn and hulling mill from 1854; Dijkstra, which is 25 m (82 ft) in height and dates from 1862; and Edens, a corn and hulling mill from 1761. The interesting **Museum Stoomgemaal** contains a steam-powered pump from 1878 which was used to drain the flooded polderland.

🏛️ **Museum Stoomgemaal**
Oostereinde 4. **Tel** 0597-425070.
Open call for timings. 🅿️

Environs
In Heiligerlee stands a monument to the Battle of Heiligerlee in 1568. This battle is famous for being over in just two hours and for the death of Count Adolf of Nassau. The **Museum "Slag bij Heiligerlee"** has an exhibition dedicated to the bloody battle.

🏛️ **Museum "Slag bij Heiligerlee"**
Provincialeweg 55. **Tel** 0597-418199.
Open Apr & Oct: 1–5pm Tue–Sun; May–Sep: 10am–5pm Tue–Sat, 1pm–5pm Sun. **Closed** public hols. 🅿️

The historical castle of Fraeylemaborg at Slochteren

⓬ Veendam

Road Map E2. 🚗 28,500. 🚌 71, 73.
ℹ️ Museumplein 5b (0598-364224).
🛒 Mon am, Thu pm.

Parkstad Veendam (Veendam Garden City) is so called for the lush greenery in the town, which for centuries was the industrial heart of the peat colonies. However, at the end of the 19th century, peat-cutting fell into decline. Although shipping grew in importance – Veendam even had its own maritime school – the town retained its character as a peat-cutting centre.

The **Veenkoloniaal Museum** (peat colony museum) offers a permanent exhibition illustrating the history of peat-cutting, navigation, agriculture and industry in the Groningen peatlands.

The most renowned inhabitant of Veendam was Anthony Winkler Prins (1817–1908), who wrote the famous encyclopaedia which is still associated with his name.

🏛 **Veenkoloniaal Museum**
Museumplein 5. **Tel** 0598-364224.
Open 11am–5pm Tue–Thu, 1–5pm Fri–Mon. **Closed** public hols. ♿

⓭ Bourtange

Road Map E2. 🚗 600. 🚌 70, 72.
ℹ️ Willem Lodewijkstraat 33 (0599-354600). 🌐 **bourtange.nl**

Right at the German border is the magnificent fortified town of Bourtange, whose history dates back to 1580, when William of Orange ordered that a fortress with five bastions be built here on what had once been swampland. The defence works were continuously upgraded, until the fort gradually lost its defensive functions. It has now been painstakingly restored to its 18th-century appearance. **Museum "De Baracquen"** exhibits artifacts excavated in the fort.

The charming town itself lies within a star-shaped labyrinth of moats.

Grand layout of the impressive fortress of Bourtange

🏛 **Museum "De Baracquen"**
Willem Lodewijkstraat 33. **Tel** 0599-354600. **Open** mid-Mar–Oct: 10am–5pm daily; Nov–mid-Mar: noon–5pm Sat & Sun. **Closed** 25 & 26 Dec. ♿

⓮ Oude en Nieuwe Pekela

Road Map E2. 🚗 13,500. 🚌 75.
ℹ️ Restaurant Het Turfschip/Flessings – terrein 3, Oude Pekela (0597-618833). 🛒 Wed pm, Thu pm.

The "old" and "new" villages of Pekela are typical ribbon developments with a marked rural, peatland character. In the 18th century, potato flour and straw-board manufacture grew in importance in the region. There are pleasant footpaths along the main canal.

⓯ Ter Apel

Road Map E2. 🚗 7,800.
🚌 26, 70, 73. ℹ️ Hoofdstraat 49a (0599-581277). 🛒 Thu.

In Ter Apel, situated in the Westerwolde region between Drenthe and Germany, is a 1465 **monastery** of the same name. In 1933, the monastery was thoroughly restored and now functions as a museum devoted to ecclesiastic art and religious history. The fragrant herb garden located in the cloisters contains a collection of nutrient-rich herbs such as birthwort and common rue.

🏛 **Museum-klooster Ter Apel**
Boslaan 3. **Tel** 0599-581370. **Open** 10am–5pm Tue–Sat, 1–5pm Sun & public hols. **Closed** 1 Jan, Mon (Nov–Mar). ♿

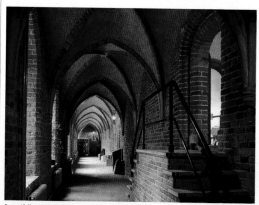
Beautifully restored cloisters at the Ter Apel monastery

FRIESLAND

Friesland, or Fryslân as it is officially called, is a remarkable province perhaps best known outside the Netherlands for its distinctive Friesian cows. Parts of it are below sea level, and its size has increased since historic times as a result of land reclamation schemes on the former Zuiderzee.

Much of the province is fenland, whose myriad canals and channels no doubt helped the freedom-loving Frisians fight off invaders. The 1345 battle of Warns, when the Frisians beat the Dutch army, is still commemorated every year. In the 7th century, the Frisians under their king, Radboud, inhabited an independent territory that stretched all the way to Flanders and Cologne (see pp48–9), and they have preserved their distinctive language to this day. Other features peculiar to this province are unique sports and recreations like sailing and racing in skûtjes (traditional Frisian boats), hunting for plovers' eggs, fierljeppen (pole-vaulting), keatsen (a ball game), and the famous Elfstedentocht, a winter ice-skating marathon around 11 Frisian towns.

The provincial capital of Leeuwarden has some interesting and unique museums, while elsewhere in the province visitors can enjoy collections consisting of items as diverse as historic costumes and hats, ceramics, letters, ice skates and sledges, vernacular paintings, bells, model boats and human mummies. Outside the towns, the landscape is interesting too, from the mud flats on the Waddenzee to the forests and heathland of the Drents-Friese Woud National Park, away to the east. Tourism is becoming increasingly important in Friesland nowadays and its inhabitants less insular. Visitors are greeted with open arms and Jo binne tige welcom – "You are heartily welcome."

Bartlehiem, the junction of the Elfsteden (11 towns) – a favourite summer destination for day-trippers

◄ Display showing the position of planets in the solar system, Planetarium Friesland

Exploring Friesland

Friesland is famous for its vast meadows and its distinctive farmhouses of the *kop-hals-romp* and *stelp* types. It also boasts a varied landscape. In the southwest are the popular *Friese meren* (Frisian lakes), while the north is typified by undulating dykes, *terp* villages and church steeples with pitched roofs. Gaasterland in the south has rolling woodlands and cliffs, whereas the *Friese wouden* (Frisian woods) in the province's southeastern corner, with their forests, heathland and drifting sands, are more reminiscent of Drenthe.

The sea dyke at Wierum

Sights at a Glance

1. Leeuwarden
2. Dokkum
3. Franeker
4. Harlingen
5. Bolsward
6. Workum
7. Hindeloopen
8. Gaasterland
9. Sloten
10. Sneek
11. Thialfstadion
12. Oude Venen
13. Beetsterzwaag
14. Appelscha

The Noorderhaven in Harlingen

Getting Around

Friesland is convenient and easy to get to. It is crossed by the A7 (east–west) and the A32 (north–south) motorways. Rail and bus links are unproblematic. Most of the larger villages and towns have a railway station; those which don't can be reached by bus. From Harlingen, Holwerd or Lauwersoog, the islands are only a short boat ride away. The province also has a good network of minor roads, walking routes and cycle tracks.

Gabled houses along Het Diep in Sloten

The *terp* of Hogbeintum, west of Dokkum, the highest in Friesland

0 kilometres 10
0 miles 5

Key

━━━ Motorway

━━━ Major road

┈┈┈ Minor road

━━━ Scenic route

╍╍╍ Main railway

─── Minor railway

━━━ Regional border

Picturesque Lindevallei at Wolvega, near Thialfstadion

The Elfstedentocht

The Elfstedentocht, or 11-town race, is a 200-km (124-mile) ice-skating marathon which passes through Leeuwarden, Skeen, IJlst, Sloten, Stavoren, Hindeloopen, Workum, Bolsward, Harlingen, Franeker, Dokkum and back to Leeuwarden. Participants are awarded the famous Elfstedenkruisje only when they have collected all the stamps on their starter's card and provided they get back to Leeuwarden before midnight. The winner of the race is guaranteed local fame.

The "Elfstedenkruisje" (Elfsteden cross) is in the shape of a Maltese cross. In the middle is an enamel coat of arms of Friesland and the inscription "De Friesche Elf Steden" –"The 11 Frisian towns".

The Tocht Der Tochten

The Tocht der Tochten (literally, "Race of Races"), as the Elfstedentocht is known, is a combination of race and touring marathon and has acquired almost mythical status in the Netherlands. The race is a real media event, keeping millions glued to their television screens. Although the marathon has been held only 15 times since 1900, the entire country falls under the spell of the event as soon as the mercury falls even slightly below zero. If there is a lasting frost, the area supervisors measure daily the thickness of the ice, as it has to be at least 15 cm (6 in) thick for the race to be held. When the magic words *It sil heve* (It shall happen) are uttered by the supervisors, Friesland is transformed, overflowing with excited crowds. Trains are packed, the roads are jammed with cars and entire villages are mobilized to provide hot tea and oranges for the skaters. Wandering musicians whip the crowd into a frenzy of enthusiasm. The Dutch language has been enriched with the Frisian word *klúnen*, which means to walk overland on skates past places where the ice is impassable.

Harns ⑨ (Harlingen)

Frjentsjer ⑩ (Franeker)

Harlingervaart

Boalsert ⑧ (Bolsward)

Workumer Trekvaart

Drylts (IJlst)

Franeker in a festive mood

Warkum ⑦ (Workum)

Hylpen ⑥ (Hindeloopen)

Starum ⑤ (Stavoren)

Dropping out is a common occurrence during the race. Despite being affected by snow blindness and symptoms of frostbite, many participants in the race attempt to complete the course. Some break down in tears when they realize that they will be unable to collect the much-coveted Elfstedenkruisje (Elfsteden cross).

The hamlet of Bartlehiem is famous for its footbridge over the Finkumervaart. Bartlehiem is the best-known skating area in all of Holland and is a psychological milestone for the skaters. Those who still must get to Dokkum may pass skaters travelling in the opposite direction, having already won their stamp from the northernmost point on the route. Many skaters have to take the Bartlehiem–Dokkum section in the dark. The Northern Lights seen at this time of year also attract thousands of spectators.

All winners of the Elfstedentocht are national heroes, but Evert van Benthem even more so. A farmer from

Two-time winner Evert van Benthem

Sint-Jansklooster, he managed to cross the finishing line at the Bonkevaart in Leeuwarden in first place twice in a row (1985 and 1986). Van Benthem's double victory gave him a legendary status throughout the Netherlands. The prize itself is a laurel wreath, both for men and for women. The names of the winners are engraved on the Elfstedenrijder monument in Leeuwarden.

The Eerste Friese Schaatsmuseum

The Eerste Friese Schaatsmuseum (first Frisian skating museum) in Hindeloopen (see p302) has among its exhibits such items as antique skates, original workshops, sleds and historical documents covering the 90 or so years that the Elfstedentocht has been held. Displays on innumerable winners, including Reinier Paping, Jeen van den Berg and Henk Angenet, are also featured here. Among the highlights of the museum's collection are the skating packs of various heroes of the event, the skates of two-time winner Evert van Benthem and the starter's card of WA van Buren. One of the most moving exhibits in the collection is the right big toe of Tinus Udding, which he lost to frostbite during the harsh race in the cold winter of 1963.

Long before sunrise, tens of thousands of skaters start off from the FEC (Frisian Exhibition Centre) in Leeuwarden.

Willem-Alexander, alias WA van Buren, in the arms of his mother, Queen Beatrix, after the 1985 race

Key

■■ Route of the Elfstedentocht

══ Road

❶ Leeuwarden

Road Map D1. 🌇 89,000. 🚌 🚉
ℹ️ Achmeatoren, Sophialaan 4 (0900-2024060). 🛍️ Fri & Sat.

Frisian capital and home to Mata Hari, Peter Jelles Troelstra and Jan Jacob Slauerhoff, Leeuwarden was also the residence of the Frisian Nassaus (1584–1747). The town park and gardens of the Prinsentuin and Stadhouderlijk Hof date back to this period.

Characteristic of Leeuwarden is the statue of **Us Mem** (our mother), honouring the famous Frisian cattle. The **Fries Museum**, situated in an 18th-century patrician house, has a large collection of items excavated from *terps*, as well as collections of clothes, art and applied arts. The same building also houses the **Verzetsmuseum Friesland**, a collection and educational facility dedicated to the Friesland resistance movement of World War II, in

Frisian coat of arms

which more than 600 Jewish people were killed, and nearly 300 members of the resistance also lost their lives. There is a chronological exhibition on World War II and its aftermath, explorations of contemporary wars and racism, and documents and artifacts from the time.

On Oldehoofsterkerkhof, the leaning tower of the **Oldehove** dominates the skyline. When building began in 1529, the church tower was going to be the tallest in the Netherlands. Unfortunately, the foundations began to sink, and so the work stopped just three years later. The tower has remained incomplete ever since. The top of the tower offers an excellent view over Leeuwarden and its environs, reaching as far as the coast.

The museum **Het Princessehof**, housed in a palace which was formerly the residence of Maria Louise van Hessen-Kassel (also known as Marijke Meu), contains a unique

Atmospheric Dokkum, a major port in the 8th century

collection of ceramics of international importance. The artifacts include Asian, European and contemporary ceramics and tiles.

The old municipal orphanage is now home to the **Natuurmuseum Fryslân** (natural history museum), whose exhibition of "Friesland underwater" is well worth a visit.

🏛️ **Fries Museum**
Wilhelminaplein 92. **Tel** 058-2555500.
Open 11am–5pm Tue–Sun. 🔲 🔲 🔲

🏛️ **Verzetsmuseum Friesland**
Turfmarkt 1. **Tel** 058-2120111.
Open 11am–5pm Tue–Sun.
Closed 1 Jan, 25 Dec.

🏛️ **Het Princessehof**
Grote Kerkstraat 11. **Tel** 058-2948958.
Open 11am–5pm Tue–Sun. **Closed** 1 Jan, 30 Apr, 25 Dec. 🔲 🔲 🔲

🏛️ **Natuurmuseum Fryslân**
Schoenmakersperk 2. **Tel** 058-2332244.
Open 11am–5pm Tue–Sun. 🔲 🔲

The leaning tower of the Oldehove (1529), still incomplete

❷ Dokkum

Road Map D1. 🌇 13,000. 🚌 ℹ️ Op de Fetze 13 (0519-293800). 🛍️ Wed.

The trading and garrison town of Dokkum was the headquarters of the Frisian Admiralty between 1596 and 1645, though it owes its fame above all to the killing here of St Boniface by pagan Frisians in AD 754 *(see pp48–9)*. The local history museum, the **Admiraliteitshuis**, has an exhibition on the life of the saint. Other exhibits include artifacts excavated from *terps*, costumes, silverware, handicrafts and folk art. In addition to the **Bonifatiuskerk**, Dokkum has a park for religious processions with the stations of the cross and a chapel. Water drawn from the well of **Bonifatiusbron** is believed to have therapeutic qualities. Near the well is a statue of the saint after whom it is named. Saint Boniface was actually an Englishman, born in 675, who came to the region on a mission to convert the Frisians. Heathens attacked Boniface and his companions. Despite holding a bible in front of his face, Boniface was killed by a sword.

In the centre, **Natuurmuseum Dokkum** explores all aspects of the natural world in Friesland, both living and inanimate. There are cabinets of rocks, stones, shells and insects, and there is a "sound cabinet" that plays the songs of various birds from the area.

On the former **town walls**, now a park, are two

19th-century **stellingmolen**-type mills known as *De Hoop* and *Zeldenrust* (see p29).

🏛 Admiraliteitshuis
Diepswal 27. **Tel** 0519-293134.
Open Apr–Oct: 1–5pm Tue–Sat. 📷
W museumdokkum.nl

🏛 Natuurmuseum Dokkum
Kleine Oosterstraat 12.
Tel 0519-297318. **Open** Oct–May:
Sat & Sun; Jun–Sep: Mon–Sat.
Closed public hols.

❸ Franeker

Road Map C1. 🏘 13,000. 🚌 🚆
ℹ Voorstraat 35 (058-2572590).
🛒 Wed & Sat.

Franeker was a university town from 1585 to 1811. Today, it is the centre of skating in Friesland. In and around the Voorstraat are several monumental buildings, including the 15th-century Martenahuis. The Cammingahuis, which dates from the 14th century, now houses the **Kaatsmuseum** (skating museum). The **Museum Martena**, in a fine 18th-century building, has a collection about the former university. The Renaissance **Stadhuis** (town hall) has an ornate façade. Opposite is the **Planetarium Friesland** (1781), built by wool industrialist Eise Eisinga. For two centuries, the planets have rotated around its ceiling. Beside the Sjûkelân, a sacred place for Frisian skating, is the Bogt fen Guné (16th century), Holland's oldest student residence.

Planetarium Friesland

🏛 Kaatsmuseum
Voorstraat 2. **Tel** 0517-393910. **Open**
15 May–Sep: 1–5pm Tue–Sat. 📷

🏛 Museum Martena
Voorstraat 35. **Tel** 0517-392192.
Open 10am–5pm Tue–Fri, 1–5pm Sat
& Sun. 📷

🏛 Planetarium Friesland
Eise Eisingastraat 3. **Tel** 0517-393070.
Open 10am–5pm Tue–Sun, 1–5pm Sun
(also Apr–Oct: 1–5pm Mon). 📷 📷

❹ Harlingen

Road Map C2. 🏘 14,500. 🚌 🚆
ℹ Grote Bredeplaats 17b
(0517-430207). 🛒 Wed am, Sat.

The port town of Harlingen retains much of its old charm. The **Zoutsloot** and **Noorderhaven** have been painstakingly restored. A statue of **Hans Brinker** (see p27) stands at the ferry port. South of

Harlingen is **Pingjum**. Menno Simons (1496–1561), the evangelical preacher after whom many of the Dutch Anabaptists named themselves, started his religious life here. Mennonites from all over the world now visit.

❺ Bolsward

Road Map C2. 🏘 10,000. 🚌 ℹ
Wipstraat 6 (0515-577701). 🛒 Thu.

Modest Bolsward first arose in the 11th century as a trading post, enjoying the height of its development in the 15th century. **Martinikerk**, a pseudo-basilica whose tower features a saddleback roof, was built during this period. The **Stadhuis** (town hall), with its local history museum, the **Oudheidkamer**, is the town's centrepiece.

Bolsward town hall

Local brews can be sampled at the **Us Heit Bierbrouwerij**, the smallest brewery in the country. A museum has displays of beer-making equipment while a guided tour shows how the beer is made. Attached to the brewery is a bar selling the house ales, with plenty available by the bottle to take away as souvenirs.

🏛 Oudheidkamer
Jongemastraat 2. **Tel** 0515-578787.
Open Apr–Oct: 9am–noon & 2–4pm
Mon–Thu. 📷

🏛 Us Heit Bierbrouwerij
Snekerstraat 43. **Tel** 0515-577449.
Open Mon, Tue, Thu–Sat (call ahead).

Mata Hari

Margaretha Geertruida Zelle (1876–1917), who became known to all the world as Mata Hari (Malaysian for "eye of the day"), grew up in Leeuwarden. Her life came to a tragic end in Vincennes outside Paris, where she was executed by a firing squad after a French tribunal found her guilty of spying for the Germans. The Fries Museum tells you more about this legendary woman, who has gained international notoriety through films and books about her life. The house where she lived with her parents from 1883 to 1890 on Grote Kerkstraat 212 now houses the Frysk Letterkundig Museum (Frisian museum of letters).

❻ Workum

Road Map C2. 🏠 4,000. 🚌 🚉
ℹ️ Merk 4 (0515-541045).

The elongated Zuiderzee town of Workum flourished around 1300. Workum is known for the fine façades of its houses and its unfinished 16th-century church, the **Grote of Gertrudiskerk**. Beside the lock is the centuries-old wharf of **de Hoop**, where traditional boats are still built. The most popular attraction in Workum is **Jopie Huisman Museum**, which is the most-visited museum in Friesland. It features the autodidactic art of painter and scrap-metal merchant Jopie Huisman (1922–2000). His drawings and paintings tell the stories of the daily grind and poverty, the drudgery and toil of the tradesman, the housewife and the ordinary person.

The picturesque 17th-century weigh house contains the **Museum Warkums Erfskip**. This museum delves into the history of Workum, and, principally, that of its shipping and pottery industries.

🏛 **Jopie Huisman Museum**
Noard 6. **Tel** 0515-543131. **Open** Apr–Oct: 10am–5pm Mon–Sat, 1–5pm Sun; Mar & Nov: 1–5pm daily. 🗖 ♿

🏛 **Museum Warkums Erfskip**
Merk 4. **Tel** 0515-543155. **Open** Apr–Oct: 10am–5pm Mon–Sat, 1:30–5pm Sun; Nov–Dec & mid-Feb–Mar: 1–5pm daily. 🗖

The Football Boots of Abe Lenstra by Jopie Huisman

❼ Hindeloopen

Road Map C2. 🏠 850. 🚌 🚉
ℹ️ Nieuwstad 26 (0514-851223).

Hindeloopen plays a special role in Friesland. This picturesque old town of seafarers and fishermen has its own dialect, its own costume and its own style of

A sea-rescue centre with its inviting bench, in Hindeloopen

painting. The town is full of little canals with wooden bridges and a variety of pretty captains' houses, with their characteristic façades. One of the most distinctive spots is the picturesque 17th-century lock-keeper's house by the port, with its wooden bell-tower.

In the **Museum Hidde Nijland Stichting** (museum of the Hidde Nijland foundation), the life of the wealthier citizens of Hindeloopen during the 18th century is showcased. Well-appointed period rooms show the colourful clothes and the now-famous painted furniture of the time. A substantial exhibition of paintings vividly illustrates the development of painting in Hindeloopen.

The **Eerste Friese Schaatsmuseum** (first Frisian skating museum) *(see p299)* offers a unique collection of old skates. It also has a fine exhibition dedicated to the Elfstedentocht and various traditional workshops (such as a smithy and a carpenter's), as well as a comprehensive collection of sledges and historical material such as old tiles and prints.

🏛 **Museum Hidde Nijland Stichting**
Dijkweg 1. **Tel** 0514-521420. **Open** Mar–Oct: 11am–5pm Mon–Fri, 1:30–5pm Sat, Sun & public hols. 🗖

🏛 **Eerste Friese Schaatsmuseum**
Kleine Weide 1–3. **Tel** 0514-521683. **Open** 10am–6pm Mon–Sat, 1–5pm Sun. 🗖

❽ Gaasterland

Road Map C2. 🚌 ℹ️ De Brink 4, Oudemirdum (0514-571777).

This area of fine, rolling woodlands in the southwestern corner of Friesland offers many opportunities for walking and cycling. The region's name comes from the word "gaast", which refers to the sandy heights formed during the last two Ice Ages.

At the edge of Gaasterland are a number of steep cliffs, such as the **Rode Klif** and the **Oudemirdumerklif**, formed when the Zuiderzee eroded the coastline. On the Rode Klif at Laaxum is an enormous boulder bearing the inscription *Leaver dea as slaef,* or, *Rather dead than a slave,* a memento of the 1345 Frisian victory over the Dutch. The **Rijsterbos** wood, with its abundant bracken, dates from

A cyclist in Gaasterland

the 17th century and once consisted mainly of oak. The little river of Luts, which is now known because of the Elfstedentocht, was used for the transport of oak logs and oak bark for tanneries. In the village of **Oudemirdum** is a hostel, shops and an old pump. **Informatiecentrum Mar en Klif** (Sea and Cliff Information Centre) has information about how the landscape was formed and about local flora and fauna. Special attention is paid to badgers, and in the wild garden, a bat tower has been built.

The Luts river in **Balk**, flanked by linden trees, inspired the poem *Mei* by Herman Gorter (1864–1927).

Informatiecentrum Mar en Klif
De Brink 4, Oudemirdum. **Tel** 0514-571777. **Open** Apr–Oct: 10am–5pm Mon–Sat, 11am–5pm Sun.

❾ Sloten

Road Map C2. 650.
Museum Stedhûs Sleat, Heerenwal 48 (0514-531541).

The smallest town in Friesland, replete with pretty canals, embankments and water-gates, was designed by famous Frisian military engineer Menno van Coehoorn. Built at a junction of roads and waterways, it was at the height of its development in the 17th and 18th centuries. On either side of the town are old cannons. The old fortress mill at the Lemsterpoort is an

octagonal *bovenkruier*-type mill from 1755. The **Museum Stedhûs Sleat** houses the **Laterna Magica**, a museum of magic lanterns, an antique museum and a collection of costumes, hats, fans and bells.

Museum Stedhûs Sleat
Heerenwal 48. **Tel** 0514-531541. **Open** Apr–Oct: 11am–5pm Tue–Fri, 1–5pm Sat & Sun.

❿ Sneek

Road Map C2. 31,600.
Marktstraat 20 (0515-750678). Tue am, Sat.

Sneek's centrepiece is the Waterpoort (water-gate) dating from 1613. Sneekweek is the name of a popular sailing event that in early August brings together amateur sailors and partygoers from all over the country. **Fries Scheepvaart**

Typical stepped gables in Sloten, the smallest town in Friesland

Mummy in Wieuwerd, a small village in Littenseradiel

Museum focuses on the history of navigation and shipbuilding. Its exhibits include a *skûtje* deckhouse, the cabin of a *boeier* yacht and approximately 200 model ships. The *zilverzaal* (silver room) houses one of the richest collections of Frisian silver.

Fries Scheepvaart Museum
Kleinzand 14. **Tel** 0515-414057. **Open** 10am–5pm Mon–Sat, noon–5pm Sun. **Closed** public hols. partly.

Environs
The village of **Wieuwerd**, north of Sneek, is known for the human mummies in its 13th-century St Nicholas church (open in summer). They were discovered by chance in 1765 and the reason for their mummification is not known.

Schuitje Sailing

Schuitje sailing, *or skûtsjesilen,* is a sport which has gained great popularity in the lakes of Friesland, *skûtje* being the name of the typical local spritsail barges. Originally used for the carriage of goods and as ferries, these boats are raced by representatives of various towns and villages. The result is a series of spectacular events held in July and August in various places, each time on a different lake and from a different base. Every day certain prizes are won, and on the last day, in Sneek, the champion of the year is announced and fêted. The races are held over the course of 11 racing days and three rest days.

⓫ The Thialfstadion

The Thialfstadion in Heerenveen, completely renovated in 2001, is regarded as the temple of Dutch ice-skating and has international renown. The exuberant crowds that converge on the stadium for international events create a unique atmosphere. Skating heroes such as Marianne Timmer, Gunda Niemann and Rintje Ritsma have all experienced emotional highlights in their sporting careers here.

VISITORS' CHECKLIST

Practical Information
Pim Mulierlaan 1, Heerenveen.
Tel 0513-637700/0900-2020026.
Open timings vary, call ahead or check website for exact opening hours. **Closed** Apr–Sep. 📷 ▣
🆆 thialf.nl

Transport
🚌 Heerenveen.

The Art of Ice-making

Making a good ice surface is an art. The Thialf ice-makers strive to strike a balance between deformation – the extent to which the ice breaks down under the pressure of the skate – and the smoothness of the ice.

Thialf Spectators
The fans here are famous for their colourful garb and their imaginative banners.

Underneath the ice are 70 km (43 miles) of cooling elements.

The great hall covers an area of 15,000 m² (17,950 sq yd) and can accommodate 13,000 spectators.

The ice hockey hall is 1,800 m² (2,150 sq yd) and has room for 4,000 spectators.

Triumph
The climax of every major skating event in the Thialfstadion is the procession of winners through the stadium on a special sleigh drawn by a Frisian horse.

Hinged Skates
Skates which have a hinge between the shoe and the blade give significantly better results. All new world records have been achieved with the help of *klapschaatsen* (hinged skates).

Stately Lauswolt, now a luxury hotel with a restaurant

⑫ Oude Venen

Road Map D2. 🏞️ ℹ️ P Miedemaweg 9, Earnewâld (0511-539500).

This region, whose name literally means "the old fens", is a fine area of peat-marshes with reedlands, swampy woodlands and sunken polders between Earnewâld and Grou. The lakes

The swampy marshes of Oude Venen

were formed in the 17th and 18th centuries by peat-cutting and now offer a home to over 100 species of birds and approximately 400 plant species. There is a large colony of great cormorants and various rare birds such as the spotted crake, the purple heron, the white-fronted goose, the barnacle goose, the Eurasian wigeon and the ruff, all of which are best watched in spring.

In and around the water are water lilies, yellow water lily, marsh lousewort and cotton-grass. The area's hayfields are yellow with marsh marigold in spring.

Reidplûm visitors' centre of *It Fryske Gea* at Earnewâld provides information on the surrounding area and is a good starting point for hiking and sailing expeditions. Beside the centre is the Eibertshiem, a breeding centre for storks.

A great deal of attention has been paid to water cleanliness in the region, and now otters have returned to breed. In winter, the area hosts many skating tours.

🏛️ **Bezoekerscentrum De Reidplûm**
Ds v.d. Veenweg 7, Earnewâld.
Tel 0511-539410.
Open mid-Apr–Sep: 1–5pm daily.

⑬ Beetsterzwaag

Road Map D2. 🏞️ 3,700. 🚌
ℹ️ Hoofdstraat 67 (0512-381955).

This village was once one of the seats of the Frisian landed gentry and so has a number of stately homes and gardens. Fine examples of these are **Lauswolt**, the **Lycklamahuis** and the **Harinxmastate**. Beetsterzwaag is surrounded by a varied

countryside, with coniferous and deciduous forests, heath and fens offering ample opportunities for a leisurely afternoon of rambling and cycling.

⑭ Appelscha

Road Map D2. 🏞️ 4,500. 🚌
ℹ️ Boerestreek 23 (0516-431760).

The vast coniferous forests, drifting sands and colourful heath and fen areas around Appelscha form stunning surroundings. The village was created in the 19th century when the main industry was peat-cutting and is now on the edge of the **Nationaal Park Drents-Friese Woud**.

A favourite place with visitors is the **Kale Duinen** area of drifting sands. On the Bosberg – at 26 m (85 ft) above sea level, the highest spot in the area – is a viewing tower and information centre.

A distinctive phenomenon in southeast Friesland is the **Klokkenstoel** (bell stool). This "poor men's church tower" was a provisional church tower built when funds were low; it was usually situated in the churchyard. In Appelscha you will find a *klokkenstoel* dating from 1453. Langedijke is home to what is presumed to be the oldest bell in the Netherlands, dating from 1300.

Environs
At Ravenswoud, 5 km (3 miles) northeast of Appelsche, an 18-m (59-ft) observation tower provides outstanding views.

Drifting sand dune near the small town of Appelscha

For hotels and restaurants in this region see p399 and p413

DRENTHE

Drenthe was once a free republic of farmers, and its inhabitants have always lived close to the land. Although the region has no cities and few towns, the rural poverty that once prevailed is no more, and tourists, especially those interested in archaeology and nature, are arriving in increasing numbers.

Drenthe, whose landscape is a product of the last Ice Age, has managed to keep time at bay by holding on to its character, reputed by the rest of the country to have been born of peat, gin and suspicion. Moraines and megaliths dot the countryside. The extensive woodland, heathland and peat bogs have a primeval atmosphere, although this does not mean that there has been no human intervention. The top level of peat has been largely removed, while the traditional *esdorps,* the local hamlets, have modern outskirts. However, peat moors and forests, ancient burial mounds, canals, flocks of sheep and green fields are the principal features here.

There are more than 50 megaliths in Drenthe, the remains of tombs dating from the Neolithic era; information about this period, with archaeological finds, is displayed in the museum at Borger. Other museums in the region feature glass blowing, artworks, natural history and paper-cutting. Orvelte boasts a fine open-air museum with Saxon farmhouses and traditional crafts, while Dwingeloo looks to the future at the Planetron observatory and planetarium.

Visitors come to Drenthe for peace and quiet after the rigours of city life. But this does not mean there are no facilities – local centres such as Assen, Emmen and Hoogeveen are urbanized areas that grew out of villages, and there is a variety of hotels, guesthouses and restaurants throughout the region.

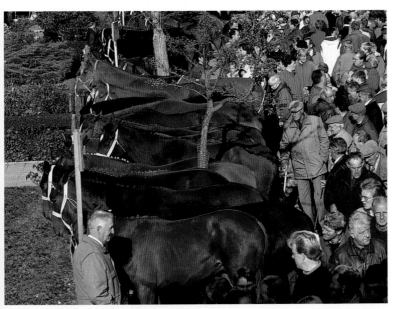

The largest horse market in western Europe, at Zuidlaren

◀ Papeloze Kerk, a megalith near Schoonoord in Drenthe

Exploring Drenthe

The finest natural areas of Drenthe are the Hondsrug ridge, between Zuidlaren and Emmen, and the Ellertsveld region between Assen and Emmen. The areas around Diever, Dwingeloo and Norg are a resplendent green (or purple, when the heather is in bloom). The eastern part of the region, with its endless excavated peatlands and the wilderness of the Amsterdamsche Veld, is relatively unknown. The provincial capital of Assen is also a regional centre, as is Emmen, where Noorder Dierenpark Zoo, in the middle of the town, has become one of the most-visited attractions in Holland. The megaliths are concentrated around Emmen, along the Hondsrug and at Havelte.

Sights at a Glance

② Assen
③ Norg
④ Eelde-Paterswolde
⑤ Zuidlaren
⑥ Hondsrug
⑦ Rolde
⑧ Borger
⑨ Orvelte
⑩ Westerbork
⑪ Dwingeloo
⑫ Diever
⑬ Coevorden
⑭ Emmen

Tour

❶ The Megalith Route
pp310–11

The 14th-century Siepelkerk at Dwingeloo

The broad and silent heath

Key

━━ Motorway
━━ Major road
═══ Minor road
━━ Scenic route
╍╍╍ Major railway
──── Minor railway
━━ Regional border
━━ International border

Thatcher at work in Havelte

For map symbols *see back flap*

0 kilometres 10
0 miles 5

The landscape reserve of the Drentse Aa river, an exceptionally peaceful hiking area near Hondsrug

Historical wooden walkway through the peatland (Valthe)

Getting Around

Every year in July, Drenthe is the venue of the *Rijwielvierdaagse*, a four-day cycle tour that attracts more than 25,000 participants. There are 500 km (310 miles) of marked cycle routes in the region. The A28 motorway crosses the province through Meppel, Hoogeveen and Assen, and the railway follows the same route. Other motorways include the N371 from Meppel to Assen along the Drentse Hoofdvaart, the N37 Hoogeveen-Emmen and the N34 Emmen-Zuidlaren. Emmen is also the last stop on the railway to Zwolle via Coevorden. Bus service is limited, particularly in the evenings and on weekends.

For hotels and restaurants in this region see pp399–400 and p413

❶ The Megalith Route

Of the 54 Megaliths in Holland, 52 are in Drenthe and the remaining two are in Groningen. These megaliths, or *hunebedden,* are the remains of ancient tombs built of boulders some 5,000 years ago by the Neolithic Beaker People. What can be seen today are only the frameworks of the tombs, which were all hidden underneath sandhills. It is still not known whether these were common graves or the tombs of prominent individuals.

At Diever and Havelte are three megaliths which are not on the route described here. The largest consists of 23 upright stones, 9 top stones, 2 keystones and a gate of 4 uprights and 2 top stones. At least 665 ancient pots have been found here. In World War II, the megalith was demolished to make way for an airfield. It was reconstructed in 1950.

⑨ Megalith at Loon
One of the best-preserved megaliths in Holland is at Loon, northeast of Assen. Before 1870 it was in even better condition, when the original top stone was still in place.

① **Witte Wieven** are ghosts that inhabit the tumuli, such as the Negen Bergen at Norg. They come out at midnight – particularly when it is misty – to dance.

NOORDENSEVELD   Tynaarlo
Norg   ①   N386
Negen Bergen   Vries
GASTERS DUINEN
NOORDENVELD
Loon
A28
N373   ⑨
ASSEN
N376
N371
N33

⑧ **The Great Megalith** of Balloo is at the end of a sandy path in the Tumulibos woods, an area which abounds with tumuli.

Key

▆▆	Tour route
═══	Other road
▬▬	Railway
🪨	Megalith

0 kilometres   5
0 miles   5

⑦ **De Zeven Marken**, the open-air museum of Schoonoord, tells you about such things as the legend of the giants Ellert and Brammert.

Building the Megaliths

Until the 19th century, it was believed that the megaliths were built by the *huynen*, giants of great strength and after whom the *hunebedden* are named. Modern historians believe that the boulders were placed with their flat edges on rollers, which thus allowed them to be moved to the site of the tomb. The upright stones were placed in pits dug beforehand. A gentle slope of earth was then made to allow the top stones to be dragged up. There is, however, no explanation of how the people of the Stone Age managed to organize such large-scale projects.

A 17th-century depiction of megalith builders

Typical beakers
after which the Beaker People are named. Pottery shards of these containers are the most common finds in the megaliths.

Beaker

Pitcher

Collared flask

② **Anloo** is one of the most picturesque Drenthe villages.

③ **The largest megalith in Holland** measures 22.5 m (74 ft), has 9 top stones and 26 upright stones. Excavations were carried out in Borger in 1685, but none of the finds has been preserved.

④ **Het Flint'n Hoes, the Nationaal Hunebedden Informatiecentrum**, (National Megalith Information Centre), has been set up beside Holland's largest megalith.

⑤ **The Exloo Necklace** was found in the peat in 1881. It is made of beads of tin, faience, bronze and amber, which is evidence of trading links between prehistoric Drenthe and the Baltic countries, Cornwall and even Egypt.

Flint was the main material used by the hunter-gatherers of prehistoric Drenthe to make such items as knives, axes, scrapers and arrowheads.

Tips for Drivers

Length: 95 km (60 miles)
Stopping-off places: All villages on the route offer refreshments and meals. To see most megaliths you will need to leave your car and walk, as only a few are by the roadside. They are almost invariably well sign-posted and make excellent picnic spots.

Megaliths (hunebedden)

There are no longer any complete megaliths. Until 1734, when trading in boulders was forbidden, thousands of megaliths were hacked up to be used as building material. There are definite traces of 88 megaliths, 82 of them in Drenthe. The 54 surviving megaliths are all restorations. The most common finds from excavations are pottery shards. Scrapers, axes, arrowheads, and amber and copper jewellery – all extremely valuable trading goods in Drenthe in 3000 BC – are much rarer finds.

⑥ **De Papeloze Kerk** (the Popeless Church) This megalith is so called because of the Calvinist sermons that were held here in the early 16th century against the "popish" (Catholic) faith. In 1959, the megalith was restored to its original state, to the extent of covering half of the tomb with sand.

❷ Assen

Road Map D2. 🗻 61,500. 🚍
ℹ️ Marktstraat 8 (0592 243788).
🛒 Wed, Sat.

Assen is the capital of Drenthe, although it was only upgraded from a village to a town in 1809. The **cloister** of the abbey church of Maria in Campis (1258–1600) now forms part of the Rijksarchief (national archive) on the Brink. Also on the Brink is the **Drents Museum** of local history, which is housed in the abbey church, the Ontvangershuis (1698), the Drostenhuis (1778) and Provinciehuis (1885). The museum contains a wealth of exhibits on prehistoric times and the town's history as well as a "discovery room" for children. There are also collections of local art, including works by Bernard Von Dülmen-Krumpelmann (1897–1987).

The controversial finds of Tjerk Vermaning (1929–87), who in the 1960s extended the history of human habitation in Holland by tens of thousands of years, are in a separate display case: disputes on the authenticity of the flint

tools he found have not yet been resolved.

Outside the formal gardens of the Drostenhuis is the town's trademark **Bartje**, a statue of the little peasant boy from Dutch author Anne de Vries' book (1935) who did not want to pray before his daily meals of brown beans. The Vaart and the Markt have the characteristic stately white houses of Assen, which were built in the late 18th to the early 19th centuries.

Bartje

Between Markt and Brink is the commercial centre with its pedestrian precinct and excellent facilities. Modern-day Assen comes to life when the **circuit van Assen** TT motorcycle racing event is held here each year on the last Saturday in June. Around 100,000 spectators descend on the town, which is home to the only remaining circuit from the championship's inaugural season in 1949. Younger children who have gained a taste for speed and bikes at the TT circuit will enjoy a visit to **Verkeerspark Assen**. This is a "traffic park" for children, where they can learn the rules of the road while driving

The 13th-century Romanesque church on the Brink of Norg

miniature cars and scooters around an artificial town, complete with traffic lights, road signs and traffic police. Older children can use quad bikes and go-karts. Other attractions include a boating lake, mini-golf and a climbing tower.

🏛️ **Drents Museum**
Brink 1–5. **Tel** 0592-37773.
Open 11 am–5pm Tue–Sun (Mon on public hols). **Closed** 1 Jan, 25 Dec. 🅿️
♿ 📷 🏠

🎡 **Verkeerspark Assen**
De Haar 1–1a. **Tel** 0592-350005.
Open Apr: days vary; May–Aug: daily; Sep & Oct: days vary. **Closed** 29 Nov–Mar. 🆆 **verkeersparkassen.nl**

❸ Norg

Road Map D2. 🗻 3,500. 🚍 ℹ️ Brink 1 (0592-613128). 🛒 Wed.

The Romanesque church on the Brink dates from the 13th century. The unique frescoes in the choir have barely survived through the centuries and are in very poor condition.

Environs
The area around Norg is steeped in prehistory. Three megalithic tombs are to be found there, while in the Noorderveld are Bronze Age tumuli (the **Negen Bergen**). Norgerholt is the name given to the oak woods where the local people used to assemble during the Middle Ages.

Children Bathing in a Stream (c.1935) by Von Dülmen-Krumpelmann

❹ Eelde-Paterswolde

Road Map D2. 🚹 10,500. 🚌 52.
ℹ B Boermalaan 4 (050-3092136).
🛒 Wed.

Two villages merge together at Eelde-Paterswolde and are squeezed between the **Paterswoldse Meer** lake and **Groningen Airport**, which, despite its name, is in Drenthe not Groningen. The lake is popular among watersports enthusiasts. The airport serves mainly domestic flights (it is a half-hour flight to Schiphol) and flying enthusiasts.

The distinctive modern brick building housing the **Museum De Buitenplaats** (De Buitenplaats museum of figurative art) was designed by the architects Alberts and Van Huut. It is a fine example of their organic architecture. In addition to hosting changing exhibitions, the museum is used as a concert hall. There are also formal and landscape gardens, the former fronting the 17th-century curator's residence, the **Nijsinghuis**. Since 1983 the house has been painted by figurative artists and is periodically opened to visitors by arrangement.

The Eelde part of town is home to the **Internationaal Klompenmuseum (Gebroeders Wietzes)**. Named in honour of the last two clog-makers to live in the village, the museum gives an overview of the development of the clog. It displays examples of clogs from around the world. Most visitors, however, come to see the world's largest clog, which is 6.5 m (21 ft) long.

Dense woodland in the Hondsrug area

🏛 **Museum De Buitenplaats**
Hoofdweg 76. **Tel** 050-3095818.
Open 11am–5pm Tue–Sun, Easter Sun & Easter Mon. **Closed** 1 Jan, 25 Dec. 🅿 💻

🏛 **Klompenmuseum Gebroeders Wietzes**
Wolfhorn 1a. **Tel** 050-3091181.
Open Apr–Oct: Tue–Sun 2–5pm.

❺ Zuidlaren

Road Map E2. 🚹 10,000. 🚌 ℹ
Stationsweg 69 (050-4092333). 🛒 Fri.

The colourful Zuidlaren **horse market**, now the largest in Western Europe, predates even the 13th-century church which stands on the Brink. The market is held in April and October. The 17th-century **Havezathe Laarwoud** was built on the remnants of the fortified residence of the counts of Heiden, who ruled the region in the 14th century. Today it is the town hall. The **Zuidlaardermeer** lake offers everything that watersports enthusiasts may require. Children will especially enjoy

the subtropical swimming complex of Aqualaren, as well as De Sprookjeshof recreation centre with playpark; they can be combined on a round tour.

❻ Hondsrug

Road Map E2. 🚌 ℹ VVVs in Zuidlaren (050-4092333), Rolde, Gieten, Exloo (0591-549515), Borger, SchoonoOord (0591-381242) and Emmen.

Between the Drentse sand plateau in the west and the Drents-Groningen peat moors in the east lies the Hondsrug ridge. Prehistoric people found it a safe place to settle, and it is the area where the megaliths now stand (*see pp310–11*).

The Drentse Aa river basin, the old villages of Gieten, Gasselte, Exloo and Odoorn, the drifting sand areas of the Drouwenerzand and the heathland of Ellertsveld are particularly attractive hiking areas, with plenty of streams in which to cool off.

In the centre of Eexloo, the **Bebinghehoes** is a cultural museum in a beautiful 18th-century, thatched farmhouse. The house itself gives an impression of farming life 200 years ago, while the coach house presents a display of carriages from the age of horse-drawn transport. There is also a children's farm, with goats, sheep, chickens and ducks, and a petting area.

🏛 **Bebinghehoes**
Zuiderhoofdstraat 6. **Tel** 0591-549242.
Open 1 Apr–1 May: Wed–Sat; May, Jun & Sep: Tue–Sat; Jul & Aug: daily.

Colourfully decorated Klompenmuseum Gebroeders Wietzes

❼ Rolde

Road Map E2. �︎ 6,200. 🚌
ℹ Onder de Molen, Grote Brink 22
(0592-241502).

Rolde was important for a
considerable time. There are
prehistoric tumuli (in the
Tumulibos woods), and three
megaliths, two of which are on
the mound directly behind the
church. During the Middle Ages,
people were tried at the
Ballooërkuil; if guilty they were
held prisoner in the 15th-century
church, a magnificent Gothic
edifice. Forests, peatland and
drifting sands surround the village.
Sheep graze on the Ballooërveld.

❽ Borger

Road Map E2. 🚫 4,700. 🚌 59. ℹ
Grote Brink 2a (0599-234855). 🛒 Tue.

Borger is the capital of the
hunebeddengebied, or megalith region. There are eight
megaliths in and around the
town, including the largest in
Holland. Nearby is the **Nationaal
Hunebedden Informatiecentrum**
('t Flint'n Hoes), with a fine exhibition about the Beaker People
and a stone casket from the
most recently excavated megalith, which was discovered in
1982 in Groningen.

🏛 Nationaal Hunebedden
Informatiecentrum
Bronnegerstraat 12. **Tel** 0599-236374.
Open daily. **Closed** 1 Jan, 25 Dec.
🐾 ♿ 💻

Environs
Drents Boomkroonpad (tree-
top walk), 2 km (1 mile) down
the "Staatsbossen" turn-off on
the Rolde-Borger road, is an

Boomkroonpad's tree-top walkway, a
well-known tourist attraction

interesting attraction. The walk
starts at the roots, with a 23-m
(75-ft) tunnel. This leads into a
125-m (410-ft) ascent to a height
of 22.5 m (74 ft), affording a
fascinating view of the forest.

🌳 Drents Boomkroonpad
Bezoekerscentrum, Drents
Boomkroonpad, Steenhopenweg 4,
Drouwen. **Tel** 0592-377305.
Open daily. **Closed** 1 Jan. 🐾 💻

❾ Orvelte

Road Map E2. 🚫 90. 🚌 22, 23.
ℹ Dorpsstraat 1a (0593-322335).

The whole of Orvelte is in effect
an open-air museum. In the
restored Saxon farmhouses
from the early 19th century,
there are exhibits on agriculture
and displays of traditional crafts.
Cars are banned from the area,
but tours in horse-drawn trams
or covered wagons are offered.
The more interesting attractions of the town include a
tinsmith's shop.

🏛 Bezoekerscentrum
Dorpsstraat 3. **Tel** 0593-322335.
Open Apr–Oct daily. 🐾 🛒 ♿
🚲 💻

Farmers at work in the Orvelte open-air museum

❿ Westerbork

Road Map E2. 🚫 8,000. 🚌 22.
ℹ BG van Wezelplein 10 (0593-
331381).

The Hoofdstraat (main street)
features a Late Gothic 14th-century
church, which now houses the
Museum voor Papierknipkunst
(paper-cutting museum) and
Saxon farmhouses which bear
witness to a prosperous past.
However, Westerbork is visited
primarily for its more recent history.
In World War II, the Westerbork
Transit Camp stood here. It was
from this camp that 107,000 Jews,
Gypsies and resistance fighters
were held before deportation to
the Nazi concentration camps.
Anne Frank *(see pp112–13)* was
one of its inmates.

🏕 Herinneringscentrum
Kamp Westerbork
Oosthalen 8, Hooghalen.
Tel 0593-592600. **Open** daily. 🐾 ♿

⓫ Dwingeloo

Road Map: D2. 🚫 1,800. 🚌 20.
ℹ Brink 4b (0521-591000). 🛒 Tue.

The first thing that strikes
visitors about Dwingeloo is
the onion dome of the
14th-century church tower
(the **Siepelkerk**). You can read
about the legend behind this
oddity on the information
board located nearby.
There is some impressive
countryside around the town.
The **Dwingelderveld** is a
national park and the
krentenbossen (currant
plantations) which flower in
April and May – the fruit
ripening in July or August – are
delightful in every respect: they
are pleasant to the eye and to
the taste buds. At the edge of
the Dwingelose Heide heath is a
radio-telescope.
The interesting and child-
friendly **Planetron** nearby is an
observatory where there is a
planetarium as well as an
electronic games area.

🔭 Planetron
Drift 11b. **Tel** 0521-593535. **Open** daily
during school hols. **Closed** 1 Jan, Mon
outside school hols. 🐾 🚲 💻

⓬ Diever

Road Map D2. ⚊ 3,700. 🚌 20.
ℹ Bosweg 2a (0521-591748).

Diever was an important centre from prehistoric times to the Middle Ages. Tumuli, megaliths and remains of the 9th-century wooden foundations of the village church lend it historical importance. The church features a 12th-century Romanesque tower of tufa stone. Diever is in the middle of the **Nationaal Park Het Drents-Friese Woud**: the town is now synonymous with cycling and rambling.

In summer, the **Shakespeare-markten** (Shakespeare fair) is held during performances of the playwright's works in the open-air theatre.

Environs

In **Vledder**, 10 km (6 miles) west of Diever, is a **museum** of graphic art and glass-blowing and art forgery.

🏛 **Museum voor Valse Kunst/ Museum voor Hedendaagse Grafiek/ Museum voor Glaskunst**

Brink 1, Vledder. **Tel** 0521-383352. **Open** Apr–Oct: 11am–4pm Wed–Sun; Nov–Dec: 11am–4pm Sat & Sun. 🅿 🎫

Lime kilns at in the village of Diever

⓭ Coevorden

Road Map E3. ⚊ 34,000. 🚌 🚉
ℹ Kerkstraat 2 (0524-525150).
🚍 Mon.

The castle here dates from around 1200. The star-shaped moat and surviving bastions and town walls define the look of the town, while the façades of the Friesestraat and Weeshuisstraat are telling of

Brown bears in the popular Noorder Dierenpark in Emmen

past centuries. **Stedelijk Museum Drenthe's Veste** highlights the town's history.

🏛 **Stedelijk Museum Drenthe's Veste**

Haven 6. **Tel** 0524-516225. **Open** 9:30–5pm Tue–Sat, noon–5pm Sun. 🅿 💻

⓮ Emmen

Road Map E2. ⚊ 105,000. 🚌 🚉
ℹ Hoofdstraat 22 (0591-649712).
🚍 Fri am.

A modern town, Emmen is the result of the amalgamation of several former villages. Eleven megaliths, including **Langgraf op de Schimmer Es** or long barrow on the Schimmer Es, the urn-fields (*see p47*) and prehistoric farmland (the **Celtic Fields**) in the vicinity and the 12th-century tower on the Hoofdstraat reflect the district's history. At **Noorder Dierenpark**, animals roam freely. The Biochron museum and Vlindertuin butterfly gardens are also here.

🦁 **Noorder Dierenpark**

Hoofdstraat 18. **Tel** 0591-850855.
Open daily. 🅿 ♿ 💻 ✏
🌐 dierenparkemmen.nl

Environs

Roughly 10 km (6 miles) east of Emmen are the **Amsterdamsche Veld** upland peat marshes, perhaps the loneliest place in Holland. In Barger-Compascuum, **Veenpark** re-creates the times when the people of Drenthe lived in poverty, cutting peat. In 1883, Vincent van Gogh stayed at the Scholte ferry-house in Veenoord (Nieuw-Amsterdam). At the **Van Gogh House**, his room on the first floor has been restored to the way it was in 1883, as has the café-restaurant below.

🏛 **Veenpark**

Berkenrode 4, Barger-Compascuum. **Tel** 0591-324444. **Open** Apr–Nov: 10am–5pm daily. 🅿 ♿ 💻

🏛 **Van Gogh Huis**

Van Goghstraat 1, Nieuw-Amsterdam. **Tel** 0591-555600. **Open** 1–5pm Tue–Sun. 💻 ✏ 📷

Van Gogh's *Peat Boat with Two Figures* (1883) in Drents Museum, Assen

OVERIJSSEL

Overijssel, a province in the east of Holland, has many areas of natural beauty and lovely old towns. In a sense it is a province of two halves, divided by the heathland and woods of the Sallandse Heuvelrug near Nijverdal, which separate the eastern district of Twente from the rest of the province.

This division is noticeable in many ways. The two halves differ in their spoken dialect, and they each have their own cultural traditions. There are also religious differences, with Twente being mainly Catholic while the rest of the province is strictly Protestant. Twente, with its larger towns, has a more modern appearance, and Enschede, for example, is livelier than western towns like Zwolle and Deventer.

Zwolle, however, is the capital of the province, a charming town dating back to the 13th century, when its port at a busy river junction led it to join the powerful Hanseatic League, growing rich from trade with England and the Baltic. Kampen and Deventer, on the IJssel river, were later members of the same league.

Overijssel's numerous unique museums and attractions highlight local history and printing, tobacco, salt and farmhouses, as well as traditional costumes, tin soldiers, Dutch painting and modern art. For children, the Hellendoorn adventure park (see p426), the Los Hoes open-air museum and Ecodrome Park are always popular.

Apart from these activities, however, the principal attraction in Overijssel is the countryside, which is ideal for walking, hiking and touring by bicycle. In places like Giethoorn you can tour the rivers, lakes and canals by boat, while the Weerribben wetlands in the northwest offer opportunities for nature rambles and watersports.

Open-air dining at a restaurant in the historic town of Zwolle in Overijssel

◀ Blue boats line a canal in the village of Giethoorn, Overijssel

Exploring Overijssel

The impressive historical monuments of Deventer and Kampen recall their prosperous pasts as Hanseatic cities. However, Overijssel has plenty to offer those who are interested in more than splendid old buildings. Those who enjoy peace and natural surroundings will find some of the finest spots in Holland. The peaceful countryside of the Sallandse Heuvelrug is ideal for rambling, while De Weerribben is suitable for yachting. There are many picturesque spots, such as Ootmarsum, Delden and Giethoorn, and children will love the amusement part at Hellendoorn *(see p426)*. In addition to this, Overijssel also has many interesting museums, such as the national tin figure museum in Ommen.

The quiet port of Blokzijl near Vollenhove

Overijssel at a Glance

1. Zwolle
2. Kampen
3. Vollenhove
4. De Weerribben
5. *Giethoorn pp322–3*
6. Staphorst
7. Ommen
8. Deventer
9. Nijverdal
10. Delden
11. Enschede
12. Ootmarsum

The IJssel north of the old Hanseatic city of Deventer

Getting Around

Overijssel can be explored easily by car, bicycle or on foot. Large parts of the region are also well connected by public transport. Note, however, that bus timetables are sketchier on weekends than on weekdays. Areas of natural beauty such as De Weerribben, for example, are not easy to reach by public transport on weekends. In some places, too, buses operate only during the daytime.

Key

▬▬ Motorway
▬▬ Major road
···· Minor road
▬▬ Scenic route
▬▬ Major railway
▬▬ Minor railway
▬▬ Regional border
▬▬ International border

Kasteel Rechteren by Dalfsen, near Zwolle

Farmhouse by the River Reest, separating Drenthe from Overijssel

For hotels and restaurants in this region see p400 and pp413–14

❶ Zwolle

Road Map D3. ⛰ 107,000. 🚅
ℹ️ Grote Kerkplein 15 (0900-
1122375). 🏛 Fri (cattle market), Sat.

In the Middle Ages, Zwolle,
capital of the province of
Overijssel, was, along with towns
such as Deventer, Kampen and
Zutphen, a city of the Hanseatic
League, a network of trading
cities. Its past is evident in the
relatively large historical centre.
The finest buildings in Zwolle,
which was granted its city
charter in 1230, are largely to
be found in the area that used
to fall within the city fortifications, which can still be seen in
the form of a moat. However,
only a few dozen metres of these
ancient fortifications are left
standing, along with the fine
Sassenpoort gate, dating from
1406, and the Late Gothic
15th-century Pelsertoren tower.

On one side of the Grote
Kerkplein is a sculpture by
Rodin entitled *Adam*, while
on the Grote Markt stands the
magnificent building of the
Hoofdwacht (guard house),
which dates from 1614.

The **Grote Kerk**, also known
as **St Michaelskerk**, is worth
a visit as well. The original
Romanesque church, built in
1040, was enlarged in 1370
and again in 1452 to become
the present-day three-naved
Gothic church.

The most recent addition
to Zwolle's cultural landscape
is the **Paleis aan de Blijmarkt**, a
contemporary art museum that
opened in 2005. Housed in a
grand Neo-Classical building
dating from 1838, the renovated
light-filled galleries hold works

View of Zwolle during the Hanseatic Period (anonymous, c.14th century)

by the likes of Van Gogh, Picasso
and Mondrian.

The **Stedelijk Museum
Zwolle** (Zwolle local history
museum) features, among its
other interesting exhibits on
local history, an 18th-century
kitchen and a Renaissance room
from Blokzijl. The fine façade of
the old part of the building, which
dates from 1741, is impressive.

The town is also home to
the **Ecodrome Park**, which
is dedicated to the natural
environment in the past,
present and future.

🏛 **Stedelijk Museum Zwolle**
Melkmarkt 41. **Tel** 038-4214650.
Open 11am–5pm Tue–Sun. **Closed**
public hols. 🛒 📷 🎒 ♿ 🏛

🦎 **Ecodrome Park**
Willemsvaart 19. **Tel** 038-4237030.
Open Nov–Mar: 10am–5pm Wed, Sat
& Sun; Apr–Oct: 10am–5pm daily. 🛒

🏛 **Paleis aan de Blijmarkt**
Blijmarkt 20. **Tel** 0572-388188.
Open 11am–5pm Tue–Sun.

Environs
The Kunstwegen (Art Paths)
are outdoor sculpture installations on the country estate of
Landgoed Anninghof. The
five-hectare open-air sculpture
park was the brainchild of art
collector Hib Anninga and
contains dozens of works, from
bright-blue ceramic dogs to
giant iron hoops, by around 80
contemporary Dutch sculptors.
The work is spread throughout
meadows and landscaped
gardens, and exploring
them makes for a pleasant
afternoon's stroll.

🏛 **Landgoed Anninghof**
Hessenweg 9. **Tel** 038-4534412.
Open May–Oct: Wed–Sun.

❷ Kampen

Road Map D3. ⛰ 48,000. 🚅
ℹ️ Oudestraat 41 (038-3313500).
🏛 Mon am.

Kampen, known for its
theological university where
Protestant theologians are
educated, is a pleasant and
lively town containing 500
historic buildings. The beauty
of this former Hanseatic city is
immediately apparent from
the IJssel riverfront. The fact
that the town used to be
well fortified is evident from
the three remaining town
gates: the Koornmanspoort,
the Broederpoort and the
Cellebroederspoort. The area
inside the old fortifications

The grand Neo-Classical façade of the Paleis aan de Blijmarkt

For hotels and restaurants in this region see p400 and pp413–14

The waterfront of the magnificent, well-preserved Hanseatic city of Kampen on the river IJssel

features the magnificent Dutch Reformed church St Nicolaaskerk, and the Gotische Huis, which now houses the **Stedelijk Museum Kampen**, the town's local history museum. Particularly noteworthy is the old town hall, or Oude Raadhuis, with a façade decorated with fine sculptures.

Kampen, which is first mentioned in documents in 1227, is also famed for its cigars, which explains why the **Kamper Tabaksmuseum** (Kampen tobacco museum) is located here. A rather more surprising find is the **Ikonenmuseum**, a collection of religious icons and the only museum of its kind in the Netherlands. The museum is housed in a former cloister, and is home to 150 mainly Russian and Greek Orthodox painted icons, spanning the 16th to 19th centuries. It also hosts temporary exhibitions.

Kampen was at the height of its development between 1330 and 1450. It revived its fortunes only when the Flevoland and Noordoostpolder regions were reclaimed and it acquired the function of regional centre. However, Kampen was never a mighty city because it did not have any powerful ruler. Kampen did not apply to join the Hanseatic League until relatively late – 1440. At that time, the Netherlands was involved in a war with the Hanseatic League, and Kampen joined the powerful league for the sake of security.

Ⅲ Stedelijk Museum Kampen
Oude Straat 133. **Tel** 038-3317361.
Open 11am–5pm Tue–Sat.

Ⅲ Kamper Tabaksmuseum
Botermarkt 3. **Tel** 038-3315868.
Open by appointment only.

Ⅲ Ikonenmuseum
Buitennieuwstraat 2. **Tel** 038-3858483.
Open 1 Apr–1 Nov: Tue–Sat;
1 Jun–1 Sep: daily.

Religious image at the Ikonenmuseum

Environs
Five km (3 miles) south of the town, in Kamperveen, is the **Hertenhouderij Edelveen**, a working deer farm that welcomes visitors. The owners give guided tours of their farmland, explaining their jobs and allowing visitors to see their herds close up. The farmers also sell venison, pâté and sausages.

Ⅲ Hertenhouderij
Edelveen: Leidijk 10a. **Tel** 0525-621564. **Open** by appointment only.

---

❸ Vollenhove

Road Map D2. 🚌 71, 171. ℹ️ Aan Zee 2–4 (0900-5674637). 🛍️ Tue.

Vollenhove is a picturesque place which was once known as the town of palaces due to the many nobles who lived here. The aristocratic residences are known as *havezaten*, or manors. The large 15th-century church is variously referred to as the **Grote Kerk, St Nicolaaskerk** or **Bovenkerk**.

❹ De Weerribben

Road Map D3.

De Weerribben is an unspoiled area of wetlands at the northwestern end of Overijssel. There is plenty for cyclists, walkers and also canoeists to do in this beautiful nature reserve.

Ⅶ Natuuractiviteitencentrum De Weerribben
Hoogeweg 27, Ossenzijl. **Tel** 0561-477272. **Open** Apr–Oct: daily; Nov–Mar: Tue–Fri & Sun. 🚫 🖥️

Water lilies in the nature reserve of De Weerribben

❺ Street-by-Street: Giethoorn

If any village were to be given the title "prettiest village in Holland", quaint Giethoorn would be the one. This well-deserved accolade is due to the village's picturesque canals which are flanked by numerous farmhouse-style buildings. A few of these buildings now contain interesting, if small, museums. The village of Giethoorn can be easily explored both by boat and by bicycle. Founded in 1230 by religious refugees, the village's distinctive form came about from peat-cutting, eventually resulting in the formation of ponds and lakes. The small canals were used for transporting peat.

Giethoorn is also known as the Green Venice because of its abundant natural beauty. Several ponds and lakes surround this charming town. The best way to enjoy the area is by hiring a small boat.

★ **Tjaskermolen**
This windmill, which turns an Archimedes' screw, is located in Giethoorn-Noord. Another one can be seen in the Olde Maat Uus museum.

BINNENPAD

★ **Olde Maat Uus**
This pleasant farmhouse which has been converted into a museum should definitely not be missed. It illustrates life in Giethoorn as it used to be.

Key

— Walking route

▬ Boat route

▬ Waterway

The delightful houses of Giethoorn contain numerous and varied tourist attractions, giving visitors plenty to do on each visit.

0 metres	50
0 yards	50

Islands in the area are a direct result of peat-cutting, which led to the creation of lakes and canals, giving Giethoorn its many little islands, connected by the village's characteristic footbridges.

VISITORS' CHECKLIST

Practical Information
Road Map D2.
🚆 2,500. 🛈 Eendrachtsplein 1 (0521-362124). 🎭 Street Theatre Festival: Jun; Rock Around Giethoorn Punt Race: Jul; Gondola Regatta: various times; Sailing Punt Race, Blues Festival, Punt Race: Aug; Slag op 't Wiede: Sep; Christmas Fair & Story Telling Festival: Dec.

Transport
🚌 70, 79.

★ Punts
Punts were formerly used to carry peat along the canals of Giethoorn. They are now used for tourist trips; you can also occasionally catch glimpses of them in the village's old ditches and channels.

Reeds
The countryside around Giethoorn abounds with lakes and ponds. The reeds which grow along their banks are used to make cane furniture and to thatch roofs.

Tourist Boats
There are many places in Giethoorn where you can hire quiet, electrically powered boats.

Deventer, larger than Amsterdam in its heyday

❻ Staphorst

Road Map D3. 🄐 15,000. 🚌 40.
🛈 Binnenweg 26 (0522-467400).
✉ Sun. 🛒 Wed am.

Staphorst is known throughout Holland as a stronghold of strict Christian beliefs. It was where the Gereformeerde Bond (reformed union), one of the strictest embodiments of Protestantism, ruled within the Dutch Reformed Church. Many of the lovely old farmhouses, painted in a characteristic green and blue, are monumental buildings. To get an idea of what they once looked like, visit the **Museum Staphorst**.

The townspeople continue to wear traditional dress, a custom which has practically vanished elsewhere in the country. Throughout Staphorst you will see women, especially elderly women, wearing the blue and black outfits.

🏛 **Museum Staphorst**
Gemeenteweg 67. **Tel** 0522-462526.
Open Apr–Oct: 10am–5pm Tue–Sat.
Closed Sun, Mon & hols. 🖼
🌐 museumstaphorst.nl

❼ Ommen

Road Map D3. 🄐 17,000. 🚌
🛈 Kruisstraat 6 (0900-1122375).
🛒 Tue am.

The district of Ommen lies in stunningly beautiful countryside extending from the town to nearby villages and hamlets. One-third of its total area of 18,000 ha (44,500 acres) is covered by nature reserves and forests. A former Hanseatic city, Ommen itself is home to a few interesting museums, including the **Nationaal Tinnen Figuren Museum** (national tin models museum).

🏛 **Nationaal Tinnen Figuren Museum**
Markt 1. **Tel** 0529-454500.
Open Apr–Oct: 11am–5pm Tue–Sat, 1–5pm Sun & hols; Nov–Mar: 11am–5pm Sat, 1–5pm Sun & hols.
Closed 1 Jan, 25 Dec. 🖼

Environs
To find out more about the nature reserves in Ommen, visit the **Natuurinformatiecentrum Ommen**, which houses a permanent exhibition illustrating the cultural history of the surrounding countryside. Particularly worth seeing are the typical Saxon farmhouses at Beerze, Junne, Stegeren, Besthem and Giethmen.

🏞 **Natuurinformatiecentrum Ommen**
Hammerweg 59a. **Tel** 0529-450702.
Open May–Oct: 1–5pm Wed–Sun; Nov–Apr: 1:30–4pm Wed, Sat & Sun.

❽ Deventer

Road Map D3. 🄐 86,000. 🚌
🛈 Brink 56 (0570-710120).
🛒 Fri am & Sat.

The lively centre of the old Hanseatic city of Deventer features numerous medieval houses, including the oldest stone house in Holland today. Buildings worth seeing in particular are those situated on the pleasant Brink (green) and the Bergkerk. In the middle of the Brink stands the impressive Waag (weigh house) from 1528, which now contains the VVV and the renovated **Historisch Museum de Waag**, with exhibits that illustrate the town's history. On the first Sunday of August, the town holds the **Deventer Boekenmarkt** (book fair), the largest in Europe. It is preceded by a poetry festival.

A tin soldier

🏛 **Historisch Museum de Waag**
Brink 56. **Tel** 0570-693783. **Open** 10am–5pm Tue–Sat, 1–5pm Sun.
Closed public hols. 🖼 🎦

❾ Nijverdal

Road Map D3. 🄐 23,500.
🚌 🛈 Willem Alexander Straat 7c (0540-612729). 🛒 Sat.

The impressive beauty of the **Sallandse Heuvelrug**, with its fine heathland and woodland, is especially apparent at Nijverdal. This is the last remaining breeding ground in the Netherlands for black grouse. An interesting exhibition on the Heuvelrug region can be seen at the

Flock of sheep in Sallandse Heuvelrug

Bezoekerscentrum Sallandse Heuvelrug (Sallandse Heuvelrug visitors' centre), with its clever and unusual "Forester's Corner".

 Bezoekerscentrum Sallandse Heuvelrug
Grotestraat 281. **Tel** 0548-612711. **Open** Apr–Oct: 10am–5pm Tue–Sun; Nov–Mar: 10am–4pm Tue–Sun. **Closed** Mon, 1 Jan, 25 & 31 Dec.

Environs
Avonturenpark Hellendoorn (Hellendoorn adventure park) *(see p426)* is great for children.

⑩ Delden

Road Map E3. 7,000. Langestraat 29 (074-3761363). Fri afternoon.

Delden is a pretty residential village, ideal for walks. This Twente hamlet has a number of attractions, including the **Zoutmuseum** (salt museum) and the 12th-century **Oude Blasiuskerk**.

Zoutmuseum
Langestraat 30. **Tel** 074-3764546. **Open** May–Sep: 11am–5pm Mon–Fri, 2–5pm Sat & Sun; Oct–Apr: 2–5pm Tue–Fri & Sun.

Environs
Some 2 km (1.2 miles) northeast of Delden are the lovely gardens of **Kasteel Twickel**.

Tuinen Kasteel Twickel (Kasteel Twickel Gardens)
Twickelerlaan 1a, Ambt Delden. **Tel** 074-3761020. **Open** May–Oct: 10am–5pm Wed–Sun.

⑪ Enschede

Road Map E3. 150,000. Stationsplein 1a (053-4323200). Tue, Sat.

Enschede is regarded as the capital of Twente, as it is the largest town in Overijssel. It was devastated in 1862 by a fire – little of the old town survived. One of the few historical buildings that can still be seen in the otherwise pleasant centre is the **Grote Kerk** on the Oude Markt.

In addition to this centre, with its theatres, concert halls and cinemas, Enschede has a number of museums, of which the **Rijksmuseum Twenthe** should not be missed. The exhibits here range from manuscripts and paintings to modern, primarily Dutch, art.

Miracle Planet Boulevard, just outside town, offers non-stop entertainment in three mega-complexes.

Rijksmuseum Twenthe
Lasondersingel 129–131. **Tel** 053-4358675. **Open** 11am–5pm Tue–Sun & hols. **Closed** 1 Jan, 25 Dec.

⑫ Ootmarsum

Road Map E3. 4,000. 64 from Almelo. Markt 9 (0541-291214). Thu am.

The village of Ootmarsum is one of the prettiest places in all of Holland. On the map since 900, Ootmarsum was granted its town charter in 1300. It has grown little since then; indeed, not much has changed here at all, making it quite suitable

Stained glass in the 13th-century Catholic church at Ootmarsum

for an open-air museum. Places of interest not to be missed include the Roman Catholic church, the only Westphalian hall-type church in Holland, built between 1200 and 1300. Here you can see the burial vaults and some impressive works of art. The rococo former town hall dates from 1778 and is now the VVV (tourist) office. There are also some interesting old draw-wells.

The **Openluchtmuseum Los Hoes** (Los Hoes open-air museum), showing what life was once like in Twente, is also worth a visit.

Openluchtmuseum Los Hoes
Smithuisstraat 2. **Tel** 0541-293099. **Open** 10am–5pm daily (Dec–Jan: weekends only & Christmas hols).

Environs
Nature lovers will find plenty to do in the countryside surrounding Ootmarsum, which is located in one of the finest parts of Twente. The landscape offers an ever-changing scenery, with its rushing brooks, old watermills, woodland paths, prehistoric tumuli and Saxon farmhouses.

The viewing point on the Kuiperberg affords a stunning vista over the entire Twente region and provides the place names of the various sights.

The half-timbered Stiepelhoes in Ootmarsum, dating from 1658

FLEVOLAND

Flevoland is Holland's youngest province, constructed by the Dutch entirely out of water, sandbanks and mud flats, thanks to massive reclamation schemes which created dykes and polders (reclaimed land, sometimes below sea level) from the turbulent Zuiderzee following an Act of Parliament in 1918.

This act provided funds for damming the northeastern part of the Zuiderzee and reclaiming the land behind the dykes. When the Afsluitdijk was completed in 1932, drainage works on the Noordostpolder began and, with the seawater pumped out, the islands of Urk and Schokland and the town of Emmeloord became by 1942 a part of the mainland. Further schemes to the south and southwest were completed in 1957 and 1968 respectively, and since 1986 these three new polders have officially constituted the Netherlands' newest province, named Flevoland after "Flevo Lacus", the original name given to the Zuiderzee by the Roman historian Pliny nearly 2,000 years ago.

Initially, the idea had been to use the polders as farmland only, with the occasional village here and there. However, as the built-up areas around Amsterdam and Utrecht became increasingly congested, new towns have grown up. The conurbation around Almere, with its highly impressive modern architecture, is among these. Other towns include Lelystad, with its several modern museums, and Dronten, where the Walibi World amusement park proves an irresistible magnet for younger visitors. Lelystad, whose name honours Cornelius Lely, the genius behind the massive land creation project *(see p330)*, is the provincial capital. There are many other attractions for visitors to this compact and attractive region, including a number of fascinating museums featuring subjects as varied as archaeology and World War II.

The exotic spoonbill, an icon of the new wildlife in Flevoland

◀ Farms and polder landscape in Emmeloord

Exploring Flevoland

The Noordoostpolder, which is the northernmost part of
Flevoland, is distinguished by its polder landscape and its
rich farmland, fruit orchards and bulb fields. There are also
many young forests, which are good for walking in. Apart
from the main town of Emmeloord, there are a number of
small new villages, as well as the old fishing village of Urk.
Oostelijk (eastern) and Zuidelijk (southern) Flevoland are
relatively sparsely populated and have a lot of greenery.
Between Almere, the largest town of Flevoland, characterized
by modern architecture, and Lelystad, the provincial capital,
there stretches a fine nature reserve known as the
Oostvaardersplassen, or Oostvaarder lakes. The coastal
lakes have inviting sand beaches and marinas.

The picturesque harbour of the fishing
village of Urk

Sights at a Glance

1. Emmeloord
2. Urk
3. Nagele
4. Schokland
5. Swifterbant
6. Dronten
7. Lelystad
8. Bataviawerf
9. Oostvaardersplassen
10. Knardijk
11. Zeewolde
12. Almere

Boats moored at Almere harbour

Key

━━━ Motorway
━━━ Major road
┄┄┄ Minor road
━━━ Scenic route
──── Minor railway
━━━ Regional border

0 kilometres 10
0 miles 10

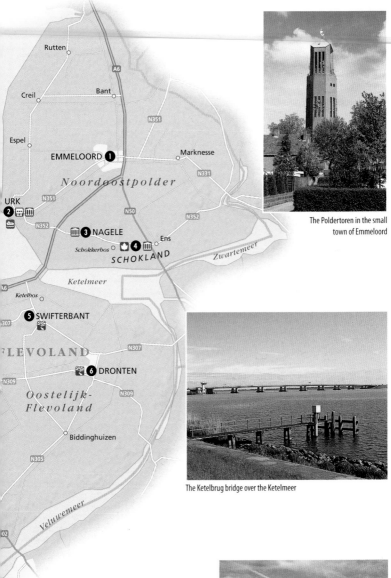

The Poldertoren in the small town of Emmeloord

The Ketelbrug bridge over the Ketelmeer

Getting Around

Flevoland has an efficient road network. All the municipalities in the region are easily accessible by car or bus. Long-distance coaches cover both the Lelystad-Emmeloord and Lelystad-Dronten routes. Almere and Lelystad can also be reached by train, and a ferry links Urk and Enkhuizen during July and August. The flat, expansive landscape of Flevoland also makes exploration by bicycle ideal. Numerous excellent cycling and hiking routes have been laid out throughout the province.

Flat farmland of Flevoland

For hotels and restaurants in this region see p400 and p414

❶ Emmeloord

Road Map D2. Noordoostpolder.
🗺 25,600. 🚌 ⓘ De Deel 25a
(0527-612000). 🛒 Thu am.

When the oldest polder
in Flevoland was drained,
Emmeloord sprang up like a
pioneer settlement. Over the
years it has developed into a
pleasant town. It is the main town
of the municipality of Noordoostpolder, encompassing *groen-
dorps* (green villages). Emmeloord
is known mainly for its octagonal
Poldertoren, a water tower
topped by a 5-m (16-ft) wind
vane in the shape of an old
merchant ship; the tower is 65-m
(214-ft) high and was built in 1959.
The carillon, one of Holland's
biggest, has 48 chimes. The viewing
platform (open in summer) offers
a view of the polder.

❷ Urk

Road Map C3. 🗺 20,000. ⛴ from
Enkhuizen, summer only. 🚌 ⓘ Wijk
2–3 (0527-684040). 🛒 Sat am.

The fishing village of Urk attracts
many tourists with its sloping
alleys and charming fishermen's
cottages. Until the Zuiderzee
was drained, Urk was an island.
Some 1,000 years ago, the island
was much larger and had five
villages; flooding gradually
reduced its size. The townspeople moved to the highest
point on the island, a hill of

boulder clay. Even after the polder
was drained, Urk managed to
retain its character in the middle
of the new land surrounding it.
Some of the older residents wear
the traditional dress, though this
is increasingly rare.

Beside the old village centre,
the fishing quay, the lighthouse
(1844) and the little church (1786)
are worth a look. In the **Museum
Het Oude Raadhuis**, situated in
the old town hall, you can find
out about the history of Urk and
the fishing industry.

🏛 **Museum Het
Oude Raadhuis**
Wijk 2–3. **Tel** 0527-683262.
Open Apr–Oct: 10am–5pm Mon–Fri,
10am–4pm Sat; Nov–Mar: 10am–4pm
Mon–Sat. 🅿 ♿ 📷 🎟

❸ Nagele

Road Map D3. 🗺 1,900. 🚌
ⓘ Emmeloord (0527-612000).

This village was built in the
1950s to designs by the De
Acht en de Opbouw, a group
of architects which included the
famous Rietveld, Van Eyck and
van Eesteren, who represented
the Nieuwe Bouwen movement.
The flat-roofed residential
buildings surround a park-like
centre with shops, schools and
churches. The village is surrounded
by a belt of woodland. **Museum
Nagele** provides information
about the village's architecture.

Schokland before land
reclamation

Schokland after land
reclamation

🏛 **Museum Nagele**
Ring 23. **Tel** 0527-653077.
Open 1–5pm Thu–Sun. **Closed** 1 Jan,
25, 26 & 31 Dec. 🅿 ♿ 📷 🎟

❹ Schokland

Road Map C3. 🚌 ⓘ see museum.

Like Urk, Schokland was
once an island. Archaeological
finds show that the site was
inhabited in prehistoric times.
In 1859, the population had to
abandon the island because it
was disappearing into the sea.
Today the "island" is so tiny that
it can barely be seen.

Museum Schokland,
consisting of the restored
church and reconstructions
of fishermen's cottages, is
dedicated to geology and
local history from the Ice
Age up until the land was
reclaimed. At the south end
of the village are the ruins
of a medieval church. In the
Schokkerbos forest to the
west is the **Gesteentetuin**,
gardens featuring Ice
Age boulders.

🏛 **Museum Schokland**
Middelbuurt 3, Ens. **Tel** 0527-251396.
Open Apr–Oct: 11am–5pm Tue–Sun
(Jul & Aug: daily); Nov–Mar: 11am–
5pm Fri–Sun. **Closed** 1 Jan, 25 Dec.
🅿 ♿ 🎟

Cornelis Lely (1854–1929)

Flevoland has come into existence thanks largely to the
plans and ambitions of civil engineer Cornelis Lely.
From 1885 to 1891, as a member of the
Zuiderzeevereniging (Zuiderzee Society), he
was responsible for studying the possibility
of closing off and draining the Zuiderzee.
His appointment as minister for trade and
industry in 1891 gave him the chance to
convince the government and parliament
how necessary it was to tame the
unpredictable Zuiderzee, though it was
not until his third term in office (1913–18)
that the law for retaining and draining the
Zuiderzee was finally passed. Apart from the
Zuiderzee projects, Lely worked to improve
the Noorzeekanaal. From 1902 to 1905 he
was governor of Suriname. He died in
1929, but his name lives on in that of
Flevoland's capital, Lelystad.

Statue of Lely

❺ Swifterbant

Road Map C3. 🅰 6,500. 🚌
🛈 De Rede 80–82, Dronten (0321-
313802). 🅰 Tue pm.

This young village is known
primarily to archaeologists
for the flint tools and earthenware of the **Swifterbant
culture** that were unearthed
here. The Swifterbant culture
inhabited the region in the
4th millennium BC.
    In spring, flower enthusiasts
can enjoy the riot of vivid
colour in the nearby bulbfields.

Environs
The Swifterbos forest nearby is
an excellent spot for recreation.
The Ketelbos is a resting place
for migrant bird species.

❻ Dronten

Road Map D3. 🅰 22,500. 🚌
🛈 De Rede 80–82 (0321-313802).
🅰 Wed.

Dronten is well-endowed
with greenery and recreation
facilities. The Meerpaal Complex
here combines a theatre,
cinema and events venue.
Outside the town hall stands
the Airgunnersmonument,
honouring airmen who lost
their lives in World War II.

Environs
Around Dronten are many
pretty woods and recreation
areas that offer opportunities
for walking and cycling.

❼ Lelystad

Road Map C3. 🅰 67,000. 🚌 🚉
🛈 Bataviaplein 60 (0320-292900).
🅰 Sat (Gordiaan), Tue (Lelycentre).

Lelystad, a provincial capital,
has a modern centre with a
number of outstanding buildings.
The cylindrical **Nieuw Land
Erfgoedcentrum** has models
and audiovisual materials
illustrating the history of the
fight against the sea, of the
land reclamation and of the
culture of the Zuiderzee.
    On the Airship Plaza is the
Zepallon museum of balloon
and airship flight. East of the
town is **Natuurpark Lelystad**,
where there are animals
such as bison and Przewalski
horses. As well as cycling
and pedestrian paths, the
park boasts a shipwreck
and a reconstructed prehistoric
village. The **Nationaal Luchtvaart
Themapark Aviodrome**, at
Lelystad airport, has historic
aircraft, a cinema and a
reconstruction of Schiphol
Station from 1928.

🏛 **Nieuw Land Erfgoedcentrum**
Oostvaardersdijk 113. **Tel** 0320-
225900. **Open** 10am–5pm Tue–Fri,
11:30am–5pm Sat & Sun.
Closed 1 Jan, 25 Dec.
🚫 🅿 🔲 🔲 🚫 ♿

🔲 **Natuurpark Lelystad**
Vlotgrasweg 11. **Tel** 0320-286111.
Open sunrise–sunset daily.
🚫 by appt. 🅿 🔲

🔲 **Nationaal Luchtvaart
Themapark Aviodrome**
Pelikaanweg 50, Luchthaven Lelystad.
Tel 0320-289842. **Open** 10am–5pm
Tue–Sun (Mon in Jul, Aug & school
hols). **Closed** 25 Dec. 🚫 🅿 🔲 ♿

❽ Bataviawerf

Road Map C3. Oostvaardersdijk 01–09,
Lelystad. **Open** 10am–
5pm daily. **Closed** 1 Jan, 25 Dec. 🚫
🅿 🔲 🔲 🌐 **w** bataviawerf.nl

From 1985 to 1995, a replica of
the Dutch East India Company
ship *Batavia (see p262)* was
built at the Bataviawerf on the
Oostvaardersdiep. The shipyard's
current project is a replica of
the 17th-century *De Zeven
Provinciën*. Visit the sailmaking
and woodcarving workshops.
The entry ticket is also valid for
NISA, the Netherlands Institute
for Submarine Archaeology,
with its fascinating display
on shipwrecks.

The *Batavia*, which went down off the Australian coast in 1629 with 341 people on board

Observation huts on the Oostvaardersplassen lakes, situated amid abundant bird populations

❾ Oostvaarders-plassen

Road Map C3. ℹ️ Staatsbosbeheer, Bezoekerscentrum, Kitsweg 1, Lelystad (0320-254585).

Between Lelystad and Almere is internationally renowned marshland covering 6,000 ha (14,825 acres). The land was originally earmarked as an industrial area. When Zuidelijk Flevoland was drained, the low-lying area beyond the Oostvaardersdijk remained a wetland. Plans to drain this area were put forward but were ultimately dismissed because the place had by this time become an area of unique natural interest.

The nature reserve includes lakes, mud flats, marshes, willow thickets and grasslands and serves as a port of call for hundreds of species of birds that come here to forage and feed. Indeed, some birds which have been unable to settle elsewhere have found their place here, including the hen harrier (the symbol of Flevoland) and the great cormorant. Other birds seen here include the great bittern, the Eurasian spoonbill, heron, rail and, more recently, the sacred ibis. The many grey geese that forage here, along with the wild cattle, wild horses and red deer that occur here, have helped the region's vegetation to proliferate.

The marshland is largely off-limits to visitors, but some fine views are to be had from the edge of the swamp, the Oostvaardersdijk and the Knardijk. Additionally, the region of **De Driehoek** has a 5-km (3-mile) walking route, open sunrise to sunset. The route starts at the information centre and passes by natural woodland, lakes and observation huts.

❿ Knardijk

Road Map C3. ℹ️ Staatsbosbeheer (0320-254585).

The Knardijk marks the border between Oostelijk and Zuidelijk Flevoland (eastern and southern Flevoland). It was built in the 1950s between the island of Lelystad-Haven and Harderwijk to enable the entire area to be placed within a polder at one time. After Oostelijk Flevoland had been dried out, it formed the south-western ring dyke of this polder. The Knardijk is of great interest

Hen harrier

to nature lovers, as it offers a fine view of the Oostvaardersplassen lakes. A great many birds live at the foot of the dyke, including hen harriers and marsh harriers. Two bird-watching huts can also be reached along the dyke. The dyke leads in a southeasterly direction along the nature reserve known as the **Wilgenreservaat**, which has evolved naturally into a mixture of woodland and clearings. Many songbirds, woodland birds, and birds of prey are to be found here, as are deer, foxes, polecats and ermines. Part of the reserve can be seen via a circular path. Nearby is the Knarbos forest, also boasting a variety of flora and fauna. A 6-km (4-mile) hiking route has been marked out.

The Knardijk, looking out over a variegated natural landscape

⓫ Zeewolde

Road Map C3. 🏠 19,400. 🚌
ℹ️ Raadhuisstraat 1 (036-5221405).
🍴 Fri.

With its picturesque marina, this village on the Wolderwijd coastal lake is a popular recreational spot. Zeewolde is the youngest town in Flevoland, having officially become a municipality in 1984. Its youth is evident from the imaginative architecture, particularly that of the town hall, library and church. An enjoyable 7-km (4-mile) walking route has been laid out in and around Zeewolde, with landscape art along the way (for information, call De Verbeelding, 036-5227037).

Environs
South of Zeewolde is the **Horsterwold**, which is the largest deciduous forest in Western Europe.

⓬ Almere

Road Map C3. 🏠 176,000. 🚌 🚉
ℹ️ De Diagonaal 199 (036-5485041).
🍴 Wed & Sat (Almere-Stad), Thu (Almere-Buiten), Fri (Almere-Haven).

Almere is Holland's fastest-growing town. Its name recalls the 8th-century name for the Zuiderzee. The earliest signs of habitation date from 65 centuries

Almere, a laboratory for modern architects

earlier. Almere today consists of three centres: Almere-Stad, which is undergoing major renovation and is where all the facilities are; Almere-Buiten, which is a green suburb; and Almere-Haven, with its lovely marina. If you are interested in modern and unusual architecture, the districts to visit are Muziewijk, Filmwijk and Stedenwijk in Almere-Stad, and the colourful Regenboogbuurt (rainbow neighbourhood) in Almere-Buiten. Also worth a visit are the town hall, and the Almeers Centrum Hedendaagse Kunst **ACHK – De Paviljoens** (Almere centre for modern art), with works by late 20th-century Dutch and foreign artists.

Environs
Near Almere are many recreation areas and nature reserves: the Weerwater; the Leegwaterplas lake; the Beginbos forest, with walking, cycling and bridleways; the Buitenhout; the Kromslootpark, with its polder vegetation; the lakes of Noorderplassen; **Lepelaarsplassen**, where rare wading birds occur; and the Oostvaardersplassen.

ACHK – De Paviljoens
Odeonstraat 3–5.
Tel 036-5450400. **Open** noon–5pm Wed–Sun (to 9pm Thu & Fri).
Closed 1 Jan, 25 Dec.

Landscape Art

In the countryside around Flevoland you will come across unusual and distinctive works of "landscape art". These are associated with various features of the landscape. East of Almere-Haven, for instance, is the *Groene Kathedraal (Green Cathedral)* (top photo), designed by Marinus Boezem and consisting of 178 Lombardy poplars planted to re-create the outline and pillars of Reims Cathedral. The *Observatorium Robert Morris* (bottom photo) consists of two round earth embankments, with three notches in them from which the sunrise can be observed when the seasons change. On the Ketelmeerdijk, you will find Cyriel Lixenberg's *Wachters op de Dijk (Watchmen on the Dyke)*, consisting of a circle, a triangle and a square. Piet Slegers' *Aardzee (Earth Sea)*, situated between Zeewolde and Lelystad, consists of a series of elongated artificial ridges resembling waves.

GELDERLAND

Gelderland is the Netherland's largest province. Its name derives from the 11th-century county of Gelre, which was linked with the town of Geldern, just over the border in Germany. The town was the fiefdom of Gerard de Rossige, whose grandson Gerard II of Wassenberg pronounced himself Count of Gelre in 1104.

Succeeding counts skilfully expanded their territory to include the Veluwe region to the north, the Betuwe in the southwest and the county of Zutphen *(see p345)*. When, in 1248, the imperial town of Nijmegen was annexed, Gelre became a power to be reckoned with. A number of its towns joined the Hanseatic League, and in 1339 the county was promoted to a duchy by the German emperor. The increasing power of the Habsburgs threatened the independence of the Gelders, eventually leading to the duke having to cede the territory in 1543 to Charles V. Gelderland thus became part of the Netherlands.

This colourful history is manifest today in the number of medieval buildings, churches, castles and fortified towns that welcome visitors throughout the province. In more recent times, the region, and especially the strategically located towns of Arnhem and Nijmegen, saw heavy fighting towards the end of World War II. The heroic action at Arnhem is remembered in the town's Airborne Museum, while the museum in Nijmegen recalls this town's long history from pre-Roman times to the tyranny of the Holy Roman Empire.

While visitors can enjoy many modern attractions, perhaps Gelderland's greatest asset is its contrasting natural scenery, which ranges from heaths and woodlands in the north to the beautiful Betuwe river valley and the pretty agricultural region of the Achterhoek.

A 17th-century granary near Winterswijk

◄ A glimpse into the old Dutch city of Nijmegen

Exploring Gelderland

Gelderland is made up of three distinct regions. In the north is the Veluwe, an extensive natural area of woodland, heaths and large tracts of drifting sand, where those looking for peaceful natural surroundings can find exactly that. To the east is the Achterhoek. This region, too, is rich in natural beauty but has a completely different character: it consists of small fields with wooden fences, old farms, stately homes and castles. In the southwest of the province, between the Rhine, the Maas and the Waal rivers, is the river-valley region of the Betuwe. This area is distinguished by its many small dykes and river banks, which offer ample opportunities for cycling and walking.

The Dolphinarium in Harderwijk

Sights at a Glance

① *Paleis Het Loo pp338–9*
② Apeldoorn
③ Hattem
④ Elburg
⑤ Nunspeet
⑥ Harderwijk
⑦ Nijkerk
⑧ Barneveld
⑨ Wageningen
⑩ *Kröller-Müller Museum pp342–3*
⑪ Nationaal Park De Hoge Veluwe
⑫ Arnhem
⑬ Zutphen

⑭ Bronkhorst
⑮ Vorden
⑯ Lochem
⑰ Winterswijk
⑱ 's-Heerenberg
⑲ Montferland
⑳ Doesburg
㉑ *Nijmegen pp346–7*
㉒ Gelderse Poort
㉓ Groesbeek
㉔ Tiel
㉕ Culemborg
㉖ Buren
㉗ Zaltbommel

ELBURG

Veluwemeer

NUNSPEET ⑤

HARDERWIJK ⑥

Ermelo

N310

Elspee

N302

Putten

A28

⑦ NIJKERK

N303

N344

Voorthuizen

BARNEVELD ⑧

N312

Hoevelaken

A1

KRÖLLER-MÜLLER MUSEUM

Scherpenzeel

Lunteren

Otterlo

⑩

A30

NATIONAAL PARK D HOGE VELUW

Ede

A12

N224

Bennekom

Renkum

Lek

WAGENINGEN ⑨

CULEMBORG ㉕

N320

Maurik

N320

Neder Rijn

A50

Kesteren

A15

Zetten

Elst

A2

BUREN ㉖

Druten

Waal

Asperen

Geldermalsen

㉔ TIEL

Beneden-Leeuwen

Beuningen

Brakel

Waal

Bergse Maas

NIJMEGEN

ZALTBOMMEL ㉗

Megen

Wijchen

A2

Kerkdriel

A50

Malde

Ammerzoden

Grave

0 kilometres   10

0 miles   5

The majestic red deer – king of the Veluwe

Getting Around

Gelderland has an excellent road network. A number of major motorways pass through the province, including the A2 and the A50. Public transport is also good. Many towns have rail links, and the bus will even take you deep into the Nationaal Park De Hoge Veluwe. The numerous bicycle tracks and footpaths allow the province to be conveniently explored either on foot or by bicycle. Cycling routes of varying lengths are well marked, and there are several walking routes across the province, including the very scenic Maarten van Rossum route.

The Veluwe, characterized by large sandy areas

HATTEM ❸
Wezep

A50

Heerde

Vaassen

PALEIS HET LOO

A1

PELDOORN
N345

Gorssel   Laren
N348

Voorst   ❶❻ **LOCHEM**   Neede
                              N346
ZUTPHEN ❶❸   N315
                                            Borculo   Eibergen
Eerbeek   N348   ❶❺ **VORDEN**   N18
               ❶❹ **BRONKHORST**   Ruurlo
                              N319
ELDERLAND   N316   Groenlo
Dieren   N314   Hengelo
Rheden   Zelhem   Lievelde   N319
lp   ❷❶ **DOESBURG**   N330
RNHEM   IJssel   N317   Doetinchem   Lichtenvoorde   **WINTERSWIJK**
                                                              ❶❼
Duiven   A12   Didam   A18   Varsseveld   N318
Zevenaar   **MONTFERLAND**   Aalten
         Beek ❶❾   Terborg
              Zeddam   N317
❷❷ **GELDERSE**   ❶❽ **'s-HEERENBERG**   Dinxperlo
POORT
Millingen
aan den Rijn

GROESBEEK

Key

━━━ Motorway
━━━ Major road
⋯⋯ Minor road
━━━ Scenic route
─┼─ Main railway
─── Minor railway
━━━ Regional border
▬▬▬ International border

Bronkhorst, the Netherlands' smallest town

For hotels and restaurants in this region see pp400–401 and p414

❶ Paleis Het Loo

The Stadholder William III built the elegant palace of Het Loo in 1692 as a hunting lodge. For generations, the Orange family used it as a summer residence. Its pomp and splendour have led to it being dubbed the "Versailles of the Netherlands". Its main architect was Jacob Roman (1640–1716); the interior and the gardens were designed by Daniel Marot (1661–1752). The severe Classical façade belies the ornate interior. After intensive restoration work was carried out, the palace is now open as a museum.

Coat of Arms (1690) of William and Mary, future king and queen of England.

★ **Bedroom of the Stadholder William III** (1713)
The wall coverings and draperies in this bedroom are of rich orange damask and purple silk.

KEY

① William III's bedroom

② **Closet of the Stadholder William III** (1690) The walls of William's private chamber are covered in scarlet damask. His paintings and Delftware are on display here.

③ King's Garden

④ Mary II's bedroom

⑤ Queen's Garden

⑥ **The throne room** now contains the original designs for the gardens.

⑦ Library

⑧ Picture gallery

Vintage Cars
This 1925 Bentley, nicknamed Minerva, was owned by Prince Hendrik, husband of Queen Wilhelmina. It is one of the royal family's many old cars and carriages on display in the stables.

★ **Dining Hall** (1686)
The marble-clad walls are hung with tapestries depicting scenes from Ovid's poems.

VISITORS' CHECKLIST

Practical Information
Road map D3. Koninklijk Park 1 (Amersfoortseweg), Apeldoorn.
Tel 055-5772400.
W paleishetloo.nl
Open 10am–5pm Tue–Sun & hols. **Closed** 1 Jan. 🚫 gardens only. 🎫 📷 ♿ 📧

Transport
🚆 Apeldoorn, then bus to palace and gardens.

Main entrance

★ **The Formal Gardens**
The gardens are a combination of vegetation, stone carvings and fountains in Classical style. The Fountain of the Celestial Sphere stands in the Lower Garden.

Lower Garden · Queen's Garden · Paleis Het Loo · Upper Garden · King's Garden

Plan of the formal gardens

The Formal Gardens

When the formal gardens on the land behind the palace were reconstructed, garden designers based their designs on old illustrations, prints, documents and plans. In the 18th century, the original ornamental gardens had been grassed over. In 1983, the intricate patterns of the original gardens were restored and planting began. The Het Loo gardens are typical of a formal garden in the 17th century in which the ideal was the harmonization of art and nature.

Stroking monkeys in Apenheul, a zoo in the Berg en Bos nature park

❷ Apeldoorn

Road Map D3. 🔼 152,000. 🚗 🚌
ℹ️ Deventerstraat 18 (526-0200).

Apeldoorn is first mentioned as Appoldro in 793, and for centuries it was a small rural town in the Veluwe. This was changed by William III in 1692 when he built his hunting lodge Het Loo *(see pp338–9)* here. Many wealthy burghers followed William's example and set themselves up in Apeldoorn. The engaging **Historisch Museum Apeldoorn** gives a good overview of the area's history.

The **Apenheul Primate Park** is a special zoo situated in the Berg en Bos nature park, where more than 30 species of monkeys run free among the visitors. The gorillas live on wooded islands that separate them from both the monkeys and visitors.

🦍 **Apenheul Primate Park**
JC Wilslaan 21. **Tel** 055-3575757.
Open Apr–Oct: 10am–5pm; Jul–Aug: 10am–6pm. 🚫 ♿

❸ Hattem

Road Map D3. 🔼 12,000. 🚌
🍴 Wed pm.

The picturesque town of Hattem (first mentioned in 891) was granted its town charter as early as 1299, joining the Hanseatic League in the 15th century. Its monumental buildings, such as the house of Herman Willem Daendals, later the governor-general of the Dutch Indies, bear witness

to Hattem's eventful and prosperous past. St Andreaskerk (St Andrew's Church) is particularly remarkable, its oldest part dating from 1176. The **Anton Pieck Museum** is dedicated to the Dutch painter and graphic artist Anton Pieck (1895–1987); it has been merged with the **Voerman Museum**, which showcases the IJssel painter Jan Voerman and his son, who illustrated the famous Verkade card albums.

🏛 **Anton Pieck Museum/ Voerman Museum**
Achterstraat 46–48. **Tel** 038-4442192 & 038-4442897. **Open** 10am–5pm Tue–Sat (Jul & Aug also open 1–5pm Sun & Mon). **Closed** 1 Jan, 9–31 Jan, 30 Apr, 25 Dec; Nov–Apr: Mon. 🚫 ♿

❹ Elburg

Road Map D3. 🔼 21,500. 🚌
ℹ️ Jufferenstraat 8 (0525-681520).
🍴 Tue.

Elburg is the best-preserved fortified town on the former Zuiderzee. The prosperity of this old town is illustrated in the 14th-century St Nicolaaskerk, with its imposing Quellhorst organ. From the 38-m (125-ft) tower you can clearly make out the medieval rectangular street pattern.

Beside the **Vischpoort** (fish gate), a former defence tower, is the oldest ropemaker's workshop in Holland. Elburg was once much nearer to the coast, but in the late 14th century the flood-plagued

town was moved well away from the sea. The interesting local history museum, the **Gemeentemuseum**, is in a 15th-century monastery.

🏛 **Gemeentemuseum Elburg**
Jufferenstraat 6–8. **Tel** 0525-68 1341. **Open** 11am–5pm Tue–Sat.
🚫 🚫

The Oudheidkamer at Nunspeet, a town in Gelderland province

❺ Nunspeet

Road Map D3. 🔼 26,000. 🚗 🚌
ℹ️ Stationsplein 1 (0341-274740).
🍴 Thu am.

Nunspeet is a good starting point from which to explore the nearby wooded countryside. Nunspeet's history comes to life in the **Oudheidkamer**. The nearby **Veluwemeer** lake is a popular watersports centre.

Environs
Some 15 km (9 miles) south of Nonspeet is the idyllic **Uddelermeer** lake, a remnant from the last Ice Age.

The pleasant market square of Hattem, with its 17th-century town hall

❻ Harderwijk

Road Map C3. 🚲 38,500. 🚍 🚌
ℹ️ Academiestraat 5 (085-2733575).
📅 Sat am.

The eel-smoking frames may
have disappeared from the
streets, but the Zuiderzee town
of Harderwijk is still a pleasant
place to wander around. The
town has an interesting history.
In the 13th century it had
become so important through
fishing and the trade in dyes that
in 1221 Count Otto II of Gelre
granted it a town charter and
ordered fortifications to be built.
Remnants of the old fortifications
are still intact in places, including
the **Visschpoort** gate. Between
1647 and 1811 Harderwijk even
had a university, from which
the Swedish scholar Linnaeus
graduated in 1735. Harderwijk's
main attraction is the
Dolfinarium *(see p426)*,
Europe's largest zoo for
marine animals. The
Veluws Museum
of local history in
the Donkerstraat
is also worth visiting.

Boats moored at the harbour of Harderwijk

❼ Nijkerk

Road Map C3. 🚲 27,000. 🚍 🚌
ℹ️ Verlaat 13 (055-5260200). 📅 Fri pm.

Nijkerk is a pleasant old town
with many shops, restaurants
and open-air cafés. The tobacco
industry made the town rich in
the 18th century. The Grote Kerk
features the tomb of Kiliaen van
Renselaer, one of the founders
of New York. Just outside
Nijkerk, on the Arkemheem
polder, is the **Hertog Reijnout**
stoomgemaal, a paddle-
wheeled steam pumping-
station, the last functioning one
of its kind in Europe. Even today
it is used to pump water out
at times of flooding.

Environs
On the road to Putten is the
Oldenaller estate with a castle
from 1655. The cycling and
walking area is open to the
public. In **Putten** itself you can
visit **De Gedachenisruimte** (hall
of remembrance) in honour of
the 600 men who in October

1944 were taken from the
village to the Neuengamme
concentration camp,
from where only 50
returned alive.

Ray

🏭 **Stoomgemaal
Hertog Reijnout**
Zeedijk 6. **Tel** 065-3225997.
Open Apr–Sep: 10am–4pm Tue–Fri,
10am–1pm Sat, 11am–4pm Sun.
Closed Mon. 🅿️ 🚫

❽ Barneveld

Road Map D4. 🚲 47,000. 🚍 🚌
ℹ️ Langestraat 85a (0342-420555).
📅 Thu, Sat am.

Barneveld owes its place in
history books to one individual:
Jan van Schaffelaar,
commander-in-chief of the
armed forces, who on 16 July
1482 chose suicide rather than
surrender and leapt from the
tower of today's Nederlands
Hervormde kerk (Reformed
church). The **Nairac** museum
of local history devotes
considerable attention to
this event. Today Barneveld
is known as a poultry centre.
The local **Pluimveemuseum**
(poultry museum) shows
how this industry has
developed here.

🏛️ **Pluimveemuseum**
Hessenweg 2a. **Tel** 0342-400073.
Open Apr–Oct: 10am–5pm Tue–Sat.
🅿️ ♿

❾ Wageningen

Road Map C4. 🚲 33,000. 🚌
📅 Wed am, Sat.

Wageningen, at the southwestern
edge of the Veluwe, is a
pleasant town that is home to
the local Landbouwuniversiteit
(agricultural university). The
university's botanical gardens
are open to the public. The
town played an important
role at the end of World
War II; the Germans signed
the official surrender in the
Hotel de Wereld.

🏨 **Hotel De Wereld**
5 Mei Plein 1. **Tel** 0317-460444.
Open Call ahead to book.

The leap of Jan van Schaffelaar

⑩ Kröller-Müller Museum

This museum owes its existence above all to one person: Helene Kröller-Müller (1869–1939). In 1908, with the support of her industrialist husband Anton Kröller, Helene Kröller-Müller started to collect modern art. In 1935, she donated her entire collection to the state, and a special museum was built to house it. As well as its large collection of modern art, which includes 278 works by Vincent van Gogh, the museum is renowned for its unique sculpture garden, the Beeldentuin.

★ Beeldentuin
Jardin d'Email by Jean Dubuffet is one of the most distinctive sculptures in the 25-ha (62-acre) sculpture garden. The garden provides a natural backdrop for works by sculptors such as Auguste Rodin, Henry Moore, Barbara Hepworth and Richard Serra.

Mondriaan
In addition to old Flemish masters, the Kröller-Müller also has a major collection of 19th- and 20th-century French paintings and a dozen abstract paintings by Piet Mondriaan.

Entrance to the Beeldentuin

Shop

Main entrance

Jachthuis St Hubertus
This hunting lodge, built from 1914 to 1920 by the architect HP Berlage, was commissioned by the Kröller-Müller family.

The Studio Boat
Claude Monet's 1874 painting is in the 19th- and 20th-century French collection.

Practical Information

Kröller-Müller Museum:
Tel 0318-591241.
Open 10am–5pm Tue–Sun &
public hols; sculpture garden
10am–4:30pm. **Closed** 1 Jan.
🖥 🅿 Jachthuis St Hubertus:
🎫 daily (Jan: open Sat & Sun
only). Reserve tickets at the visitors'
centre (see column at right).

staurant

Information
centre

★ **Van Gogh Collection**
Café Terrace at Night (1888). Van Gogh's
huge collection of drawings, paintings
and prints are the heart of the museum.

Museum Guide

*The museum, together with
the sculpture garden, gives
expression to the notion
that nature, architecture
and art should be
combined to form a whole.*

Key to Floorplan

☐ Exhibition rooms

⓫ Nationaal Park De Hoge Veluwe

Road map D4. Houtkampweg,
Otterlo. Tel 055-378 8100. 🚌 Ede,
Apeldoorn. **Open** 9am–6pm daily.

Like the Kröller-Müller Museum,
De Hoge Veluwe is also the
result of a collector's ambition.
The Kröller-Müllers collected
plots of unused land in the
Veluwe until they possessed
one single tract of natural land.
They even bought, in 1914, the
public road between Otterlo
and Hoenderlo. The 5,500 ha
(13,600 acres) of woodland,
marshland, heath and drifting
sand now make up the largest
nature reserve in Holland. The
park is a treasure trove for all
kinds of wildlife: rare birds,
butterflies, plants and fungi.
Red deer, roe deer and
moufflon sheep still live freely
here. If you are lucky, you may
be able to catch a glimpse of a
wild boar or a stag (they are
very shy animals). Bicycle and
pedestrian paths have been
laid out everywhere, and at the
visitors' centre you can borrow
a white bicycle free of charge.

Underneath the visitors'
centre is the world's first
underground museum, the
Museonder, giving visitors an
idea of what life is like below
the earth's surface. You can
see the roots of a 140-year-old
beech tree, experience a
recreated earthquake and
drink ancient Veluwe groundwater. The park has two
restaurants: the Rijzenburg at
the Schaarsbergen entrance
and the De Koperen Kop
café-restaurant located in
the visitors' centre.

Museonder, the world's first
underground museum

⑫ Arnhem

Road Map D3. 🚇 136,500. 🚉 🚌
ℹ️ Stationsplein 13 (0481-366250).
🗓️ Fri, Sat (Kerkplein).

Arnhem, the capital of the province of Gelderland, was declared the centre of the regional government back in 1544 by Charles V. In September 1944, the town suffered serious damage in the Battle of Arnhem, one of the most notorious battles of World War II. All the townspeople were forced to abandon their homes and were not able to return until 1945, when the war ended. Arnhem rose again from the ashes and is now sprucing itself up rapidly. The monuments that have been restored include the **Eusebiuskerk** from 1560, which

Traditional houses in the Openluchtmuseum

Allied troops landing in Arnhem on 17 September 1944

was almost totally destroyed during the war. The tower, at 93 m (305 ft), is now taller than it ever was and has a glass lift which affords visitors a stunning view of the Rhine valley. The **Duivelshuis**, built in 1545 by Maarten van Rossum *(see p349)*, is an outstanding example of Dutch Renaissance architecture. Arnhem is also known for its monumental parks, such as the **Sonsbeek**, a romantic landscape park, and **Zypendaal**. In **Bronbeek**, a home for ex-servicemen, there is an exhibition dedicated to the former Dutch Indies. It is

also worth allowing time for a visit to the **Burgers' Zoo** *(see p426)* and **Openluchtmuseum** (open-air museum), where the staff, dressed up in traditional costume, illustrate the rural way of life, handicrafts and industry in the Netherlands of the 19th century.

🏛️ **Openluchtmuseum**
Schelmseweg 89. **Tel** 026-3576111.
Open Apr–Oct: 10am–5pm daily. 🐾

Environs
The **Posbank** at Rheden is an example of the lateral moraine landscape of Veluwe.

Arnhem Town Centre

① Koepelkerk
② Post Office
③ Eusebiuskerk
④ Sabelspoort
⑤ Provinciehuis
⑥ Stadhuis
⑦ Stadsschouwburg
⑧ Musis Sacrum

0 metres   200
0 yards   200

Old book at the St Walburgskerk library, built in 1564

⑬ Zutphen

Road Map D4. 👥 36,000. 🚉
ℹ️ Stationsplein 39 (0575-519355).
🛍️ Thu am, Sat.

The hanseatic town of Zutphen is one of the Netherlands' oldest historical towns. One of the most distinctive features of the town, which is first mentioned in 1030, is the preserved medieval street layout. The main sights of Zutphen are the **St Walburgskerk**, the church square and the remains of the fortifications. They include the **Drogenapstoren** tower, which dates from 1444.

Zutphen has a number of interesting museums, including the informative **Stedelijk Museum** (local history museum) and the **Grafisch Museum** (graphic art museum), which is highly recommended.

Definitely worth visiting is the reading room of the unique **Librije** (library) of the St Walburgskerk. All of the 750 books in it date from before 1750 and include 80 incunabula printed before 1500. The books in the library, which was built in 1564, are chained to the desks. This is because it was a public library, which was unsupervised at the time. There are only four other libraries of this kind in the world: two are in England and two are in northern Italy.

🏛️ **St Walburgskerk and Librije**
Kerkhof 3. **Tel** 0575-514178. **Open** Jun: 1:30–4:30pm Tue–Sat; Jul–early Sep: 10:30am–4:30pm Tue–Sat. ♿

⑭ Bronkhorst

Road Map D4. 👥 160. 🚌 52 from Zutphen train station.

Bronkhorst's 160 inhabitants make it the smallest town in the Netherlands. The lords of Bronkhorst were granted a town charter in 1482. This very rural town, which once stood in the shadow of a castle (the castle no longer exists), never really flourished and has remained a village of farmsteads. It has many restored farmhouses, operates strict conservation rules forbidding new development and prohibits motor vehicles, which means cars must be left in a car park outside the town. All that remains of the once-mighty castle of the Lords of Bronkhorst, which had fallen into disrepair by the 17th century, is the *kasteelheuvel* (castle hill).

The Lords of Bronkhorst, together with the noble Bergh, Baer and Wisch families, belonged to the *Baanderheren*. They were nobles who were allowed to wage war under their own flag, which was an old hereditary right.

⑮ Vorden

Road Map D4. 👥 8,400. 🚉
ℹ️ Kerkstraat 1b (0575-553222).
🛍️ Fri am.

There is mention of a Huis Vorden (Vorden house) as early as 1208; the first record of the family dates from 1315. The **Nederlands-herformde kerk**, which dates from around 1300, is well worth a visit. The best-known figure to come from Vorden is the poet of Achterhoek **ACW Staring** (1767–1840), who lived in De Wildenborch castle from 1791 until his death.

Environs
Around Vorden are eight castles in very picturesque surroundings. A bicycle trip of the area, passing farms and country estates, is definitely worth the effort.

An ancient watermill at Vorden, a town in eastern Netherlands

⑯ Lochem

Road Map D4. 👥 19,000. 🚉
ℹ️ Tramstraat 4 (0573-251898).
🛍️ Wed am.

Lochem, one of the oldest villages in the Achterhoek to have its own parish church, was granted its town charter in 1233. During the Dutch War of Independence, the town was often besieged. It was razed to the ground in 1615. Only the **Grote kerk**, also known as **St Gudulakerk**, with its 56-m (185-ft) steeple, was spared. This 14th-century hall-type church has fine murals from Catholic times (it is now a Reformed Church). The **Stadhuis** (town hall), across from the church, dates from 1615.

Bronkhorst, a tiny, picturesque village of farmsteads

A charming old farmhouse near Winterswijk

⓱ Winterswijk

Road Map E4. 🚗 28,000. 🚆
ℹ️ Mevr, Kuipers Rietbergplein 1
(0543-512302). 🅿️ Wed am, Sat.
🌐 winterswijk.nl

The 20th century was not kind to
the town of Winterswijk and the
grand railway station bears
witness to better times. There is
now only a single railway track,
although it is evident that in the
past the rail traffic was much
heavier. The **Museum Freriks** is
interesting, with its exhibits
relating to the textile industry that
flourished here before World War
II. The museum also has prints
by Pieter Mondriaan Sr, whose
famous painter son Piet spent his
childhood in Winterswijk.
    On the outskirts of the town
lies a pleasant sculpture park, **De
Beeldtuin**. Set out in the shady
mature orchards of an old farm,
there are also meadows and
wooded areas. The works of art, by
contemporary, mainly Dutch
sculptors, are dotted all over the
grounds, and represent just about
every genre, from Pop Art through
traditional to highly abstract.
The park also hosts changing
temporary exhibitions of 3D art.

🏛️ **Museum Freriks**
Groenloseweg 86. **Tel** 0543-533533.
Open 10am–5pm Tue–Fri,
2–5pm Sat & Sun. 🚫

🏛️ **De Beeldtuin**
Steggemansweg 1. **Tel** 0543-521034.
Open phone ahead.

⓲ 's-Heerenberg

Road Map D4. 🚗 18,000.
🚌 24. ℹ️ Hofstraat 1 (0316 -291391).
🅿️ Thu.

The old castle town of
's-Heerenberg and the area

surrounding it are among the
prettiest corners of Achterhoek.
The little town, which was
granted its charter in 1379,
retains its historical centre, with
buildings from the 15th and 16th
centuries. **Huis Bergh** is one of
Holland's finest castles and
houses the art collection of the
textile magnate JH van Heek.

🏛️ **Kasteel Huis Bergh**
ℹ️ Hof Van Bergh 8 (0314-661281).
Open May–Oct: 12:30–4:30pm Tue–
Sun. **Closed** 1 Jan, 24, 25 & 31 Dec. 🚫

⓳ Montferland

Road Map D4. ℹ️ Hofstraat 1,
's-Heerenberg (0316-291391).

Montferland, one of the few
hilly areas in the Netherlands,
is exceptionally attractive.
Apart from **'s-Heerenberg** *(see
above)*, there is a number of
other attractions, such as
Zeddam, Beek and nature
reserves where you can walk,
cycle, swim or even dive. The
natural spring in Beek, "het

Peeske", and the historic
farmhouses along the
Langeboomseweg in
Velthuizen are worth seeing.

⓴ Doesburg

Road Map D4. 🚗 11,000. 🚌 27/29
Arnhem & 26/28 Dieren.
ℹ️ Gasthuisstraat 13 (0313-479088).
🅿️ Wed am, Sat.

Doesburg is a snug Hanseatic
town on the IJssel. Granted its
town charter in 1237, this small
town's well-preserved old centre
has had listed status since 1974.
Doesburg contains at least 150
national monuments, including
a Late Gothic town hall, one of
the earliest in Holland. The
Grote or Martinuskerk, a Late
Gothic basilica with a 97-m
(320-ft) tower, is another of the
town's noteworthy buildings,
along with the local museum
De Roode Toren.

🏛️ **De Roode Toren**
Roggestraat 9–13. **Tel** 0313-474265.
Open 10am–noon, 1:30–4:30pm Tue–
Fri, 1:30–4:30pm Sat & Sun (Nov–Mar:
pm only).

㉑ Nijmegen

Road Map D4. 🚗 152,000. 🚆
ℹ️ Keizer Karelplein 32 (0481-366250).
🅿️ Mon, Sat.

Nijmegen is one of the oldest
towns in Holland. Archaeological
remains show that the Batavians
were settled here even before

Huis Bergh, one of Holland's finest castles

the first millennium BC, while the Romans had a fort here from 12 BC. In AD 104, the emperor Trajan granted trading rights to a new settlement west of present-day Valkhof. The town's ancient name of Ulpia Noviomagus Batavorum is presumably also from this time.

Nijmegen owes its existence to its strategic position on the river Waal. A fort has stood here since early times, and even in World War II, the town was a significant battle scene. The most important sights include the **Valkhof**, with its new **museum**, which stands on the spot where the fort of the Batavians, Roman engineering works and, later, one of Charlemagne's palaces stood. All that remains of the palace which was rebuilt by Frederick Barbarossa is the **St Maartenskapel** from 1155 and the **St Nicolaaskapel**, one of the earliest stone buildings in all of Holland. This chapel (part of which dates back to 1030) is a rare example of Byzantine architecture in northern Europe. Other noteworthy buildings include the St Stevenskerk, the construction of which began in 1254, the **Waag** (weigh house) and the **Kronenburgerpark**, with the remnants of fortifications (the Kruittoren tower).

A fascinating insight into the Dutch national obsession with all things two-wheeled can be found at **Velorama**, the bike museum. Spread over two floors, there are examples from the entire history of cycling,

Nijmegen's Waag, dating from 1612

from the earliest "hobby horse"-type bikes that date back to 1817. The upstairs room is devoted to the bicycle's modern incarnation, with beautifully shiny examples of racers, recumbents and everyday bikes. Star of the show, however, is the bicycle that belonged to Queen Wilhelmina in the 1940s and 1950s.

Nijmegen is perhaps best known for its annual four-day rambling meet, the **Vierdaagse**, in which tens of thousands of ramblers take part. With its many cafés, the town also has a vibrant nightlife.

Each July, **de-Affaire**, a week-long festival of music, accompanies the Vierdaagse long-distance marches *(see box)*. Events take place all over town, but many are focused around the Waalpark. Featuring around 100 acts, international cutting-edge rock and pop bands play alongside DJs and world musicians. There are also workshops on such activities as Latin music and dancing.

⚏ Museum Het Valkhof
Kelfkensbos 59, Nijmegen.
Tel 024-3608805. **Open** 10am–5pm Tue–Sun. **Closed** 25 Dec. 🅿 □ 🏛

⚏ Velorama National Bicycle Museum
Waalkade 107. **Tel** 024-3225851.
Open 10am–5pm Mon–Sat, 11am–5pm Sun. **Closed** 1 Jan, 25 Dec.

Environs
Close to Nijmegen is the Ooypolder, a beautiful, relaxing oasis for nature lovers. Here you can cycle and walk.

Ruins of the Valkhof in Nijmegen, one of the oldest towns in Holland

Nijmegen's Four Days Marches

In mid-July thousands of people from all around the Netherlands (and beyond) descend on the city to take part in the annual De Vierdaagse, the Four Days Marches. This is a series of hikes in and around Nijmegen, divided into daily legs of 30 km (20 miles) to 50 km (30 miles). The walks began in 1909 as a military exercise for soldiers, who marched from Nijmegen's garrison to Breda's, where they participated in a sports tournament. In that year, 309 soldiers completed the 150 km route. After a few years, civilians began to join in, until the march became a highlight of the national sporting calendar. In recent years, the number of participants has topped 45,000. Those who complete the walk receive a commemorative medal.

Walkers tackling the Four Days Marches

Beavers introduced to the Gelderse Poort now thrive

㉒ Gelderse Poort

Road Map D4. **ℹ** Arnhem
(0481-366250).

At the point where the Rhine
enters the Waal, the IJssel and
the Neder-Rijn (Lower Rhine) is
the Gelderse Poort. This is a
protected area where the flora
and fauna have been allowed
to grow freely. At the heart of
it is the Millingerwaard, where
the currents are particularly
strong and where, at high
water, the surrounding area
regularly floods. The river
banks, woodlands and marshes
provide ideal breeding grounds
for endangered species of
birds such as the corncrake
and the penduline tit.

Gelderse Poort Visitors' Centre
Gerard Noodtstraat 121. **Tel** 024-3297
070. **Open** Apr–Oct: 9am–5pm daily.

㉓ Groesbeek

Road Map D4. 19,000.
ℹ Dorpsplein 1a (024-3977118).

Its hilly woodland surroundings
make Groesbeek an attractive
place for cyclists and hikers. The
route of the four-day annual
hike (Vierdaagse) follows the
Zevenheuvelenweg from
Groesbeek to Berg en Dal, past
the Canadian war cemetery.
Groesbeek was subjected to
heavy bombardment at the
end of World War II. The
Bevrijdingsmuseum (liberation

museum) illustrates the
development of Operation
Market Garden (1944) and
Operation Veritable (1945),
which brought about the final
liberation of Holland. Groesbeek
has two other popular
museums: the **Bijbels
Openluchtmuseum** and the
Afrika Museum.

⋔ Bevrijdingsmuseum 1944
Wylerbaan 4. **Tel** 024-3974404. **Open**
10am–5pm Mon–Sat, noon–5pm Sun
& hols. **Closed** 25 Dec, 1 Jan.

㉔ Tiel

Road Map C4. 36,500.
ℹ Plein 63 (0344-633030). Mon
pm, Sat.

Tiel, situated on the Waal, is an
ancient town that flourished
during the Middle Ages
because of its strategic location
on the trading routes to and
from Cologne. One of the best-
preserved monuments from this
time is the **Ambtmanshuis**,
dating back to 1525. The town
also has the oldest elm tree in
the country. The local history
museum, **De Groote Sociëteit**
on the Plein, is worth a visit. Tiel
is the centre of fruit farming in
the Betuwe region. On the
second Saturday in September
of each year, it also becomes
the centre of the **Fruitcorso** (see
p38), as a procession of floats

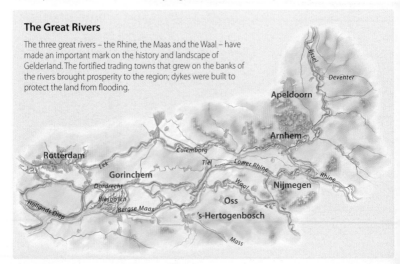

The Great Rivers

The three great rivers – the Rhine, the Maas and the Waal – have
made an important mark on the history and landscape of
Gelderland. The fortified trading towns that grew on the banks of
the rivers brought prosperity to the region; dykes were built to
protect the land from flooding.

Dyke house on the Linge

decorated with fruit winds through the streets of the town. Tiel is also renowned for its tinsmith industry.

Environs
Asperen is a peaceful little town on the River Linge. On the Lingedijk is **Fort Asperen**, which is part of the Nieuwe Hollandse Waterlinie. Farther upstream is the little town of **Acquoy**, with its crooked 15th-century tower. A Lady Pisa is buried in the churchyard, but there is no connection to the Leaning Tower in Italy.

㉕ Culemborg

Road Map C4. 24,000. Camping de Hogekuil, Achterweg 4 (0345-515701). Tue.

The old "Driestadje" (triple town) of Culemborg, formerly consisting of three walled towns, is picturesquely situated on the River Lek. It is a great place to wander around. If you enter the former fortress through the old Binnenpoort gate, you'll reach the Markt. Here is the Late Gothic Stadhuis (town hall), built by Flemish masterbuilder Rombout Keldermans for Vrouwe Elisabeth van Culemborg (1475–1555). Her estate was sufficient to finance the **Elisabeth Weeshuis** (1560), which is now operated as a historical museum.

Other well-preserved buildings in Culemborg are the Huize de Fonteyn in the Achterstraat and the house where Jan van Riebeeck, who founded Cape Town, South Africa, was born. The large

clock in the Grote Kerk was a gift from South Africa. Even today, the "papklok" bell, which is used to announce the closing of the town gates, is tolled each and every evening at 10 o'clock.

🏛 Museum Elisabeth Weeshuis
Herenstraat 29. **Tel** 0345-513912. **Open** Apr–Oct: 1–5pm Tue–Fri, 2–5pm Sat & Sun.

㉖ Buren

Road Map C4. 1,800. Markt 1 (0344-571922). Fri.

On the main road between Tiel and Culemborg is Buren. This little town is known for its historic links with the House of Orange, and the entire town has been listed. One of the most beautiful houses is the **Koninklijk Weeshuis** (Royal Orphanage), which was built in 1613 by Maria of Orange. The Late Gothic **Lambertuskerk** is also worth seeing.

㉗ Zaltbommel

Road Map C4. 11,000. Markt 15 (0418-518177). Tue, Sat.

Bommel, as its inhabitants say, is more than 1,000 years old. During the 80 Years War (see p53), it was an important mainstay of the Republiek der Zeven Verenigde Nederlanden (Republic of the Seven United Netherlands). The town is surrounded by two well-preserved sets of walls, which have now been laid out as a park. Within the town walls, the first building worth mentioning is the 15th-century **St Maartenskerk**, whose low towers give the town its distinctive skyline. The interior of the church is worth a look.

Another worthwhile stop is at the house of the Gelderland commander-in-chief **Maarten van Rossum** (1478–1555), who is known for plundering The Hague in 1528. The house is now an intimate museum with a large collection of drawings and prints from the region; it also hosts visiting exhibitions.

🏛 Maarten van Rossummuseum
Nonnenstraat 5. **Tel** 0418-512617. **Open** Apr–Oct: 10am–5pm Tue–Sun.

The house of Maarten van Rossum in Nonnenstraat, Zaltbommel

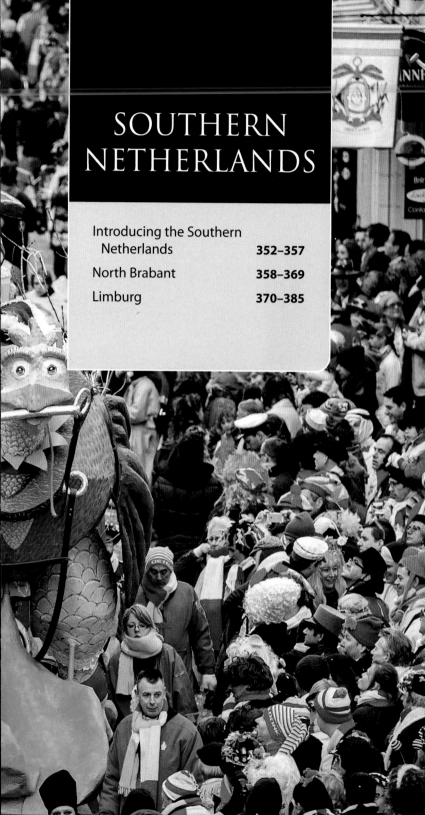

SOUTHERN NETHERLANDS

Southern Netherlands at a Glance

South of Holland's great rivers lie the provinces of North Brabant and Limburg, where industry and countryside coexist in harmony, though the coal fields are long gone. As with the rest of the Netherlands, eating and drinking well are held in high regard here. Visitors to the Southern Netherlands will also find cities with historical centres, such as Den Bosch, Breda, Thorn and Maastricht; the beautiful countryside of Kempen, Peel and the hills of Zuid Limburg; thriving modern towns; and peaceful rural villages.

The Gothic Church of Sint Jan *(see pp364–65)* in Den Bosch was started in the late 14th century and completed in the 1500s.

Heusden

Oosterhout

's-Hertogenbos

Breda

Tilburg

Box

Roosendaal

NORTH BRABA
(See pp358–69)

Bergen op Zoom

Zundert

The construction of the Grote or Onze Lieve Vrouwe-kerk (Church of Our Lady) *(see p366–7)* in Breda began in 1410. The church, which is finished in the Brabant Gothic style, has a 97-m (318-ft) tower, offering a stunning view over the town and the surrounding countryside.

0 kilometres   20

0 miles   20

The Van Abbemuseum *(see p368)* in Eindhoven has undergone extensive renovation. Architect Abel Cahen has preserved the old builing while creating light-filled spaces in the angular, slanting new wing. A large collection of modern art, including video and other installations, is on display.

◀ Revellers take part in carnival celebrations in Den Bosch, North Brabant

The Kasteeltuinen, the gardens of the 17th-century Castle Arcen (*see p374*), in the town of the same name on the River Maas, have a lovely rose garden, as well as subtropical gardens, a forest of Scots pines and a golf course.

The Bonnefantenmuseum (*see pp378–9*) in Maastricht is housed in a striking building designed by the Italian architect Aldo Rossi. The collections of old works of art and contemporary international art are impressive.

Oss

Gennep

Uden

Venray

uenen   Helmond

Eindhoven

Valkenswaard

Venlo

Tegelen

Weert

LIMBURG
(See pp370–85)

The Van
Abbemuseum

Roermond

Maasbracht

Sittard

Geleen

Heerlen

Maastricht

Eijsden

The route through the Heuvelland (*see pp384–85*) passes among hills and dales and by meandering rivers, their banks dotted with old castles. Outstanding examples of these are the 17th-century Kasteel Eijsden and Kasteel Schaloen in Valkenburg.

Catholicism and Devotion

One of the main reasons for the differences between Holland's southern and northern provinces is the marked presence of Catholicism in the south, even in these secular times. Religious imagery is a common sight here. The churches in the Brabant Gothic or Neo-Gothic style are decorated flamboyantly and many host traditional processions throughout the year.

SANCTA MARIA ORA PRO NOBIS
MDCCCLIII   J.J. BOSTEN PASTOR

Religious images, usually of the Madonna and Child, are a common roadside sight in Limburg. This one is set into the façade of a house in Mechelen.

The Maria Magdalena Chapel (1695) in Gemert is also known as the Spijkerkapelleke ("nail chapel") because people made offerings of nails here in the hopes of having their skin disorders cured. Every 22 July, which is the day of Mary Magdalene, an open-air mass is held here.

Decorative carving

Candles abound around images of St Mary.

Detail from the retable of the Holy Family in the Basilica of the Holy Sacrament in Meerssen, Limburg. It depicts Mary, Joseph and the infant Jesus fleeing to Egypt. This fine altar is richly decorated with scenes from the life of the Holy Family. The Holy Sacrament is honoured in the church. The host is kept in the Unique Sacramentstoren (sacrament tower) in the choir. The church itself is an example of Maasland Gothic and part of it (the nave and the choir) dates from as far back as the 14th century.

This tomb in the Late Romanesque/Early Gothic Onze-Lieve-Vrouwemunsterkerk (Minster Church of Our Lady) in Roermond dates from the 13th century. Inside the tomb lies Count Gerard van Gelre and his wife Margaretha van Brabant. At the time, Roermond was part of the duchy of Gelre.

St Anna-te-Drieën – the trinity of Anna, her daughter Mary and the infant Jesus – is a familiar image in religious art. This statue from Mechelen incorporates the town's coat of arms.

The Basiliek van de HH Agatha en Barbara (Basilica of SS Agatha and Barbara) in Oudenbosch is a copy of St Peter and St John of the Laterans in Rome. The picture on the right shows the façade. The interior of the church is richly decorated, though appearances are deceptive: what appears to be marble is actually painted wood.

Statue of St Mary in the Onder de Linden Chapel in Thorn (Limburg).

Onder De Linden Chapel in Thorn

The Onder de Linden Chapel, located just outside the town of Thorn in Limburg, was founded in 1673 by Clara Elisabeth van Manderscheidt-Blankenheim, who lies buried in the parish church of Thorn. This chapel, dedicated to St Mary, is opulently decorated with carvings and Baroque paintings depicting scenes of the life of the Virgin Mary. Shown in the picture on the left is the Onze-Lieve-Vrouwebeeld (statue of Our Lady). St Mary's Chapel is also called the Loretokapel, after the Holy House of Nazareth in the Italian town of Loreto, on which the earlier 17th-century part of the chapel is based.

The 15th-century tower of the Michielskerk is all that remains of the North Brabant Sint-Michielsgestel. The medieval church was built in honour of the archangel Michael. The village, also named after the saint, grew up around the church. Neglect and the elements have meant that the church building itself has been levelled to the ground, but the solid tower has withstood the ages.

The church of Rolduc, a former canon's abbey at Kerkrade which today houses a Catholic middle school and a training school for priests, has a fine altar depicting the Lamb of God. The Lamb of God represents Christ, who was sacrificed in the same way as a lamb, in order to take away the sins of the world.

Carnival

Every year in February, in the week before Ash Wednesday, carnival breaks out in the towns south of the great rivers. While life goes on as usual in the north of the country, people in the south celebrate this old tradition, which is also honoured in other parts of the Catholic world. A festive mood abounds everywhere, with the best-known celebrations being held in Den Bosch, Bergen op Zoom and Maastricht. For days on end, there is drinking, singing and dancing all over Brabant and Limburg.

Carnavalsstokken (carnival rods) are brightly decorated. They are carried by the Prince of the Carnival when he passes through the streets on his float.

Music plays an important role at carnival time. Every year, the associations choose the official carnival anthem that will be played over and over again. The Zaate Herremienekes of Maastricht (pictured left) are among the better-known bands. Dozens of its members march through the streets blaring out enthusiastically; what their music may lack in elegance is made up for by their verve. On Shrove Tuesday they compete in the Herremienekes competition.

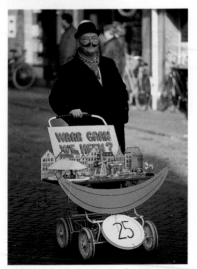

Although in high spirits, his question is profound (the sign on the pram reads, "Where are we going?")

Carnival – Putting Your Worries Aside

The carnival season officially starts on 11 November – the eleventh of the eleventh – or "day of fools", when the Council of Eleven names the Prince of the Carnival. From then on, the municipalities are busy with preparations, and on the Sunday (in many places now on the Friday) before Ash Wednesday, the festivities begin. Wild celebrations are held throughout North Brabant and Limburg, and most public institutions are closed. Long processions with floats parade through the towns. People dress up festively: the more colourful and exuberant the costume, the better. "Dansmarietjes" (dancing girls) accompany the floats in their colourful costumes, and the mood everywhere is upbeat. All the merriment comes to an end after Shrove Tuesday, the climax of the carnival.

Refreshments both indoors and outdoors at carnival time

Carnival Floats

At carnival time, long processions with extravagantly decorated floats wind their way through the main streets of towns and villages. Months of preparation often go into creating the floats, and secrecy prevails during their preparation. The decoration of the float is usually on an upbeat and amusing theme, but current events are sometimes illustrated in imaginative ways. When leading politicians are featured, they are more often than not caricatured mercilessly, and social ills are exposed, often using costumed participants in *tableaux vivants*.

A festive float

The Raad van Elf (Council of Eleven) is the central office of the local carnival organization. Every year, the council appoints a Prince of the Carnival, who holds power in a municipality on the days of the carnival. The council's ritual number is 11, which is considered the number of fools. From 11 November onwards, the Raad van Elf is busy preparing carnival events. At the lively meetings, many a beer is drunk to a call of "Alaaf!" ("Eleven!").

Prince Carnival's adjutant

Characteristic carnival cap with feather

Prince Carnival

Colourful fool

Silly clothes are mandatory at carnival time. In earlier times it was customary to put on masks, whereas today the trend is to dress up in as unusual a way as possible. The northerners' belief that it is enough to put on a peasant's smock to be properly dressed is a misconception.

NORTH BRABANT

The Netherland's second-largest province is distinguished primarily by its natural beauty. In the south and southeast are the relatively high elevations of Kempen and the Peel; in the northwest, the watery Biesbosch. Here, arms of the Waal and Maas rivers converge through a wilderness of sandbanks.

North Brabant has been inhabited by humans since the earliest times. The Celts settled here in the 7th century BC and stayed for many centuries. They were defeated by Julius Caesar *(see pp46–7)*, who describes them as the "Belgae" in his writings. The Rhine became the northern frontier of the Roman Empire and Roman remains have been found in the area. When the Romans left, the Franks took charge of Toxandria, as the region was known in those days. Under Charlemagne *(see p48)*, this region grew in importance as new towns expanded at points along trade routes, and in the 12th century became part of the Duchy of Brabant. The Dukes of Brabant, among them Godfried III and Henry I, expanded their territory

and founded towns such as Breda and 's-Hertogenbosch. The Duchy flourished until the 16th century, when the 80 Years War left the south of Brabant under Spanish rule and the north under the rule of the Netherlands.

Although North Brabant has its fair share of commerce and industry, and Eindhoven is a major manufacturing centre, tourism has become increasingly important. The region's colourful history is evident from the medieval buildings and bastions in many of the towns, and the castles dotted around the countryside, with a range of fine exhibits in churches and museums. For younger visitors the highlight is the fairytale theme park De Efteling at Kaatsheuvel, northeast of Breda.

Het Grote Peel, an area of outstanding natural beauty in North Brabant

◀ The beautiful ceiling of the basilica in Oudenbosch

Exploring North Brabant

North Brabant's rich historic past and unspoiled
countryside have given the province its unique
character. The centres of 's-Hertogenbosch and Breda
and the picturesque fortified towns of Heusden and
Willemstad are of great historical interest. The beautiful
natural areas of the Loonse and Drunense dunes, Peel,
Kempen and Biesbosch areas provide opportunities
for various tours. Van Abbemuseum in Eindhoven, De
Wieber in Deurne and the many other museums in the
region offer a great deal of cultural interest. De Efteling
is one of Europe's best-known theme parks.

The Markiezenhof in Bergen op Zoom,
dating from 1511

Sights at a Glance

1. 's-Hertogenbosch pp362–6
2. Heusden
3. Tilburg
4. Breda
5. Oudenbosch
6. Willemstad
7. Bergen op Zoom
8. Eindhoven
9. Heeze
10. Nuene
11. Helmond
12. Deurne
13. Gemert

Drifting sands and conifers in the Loonse and the
Drunense dunes, east of Kaatsheuvel

Key

— Motorway
— Major road
⋯ Minor road
— Scenic route
⋯ Main railway
— Minor railway
— Regional border
— International border

For map symbols *see back flap*

Getting Around

North Brabant has an excellent transport infrastructure. All the larger towns, as well as many smaller towns and villages, can be reached easily by train. There is an extensive network of long-distance buses, which will take you to even the smallest village. The province can be explored by car with great ease thanks to its dense motorway network, which includes the A2 and the A58, as well as its many good major roads. Areas of natural beauty, such as the Peel and Kempen, are ideal countryside for cycling.

The 14th-century Kasteel Heeswijk, rebuilt numerous times during its lifetime

Sheep on the Strabrechtse Heide, near Heeze

For hotels and restaurants in this region see p401 and pp414–15

❶ Street-by-Street: 's-Hertogenbosch

In 1185, Henry I of Brabant founded the town of 's-Hertogenbosch. The strategically positioned town – usually called Den Bosch – grew rapidly. From the 16th century, however, its prosperity waned, when the States General ignored Brabant and chose to favour other regions. Its prestige rose again after 1815, when it became the capital of North Brabant. Today, it is a vibrant, lively town.

Stone Plaque with Swan
Such plaques are a common sight in the city centre.

De Moriaan
The medieval building known as De Moriaan, with its stepped gable, is the town's oldest building. It now houses the town's tourist office.

0 metres 100
0 yards 100

★ Binnen-Dieze
The Binnen-Dieze, the city's inner canal, runs partly underground. It is possible to make a spectacular round trip along the restored town walls.

★ Sint Jan
The flying buttresses of the Sint Jan Church (see pp364–5) are decorated with a variety of figures.

Statue of Jeroen (Hieronymus) Bosch The painter Jeroen Bosch (c.1450/1460–1516), is the city's most renowned figure.

Medieval Well Restored to its former glory, this well is located in the Markt.

HINTHAMERSTRAAT

MARKT

KERKSTRAAT

KOLPERSTRAAT

RIDDERSTRAAT

FONTEINSTRAAT

ER HET STADHUIS

VERWERSSTRAAT

WATERSTRAAT

Stadhuis
The Neo-Classical town hall, built in 1670, stands in the Markt. The figures of horsemen beneath the tympanum spring to action twice every hour.

Zwanenbroedershuis
The Zwanen brothers (14th century) did much charity work but are best known as gourmands. Their house is now a museum.

Noordbrabants Museum
The North Brabant museum is housed in the monumental former government building.

Key

— Recommended route

Sint Jan

There was a church of Sint Jan (St John) in Den Bosch as early as the beginning of the 13th century, although nothing of the original Romanesque church exists today. The present-day Gothic church was built from the late 14th to the 16th century. The majestic cathedral survived the Iconoclastic Riots of 1566 *(see p56)* and a devastating fire in 1584. The damaged building is undergoing continuous restoration.

★ Organ
The great organ (1617) was fully refurbished in 1985 and restored to its original state.

Statue of St Mary
The 13th-century miracle-working figure of the Zoete Lieve Vrouw of Den Bosch (Our Good Lady of Den Bosch) was for centuries kept in Brussels, but was returned to Sint Jan in 1853.

KEY

① **The ornamental south portal** is dedicated to Saint John the Evangelist.

② **Flying buttresses** are designed to strengthen the structure of the building. They are richly ornamented with saints, angels and other figures.

③ **The gargoyles** are designed to channel rainwater pouring off the roof. Here, the drain pipes are encased by the head of mythical animals.

④ **The stained-glass window frame** depicts the woman and the dragon from *The Book of Revelation*.

⑤ **The seven radiating chapels** around the choir form an elegant crown.

Baptistery
The baptismal font in the baptistery dates from 1492. The figures on the cover depict the baptism of Jesus by St John.

Baldachin
The revolving baldachin in the middle of the cathedral is ascribed to Alart Duhameel. The all-seeing eye looks down from the vaults.

Antoniuskapel
The Chapel of St Anthony contains a spectacular Passion altar made by a studio in Antwerp. The Church of Sint Jan managed to buy the retable in 1901 for one guilder.

★ Stained-Glass Windows
The Church of Sint Jan was restored in Neo-Gothic style during the 19th century. A great deal was changed, including the lively and colourful stained-glass windows.

★ Sanctuary
The sanctuary was built from 1380 to 1425 by Willem van Kessel. The vaults are painted with a variety of religious scenes, among them the coronation of St Mary.

Exploring 's-Hertogenbosch

Along with a large number of historical buildings and interesting museums, the town of 's-Hertogenbosch offers a wide choice of fine restaurants. The excellent Noordbrabants Museum has an excellent exhibition of art from the Southern Netherlands from 1500 to the present. The most striking building in 's-Hertogenbosch is the majestic Gothic church of Sint Jan. The historic district of Uilenburg offers ample opportunities to while away the time with a drink or a bite to eat in a café.

Four putti (1731) by Walter Pompe, Noordbrabants Museum

The splendid church of Sint Jan (*see pp364–5*) is Den Bosch's crowning glory. In the Markt stand historical buildings such as **De Moriaan** (parts of which date back to the 12th century) and the town hall, dating from 1670. A statue of the great painter Hieronymus Bosch (c.1453–1516) stands between the two grand buildings. Born in 's-Hertogenbosch, Bosch spent most of his life here. In the town's historical district of Uilenburg, beyond the Markt, are plenty of good cafés and restaurants. The **Binnen-Dieze**, the city's inner canal, surfaces at this point; houses here stand directly in its water. Right by Sint Jan is the majestic **Zwanenbroedershuis** (*see p363*), as well as the Museum Slager, which showcases paintings by the Slager family.

🏛 Noordbrabants Museum
Verwersstraat 41. **Tel** 073-6877877.
Open 11am–5pm Tue–Sun.
Closed 1 Jan, 25 Dec. 🖼 ♿ 🖵
The excellent Noordbrabants Museum displays art by renowned artists such as Pieter Brueghel and Teniers, as well as modern artists such as Van Gogh, Mondriaan and Sluyters. The museum also features exhibits on the history of the province of North Brabant, from prehistoric times to the present.

❷ Heusden

Road Map C4. 🏔 43,000. 🚌 🛈
Pelsestraat 17 (0416-662100). 🏪 Thu.

After a thorough refurbishment that started in 1968 and lasted for decades, the picturesque ancient fortified town of Heusden on the River Maas has been restored to its former glory. That Heusden fell victim to the redevelopment craze of the 1960s matters little. Walls, houses, moats, the **Veerpoort** (ferry gate) and the **Waterpoort** have all been restored in the old style. As advertising is banned in Heusden, it is easy to imagine that time has stood still here, save for the fact that motor vehicles are allowed into the fortress.

❸ Tilburg

Road Map C5. 🏔 213,000. 🚗 🚌
🛈 Nieuwlandstraat 34 (0900-2020815). 🏪 Tue–Sat.

Tilburg, the sixth-largest town in Holland, once had a flourishing textile industry. The interesting **Nederlands Textielmuseum**, which is housed in a former textile mill, illustrates the history of the country's textile industry and explains how textiles were produced. The **kermis van Tilburg** (Tilburg fair), held each year at the end of July, is the biggest fair in Holland. The entire town puts all its energy into the event, and people come from far and near to attend.

🏛 Nederlands Textielmuseum
Goirkestraat 96. **Tel** 013-5367475.
Open 10am–5pm Tue–Fri, noon–5pm Sat & Sun. **Closed** most public hols.
🖼 ♿ 🖵 by appointment.
🖵 🖼 📷

Environs
Kaatsheuvel is home to **De Efteling**, the famous theme park where all kinds of fairytale personalities come to life (*see p427*).

❹ Breda

Road Map B5. 🏔 182,100. 🚗 🚌
🛈 Willemstraat 17–19 (0900-5222444). 🏪 Tue & Fri am, Sat.

The Old Bastion of Breda was built at the confluence of the rivers Aa and Mark around the **Kasteel van Breda**, where the Koninklijke Militaire Academie (royal military academy) is now established. Breda was granted its town charter in 1252.

A walk through the old centre will take you to the **Grote Kerk**, also known as the Onze Lieve Vrouwe Kerk (Church of Our

Mills on the bastion of the old fortified town of Heusden

Lady). It is prominent on the Grote Markt and cannot be missed. Construction of this magnificent Brabant Gothic-style church began in 1410; in 1995–8 it underwent restoration.

At the Spanjaardsgat water-gate, near the castle, legend has it that in the 16th century, during the 80 Years War of independence from Spain, Adriaen van Bergen tricked his way past the Spanish with a peat barge full of soldiers and liberated the town.

Breda's Museum is housed in the old barracks of the Chassékazerne. The museum displays interesting exhibits that illustrate local history.

🏛 **Breda's Museum**
Parade 12–14. **Tel** 076-5299300. **Open** 10am–5pm Tue–Sun. 🔲 🔲 🔲

❺ Oudenbosch

Road Map B5. 🔼 13,000 (municipality of Halderberge).
🔲 🔲 🛈 Parklaan 15 (0165-390555).
🔲 Tue pm.

Between 1860 and 1870, Oudenbosch was the point from which the Zouaves set out on their journey to Rome to defend the pope against Garibaldi. Upon their return, they had the architect PJH Cuypers (*see p375*) build a miniature replica of St Peter's basilica in Rome, the **Basiliek van de HH Agatha en Barbara** (Basilica of SS Agatha and Barbara).

❻ Willemstad

Road Map B4. 🔼 2,300.
🔲 🛈 Lantern Dijk 12. 🔲 Mon.

The Bastions of Willemstad were built in 1583 by William of Orange. The Mauritshuis (1623), the former hunting lodge of Maurice, Prince of Orange, is today a museum. The influence of the Oranges can also been seen in the white Oranjemolen mill (1734). There is a pleasant harbour and a tree-lined "Wedding Walk", which leads to a domed church, the Koepelkerk.

The basilica of Oudenbosch, a miniature copy of St Peter's in Rome

❼ Bergen op Zoom

Road Map B5. 🔼 66,200. 🔲 🔲
🛈 Korte Meesstraat 19 (0164-277482). 🔲 Thu.

The old town of Bergen op Zoom grew around a chapel that was dedicated to St Gertrude. In 1260, Bergen op Zoom was granted its town charter, after which it enjoyed a period of prosperity. The 15th-century **St Geertruids-kerk**, with its striking tower, stands on the site of the original chapel. The lords of Bergen op Zoom built the **Markiezenhof**, which was finally completed in 1511. The castle is today a museum, with period rooms and an unusual collection of fairground items. There are also changing exhibitions, which vary from cultural history to modern art.

🏛 **Markiezenhof**
Steenbergsestraat 8. **Tel** 0164-277077.
Open 11am–5pm Tue–Sun.
🔲 🔲 🔲

The Surrender of Breda

During the 80 Years War, Breda was kept under siege by Spain for ten months, before finally surrendering to Ambrosio Spinola's troops on 5th June 1625. The moment of capitulation is captured in Velázquez's painting, known as both *The Surrender of Breda* and *Las Lanzas* – the lances – after the line of weapons that dominate the background. Velázquez, the great court painter of King Philip IV, is said to have painted the scene from memory. His picture shows the moment when the commander of the Dutch troops, on the left of the picture in a supplicating position, hands the key of the Dutch fortress to a straight-backed Spinola. The painting is famous for its composition, with the canvas divided into two balanced parts: left and right contain a group of soldiers and a horse, while the fore- and background are split into human activity and the smouldering city behind. The work is also noted for the lively way it portrays the men, several of whom look the viewer directly in the eye. The painting now hangs in Madrid's Museo del Prado.

The Surrender of Breda by Velázquez

Woman in Green (1909) by Picasso, Van Abbemuseum (Eindhoven)

❽ Eindhoven

Road Map C5. 🏛 224,800. 🚉 🚌
ℹ Stationsplein 17 (040-2979115).
🎪 Tue, Wed, Sat & Sun.

The old market town of Eindhoven was merged with the villages of Strijp, Woensel, Tongelre, Stratum and Gestel in the 19th century. The municipality of Eindhoven grew enormously in the last century when Philips, the electronics company, sited its factory there. Philips's best-known building, the distinctive **Witte Dame** (White Lady) was built in 1922 by architect Dirk Rozenberg; it has now been sold and converted into a design college, library and centre for artists. The former Philips area in Strijp is also being developed into a residential area with shops, restaurants and theatres.

The city centre was heavily bombed in World War II and as a result very few old buildings have survived. In their place

are a clutch of striking modern buildings, including the Stadhuis, an imposing structure, surrounded by a large empty space, the Stadhuis Plein, and the more appealing train station with its slender tower and glassy frontage.

The **Philips Museum**, in the city centre, holds a fascinating collection of electrical objects dating back to the earliest days of the company. On display are dozens of the very first light bulbs dating from the 19th century, beautiful bakelite radios and hulking cabinets from the birth of broadcasting. Visitors can learn about the history of light-bulb making, from hand-made to mass-produced, and how the light bulb transformed Eindhoven from a small town into an industrial giant.

A rather more surprising find in the centre of this industrial city is the **Eindhoven Museum**. This open-air museum in the middle of the Genneper Park contains reconstructions of an Iron Age village, a Viking settlement and a medieval town. Actors in costume people the scene, and are on hand to answer questions. There's also a restaurant where visitors can eat meals based on ancient recipes, like grain stew and lentil pâté.

Looming over the railway station is the space-age **Philips Stadion**, home of the PSV Eindhoven football team. The stadium, although ultra-modern these days, still stands on the spot where the first pitch

was laid out for the team in 1913. Guided tours allow visitors to enter the players' changing rooms and to walk down the tunnel onto the pitch.

Eindhoven's most important sight, however, is the **Van Abbemuseum**, which is

Eindhoven Museum, one of the town's main attractions

devoted to modern art. The original building was designed in 1936 by AJ Kropholler and has been described as a "brick castle". In the 1990s, architect Abel Cahen was commissioned to expand the museum. Cleverly integrating the existing building into a large new wing, he quadrupled the exhibition space and added a restaurant and multimedia centre. Queen Beatrix opened the museum in January 2003. The collection contains works by Chagall, Lissitzky and Beuys, and is particularly known for Picasso's *Woman in Green* (1909).

🏛 **Philips Museum**
Emmasingel 31. **Tel** 040-2359030.
Open 11am–5pm Tue–Sun.

🏛 **Eindhoven Museum**
Boutenslaan 161b. **Tel** 040-2522281.
Open Apr–Oct: 11am–5pm Tue–Sun.

🏛 **Philips Stadion**
Frederiklaan 10a. **Tel** 040-2505505.
🎫 booking essential.

🏛 **Van Abbemuseum**
Bilderdijklaan 10. **Tel** 040-2381000.
Open 11am–5pm Tue–Sun. 🎪 ♿
📷 Ⓦ vanabbemuseum.nl

Philips Stadion, home to the football team PSV Eindhoven

❾ Heeze

Road Map C5. ⚹ 15,700. 🚌 🚆
ℹ Schoolstraat 2 (040-2260644).
🏠 Thu am.

The 17th-century castle of
Kasteel Heeze is the centrepiece
of this small Brabant town, just
outside Eindhoven. Designed by
Pieter Post, it stands amid lovely
streams, woods and meadows.
Among the many exhibits set out
in the castle's 30 halls are valuable
Gobelin tapestries.

🏠 **Kasteel Heeze**
Kapelstraat 25. **Tel** 040-2261431.
Open May–Sep. 🅿 🔲 May–Sep:
2pm Wed, 2 & 3pm Sun (Jul & Aug:
also 2pm Wed).

❿ Nuenen

Road Map C5. ⚹ 22,700. 🚆 ℹ
Berg 29 (040-2839615). 🏠 Mon pm.

Nuenen, northeast of Eindhoven,
is the village where Van Gogh
lived from 1883 to 1885. The
Vincentre in Van Gogh Village
deals comprehensively with his
time in Nuenen.

The magnificent 17th-century
Kasteel Heeze

The vast Strabrechtse Heide at Heeze and Geldrop

🏛 **Vincentre**
Berg 29. **Tel** 040-2839615.
Open 10am–5pm Tue–Sun (Mon in
summer only). 🅿 some public hols.

⓫ Helmond

Road Map C5. ⚹ 90,100. 🚌 🚆
ℹ Watermolenwal 11 (0492-522220).
🏠 Wed am, Sat am.

The most outstanding feature
of Helmond is the castle
dating from 1402, today the
Gemeentemuseum (local
history museum). The museum
has many historical artifacts and
a fine collection of modern art,
including works by Breitner and
Charley Toorop.

🏛 **Gemeentemuseum**
Kasteelplein 1. **Tel** 0492-845980.
Open 10am–5pm Tue–Fri, noon–5pm
Sat & Sun. 🅿 ♿ 🔲 🖥

⓬ Deurne

Road Map D5. ⚹ 32,000. 🚌 🚆
ℹ Markt 14 (0493-323655). 🏠 Fri pm.

The relaxing town of Deurne
is an artistic centre. The house
(1922) of the extravagant
doctor and painter Henrik
Wiedersma, who used to make
house calls on his motorcycle,
is now a **museum** of
expressionist works by the
doctor and his avant-garde
friends, including Ossip Zadkine,
who often stayed with him.
Poets such as Roland Holst,
Nijhoff and Bloem were also
regular visitors to the house.

🏛 **Museum De Wieger**
Oude Liesselseweg 29. **Tel** 0493-322930.
Open noon–5pm Wed–Sun. **Closed**
Mon, Tue & most public hols. 🅿 🖥

⓭ Gemert

Road Map C5. ⚹ 27,300 (community
of Gemert-Bakel). 🚆 ℹ Ridderplein
49 (0492-366606). 🏠 Mon pm.

Gemert is a town of historical
importance; its nickname was
once "Heerlijkheid Gemert"
("glorious Gemert"). Until 1794
it was ruled by the Knights of
the Teutonic Order: their **castle**
still stands and is now used
as a monastery.
The **Boerenbondmuseum**
(agricultural museum) is in a
farmhouse dating from the
beginning of the 20th century;
the displays portray what rural
life was like at that time.

Van Gogh in Brabant

Vincent van Gogh was born in 1853
in Zundert, south of Breda. There, in the
Cultureel Centrum, you can learn about
his childhood. In 1883, he moved to
Nuenen, where his father was rector.
He stayed there until 1885, when he
moved on to Antwerp. The Nuenen
period was very prolific for Van Gogh.
Rural life in Brabant inspired him, and he
painted farms, labourers and weavers in
the blue and brown tones that are so
characteristic of his Nuenen work.
A famous painting dating from this
period is *The Potato Eaters* (1885).

Statue of Van Gogh in Nuenen

LIMBURG

Limburg is the Netherlands' southernmost province, squeezed by the course of history into its present unusual shape – its boundaries defined by Belgium to the south and to the west and by Germany to the east. Yet its outline is not the only remarkable thing about this delightful multilingual province.

From a geological point of view, Limburg is much older than the rest of Holland, sitting on coal deposits that are around 270 million years old. In the mining museum at Kerkrade, east of Maastricht, you can see how coal used to be mined in this region. The caves that can be seen in many places in South Limburg are also mines, albeit for the local limestone laid down between 60 and 70 million years ago. The best-known cave systems, parts of which date from the Roman era, are at Valkenburg and at St Pietersberg near Maastricht.

The Maas river valley has been attractive to settlers since the last Ice Age. There is evidence of early nomads, followed by the remains of successive sedentary societies such as the "Bandkeramikers" and the Beaker Folk (see p46). The Romans were here for around 400 years and Maastricht, which they founded, has much evidence of their impressive buildings. Heerlen was also an important Roman crossroads and the bathhouse museum here makes an excellent and informative visit. In the Middle Ages, Limburg was split up and fought over at various times by the German Empire, Gelder, Liège, Brabant and the Spanish. It acquired its present borders in the 19th century. Nowadays it has plenty to offer visitors, from historic towns with fine architecture, shops and nightlife to countryside dotted with half-timbered houses, farms, water mills in the rivers, and countless castles and country houses.

Half-timbered houses in the South Limburg town of Cottessen

◀ Statues on the estate of one of the castles in Valkenburg

Exploring Limburg

Noord Limburg is made up of the Peel and the Maas
regions. Between the River Maas and the German border
are nature reserves with fens, woodland, heathland and
river dunes. The former wilderness known as the
Peelgebied is on the border with North Brabant. Middle
Limburg is the section from the Maasplassen lakes,
which were created by the digging of gravel pits. It is
now one of the most important watersports areas in the
country. Zuid Limburg consists of Maastricht, the
Mijnstreek (mining country) and the pretty chalk-hill
landscape to the south.

Picking asparagus in Noord Limburg

National park of De Grote Peel

Getting Around

Limburg is easily reached by rail and by road,
which are also the best ways to explore it. The
motorways and railways invariably follow the
same routes, that is to say: Nijmegen–Venlo–
Roermond–Geleen–Maastricht, Weert–
(Roermond)–Geleen–Maastricht and, finally, the
triangle Maastricht–Geleen–Heerlen. For cyclists
there are long sections of cycle paths along the
Julianakanaal and the Zuid-Willemsvaart. The
south of Zuid Limburg in particular is simply
ideal for cycling (including racing) and rambling.
The tourist railway or "environmental line" from
Schin near Geul to Kerkrade via Wijlre, Eys and
Simpelveld operates from April to October on
Sundays and most Wednesdays and Thursdays,
with two steam trains and a "rail-bus".

0 kilometres   10

0 miles   10

Limestone quarry with old passageways

For map symbols see back flap

MOOK

Meijel
*Nationaal
Park de
Grote Peel*

Nederweert

WEERT ⑤ 🏠

LIM

Stramproy

🏠

THORN ⑨

Maasbrach

Susteren

SITTARD ⑩

Stein

Geleen

ELSLOO ⑮

Beek

Nuth

Meerssen

VALKENBURG ⑬

MAASTRICHT ⑧

Wijl

GULPEN

HEUVELLA

EIJSDEN ⑯   ⑱

Sights at a Glance

1 Mook
2 Venray
3 Arcen
4 Venlo
5 Weert
6 Roermond
7 De Meinweg
8 *Maastricht pp376–81*
9 Thorn
10 Sittard
11 Hoensbroek
12 Heerlen
13 Valkenburg
14 Gulpen
15 Elsloo
16 Eijsden
17 Vaals

Tour

18 *Heuvelland pp384–5*

Field chapel in Heuvelland

Gennep

Nieuw-Bergen

Well

VENRAY

N270

ARCEN 3

Horst

N271

num

A67

Blerick

asbree

VENLO 4

anningen

Tegelen

Maas

A73

N273

Reuver

URG

Swalmen

6 **ROERMOND**

7

DE MEINWEG

Posterholt

Key

— Motorway
— Major road
⋯ Minor road
— Scenic route
⁓ Major railway
— Minor railway
▬ Regional border
▬ International border

runssum

SBROEK

Landgraaf

HEERLEN

Kerkrade

Simpelveld

A76

3

17 **VAALS**

Kasteel Schaloen at Valkenburg (13th century), rebuilt in the 17th century

For hotels and restaurants in this region see p401 and p415

❶ Mook

Road Map D4. 🖼 825. 🚍 83.
ℹ Witteweg 10, Plasmolen
(024-6961762).

The village of Mook is on the
River Maas in the very north
of Limburg. On 14 April 1574,
the Prince of Orange's army
was routed on the nearby
Mookerhei by the Spanish. The
star-shaped fortifications of the
Heumense Schans from the 80
Years War stand atop a 43-m
(141-ft) ridge from the Saalian
Ice Age. It offers a fantastic
vantage point from which to
view the Maas valley.

South of Mook is the recreation
area of the Mookerplas lake
and the fine estate of **Sint
Jansberg**, where the Bovenste
Plasmolen, an ancient watermill,
has been restored.

❷ Venray

Road Map D5. 🖼 43,000. 🚍 27, 29,
30, 39. ℹ Passage 4, Venray (0478-
510505). 🛒 Mon pm.

During World War II, Noord
Limburg was the scene of heavy
fighting. An English and a
German (at Ysselsteyn) military
cemetery lie near the town.
Nearby Overloon is home to the
Oorlogs-en Verzetsmuseum
(War and Resistance Museum).
In 1944, Venray was largely
destroyed. The 15th-century
basilica of **St Petrus Banden**,
with its magnificent interior,
was given a new 80-m (262-ft)
tower in restoration works. The
Geijsteren estate on the Maas,
where old Maas terraces are
visible in the terrain, is an
outstanding rambling area.

❸ Arcen

Road Map D5. 🖼 9,000. 🚍 83.
ℹ Klasstraat 17, Bookstore Koops
(077-3543800).

The main attraction of Arcen,
picturesquely located on the
Maas, is the finely restored
17th-century Arcen castle with its
Kasteeltuinen (castle gardens).
They incorporate a rose garden,
subtropical gardens, Eastern
gardens, a pine forest and a golf

course. You can also take the
waters at the **Thermaalbad
Arcen** spa; its mineral-rich water
is extracted from 900 m (2,955 ft)
underground. Other local delights
include special Arcen beer,
asparagus (with an asparagus
market on Ascension Day), and
the drink distilled by the Branderij
De IJsvogel, housed in the 17th-
century **Wijmarsche water mill**.
Outside Arcen is the **Nationaal
Park Landgoed de Hamert**.

❁ Kasteeltuinen
Lingsforterweg 26. **Tel** 077-4736010.
Open Apr–late Oct: 10am–6pm
daily. **Closed** rest of the year. 🐾

Exquisite gardens of the 17th-century
Arcen castle

The magnificent 16th-century Venlo town hall in the Markt

❹ Venlo

Road Map D5. 🖼 100,000. 🚍
ℹ Klasstraat 17, Bookstore Koops
(077-3543800). 🛒 Fri pm, Sat.

The combined city of Venlo/
Blerick began as a Roman
settlement. In the Middle Ages
it grew rich on trade. The
15th-century St Martinuskerk, a
Gothic hall-type church, and Ald
Weishoes, a Latin school built in
the Gelderland Renaissance style
dating from 1611, are among
the few historical buildings to
have survived World War II. The
town hall was designed between
1597 and 1600 by Willem van
Bommel. The local **Museum
Van Bommel-Van Dam** features
modern art; the **Limburgs
Museum**, archaeological finds.

▥ Museum Van Bommel-
Van Dam
Deken van Oppensingel 6. **Tel** 077-
3513457. **Open** 11am–5pm Tue–Sun.
Closed Mon, 1 Jan, Carnival, 25 Dec.

▥ Limburgs Museum
Keulsepoort 5. **Tel** 077-3522112.
Open 11am–5pm Tue–Sun.
Closed 1 Jan, Carnival, 25 Dec.
🖥 **limburgsmuseum.nl**

For hotels and restaurants in this region see p401 and p415

❺ Weert

Road Map C5. 🏔 49,000. 🚉
ℹ️ Markt 11 (0495-534211). 🛍 Sat.

The jewel of Weert is the
St Martinuskerk, one of the few
Late Gothic hall-type churches
in Holland (in hall-type churches,
the side aisles are equal in height
and width to the nave). When
restoration works were carried
out around 1975, paintings from
the 15th and 16th centuries
were discovered beneath the
layers of whitewash on the
vaulted ceilings. Before the high
altar (1790), by Italians Moretti
and Spinetti, lies the tomb of the
lord of Weert, beheaded in 1568
on the order of Alva in Brussels.
Not far from the church is the
Ursulinenhof, an example of a
new building successfully
integrated into a
historical centre.
    Surrounding areas
such as Weerterbos
forest and the
**Nationaal Park
De Grote Peel** are
remnants of a region
of peat moors.

Limburg asparagus

❻ Roermond

Road Map D5. 🏔 57,000.
🚉 ℹ️ Markt 17 (0475-335847).
🛍 Wed pm, Sat.

The oldest church in the see
of Roermond is the 13th-
century Late Romanesque,
Early Gothic **Onze-Lieve-
Vrouwemunsterkerk** (minster

Interior of the Onze-Lieve-Vrouwemunsterkerk in Roermond

church of Our Lady), which
was originally the church of a
Cistercian abbey. The interior of
the church is worth a visit. The
St Christoffelkathedraal, a
Gothic cruciform basilica
with a gilded statue of
St Christopher on the
tower, dates from the
early 15th century. The
church's stained-glass
windows are by the local
glazier Joep Nicolas.
    Roermond is by the
Maasplassen lakes, one of
the country's largest areas for
watersports. The lakes cover
more than 300 ha (740 acres)
and have a length of approximately 25 km (15 miles). The
Maasplassen were created
through large-scale gravel
quarrying in the Maas valley,
which went on as far as
Maaseik in Belgium.

❼ De Meinweg

Road Map D6. 🏔 none. 🚌 78, 79.
ℹ️ Beheerseenheid De Meinweg,
Bezoekerscentrum, Meinweg 2,
Herkenbosch (0475-528500).

The national park of De Meinweg
in the east of the province possesses a unique natural beauty.
Nine hiking routes have been
laid out here. You can also tour
the park by horse-drawn cart,
accompanied by expert guides.

Dr PJH Cuypers

Architect Pierre Cuypers was
born in Roermond in 1827. He
lived and worked both in his
hometown and in Amsterdam.
One of Cuypers' sons and one
of his nephews also became
renowned architects.
Considered one of the prime
representatives of the
Netherlands Neo-Gothic,
Cuypers designed the Central
Station and the Rijksmuseum
in Amsterdam, and De Haar
castle in Haarzuilens. He was
also the architect and restorer
of countless churches,
including the *munsterkerk*
(minster church) in Roermond.

Munsterkerk in Roermond

The 1,600-ha (3,955-acre) De Meinweg national park

❽ Street-by-Street: Maastricht

Maastricht emerged in Roman times at a point along the River Maas which could be crossed on foot (Mosae Traiectum), on the Roman road that led from Colonia Agrippina (Cologne) to Bononia (Boulogne). The founder of Christian Maastricht was St Serviatus, bishop of Tongeren, who died in AD 384 in Maastricht and was buried in the cemetery then located outside the town walls. The magnificent basilica of St Servaas was built over his tomb. In addition to the basilica, another fine church is the Romanesque Onze-Lieve-Vrouwebasiliek.

Sculpture of Pieke
This sculpture in Stokstraat is of Pieke and his dog, from a book by Ber Hollewijn.

The Generaalshuis
Now the Theater aan het Vrijthof, this Neo-Classical palace was built in 1809. General Dibbets, who succeeded in keeping Maastricht part of the Netherlands, lived here around 1830.

Key

— Recommended route

```
0 metres        100
0 yards         100
```

GROTE GRACHT

HELMSTRAAT

STATENSTRAAT

VRIJTHOF

In den Ouden Vogelstruys
One of the many street cafés flanking the Vrijthof, this lively, popular spot serves a small selection of meals.

★ Cemetery
Now one of the city's main squares, the cemetery was located outside the town walls when the construction of St Servaas began.

★ Stadhuis

The town hall on the Markt was built in 1559–1664 and is a masterpiece by Pieter Post of the Northern Netherlands. The lobby is open to visitors.

VISITORS' CHECKLIST

Practical Information
Road Map C6. 122,500.
Kleine Staat 1 (043-3252121).
Mon–Sat. Amstel Gold Race (cycling classic): Apr; Vrijthof Fair; St Servaas procession: May; Preuvenemint culinary festival: end of Aug.

Transport
Stationsplein.
Stationsplein.

St Servaasbrug
This bridge is a solid yet elegant structure of seven semicircular arches dating from 1280. Ships can reach the Wyck side through a modern section.

★ Onze-Lieve-Vrouwebasiliek
In one of the chapels of this Romanesque cruciform basilica is the votive statue of Our Lady "Sterre der Zee".

The Wall Lizard
This animal can be seen in parts of Maastricht, the only Dutch town it occurs in.

Bonnefantenmuseum

The Bonnefantenmuseum is one of Maastricht's most prominent landmarks, situated on the right bank of the Maas in a distinctive building designed by the Italian architect Aldo Rossi. The museum's exhibits include old masters, painting and sculpture from the medieval period to 1650, and a celebrated international collection of modern art.

★ Cupola by Aldo Rossi
The tower houses a restaurant and an exhibition hall.

La Natura è l'Arte del Numero
This installation, designed by Mario Merz, consists of tables covered with glass, branches, stones, vegetables and numbers fashioned out of fluorescent tubes.

Cimon and Pero
Peter Paul Rubens (1577–1640) depicted Pero feeding her starving father Cimon while he awaited execution in prison.

KEY

① **Plattegronden** by René Daniels (b. 1950) is a simplified re-creation of a museum hall. Daniels painted yellow rectangles over the red flat paintings, which are out of sync with the perspective of the hall, thus creating a disorienting effect.

② **Terrace**

③ **Domed hall**

④ **Inner tower**

★ Wood Carvings
The fine collection of medieval wood carvings includes *St Anna-te-Drieën*, a walnut sculpture by Jan van Steffeswert (1470–1525).

Bonnefantopia
The Rotterdam group of artists Atelier van Lieshout created this large installation in 2002. It features stylized polyester bodies hanging, squatting and lying down throughout the structure.

VISITORS' CHECKLIST

Practical Information
Avenue Céramique 250.
Tel 043-3290190.
🌐 **bonnefanten.nl**
Open 11am–5pm Tue–Sun & public hol Mon. **Closed** 1 Jan, Carnival, 25 Dec. 📷 for temp exhibits. 🅿 ✏ 🖥

Transport
🚌 1, 3, 50, 53, 54, 57.

View on a City from a River
by Jan Brueghel the Elder (1568–1625).

Entrance

Museum Guide

The Bonnefantenmuseum was designed by Aldo Rossi. It has a permanent collection of early and contemporary art; in addition, a range of temporary exhibitions are organized. The highlight of the museum is its magnificent collection of medieval wood carvings.

★ Staircase
The monumental staircase runs through the middle of the museum and leads into the different wings and floors of the museum.

St Stephen
Giovanni del Biondo (1356–99) painted this work, thought to be part of a triptych, as the panel has signs of being cut with a saw.

Exploring Maastricht

Maastricht is considered to be one of the oldest towns in Holland. It was the seat of the country's first bishopric and an impressive fortress. It has some outstanding historical monuments, including the Romanesque Onze-Lieve-Vrouwebasiliek (Basilica of Our Lady); the Romanesque St Servaas Basilica, with a very old crypt and a carved Gothic portal (early 13th century); a scattering of Gothic churches; a Baroque church formerly belonging to the Augustine order (1661); and a Walloon church from 1733. A great deal remains of the fortifications, including Roman foundations, part of the medieval wall, a 17th-century bastion, and 18th- and 19th-century reinforcement works.

The medieval Helpoort gate, the oldest city gate in the country

🏛 Natuurhistorisch Museum

De Bosquetplein 7. **Tel** 043-3505490. **Open** 11am–5pm Tue–Fri, 1–5pm Sat & Sun. **Closed** some public hols. 🅿

This attractive natural history museum showcases the natural history of the south of Limburg through the ages. Highlights of the museum include the remains of the enormous mosasaur and giant tortoises found in the limestone strata of St Pietersberg.

🏛 Roman Foundations of the Tower

OL Vrouweplein. **Tel** 043-3251851. **Open** timings vary, call to check.

In the courtyard of the Onze-Lieve-Vrouwebasiliek you can see the foundations of a Roman tower which was once part of the Roman *castellum*. The *castellum* stood on the banks of the River Maas, just south of the St Servaasbrug bridge, where

the Romans settled in 50 BC and where the district of Stokstraat, with its medieval and Golden Age buildings, now lies. The pavement of Op de Thermen, a small and peaceful square in this district where the original Roman fort once was, has been marked with the outlines of the old Roman baths. The first medieval wall around Maastricht dates from around 1229. Of these, the Onze-Lieve-Vrouwewal – which has cannons standing in front of it – and the Jekertoren tower can still be seen.

Mosasaurus hofmanni in the natural history museum, known locally as the terrible Maas lizard

🏛 Helpoort

St Bernardusstraat 24b. **Tel** 043-3212586. **Open** Easter Day–Oct, 12:30–4:30pm daily. 🅿 voluntary donation.

The Helpoort gate, dating from the early 13th century, also forms part of the early medieval town fortifications. It stood at the southern end of the town and is the oldest surviving town gate in Holland, and the only one still standing in Maastricht.

Other structures from this period can be seen across the River Maas in Wyck: the Waterpoortje gate, the Stenen Wal (wall) along the river, and the Maaspunttoren. The second medieval fortifications, made necessary by the rapid growth of the city, were built around 1350. Of these, the Pater Vinktoren near the Helpoort gate, and the romantic embankment wall and the semicircular towers known as De Vijf Koppen and Haet ende Nijt continue to survive to this day.

The impressive Pater Vink tower

🏛 Museum Spaans Gouvernement

Vrijthof 18. **Tel** 043-3211327.
Open 10am–6pm Tue–Sun.
Closed public hols.

This museum, housed in a 16th-century chapterhouse, features period rooms from the 17th and 18th centuries, and Dutch paintings from that era.

🏛 Centre Céramique

Avenue Céramique 50. **Tel** 043-350 5600. **Open** call ahead or check website. **Closed** Mon & public hols.
🎫 📷 🌐 **centreceramique.nl**

This information centre has a library, archive, cafés and the European Journalism Centre.

🏛 Grotten St-Pietersberg

Luikerweg. 📞 phone for details (043-3252121). 🎫 📷 ♿

The famous St Peter's caves were created when limestone was quarried through the centuries. Eventually a maze of over 20,000 passageways came into being. Some of the inscriptions on the walls are very old, and reveal artistic skills of the miners.

The Gothic Bergportaal (15th century) of the St-Servaasbasiliek

🏛 St-Servaasbasiliek

Keizer Karelplein 7. **Tel** 043-3212082.
Open 10am–5pm Mon–Sat, 12:30–6pm Sun. **Closed** 1 Jan, Carnival, 25 Dec.

Construction on St Servatius Basilica began around the year 1000 on the spot where the saint was buried (upon which stood an earlier church). The nave, the crypt, the transept and the chancel are the oldest parts of the basilica, dating back to the 11th century. The apse and the two chancel towers were built in the following century. The western end also dates from the 12th century. The southern Bergportaal gate dates from the early 13th century, and is one of the

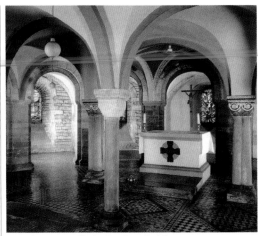

Crypt in the eastern part of the Onze-Lieve-Vrouwebasiliek

earliest Gothic buildings in the Maasland region. This portal is dedicated to St Mary, with representations of her life, death and Assumption in the arch. The side chapels and the Gothic transept date from approximately 1475.

Highlights of the basilica's treasury are the 12th-century reliquary containing the relics of St Servatius and St Martin of Tongeren, and the golden bust of St Servatius. The latter was donated to the town by the Duke of Parma when Maastricht was captured by the Spaniards in 1579.

During the 19th century, thorough restoration works were undertaken by Pierre Cuypers. He restored the western end to its original Romanesque splendour, as

well as commissioning new murals and ceiling paintings. These were repainted during a subsequent restoration, which was completed in 1990.

🏛 Onze-Lieve-Vrouwebasiliek

O-L-Vrouweplein. Treasury: **Tel** 043-3561330. **Open** timings vary, call to check. Church: **Closed** during services.

Construction of Onze-Lieve-Vrouwebasiliek began around 1000. The oldest part of the basilica is the imposing west façade. Once this was completed, work began on the nave and transept. The chancel followed in the 12th century, built over an 11th-century crypt. The apse pillars, made from limestone, are crowned with lavishly sculpted capitals, such as the renowned Heimokapiteel.

The Reliquary of St Servatius

The magnificent restored reliquary is a monumental shrine containing the relics of St Servatius and St Martin of Tongeren. It is made of wood covered with embossed gilded copper plate in the shape of a house. It dates from about 1160 and was built by artists from the Maasland region. The front of the reliquary depicts Christ, with the 12 apostles along the sides, and St Servatius surrounded by angels on the back. The "roof" of the "house" is decorated with scenes from the Last Judgement.

The 12th-century reliquary

The impressive medieval Kasteel Hoensbroek

❾ Thorn

Road Map D5. 🏛 2,600. 🚌 72, 73, 76.
ℹ Wijngaard 8 (0475-561085).

Southeast of Weert on the A2 is the little town of Thorn, which with its picturesque narrow streets and houses, historical farm buildings and monumental **Abbey Church** looks like an open-air museum. For some 800 years, until 1794, Thorn was the capital of an autonomous secular foundation headed by an abbess. The Wijngaard, the village square, is surrounded by whitewashed houses where the noble ladies of the foundation once lived. The 14th-century abbey church with its 18th-century interior was thoroughly restored at the

A whitewashed house in Thorn

end of the 19th century by renowned architect Pierre Cuypers, who also added a splendid Gothic tower. Clara Elisabeth van Manderscheidt-Blankenheim, a canoness of the foundation, founded the **Kapel van O-L-Vrouwe onder de Linden** (Chapel of Our Lady under the Linden) north of the town in 1673.

❿ Sittard

Road Map D6. 🏛 46,500. 🚌
ℹ Kitzraedthuis, Rosmolenstraat 2 (0900-5559798). 🚩 Thu am, Sat.

In the 13th century, Sittard was granted its town charter and built its defensive walls, of which considerable sections remain intact, including **Fort Sanderbout**. The Grote Kerk, or St Petruskerk, built around 1300, is worth a visit. The 80-m (262-ft) tower is built of layers of alternating brick and limestone blocks, or "speklagen" (bacon layers). In the Markt is the 17th-century Baroque **St Michielskerk**; Our Lady of the Sacred Heart basilica stands in the Oude Markt. The oldest house in Sittard is the half-timber house built in 1530 on the corner of the Markt and the Gats and containing the De Gats coffee house. The Jacob Kritszraedthuis, a patrician house, was built in 1620 in Maasland Renaissance style.

⓫ Hoensbroek

Road Map D6. 🏛 25,500. 🚌
ℹ Bongerd 19, Heerlen (0900-5559798). 🚩 Fri am.

Before the state-run Emma mine was opened here in 1908, Hoensbroek was a sleepy farming town. It subsequently grew into the centre of the Dutch coal-mining industry. Its industrial importance waned with the closing of the mines.

Kasteel Hoensbroek was built in the Middle Ages. All that remains of the original castle is the round corner-tower. The wings and towers around the rectangular inner courtyard date from the 17th and 18th centuries. The castle is moated and today functions as a cultural centre.

Thermae at the Thermenmuseum

⓬ Heerlen

Road Map D6. 🏛 87,500. 🚌
ℹ Bongerd 19 (0900-5559798).
🚩 Tue, Thu am & Fri.

The Roman town of Coriovallum has been discovered beneath Heerlen. The **Thermenmuseum** contains the foundations of the ancient *thermae* and many everyday items from Roman times. Romanesque **St Pancratiuskerk** dates back to the 12th century. In the 20th century, until 1974, Heerlen was the centre of coal mining in Limburg. FPJ Peutz built the town hall and Schunck department store (known as the *Glaspaleis*, or crystal palace) in the 1930s.

🏛 **Thermenmuseum**
Coriovallumstraat 9. **Tel** 045-5605100.
Open 10am–5pm Tue–Fri, noon–5pm Sat, Sun & public hols. **Closed** 1 Jan, Carnival, 24 & 25 Dec. 🐾 🎫 🏛 🗣

⓭ Valkenburg

Road map D6. 🚶 5,500. 🚉 🚌 36, 47, 63. **ℹ** Th. Dorrenplein 5 (0900-5559798). 🛍 Mon am, Tue am.

The old fortified town of Valkenburg, situated in an area dotted with castles, is popular with visitors. In addition to sights such as the old gates of Berkelpoort and Grendelpoort, a 13th-century Romanesque church and the ruins of a 12th-century castle, there are many new attractions, such as a casino, catacombs, the Fluweelen cave, **Gemeentegrot** (a Roman quarry and cave complex), a cable car, the Prehistorische Monstergrot and the **Steenkolenmijn** (coal mine).

🏠 Gemeentegrot

Cauberg 4. **Tel** 043-6012271. **Open** 11am–5pm daily **Closed** 1 Jan, Carnival, 25 Dec. 🔲 🔳 guided tours only. 🚶

⓮ Gulpen

Road Map D6. 🚶 7,500. 🚌 150. **ℹ** Dorpsstraat 27 (0900-5559798). 🛍 Thu morning.

Gulpen lies at the confluence of the Geul and Gulp streams. The town's surrounding countryside, with its half-timbered houses, water mills and orchards, is probably the prettiest in Limburg. Hiking routes are marked. The 17th-century Kastell Neubourg,

Picturesque sloping streets of the Maasland village of Elsloo

built on the site of a Roman temple from 2,000 years ago, is now a hotel and restaurant. Beside the castle is the Neubourgermolen mill, with a fish ladder for trout. The Gulpen brewery is worth a visit. The common kingfisher can be seen here.

⓯ Elsloo

Road Map D6. 🚶 8,650. 🚉 🚌 93. **ℹ** Kitzraedhuis, Rosmolenstraat 2, Sittard (0900-5559798).

Artifacts from the prehistoric pottery culture found at Elsloo are on display in the Maasland local history museum, De Schippersbeurs. In the Waterstaatskerk, dating from 1848, is the 16th-century **St-Anna-te-Drieën** by the

Master of Elsloo. Remnants of Elsloo's earliest castle can be seen in the middle of the river at low water. Of the later Kasteel Elsloo, only one tower survives.

⓰ Eijsden

Road Map C6. 🚶 4,800. 🚉 🚌 58, 59. **ℹ** Diepstraat 31 (0900-5559798). 🛍 Thu pm.

Eijsden, the southernmost municipality in the Netherlands, is a protected rural area. There is a pleasant walk to be had along the Maas quay. Kasteel Eijsden was built in 1636 in the Maasland Renaissance style on the foundations of an earlier stronghold. The castle is not open to the public, but the park makes for a nice stroll.

Kingfisher

⓱ Vaals

Road Map D6. 🚶 9,600. 🚌 50. **ℹ** Landal Maastrichterlaan 73a (0900-5559798). 🛍 Tue am.

Vaals' wooded countryside is known for the Drielandenpunt, from which three countries are visible. At 322 m (1,058 ft), it is also the highest point in Holland. Worth visiting are Kasteel Vaalsbroek and the Von Clermonthuis; both date from the 18th century. De Kopermolen, once a church, is now a museum.

Limburg's scenic countryside, with the meandering Jeker river

⑱ Heuvelland

In the Zuid Limburg region of Heuvelland, the hills and the river valleys are covered with fertile loess soil, which occurs nowhere else in Holland. In the peaceful rolling countryside, with its stunning views, is a region of wooded banks, orchards and fields, dotted with picturesque villages and castles, and criss-crossed by narrow roads passing through cuttings with roadside shrines and field chapels. Heuvelland just may be one of the prettiest parts of Holland.

③ **The orchid garden** in the traffic-free Gerendal, a dry valley between Schin op Geul and Scheulder, is the pride of the region. The garden was laid out by the national forestry commission and is situated behind the forester's lodge. Twenty varieties of wild orchid grow here.

② **The Basilica of the Holy Sacrament** in Meerssen, built in the late 14th century of limestone in Maasland Gothic style, is one of the most elegant churches in all of Holland. The chancel features a lavishly decorated tabernacle.

⑧ **Kasteel Eijsden** was built in the Maasland Renaissance style in 1636. This style is easily distinguished by its combined use of brick and stone masonry, with stone being used to frame doors and windows.

Tips for Drivers

Tour length: 80 km (50 miles). Part of the route passes through hilly areas with narrow roads.
Stopping-off points: especially good viewing points are to be found at Noorbeek, Slenaken and Epen.

① Grape-growing in Zuid Limburg

In the past, grape-growing and wine-making was more widely practised in Zuid Limburg than it is today. For example, in the 18th century, there were at least 200 ha (495 acres) of vineyards on and around St-Pietersberg. Today, a few small professional vineyards can still be found in the region, the most famous being the Apostelhoeve. On this vine-growing estate situated to the the south of Maastricht on the Louwberg above the de Jeker valley, white wine is made from Müller-Thürgau, Riesling, Auxerrois and Pinot Gris grapes.

Grapes from Limburg

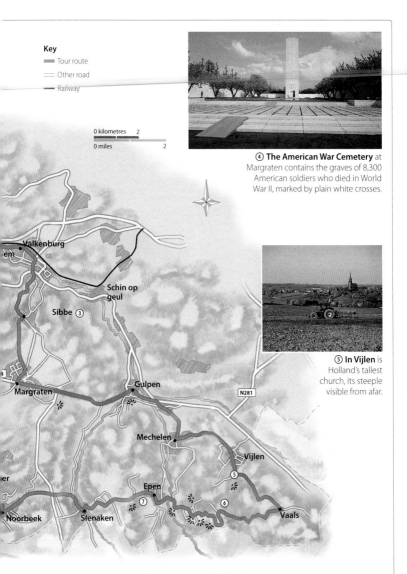

Key

━━ Tour route

═══ Other road

━━ Railway

0 kilometres 2

0 miles 2

④ **The American War Cemetery** at Margraten contains the graves of 8,300 American soldiers who died in World War II, marked by plain white crosses.

⑤ **In Vijlen** is Holland's tallest church, its steeple visible from afar.

⑥ **Large stretches of forest** are rare in Zuid Limburg. Exceptions are the Boswachterij Vaals with the Vijlenerbos forest, and the forests by the Brunsummerheide (Brunsummer heath). Here the woods cover the landscape and there are lots of springs.

⑦ **Rambling in the Geuldal**
At Epen, turn off towards Plaat and take the road to the fulling mill in Geul. Carry on after the bridge. A path on the opposite side follows the river upstream into Belgium. Along the Geul are poplars with mistletoe growing in the branches, which can be seen particularly well in winter. The path leads past the Heimansgroeve, a quarry for rock from the Carboniferous period.

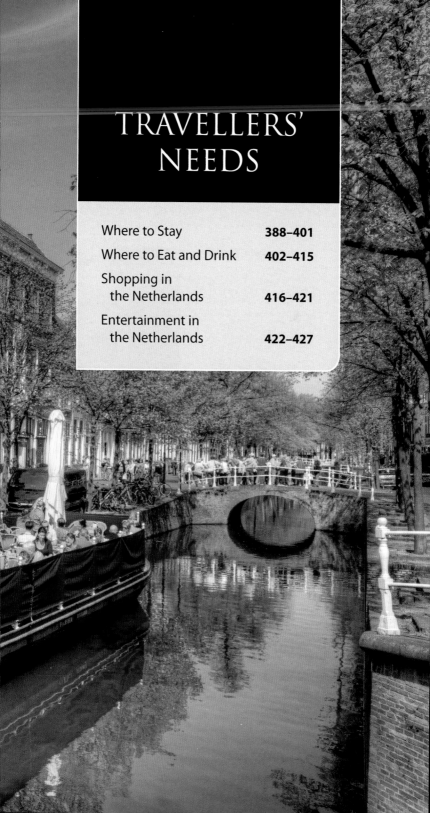

TRAVELLERS' NEEDS

WHERE TO STAY

The Netherlands offers a variety of accommodation to suit every traveller's tastes and needs, ranging from inexpensive backpacker hostels to pricey château living. Visitors can choose to stay in one of the luxury chain hotels here, which vary from bland to spectacular, but there is also good accommodation to be found in historical castles, convents, prisons, mansions – and in one case, a harbour crane – that have been converted into hotels, hostels or B&Bs. Campers, too, will be spoiled for choice here, with numerous campsites and caravan parks, often situated in stunning locations. For those who intend to stay in a particular area over a longer period of time, camping is an especially economical option. Visitors who need more spacious or convenient accommodation can book one of the 350-odd bungalow parks in the country, or rent an apartment in one of the many coastal towns.

Hotel Types

There is a huge variation in the price, quality and facilities offered by different hotels. The choice is greatest in Amsterdam and the larger cities, where there is something to suit every traveller's pocket. There are also plenty of choices further afield, generally at lower rates. After hotels, bed-and-breakfast (B&B) accommodation is also plentiful. As these lodgings are offered by individuals rather than by chains, this type of accommodation may vary greatly in nature and level of comfort – one night you might be staying in a family home, and the next in a chic country estate. The least expensive form of overnight accommodation is in a hostel. **Stayokay** runs 25 well-appointed hostels throughout the country, ranging from a house on the top of a dune to a medieval castle, and featuring dormitories or private rooms.

Hotel Chains

Most major hotel chains are represented in the Netherlands, including **Best Western**, **Golden Tulip**, **Hilton**, **Holiday Inn**, **Mercure**, **NH** and **Radisson**. Most of these can be found in the bigger cities, although some are situated in country areas also. Chain hotels range in quality from fair to excellent, and in size from large to massive, and cater to tourists and business travellers alike. Their scale, and often their internationally recognized style, mean that chain hotels are generally less personal than individually operated hotels, but when you spend the night in one of these, you are usually assured of a competitively priced and hassle-free stay.

Stylish interiors of the Het Arresthuis, Roermond *(see p401)*

Categories

All hotels in the Netherlands are categorized according to international standards under the Netherlands Hotel Classification system, which awards each hotel with one to five stars. Hoteliers class their hotels themselves, after which an inspection is carried out by an independent organization. The number of stars awarded to each hotel depends on the facilities it offers: the more stars it has, the more luxurious it is. A one-star hotel is basic and may or may not offer breakfast. In two-star hotels, at least 25 per cent of the rooms will have their own bathroom or shower and WC. These hotels will also have a guest lounge, and a lift if they are more than three storeys high. Three-star hotels are considered middle of the range. Their rooms have central heating, and at least half have their own bathrooms. Four-star hotels will have a night bar; also 80 per cent of their rooms will have en suite bathrooms, and all of them have

Château De Havixhorst *(see p400)* in De Schiphorst

◄ A typical boat restaurant in South Holland

Colourful decor at Harbour Crane *(see p399)*, Harlingen

telephones. A five-star hotel will belong to the deluxe category, with 24-hour service, large rooms with en-suite facilities, a restaurant and so on.

Although this classification system does provide an insight into the hotel's level of amenities, it looks exclusively only at the facilities and amenities provided by the hotel.

Apartments

Staying in a self-catering apartment or holiday home is an increasingly popular alternative to hotels or hostels and can be an economical choice, particularly if you are travelling in a group. Accommodation ranges from a private room in the countryside with basic and sometimes shared facilities to a sleek city loft with five-star amenities. Some apartments might require a minimum stay, especially in high season, and it is always a good idea to inquire if there are any additional or hidden fees, such as key money or cleaning cost. On the coast and on the islands there are "apartment-hotels", which are apartment buildings with hotel facilities, such as a reception, restaurant and swimming pool.

Prices

Room prices always include VAT ('BTW'). Tourist tax (*toeristenbelasting*) varies by municipality and is often but not always included. Breakfast is often included, but this should be specifically stated. If not, do check, as breakfast in a luxury hotel can be expensive.

Obviously, a five-star hotel is pricier than a three-star. Hotels in larger cities, in Amsterdam in particular, are relatively more expensive than those further afield, although in the city it is easier to find hotels in wider-ranging price categories and good deals can be found off-season.

As many hotels have abolished dedicated single rooms, solo travellers often end up paying only slightly less than the same accommodation would cost two people sharing. Kids under the age of 12 can usually stay free of charge or at a much reduced rate, if they share their parents' room.

Booking Accommodation

High season runs pretty much year-round in Amsterdam. In winter, with the exception of Christmas and New Year's, visitors will manage to find a room, but at all other times it is wise to book well in advance. In other major cities, high season runs from spring until autumn or further afield from late spring until early autumn. On the coast and on the islands, any month other than July or August is considered off-season.

Bookings can be made directly with the hotel by telephone or email, or in person at the reception, although this often means you pay the standard room price, which is usually higher than the more competitive rates found online. Unless a hotel or chain offers a "best rate guarantee" when booking through their website, the lowest rates are often found through dedicated hotel-booking websites like Expedia.nl, Hotels.nl and Booking.com. The best way of searching for individual hotels or a particular chain is by name. The price differences found on different websites for the same room in the same hotel at the same dates can be astounding; it pays to compare prices through a meta search engine such as Travelsupermarket.com, Lookingforbooking.com or Hotelscombined.com – the latter also has a clever iPhone app.

No-frills hotels, such as CitizenM, Yotel, Qbic and easyHotel, that offer tiny yet smart rooms at the lowest possible price, can usually be booked only through their own respective websites.

Stayokay hostels can be booked through their own website, Stayokay.nl, while a wider choice of International Youth Hostel Federation (IYHF) and non-IYHF hostels around the country can be booked through Hostels.com, Hostelbookers.com or Hostelworld.com.

Many B&Bs can be booked through Bedandbreakast.nl. Airbnb.nl offers an equally wide range of B&Bs, plus private rooms, apartments and holiday homes.

The "VVV" tourist information offices around the country can also assist visitors in booking suitable accommodation.

Façade of Stempels *(see p397)* in Haarlem

The bar of the Hotel Van der Werff *(see p398)* on Schiermonnikoog

Payment

Major credit cards are accepted at almost every hotel. If you provide your credit card details at the time of booking, it is usually used as a guarantee and your card will not be actually charged until checkout. However, advance payment may be required in some cases, for example when booking at a highly discounted rate or special package, in which case your credit card will be charged immediately. Most hotels will charge a no-show fee, up to or even extending the full room rate, if you do not show up without prior cancellation. As always, watch out for any hidden charges, especially when using the "express checkout" service that many hotels offer.

Discounts

Many hotels and chains offer "early bird" discounts for rooms booked well in advance. Hotels that cater mainly to business travellers during the week, will often offer discounts to leisure travellers over the weekend and conversely, hotels that are usually full with tourists at the weekends may offer reductions on weekdays.

Packages

Many hotels offer special packages of one or two nights, with breakfast and dinner included. These packages are often based on a particular theme; for example, a cycling or rambling package may include cycle hire, or a wellness package may include a couple's massage at the hotel spa. Such packages can be an economical choice. Packages can be booked through the hotel booking websites mentioned in the directory. Attractive deals can also be found through group deal websites like Groupon.com and LivingSocial.com, although you need to be flexible, as the timeframes for booking and travelling are usually limited.

Travellers with Disabilities

Many large hotels are fully accessible for wheelchairs. Smaller hotels may be less accessible, particularly those in historic buildings where steps and stairs prevent this. Hotels that do have wheelchair access, but no lifts, will have some accessible rooms on the ground floor. Some websites, like Hotels.com and Booking.com, allow you to search for or filter by hotels with facilities for people with disabilities. However, it is always best to consult the hotel directly before you book.

Gay Hotels

The days of Amsterdam being the "gay capital of Europe" may be gone, according to many locals, but the city still has a lot to offer to gay and lesbian travellers. A number of hotels cater exclusively to gay guests, of which the **Amistad**, with its fresh interior and smart rooms, and **Quentin Golden Bear Hotel**, with comfortable rooms (although some with shared facilities), are great choices.

Then there is a choice of hotels that are regarded as gay-friendly by the International Gay & Lesbian Travel Association (Iglta.org), including the hip Lloyd and the posh Grand. No hotel in Amsterdam would turn away a same-sex couple, but another particularly welcoming lodging, that is popular with women, is the **Quentin**.

At gay tourist information centres, such as **Gaytic** on Spuistraat, visitors can pick up a free gay tourist kit and

InterContinental Amstel *(see p397)* in Amsterdam (right), with its picturesque location

get more information on gay-friendly hotels as well as the gay scene in the city.

Recommended Hotels

The hotels listed on pages 396–401 vary significantly in both class and cost, and are considered the best choice in terms of price, charm or location. To help you find accommodation that suits your personal taste, we have divided the entries into six categories: Charming, Hotels with Character, Historic, Family-friendly, Design and Luxury. Some hotels are better than others and a few stand out for a particular reason, such as a romantic atmosphere, a fantastic spa or a stunning location. For each region we have handpicked one such exceptional lodging, ranging from an inexpensive hostel in a bunch of peculiar

Grand Hotel de Kromme Raake *(see p399)* in Eenrum, with a traditional in-built bed

cube houses or a hotel that consists of individually decorated rooms spread out over several private homes, to a deluxe suite in a converted Ilyushin airliner or a room with a dazzling view in a dockside crane. Here you will not only be guaranteed a comfortable night's sleep, but

also gain a memorable experience. These highly recommended hotels are marked as "DK Choice". The "DK Choice" hotels are extra special. These hotels may have above average standards, or a breathtaking location, or they may simply have a charm that sets them apart.

DIRECTORY

Hotel Types

Stayokay
W stayokay.com

Hotel Chains

Best Western
W bestwestern.nl

Golden Tulip
W goldentulip.com

Hilton
W hilton.com/netherlands

Holiday Inn
W holidayinn.nl

Mercure
W mercure.com

NH Hotels
W nh-hotels.com

Radisson Blu
W radissonblu.com

Booking Accommodation

B&B booking websites
W bedandbreakfast.nl
W airbnb.com

Compare prices

W travelsupermarket.com

W lookingforbooking.nl

W hotelscombined.com

Dutch Tourist Office
W holland.com

Hostel booking websites

W stayokay.com

W hostels.com

W hostelbookers.com

W hostelworld.com

Hotel booking websites

W hotels.nl

W booking.com

W expedia.nl

VVV Netherlands BV
Umbrella organisation for Dutch tourist offices.
W vvv.nl

Gay Hotels

Gaytic Information Centre
Spuistraat 44
1012 DV Amsterdam.
Tel (020) 330 1461
W gaytic.nl

Hotel Amistad
Kerkstraat 42
1017 GM Amsterdam.
Tel (020) 624 8074.
W amistad.nl

Quentin Amsterdam Hotel
Leidsekade 89
1017 PN Amsterdam.
Tel (020) 626 2187.
W quentinamsterdam.com

Quentin Golden Bear Hotel
Kerkstraat 37
1017 GB Amsterdam.
Tel (020) 624 4785.
W quentingoldenbear.com

Sir Albert
Albert Cuypstraat 2,
De Pijp, 1072 CT
Amsterdam.
Tel (020) 305 3020.
W siralberthotel.com

Bungalow Parks

The Netherlands has at least 350 holiday villages ("bungalowparken"), with dozens to hundreds of bungalows or cabins, many designed for four to eight persons, together with numerous facilities such as supermarkets and restaurants. They also provide many recreation facilities, some open-air and others indoors for days when the weather is not at its best. Rental is by the week, midweek or weekend, with arrival and departure on set days. The parks are often situated in areas of natural beauty and offer plenty to do in the surrounding area. A selection of the best parks in the country is given here.

Efteling Village Bosrijk
This leafy holiday park is set in woodland next to the country's biggest theme park. Cottages sleep six to eight, while apartments (in a faux manor house or gatehouse) have room for four.

Port Zélande
This Mediterranean-style CenterParcs Park at Lake Grevelingen features numerous recreation facilities and comfortable bungalows.

0 kilometres 40
0 miles 40

TERSCHELLIN
WEST FRISIA
ISLANDS
VLIELAND
SLUFTERVALLEI
KRIM
PARC TEXEL *TEXEL*
CREATIEF BEACH
CALIFORNIË PARK TEXEL

NORTH
HOLLA

AMSTERDAM
ZANDVOORT
Haarlem
SOLLASI
'T EEKHOORNNES
UTRECH
Den Haag
KIJKDUINPARK **Utrech**
SOUTH
HOLLAND
Rotterdam
TOPPERSHOEDJE
PORT ZÉLANDE
DUINOORD PARK PORT GREVE
PARC EFTELING
BURGH-HAAMSTEDE DROOMRIJK
DE SCHOTSMAN NOOR
Middelburg DE ROSE
DE FLAASBLOEM BRAB
HOF VAN ZEELAND BOERDERIJ
ZEEBAD ZWAR
PANNENSCHUUR ZEELAND
HET VENNENBOS
B E L G I U M

De Flaasbloem
The initially (and still mildly) Christian RCN recreation parks offer relatively inexpensive bungalows and plenty to do for children.

Key and Contact Details

- Europarcs (088-0708090)
- Zilverberk (zilverberkvakanties.nl)
- CenterParcs (0900-6606600)
- Landal GreenParks (070-3003506)
- Holidaypark Molke (0584-512743)
- RCN-recreatiecentra (0343-513547)
- Hogenboom Vakantieparken (0900-2002002)
- Other parks

SCHIERMONNIKOOG

NPARK BLIEKE   AMELAND

BOOMHIEMKE   CREATIEF NATUURDORP SUYDEROOGH

GRONINGEN

Groningen

Leeuwarden

IT WIID

FRIESLAND

DE POTTEN   WITTERZOMER   PARC STADSKANAAL

DE ROGGEBERG   Assen   PARC BORGER

BOSMEER

DE NOORDSTER   AELDERHOLT

DRENTHE   HET ZUIDERVELD

VAKANTIEPARK DE WILTZANGH

DE HUTTENHEUGTE

HET STOETENSLAGH

OVERIJSSEL

Lelystad   Zwolle   CREATIEF VILLAPARK DE VLEGGE

VOLAND

HOOGWOLDE   GERNER

DE JAGERSTEE   HOGE HEXEL

PARC EPE   B.C. HELLENDOORN
ZILVERBERK HELLENDOORN
EMHOF   SALLANDSHOEVE

ZEEWOLDE   LANDGOED 'T LOO   VAKANTIEPARK DE PRINS

AS   TWENHAARSVELD

RABBIT HILL   ELDORADO   RUIGHENRODE

IGGELENBERG   PARC BEEKBERGEN
HEIDEHEUVEL   'T STIEN 'N BOER

ROTE BOS   COLDENHOVE

KELDUIN   GELDERLAND

Arnhem   'T ZONNETJE

togenbosch   SCHUTTERSOORD

ANT   HET HEIJDERBOS

G E R M A N Y

ARCEN

LOOHORST
HET MEERDAL

PARC VLIERDEN

EMPERVENNEN   DE LOMMERBERGEN

WEERTERBERGEN

LIMBURG

HOMMELHEIDE

tricht   SIMPELVELD

DE MECHELERHOF

HOOG VAALS

Aqua Mundo
The spectacular subtropical paradise at De Eemhof (and other CenterParcs) offers a wonderful and wet time for all.

Landal Hoog Vaals
In the rolling landscape of Limburg, Landal combines beautiful countryside with a plethora of activities.

Camping

Many people regard camping as the ideal way to take a holiday. It is inexpensive, you are out in the open air, often in beautiful natural locations. Camping comes in many shapes and sizes: settling in one place for the whole holiday or hopping from one campsite to the next; you can camp in a tent, a caravan, a tent-trailer or a camper van; you can camp in nature, on a farm or in a holiday park. The Netherlands, with its many different types of campsites, has something for everyone.

Camping at one of Holland's many nature sites

De Roos campsite at Beerze, located on the River Vecht

Types of Campsite

Campsites in the Netherlands fall into two main categories. There are *natuurterreinen,* (nature sites), which are small or medium-sized campsites with basic facilities, often situated in the most spectacular countryside that the Netherlands has to offer. The other group consists of larger campsites with a good range of facilities, often near recreation areas or other attractions. Both types of campsite are to be found throughout the Netherlands, and on both you can either set up your own tent and caravan or you can rent

accommodation. The advantage of renting, of course, is that you travel lighter.

Nature Camping

Dutch law prohibits rough camping – ie off designated campsites. However, there are plenty of campsites that give you a true sense of camping in nature. These natural campsites, *natuur-kampeerterreinen*, are small-scale and often situated in scenic locations, with plenty of countryside around for exploring on foot or by bicycle. You can pitch a tent or park your caravan, tent-trailer or camper here. There are no fixed pitches, sanitary arrangements are fairly basic but good, and there is usually a children's play area. Staying here requires a membership card from **Stichting Natuur-kampeerterreinen**, which includes a booklet listing all

130-plus official natural camping sites.

The campsites of the **Vereniging Gastvrije Landgoederen** combine the attraction of natural surroundings with that of cultural history. These sites are situated on private estates, usually on the grounds of a castle or stately home. The association's 20-odd sites are distinguished by their peace, atmosphere and spaciousness, and offer abundant opportunities for rambling, cycling or horse riding.

Camping on a farm means you will be assured of a tranquil rural atmosphere. There are hundreds of **VeKaBo** farm campsites, usually small and with limited facilities, but offering a variety of

Camping in Zeeland, popular among Dutch and foreign holidaymakers alike

experiences; you will often be able to help the farmers feed the animals, milk the cows or harvest the crops.

Another excellent way of experiencing the countryside is by using hikers' cabins, *trekkershutten*, designed for use by walkers on multiple-day hiking-trips. They offer basic accommodation for up to four people and are often situated at campsites whose facilities are available to the hikers. Bring your own kitchen utensils and bedding.

Hanging the laundry to dry among the fragrant blossoming trees

Large Family Campsites

Large family campsites or *gezinscampings* are popular among Dutch holidaymakers taking a break in their own country. Social life is an important aspect of these campsites, with plenty of opportunities to meet your fellow campers through an abundance of activities, such as barbecues, karaoke, games, competitions and sports events. Children also get to meet others of their age and there is plenty of room for running around and playing.

The largest campsites have extensive sanitary facilities and hot water. They also provide electrical hook-ups for caravans, as well as running water and sewage connections. Campsite shops mean that you can do most of your shopping on-site, and if you don't feel like cooking your own food, there is often a restaurant or snack bar. Launderettes and dry-cleaning services are also often available. Many have a swimming pool and other

recreation facilities such as tennis courts, mini-golf and so on.

The Dutch Automobile Club, **ANWB**, has awarded the best campsites in Europe with their quality label "Best Camping". These offer an exceptionally great terrain with large pitches, extensive facilities and terrific service. Over thirty such campsites are located in the Netherlands, and are listed in their camping guides and online, albeit in Dutch only: www. anwb.nl/vakantie/camping.

DIRECTORY

Nature Camping

Vereniging Gastvrije Landgoederen
Tel 0318-578555.
W gastvrije landgoederen.nl

Karaktervolle Groene Campings
W kgc.nl

Nivon Natuurvrienden
W nivon.nl

Stichting Natuur-kampeerterreinen
Tel 030-6033701.
W natuur kampeerterreinen.nl

SVR (Stichting Vrije Recreatie)
W svr.nl

Trekkershutten
Tel 030-6033701.
W trekkershutten.nl

VeKaBo (Vereniging van Kampeerboeren)
Tel 0900-3336668.
W vekabo.nl

Family Campsites

Roompot Parken
Tel 0113-374297.
W roompot.nl

Vacansoleil
Tel 0900-9899.
W vacansoleil.nl

Guides

ANWB online booking
W anwbcamping.nl/nederland.html
(Dutch only)

ANWB Voordeel Campinggids 1 & 2
Both list hundreds of campsites in the Netherlands, and thousands in the rest of Europe (Dutch only).

Online camping guides
Lists over 750 campsites inspected by the ANWB.
W en.camping.info/netherlands

W alanrogers.com
W europe-camping-guide.com/en/list/netherlands
W eurocampings.eu/en/europe/netherlands

Where to Stay

Amsterdam

Oude Zijde

The Grand €€€
Luxury **Map** 5 A1
Oudezijds Voorburgwal 197, 1012 EX
Tel *(020) 555 3111*
[w] sofitel.com
A World Travel award nominee,
The Grand has a lush courtyard
enclosed by a 17th-century town
hall. Rooms have modern decor.

DK Choice

Hôtel Droog €€€
Hotels with Character **Map** 5 A2
Staalstraat 7B, 1011 JJ
Tel *(020) 523 5059*
[w] hoteldroog.com
Hôtel Droog's designers offer
a hospitality experience with
a twist. There's only one room here
but with a few extras – an art
gallery, beauty salon, fashion
boutique, indoor garden, tea
room/café and design store.

---

misc eatdrinksleep €€€
Waterside **Map** 5 A1
Kloveniersburgwal 20, 1012 CV
Tel *(020) 330 6241*
[w] misceatdrinksleep.com
Six miscellaneously-themed rooms
(e.g. Rembrandt, Baroque) offer
amenities such as rain showers,
espresso machines or free minibar.

Nieuwe Zijde

Hotel Des Arts €€
Family-friendly **Map** 4 F1
Rokin 154–156, 1012 LE
Tel *(020) 620 1558*
[w] hoteldesarts.nl
Intimate single, family and group
rooms are on offer here; some
with lovely canal views.

Hotel Sint Nicolaas €€
Hotels with Character **Map** 2 D4
Spuistraat 1A, 1012 SP
Tel *(020) 626 1384*
[w] hotelnicolaas.nl
Housed in a former harbour
office and mattress factory, this
quirky hotel has oddly-shaped en-
suite rooms. Breakfast included.

DoubleTree €€€
Business **Map** 2 F4
Oosterdoksstraat 4, 1011 DK
Tel *(020) 530 0800*
[w] doubletree3.hilton.com
This large hotel with harbour views
features 16 conference halls, free
Wi-Fi, remote printing facilities,
fitness rooms and a DVD library.

Western Canal Ring

The Times Hotel €€
Waterside **Map** 1 C4
Herengracht 135–137, 1015 BG
Tel *(020) 330 6030*
[w] thetimeshotel.nl
Set in combined canal houses
dating from 1650, this hotel
blends modern comfort with
old Dutch tradition.

The Dylan €€€
Luxury **Map** 1 B5
Keizersgracht 384, 1016 GB
Tel *(020) 530 2010*
[w] dylanamsterdam.com
Refined and tasteful, each room
and suite at The Dylan is unique.
Michelin-starred restaurant.

The Toren €€€
Luxury **Map** 1 C4
Keizersgracht 164, 1015 CZ
Tel *(020) 622 6352*
[w] thetoren.nl
This Travellers' Choice award
winner features garden-side
suites with two-person Jacuzzis.

Central Canal Ring

Acostar Hotel €€
Charming **Map** 4 E1
Kerkstraat 45–49, 1017 GB
Tel *(020) 330 0242*
[w] acostarhotel.com
Located near Leidseplein, this
hotel offers 30 rooms on five floors.
Bike hire and laundry service.

Hotel Pulitzer €€€
Luxury **Map** 1 B5
Prinsengracht 315, 1016 GZ
Tel *(020) 523 5235*
[w] pulitzeramsterdam.com
Stay in 17th- and 18th-century
restored canal houses. There are

Brick exterior of Hôtel Droog
in Amsterdam

---

three gardens, a restaurant, bar
and wine salon. Guests can take
saloon boat tours of the canals.

Eastern Canal Ring

DK Choice

Banks Mansion €€€
Waterside **Map** 5 A2
Herengracht 519–525, 1017 BV
Tel *(020) 420 0055*
[w] carlton.nl/banksmansion
This monumental former bank-
cum-mansion is a Travellers'
Choice award winner. Rooms
are lovely, with Frank Lloyd
Wright-inspired decor.
Everything is included in the
price: breakfast, movies, self-
service bar, even iPad loans.

Museum Quarter

Stayokay City
Hostel Vondelpark €
Family-friendly **Map** 4 D2
Zandpad 5, 1054 GA
Tel *(020) 589 8996*
[w] stayokay.com/vondelpark
This sprawling hostel offers great-
value rooms ranging from 20-
bed dorms to double rooms.

Conscious Hotel
Museum Square €€€
Design **Map** 4 D4
De Lairessestraat 7, 1071 NR
Tel *(020) 671 9596*
[w] conscioushotels.com
An eco-friendly "Green Key" gold
certificate holder, this modern
hotel features a gorgeous garden.

DK Choice

Conservatorium €€€
Luxury **Map** 4 D3
Van Baerlestraat 27, 1071 AN
Tel *(020) 570 0000*
[w] conservatoriumhotel.com
Housed in a former music
conservatory, the space has
been imaginatively reused. It has
high ceilings and a beautiful
atrium designed by Piero Lissoni.
Almost half the rooms are
duplexes, with amazing views.

Plantage

Hermitage €€
Waterside **Map** 5 B3
Nieuwe Keizersgracht 16, 1018 DR
Tel *(020) 623 8259*
W hotelhermitageamsterdam.com
A converted 1733 canal house
with a garden, Hermitage is a
good option for groups or families.

DK Choice

Amsterdam House €€€
Family-friendly **Map** 5 A2
's-Gravelandse Veer 3–4, 1011 KM
Tel *(020) 626 2577*
W amsterdamhouse.com
Enjoy a true Amsterdam on-the-
water experience. Stay on a
houseboat with a well-equipped
kitchen and bathrooms. Rooms
and apartment are warm, bright,
modern, and great for groups.

**InterContinental Amstel
Amsterdam** €€€
Luxury **Map** 5 B4
Professor Tulpplein 1, 1018 GX
Tel *(020) 622 6060*
W amsterdam.intercontinental.com
This rock star favourite offers
great views over the Amstel
river. First class service. Michelin-
starred restaurant.

Further Afield

Lloyd Hotel €€
Hotels with Character
Oostelijke Handelskade 34, 1019 BN
Tel *(020) 561 3636*
W lloydhotel.com
Rooms vary from simple to luxur-
ious at this industrial-chic hotel
located in a former borstal. Unique
focus on culture and events.

North Holland

BERGEN AAN ZEE: Blooming €€
Design **Map** B3
Duinweg 5, 1861 GL
Tel *(072) 582 0520*
W blooming-hotels.com
This hip hotel is set in 11 ha
(27 acres) of private woodland and
dunes. Rooms range from tiny
singles to bright and airy suites.

**BROEK IN WATERLAND: Inn on
the Lake** €€
Charming **Map** C3
Kerkplein 11, 1151 AH
Tel *(020) 331 8573*
W innonthelake.nl
Housed in a former vicarage dating
back to the 17th century, this B&B
offers four uniquely-styled rooms
with five-star amenities.

HAARLEM: Stempels €€
Historic **Map** B3
Klokhuisplein 9, 2011 HK
Tel *(023) 512 3910*
W stempelsinhaarlem.nl
Once the venue for the royal
banknotes printing company,
the building is now home to
Stempels, a boutique hotel with
modern amenities.

HEEMSKERK: Stayokay €
Historic **Map** B3
Tolweg 9, 1967 NG
Tel *(0251) 232 288*
W stayokay.com
Enjoy the experience of staying
in a medieval castle with turrets,
towers, moat and gardens at this
hostel. Shared and private rooms.
Bike rental service.

DK Choice

ZAANDAM: Inntel €€
Design **Map** B3
Provincialeweg 102, 1506 MD
Tel *(075) 631 1711*
W inntelhotels.nl
The unique building of this
four-star hotel resembles the
famous wooden houses of
the nearby Zaanse Schans.
The contemporary rooms are
inspired by the town's history
or pay homage to its residents.

**ZUIDOOSTBEEMSTER: Fort
Resort Beemster** €€
Hotels with Character **Map** C3
Nekkerweg 24, 1461 LC
Tel *(0299) 682 200*
W fortresortbeemster.nl
This hotel is housed in a historic
building that was once a part of
the Defence Line of Amsterdam,
a UNESCO World Heritage Site.
Great spa and wellness facilities.

Utrecht

AMERONGEN: Buitenlust €
Charming **Map** C4
Burg Jhr H v d Boschstraat 13, 3958 CA
Tel *(0343) 451 692*
W buitenlust-amerongen.nl
Located near Utrechtse Heuvelrug
National Park, Buitenlust is a great
option to explore the surrounding
area. Cheerful, spacious rooms.

**AMERSFOORT: Logies
de Tabaksplant** €
Historic **Map** C4
Coninckstraat 15, 3811 WD
Tel *(033) 472 9797*
W tabaksplant.nl
Rooms are spread over several
medieval buildings, with a lovely
restaurant and courtyard.

Simple, subtle decor at Stempels hotel
in Haarlem

UTRECHT: Mary K €€
Charming **Map** C4
Oudegracht 25, 3511 AB
Tel *(030) 230 4888*
W marykhotel.com
Located at the quiet end of the
Oudegracht, the quirky Mary K
offers rooms of all sizes, each
designed by a local artist.

DK Choice

UTRECHT: Dom €€€
Design **Map** C4
Domstraat 4, 3512 JB
Tel *(030) 232 4242*
W hoteldom.nl
Contemporary restyling has
transformed this 18th-century
building into a luxury hotel.
Stay in one of their state-of-
the-art rooms with Auping
beds, Nespresso machines
and yoga mats. The hotel also
has a coveted restaurant and
a cocktail bar out of a Bond
movie. Quite an experience.

ZEIST: Kasteel Kerckebosch €€
Historic **Map** C4
Arnhemse Bovenweg 31, 3708 AA
Tel *(030) 692 6666*
W kasteelkerckebosch.nl
This castle in the woods has
modern rooms and an excellent
restaurant. Amenities include bike
rental and packed lunch boxes.

South Holland

**DELFT: De Bieslandse
Heerlijkheid** €€
Charming **Map** B4
Klein Delfgauw 61, 2616 LC
Tel *(015) 310 7126*
W bieslandseheerlijkheid.nl
Surrounded by acres of polderland,
this rustic B&B is set in a converted
farmhouse. The main building
has four comfortable rooms, plus
a cosy garden house.

For more information on types of hotels *see page 391*

Tables awaiting diners at the lovely "market café" at Villa Augustus, Dordrecht

DORDRECHT: Villa Augustus €€
Design **Map** B4
Oranjelaan 7, 3311 DH
Tel *(078) 639 3111*
W villa-augustus.nl
A boutique hotel housed in a
castle-like water tower, this place
offers great views, a huge garden,
a "market café" and a restaurant.

DK Choice

ROTTERDAM: Stayokay €
Hotels with Character Map B4
Overblaak 85–87, 3011 MH
Tel *(010) 436 5763*
W stayokay.com
Located in the Cube Houses built
by Piet Blom in the 1980s, this
hotel looks distinctly quirky. The
comfortable rooms, however,
ensure a pleasant stay. There are
cafés and restaurants nearby,
along with good transport links.

ROTTERDAM: SS Rotterdam €€
Design **Map** B4
3e Katendrechtsehoofd 25, 3072 AM
Tel *(010) 297 3090*
W ssrotterdam.nl
Holland America Line's former
flagship, SS Rotterdam is now
a floating hotel in 1950s style.

SCHEVENINGEN: Strandhotel €
Charming **Map** B4
Zeekant 111, 2586 JJ
Tel *(070) 354 0193*
W strandhotel-scheveningen.nl
This small, family-run hotel on
the beach features basic budget
rooms and pleasant sea-view
rooms. Picnic baskets available.

THE HAGUE: Mozaic €€
Design **Map** B4
*Laan Copes van Cattenburch 38–40,
2585 GB*
Tel *(070) 352 2335*
W mozaic.nl
Stay in trendy, well-appointed
rooms in this boutique hotel set
in an elegant neighbourhood.

Zeeland

**CADZANDBAD: De
Blanke Top**
Family-friendly **Map** A5
Boulevard de Wielingen 1, 4506 JH
Tel *(0117) 392 040*
W blanketop.nl
Pretty views at this resort are as
inviting as the delectable food at
its fine-dining restaurant. There's
an ongoing renovation, but the
main building remains open.

DOMBURG: Hotel ter Duyn €€
Charming **Map** A5
PJ Eloutstraat 1, 4357 AH
Tel *(0118) 584 400*
W hotelterduyn.nl
Just a stone's throw away from
the beach, this pleasant hotel
has suites only, each with a
small kitchen.

**KRUININGEN: Manoir
Inter Scaldes** €€€
Luxury **Map** B5
Zandweg 2, 4416 NA
Tel *(0113) 381 753*
W interscaldes.eu
This Relais & Châteaux member
has 12 stylish rooms in a
thatched villa, and a Michelin-
starred restaurant.

DK Choice

**MIDDELBURG: Aan
de Dam** €€
Historic **Map** A5
Dam 31, 4331 GE
Tel *(0118) 643 773*
W hotelaandedam.nl
Originally built in the 17th
century, this historic mansion
now houses a charming hotel
with guest rooms that recall
the Golden Age. Contemporary
furnishings complement
the vintage ambience of the
tastefully decorated rooms.
Enthusiastic staff.

SINT MAARTENSDIJK: Kom! €€
Charming **Map** B5
Markt 58, 4695 CH
Tel *(0166) 663 000*
W hotelkom.nl
Behind a 16th-century façade is
a boutique hotel with modern
rooms. Good, affordable restaurant.

**SLUIS: Gasthof d'Ouwe
Schuure** €
Charming **Map** A5
St Annastraat 191, 4524 JH
Tel *(0117) 462 232*
W ouweschuure.nl
This B&B on the Belgian border
has seven rooms and a farm-
house converted into a restaurant.

West Frisian Islands

DK Choice

AMELAND: Nobel €€
Design **Map** C1
*Gerrit Kosterweg 16, Ballum
9162 EN*
Tel *(0519) 554 157*
W hotelnobel.nl
Stay in stylish, futuristic-looking
rooms at this smart contemporary hotel. It also has a fine-
dining restaurant – a modern
take on the old brown café, a
liquor store with an impressive
wine list and its own distillery.

**SCHIERMONNIKOOG: Van
der Werff** €€
Historic **Map** D1
Reeweg 2, 9166 PX
Tel *(0519) 531 203*
W hotelvanderwerff.nl
This legendary inn, reached by
ferry and vintage omnibus, has
neat, modern rooms on offer.

TERSCHELLING: Stayokay €
Charming **Map** C1
't Land 2, West Terschelling, 8881 GA
Tel *(0562) 442 338*
W stayokay.com
Enjoy pleasant views of the
Wadden Sea from this hostel
situated on a dune top. Shared
and private rooms. Good for biking.

**TERSCHELLING: Sandton
Paal 8 aan Zee** €€€
Luxury **Map** C1
*Badweg West 4, West Terschelling,
8881 HG*
Tel *(0562) 449 090*
W sandton.eu/nl/terschelling
Well-furnished rooms with great
views await visitors at this four-
star resort on a dune top. Pool,
sauna and bike rentals are
among the amenities offered.

TEXEL: Zeerust €€
Charming   Map B2
Boodtlaan 5, De Koog, 1796 BD
Tel *(0222) 317 261*
W hotelzeerust.nl
This up-to-date, small hotel is ideally located between village, woods and beach. Fresh breakfasts available.

TEXEL: Bij Jef €€€
Design   Map B2
Herenstraat 34, Den Hoorn, 1797 AJ
Tel *(0222) 319 623*
W bijjef.nl
Set in a former vicarage, this luxurious B&B comes with five-star amenities and fine views. Michelin-starred restaurant.

VLIELAND: WestCord Residentie Vlierijck €€€
Luxury   Map C1
Willem de Vlaminghweg 2, 8899 AV
Tel *(0562) 453 840*
W residentie-vlierijck-vlieland.nl
Balconied self-catering apartments with a bar, restaurant, pool and sauna are on offer at this smart apartment-hotel. Close to the ferry.

Groningen

DEN HAM: Piloersemaborg €€
Historic   Map D3
Sietse Veldstraweg 25, 9833 TA
Tel *(050) 403 1362*
W piloersema.nl
Stay in a well-preserved 17th-century grange that features five luxurious rooms and a first-rate restaurant.

EENRUM: Grand Hotel de Kromme Raake €€
Historic   Map D1
Molenstraat 5, 9967 SL
Tel *(0595) 491 600*
W hoteldekrommeraake.nl
This is officially the world's smallest hotel, with only one room, but that one has hosted many celebrities.

DK Choice

GRONINGEN: Stee in Stad €
Charming   Map D1
Floresstraat 75, 9715 HR
Tel *(050) 577 9896*
W steeinstad.nl
Three homes located in a residential neighbourhood have been lovingly converted into a characterful B&B, which serves as a work project for disadvantaged people. All nine rooms (singles and doubles) have been individually decorated based on themes.

GRONINGEN: Asgard €€
Design   Map D1
Ganzevoortsingel 2–1, 9711 AL
Tel *(050) 368 4810*
W asgardhotel.nl
Minimalist rooms with floor heating and rain showers are on offer at this revamped 1930s deaconess hospital.

GRONINGEN: Prinsenhof €€
Historic   Map D1
Martinikerkhof 23, 9712 JH
Tel *(050) 317 6550*
W prinsenhof-groningen.nl
A 15th-century palace makes for stunning grandeur in conversion. Beautiful gardens. Elegant restaurant and an equally refined café.

LUTJEGAST: Erfgoed Rikkerda €€
Charming   Map D1
Abel Tasmanweg 28, 9866 TD
Tel *(0594) 612 928*
W rikkerda.nl
This stylish B&B features spacious accomodation and a charming garden. Stabling facilities available.

WARFHUIZEN: De Theaterherberg €
Design   Map D1
Baron van Asbeckweg 42, 9963 PC
Tel *(0595) 572 742*
W theaterherberg.nl
The "Theatre Inn" houses a tiny theatre and, in the former 19th-century wine barn, four literary-themed rooms.

Friesland

HARICH: Welgelegen €
Charming   Map C2
Welgelegen 15, 8571 RG
Tel *(0514) 605 050*
W hotelwelgelegen.nl
Inside a 19th-century farmhouse, Welgelegen offers a romantic bridal suite upstairs.

DK Choice

HARLINGEN: Harbour Crane €€€
Hotels with Character   Map C2
Dokkade 5, 8862 NZ
Tel *(0517) 414 410*
W havenkraan.nl
An old harbour crane has been painstakingly converted into a contemporary hotel room: the bed is 17 m (56 ft) above ground and the crane revolves 360 degrees for a constantly changing, panoramic view of Friesland and the Wadden Sea.

KOUDUM: Galamadammen €€
Charming   Map C2
Galamadammen 1–4, 8723 CE
Tel *(0514) 521 346*
W galamadammen.nl
Set beside the marina, this hotel calls for exploring the Frisian lakes by rental boat.

LEEUWARDEN: Grand Hotel Post Plaza €€
Luxury   Map D1
Tweebaksmarkt 25–27, 8911 KW
Tel *(058) 215 9317*
W post-plaza.nl
Plush accomodation in an 18th-century former bank building, this centrally located hotel has modern rooms and a spa.

STAVOREN: De Vrouwe van Stavoren €
Design   Map C2
Havenweg 1, 8715 EM
Tel *(0514) 681 202*
W hotel-vrouwevanstavoren.nl
Sleep in a Swiss wine cask – complete with sitting area, private bath and twin beds. Quite an extraordinary accommodation.

TERNAARD: Herberg de Waard van Ternaard €€
Charming   Map D1
De Groedse 3, 9145 RG
Tel *(0519) 571 846*
W herbergdewaard.nl
This inn in an 1860s mansion, now transformed into a boutique hotel, offers rooms decorated in wood and marble.

Drenthe

COEVORDEN: Kasteel Coevorden €€
Design   Map E2
Het Kasteel 29, 7741 GC
Tel *(0524) 522 009*
W kasteelcoevorden.nl
Right at the town centre, this hotel is housed in a beautifully preserved century-old warehouse.

Grand entrance to the Prinsenhof hotel in Groningen

For more information on types of hotels *see page 391*

DE SCHIPHORST: Château De Havixhorst €€€
Luxury Map D3
De Schiphorsterweg 34–36, 7966 AC
Tel *(0522) 441 487*
W dehavixhorst.nl
Stay in lavish suites in a romantic 17th-century manor house on an estate with Baroque gardens.

NORG: De Eshof €
Charming Map D2
Esweg 25, 9331 AP
Tel *06 2169 0092*
W eshofnorg.nl
Three rooms, a sauna and a pool are on offer at this B&B in a converted 18th-century Saxon farm.

DK Choice

VEENHUIZEN: Bitter & Zoet €€
Historic Map D2
Hospitaallaan 16, 9341 AH
Tel *(0592) 385 002*
W bitterenzoetveenhuizen.nl
"Dedication", "Obligation" and "Bitter & Sweet" – the three buildings of a monumental 19th-century hospital complex now make for a boutique hotel with stylish rooms and apartments, a sauna, restaurant and bakery.

ZEEGSE: De Zeegser Duinen €€
Charming Map D2
Schipborgerweg 8, 9483 TL
Tel *(0592) 530 099*
W hoteldezeegserduinen.nl
This four-star hotel is set in a wooded nature reserve. Check in, go cycling and return to unwind.

Overijssel

BLOKZIJL: Kaatjes Résidence €€€
Design Map D2
Brouwerstraat 20, 8356 DV
Tel *(0527) 291 833*
W kaatje.nl
Located on a pretty square, this luxurious B&B has modern rooms and a Michelin-starred restaurant.

DK Choice

HENGELO: Tuindorphotel 't Lansink €€
Hotels with Character Map E3
C T Storkstraat 18, 7553 AR
Tel *(074) 291 0066*
W hotellansink.com
Built a century ago as part of a garden village for Stork factory workers, this small-scale grand hotel once hosted famous (and royal) guests. Today, it has heaps of character, a fine-dining restaurant and contemporary rooms.

Beautifully decorated guest room at Modez in Arnhem

HOLTEN: Hoog Holten €€
Charming Map D3
Forthaarsweg 7, 7451 JS
Tel *(0548) 361 306*
W hoogholten.nl
Wonderful hideaway in a former hunting lodge, Hoog Holten features well-furnished rooms, a pleasant terrace, wine bar and a restaurant.

LATTROP: Landgoed de Holtweijde €€
Luxury Map E3
Spiekweg 7, 7635 LP
Tel *(0541) 229 234*
W holtweijde.nl
The tranquil setting adds to the charm of this five-star resort. There are suites and private cottages, as well as a spa, tennis courts and driving range.

TUBBERGEN: Droste's €
Design Map E3
Uelserweg 95, 7651 KV
Tel *(0546) 621 264*
W drostes.nl
A cosy, contemporary inn with a restaurant, Droste's is set amid rolling meadows. Rooms are comfortable; some feature a balcony or terrace.

ZWOLLE: Hampshire Hotel Lumen €€
Design Map D3
Stadionplein 20, 8025 CP
Tel *(088) 147 1471*
W hotellumen.nl
Four-star hotel with an odd soccer stadium location, but stylish lobby, lounge and restaurant.

ZWOLLE: De Koperen Hoogte €€
Design Map D3
Lichtmisweg 51, 8035 PL
Tel *(0529) 428 428*
W dekoperenhoogte.nl
Rooms are kitschy, but luxurious at this hotel housed in a former water tower. There's a revolving restaurant offering great views.

Flevoland

EMMELOORD: Hotel Emmeloord €
Business Map D2
Het Hooiveld 9, 8302 AE
Tel *(0527) 612 345*
W hotelemmeloord.nl
This great-value hotel is located beside a marina, 20 minutes from the national park.

LELYSTAD: Waterlodge de Aalscholver €
Design Map C3
Rijksweg A6, Parkeerplaats "de Aalschover", 8218 PW
Tel *(036) 523 9273*
W haje.nu
Accommodation at this offbeat roadside restaurant is in rooms in a floating "hotel ark" on the water.

LELYSTAD: De Groene Watertuinen €€€
Luxury Map C3
Groene Velden 154, 8211 BD
Tel *(0320) 263 310*
W groenewatertuinen.nl
Set in a leafy suburb, this hotel features two suites, plus a pool, jacuzzi and sauna.

DK Choice

URK: Pension het Anker Wijk €
Charming Map C3
4–13/Prins Hendrikstraat 13, 8321 GC
Tel *(0527) 685 307*
W overnachteninurk.nl
One of Urk's best B&Bs, this snug, little place is housed in a former fisherman's cottage in the older part of the village. It's here that guests can get an experience of how the fishing village traditionally looked.

Gelderland

ARNHEM: Modez €€
Design Map D4
Elly Lamakerplantsoen 4, 6822 BZ
Tel *(026) 442 0993*
W hotelmodez.nl
This striking hotel is decorated by 30 designers under the guidance of fashion illustrator Piet Paris.

BRUMMEN: Het Oude Postkantoor €€
Charming Map D4
Zutphensestraat 6, 6971 EM
Tel *(0575) 566 781*
W hetoudepostkantoor.nl
The village post office has been converted into a small hotel with authentic details.

DOETINCHEM: Villa Ruimzicht €€
Charming   Map D4
Ruimzichtlaan 150, 7001 KG
Tel *(0314) 320 680*
🆆 *hotelvillaruimzicht.nl*
Adventurous cooking, designer furniture and art come together at this 19th-century manor.

HARDERWIJK: Harderwijk op de Veluwe €€
Luxury   Map C3
Leuvenumseweg 7, 3847 LA
Tel *(0341) 801 010*
🆆 *hotelharderwijk.com*
All smartly furnished rooms have Jacuzzis and rain showers at this four-star hotel.

NIJMEGEN: Manna €€
Design   Map D4
Oranjesingel 2C, 6511 NS
Tel *(024) 365 0990*
🆆 *manna-nijmegen.nl*
Individually decorated suites and studios are on offer at this stylish boutique hotel.

OTTERLO: Sterrenberg €€
Design   Map D4
Houtkampweg 1, 6731 AV
Tel *(0318) 591 228*
🆆 *sterrenberg.nl*
This wonderful hideaway is close to the Hoge Veluwe national park. Great restaurant, indoor pool, spa.

DK Choice

TEUGE: Airplane Suite €€€
Hotels with Character   Map D3
De Zanden 61B, 7395 PA
Tel *06 1938 8603*
🆆 *vliegtuighotel.nl*
An Ilyushin 18 aircraft that flew Communist Party moguls in the 1960s has been converted into a suite for two with an Auping bed, pantry, sauna and jacuzzi. The cockpit is still fully equipped.

North Brabant

BREDA: Bliss €€€
Design   Map B5
Torenstraat 9–11, 4811 XV
Tel *(076) 533 5980*
🆆 *blisshotel.nl*
Nine themed suites come with Jacuzzis, fireplaces, workstations or terraces.

GELDROP: Nijver €
Design   Map D5
Heuvel 1A, 5664 HJ
Tel *(040) 286 7000*
🆆 *hotelnijver.nl*
Nijver is a boutique hotel that pays tribute to the textile industry with its nine stylishly decorated suites.

KAATSHEUVEL: Efteling Hotel €€€
Design   Map D5
Horst 31, 5171 RA
Tel *(0416) 537 777*
🆆 *efteling.com*
Four-star hotel in a cloud castle near a well-known amusement park. Fairytale-themed rooms.

DK Choice

NIEUWENDIJK: Fort Bakkerskil €
Historic   Map C4
Kildijk 143, 4255 TH
Tel *06 4593 4892*
🆆 *bakkerskil.nl*
Part of the 19th-century New Dutch Water Line, this sturdy fort has now been converted into a B&B: choose between a bed in the sickbay, powder magazine or explosives storage.

OISTERWIJK: Stille Wilde €
Family-friendly   Map C5
Scheibaan 11, 5062 TM
Tel *(013) 528 2301*
🆆 *stillewilde.nl*
Comfortable rooms with terrace or balcony are on offer here. Ample recreational opportunities.

OSSENDRECHT: De Volksabdij €
Historic   Map B5
Onze Lieve Vrouwe ter Duinenlaan 199, 4641 RM
Tel *(0164) 672 546*
🆆 *devolksabdij.nl*
The well-appointed rooms of this heritage hotel occupy a former monastery, set in a nature reserve.

'S-HERTOGENBOSCH: Stadshotel Jeroen €€
Charming   Map C4
Jeroen Boschplein 6, 5211 ML
Tel *(073) 610 3556*
🆆 *stadshoteljeroenbosch.nl*
This stylish hotel is named after painter Hieronymus Bosch. Choose

Airplane Suite, Teuge, set in a disused Ilyushin 18 aircraft

between four characterful rooms and two spacious suites. There's also a parlour and a terrace.

Limburg

KERKRADE: Abdij Rolduc €
Historic   Map D6
Heyendallaan 82, 6464 EP
Tel *(045) 546 6888*
🆆 *rolduc.com*
A 900-year-old abbey that now houses a conference centre, restaurant and hotel.

MAASTRICHT: Zenden €
Design   Map C6
Sint Bernardusstraat 5, 6211 HK
Tel *(043) 321 2211*
🆆 *zenden.nl*
Minimalist rooms with Auping beds, Vitra furniture, Alessi baths.

MAASTRICHT: Kruisherenhotel €€€
Luxury   Map C6
Kruisherengang 19–23, 6211 NW
Tel *(043) 329 2020*
🆆 *chateauhotels.nl*
Design hotel with individually decorated rooms.

DK Choice

ROERMOND: Het Arresthuis €€
Hotels with Character   Map D5
Pollartstraat 7, 6041 GC
Tel *(0475) 870 870*
🆆 *hetarresthuis.nl*
The cells of this 19th-century prison have been converted into "comfort cachots". The warden's office is now a luxury suite, the yard has become a patio, and instead of roll calls, there are six-course dinners.

SITTARD: Merici €€
Historic   Map D6
Oude Markt 25, 6131 EN
Tel *(046) 400 9002*
🆆 *hotelmerici.nl*
Merici is a charming four-star hotel set inside a 19th-century Ursuline boarding school.

VALKENBURG AAN DE GEUL: Dieteren €€
Charming   Map D6
Neerhem 34, 6301 CH
Tel *(043) 601 5404*
🆆 *hoteldieterenvalkenburg.nl*
Located beside the cable car in a picture-perfect town, Dieteren offers comfortable rooms with balcony or terrace. There's also a pool and a garden.

For more information on types of hotels *see page 391*

WHERE TO EAT AND DRINK

The Dutch are innovative people, and this quality is reflected in their cooking. Old colonial ties have long influenced Dutch cuisine and its restaurant scene, so Surinamese and especially Indonesian restaurants are aplenty. More recently, as the Dutch have been introduced to the cooking skills of immigrants into the area, Turkish snack bars and Moroccan restaurants are popping up.

The Dutch restaurant scene leans heavily on international influences. Especially in the bigger cities, visitors can choose between exotic flavours from countries as diverse as Spain, Greece, Israel, Lebanon, Sweden, Ethiopia, India, Thailand, Vietnam and Japan. A popular Dutch phenomenon is the *eetcafé*,

or bar, where diners can order meals from a limited menu, featuring at least one inexpensive, daily-changing set menu (*dagmenu*).

Although many Dutch have forgotten, there is such a thing as "traditional Dutch cooking", which is now being rediscovered. A growing number of chefs are serving new takes on traditional Dutch fare, involving meat or fish, potatoes and more elaborate sauces. Eating out has long been considered something people hastily do in between appointments or before going to the theatre, but the Dutch are now taking it more seriously and the number of Michelin-starred restaurants is on the rise.

Eating out is an increasingly popular pastime in the Netherlands

Types of Restaurant

The Netherlands boasts a wide variety of restaurants. Amsterdam is one of the best places in Europe to try the diverse flavours of Indonesia, and Chinese restaurants and pizzerias have also spread far and wide across the country. Indeed it is difficult to find a country whose cuisine is not represented by some restaurant in the Netherlands. There is also an infinite variety in the range of dishes, ingredients, presentation and price.

Traditional Dutch cooking is best described as simple and straightforward. As a maritime nation, the Netherlands does have many fish restaurants, particularly along the coast. A large number of restaurants serve French cuisine, and their quality is consistently improving. Chefs frequently add local ingredients to French recipes,

such as fennel or asparagus. This means that you can eat wild duck on endive *stamppot* (mashed potato and cabbage), a combination unheard of in France. It is in areas such as these that Dutch chefs are showing increasing inventiveness.

Eetcafés

Eetcafés (eating cafés) are a popular phenomenon in the Netherlands. The term *eetcafés* is most commonly applied to traditional brown cafés. Initially, some cafés and bars sold snacks to go with their drinks, such as an appetizer, a sandwich or a meatball. These snacks have since been refined to a growing extent. Bars and cafés have gradually evolved into *eetcafés* where diners can enjoy sandwiches at

lunchtime and cheap, often very decent, meals in the evenings, usually at much lower prices than those in traditional restaurants.

Vegetarian Restaurants

Most restaurants have several vegetarian dishes on their menus. This applies both to Dutch/French restaurants and to ethnic restaurants. There is also an increasing number of restaurants that cater exclusively to vegetarian diners.

Opening Hours

The Netherlands does not have a tradition of lunching, but this is gradually changing, with more restaurants now opening at lunchtime, usually from noon to 2pm. In the evenings, the

An *eetcafé*, one of the many in Holland serving increasingly refined meals

Vibrant interiors at Eetbar Dit *(see p415)* in 's-Hertogenbosch

majority of restaurants open at 6pm and the kitchens usually close around 10pm. An increasing number of restaurants stay open all day, serving breakfast, lunch and dinner and light meals or snacks in between.

In the cities, night restaurants are on the rise, with kitchens staying open until midnight or later, allowing you to round off a visit to the theatre or movies with a late dinner.

Traditionally, many restaurants do not open on Mondays, though this is also changing.

Reservations

Anybody wishing to eat in one of the country's more renowned restaurants would do well to book, and sometimes booking a few days in advance – or weeks for the most acclaimed restaurants – is advisable. *Eetcafés* and other informal eateries can get crowded in the evenings, but reservations are usually accepted only for large groups, if at all.

Tipping

It is customary to leave a tip of roughly 10 per cent by rounding up the amount. If you pay by credit card, you can either add the tip to the bill or leave change on the table. Leaving no tip at all is usually done only when you are particularly dissatisfied with the service provided. At very informal places, such as takeaways or snack bars, tipping is not expected.

Etiquette

The atmosphere at many Dutch restaurants is fairly informal, and you can generally wear what you like; smart casual dress is suitable almost everywhere. In upmarket restaurants, however, dressing smartly is appropriate. Smoking is banned in all restaurants. It is considered impolite to use your mobile phone while at the table.

Prices

Restaurants are legally obliged to display their menu outside, with prices, inclusive of VAT

A snack bar, ideal for a quick but satisfying bite to eat

("BTW") and service. Prices can vary markedly, and a restaurant can be found in each price class: you can find many establishments where you can eat for less than €25; in top restaurants, however, you should not be surprised if your bill exceeds €70, excluding wine. The cost of drinks is invariably extra and the mark-up levied by a restaurant, especially on house wine and table water, can be high.

Travellers with Disabilities

Many restaurants are accessible for wheelchairs, but even if they are, toilet facilities may still pose a problem, as they are often reached via stairs and therefore not easily accessible.

Drinks

All but the most informal restaurants will have a wine list offering a range of fine wines to accompany your meal. Although French wines are still the staple, New World wines have become increasingly popular. Upmarket restaurants will have a sommelier to help you with your choice, and many offer a wine package, serving a glass of carefully paired wine with your meal.

Typically Dutch brown cafés are making way for airy grand cafés and sleek cocktail bars, offering a long list of exotic aperitifs. However, for most Dutch, beer is still the tipple of choice, with Heineken or any other Dutch lager on tap everywhere.

Recommended Restaurants

The restaurants listed on pages 406–415 have been selected not only for the quality of food served, but also on the basis of value for money, atmosphere, location and service. Obviously, some restaurants are better than others and a few stand out for a particular reason, such as their innovative chef, pleasant waterside terrace or romantic atmosphere. For each region we have have handpicked one such exceptional restaurant, ranging from a year-round beach club at the quiet end of Zandvoort beach, via a tiny Italian trattoria dishing out fantastic king crab cannelloni, to a Michelin-starred restaurant in a fairytale castle, with a terrace that seems to float in the moat. Here you will not only be guaranteed a decent meal, but also gain a memorable experience. Our highly recommended restaurants are marked as "DK Choice".

The Flavours of the Netherlands

The typical Dutch menu offers good, solid fare. Pork, hams and all kinds of sausages are popular, while the North Sea provides plenty of fresh fish, especially cod, herring and mackerel, as well as its own variety of tiny brown shrimps. Leafy green vegetables, such as cabbage, endive (chicory) and curly kale make regular appearances, frequently mashed with the ubiquitous potato. Sauerkraut arrived from Germany long ago and is now considered a native dish. The world-famous Gouda and Edam cheeses are sold at various stages of maturity, and with flavourings such as cloves, cumin or herbs.

Edam cheese

Sampling pickled herring at one of Amsterdam's many fish-stalls

Amsterdam's Culinary Influences

Traditional Dutch cuisine may be simple, wholesome and hearty, but the variety of food on offer in Amsterdam is huge and influenced by culinary styles from across the globe. The Netherlands was once a major colonial power and its trading ships brought back exotic ingredients, ideas and people from former colonies to settle. Dutch chefs branched out and tried new flavours, and as such, "fusion" food has long been a feature of Amsterdam's menus. From its street-corner fish-stalls to its cafés and top-flight gourmet restaurants, eating out in Amsterdam can be full of surprises. Over 50 national cuisines are represented, offering a sometimes bewildering variety of choice and good value for money.

The Melting Pot

Amsterdam has long had a reputation for religious and political tolerance. Refugees who found a safe haven there brought along their own styles of cooking. In the 16th century, Jews fleeing

Fried tofu with sambal oelek (chilli sauce)

Bami goreng (fried noodles with chicken and pork)

Steamed rice

Prawn crackers

Gado gado (vegetable salad with peanut sauce)

Satay ayam (chicken satay)

Selection of typical *rijsttafel* dishes

Local Dishes and Specialities

Erwtensoep is a thick pea and smoked sausage soup, which is often served with rye bread and slices of bacon.

Brown shrimp

Dining out in the Netherlands is almost guaranteed to come up with some curious quirks. Cheese, ham and bread are standards at breakfast, but you may also find *ontbijtkoek* (gingerbread) and *hagelslag* (grains of chocolate) to sprinkle over bread. Ham and cheese are also lunchtime staples, often served in a bread roll with a glass of milk, though more adventurous sandwiches and salads are also common nowadays. In Amsterdam, pancake houses provide both sweet and savoury snacks throughout the day. The evening is the time when Amsterdam's eateries have the most to offer. The soups and mashed vegetables of Dutch farmhouse cooking sit alongside spicy Indonesian delights, as well as innovative cuisine from some of Amsterdam's fine chefs.

Baskets of wild mushrooms at an organic market

persecution in Portugal and Antwerp were some of the first foreigners to make their home in the city. Today, Amsterdammers count as their own such Jewish specialities as *pekelvlees* (salt beef), pickled vegetables (often served as salad) and a variety of sticky cakes, now found mostly in the more old-fashioned tea-rooms.

The 20th century saw an influx of immigrants from Turkey and several North African countries. Large Arab and Turkish communities have become established in Amsterdam. As a result, restaurants with menus that feature Middle-Eastern style stuffed vegetables, succulent stews and couscous, are almost everywhere. *Falafel* (fried chickpea balls) are readily available from road-side take-aways and are now one of the

city's favourite late-night snacks. Ethiopians, Greeks, Thais, Italians and Japanese are among other waves of immigrants to make their culinary mark, and most recently traditional British fare has become popular.

Gouda on offer in an Amsterdam cheese shop

Indonesian Legacy

The Dutch began colonizing Indonesia in the 17th century and ruled the southeast Asian archipelago right up until 1949. Indonesian cuisine has had a marked influence on eating habits in the Netherlands. Ingredients once regarded as exotic have crept into Dutch dishes. It is now commonplace to spice up apple pies and biscuits with cinnamon, which is sometimes even used to flavour vegetables. Coconut and chillis are very popular flavourings, too, and sampling a *rijsttafel* (see below) is considered one of the highlights of any trip to the country.

THE RIJSTTAFEL

Dutch colonialists in Indonesia often found that the modest local portions failed to satisfy their hunger. To match their larger appetites, they created the *rijsttafel* (literally "rice-table"). It consists of around 20 small spicy dishes, served up with a shared bowl of rice or noodles. Pork or chicken *satay* (mini kebabs with peanut sauce) and *kroepoek* (prawn crackers) usually arrive first. A selection of curried meat and vegetable dishes follows, with perhaps a plate of fried tofu and various salads, all more or less served together. A sweet treat, such as bananas fried in batter, rounds it all off.

Shrimp croquettes are shrimps in a creamy sauce, coated in breadcrumbs and deep-fried.

Stamppot is a hearty dish of curly kale or endive (chicory) and crispy bacon mixed with mashed potato.

Nasi goreng, an Indonesian-style dish of egg-fried rice with pork and mush-rooms, is also popular for a *rijsttafel*.

Where to Eat and Drink

Amsterdam

Oude Zijde

De Bakkerswinkel　　　　€
Bakery　　　　　**Map** 2 D4
Warmoesstraat 69, 1012 HX
Tel *(020) 489 8000*
Try traditional English scones
with cream (not clotted, sadly)
or lemon curd. Serves breakfast,
lunch and has a high tea menu.

Café de Engelbewaarder　　€
Brown Café　　　　**Map** 5 1A
Kloveniersburgwal 59, 1011 JZ
Tel *(020) 625 3772*
The daily-changing menu at this
laid-back, traditional Dutch pub
is mostly European and seasonal.
Vegetarian options are also
available. Live jazz on Sundays.

Éenvistwéévis　　　　€€
Seafood　　　　　**Map** 5 C1
Schippersgracht 6, 1011 TR
Tel *(020) 623 2894*　　**Closed** *Sun &*
Mon
A paradise for fish lovers, the
menu here depends on the daily
catch and seasons. Organic,
sustainable ingredients. Intimate
decor. No credit cards.

In de Waag　　　　　€€
Fusion　　　　　**Map** 5 B1
Nieuwmarkt 4, 1012 CR
Tel *(020) 422 7772*
This restaurant is located in a 1488
guildhouse, on the top floor of
which Rembrandt once took
anatomy lessons. Informal interior
lit by 300 candles. Eclectic menu,
divine desserts. Book ahead.

Kilimanjaro　　　　€€
African　　　　　**Map** 5 C1
Rapenburgerplein 6, 1011 VB
Tel *(020) 622 3485*　　**Closed** *Mon*
Sample West-African antelope
stew or Senegalese crocodile

yassa at this Pan-African restaurant
serving specialities from across
the continent. Warm decor, with
African artwork. No credit cards.

Blauw aan de Wal　　　€€€
Fusion　　　　　**Map** 5 A1
Oudezijds Achterburgwal 99, 1012 DD
Tel *(020) 330 2257*　　**Closed** *Sun*
Set in an ancient warehouse, this
place features rustic decor, brick
walls and wooden beams. It
serves modern Mediterranean
delights, with a menu that
changes every week. Outstanding
wine list. Reservations essential.

Nieuwe Zijde

Catala　　　　　€
Spanish　　　　　**Map** 1 C5
Spuistraat 299, 1012 VS
Tel *(020) 623 1141*
Sample authentic Catalonian
tapas in the warm rustic interior
of this restaurant. Popular fish
dishes include rice with shellfish,
grilled swordfish and monkfish. Or,
try the famous Pata Negra *jamon*.

Getto Food & Drinks　　€
Café/Bar　　　　**Map** 2 E4
Warmoesstraat 51, 1012HW
Tel *(020) 421 5151*　　**Closed** *Mon*
This gay-friendly bar-restaurant,
offers home-style cooking.
Burgers are a speciality here,
and are named after famous
Amsterdam drag queens, like the
"Jennifer Hopelezz".

Kam Yin　　　　　€
International　　　　**Map** 2 E4
Warmoesstraat 6, 1012 JD
Tel *(020) 625 3115*
An Amsterdam institution, Kam
Yin serves Chinese and Surinamese

cuisine. The extensive menu
makes it a great place for quick,
delicious food. There is an attached
snackbar. Well worth a visit.

Tibet　　　　　€€
Tibetan/Chinese　　**Map** 2 E4
Lange Niezel 24, 1012 GT
Tel *(020) 624 1137*
Choose from a variety of Chinese
Szechuan dishes, as well as staple
Tibetan fare. Asian lunch (rice,
noodle dishes) is also served
here. Eclectic Tibetan decor and
relaxed service.

ANNA　　　　　€€€
European　　　　**Map** 2 D4
Warmoesstraat 11, 1012 JA
Tel *(020) 428 1111*　　**Closed** *Sun*
This upmarket restaurant is housed
in two renovated buildings. Serves
European cuisine with a twist –
including dishes like pan-fried
corvine fillet and braised quail.

D'Vijff Vlieghen　　　€€€
Traditional　　　　**Map** 1 C5
Spuistraat 294–302, 1012 VX
Tel *(020) 530 4060*
Dine surrounded by original
Rembrandt etchings and 17th-
century furnishings. Try lightly
smoked duck breast, or the
"surprising" chef's menu.

Central Canal Ring

Goodies　　　　　€
Mediterranean　　　**Map** 4 E1
Huidenstraat 9, 1016 ER
Tel *(020) 625 6122*
An informal diner, Goodies serves
great food made from organic

Elegant, bistro-style decor at Visrestaurant
Lucius, Amsterdam

ingredients. Try bruschettas or the meal-sized salads. The menu also includes tapas-style dishes and delectable home-made cakes.

Pancakes! €
Bakery   **Map** 1 B5
38 Berenstraat, 1016 GH
Tel *(020) 528 9797*
Dutch and international pancakes are served in grand style. The flour is specially milled from the Dutch grain mill, de Korenmolen. Sustainably sourced ingredients.

Balthazar's Keuken €€
International   **Map** 1 B5
Elandsgracht 108, 1016 VA
Tel *(020) 420 2114*   **Closed** *Sun–Tue*
An open kitchen gives the feeling of dining at someone's home. Try the weekly changing three-course menu with up to five appetizers and pre-chosen wine.

Portugália €€
Portuguese   **Map** 4 E1
Kerkstraat 35, 1017 GB
Tel *(020) 625 6490*
This family-run restaurant serves simple cuisine with an emphasis on fish and meat. Try the single-pan dishes (*Cataplana*), like the monkfish, clams, shrimp and potatoes in a cream sauce.

Salmuera €€
International   **Map** 1 A5
Rozengracht 106, 1016 NH
Tel *(020) 624 5752*
Taste Latin-inspired international dishes at this popular restaurant. Try the classic ceviche or feast on the streetfood platter.

Struisvogel €€
International   **Map** 1 B5
Keizersgracht 312, 1016 EX
Tel *(020) 423 3817*
In the cellar of a canal house, Struisvogel serves French organic cuisine. Try the value-for-money set menu, accompanied by apple-orange crumble with vanilla ice cream.

DK Choice

Restaurant Vinkeles €€€
French   **Map** 1 B5
Keizersgracht 384, 1016 GB
Tel *(020) 530 2010*   **Closed** *Sun*
At this world famous, Michelin-starred restaurant, ask to be seated amid 18th-century bakery ovens, or dine on a 19th-century salon boat. Be prepared for the finest of fine-dining experiences, featuring the best in French cuisine. The *anjou duif* (pigeon) is particularly recommended.

A beautifully laid table at Balthazar's Keuken, Amsterdam

Eastern Canal Ring

Kingfisher €
International   **Map** 4 F4
Ferdinand Bolstraat 24, 1072 LK
Tel *(020) 671 2395*
Good food, ranging from snacks (shrimp croquettes) to lunch (Ploughman's sandwich or grilled pork belly) to a day menu (fish, meat or vegetarian) is on offer here. Free Wi-Fi. Excellent value.

Buffet van Odette €€
Brasserie   **Map** 4 F2
Prinsengracht 598, 1017 KS
Tel *(020) 423 6034*   **Closed** *Tue*
Light and sunny with a great terrace, this place serves breakfast, lunch and dinner. Ingredients are mostly organic and locally sourced. Popular choices: the truffle cheese omelette and steak sandwich.

John Dory €€
Seafood   **Map** 5 A3
Prinsengracht 999, 1017 KM
Tel *(020) 622 9044*   **Closed** *Sun & Mon*
Housed in a restored warehouse dating back to 1860, this comfortable restaurant offers three- to seven-course menus. Good selection of wines. Attentive staff.

Rose's Cantina €€
South American   **Map** 4 F1
Reguliersdwarsstraat 38–40, 1017 BM
Tel *(020) 625 9797*
The menu at this established, sprawling South American restaurant focuses on tacos, enchiladas and quesadilla. Also try Rose's house burger. Great cocktails, and a "tequila library". DJs on weekend.

Steakhouse Piet de Leeuw €€
Traditional   **Map** 4 F2
Noorderstraat 11, 1017 TR
Tel *(020) 623 7181*
Open since 1949, this eatery is famous for its steaks (beef and horse) and fish (sole, salmon). Frequented by locals who praise the food as well as the brown café decor.

De Waaghals €€
Vegetarian   **Map** 4 F3
Frans Halsstraat 29, 1072 BK
Tel *(020) 679 9609*
Beautifully prepared creative cuisine featuring organic produce attracts diners here. The menu changes twice a month and always features one international special of the month.

Sluizer €€€
International   **Map** 5 A3
Utrechtsestraat 41–45, 1017 VH
Tel *(020) 622 6376*
Two restaurants operate under one roof: Specialties and Fish. Extensive à la carte and changing choice menus, with international meat, fish and vegetarian options.

Museum Quarter

Het Blauwe Theehuis €
Fusion   **Map** 3 C3
Vondelpark 5, 1071 AA
Tel *(020) 662 0254*   **Closed** *winter*
Housed in a 1937 circular building with a huge terrace, the "Blue Teahouse" overlooks the charming Vondelpark. The breakfast and lunch menus are European, French or Mediterranean based.

Café Toussaint €€
International   **Map** 4 D1
Bosboom Toussaintstraat 26, 1054 AS
Tel *(020) 685 0737*
This small café with an open kitchen is an absolute gem. Focus is on healthy, international fare: soups, sandwiches and tapas. Good range for vegetarians.

Due Napoletani €€
Italian   **Map** 4 E4
Hobbemakade 61–63, 1071 XL
Tel *(020) 671 1263*   **Closed** *Tue*
Chic Italian cuisine is served in an informal setting. The pasta al parmigiano is a popular dish. Staff here are so accomodating that if you call ahead, they will also open for lunch.

For more information on types of restaurants *see page 402*

The Seafood Bar   €€
Seafood   **Map** 4 D3
Van Baerlestraat 5II, 1071 AL
Tel *(020) 670 8355*
This sleek and trendy seafood
bar is open for lunch and dinner.
The menu changes every three
months, although some favourites
remain. Popular dishes include
fruits de mer and fish and chips.

Srikandi   €€
Indonesian   **Map** 4 E2
Stadhouderskade 31, 1071 ZD
Tel *(020) 664 0408*
Art and music create an authentic
atmosphere at this traditional
Indonesian restaurant. Known for
its version of a *rijsttafel* (rice table)
with 18 dishes. Good vegetarian
options. Book ahead.

The College Hotel   €€€
Modern Dutch   **Map** 4 E5
Roelof Hartstraat 1, 1071 VE
Tel *(020) 571 1511*
Housed in a former 1895 school
building, this elegant venue
combines a restaurant, hotel and
lounge bar. Known for its classic
Dutch cuisine with a modern
twist. Lovely courtyard.

Le Garage   €€€
International   **Map** 4 E4
Ruysdaelstraat 54–56, 1071 XE
Tel *(020) 679 7176*   **Closed** *Sun;*
Sat lunch
Le Garage is an elegant bistro
with plush red seating, set in a
renovated garage. French and
international fare on offer, with an
emphasis on organic ingredients.

Plantage

Aguada   €
International   **Map** 5 C3
Roetersstraat 10-W, 1018 WC
Tel *(020) 620 3782*
This tiny, family-run café-restaurant
offers "home-cooked" food in
an informal atmosphere. Cheese
fondue is their speciality, but

they also serve Dutch wild boar
and Italian, Indonesian and Indian
fare. Credit cards are not accepted.

Bloem   €
European   **Map** 6 D2
Entrepotdok 36, 1018 AD
Tel *(020) 330 0929*
Almost all the bread, fruit,
vegetables and meat served here
are organic, and locally sourced
wherever possible. Delicious, as
well as healthy.

De Pizzabakkers Plantage   €
Italian   **Map** 5 C2
Plantage Kerklaan 2, 1018 TA
Tel *(020) 625 0740*
Come here for authentic Italian
pizza, made with locally sourced
ingredients, and baked in a wood
oven. Good range of antipasti,
vegetarian choices and desserts.
Cash not accepted.

Paerz   €€
European   **Map** 6 D2
Entrepotdok 64, 1018 AD
Tel *(020) 623 2206*   **Closed** *Mon & Tue*
Choose from the chef's menu
with three or four courses or the
à la carte menu. Both are inspired
by classic French cuisine and
feature seasonal produce. In
summer, the seating beside the
water is particularly pleasant.

De Plantage   €€
International   **Map** 5 C2
Plantage Kerklaan 36, 1018 CZ
Tel *(020) 760 6800*
This industrial-chic restaurant, next
to the zoo, offers breakfast, lunch
and dinner. Try the daily changing
Plats Plantage (mixed plate of
meats or vegetarian options)
or the juicy Burgos lamb.

Tempura   €€
Japanese   **Map** 5 C2
Plantage Kerklaan 26, 1018 TC
Tel *(020) 428 7132*   **Closed** *Mon*
Extensive sushi, yakatori, tempura,
as well as grilled and vegetarian

dishes and set menus are on offer
at this neighbourhood Japanese-
style brasserie. The squid and the
St Jacques sashimi are wonderful.
Credit cards not accepted.

DK Choice

La Rive   €€€
Mediterranean   **Map** 5 B4
Amstel Hotel, Professor Tulpplein 1,
1018 GX
Tel *(020) 520 3264*   **Closed** *Mon,*
lunch on Sat
La Rive offers beautiful, elegant
cuisine elevated to the level
of art. This Michelin-starred
restaurant is located in the
ultra-lux Amstel Hotel, and
serves dishes inspired by
French and Mediterranean
flavours, created using high-
quality seasonal produce.
It also has a selection of
outstanding wines. Reserve
the Chef's table.

Western Canal Ring

De Bolhoed   €
International   **Map** 1 B3
Prinsengracht 60–62, 1015 DX
Tel *(020) 626 1803*
Enjoy pleasant views from the
canalside terrace at this popular
vegetarian restaurant. It serves
imaginative international dishes
(Mexican, Mediterranean, Asian,
African) with a daily vegan choice.
Mostly organic and seasonal
ingredients, along with delicious
desserts. Book ahead.

Greenwoods   €
Tearoom   **Map** 1 C4
Singel 103, 1012 VG
Tel *(020) 623 7071*
Opt for a full English breakfast
(served all day) or a more delicate
high tea at this welcoming
English-style tearoom. Another
branch, on the Keizersgracht 465,
also serves dinner (fish and chips).

Pancake Bakery   €
Bakery   **Map** 1 C3
Prinsengracht 191, 1015 DS
Tel *(020) 625 1333*
This family-run eatery serves a
variety of pancakes. Favourites
include Egyptian (lamb, paprika,
garlic sauce), Caprese (mushrooms,
mozzarella, basil pesto, sundried
tomatoes) and the classic Dutch
(syrup, powdered sugar or bacon).

Piqniq   €
Café   **Map** 1 C3
Lindengracht 59,1015 KC
Tel *(020) 320 3669*   **Closed** *Tue*
Piqniq offers a selection of
miniature homemade goodies:

Elegant interiors at the Michelin-starred La Rive in Amsterdam mini-sandwiches, soups, bite-sized quiches and cakes. Order a selection or try the fixed menu. High tea, gluten-free options.

Black and Blue €€
Steakhouse   Map 1 B4
Leliegracht 46, 1015 DH
Tel *(020) 625 0807*
Meat lovers head to this steakhouse for a fine selection of organic steaks and Angus beef burgers from a charcoal grill/oven. Or try the Cornish hen with thyme and lemon. Small terrace.

Chez Georges €€
French   Map 1 C3
Herenstraat 3, 1015 BX
Tel *(020) 626 3332*   **Closed** *Sun*
A must for gourmands, Chez Georges dishes up a seasonal Burgundian menu. Sample the daily changing five-course set meal and dessert. Ask for vegetarian options. Fine wine selection. Book ahead.

Stout! €€
Fusion   Map 1 C3
Haarlemmerstraat 73, 1013 EL
Tel *(020) 616 3664*
Indulge in international cuisine with inspired flavour combinations. "Stout Plateau" offers ten small treats, or try the fresh "Catch of the Day". Pleasant terrace for people-watching while having lunch.

Further Afield

Azmarino €
East African   Map 5 A5
Tweede Sweelinckstraat 6, 1073 EH
Tel *(020) 671 7587*   **Closed** *Mon*
This restaurant, with traditional African furnishings, serves a classic menu: *enjera* (pancakes), a choice of meats (mild to spicy), and some vegetarian options. Try eggs in red sauce, or *enjera* with meat or vegetable sauces. Open on weekends for breakfast and lunch.

Blauw €€
Indonesian   Map 3 A4
Amstelveenseweg 158, 1075 XN
Tel *(020) 675 5000*
Blauw is one of the better-known and beloved Indonesian restaurants in town. The decor is stylish and intimate, without a hint of kitsch. Order the enormous *rijsttafel*. Worth the trip.

Ciel Bleu €€€
French
Okura Hotel, Ferdinand Bolstraat 333, 1072 LH
Tel *(020) 678 7111*   **Closed** *Sun*
Awarded a second Michelin star in 2011, this French restaurant

is renowned for its creative, innovative dishes, and terrific views of Amsterdam. The place to make an impression.

DK Choice

De Kas €€€
Organic
Kamerlingh Onneslaan 3 1097 DE
Tel *(020) 462 4562*   **Closed** *Sun*
Dine in a lush oasis surrounded by plants at this restaurant set in a 1920s greenhouse, or reserve the frantic Chef's Table in the kitchen. The Michelin-starred chef and owner offers a fixed three-course menu (vegetarian options available) based on the seasonal produce cultivated in the adjacent nursery or sourced from local growers of organic food, as well as meat and fish producers.

North Holland

BLARICUM: Tafelberg €
International   Map C3
Oude Naarderweg 2, 1261 DS
Tel *(035) 538 3975*
Opened in the 1930s as a teahouse on the heath, Tafelberg is now a full-fledged restaurant with a large terrace that serves as an idyllic resting spot after a walk in the woods. Expect the odd Dutch celebrity.

DK Choice

HAARLEM: De Jopenkerk €€
Traditional   Map B3
Gedempte Voldersgracht 2, 2011 WB
Tel *(023) 533 4114*
This century-old church has been stunningly transformed into a grand café (on the ground floor) and a restaurant (upstairs) with an in-house brewery. Most of the mainly Dutch meat and fish dishes are cooked with beer, and every course comes with a beer recommendation. A favourite among locals, the restaurant can get noisy, especially on weekend nights.

HAARLEM: Specktakel €€
Fusion   Map B3
Spekstraat 4, 2011 HM
Tel *(023) 532 3841*
Expect organic meat, fresh seafood and exotic game prepared in Japanese, Chinese, Italian or French style with Australian, African, American

Grand interior of De Jopenkerk, Haarlem, which was once a church

and Creole influences at this intimate restaurant on "Bacon Street". Order the Umami menu.

HAARLEM: Ratatouille €€€
International   Map B3
Spaarne 96, 2011 CL
Tel *(023) 542 7270*   **Closed** *Sun & Mon; Wed–Sat lunch*
Michelin-starred chef Jozua Jaring proves that it's possible to prepare delectable and subtly flavoured dishes using ordinary, affordable ingredients. Choose from two to eight courses accompanied by wine.

HEEMSTEDE: Southern Cross €€
Australian   Map B3
Zandvoortselaan 24, 2106 CP
Tel *(023) 521 9992*   **Closed** *Mon*
There is no clearly defined "Australian cuisine", so except for the grilled crocodile and roasted kangaroo, this restaurant serves world food with a distinct Aussie touch. On balmy summer nights, book a table on the patio.

HILVERSUM: Surya €
Indian   Map C3
Langestraat 126, 1211 HC
Tel *(035) 631 9420*   **Closed** *Mon*
Not your average curry house: this eatery features colourful decor and long benches with lots of cushions. Serves a plethora of Indian and Nepalese specialities, such as chicken *tikka* and lamb *vindaloo*, as well as vegetarian dishes.

HILVERSUM: Rex €€
International   Map C3
Groest 23, 1211 CZ
Tel *(035) 631 9529*
Former 1920s Art Deco cinema turned into a hip club, lounge and restaurant, Rex dishes up salads, pasta and fish, but is best known for the dry-aged steaks. Side dishes are extra. Dine on the terrace in the summer.

HOOFDDORP: Vork en Mes €€
Creative   **Map** B3
Paviljoenlaan 1, 2131 LZ
Tel *(023) 557 2963*   **Closed** *Sun*
Futuristic pavilion on the lake
provides a unique setting for a
leisurely meal. The chef was trained
at Michelin-starred restaurants
and cooks up a changing five-
course surprise menu.

MONNICKENDAM:
Posthoorn €€€
French   **Map** C3
Noordeinde 43, 1141 AG
Tel *(0299) 654 598*   **Closed** *Mon*
Delicate French food is served in
two of the prettiest houses in this
fairytale town. The decor meticu-
lously matches old-world charm
with modern comforts. One
Michelin star.

OUDERKERK AAN DE
AMSTEL: Lute €€€
French   **Map** C3
De Oude Molen 5, 1184 VW
Tel *(020) 472 2462*   **Closed** *Sun;*
Sat lunch
Set in an 18th-century gunpowder
mill, Lute makes the most of its
location by the Amstel river, with
sophisticated dishes served in
the stables, the greenhouse or
on the terrace.

SANTPOORT: Brasserie DenK €€
French   **Map** B3
Duin en Kruidbergweg 60, 2071 LE
Tel *(023) 512 1800*
This sleek lounge bar and brasserie
is housed in a Neo-Renaissance
castle-like country estate. The bar
menu offers brasserie food, while
the brasserie itself has a decent
restaurant menu.

ZANDVOORT: Tijn Akersloot €€
International   **Map** B3
Boulevard Paulus Loot 1B, 2042 AD
Tel *(023) 571 2547*
At the quiet end of the popular
Zandvoort beach, this beach club

Atmospheric interiors at Badhu, an Arabian
restaurant in Utrecht

serves sandwiches, soup and
snacks by day, and stone oven
pizzas, steaks and more
sophisticated dishes at night.

Utrecht

AMERSFOORT: Hop en Hen €
International   **Map** C4
Hof 8, 3811 CJ
Tel *(033) 737 0005*   **Closed** *Mon*
Chicken and beer feature
prominently on the menu at this
cheerful eatery, where tables at
the back even have their own
beer tap. Guests can also opt to
sit on the terrace that overlooks
the bustling town square.

AMERSFOORT: De Saffraan €€€
French   **Map** C4
Kleine Koppel 3, 3812 PG
Tel *(033) 448 1753*   **Closed** *Sun &*
Mon; Sat–Wed lunch
A century-old clipper on the Eem
river has been transformed into
an intimate and stylish restaurant.
Alfresco dining on the deck in
the summer.

BAARN: Pomodori €
Italian   **Map** C3
Laandwarsstraat 15, 3743 BS
Tel *(035) 541 4013*   **Closed** *Sun,*
Mon–Wed lunch
Tiny restaurant in an even tinier
back alley, Klein Fornuis prepares
classic dishes with an imaginative
twist. Weekly changing set
menus on offer.

HOUTEN: Kasteel
Heemstede €€€
French   **Map** C4
Heemsteedseweg 20, 3992 LS
Tel *(030) 272 2207*   **Closed** *Sun &*
Mon
Housed in a romantic 17th-century
castle, this Michelin-starred restaur-
ant has a terrace that seems to
float on the moat surrounding the
castle. Fine dining, great service
and an excellent wine list.

LEUSDEN: Bistro Bling €€
French   **Map** C4
Waarden 25B, 3831 HA
Tel *(033) 433 2070*   **Closed** *Mon*
The interior lives up to the name
with cheap chandeliers, glass
curtains and baroque mirrors,
but the service is friendly and
the bistro fare is well done.

MAARSSEN: Delice €€
North African   **Map** C4
Kaatsbaan 25, 3601 EB
Tel *(0346) 284 4534*   **Closed** *Sun*
& Mon
North African dishes, great wines,
contemporary interiors and a

relaxed atmosphere prove to be
a winning combination. Try the
lamb with apricots, sesame and
seasonal vegetables.

MAARSSEN: De Nonnerie €€
French   **Map** C4
Langegracht 51, 3601 AK
Tel *(0346) 562 201*   **Closed** *Sun; lunch*
Creative cooking guarantees a
great dining experience at this
beautifully restored former
nunnery by the Vecht river. The
three- to five-course set menus
are good value for money.

DK Choice

UTRECHT: Badhu €
Arabian   **Map** C4
Willem van Noortplein 19, 3514 GK
Tel *(030) 272 0444*
As befits a restaurant set in a 1920s
bathhouse, Badhu's interior is
inspired by an Arabian *hamam*.
The restaurant is very popular
and is open all day, serving
Arabian breakfast, *meze* (small
Arabian dishes to share) for lunch,
afternoon *chai* (high tea Arabian
style) and evening cocktails in a
thousand-and-one-nights setting.

UTRECHT: De Keuken
van Gastmaal €€
French   **Map** C4
Biltstraat 5, 3572 AA
Tel *(030) 233 4633*   **Closed** *Sun & Mon*
Just a few tables are centred
around an open kitchen, in
which the chef works wonders
with sustainable fish, organic
meat and regional vegetables.
Dishes are paired with fine wines.

VREELAND AAN DE VECHT:
De Nederlanden €€€
French   **Map** C3
Duinkerken 3, 3633 EM
Tel *(0294) 232 326*   **Closed** *Mon;*
Sat lunch
Set in a monumental mansion,
this boutique hotel and Michelin-
starred restaurant serves refined
French cuisine along with a
500-bottle wine list. Fantastic
terrace and kitchen garden.

South Holland

DELFT: La Tasca €€
Mediterranean   **Map** B4
Voldersgracht 13B, 2611 ET
Tel *(015) 213 8535*   **Closed** *Sun*
Don't look for the menu – there
isn't one. Guests are invited to
tell the chef what they don't like,
and then wait as he cooks up
a three- to five-course surprise
meal for them.

LEIDEN: Buddhas   €€
Thai   Map B3
Botermarkt 20, 2311 EN
Tel *(071) 514 0047*
Huge golden Buddha statues line
the walls of this contemporary
restaurant. There is an extensive
menu, and the generous portions
make it good value for money.

DK Choice

NOORDWIJK: Bries   €€
International   Map B3
*Koningin Astrid Boulevard 102,
2202 BD*
Tel *(071) 361 7891* **Closed** *winter*
Bries is not your average
makeshift beach club, but a
well-designed and spacious
pavilion, fitted out with stylish
furniture. There are loungers
and cabanas, plus massage
and yoga on the beach. The
full-fledged menu leans
heavily towards fresh seafood.
Pick your choice of fish at the
Wednesday fish market. Open
in the summer only.

OOSTVOORNE: Aan Zee €€
Traditional   Map B4
Strandweg 1, 3233 CW
Tel *(0181) 820 990* **Closed** *Mon & Tue*
This striking pavilion in the dunes
is truly sustainable: it is built of
untreated wood, fed by solar and
wind energy and uses dune water.
Round off your meal with breath-
taking views from the watchtower.
Open for lunch daily from May to
September if the weather is sunny.

ROTTERDAM: Bird   €€
Italian/Mediterranean Map B4
Raampoortstraat 26, 3032 AH
Tel *(010) 737 1154* **Closed** *Sun & Mon*
Savour Neapolitan pizza and
Mediterranean comfort food at the
restaurant wing of this popular
jazz stage and nightclub. On
"culinary cinema nights", guests
are served exactly what is being
eaten on-screen. Set menus only.

ROTTERDAM: Sānsān €€
Chinese   Map B4
Hang 33, 3011 GG
Tel *(010) 411 5681* **Closed** *Tue*
A favourite among Chinese locals
and visitors, Sānsān is known
for the quality of food and
service. The traditional Sichuan
fare ranges from delicate lemon
fish to fiery sizzling beef.

ROTTERDAM: FG Restaurant €€€
International   Map B4
Katoshoek 37b, 3032 AE
Tel *(010) 425 0520* **Closed** *Sun & Mon*
After years of molecular cooking
at Heston Blumenthal's The Fat

Tables on the beach at Bries in Noordwijk

Duck, François Geurds is now
a master chef in his own right.
Vegetarians get their own multi-
course tasting menu. The Chef's
Table is a coveted spot.

ROTTERDAM: Zeezout €€€
Seafood   Map B4
Westerkade 11B, 3016 CL
Tel *(010) 436 5049* **Closed** *Mon;
Sun lunch*
Fabled fish restaurant, Zeezout
is situated in the fisherman's
quarter of arguably the world's
biggest seaport. Fresh fish only,
with seasonally changing menus.
Great in summer, with panoramic
views over the Maas river.

SCHEVENINGEN: At Sea €€€
Mediterranean   Map B4
Heilingweg 138, 2583 DX
Tel *(070) 331 7445* **Closed** *Mon &
Tue; Sat & Sun lunch*
This sleek restaurant in an old
fishing port dishes out delicious
seafood (but also meat and game)
paired with fine wines. Order
à la carte, go for the five-course
Chef's Choice or choose from
set menus that change daily.

SCHIPLUIDEN: Aan de Zweth €€€
French   Map B4
Rotterdamseweg 480, 2636 KB
Tel *(010) 470 4166* **Closed** *Tue;
Sat lunch*
Exclusive restaurant with two
Michelin stars – and food, prices,
ambience and service to match.
Set in a picturesque house along
the Schie creek. A seat at the
Chef's Table includes an aperitif
aboard the restaurant's own sloop.

**STREEFKERK: De
Limonadefabriek**   €€
Creative   Map B4
Nieuwe Haven 1, 2959 AT
Tel *(0184) 689 335* **Closed** *Mon &
Tue; Oct–Apr: Sat lunch*
Despite its name and appearance,
this is not a lemonade factory,
but a strikingly modern floating
restaurant on the Lek river,

serving equally modern and
well-presented food. The
adjacent bistro is also superb.

THE HAGUE: HanTing Cuisine €€
Fusion   Map B4
Prinsestraat 33, 2513 CA
Tel *(070) 362 0828* **Closed** *Mon; lunch*
Chinese chef Han expertly fuses
traditional French cooking with
oriental flavours, creating dishes
that please the eye as well as the
palate. The rice-paper lanterns
are pretty too. One Michelin star.

THE HAGUE: Logisch €€
Organic   Map B4
Maliestraat 9, 2514 CA
Tel *(070) 363 5259* **Closed** *Sun & Mon*
Organic food that is cheerful
and good value. Choose from
set menus inspired by the sea,
woods or garden. Or opt for à
la carte – black Angus steak with
asparagus and mushrooms or
steamed sea catfish with herbs.

THE HAGUE: The Penthouse €€€
International   Map B4
Rijswijkseplein 786, 2516 LX
Tel *(070) 305 1000*
This is probably the poshest spot
in town, although not for those
afraid of heights. Packs a terrace
café, skybar, restaurant and nightclub all in one, with a smashing
view from the 42nd floor of
a skyscraper.

Zeeland

**BURGH-HAAMSTEDE:
Pannekoekenmolen
De Graanhalm**   €
Bakery   Map A4
Burghseweg 53, 4328 LA
Tel *(0111) 652 415*
This pancake house in a working
windmill serves pancakes in
35 sweet and savoury varieties,
such as sugar and syrup, bacon
and cheese or strawberries and
whipped cream.

For more information on types of restaurants *see page 402*

CADZAND: Pure C   €€€
Mediterranean   **Map** A5
Boulevard de Wielingen 49, 4506 JK
Tel *(0117) 396 036*   **Closed** *Mon & Tue*
Latest venture of celebrity chef
Sergio Herman, this restaurant
was awarded a Michelin star
soon after opening. Great food,
relaxed atmosphere.

DK Choice

**DOMBURG: Het
Badpaviljoen**   €€€
Seafood   **Map** A5
Badhuisweg 21, 4357 AV
Tel *(0118) 582405*   **Closed** *Tue &
Wed*
In a fairytale turn-of-the-century
bathing pavilion on a dune top,
this fine-dining restaurant has
a clean-cut interior and serves
anything fishy, from the freshest
Zeeland oysters and mussels
to North Sea crab and whole
lobsters. Order a seafood plate
for two and dine alfresco on
the seaside terrace.

GOES: Jan   €€
Seafood   **Map** A5
Bierkade 3A, 4461 AV
Tel *(0113) 219 974*   **Closed** *Tue & Wed*
This fish restaurant in the old
harbour features a chic interior.
The chef's speciality is classically
cooked shellfish: oysters, crab and
clams galore. Quayside terrace.

**HOOFDPLAAT: De Kromme
Watergang**   €€€
Regional   **Map** A5
Slijkplaat 6, 4513 KK
Tel *(0117) 348 696*   **Closed** *Mon &
Tue; first two weeks in Jun; last week
Sep–first week Oct*
Adventurous cooking with an
emphasis on seafood is the high-
light of this two-star restaurant
located in a hamlet called Slijkplaat,
or "mud plate". Food comes straight
from the silty clay of Zeeland.

MIDDELBURG: Scherp   €€
Regional   **Map** A5
Wijngaardstraat 1–5, 4331 PM
Tel *(0118) 634 633*   **Closed** *Sun & Mon;
end Jul–mid-Aug; end Dec–mid-Jan*
Chef Scherp serves dishes such
as Zeeland oysters with wasabi
cream, cucumber, passion fruit
foam and chardonnay vinegar.
Regional delicacies, some meat
and game, but mainly seafood.

OUWERKERK: De Vierbannen   €€€
French   **Map** A5
*Weg van de Buitenlandse Pers 3,
4305 RJ*
Tel *(0111) 647 547*   **Closed** *Mon & Tue*
Housing a brasserie and restaurant,
this building has a terrace with

Lovely table setting at Herberg Onder
de Linden, Aduard

superb views of the surrounding
creeks and the Oosterschelde.
Serves mainly seafood.

West Frisian Islands

AMELAND: Boerenbont   €€
Modern Dutch   **Map** C1
Strandweg 50, 9163 GN Nes
Tel *(0519) 542 293*
A mix of old and new: the cuisine
is traditional – with a touch of the
modern – served on the classic
painted crockery from which the
restaurant takes its name. Old
Dutch texts on the walls temper
the contemporary decor.

**SCHIERMONNIKOOG:
Ambrosijn**   €€
Regional   **Map** D1
Langestreek 13, 9166 LA
Tel *(0519) 720 261*
This intimate place serves salads
and sandwiches by day, and
three- to five-course set menus
for dinner. "Ambro" is the name of
the wild apples that grow all over
the island, and which the restaurant puts in its crunchy apple pie.

TERSCHELLING: Loods   €€
International   **Map** C1
Willem Barentszkade 39, 8881 BD
Tel *(0562) 700 200*
Comfort food is dished up in a
light-flooded dining room with
an industrial feel. Scaffolding
wood tables, designer chairs and
large metal lamps constitute the
interior. Pleasant seaview terrace.

TEXEL: Topido   €€
Regional   **Map** B2
Kikkertstraat 23, 1795 AA De Cocksdorp
Tel *(0222) 316 227*   **Closed** *Mon*
Head here to get a taste of Texel:
lamb, goat and beef from the

island, shrimp from the Wadden
Sea and fish from the North Sea,
cheese from a nearby sheep farm
and locally brewed beer.

DK Choice

**VLIELAND: Uitspanning Het
Armhuis**   €€€
International   **Map** C1
Kerkplein 6, 8899 AW
Tel *(0562) 451 935*   **Closed** *Mon &
Tue*
This monumental 17th-
century almshouse once
sheltered orphans, the elderly,
the poor and the needy. It is
now home to the island's best
restaurant. A bistro by day,
it serves three- or four-course
set menus for dinner. Enjoy
refined, classically cooked
dishes either indoors or
outside in the garden.

Groningen

**ADUARD: Herberg Onder
de Linden**   €€€
French   **Map** D1
Burg. van Barneveldweg 3, 9831 RD
Tel *(050) 403 1406*   **Closed** *Sun–Tue*
The chef has kept his Michelin
star rating for nearly three
decades, so expect good quality
and prices to match. Limited but
mouth-watering set menus.

**GRONINGEN: Het
Goudkantoor**   €
Mediterranean   **Map** D1
Waagplein 1, 9712 JZ
Tel *(050) 589 1888*   **Closed** *Sun
dinner*
The "Gold Office" is where taxes
were collected during the
Golden Age. It now houses
a fine restaurant, serving
Mediterranean fare for the
local palate.

DK Choice

GRONINGEN: WEEVA   €
Regional   **Map** D1
*Gedempte Zuiderdiep 8–10,
9711 HG*
Tel *(050) 588 6555*
This "Living and Eating House
for All" retains the original
atmosphere of the 1871
soup kitchen it once was,
even though the clientele
is greatly changed. It serves
good comfort food, prepared
with regional and healthy
ingredients, at affordable
prices – such as the dish of
the day for under €10.

GRONINGEN: Flinders Café €€
International **Map** D1
Nieuweweg 2/Schuitendiep 54,
9711 TD
Tel *(050) 737 0242* **Closed** *dinner*
Located in Noorderplantsoen
park, this ship-shaped Art Deco
pavilion serves breakfast, lunch,
snacks and dinner. Diners can
choose from soups and salads to
full-fledged meals.

NOORDLAREN:
De Waterjuffers bij Vos €€
Regional **Map** E2
Osdijk 4, 9479 TC
Tel *(050) 711 9310* **Closed** *winter:*
Mon–Fri
This restaurant with a waterside
terrace is set on the banks of the
Zuidlaardermeer in a nature
reserve. Serves eel and zander
straight from the lake, but also
vegetarian and meat dishes.

Friesland

DK Choice

HARLINGEN: Anna
Casparii €€
Seafood **Map** C2
Noorderhaven 67–71, 8861 AL
Tel *(0517) 412 065*
Housed in a historic building
dating back to the 18th century,
this traditional in-house restaurant of Hotel Anna Casparii
offers an extensive selection of
fresh seafood and an impressive
range of beers. The attractive
canalside setting provides
the ideal backdrop to enjoy
a leisurely meal.

HEERENVEEN: Het Ambacht €€
International **Map** D2
Burg. Falkenaweg 56, 8442 LE
Tel *(0513) 232 172* **Closed** *Sun &*
Mon; Sat lunch
Chef Henk Markus, dubbed "the
Frisian Jamie Oliver", transformed a
century-old technical school into
a trendy restaurant that employs
disadvantaged youth. Sample
local delicacies like monkfish,
wagyu beef and ringneck dove.

LEEUWARDEN: De Walrus €
International **Map** D1
Gouverneursplein 37, 8911 HH
Tel *(058) 213 7740*
Spreading over three floors, this
grand café is a go-to place for
dinner or just drinks. The menu
is international, ranging from popular Dutch staples to Thai-style
curries. Welcoming pavement
terrace and lively atmosphere.

MAKKUM: De Prins €
Traditional **Map** C2
Kerkstraat 1, 8754 CN
Tel *(0515) 231 510* **Closed** *Tue;*
Mon & Wed lunch
Established in 1760, De Prins has
been run by the same family for
three generations. The taproom
features handpainted tiles on the
walls. Old-fashioned Dutch dining.

SNEEK: Cook & Ny €
International **Map** C2
1e Oosterkade 24, 8605 AA
Tel *(0515) 433 019* **Closed** *Mon*
This eatery has everything to
attract diners: a sleek interior, an
international-sounding name
and great tapas, from *patatas*
bravas and vegetable-filled filo to
garlic snails and catfish *saté*.

Drenthe

ASSEN: Touché €€
Fusion **Map** D2
Markt 20, 9401 GT
Tel *(0592) 769 069* **Closed** *Mon*
The chef cooks up modern takes
on traditional dishes here, such
as slowly braised duck glazed
with hoisin sauce and star anise.
Set in the town's prettiest square.

DK Choice

BORGER: Villa van Streek €€
Regional **Map** E2
Torenlaan 13, 9531 JH
Tel *(0599) 657 007* **Closed** *Mon*
In the dolmen capital of Drenthe,
a former Royal Marshals barracks
now houses this artistically
decorated eatery. Open all day
for brunch, lunch and dinner,
it offers a changing menu of
regionally harvested dishes at
affordable prices. The adjacent
shop and tourist info sells maps
for touring the nearby dolmens.

Smoked salmon, one of the dishes that
visitors can sample in Friesland

RODEN: Cuisinerie
Mensinge €€
French **Map** D2
Mensingheweg 1, 9301 KA
Tel *(050) 501 3149* **Closed** *Mon &*
Tue
The coach house and stables
of a 600-year-old manor tucked
away in a nature reserve now
house a wonderfully romantic
bistro and restaurant. No à la
carte at dinner.

RODERESCH: Herberg
van Es €€
International **Map** D2
Hoofdweg 1, 9305 TD
Tel *(050) 501 2660* **Closed** *Mon &*
Tue
The natural area surrounding this
restaurant is popular among hikers
and bikers. Extensive menus for
lunch and dinner, and a game
menu (in season) featuring deer,
hare, boar and more.

ZUIDLAREN: De Vlindertuin €€€
French **Map** E2
Stationsweg 41, 9471 GK
Tel *(050) 409 4531* **Closed** *Sun &*
Mon
The Michelin-starred "Butterfly
Garden" is one of Drenthe's finest
restaurants, serving refined French
food with a modern twist in a
300-year-old farmhouse. Order
the eight-course tasting menu.

Overijssel

DK Choice

DE LUTTE: De
Bloemenbeek €€€
French **Map** E3
Beuningerstraat 6, 7587 LD
Tel *(0541) 551 224*
Located in the gently rolling
landscape of the Dinkel valley,
Michelin-starred "The Flower
Stream" is a fine dining restaurant
attached to a country house
hotel. The cuisine is a delightful
amalgamation of French and
Dutch styles, but the extensive
and well-chosen wine list is
very French.

DEVENTER: Jackies
NYCuisine €€
International **Map** D3
Grote Poot 19, 7411 KE
Tel *(0570) 616 666*
This contemporary eatery is
inspired by the style of Jackie O
and the cuisine of New York City,
including Chinatown. Spot on,
with great food and attentive
service in a stylish setting.

For more information on types of restaurants *see page 402*

ENSCHEDE: Yuen's Oriental Bistro €€
Asian **Map** E3
Noorderhagen 9, 7511 EJ
Tel *(053) 911 887* **Closed** *Sun & Mon*
The chef fuses fresh organic ingredients and Japanese, Thai, Mongolian, Cantonese and Korean flavours into an affordable surprise menu at this modern Asian restaurant with an open kitchen.

ZWOLLE: Librije's Hotel €€€
Modern Dutch **Map** D3
Spinhuisplein 1, 8011 ZZ
Tel *(038) 421 2083* **Closed** *Mon lunch*
This hotel has two award-winning restaurants, both offering inventive menus. Set menus rule the roost; try the elaborate seven-course dinner. There is an atelier where groups can cook their meals under a chef's supervision. Book ahead.

Flevoland

ALMERE-HAVEN: Bij Brons €€
French **Map** C3
Sluis 3, 1357 NZ
Tel *(036) 540 1126* **Closed** *Mon*
Right in the marina, this restaurant has tables centred around the open kitchen. Fresh, mostly organic and seasonal ingredients. The five-course surprise menu with paired wines is a good deal.

BIDDINGHUIZEN: Beachclub NU €
International **Map** C3
Bremerbergdijk 10, 8256 RD
Tel *(0321) 331 629* **Closed** *winter: Mon & Tue*
Set on a pretty stretch of sand along Lake Veluwe, this smart beach club offers barbecue, tablegrill and a limited menu in the ground-floor lounge and terrace. For à la carte head upstairs, where lake views are an added attraction.

DK Choice

URK: Restaurant De Boet €
Seafood **Map** C3
Wijk 1–61, 8321 EM
Tel *(0527) 688 736* **Closed** *Sun; Sat & Mon lunch*
This is the smartest restaurant in the village of Urk, occupying two old harbourside buildings – an old warehouse and a steamship office. The menu changes daily and offers the freshest of seafood. Try the fried plaice, with scallops, mashed potatoes, string beans, zucchini and sweet onion sauce with mustard.

Charming dining area with neatly laid out tables at Librije's Hotel, Zwolle

Gelderland

ARNHEM: ZafVino €€
Mediterranean **Map** D4
Zwanenstraat 22, 6811 DD
Tel *(026) 379 0009* **Closed** *Tue & Wed*
Sit wherever there is room, including communal tables, at this atmospheric eatery. There is no fixed menu; choose from dishes listed on the blackboard.

BARNEVELD: De Oranjerie €€
International **Map** D4
Stationsweg 4A, 3771 VH
Tel *(0342) 419 601* **Closed** *Sun & Mon*
In the grounds of a mock Tudor castle, this fine-dining restaurant is an accurate replica of a 19th-century greenhouse. The food, from local roe to whole lobsters, matches the ambience.

BEEKBERGEN: Het Ei van Columbus €€
French **Map** D4
Stoppelbergweg 63, 7361 TE
Tel *(055) 506 1498* **Closed** *Mon & Tue*
"The Egg of Columbus" offers a limited, exquisite but affordable menu, in the midst of the leafy Veluwe nature reserve. Three-course set menu for under €30.

BERG EN DAL: PUUR M €€
International **Map** D4
Zevenheuvelenweg 87, 6571 CJ
Tel *(024) 684 1452* **Closed** *Tue*
This stylish wine bar-restaurant has a hundred wines on the list and about two-dozen by the glass, along with a plethora of starters, comparable to Spanish tapas and *raciones*.

ERMELO: Boshuis Drie €€
Traditional **Map** C3
Sprielderweg 205, 3852 MK
Tel *(0577) 407 206* **Closed** *Mon*
A beautifully preserved thatched farmhouse in the midst of the 'Forest of the Dancing Trees',

Boshuis Drie dishes up evergreen Dutch favourites, such as pancakes for lunch and shrimp cocktail, game stew or juicy steaks for dinner.

DK Choice

NIJMEGEN: De Nieuwe Winkel €€
Fusion **Map** D4
Hertogstraat 71, 6511 RW
Tel *(024) 322 5093* **Closed** *Sun & Mon*
Radish in "edible soil" served in a flowerpot, followed by a "golden egg" filled with poached yolk – and these are only the appetizers. Besides a mad chef, "The New Shop" boasts a modern decor, friendly atmosphere, a minimal menu and food that is a feast for the eyes as much as the taste buds.

North Brabant

BERGEN OP ZOOM: Le Bouleau €€
International **Map** B5
Bemmelenberg 16, 4614 PG
Tel *(0164) 258 782* **Closed** *Mon & Tue*
In a romantic spot in the woods, this restaurant serves international dishes such as garlic *gambas* and grilled ribeye. The attractively priced three-course market menu is a good choice.

BREDA: Wolfslaar €€€
French **Map** B5
Wolfslaardreef 100–102, 4834 SP
Tel *(076) 560 8000* **Closed** *Sun; Sat lunch*
Set in the converted coach house of a chic country estate, this Michelin-starred restaurant offers modern takes on classic dishes using sustainable and organic ingredients, like quail with foie gras or halibut with mussels.

DK Choice

EINDHOVEN: Kreeftenbar €
Seafood **Map** C5
Kleine Berg 21, 5611 JS
Tel *(040) 236 4440* **Closed** *Mon*
Discover lobster for the masses: lobster soup, lobster salad, lobster rolls and half and whole lobsters, either cooked or gratin, along with a good choice of Asian dishes, from sushi to king crab and Peking duck. The prices here are easily affordable, with a three-course lobster dinner for under €30.

EINDHOVEN: Smeagol €
Argentinian **Map** C5
Kerkstraat 10, 5611 GJ
Tel *(040) 737 0298*
Enjoy juicy steaks straight from the Argentinian pampas. Other dishes include empanadas and fajitas, garlic *gambas* and mixed grill. Modern interior.

EINDHOVEN: Piet Hein Eek €€
Creative **Map** C5
Halvemaanstraat 28, 5651 BP
Tel *(040) 400 9005* **Closed** *Mon*
A beautifully revamped former Philips factory now houses Dutch designer Piet Hein Eek's flagship store, workshop, art gallery and restaurant. Design lover's paradise.

KAATSHEUVEL: De Molen €€€
International **Map** C4
Vaartstraat 102, 5171 JG
Tel *(0416) 530 230* **Closed** *Mon*
Expect adventurous Michelin-starred cooking at this windmill on the edge of a national park. The ten-course tasting menu is absolutely amazing.

NUENEN: Olijf €€
Mediterranean **Map** C5
Berg 18, 5671 CC
Tel *(040) 291 3476* **Closed** *Wed; Jul & Aug: also Tue*
This restaurant is located in the village where Van Gogh painted *The Potato Eaters*. Serves mostly Mediterranean seafood. Affordable set menus with paired wines.

**'S-HERTOGENBOSCH:
Eetbar Dit** €
International **Map** C4
Snellestraat 24–26, 5211 EN
Tel *(073) 614 1015*
Try a modern take on the old Dutch *eetcafé* here. Tapas-like small dishes such as shrimp croquettes, burgers and *rendang* that are meant to be shared.

'S-HERTOGENBOSCH: De Verkadefabriek €€
International **Map** C4
Boschdijkstraat 45, 5211 VD
Tel *(073) 681 8170*
This former cookie factory now houses a theatre, cinema and restaurant. Enjoy lunch, tapas and dinner in an industrial setting.

Limburg

GULPEN: L'Atelier €€€
French **Map** D6
Markt 9, 6271 BD
Tel *(043) 450 4490* **Closed** *Tue & Wed; Sat lunch*
L'Atelier has to be rated one of Limburg's best restaurants.

Expect fine dining, a warm, intimate atmosphere, friendly service and an excellent wine list.

MAASBRACHT: Da Vinci €€€
French **Map** D6
Havenstraat 27, 6051 CS
Tel *(0475) 465 979* **Closed** *Mon & Tue; Sat lunch*
Not a pizzeria but a French restaurant, this place is run by the only Dutch female chef with two Michelin stars. Expect fine French fare with meticulously paired wines, stiff linen and ditto prices.

DK Choice

MAASTRICHT: Umami €
Chinese **Map** D6
Stationsstraat 12, 6221 BP
Tel *(043) 351 0006* **Closed** *Mon & Tue lunch*
This is one of a small chain of decidedly modern conceptual Chinese eateries (there are six other Umamis around the country), the side project of chef Han of Michelin-starred restaurant HanTing in The Hague. Michelin-star quality at bargain prices: choose seven dishes in three courses for around €20.

MAASTRICHT: SoFa €€
Mediterranean **Map** D6
Hoge Weerd 6, 6229 AM
Tel *(043) 367 1337* **Closed** *Sun & Mon*
Short for "sounds fantastic", SoFa is set inside the coach house of a 15th-century castle on a peninsula in the Maas river. Serves sunny Mediterranean food inside and out on the terrace.

MAASTRICHT: Beluga Loves You €€€
International **Map** D6
Plein 1992 12, 6221 JP
Tel *(043) 321 3364* **Closed** *Sun*
Visit this star-studded restaurant, both in terms of Michelin stars (two) and visiting celebrities (many), in a striking modern

building right on the edge of the Maas river. Great looks, spectacular tastes.

SLENAKEN: De La Frontière €€
South African **Map** D6
Grensweg 1, 6277 NA
Tel *(043) 457 4302* **Closed** *Mon & Tue*
Experience a slice of South Africa in south Limburg, complete with zebra skins, pottery and colourful art, Cape wines and dishes like biltong pâté and Kalahari kudu.

UBACHSBERG: De Leuf €€€
Creative **Map** D6
Dalstraat 2, 6367 JS
Tel *(045) 575 0226* **Closed** *Sun & Mon; Sat lunch*
This fine-dining restaurant with two Michelin stars serves creatively cooked dishes like sea urchin with avocado, and pigeon with liquid black pudding.

VALKENBURG AAN DE GEUL: Tapas BarCelona €
Spanish **Map** D6
Berkelstraat 6, 6301 CC
Tel *(043) 852 4524* **Closed** *Mon & Tue*
The menu at this tapas bar ranges from garlic bread and spicy potatoes to bacon-wrapped dates and *pata negra* ham. Gaudí-inspired pillars, Andalusian lamps and a big Osborne bull on the wall.

VALKENBURG AAN DE GEUL: Aan de Linde €€
French **Map** D6
Jan Deckerstraat 1B, 6301 GX
Tel *(043) 601 0577*
A brasserie by day and a restaurant in the evening, this attractive, popular local eatery has taken over what was once a historic and eclectic casino hotel.

WELL: Brienen aan de Maas €€€
French **Map** D5
Grotestraat 11, 5855 AK
Tel *(0478) 501 967* **Closed** *Mon & Tue*
The scenic setting of this Michelin-starred restaurant along the Maas river is matched by its regionally influenced cooking. The à la carte menu focuses mainly on seafood.

Diners at the popular Verkadefabriek in 's-Hertogenbosch

For more information on types of restaurants *see page 403*

SHOPPING IN THE NETHERLANDS

Throughout the Netherlands you will find a huge range of shops and markets. Many towns will have large retail chains, but you will also find unique independent shops selling clothes, everyday goods and knick-knacks. Large specialized shops such as furniture stores, factory outlets and garden centres are usually on the outskirts of towns and sometimes grouped together in retail parks with parking facilities, child-care facilities and a cafeteria. Most are open, and at their busiest, on public holidays. Recent fashion items can often be picked up cheaply at street markets and second-hand shops.

Shop selling antiques and curios

Markets

Practically every town and village holds a general market at least once a week. There are also specialized markets, for example, the farmers' markets, where you can buy fresh farm produce, as well as antique markets and book fairs. Famous specialized markets include the cheese markets of Alkmaar, Edam and Gouda. Then there are also flea markets, where traders and individuals alike sell second-hand goods.

The Netherlands' biggest flea market takes place on Koninginnedag (Queen's Day) *(see p36)*, when practically half of the country tries to get rid of unwanted goods on the street. Fairs are also popular and are held twice a year. Most markets start at 9:30am and end at 4pm or 5pm, while some are open either in the mornings or the afternoons only.

Antiques

Antique collectors will find plenty to occupy themselves with in the Netherlands. If you are fortunate, you may strike it lucky in second-hand shops or at flea markets, but your best bet is to go to an authentic antique dealer. Many antique dealers specialize in a particular period or field – prints or clocks, for instance. If you prefer buying antiques at auctions, you would probably do best to visit the branches of the international auctioneers **Sotheby's** or **Christie's**. In smaller auction houses too, interesting pieces often go under the hammer. Another way of buying antiques is to visit the antique markets and fairs that are held regularly throughout the country.

Amsterdam's Nieuwe Spiegelstraat is the place for antique collectors. Vendors include antique dealers specializing in ceramics, glass, antique prints, paintings and nautical memorabilia.

Haarlem, Middelburg and 's-Hertogenbosch have large numbers of antique shops; these are often located in old farmhouses. The most common pieces on sale are pine or oak furniture. The MECC in Maastricht and the **Brabanthallen** in 's-Hertogenbosch are the venues of annual antique fairs, such as the renowned **TEFAF**, the world's biggest art and antique fair. Antique dealers from around the world come here to trade.

Antique dealer's shop sign

Fashion

The Dutch are spending more and more of their incomes on good-quality fashionable clothing. Besides internationally renowned couturiers, many up-and-coming fashion designers have set up their own boutiques. Their clothes are often handmade and fairly pricey. More affordable clothes are available at the larger fashion retailers, both home-grown and international. A typical Dutch way of being fashionable is to combine a new and expensive garment with second-hand clothes. To see the designs of the most famous couturiers, it is best to go to Amsterdam. On the PC Hooftstraat you will find clothes by Hugo Boss, Armani and Yves Saint-Laurent, while classical English clothing and shoes are to be found in the shops on the Haagse Noordeinde in The Hague. Chains such as Vera Moda sell everyday and durable clothing.

One of the country's many antique and second-hand shops

A trendy clothing boutique featuring the very latest in Dutch fashion

Retail Stores and Shopping Centres

The most upmarket retail store in the Netherlands is the **Bijenkorf**, which offers contemporary furniture, the latest names in fashion, a huge book department and all major cosmetics brands. The Vroom & Dreesmann department stores are slightly smaller and offer lower prices than the Bijenkorf. One step lower on the prices scale is Hema, which offers a wide and remarkably trendy range of things such as lighting accessories and household goods. At most shopping centres you will find the same names, although some centres are reserved for more exclusive shops. One of these is the **Magna Plaza** in Amsterdam, where you will find upmarket boutiques and jewellers' shops. De Groene Passage in Rotterdam is a covered shopping centre dedicated to the environment, selling items ranging from organic meat to New Age books.

La Vie in Utrecht has a good range of shops; in The Hague, **De Passage** is the prime shopping centre. Batavia Stad Outlet Shopping centre in Lelystad is a shopping village built to resemble a 17th-century town. Here manufacturers of expensive brands sell end-of-line products, in particular clothes, at heavy discounts. The designer outlet park in Roermond is a similar place to find bargains.

Furniture

The Netherlands' top furniture designer, Jan des Bouvrie, has his own shop in a converted arsenal in Naarden called **Studio het Arsenaal**. At **Van Til Interior** in Alkmaar you can buy designer furniture. In Amsterdam-Zuidoost, you can spend a day viewing furniture in the 75 shops of the **Villa Arena**. Woonthemacentrum De Havenaer in Nijkerk and Palazzo Lelystad also offer interesting collections. You will find "meubelboulevards", shopping streets of furniture stores, throughout the country.

Auction and Sales Houses

The famous British auction houses **Sotheby's** and **Christie's** have branches in Amsterdam, where international collections in particular are auctioned. The **Eland De Zon Loth Gijselman** in Diemen, deals in antiquities and art and auctions furniture and estates. **Holbein** in Rijssen sells art and antiques, the **Veilinghuis de Voorstraat** in Zwolle specializes in stamps and coins.

Garden Centres

Dutch garden centres sell plants, seeds, bulbs, soil, compost and garden furniture. For more unusual plants go to specialist growers, of which there are many in the Netherlands. Garden centres are usually on the edge of towns or just outside them. They are usually open for business on Sundays and public holidays.

An abundance of flowers at a Dutch garden centre

Chocolate

Verkade and Droste are the Netherlands' best-known chocolate makers, and you can find their products everywhere. Many towns now have specialized confectioners' shops. The renowned Belgian confectioner **Leonidas** has numerous outlets in the country. **Puccini Bomboni** produce exceptional chocolates, sold individually.

Tea and Coffee

The Netherlands has been a tea and coffee importer for centuries, and you can find specialist tea and coffee shops everywhere; many still roast their own coffee. In Amsterdam, **Simon Levelt** always has at least 25 varieties of coffee and 100 tea blends on sale. **Geels & Co Koffiebranderij**, an old family business, has a roasting house and museum.

Magna Plaza (*see p94*), open for Sunday shopping

What to Buy in Holland

In the cities and tourist resorts, souvenir shops are not difficult to find. But if you are looking for something out of the ordinary, either for yourself or as a gift, you can often find something in more specialized shops, or even in a supermarket. Flowers and Delftware never fail to delight. For other things worth taking home, for example, local delicacies such as Dutch cheese and *speculaas*, or drinks such as *jenever* gin *(see p420)*.

Souvenir Dolls
Dutch national costume is hardly worn in the Netherlands any more, except by souvenir dolls such as this trio from Volendam.

Miniature Houses
Painted miniature pottery houses (often Delft blue) are a popular souvenir. Some are designed to be filled with *jenever* gin, while others are purely ornamental.

Painted Wooden Clogs
The traditional wooden clog has come to symbolize Holland. They can be bought in all colours and sizes. They can also be ordered online at www.woodenshoes.com

Dutch bulbs

Red Coral
Necklaces of red coral are often part of traditional costume in places such as Volendam. However, they also add a nice touch when worn with modern clothing.

Gouda Pipes
Long-necked clay pipes from Gouda, known as Grouwenaars *(see p243)*, have been made here since the beginning of the 17th century and make a nice gift for smokers and non-smokers alike.

Flowers
Bulbs and cut flowers are available all the year round in the innumerable flower shops, flower stalls and garden centres that are easily found throughout the Netherlands.

Prints of Dutch windmills

Old Maps and Prints

Amsterdam in particular has made its mark in the field of cartography. Many antique shops sell atlases and books of prints.

Reproductions of maps of Amsterdam and Russia

Inlaid diamond necklace

Diamonds

Diamonds were cut in Amsterdam as early as the 16th century, and the town continues to be one of the main diamond centres of the world. Many jewellers sell uncut diamonds and second-hand diamond rings.

Diamond brooch

Diamonds of different colours

Delftware mugs

Modern Delftware

Modern blue Delftware items decorated with windmills or other images of Holland are available in the form of tea sets, sculptures, vases and even royal Delft ashtrays. When buying, make sure that there is a certificate of authenticity *(see p32)* to go with it.

Makkum Pottery

This colourful earthenware, primarily tiles, plates and bowls, is still produced by the Tichelaar factory *(see p33)* at Makkum in Friesland.

Speculaas
These biscuits, flavoured with cinnamon, cloves and ginger, are eaten mainly around St Nicholas's day.

Speculaas

A distinctive Edam cheese

Edam Cheese
The world-famous Edam cheese *(see p178)* has an excellent taste and makes a good souvenir.

Speculaas Board
Mould your own speculaas biscuits in these biscuit moulds, or use them for attractive wall ornaments.

Haagse Hopjes
These coffee-flavoured sweets were first made at the end of the 18th century at the inspiration of a Baron Hop of The Hague.

Zeeland Butter Candies
These butter-flavoured sweets from Zeeland, made of glucose sugar syrup and butter, are delicious.

Butter candies

Hopjes

Dutch Beer
The Dutch are renowned beer-drinkers. In addition to the three brands depicted here, there are countless other varieties available.

Zaans Mustard
This coarse mustard is made at De Huisman mustard plant on the Zaanse Schans *(see p179)*.

Jonge grain jenever

Sonnema herenburg

Zwarte Kip advocaat

Gingerbread

Spirits
Renowned Dutch spirits include *jenever*, a kind of gin sold in glass or stoneware bottles (there are four basic kinds, including "young" and "old"), *berenburg*, the Frisian distilled herbal drink and *advocaat*, made of brandy and eggs.

Gingerbread
This scrumptious bread comes in a variety of regional variations, and is excellent at breakfast or even as a snack – especially with a thick layer of butter.

Liquorice Drops
The ubiquitous liquorice drops are sold either salted or sweet.

DIRECTORY

Antiques

Brabanthallen
Diezekade 2,
's-Hertogenbosch.
Road Map C4.
Tel 073-6293911.
Spring antique fairs.

Le Collectionneur
Damplein 5, Middelburg.
Road Map A5.
Tel 0118-638595.

EH Ariëns Kappers
Keizersgracht 208,
Amsterdam.
Map 1 B4.
Tel 020-6235356.
(call for appointment)

Emmakade 2 Antiek
Emmakade 2,
Leeuwarden.
Road Map D1.
Tel 058-2153464.

**Jan de Raad
Antiquiteiten**
Hekellaan 10,
's-Hertogenbosch.
Road Map C4.
Tel 065-3177494.

TEFAF Maastricht
Art and Antiques Fair
(Mar), Maastricht.
Road Map D6.
W tefaf.com

De Tijdspiegel
Nieuwstraat 17,
Middelburg.
Road Map A5.
Tel 0118-627799.

Retail Stores and Shopping Centres

De Bijenkorf
Dam 1, Amsterdam.
Map 2 D3.
Tel 0800-0818.
Ketelstraat 45, Arnhem.
Road Map D4.
Tel 0800-0818.
Wagenstraat 32,
The Hague.
Road Map B4.
Tel 0800-0818.
Piazza 1, Eindhoven.
Road Map C5.
Tel 0800-0818.

Coolsingel 105,
Rotterdam.
Road Map B4.
Tel 0800-0818.
Sint-Jacobsstraat 1a,
Utrecht.
Road Map C4.
Tel 0800-0818.
W bijenkorf.nl

Magna Plaza
Nieuwez. Voorburgwal
182, Amsterdam.
Map 1 4C
Tel 020-5703570.

De Passage
Passage, The Hague.
Road Map B4.
Tel 030-2565165.

**La Vie
Shoppingcentre**
Lange Viestraat 669,
Utrecht.
Road Map C4.
Tel 030-2340088.

Furniture

Studio het Arsenaal
Kooltjesbuurt 1,
Naarden-Vesting.
Road Map C3.
Tel 035-6941144.

Van Til Interieur
Noorderkade 1038,
Alkmaar.
Road Map B3.
Tel 072-5112760.

Villa Arena
Arena Boulevard,
Amsterdam-Zuidoost.
Tel 0800-8455227.
W villaarena.nl

Auction and Sales Houses

Christie's
Cornelis Schuytstraat 57,
Amsterdam.
Map 3 4C
Tel 020-5755255.

**De Eland De Zon
Loth Gijselman**
Industrieterrein Verrijn
Stuart, Weesperstraat
110–112, Diemen.
Road Map C3.
Tel 020-6230343.

**Holbein Kunst- en
Antiekveilingen**
Jutestraat 31, Rijssen.
Road Map D3.
Tel 0548-541577.

Sotheby's
Emmalaan 23,
Amsterdam.
Tel 020-5502200.

**Veilinghuis de
Voorstraat**
Voorstraat 23, Zwolle.
Road Map D3.
Tel 038-4211045.

Chocolates

Huize van Wely
Beethovenstraat 72,
Amsterdam.
Map 4 D5.
Tel 020-6622009.
Hoofdstraat 88,
Noordwijk (ZH).
Road Map B3.
Tel 071-3612228.

Leonidas
Stationsplein 34,
Amsterdam.
Map 2 E3.
Tel 020-3305261.
Rembrandthof 55,
Amstelveen.
Road Map B3.
Tel 026-2320000.
Radboudkwartier 4,
Utrecht.
Road Map C4.
Tel 030-2110011.
Ds. Jan Scharpstraat
298–81, Rotterdam.
Road Map B4.
Tel 010-4048210.
Gentsestraat 8, Hulst.
Road Map B5.
Tel 0114-321848.
Oude Kerkstraat 35, Sluis.
Road Map A5.
Tel 0117-760003.
Huevelgalerij 131b,
Eindhoven.
Road Map C5.
Tel 040-3070000.

Puccini Bomboni
Staalstraat 17,
Amsterdam.
Map 5 A2
Tel 020-6265474.
Singel 184, Amsterdam.
Map 1 4C
Tel 020-4278341.

Tea and Coffee

Droom van Utrecht
Schoutenstraat 6, Utrecht.
Road Map C4.
Tel 030-2316934.

**Geels & Co
Koffiebranderij**
Kikkertweg 22, 1521 RG
Wormerveer.
Road Map B3
Tel 075-2340747.

Het Klaverblad
Hogewoerd 15, Leiden.
Road Map B3.
Tel 071-5133655.

**Koffiebrander
Blanche Dael**
Wolfstraat 28, Maastricht.
Road Map C6.
Tel 043-3213475.

**Simon Levelt koffie-
en theehandel**
Prinsengracht 180,
Amsterdam.
Map 1 4B
Tel 020-6240823.
Veerstraat 15, Bussum.
Road Map C3.
Tel 035-6939459.
Zwanestraat 38,
Groningen.
Road Map D1.
Tel 050-3114333.
Gierstraat 65, Haarlem.
Road Map B3.
Tel 023-5311861.
Botermarkt 1–2, Leiden.
Road Map B3.
Tel 071-5131159.
Vismarkt 21, Utrecht.
Road Map B3.
Tel 030-2314495.

ENTERTAINMENT IN THE NETHERLANDS

Cultural life in the Netherlands is not confined to the Randstad. Outside the big cities there is also plenty to do. There is a theatre or a cultural centre in just about every town, where theatre groups, cabaret artists, orchestras and rock bands perform. There is also a growing number of entertainment complexes, such as the Miracle Planet Boulevard centre in Enschede. You can find out what's on either by contacting the relevant venue or through the local VVV (tourist) offices; another option is the AUB Ticketshop *(see p153)* in Amsterdam. Here you can usually book tickets, or obtain more information about performances. You can also get tickets and information via the Uitlijn (0900-0191). The major national dailies publish a list of events each week. Most cities publish a weekly *uitkrant*, or entertainment guide, while the internet is another source of information.

Theatre

The Netherlands boasts a large number of theatres, concentrated mostly around Amsterdam. That city's top theatre is the Stadsschouwburg *(see p116)*, where many touring theatre companies put on performances. The Netherlands' largest theatre company, Toneelgroep Amsterdam, is based here and is now directed by Ivo van Hove.

The annual highlight for opera, theatre and dance is the Holland Festival. The best in international cultural offerings is to be had during the Amsterdam Festival. During the International Theatre School Festival in June, experimental drama is performed at venues such as De Brakke Grond *(see p151)* and **Frascati**. The **Soeterijn**, on the other hand, specializes in theatre from developing countries. The theatre company frequently wins prizes: the Theatergroup Hollandia has won great acclaim with its performances in large halls and aircraft hangars. The musical dramas of Orkater can be seen in various parts of the country at different times of the year, but mainly at the Stadsschouwburg and **Bellevue**. **De la Mar** stages big box-office hits, comedy and concerts by Dutch solo artists and groups. Youth-focused theatre is put on in **De Krakeling**. For years now the performances by the Toneelschuur in Haarlem have won critical acclaim. The De Appel group stages both experimental and repertory theatre at the **Appeltheater** in The Hague. Throughout the Netherlands there are numerous excellent theatre groups. Het Zuidelijk Toneel of Eindhoven in the south always packs theatre halls, as do the Theater van het Oosten from Arnhem in the east of the country and the Noord Nederlands Toneel from Groningen in the north.

Every year in May, the Festival aan de Werf in Utrecht presents an appealing smorgasbord of theatre and cabaret performances.

Musicals and Cabaret

The Netherlands' most outstanding musical theatres are the **AFAS Circustheater** of The Hague, the **Beatrix Theater** in Utrecht and the Koninklijk Theater Carré *(see p139)* in Amsterdam. These stage Dutch versions of big box-office hits such as *Les Misérables* and *Miss Saigon*.

De Kleine Komedie *(see p153)*, a magnificent 17th-century building on the Amstel river opposite the Muziektheater, is a favourite venue for cabaret groups. Stand-up comedy has also gained popularity mainly through this venue. Other comedy venues in Amsterdam are **Comedy Café, Toomler** and **Boom Chicago**.

Scene from the musical *Oliver!* at the Theater Carré

Dance

The Netherlands is the proud home of two world-famous ballet troupes: the Nationale Ballet and the Nederlands Dans Theater (NDT). The Nationale Ballet is based in the Musiektheater *(see p153)*, which is commonly known among Amsterdam theatre-goers as the "Stopera". This contemporary building can accommodate 1,600 people and is a significant centre both for dance and for opera. The foyer affords a pleasant view of the River Amstel.

The Nederlands Dans Theater, based in The Hague, offers a colourful programme of modern and contemporary dance and under the direction of the present choreographers has staged sold-out performances with live music. Introdans of Arnhem performs an exciting combination of jazz, flamenco and ethnic dance. The country's biggest choreo-graphers use the Holland Festival as a platform to present their new creations to the public. During the Internationale Theaterschool Festival, which also takes place in June, the proportion of dance performed is growing. The festival venue is the Nes, one of Amsterdam's oldest streets. Julidans is the name given to a summer dance festival in Amsterdam, in which contemporary dance by various international dance companies is performed.

Dr Anton Philipszaal Music Theater and Lucent Dance Opera Danstheater in The Hague

Noord Nederlands Toneel staging Anton Chekhov's *The Seagull*

Film

Going to the movies continues to be a popular pastime in the Netherlands, and you will find at least one or more cinemas in almost every town. Amsterdam alone has more than 45 cinemas. Foreign-language films are shown in the original language with subtitles. The most magnificent cinema in Amsterdam is Tuschinski, an Art Deco masterpiece built from 1918–21, with a stylish foyer and generous seating *(see p119)*. The major premieres are held here: if you want to see famous faces, the best time is Wednesday evenings at the cinema entrance.

There is a list of all films that are showing at the box office of every cinema, and such lists are also displayed in cafés and restaurants. Cinema programmes change every Thursday, so you will find a list of films that are on in Wednesday's evening papers and in Thursday's morning papers. *De Filmkrant* is a much-respected movie magazine that is published every Monday, which in addition to the week's film listings also provides background infor-mation on major films. Major film events in the Netherlands are the Nederlands Film Festival, which is held in Utrecht in September and October, where Dutch films are premiered. The award given to the winning films at this festival is the much-coveted Golden Calf statuette. The IDFA (International Documentary Film Festival Amsterdam) is the biggest of its kind, held every year in November/December. The renowned International Film Festival in Rotterdam takes place each January.

The Golden Calf statuette

Orchestral, Chamber and Choral Music

The Concertgebouw *(see p124)* in Amsterdam is traditionally the most important venue for concert music. The Grote Zaal hall is famous for its acoustics, and its resident musicians are the Koninklijk Concertgebouworkest. During the summer months, the orchestra puts on special concerts.

An outstanding orchestra is the Rotterdams Philharmonisch Orkest, whose conductor, the Czech Jirí Belohlávek, was appointed in 2012. The orchestra is based in **De Doelen** in Rotterdam. The Residentie Orkest, whose history goes back almost 100 years, performs regularly at the **Zuiderstrandtheater** in The Hague and is not to be confused with the **Muziekcentrum Frits Philips** in Eindhoven, where the Brabants Orkest is based.

The Amsterdamse Koninklijk Concertgebouworkest performing

The Gelders Orkest makes regular appearances in the **Musis Sacrum** concert hall in Arnhem. Another go-to venue offering a rich programme of music is the **TivoliVredenburg**.

Church Music

Of the many organs in the Netherlands, that of the **Grote Kerk** in Elburg is probably the best known. Every year it is used in the national amateur organist competition. The instruments in the **Oude Kerk** and the **Nieuwe Kerk** are the most famous of Amsterdam's 42 church organs. Organ concerts can be heard at the **Waalse Kerk** and also on Tuesdays at lunchtime in the **Westerkerk**.

The programme of the 17th-century **Engelse Kerk** contains a wide variety of music genres, ranging from Baroque to modern. In the **Domkerk** in Utrecht, concerts are performed on a regular basis.

Opera

Established in 1988 in Amsterdam, the **Dutch National Opera & Ballet** is the home of the Nederlandse Opera. One of Europe's most modern opera theatres, its stage has been graced by many established international companies, although it is also

used for experimental works. The Stadsschouwburg *(see p116)* on the Leidseplein is also host to a great deal of opera, although if experimental opera is your thing, the Westergasfabriek is probably the best venue. Another good venue to watch an opera is the **Wilminktheater** in Enschede.

Rock And Pop

Two venues in particular have established themselves as the most important rock venues in the Netherlands: **Ahoy'** in Rotterdam and Vredenburg in Utrecht, although international rock stars now perform in many parts of the Netherlands. With a capacity of over 5,000, the easily accessible **Heineken Music Hall** is Amsterdam's prime rock venue. It has been used for concerts by megastars such as the late Michael Jackson and the Rolling Stones. However, for locals, there are only two real rock venues: **Paradiso** and **De Melkweg**. Paradiso, in a former church near the Leidseplein, enjoys the greatest respect. The Melkweg (Milky Way), which is also near the Leidseplein, owes its name to

the fact that the building in which it is located used to be a dairy. The programme in both of these respected venues changes constantly, and all rock and pop enthusiasts will eventually find something to their taste.

Every Sunday in summer there are free open-air concerts in the Vondelpark, often with renowned bands in the line-up. Programmes are displayed at the entrances to the park. In June the world's largest free pop festival, the Haagse Zuiderpark Parkpop, is held in The Hague. Another annual festival which attracts visitors from near and far is the Pinkpopfestival in Landgraaf (Limburg).

Jazz

The foremost venue of the jazz scene in Amsterdam is the **Bimhuis**. Although the casual visitor might find the atmosphere a tad pretentious, the music here is of top quality, and the Bimhuis enjoys a reputation that goes far beyond the country's borders. There are good jazz cafés to be found all over Amsterdam, most of them featuring local jazz bands. Around the Leidseplein are the **Alto Jazz Café** and **Bourbon Street**, which is open until 4am on weekdays and until 5am on weekends. Alto is best on Wednesdays, when the "godfather" of Amsterdam jazz, Hans Dulfer, performs. His daughter Candy, who has gained international renown, sometimes plays in **De Heeren van Aemstel**. De **Engelbewaarder** is a venue for Sunday jazz. Meanwhile, in Rotterdam, the annual North Sea Jazz Festival takes place in the Congresgebouw. **Dizzy** jazz café has become a household name among jazz-lovers in Rotterdam, hosting over 100 jazz concerts every year.

Hans Dulfer

DIRECTORY

Theatres

Appeltheater
Duinstraat 6–8, The
Hague. **Road Map** B4.
Tel 070-3502200.

Arsenaaltheater
Arsenaalplein 1,
Vlissingen. **Road Map** A5.
Tel 0118-430303.

Bellevue
Leidsekade 90,
Amsterdam. **Map** 4 D1.
Tel 020-5305301/02.

Chassé Theater
Claudius Prinsenlaan 8,
Breda. **Road Map** B5.
Tel 076-5303032.

Compagnietheater
Kloveniersburgwal 50,
Amsterdam. **Map** 2 D5.
Tel 020-5205310.

Concordia
Oude Markt 15, Enschede.
Road Map E3.
Tel 053-4300999.

De Flint
Conickstraat 60,
Amersfoort.
Road Map C4.
Tel 033-4229229.

Frascati
Nes 63, Amsterdam.
Map 2 D5.
Tel 020-6266866.

De Harmonie
Ruiterskwartier 4,
Leeuwarden.
Road Map D1.
Tel 058-2330233.

De Krakeling
Nwe Passeerdersstraat 1,
Amsterdam. **Map** 4 D1.
Tel 020-6245123.

De la Mar
Marnixstraat 402,
Amsterdam. **Map** 4 D1.
Tel 0900-3352627.

Orpheus
Churchillplein 1,
Apeldoorn.
Road Map D3.
Tel 055-5270300.

Stadsschouwburg
Leidseplein 26,
Amsterdam. **Map** 4 E2.
Tel 020-6242311.

't Spant
Kuyperlaan 3, Bussum.
Road Map C3.
Tel 035-6913949.

**Theater aan het
Vrijthof**
Vrijthof 47, Maastricht.
Road Map C6.
Tel 043-3505555.

Toneelschuur
Lange Begijnestr 9,
Haarlem. **Road Map** B3.
Tel 023-5173910.

Transformatorhuis
Klönneplein 2,
Amsterdam. **Map** 1 A1.
Tel 020-5860710.

Musicals and Cabaret

AFAS Circustheater
Circusstraat 4, The Hague.
Road Map B4.
Tel 0900-1353.

Beatrix Theater
Jaarbeursplein 6, Utrecht.
Road Map C4.
Tel 0900-1353.

Boom Chicago
Rozengracht 117,
Amsterdam. **Map** 4 E2.
Tel 020-2170400.

Comedy Café
IJdok 89, Amsterdam.
Map 4 E2.
Tel 020-7220827.

Toomler
Breitnerstr. 2, Amsterdam.
Map 3 C5.
Tel 020-6707400.

Dance

**Rotterdamse
Schouwburg**
Schouwburgplein 25,
Rotterdam. **Road Map** B4.
Tel 010-4118110.

Schouwburg Arnhem
Koningsplein 12, Arnhem.
Road Map D4.
Tel 026-4437343.

Orchestra, Chamber and Choral Music

Anton Philipszaal
Spuiplein 150, The Hague.
Road Map B4.
Tel 070-8800333.

**Concertgebouw
De Vereeniging**
Keizer Karelplein,
Nijmegen. **Road Map** D4.
Tel 024-3221100.

De Doelen
Schouwburgplein 50,
Rotterdam. **Road Map** B4.
Tel 010-2171717.

Musis Sacrum
Velperbuitensingel 25,
Arnhem. **Road Map** D4.
Tel 026-3720720.

**Muziekgebouw Frits
Philips**
Jan van Lieshoutstraat,
Eindhoven.
Road Map C5.
Tel 040-2655600.

TivoliVredenburg
Vredenburgkade 11,
Utrecht. **Road Map** C4.
Tel 030-2314544.

Zuiderstrandtheater
Houtrustweg 505, The
Hague. **Road Map** B4.
Tel 070-8800333.

Church Music

Domkerk
Domplein, Utrecht.
Road Map C4.
Tel 030-2310403.

Engelse Kerk
Begijnhof 48, Amsterdam.
Map 1 C5.
Tel 020-6249665.

Grote Kerk
Van Kinsbergenstraat,
Elburg. **Road Map** D3.
Tel 0525-681520.

Nieuwe Kerk
Dam, Amsterdam. **Map** 2
D5. **Tel** 020-6386909.

Oude Kerk
Oudekerksplein 23,
Amsterdam. **Map** 2 D4.
Tel 020-6258284.

Waalse Kerk
Walenplein 157,
Amsterdam.
Tel 020-6232074.

Westerkerk
Prinsengracht 281,
Amsterdam. **Map** 1 B4.
Tel 020-624776.

Opera

**Dutch National
Opera & Ballet**
Map 5 B2.

Wilminktheater
Wenninkgaarde 40–42,
Enschede. **Road Map** E3.
Tel 053-4858500.

Rock and Pop

Ahoy'
Ahoyveg 10, Rotterdam.
Road Map B4.
Tel 010-2933810.

Heineken Music Hall
Arena Boulevard 590,
Amsterdam.
Tel 0900-6874242.

De Melkweg
Lijnbaansgracht 234 a,
Amsterdam. **Map** 4 E2.
Tel 020-5318181.

Paradiso
Weteringschans 6–8,
Amsterdam. **Map** 4 3F.
Tel 020-6264521.

Jazz

Alto Jazz Café
Korte Leidsedwarsstraat
115, Amsterdam.
Map 1 B4.
Tel 020-8454380.

Bimhuis
Piet Heinkade 3,
Amsterdam.
Tel 020-7882188.

Bourbon Street
Leidsekruisstraat 6–8,
Amsterdam. **Map** 4 2E.
Tel 020-6233440.

Dizzy
's-Gravendijkwal 127,
Rotterdam. **Road Map** B4.
Tel 010-4773014.

De Engelbewaarder
Kloveniersburgwal 59,
Amsterdam. **Map** 2 5D.
Tel 020-6253772.

**De Heeren van
Aemstel**
Thorbeckeplein 5,
Amsterdam. **Map** 5 A2.
Tel 020-6202173.

Amusement and Theme Parks

The Netherlands offers a great variety of amusement and theme parks. Whether you want to see frolicking dolphins, take a white-knuckle ride, go back to Roman times or spend the day splashing in a swimming pool, there is something for everyone. And because the Dutch weather doesn't always play along, most parks have attractions indoors. Listed below is a sample of the parks to be found in the country.

One of the rides at the Hellendoorn Adventure Park

Aqua Zoo Friesland

This watery domain near Leeuwarden shows beavers, minks, polecats, storks and other animals in their natural surroundings. Otters are a highlight here, having disappeared from the Netherlands due to pollution of their freshwater habitat. A path winds its way through the entire terrain, leading at one point through a glass tunnel that provides visitors with a close-up of the otters' underwater antics.

Archeon

This open-air archaeological park brings the past to life in captivating fashion. Visitors wander from prehistoric times, the Roman period and the Middle Ages, aided by the re-creations of actors. You can see how the hunter-gatherers lived and how farmers tilled their fields. You then explore a Roman town complete with bath-house, temple and theatre, followed by a medieval city with

working craftsmen. The hands-on fun includes a trip in a prehistoric canoe.

Het Arsenaal

A large attraction with a maritime theme has been set up at Het Arsenaal in Vlissingen. First visitors watch a naval review with models of famous ocean liners, including the *Titanic*. For those hooked on adrenaline there is a shipwreck simulator and a scary pirate cave on a treasure island. In Onderwaterwereld you can observe sharks, lobsters and other creatures of the deep. The 64-m (210-ft) tower of Het Arsenaal gives a fine view of the Westerschelde estuary.

Avonturenpark Hellendoorn

This place offers a vast range of attractions, including the Canadian River log-ride with a 12-m (39-ft) drop in a tree trunk, the Sungai Kalimantan rafting-ride, the Tornado and Rioolrat (underground) rat ride, a monorail over a dinosaur park

and Montezuma's Revenge (prepare to get wet!). Younger children will enjoy Dreumesland (Dreamland) with its play castle and much more.

Burgers' Zoo

This unusual park allows you to see animals from all over the world in their natural environments, which have been carefully re-created here.

In Burgers' Desert, in a vast hall with 20-m (65-ft) ceilings, you can wander through a rocky cactus desert with birds and an oasis. There is also a dense tropical jungle and a safari park with giraffes, rhinoceroses and lions. In the ocean section, you can stand on a tropical coral beach and peer through the glass at an undersea world.

Dolfinarium

Frolicking dolphins and seals always draw large crowds, but the Dolfinarium does one better with its Lagune, a large bay where dolphins, sea lions and fish live. In Fort Heerewich you learn how stranded dolphins are cared for. An underwater show and a 3D film provide additional excitement.

Duinrell

Nestled in the sandy woodlands of the Wassenaar region, this park has rides such as the Waterspin, toboggan runs, a frog roller coaster and a monorail. In summer there are elaborate shows such as the *Music Laser Light Show*. For the little ones there is a fairytale

Suspension bridge through the tropical rainforest in Burgers' Bush

wonderland, a large playground and numerous kids' shows. A big draw is the Tikibad, an indoor pool with spectacular slides, a surf pool and a water ballet show.

EcoMare

Located on the island of Texel, just a few kilometres away from the pretty village of de Koog, EcoMare is a fascinating sealife and marine centre dedicated to exploring the flora and fauna of Texel. It also offers a glimpse into the history of the island. Among the exhibits, there are seals and porpoises, and a good number of giant turtle and humpback whale skeletons that were discovered on the island. The road beyond the museum leads to the beach,

Stranded seals recovering their health in EcoMare on Texel

Visitors enjoying the splash ride in Duinrell

which has a café to unwind in and unlimited opportunities for dune walking.

De Efteling

This theme park in Kaatsheuvel draws on the world of fantasy. In the fairytale forest you may bump into Little Red Riding Hood, Snow White or Sleeping Beauty. The Fata Morgana is a simplified take on the Arabian Nights; here you can view the entire park from a 45-m (148-ft) Flying Temple.

Extreme thrills are provided by the Python, the Pegasus and the underground Vogel Rok roller coasters and many other rides. It's worth checking the website for "busy" days.

If a day isn't enough to explore the park, you can stay the night in Efteling Hotel.

Linnaeushof

This playground claims to be Europe's largest, with more than 350 different pieces of equipment, including a super slide, cable rides, a skate-rail, trampolines, a climbing wall, pedaloes and 360-degree swings. In the "spider's web", you risk tumbling into the water as you climb nets to the pirates' crow's nest.

Toddlers have their own special playground with a huge sandpit and road village where they can ride tricycles and toy aeroplanes. For wet weather there's an indoor playground.

Noordwijk Space Expo

This sprawling display about outer space is a treat for all ages. Some of its rockets and satellites are the real thing (as is the piece of moon rock 4 billion years old), but the replicas, such as a model lunar module, are convincing. You can visit a space station and watch multimedia presentations. Children will enjoy the treasure hunt and zero-gravity simulator.

DIRECTORY

Aqua Zoo Friesland
De Groene Ster 2, 8926 XE Leeuwarden. **Road Map** D2. **Tel** 0511-431214. **Open** 10am–4pm daily (longer in summer).
W aquazoo.nl

Archeon
Archeonlaan 1, 2408 ZB Alphen a/d Rijn. **Road Map** B4. **Tel** 0172-447744. **Open** Apr–Oct: 10am–5pm Mon, Wed & Sat, 10am–4pm Tue, Thu & Fri.
W archeon.nl

Het Arsenaal
Arsenaalplein 7, 4381 BL Vlissingen. **Road Map** A5. **Tel** 0118-415400. **Open** Apr–Oct: 10am–7pm daily; mid-Feb–Mar: timings vary, call ahead.
W arsenaal.com

Avonturenpark Hellendoorn
Luttenbergerweg 22, 7447 PB Hellendoorn. **Road Map** D3. **Tel** 0548-659159. **Open** call ahead.
W avonturenpark.nl

Burgers' Zoo
Anton van Hooffplein 1, 6816 SH Arnhem. **Road map** D4. **Tel** 026-4424534. **Open** Apr–Oct: 9am–7pm daily; Nov–Mar: 9am–5pm daily.
W burgerszoo.nl

Dolfinarium Harderwijk
Strandboulevard Oost 1, 3841 AB Harderwijk. **Road Map** C3. **Tel** 0341-467467 **Open** mid-Feb–Jun & Sep–Oct: 10am–5pm daily; Jul–Aug: 10am–6pm daily.
W dolfinarium.nl

Duinrell
Duinrell 1, 2242 JP Wassenaar. **Road Map** B4. **Tel** 070-5155255. **Open** Theme park: Apr–Oct: 10am–5pm daily (mid-Jul–Aug to 6pm).
W duinrell.nl

EcoMare
Ruyslaan 92, 1796 AZ De Koog, Texel. **Road Map** B2. **Tel** 0222-317741. **Open** 9:30am–5pm daily.
W ecomare.nl

De Efteling
Europalaan 1, 5171 KW Kaatsheuvel. **Road Map** C4. **Tel** 0416-537777. **Open** Apr–Oct: 10am–6pm daily (later in summer). Winter Efteling: open around Christmas.
W efteling.com

Linnaeushof
Glipperweg 4c, 2104 AK Heemstede. **Road Map** B3. **Tel** 023-5847624. **Open** Apr–Sep: 10am–5pm daily (Jun–Aug: to 6pm).
W linnaueshof.nl

Noordwijk Space Expo
Keplerlaan 3, 2201 AZ Noordwijk. **Tel** 071-3646489. **Open** 10am–5pm Tue–Sun (also Mon in school hols).
W spaceexpo.nl

Sports Holidays

With its abundance of water, the Netherlands lends itself to all kinds of watersports such as boating, sailing and canoeing; however, there are also plenty of opportunities for sporting activities on dry land, whether you want to kick a ball about or play golf or tennis, or even go riding. Most *VVV-gidsen* (see p432) tell you where there are golf courses and tennis courts in the locality, and they give the addresses of angling clubs, stables, boatyards, sailing schools and so on.

Ramblers in the Heuvelrug in Utrecht

Canoeists enjoying themselves on the water

Watersports

The favourite places in the Netherlands for watersports are the Frisian seas, the coastal lakes, the Plassengebied (lakelands), the southwest river delta, and the lakes of the Vechtplassen, the Maasplassen, the IJsselmeer and, of course, the North Sea. Everywhere there are abundant marinas and watersports centres, often with equipment for hire. The ANWB publishes the *Wateralmanakken*, available at ANWB and VVV offices and in bookshops, which give details of sailing regulations, bridge and lock opening times, port information and so on. The *ANWB/VVV waterkaarten* (navigation charts)

are also used by many people. You can obtain information on sailing and surfing organizations at institutions such as the **Commissie Watersport Opleidingen** (watersports training commission) and the ANWB. Surfers will find plenty to do on the North Sea and IJsselmeer coast (surfing beaches, equipment hire), and it is also possible to surf on many inland waters, including the Reenwijkse Plassen, the Randmeren and the Frisian lakes. For further information on sailing, boating and windsurfing, ask at the **Koninklijk Nederlands Watersport Verbond** (royal watersports association). Good places for diving include the Oosterschelde and Grevelingenmeer; for more information apply to the Dutch underwater-sports association, the **Nederlandse Onderwatersport Bond**.

Canoeing is another popular watersport in the Netherlands. Dozens of round trips in various craft organized in lakes, rivers and the sea are also available. The local VVV tourist office will be able to direct you further.

Rambling and Cycling

Ramblers' guides and maps can be obtained in many places, including the VVV, ANWB and bookshops. The VVV also provides information on walking tours and local events. The *Er op Uit!* booklet published by the Dutch Railways contains rambling routes from one station to another. The majority of them are 15 to 20 km (9 to 12 miles), though some two-day hikes are also described. You will find route maps at the station where the hike begins. Around 30 long-distance hiking trails have been marked out in the Netherlands. These routes, which are at least 100 km (62 miles) in length, follow mainly unmetalled tracks. A popular

Sailing

Sailing courses suitable for all ages and experience levels are widely available along the Dutch coast for practically all types of vessel. Taking lessons at a CWO registered sailing school will give you an internationally recognized CWO sailing certificate. More experienced sailors can explore the North Sea, the IJsselmeer (watch out for strong winds), the Waddenzee (where you have to watch the shallows) or the Westerschelde (which has strong tidal currents). However, you can also go for a more relaxing experience on the Vinkeveense Plassen lakes. Cruises are also widely available. Hollands Glorie (tel. 010-4156600) offers cruises on traditional sailing craft on waterways such as the IJsselmeer, the Waddenzee and the Frisian lakes.

Yachting on the Oosterschelde

Sailing dinghy

Golfers on the Lauswolt Estate in Friesland

hiking trail is the Pieterpad (LAW 9), stretching 480 km (300 miles) from Pieterburen in Groningen to the Sint-Pietersberg at Maastricht.

Wandelplatform-LAW publishes guides to the routes, with and without accommo-dation details. Many natural areas are criss-crossed by footpaths and cycle tracks, among them the Nationaal Park De Hoge Veluwe *(see p343)*. You can find out about accessibility of various areas and about enjoyable routes or excursions at VVV or ANWB tourist information offices, at the Staatsbosbeheer (forestry commission) (www.staats-bosbeheer.nl) or the Vereniging Natuurmonumenten *(see p264)*. For details on cycling, see pages 448–9.

Golf and Tennis

The Netherlands has some 160 golfing clubs, all members of the Nederlandse Golf Federatie (**NGF**). Many clubs also provide opportunities for non-members to play, although some may require proof of golfing proficiency. Many of them also offer training courses. Golf courses in the Netherlands are in dunelands, woodland and polderland.

In many areas you will find tennis clubs with outdoor and indoor courts. Most bungalow parks have tennis courts for the use of residents.

Fishing

Fishing is a popular sport in the Netherlands. In the inland waterways you can angle for bream, carp and pike, while flatfish and mackerel can be caught along the coast and in the sea. Local angling associ-ations will give you information on when and where to fish. Don't forget to obtain a fishing permit (which is compulsory for inland waters). The permits are available at VVVs or angling associations. Sometimes you also need a permit for a particular lake or river. Along the coast, angling trips are organized on the North Sea and in the Waddenzee.

Horse Riding

There are many stables where you can hire ponies for pony-trekking. Some stables hire out horses only if you have a riding permit or if you are on a guided tour (information is available from the **SVR**). For some nature reserves which allow riding you will need to get a riding permit from the organization managing the area, and you will have to keep to the bridleways. Beach riding is an unforgettable experience, but keep an eye on the signs, because some sections of beach – especially in summer – are closed to horses.

Riding on Ameland

DIRECTORY

Watersports

Commissie Watersport Opleidingen (CWO)
't Breukeleveensemeentje 4,
1231 LM Loosdrecht.
Tel 085-4015966.

Koninklijk Nederlands Watersport Verbond
Wattbaan 31-49, 3439 ML Nieuwegein.
Tel 030-7513700.

Nederlandse Onder-watersport Bond
Landjuweel 62,
3905 PH Veenendaal.
Tel 0318-559347.

Rambling and Cycling

Cycletours
Gyroscoopweg 104, 1042 AX Amsterdam.
Tel 020-5218400.

Fietsvakantiewinkel
Ⓦ fietsvkantiewinkel.nl

Koninklijke Wandel Bond Nederland (KWBN)
PO Box 1020, 6501 BA Nijmegen.
Tel 024-3655575.

NTFU
Postbus 326,
3900 AH Veenendaal.
Tel 0318-581300.

Stichting Landelijk Fietsplatform
Postbus 846, 3800 AV Amersfoort.
Tel 033-4653656.

Wandelplatform-LAW
Postbus 846, 3800 AV Amersfoort.
Tel 033-4653660.
Ⓦ wandelnet.nl

Golf

NGF
Postbus 8585, 3503 RN Utrecht.
Tel 030-2426370.

Fishing

Sportvisserij Nederland
Postbus 162, 3720 AD Bilthoven.
Tel 030-6058400.
Ⓦ sportvisserijnederland.nl

Horse Riding

SVR
De Beek 125, 3852 PL Ermelo.
Tel 088-0224399.
Ⓦ veiligpaardrijden.nl

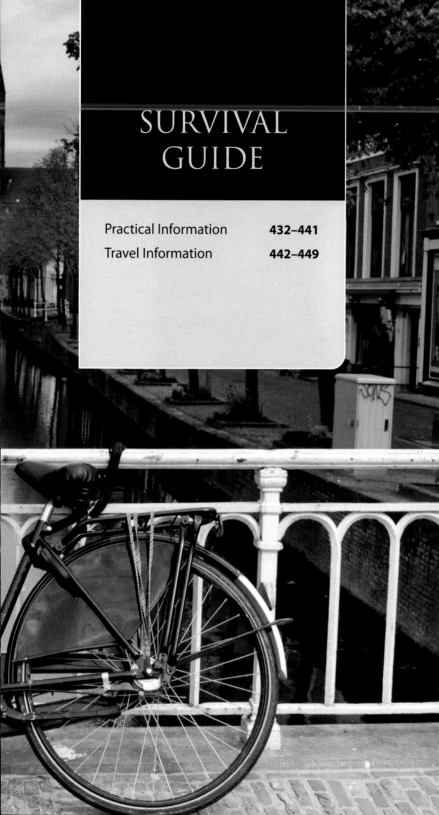

SURVIVAL GUIDE

PRACTICAL INFORMATION

The Netherlands is relatively small and has a dense road and motorway network, with good public transport, so getting around is quick and easy. Whether you are going to Amsterdam, the Veluwe, Maastricht or Zandvoort, you can get there from anywhere in the country very quickly by car or by train. The flat landscape with its many canals and dykes means that holidaymakers have plenty of opportunity to explore the countryside by bicycle *(see pp448–9)* or by boat *(see p447)*. Another option is to take a trip by steam train. The best place to find out what's available in your area – and in the country as a whole – is the local VVV (tourist information) office.

VVV and ANWB offices, which often share the same premises

Tourist Information

The best source of information for tourists is the local or regional **VVV** office. Many towns and places of interest have VVV offices where you can drop in and ask for advice and brochures about places of interest, local events, walks, cycle routes and excursions in the town or region. In addition, they can provide maps and books about other parts of the Netherlands. The VVV-*gidsen* series in Dutch is very practical, with information and facts about individual provinces and regions.

At VVVs you can also book domestic excursions, hotels, short breaks and theatre tickets anywhere in the country. Annual museum cards and CJPs are also on sale here. Smaller VVV outlets, although providing comprehensive information about their local area, do not provide other services.

ANWB offices in the Netherlands also have a selection of cycling, rambling and motoring guides, tickets, camping guides and road atlases. ANWB members have access to specialized membership information about various subjects and holiday offers. In many cases the VVV and the ANWB share the same premises. If you are travelling to the Netherlands from abroad you can obtain information in advance from the **Netherlands Board of Tourism (NBT)** in your own country.

ANWB logo

Language

The Dutch have been linguists for centuries, and most students learn English, some German and French. English is certainly very widely and fluently spoken in Amsterdam. However, it's always appreciated if you can handle a few niceties: greeting a Dutch person with "Dag" ("good day"), for example, before asking whether they speak English. The Phrase Book on pages 471–2 is a useful place to start.

Entertainment

Many VVV-*gidsen* guides have an annual review of events in a particular region or province. For up-to-date information on events, exhibitions, performances and films, it is worth looking in the entertainment supplements issued by daily papers, or ask at the local VVV office. Plays, concerts, special events and festivals are usually advertised on billboards or in cafés. Special regional and local entertainment guides are also a good source of information; for example, the monthly *Uitkrant* tells you what's on in Amsterdam in the way of the performing arts, while the weekly *Uitloper* is Utrecht's entertainment guide. These guides are distributed at many sites free of charge.

Tickets for concerts and events are available not only at the box office of the venue itself but also via the national **Ticket Service** and at VVV offices. Some towns also have their own booking bureau; for instance, in Amsterdam you can book your tickets at the AUB *(see p150)*.

Revellers at a music festival in Amsterdam

◀ The canal with the Old Church Tower of Delft in the background

The Museum Card allowing entry to a majority of museums

Museum Card

The Annual Museum Card (*Museumjaarkaart*) has quickly risen to huge popularity. It costs €59.90 for people over the age of 18, and €32.45 for under-18s. It gives the holder free entry to over 400 museums in the country. However, you often have to pay a supplement for special exhibitions. The card is available at all participating museums and at VVVs. It can also be ordered online from www. museumkaart.nl.

Travellers with Disabilities

Most public buildings have good facilities for travellers with disabilities. Museums, art galleries, cinemas and theatres generally are wheelchair-accessible. Only some establishments in very old buildings are less accessible, but there are always staff who are able to lend a hand. If you require assistance it's a good idea to phone in advance. Accessibility information for hotels is given on page 390.

In Amsterdam and other major cities, all main pedestrian crossings are equipped with sound for the blind. For disabled people travelling by train, the NS has issued a pack entitled *Gehandicapten*. This contains information on Dutch railway stations and what facilities they have, and also lists the stations (there are approximately 150 of them) where people in wheelchairs can get assistance when boarding and alighting from trains. Many trains have wheelchair-accessible doors, and most new double-decker trains have wheelchair-accessible toilets. If you need help, it's best to contact the **Bureau Assistentieverlening Gehandicapten** at least three hours before travelling.

Assistance to travellers with disabilities at wheelchair-accessible tourist office

Opening Hours

Although until recently just about every shop in the country was open from 9am to 6pm, today there is an increasing variety in shop opening hours. Many retail stores and supermarkets are open until 7pm or later. In the cities, shops tend to stay open longer. Many towns have a "shopping evening" (*koopavond*) once a week, when most shops remain open until 9pm: Thursday in Amsterdam and The Hague, Friday in Utrecht. In an increasing number of towns shops open on Sundays at least once in the month. Many shops have half-day closing one day a week, usually Monday, but varying from one region to another.

Banks are usually open on weekdays from 9am to 5pm, and VVVs are also open on Mondays to Fridays from 9am or 10am to 5pm (sometimes on *koopavond* until 9pm). On Saturdays they close early or even all day, and most are closed on Sundays. Some VVVs are closed during the winter.

Many museums are shut on Mondays, and open from 10am to 5pm for the rest of the week. On Sundays and public holidays they tend to open later. Practically all museums are closed on Christmas and New Year's Day. Open-air museums and small museums tend to close for the winter.

DIRECTORY

Tourist Information

ANWB Main Office
Wassenaarseweg 220,
2596 EC
The Hague.
Tel 088-2692222.

I Amsterdam Visitor Centre
Stationsplein 10, 1012 AB
Amsterdam.
Tel 020-7026000.

Netherland Board of Tourism
PO Box 63470, 2502 JL
The Hague.
Tel 070-370 5705.
🔲 holland.com

VVV The Hague
Spui 68. **Tel** 070-3618860.

VVV Maastricht
Kleine Staat 1.
Tel 043-3252121.

VVV Rotterdam
Coolsingel 195.
Tel 010-7900185.

VVV Utrecht
Domplein 9.
Tel 030-2360004.

Entertainment

Ticket Service
Tel 0900-3001250.
🔲 ticketmaster.nl

Museum Card

Stichting Museumjaarkaart
🔲 museumkaart.nl

Travellers with Disabilities

Bureau Assistentie-verlening Gehandicapten
🔲 avg.ns.nl

Flower seeds and bulbs, freely exported items (with certificate)

Visas and Customs

Travellers from other EU countries can travel freely in and out of the Netherlands provided they have a valid passport or European identity card. For a stay lasting up to three months, travellers from Australia, New Zealand and North America need only a valid passport.

EU residents may bring an unlimited quantity of goods into the country provided they are for their personal use. For tobacco and alcohol, the following quantities are considered limits for personal use: 800 cigarettes, 400 cigars, 1 kg of tobacco, 10 litres of spirits, 20 litres of liqueurs, 90 litres of wine (or 60 litres of fortified wine) and 110 litres of beer. Duty will be charged on quantities exceeding these specified limits.

For travellers from outside the EU, the limits are 200 cigarettes, 100 cigarillos, 50 cigars or 250 g of tobacco, 2 litres of unfortified wine plus 1 litre of spirits or 2 litres of fortified wine or liqueur wine or spirits, 50 g of perfume, 0.25l of eau de toilette and other items up to a value of €175. Residents of other EU countries may no longer import goods on which VAT has not been paid. If you are entering or leaving the EU, you can take non-VAT-paid goods with you. More details are available from

the **Customs Helpline** *(Douanetelefoon)*, which gives precise information on customs regulations. Travellers from outside the Netherlands may be able to obtain information at their local embassy.

Travel Safety Advice

Visitors can get up-to-date travel safety information from the Foreign and Commonwealth Office in the UK, the State Department in the US and the Department of Foreign Affairs and Trade in Australia.

Time

Like all its neighbouring countries, the Netherlands is on Central European Time, which is 1 hour ahead of Greenwich Mean Time. Daylight saving (1 hour) operates from the end of March to the end of October.

Sydney is 8 hours ahead, Johannesburg 1 hour (the same as the Netherlands), New York is 6 hours behind and Los Angeles 9 hours behind.

Customers showing their appreciation with a tip

Tipping

Taxi drivers expect a tip of around 10 per cent. Although a service charge is included on restaurant bills, it is customary to round the bill up slightly *(see p403)*.

In hotels you may if you like leave something for the chambermaid after a longer stay, even though it is not generally the rule.

Public Toilets

There is a limited number of public conveniences in the Netherlands. In some cities you will find toilets where you have to insert money into a slot to open the door. Popping into a café to use the toilets there is accepted practice in the Netherlands; some establishments have an attendant who should be paid a small amount. Large retail stores and stations also have toilets, and you generally need to pay a small fee to use these. The latter also have nappy-changing facilities. On motorways you will find toilets at all service stations.

Electricity

In the Netherlands the electrical voltage is 220 volts AC. Dutch plugs are of the two-pin type, and adapters are available for visitors from countries with different plugs (for example, Great Britain).

Television and Radio

The television programmes on offer in the Netherlands are undergoing a great deal of development at the moment. The traditional system was to have a large number of broadcasting networks, each with their own political or religious leanings, being given a certain amount of air-time on each of the three public TV stations (Nederland 1, 2 and 3). More recently, however, commercial television stations have emerged to compete with Hilversum (the town where the Netherlands' main networks are based, (see p195).

As well as national TV networks, the Netherlands has a number of regional and local providers, such as Omrop Fryslân, Omroep Flevoland, Omroep Gelderland and the Amsterdam local network AT5. In addition, large numbers of foreign programmes can be received on cable TV, the range varying depending on the local cable company.

The Netherlands has five national radio stations, each of them with their own "personality": Radio 1 deals mainly with current affairs and sport, Radio 2 broadcasts light music and various information programmes, Radio 3 rock and pop and Radio 4 classical music. 747 AM is a news channel.

Newspapers and Magazines

The Netherlands has five national morning newspapers (De Telegraaf, de Volkskrant, Algemeen Dagblad, NRC Next and Trouw) and two national evening papers (Het Parool and NRC Handelsblad). These tend to focus on the west of the country. Regionally, the more popular papers are the Nieuwsblad van het Noorden, Friesch Dagblad, Tubantia, De Gelderlander, Utrechts Nieuwsblad, Provinciale Zeeuwsche Courant, Brabants Dagblad and Dagblad De Limburger, which contain information on local holiday activities and events. The more famous Dutch weekly news magazines include HP/De Tijd, Elsevier and Vrij Nederland.

The major bookshops in the large cities (as well as the main railway stations) sell many major international newspapers and magazines.

Pets

If you bring your dog or cat to the Netherlands from abroad, you need to be able to prove that your pet has been immunized against rabies. This is shown by a valid pet's passport provided by your veterinarian which indicates when the animal was last vaccinated.

A selection of national and international newspapers available

Embassies and Consulates

If you are visiting from abroad and your passport gets lost or stolen, you should report it immediately either to your consulate or embassy. Most embassies are situated in the administrative capital, The Hague. A number of countries, including the UK, USA, France, Germany and Italy, also have consulates, which tend to be located in Amsterdam.

DIRECTORY

Embassies and Consulates

Australia
Embassy: Carnegielaan 4, 2517 KH The Hague.
Tel 070-3108200.
W netherlands. embassy.gov.au

Belgium
Embassy: Johan van Oldenbarneveltlaan 11, 2582 NE The Hague.
Tel 070-3123456.

Canada
Embassy: Sophialaan 7, 2514 JP The Hague.
Tel 070-3111600.
W canada.nl

France
Embassy: Anna Paulownastraat 76, 2518 BJ The Hague.
Tel 070-3125800.
W ambafrance-nl.org

Germany
Embassy:
Groot Hertoginnelaan 18–20, 2517 EG The Hague.
Tel 070-3420600.
W niederlande.diplo.de
Consulate:
Honthorststraat 36–38, 1071 DG Amsterdam.
Tel 020-5747700.

United Kingdom
Embassy:
Lange Voorhout 10, 2514 ED The Hague.
Tel 070-4270427.
W ukinnl.fco.gov.uk
Consulate General:
Koningslaan 44, 1075 AE Amsterdam.
Tel 020-6764343.

Ireland
Embassy:
Scheveningseweg 112, 2584 AE The Hague.
Tel 070-3630993/4.

New Zealand
Embassy: Eisenhowerlaan 77N, 2517 KK The Hague.
Tel 070-3469324.
Fax 070-3632983.
W nzembassy.com/ netherlands

South Africa
Embassy: Wassenaarseweg 40, 2596 CJ The Hague.
Tel 070-3924501.
W zuidafrika.nl

United States
Embassy: Lange Voorhout 102, 2514 EJ The Hague.
Tel 070-3102209.
W thehague. usembassy.gov
Consulate: Museumplein 19, 1071 DJ Amsterdam.
Tel 020-5755309.
Fax 020-5755310.
W amsterdam. usconsulate.gov

Customs Helpline
Tel 0800-0143.
Open 8am–8pm Mon–Thu, 8am–5pm Fri.

Travel Safety Advice

Australia
W dfat.gov.au
W smartraveller.gov.au

United Kingdom
W gov.uk/foreign-travel-advice

United States
W travel.state.gov

Personal Security and Health

If you keep to a few basic safety rules, you should have a trouble-free stay in the Netherlands. Obviously, it is better not to carry large amounts of cash or valuables around, and not to keep passports, cheques and credit cards together in one place. Visitors from abroad can always insure themselves against losses of money and personal items from theft. It is also a good idea to insure yourself against medical expenses. For those who do find themselves in trouble on holiday, the country has efficient emergency services and facilities.

Emergencies

The national **emergency number** for the police, fire brigade and ambulance is 112. This number must only be dialled in emergencies. For less urgent help, it is best to contact the nearest police station, hospital or a local doctor. If your car breaks down, members of the ANWB can call out the roadside assistance service of the **ANWB Wegenwacht** 24 hours a day, 7 days a week, using the roadside emergency phones or by dialling a toll-free phone number.

Personal Belongings and Safety

It is as true of the Netherlands as elsewhere in Europe that opportunity makes the thief. When in busy shopping streets or on public transport, do not leave your wallet in your back pocket, and if you need to go to the lavatory on the train or when in a restaurant, take your handbag or wallet with you. Do not leave any valuables in your car, and always make sure it has been properly locked. Large cities, particularly Amsterdam, have a big problem with bicycle theft, so a decent lock is a good investment. Muggings are rare, but at night it is better to avoid unlit

areas and parks. Women can visit cafés in the evening without risk.

Reporting Crime

If you have been the victim of theft or a mugging, report it to the nearest police station (some smaller municipalities do not have their own police station). You will need to make a verbal report describing any loss and, if necessary, injury. Many insurance companies require you to report within 24 hours of the incident taking place. If your passport is stolen, you should immediately report this to your embassy *(see p435)* as well as to the police.

Dutch police officers

Medical Treatment and Insurance

Minor medical problems can usually be dealt with at a pharmacy, though the prescription of drugs is very strict. The majority of drugs are available only on prescription. Pharmacies – which are recognizable by their snake symbol – are open on weekdays from 8:30 or 9am to 5:30 or 6pm.

If the pharmacy is closed, you will find on the door a list of the nearest pharmacies that are open. Local newspapers also give details of duty doctors, pharmacies and other health services in the town or region. In an emergency you can get treatment in hospitals, which are open 24 hours a day.

Visitors from abroad who will be carrying prescription drugs with them should ask their doctor for a medical passport. This is a document stating your condition and the medication you require for it. The passport can be shown at the customs as evidence that you are bringing the medication in for your personal use.

Travellers from European Union countries should apply for and take with them a European Health Insurance Card (EHIC). You can do this online or at post offices in the UK before you leave. It will enable you to claim for state health service treatment

Fire engine

Police car

Ambulance

in EU countries. It is also a good idea to purchase comprehensive medical insurance if it is not included in your travel insurance.

Mosquitoes

Attracted by the canals, mosquitoes can be a real irritant. Residents and regular summer visitors deal with them in various ways. Burning coils, ultra-violet tubes, mosquito nets, repellent sprays and anti-histamine creams and tablets are available from large pharmacies and supermarkets.

A crowded street festival: a place to be wary of pickpockets

Lost Property

If you lose any valuables, you can check at the police station to see whether anyone has handed them in. Local police stations usually keep articles that have been handed in before passing them on to the central police station for the district. If you lose your passport you must also inform your consulate (see p435) or embassy. If you lose something on a train,

SPOED-EISENDE HULP OPNAME

Oprijden tot de slagboom

Emergency room sign

inform the station first. Small stations keep lost property for one day. After that they are taken to the nearest main station, and finally to the **Central Lost Property Office** (Centraal Bureau Gevonden Voorwerpen) in Utrecht. By filling in a search form (available at railway stations), you can describe the items you have lost. If you lose something on a bus, tram or metro, you should contact the office of the local or regional transport organization (look for "openbaar

vervoer" (public transport) in the Yellow Pages). **Schiphol** Airport has a special lost property number.

Drugs

Although the use of soft drugs is officially illegal in the Netherlands, the police will not take action if you have a small quantity of hashish or marijuana in your possession. It is worth remembering that not every restaurant or café owner will take kindly to tourists lighting up on the premises. People caught with hard drugs will be prosecuted.

DIRECTORY

Emergency Numbers

Ambulance, Fire Brigade, Police
Tel 112. (for the deaf and hard of hearing)
Tel 0800-8112.

Safety

Police
Non-urgent matters:
Tel 0900-8844
(you will be connected to the nearest police station). For the deaf and hard of hearing
Tel 0900-1844.

Police Amsterdam-Amstelland
Head office:
Elandsgracht 117,
1016 TT Amsterdam.
Tel 0900-8844.

Hospitals in Major Cities

Amsterdam: Academisch Medisch Centrum
Meibergdreef 9.
Tel 020-5669111.

OLVG, Locatie West
Jan Tooropstraat 164.
Tel 020-5108911.

Onze Lieve Vrouwe Gasthuis (OLVG)
Oosterpark 9, 1091 AC Amsterdam.
Tel 020-5999111.

Slotervaart Hospital
Louwesweg 6.
Tel 020-5129333.

VU Medisch Centrum
De Boelelaan 1117.
Tel 020-4444444.

The Hague: Bronovo Hospital
Bronovolaan 5.
Tel 070-3124141.

MCH Hospital Westeinde
Lijnbaan 32.
Tel 070-3302000.

Rotterdam: Erasmus Medisch Centrum
's-Gravendijkwal 230,
3015 CE Rotterdam.
Tel 010-7040704

Utrecht: Academisch Hospital Utrecht
Heidelberglaan 100.
Tel 088-7555555.

Lost Property

Central Lost Property Office
Ⓦ verlorenof gevonden.nl

Schiphol – Lost Property
Tel 0900-0141/020-7940800.

Roadside Assistance

ANWB Wegenwacht
Tel 088-269-2888 (toll-free).

Banking and Local Currency

In the Netherlands, cash remains a popular means of payment, but credit cards and debit cards are now the norm. Almost all hotels, shops and restaurants accept major credit cards in payment. Other means of payment are traveller's cheques (with identification), and, occasionally, US dollars (particularly at antique and souvenir shops). In 2002, the Netherlands began to use the euro. The best place to change money is at a bank. You can take an unlimited amount of currency into the Netherlands, and you can withdraw limited amounts of cash at an ATM.

Geldautomaat

ATMs can be found outside post offices, banks and GWK offices

Bank Opening Hours

Banks are generally open on Mondays to Fridays from 9am to 4 or 5pm. Some banks remain open longer on *koopavond*, or shopping evening, often a Thursday.

These bureaux can still be found at the now unguarded border crossing points, at Amsterdam Schiphol Airport and at major railway stations. Most GWK bureaux are open daily and have extended opening hours.

GWK *(grenswisselkantoor)*, the Netherlands' official exchange bureau

Changing Money

Foreign currency can be changed at banks, post offices and American Express offices. A small commission is sometimes charged on these transactions.

In small bureaux de change (often open outside business hours), located throughout the major cities and in larger towns, you can exchange money from non-Eurozone countries, though often at unfavourable rates.

The Netherland's official bureaux de change, GWK *(grenswisselkantoor)*, is a privatized state enterprise, which gives reasonable rates of exchange and charges relatively low commissions, as well as providing various other services for travellers.

Bank and Credit Cards

You can use your bank card to withdraw money at any Dutch bank displaying your card's logo, but usually there is a substantial commission charge. You can also use bank cards to withdraw cash at ATMs 24 hours a day. These machines usually also accept Eurocard/MasterCard, American Express, Diners Club and Visa cards. When a foreign card is inserted, most ATMs will offer a choice of languages, and so should be simple to use. ATMs are plentiful and can be found outside post offices, banks and GWK offices, and within main railway stations. Shops, restaurants and hotels post signs stating whether you can pay by credit card, switch

card or chipknip/chipper (top-up cards available from Dutch banks or the Postbank). Most payphones *(see p440)* accept credit cards for calls.

All major credit cards are widely accepted in the Netherlands and, as elsewhere in Europe, have superseded many cash transactions, even though the Dutch have proved to be a little reluctant to abandon cash as compared to, for example, the British. Almost all hotels and hostels gladly accept credit card payments, but the position is more varied in restaurants. Clarify the situation before the bill arrives. It is normal to pay cash in bars, and taxi drivers would also not want to receive credit card payments. One advantage of using a credit card is that if a purchase is contested, the credit card company will usually take up the matter on your behalf. Depending on the credit card, there are generally some attached insurances as well.

The History of Dutch Currency

Before the introduction of the guilder, the Dutch national currency unit before the euro, duiten, stuivers, rijders, schellings and ducats made out of various metals were used. Until 1847, there was a double standard where the value of the coin was equal to the value of the gold or silver in it. Silver coins were minted until 1967, when nickel or bronze coins were minted. Gold and silver coins from earlier centuries are now valuable collector's items.

The Euro

The euro (€) is the common currency of the European Union (EU). It went into general circulation on 1 January 2002, initially for 12 participating countries. The Netherlands was one of those 12 countries. EU members using the euro as sole official currency are known as the Eurozone. A number of EU members have opted out of joining this common currency. Euro notes are identical throughout the Eurozone countries, each including designs of architectural structures and monuments. The coins, however, have one side identical (the value side) and one side with an image unique to each country. Both notes and coins are exchangeable in each of the participating euro countries.

Bank Notes

Euro bank notes have seven denom-inations. The €5 note (grey in colour) is the smallest, followed by the €10 note (pink), €20 note (blue), €50 note (orange), €100 note (green), €200 note (yellow) and €500 note (purple). All notes show the 12 stars of the European Union. Not all businesses in the Netherlands accept the €200 and €500 notes.

€5 note

€10 note

€20 note

€50 note

€100 note

€200 note

€500 note

€2 coin

€1 coin

50 cents

20 cents

10 cents

Coins

The euro has eight coin denominations: €2 and €1; 50 cents, 20 cents, 10 cents, 5 cents, 2 cents and 1 cent. The €2 and €1 coins are silver and gold in colour; cent coins are gold or bronze. Prices are rounded off to the nearest 5 cents; the 2- and 1-cent coins are no longer in use.

5 cents

2 cents

1 cent

Communications

Before 1989, telephone and postal services in the Netherlands were part of the same state-run company, PTT. This has now been separated into two companies – KPN Telecom and TNT Post. For some years, Telfort public telephones have also been appearing beside the KPN boxes. The Telfort telephones are mostly found at train stations.

Using the Telephone

You will find the green KPN telephone kiosks in the streets, in post offices and outside many railway stations. Most KPN telephone kiosks take both phonecards and most major credit cards (the logo on the telephone will tell you which credit cards are accepted). If you use a credit card, you need to remove it from the slot before speaking (phonecards are only removed when you have finished your call), and you have to pay a surcharge of €1.15. In KPN booths, locals can also use their bank or giro card to make phone calls, if these are fitted with a "chipper" or "chipknip" (which means you can top them up). ANWB members can also use KPN telephone kiosks to call the roadside assistance patrol (see p445).

There are no longer any solely coin-operated payphones. KPN phone boxes accept only KPN phone-cards or special kiosk-cards, available at some train stations. KPN phonecards can be purchased

Storefront of an Amsterdam telephone shop

at post offices, tobacconists, train stations and department stores, as well as at the GWK, and come in various denominations.

At train stations you will often find Telfort phone boxes, painted blue and orange. These accept Telfort phonecards, available at ticket windows and in the Wizzl station shops and also at the GWK. Telfort phones also accept coins (10, 20 and 50 cent, €1 and €2) but do not give change, credit cards (with a €1.15 surcharge) and special kiosk-cards.

Instructions on how to use KPN and Telfort telephones can be found in the booths in Dutch, English and other west European languages.

Mobile Phones

Mobile network coverage in the Netherlands is excellent and works on the 900/1800 MHz band. If necessary, contact your service provider for further information. Check your insurance policy to see if you are covered in case your phone gets stolen, and keep your network operator's helpline number handy.

To use your mobile phone abroad, you may need to enable the "roaming" function on it. It is also more expensive to make and receive calls while abroad, although roaming charges are due to be abolished within the EU in 2017. A cheaper option is often to purchase a local SIM card to use in your phone. You can only do this if your handset is "sim free" or unlocked. KPN

Finding the Right Number

• Directory enquiries for phone and fax numbers in Holland: dial 0900-8008 or 118 (only one number per call on either service).
• Directory enquiries for phone and fax numbers abroad: dial 0900-8418, or visit www.detelefoon gids.nl.
• National or international calls through the operator: dial 0800-0410.
• Collect calls in Holland or abroad: dial 0800-0101.
• National dialling codes are: Australia 61, New Zealand 64, South Africa 27, the United Kingdom 44, and the USA and Canada 1.

Hotspots gives Internet access for smart phones; send an SMS to: HOTSPOTS, number 4222 and you can log on for 15 minutes for a small fee, which is charged to your phone.

Colourful selection of Dutch pictorial phonecards

Phoning Abroad

From the Netherlands you can direct-dial almost all destinations abroad. First you need to dial the international number 00, followed by the country number, and then the local number without the first digit (usually a 0), and finally the individual number. Many country codes are listed in telephone booths. Telephone directories have more detailed lists. Directories for the whole of the country are available. Calls made from hotel rooms are usually expensive.

Internet access at OBA (Amsterdam Public Library)

Internet

Faster than a letter and cheaper than a phone call, sending and receiving email has never been easier or more convenient. As most people in the Netherlands have either ADSL or a cable connection at home, the number of internet cafés has decreased. Also, more and more hotels offer Wi-Fi for guests with laptops, and while this is not always free, rates for internet use have fallen dramatically over the last decade. It is better to check before using Wi-Fi to avoid ending up paying a heavy bill.

However, in most tourist areas you'll still find plenty of places to read and send email. Most are bars, cafés and coffee (smoking) shops, offering PCs with internet services. Opening hours vary, but cafés are often open late into the night. Not all offer headsets, so using Skype or other VoIPs to make cheap phone calls is not always possible.

A recent development is modern and trendy coffee bar franchises, like Coffee Company and Bagel and Beans, offering Wi-Fi for customers who bring their laptop. You either buy minutes or go online for a limited time for each beverage you order, using the code on your receipt to gain access.

Visitors to Amsterdam will find www.iamsterdam.com worth a look. Financed by Amsterdam city council, it offers listings and reviews in English about cultural events in the city, plus useful information on things like doctors and dentists. It also has information for expats living in the city. *Time Out Amsterdam* is a monthly listings magazine, also in English, aimed at tourists and available from newsagents in the city centre of the capital. Apart from comprehensive listings about what's on, it also offers reviews and features.

Postal Services

Post offices in the Netherlands can be recognized by the **TNT** logo. In addition to buying stamps, sending telegrams and sending mail, you can also change money and traveller's cheques, make phone calls and send faxes. Larger post offices also have photocopy services and sell stationery. Smaller municipalities sometimes have only a sub post office (in a supermarket, for example), providing basic services. There are no longer post offices in most villages.

Slot for all other destinations
Slot for local destinations
Dutch TNT postbox

TNT has closed many of the larger post offices and opened many smaller concerns inside shopping malls and shops.

Sending Mail

Most TNT postboxes have two slots. The right slot is for local mail (post codes are given above the slot), the left one is for other destinations. A sign on the box indicates when the mail is collected (a red sign means 5pm or 6pm, a blue board means 7pm). There is no Saturday mail collection.

Postcards and letters weighing less than 20 g (1 oz) cost €0.73 (or one "Nederland 1" stamp) to send to destinations within the Netherlands; those sent to European destinations cost €1.25, or one "International 1" stamp; these new "standard" stamps are widely available in small shops, for example those selling postcards. For heavier letters or to post to other parts of the world, visit a post office – but be prepared for queues. Most post offices are open from 9am to 5pm weekdays; some also open on Saturdays until 1pm.

Postcards and letters weighing less than 20 g (1 oz) to destinations within Europe are sent by priority mail. For other international mail which you want to send priority, pay extra for a priority sticker at the post office. Important documents may be sent by insured or registered mail. Urgent mail can be sent by TNT's courier service.

DIRECTORY

TNT

Tel 0800-1234 (customer service for domestic and international deliveries).

w tnt.com/express/nl_nl/site/home.html

TRAVEL INFORMATION

Almost every major European airport has direct flights to Schiphol, but this modern international airport southwest of Amsterdam also has direct connections with other airports around the world, including many in the United States. The Netherlands also has efficient rail links with neighbouring countries. Major stations are served by international trains, including the Thalys, the high-speed train from Paris. The country's comprehensive road network makes the Netherlands ideal for exploring by car or by public transport *(see pp446–7)*. Many packages and special-interest holidays are on offer, so it's worth shopping around.

Car-hire counter at Schiphol

By Air

Schiphol airport handles some 175,000 flights a year by many international carriers. To increase this volume further, there are serious plans to expand the airport. **KLM** (Royal Dutch Airlines) and its airline partners have flights to Amsterdam from over 350 cities worldwide. Northwest Airlines offers non-stop flights from Boston, Detroit and Washington, **Delta Air Lines** from Atlanta and New York (JFK) and **United Airlines** from Newark. There are many flights a day from the UK and the Irish Republic. Low-cost airline **easyJet** serves Amsterdam from London, Luton and several other British cities. To get the lowest fare, generally you must book well in advance.

Schiphol Airport

Schiphol has only one terminal. The airport signs are colour-coded, with yellow signs indicating transfer desks and gates, green ones amenities such as coffee bars, restaurants and shops. At Schiphol Plaza you can find shops, book hotels, hire a car or buy a railway ticket. Beneath it are the platforms of Schiphol railway station. From the car park there are transfer buses to take you to the terminal. The long-stay car park is served by an automatic bus, the Parking Hopper, that takes you to the transfer bus.

See Buy Fly duty-free shops

Bar

Gate E

Lounge Centre

F2/F9

See Buy Fly duty-free shops

Bar

Gate F

Lounge West

Gate G

Departures

Railway tickets

To the trains

Departures

Gate E

Arrivals

Gate F

Hotel reservations

Arrivals

Gate G

SCHIPHOL PLAZA

0 metres   100
0 yards   100

Car hire

Taxis

Meeting point

Planes at Amsterdam Schiphol Airport

Shopping

If you are leaving the country by plane, you will find the large See Buy Fly shopping centre when you leave customs control. Although travellers to other EU member states are not permitted to buy duty-free goods at the airport (see p434), it is still possible to find some bargains with the low See Buy Fly prices; only alcohol and tobacco is sold here at the same price as in local shops. Passengers to destinations outside the EU can still purchase duty-free alcohol and tobacco. The centrally located Schiphol Plaza is open to everyone, but the goods stocked here are not sold at See Buy Fly prices.

Getting to and from Schiphol

Every major city in the Netherlands can be reached by train from Schiphol Station. The journey to Amsterdam Centraal Station takes 20 minutes. Schiphol is also on the night-train network of the Western Netherlands (see p446). In addition, the airport has good bus connections with many towns. KLM runs a bus service (the KLM Hotel Shuttle), linking the airport with some 20 hotels in central and south Amsterdam. There are also abundant taxis waiting at the airport. Ask for a quote before getting in, as tourists are often overcharged.

Watch shop at Schiphol

Regional Airports

Eindhoven, Maastricht, Rotterdam and Groningen are all served by domestic flights, with flights between Eindhoven and Schiphol, Maastricht and Schiphol, Groningen and Rotterdam and Eindhoven and Rotterdam. There are direct international flights between Rotterdam and Eindhoven and Manchester and London, and between Maastricht and Munich, Berlin and London.

Map labels

Terminal
D42/D57 D62/D87
D12/D31
Entrance
E2/E13
Lounge Center
Lounge South
C3/C16
D2/D8
B1/B16
Lounge Vest
G20
P1
P2
WTC
Hilton
G1/G10
Schiphol East long-stay car park
P40
P12
Exit
A4 AMSTERDAM
Entrance
A4 THE HAGUE/ ROTTERDAM
Railway station
See Buy Fly duty-free shops
Gate B / C
Airline desks
Gate D
Arrivals
Gate B / C

Key

Public access areas
Check in/baggage pick-up
Passengers only
Customs
Passport control
No entry

Information screens at Schiphol

By Rail

The Netherlands can easily be reached by train from most European countries, although visitors from further afield may have to change trains several times en route. Eurostar runs from London via the Channel Tunnel to Brussels, where you change for Amsterdam.

There are direct trains from a number of European stations. For example, Brussels, Paris, Berlin, Zurich, Vienna and (seasonally) Milan have direct rail links to Amsterdam Centraal Station (CS) and Utrecht CS. From Brussels and from Antwerp there are trains to Amsterdam all day, stopping at Roosendaal, Rotterdam, The Hague and Schiphol, including five journeys daily by the Thalys high-speed train from Paris.

Many other towns, particularly those in the border regions of Belgium and the Netherlands, can easily be reached by train. Hook of Holland is connected by trains which connect with ferries from the UK port of Harwich.

Special Tickets

Tourists from other EU countries can purchase cards in their countries that will entitle them to special reductions. An Interrail card for people aged 26 and under, along with a slightly dearer version for the over-26s, allows travellers to use the entire European rail network at a discount. Eurail Selectpass offers unlimited

The Thalys high-speed train

Ferries serve Rotterdam, Hook of Holland and IJmuiden

travel on the national rail networks of any three to five bordering countries out of 18 European nations, including the Netherlands.

By Coach

For travellers from many European countries the cheapest way to reach the Netherlands is by coach. Most long-distance coaches have toilets and make regular stops. In summer in particular there are large numbers of coaches from other countries serving a whole range of towns in the Netherlands.

A Eurolines coach

Eurolines offers a very extensive network of coach connections. It has coaches running from many European cities to the Netherlands at least once per week. Dozens of points in the Netherlands (depending on the point of departure and route) are served by them. From Brussels and Antwerp there are coaches to places such as Breda, Rotterdam, The Hague, Utrecht and Amsterdam.

Ferries

A number of ferry companies serve routes between Britain and the Netherlands. These include **P&O Ferries** that sail between Hull and Rotterdam/Europoort, while **Stena Line** sails between Harwich and Hook of Holland. **DFDS**

Seaways serves Newcastle and IJmuiden. Other convenient ferry ports for visitors from Great Britain are Calais and Boulogne (from Folkestone and Dover) in France. Crossing times by ferry range from 16 hours (Newcastle–IJmuiden) to 75–90 minutes (Dover–Calais). Ticket prices depend on the speed of crossing. In summer it is a good idea to book in advance.

Motoring in Holland

The good system of roads in the Netherlands makes all parts of the country easy to reach by car. Beware, however, in the Randstad region: you may have to put up with traffic jams during the rush hour.

To drive in the Netherlands you need to have a valid national driving licence. In addition, if in your own car, you will need to have your vehicle log book and insurance papers with you.

Roads in the Netherlands are divided into three categories. Provincial roads are designated with the letter "N" before the road number, national motorways are designated with an "A" before the number and international highways have the letter "E" before the number. All Dutch motorways are equipped with emergency telephones from which motorists can call the **ANWB** road assistance service *(see p436)* if their car breaks down. A non-member can pay for the ANWB's services, or become a temporary ANWB member. Unless otherwise signposted, the maximum speed for cars in Holland is 120 km/h (75 mph) on motorways, 100 km/h (62 mph) on major roads, 80 km/h (50 mph) on secondary roads and 50 km/h (30 mph) in built-up areas. At unmarked junctions, give way to traffic coming from the left, except for trams, which always have right of way (except when you are driving along a road which has right of way). In built-up areas motorists must give

Emergency phone

way to buses that are leaving bus stops.

Finding somewhere to park is often a problem in the cities. As clamping is prevalent and theft rife, it is often best to look for a car park rather than to try to find street parking. When you enter a car park, take a ticket from the machine at the barrier, and pay at the payment machine before leaving. Avoid out-of-order street meters as you could get fined or your car could be clamped. You may not park on yellow lines, and on yellow broken lines you may not park even to load or unload. If you stop on a blue line, you will need to have a parking disc.

Car Hire

To hire a car you need to be at least 21 years old and have a valid driving licence. Some hire companies also require at least one year's driving experience. The main international car-hire companies such as **Avis**, **Budget**, **Europcar** and **Hertz** have offices at Schiphol and in all major cities. Local car-hire firms are often substantially cheaper. When hiring a car without a credit card, you may have to pay a hefty deposit.

A bike hooked on a car, an easy way of taking your bike along

DIRECTORY

Schiphol Airport

Information and services
Tel 0900-0141
🅦 schiphol.nl

Regional Airports

Eindhoven Airport
Tel 0900-9505.

Groningen Airport Eelde
Tel 050-3097070

Maastricht Aachen Airport
Tel 043-3589898.

Rotterdam Airport
Tel 010-4463444.

Airlines

Aer Lingus
Tel 0900-2658207.
🅦 aerlingus.com

British Airways
Tel 020-3469389.
🅦 ba.com

Delta Air Lines
Tel 020-7219128.
🅦 delta-air.com

easyJet
Tel 0900-0401048 (NL).
🅦 easyjet.com

KLM & KLM Cityhopper
Tel 020-4747747.
🅦 klm.nl

Transavia
Tel 0900-0737.
🅦 transavia.com

United Airlines
Tel 020-3469381.
🅦 united.com

Railways

NS International Support
Tel 030-2300023.

Public transport travel information
Tel 0900-9292.
🅦 9292.nl

Bus Companies

Eurolines Nederland
Stationsplein 3
(Bus station, next to Amsterdam-Duivendrecht train station).
Tel 0880-761700.
🅦 eurolines.nl

Rokin 38A, 1012 KT Amsterdam.
Tel 0880-761700.

Eurolines (UK)
Tel 08717-818177 (UK).
🅦 nationalexpress.co.uk

Ferries

DFDS Seaways
Tel 0871-5229955.
🅦 dfdsseaways.co.uk

P&O North Sea Ferries
Tel 0800-1300030.
🅦 poferries.com

Stena Line BV
Stationsweg 10, 3151 HS.
Tel 0174-389333.
🅦 stenaline.co.uk

By Car

ANWB
Tel 088-2692222.

Car Hire Firms at Schiphol

AVIS
Tel 088-2847620.

Budget
Tel 088-2847620.

Europcar
Tel 020-3164190.

Hertz
Tel 020-5020240.

Public Transport

The Netherlands has a comprehensive and efficient public transport system. Major cities can be easily reached by train, while towns and villages are served by local buses as well as a number of trains. The Randstad in particular gets fairly snarled up in the morning and evening rush hour. If you need to travel at that time, the best thing to do is to leave the car and take the train.

Dieren–Apeldoorn steam train

Steam Trains

There are many places in the Netherlands where you can take a ride in a steam train. There is, for example, the 22-km (14-mile) Dieren–Apeldoorn line, the 16-km (10-mile) Kerkrade–Schin op Geul, (the "million line", *see p372*), the 15.5-km (9.5-mile) Goes–Oudelande, around the Valkenburgse Meer lake and through the Hoogoventerrein at IJmuiden (21 km/13 miles, departing from Beverwijk Station, *see p192*). A steam train runs the 20 km (12 miles) between Hoorn and Medemblik in summer (*see p182*). Check with the VVV, as schedules vary.

Long-distance buses cover an expanding number of routes

By Bus

The Netherlands has a good network of local buses and inter-city coaches. Booklets are available giving detailed information on routes, time-tables and fares, although it is also possible to get information from **Openbaar Vervoer Reisinformatie** (0900-9292).

Operated by a number of companies, long-distance buses are very comfortable. They usually follow direct routes between places and stop less frequently than local buses (*streekbussen*). In the evenings they do not operate as late as the local buses. The timetables for buses are based on the railway timetable. Long-distance buses are green and have an information display.

By Tram

There are trams in Amsterdam, Rotterdam, Utrecht and The Hague. They generally run from 6am to midnight. On Sundays they start one or one-and-a-half hours later. Tram stops display the name of the stop, the tram numbers that stop there and show the other stops on the route. Tram shelters display maps of the tram network.

You can board or alight from any door, unless there is a conductor on the tram, when the rear door is for boarding only. Tram stops are normally announced, but if you aren't sure where to get off, you can always ask the driver to call out the stop.

By Train

The Dutch national railway company, Nederlandse Spoorwegen, or simply NS, runs a busy network which is considered one of the best in the world. Trains are clean and generally run on time, and tickets are reasonably priced. Timetables are displayed on yellow boards in stations. Rail tickets are available at ticket offices, Wizzl station shops and from ticket machines in stations, or, with a substantial supplement, from the conductor aboard the train. Dutch Railways has a wide variety of fare discounts on offer, including *Railrunner* tickets for children, and other offers for people regularly using the same route. Combined season tickets for the train and local or urban transport are also available. For information it is best to ask at ticket offices, or telephone 0900-9292.

Many railways in Friesland, Groningen and the Achterhoek are run by NordNed and Syntus. NS cards are also valid on these lines. Night trains run on the Utrecht CS-Amsterdam CS-Schiphol-Leiden Centraal-The Hague CS-Delft-Rotterdam CS lines.

An NS double-decker train speeding past tulip fields

Metro

Amsterdam and Rotterdam are the only towns in the Netherlands with a metro. Both networks are fairly extensive. Amsterdam's metro has three lines, two of which begin at the Centraal Station, and the third at Station Sloterdijk. They go as far as Gaasperplas and Gein. From Centraal Station there is also a suburban tram to Amstelveen. The Rotterdam metro system comprises two lines which cross one another, the north–south line going from Centraal Station to Spijkenisse, and the west–east line from Marconiplein to Capelle, with a branch to Ommoord-Zevenkamp. The first metro leaves the terminus at around 6am (around 7:45am on Sundays), and the last train arrives at its destination at approximately 0:15 or 0:30am.

OV-chipkaart, a smartcard required for travelling on public transport

Tram, Bus, Metro and Train Tickets

To travel on buses, trams and metro systems throughout the Netherlands you must have an OV-chipkaart: a "smartcard" that works much like a pay-as-you-go phone card, deducting the cost of each trip from the available credit. OV-chipkaarts are also available for train journeys.

The ticketing system works via the OV-chipkaart (www.wov-chipkaart.nl). They are of two types: paper and plastic. Paper OV-chipkaarts are best used for shorter journeys. These can be purchased from most tram and bus drivers, many VVVs and a few hotels. They need to be checked against an electronic reader when you enter and leave the public transport system. For longer stays, purchasing a rechargeable, plastic OV-chipkaart is advisable. It comes in two main types, personalized and anonymous and both cost €7.50. Valid for five years, these are sold at train and bus stations. Also, please note that the plastic (but not paper) OV-chipkaart can also be used on the NS train network. In order to validate a journey, users need to hold the OV-chipkaart in front of the grey card reader at metro or platform gates and on boarding a bus or tram; remember to swipe again on disembarking, or you will be charged the full fare to the terminus. Children under 4 travel free; seniors and 4–11-year-olds can claim a discount if they buy their cards in advance.

Taxis

If you need a taxi, the best thing is to either go to a taxi-stand or phone a Taxicentrale: numbers can be found in the phone directory and in the Yellow Pages. It is less common to hail a taxi in the street, although it can be done. Taxis are metered and after an initial charge, the fare depends on the distance travelled and the time. Taxis cost more at night.

A treintaxi

Rail Taxis

Around 100 Dutch railway stations operate a rail taxi, or *treintaxi*, service which enables you to travel cheaply to a destination in the same or nearby district. The price of a single ticket starts from €6 and is valid whatever the length of the journey. The taxi will also take other passengers to their destinations, and so will usually take a roundabout route.

Rail taxis operate from 7am (8am on Sundays and public holidays) until just after the arrival of the last train. You can book by phoning 0900-TREINTAXI/8734682 or via the Reisplanner Xtra travel planner app. At the station, book by pressing the button on the blue-yellow column. Information on places covered by the service is given in the NS leaflet *Treintaxi-stations op een rijtje*.

Special Outings

The Canal Bus is an excellent way to get around Amsterdam's waterways. They operate on three circular routes: the green route, the red route and the blue route, which meet at various points, including the jetty outside Centraal Station and on the Singelgracht between the Rijksmuseum and Leidseplein. There are 17 stops in all and together they provide easy access to most major sights. During high season, boats leave from opposite Centraal Station every half an hour between 9:30am and 6pm. A day ticket for all three routes, which costs €19 per adult, and €9.50 for children (aged 4–12 years), allows you to hop on and off as many times as you like. Another reasonable offer is the 24-hour ticket, which costs just €2.50 more.

The Canal Bus in Amsterdam

Cycling

The flat landscape of the Netherlands makes it a boon for cyclists. At least 85 per cent of the population has a bicycle, and there is no shortage of maps and guidebooks with interesting cycling routes. You can use the LF-routes *(see p449)* to plan your own daytrip or cycling holiday. Another possibility is to take part in an organized cycle tour, where you are awarded a souvenir medal at the end.

Guides showing cycling routes

Road Safety

The large number of cycle paths and cycle lanes, often equipped with traffic lights for cyclists, make cycling in the Netherlands a safe and enjoyable activity. However, it's worth keeping a look-out for mopeds, which frequently make use of cycle paths. Cycling in the peaceful countryside and cycling in the busy city are two quite separate experiences. In Amsterdam particularly, the traffic is fairly chaotic – mostly because of the large number of cyclists, who tend to ignore the traffic regulations. If you are unaccustomed to this, it's worth taking extra care. Front and rear lights, a rear reflector and reflective strips or reflective circles are compulsory at night. Many cyclists ride without this equipment, often leaving them almost invisible.

Cycle Hire

There are plenty of cycle hire shops in the Netherlands. You can either go to private cycle hire places or hire a bike from

some 100 railway stations with a *Rijwielshop* or *Fietspoint*. Cycle hire usually costs around €7.50 per day. Cycle hire shops also offer weekly tariffs that work out relatively cheaper. Many of them require a deposit, which can range from €30 to €145, and often want proof of identity. Tandems are also sometimes available, though they cost more, and their lack of manoeuvrability does not make them very suitable for use in city traffic.

Sign for the Rijwiel cycle hire shop, found at nearly 100 railway stations

If you are planning to make a train journey and hire a cycle from your destination, it is worth buying a *huurfietskaartje* (cycle hire ticket) when setting out. It is a good idea to reserve the bicycle by telephone in advance. The NS publishes a special pamphlet, *Fiets en Trein*, which lists stations where you

can hire bicycles. The VVV and ANWB can also direct you to cycle hire shops.

Security

Even if your bicycle is equipped with a rear-wheel lock, it's a good idea – particularly in the big cities – to secure your bicycle to a post or a bicycle rack by the front wheel. Cycle hire shops will often provide you with a lock for the bike, especially in cities where bicycle theft is a problem. At many railway stations you can leave your bicycle in a secure bicycle park for around €1. Do not leave any luggage on your bicycle if you park it somewhere, not even in a guarded bicycle park.

Bicycles and Public Transport

For an additional payment you can take your bicycle on the train, except during rush hours (Sep–Jun: 6:30–9am and 4:30–6pm Mon–Fri). To do this, you need to buy a *Dagkaart fiets* (bike ticket) from a train or metro station in addition to your ordinary train ticket. These tickets cost €6 and are valid for the whole day regardless of the length of your journey. Places for bicycles on trains are marked with stickers on the carriage. Folding cycles, when folded, may be taken on trains free of charge. Bicycles may be taken on metros and suburban (fast) trams, provided that you have a bike ticket, but they are not allowed on buses and city trams.

An organized cycling tour on the Zaanse Schans

Cycling Tours

If you want to get from point A to point B by the quickest possible route, just follow the white-and-red ANWB cycle route signposts. Maps and guides for cyclists describing routes of various lengths are available from the VVV, the ANWB and many bookstores. They often contain a variety of local background information, as well as the addresses of cycle hire shops and places to stay, such as *pensions*, camping sites and hiking huts *(see also p395)*. Useful examples are the regional *ANWB/VVV Toeristenkaarten*, which suggest some particularly enjoyable routes, and the *Dwarsstap-fiets-mappen*, which give descriptions of cycle routes, often in the area surrounding big cities, and also contain topographical maps. The regional *ANWB/VVV-fietsgiden* have maps and provide descriptions of hundreds of enjoyable cycling trips of around 25 km (15 miles), from the *Amelandroute* to the *Maasdalroute* in Limburg. Many of these routes are marked with hexagonal signs. Around 45 railway-based routes are also offered under the name *NS-Fietstocht*. Maps of the route are on sale at the relevant railway stations. NS publishes a booklet, entitled *Er op Uit!*, describing these routes. Long-distance tours of at least 200 km (125 miles) in length (for example, the

Cyclists on tour stopping to enjoy an ice cream

230-km/143-mile *Elfstedenroute* in Friesland) are described in guides such as the *ANWB/VVV Lange Fiestronde*. These routes are also signposted. Another organization, the **Stichting Landelijk Fiets-platform**, or national cycling association *(see p429)*, has a network of some 6,000 km (3,730 miles) of numbered National Cycle Routes (*Landelijke Fiestroutes*, or *"LF"*). These often follow quiet byroads and cycle tracks and are described in two of the *LF-basisgidsen*. Some are marked with square signs, such as LF-15, which is the *Boerenlandroute* (farmland route) from Alkmaar to Enschede. Guides to individual routes are also available. The *Fietsideeënkaart*, a map available from the VVV and ANWB, also provides brief descriptions of LF and other marked cycling routes around the country.

Cycle lane sign

To take part in an organized cycle tour, contact organizations such as **Cycletours** or the **Fietsvakantiewinkel** *(see p429)*, some of the main VVV offices and the ANWB (members only). These organizations can arrange cycle-tour packages, including accommodation and luggage transfer. For information on cycling in nature reserve areas, see page 429.

Cycling Events

Meimaand Fietsmaand is the year's biggest bicycle event: a whole month (May) packed with bicycle rides, meets and races throughout the Netherlands. In 2010, about 570,000 cyclists participated. Information on the various routes and events can be found at the national cycling association's website: www.fietsplatform.nl. Local cycle-touring clubs organize regular non-competitive tours through picturesque or interesting areas, although you have to pay a fee to join. For further information, apply at the Dutch cycle tour society (Nederlandse Toer Fiets Unie, or **NFTU**, *see p429*). In addition, dozens of local tours lasting several days are organized locally, such as the *Drentse Rijwielvierdaagse* in July. Participants can often choose between routes of lengths varying from 30 to 100 km (20 to 60 miles) per day. You will find an overview of these online at www.fiets4daagse.nl.

The ferry at Wijk near Duurstede, which carries bicycles

General Index

Newport Community Learning & Libraries

Page numbers in **bold** refer to main entries.

Acknowledgments

Dorling Kindersley would like to thank the following people for their help in preparing this guide:

For Dorling Kindersley
Translation from Dutch Mark Cole (Linguists for Business)
Design and Editorial Assistance Jo Cowen, Jacky Jackson, Ian Midson, Conrad van Dyk, Stewart Wild
Dtp Designers Jason Little, Conrad van Dyk
Managing Editor Helen Townsend
Publishing Manager Jane Ewart

For International Book Productions
Proofreader Maraya Radhua

Main Author
Gerard M L Harmans graduated in biology and philosophy at the Vrije Universiteit (Amsterdam), and then chose to work in publishing. He edited an encyclopaedia for Het Spectrum before setting up an independent business with Paul Krijnen in 1989 called de Redactie, boekverzorgers.

Other Contributors
All contributors were selected from de Redactie, boekverzorgers in Amsterdam. The team of authors, translators and editors share a broad field of expertise. Every member of the team made an invaluable contribution.
Anneliet Bannier graduated in translation studies from Amsterdam University. She works as a translator and sub-editor on travel guides. She lives in Zaanstreek.
Hanneke Bos is an editor and translator in the fields of linguistics, cultural history and travel literature.
Jaap Deinema, from Eindhoven, is an expert on the Netherlands. He has made numerous contributions to travel guides. He was responsible for the ATO/VVV edition Infopocket Amsterdam.
Jérôme Gommers, born in Paris, is a freelance author and lover of the Dutch landscape and its poetry. Among other things, he has conducted a comprehensive study of the construction and development of the Noordoostpolder.
Ron de Heer studied philosophy in Amsterdam. For ten years he has been working as a translator/editor, primarily of travel guides, novels and culinary publications.
Marten van de Kraats writes and translates texts in the fields of travel and automation. Every year he edits the Dutch edition of the Rough Guide Travels on the internet, the best-selling internet book on Holland and Belgium.
Paul Krijnen is a social geographer who has specialized in medieval mark organizations of the Netherlands, such as the Erfgooiers. His great passion is the Dutch borderlands.
Frans Reusink studied Dutch language. After working as a copywriter, he has been active as a photographer, written travel reports for magazines, and edited travel guides.
Theo Scholten is a Dutch scholar. He has worked on many literary publications but is currently active in non-fiction as an editor and translator. He has made previous contributions to travel guides on Belgium and France.
Ernst Schreuder, a Frisian editor, won the Elfsteden Cross for completing the Tocht der Tochten in 1986 and 1997. Travel and travel guides are his occupation and his hobby.
Catherine Smit studied Dutch language and literature at Utrecht and has contributed as editor and translator to many books, including travel guides.
Jacqueline Toscani graduated in European Studies from Amsterdam University. Since 1992 she has been working as an editor and translator of travel guides, including many titles in the Capitool and Marco Polo series. In the latest series she was co-author of the Vakantieplanner (holiday planner).

Willemien Werkman is a historian and, after studying the history of the Vecht estates, has devoted herself to translation and editing.

Additional Contributors
Paul Andrews, Hedda Archbold, Christopher Catling, Jaap Deinema, Marlene Edmunds, Adam Hopkins, Marten van de Kraats, David Lindsey, Fred Mawer, Alison Melvin, Robin Pascoe, Catherine Stebbings, Richard Widdows, Stewart Wild. Other contributions were taken from the Eyewitness Travel Guide Amsterdam by Robin Pascoe and Christopher Catling, which previously appeared in a translated and revised edition (Capitool Reisgids Amsterdam) published by de Redactie, boekverzorgers.

Additional Illustrations
Peter de Vries, Mark Jurriëns, Hilbert Bolland, Gieb van Enckevort, Armand Haye and Stuart Commercial Artists: Jan Egas and Khoobie Verwer.

Additional Photography
Max Alexander, Ian O'Leary, John Whittaker.

Editorial and Design Assistance
Louise Abbot, Willem de Blaauw, Frank Bontekoning, Lucinda Cooke, Emer FitzGerald, Willem Gerritze, Martine Hauwert, Peter Koomen, Catherine Palmi, Ron Putto, Sadie Smith, Susana Smith, Inge Tijsmans, Sylvia Tombesi-Walton, Pascal Veeger, Erna de Voos, Willeke Vrij, Gerard van Vuuren, Martine Wiedemeijer.

Picture Research
Harry Bunk; Corine Koolstra; Dick Polman; de Redactie, boekverzorgers; Rachel Barber; Ellen Root.

Revisions Team
Tora Agarwala, Madhura Birdi, Willem de Blaauw, Neha Dhingra, Sander Groen, Sumita Khatwani, Shikha Kulkarni, Phil Lee, Bhavika Mathur, Avijit Sengupta, Azeem Siddiqui, Rituraj Singh, Rachel Thompson, Ajay Verma, Gerard van Vuuren.

Special Assistance
John Bekker; Wim ten Brinke; Bert Erwich; Niek Harmans; Frits Gommers; Hans Hoogendoorn; Cathelijne Hornstra; Petra van Hulsen; Frank Jacobs; Chris de Jong; Nina Krijnen; Mies Kuiper; Louise Lang; Frank van Lier; Bas de Melker; Miek Reusink; Dick Rog; Joske Siemons; Erika Teeuwisse; Wout Vuyk, Douglas Amrine.

Picture Credits
t = top; tl = top left; tlc = top left centre; tc = top centre; tr = top right; trc = top right centre; c = centre; cl = centre left; cla = centre left above; clb = centre left below; ca = centre above; cr = centre right; cra = centre right above; crb = centre right below; bc = bottom centre; b = bottom; bl = bottom left; br = bottom right. Every effort has been made to trace the copyright holders. Dorling Kindersley apologizes for any unintentional omissions and would be pleased, in such cases, to add an acknowledgment in future editions.

The publishers are grateful to the following museums, photographers and picture libraries for permission to reproduce their photographs:

4corners images: SIME/ Pavan Aldo 151br; VAN **Abbemuseum, Eindhoven**: © Pablo Picasso Lady in Green, 1909, 1999 c/o Beeldrecht Amstelveen 364tl; **AKG, London**: 68bl, 105tr, 126ca, 221tr; **Alamy Images**: Stephen Barnes/Netherlands 447br; Tibor Bognar 74; Bertrand Collet 405tl; Keith Erskine 150br; f1 online 10bl; GAUTIER Stephane/SAGAPHOTO.CO 72cl; Hemis 86, 294; Peter Horree 306, 423tr; Horizons WWP 14tr; Joana Kruse 16br, 196; frans lemmens 17bc, 246, 260-1, 326, 371; LH Images 125bl;

David Noble 15tr; David Noton Photography 212; Ingolf Pompe 2 152bl; PjrTravel 13tr; Peter Scholey 72clb; Paul M Thompson 368bl. **Alamy Stock Photo:** Mieneke Andeweg-van Rijn 180bl; Timewatch Images 245tr. **Algemeen Rijksarchief, The Hague:** 61cra; **Amsterdam Tourism & Convention Board:** 111br, 114tl, 432bl, 447cl; **Amsterdams Historisch Museum:** 51cra, 51crb, 68-69c, 69bl, 70cla, 96tl, 96cl, 96bc, 97tl, 97crb, 97cr, 97br, 114b, 118bl; AFF/**Anne Frank foundation, amsterdam:** 112cl, 112b, 113br, 113cr (Miep Gies); **ANP:** 21b, 76tr, 139tl, 63cra; **ANWB audiovisuele dienst:** 27tr, 34clb, 39br, 52bl, 63tl, 142br, 167tr, 170bl, 170br, 171b, 172bl, 173bl, 184bl, 189b, 192tl, 192bl, 195tl, 211cra, 211br, 214tr, 224c, 228t, 228br, 234tr, 234bl, 236br, 243tr, 249tr, 253br, 255tr, 255c, 255bc, 256bc, 257tl, 283tr, 293br, 319br, 336tr, 342clb, 357bl, 364tr, 365cra, 365crb, 381br, 382cr, 394cla, 394b, 432cla, 432clb, 434cr, 434bc, 435tr, 436c, 439c; **archeologisch instituut vu/f kortlang, amsterdam:** 46-47c; **The Art Archive:** Museo del Prado Madrid The Surrender of Breda (1635) Diego Velazquez 367br; **Atlas Van Stolk:** 45clb, 51bl, 52br, 56-57c, 57tl, 57cr, 58cl, 59tl. **BADHU:** 410bl; **Balthazar's Keuken:** 407tr; **B&U international picture service:** 105bl, 109br, 167br, 216cla; **aart de bakker:** 353tr, 353br, 374tr, 377tc, 377cra, 380tr, 416cla; **bonnefantenmuseum, maastricht:** 378tr, 378cl, 378bl, © Rene Daniels Platte Gronden, 1986, 1999 c/o Beeldrecht Amstelveen 378br; 379tl, 379cra, 379bl, 379br; **henk brandsen:** 49bc, 310cla, 311tl, 311tr, 311cra; **bridgeman art library:** Christie's London, Grote Markt, Haarlem; Private collection Self-portrait © Kazimir Malevitch 133br; **Bries Noordwijk:** 411tr; **Quinta Buma:** 38t; **Harry Bunk:** 37cl, 72tr, 142cla, 143bl, 143br, 147tl, 206b, © Ossip Zadkine De verwoeste stad 1947, 1999 c/o Beeldrecht Amstelveen 234cl; 235cra, 235crb, 235bc, 241cr, © Mari Andriessen Cornelius Lely, 1983, 1999 c/o Beeldrecht Amstelveen 330bc, 417bl, 438cl, 440c; **Cees Buys:** 27tl, 51ca, 248bc, 284clb, 287c, 291b, 303c, 308cla, 319cr, 321t, 324tl, 325tr, 325bl, 329tr, 329cr, 343br, 371b, 385cra, 392cla; **George Burggraaff:** 22t, 25bl, 32tr, 36tr, 36bl, 46cl, 172tr, 172cla, 193tl, 201ca, 204cla, 220tr, 241tl, 250tr, 250br, 253crb, 258tr, 259tr, 259br, 262cr, 264clb, 265cra, 265br, 282br, 301cr, 305cl, 318cl, 321br, 322ca, 322cl, 323cr, 323br, 329br, 337bl, 340br, 347bl, 347tr, 349br, 357tl, 357tr, 362br, 365ca. **Catharijneconvent, Utrecht:** 49cra, 54bl, 56tr, 205cra, 355tl; **Centraal Museum, Utrecht:** Ernst Moritz 206br; 208cla, 208tr, 209tr, 209br; **Cleveland Museum, Cleveland:** 54-55c; **Cobra Museum, Amstelveen:** © Karel Appel Foundation, Karel Appel Questioning Children 1949, 1999 c/o Beeldrecht Amstelveen 193br. **Het Concert Gebouw:** Hans Samson 150cla; **Corbis:** Arcaid/ Alex Bartel 152tr; Dave Bartruff 404cl; Owen Franken 405cr; Frans Lemmens 268; Jean-Pierre Lescourret 64-5, 81bl; Koen Van Weel/epa 350-1. **Jan Derwig:** 103tr, 145bl; **Dreamstime.com:** Ak4masforest 145tr; Gunold Brunbauer 180tr, 180c; Rob Van Esch 38cr, 358; Patricia Hofmeester 34-5; Peter De Kievith 69cb; Ldambies 164-5; Ber Lybil 2-3; Mauvries 45br; Miv123; Neirfy 430-1; Richardt777 12bc; Robertlindeboom 280; Richard Semik 13bl; Pieter Snijder 334; Teo Stuivenberg 210bl; TasFoto 341tr; Dennis Van De Water 17tr; Rudmer Zwerver 170tr; **Jurjen Drenth:** 32cla, 34lb, 39bl, 47crb, 57bl, 71tr, 72cla, 72br, 73cra, 73cr, 73tr, 78b, 90tr, 112tr, 122tr, 390br, 403c, © Hildo Krop Berlage, 1999 c/o Beeldrecht Amstelveen 146bl; 148cl, 149cr, 151tr, 164/165, 167 tr, 170cl, 170-171c, 173br, 175b, 177cr, 178bl, 196, 197b, 198clb, 200bl, 201b, 202cl, 202br, 203br, 204bl, 205bc, 207tl, 213b, 214cla, 214clb, 217clb, 223cr, © Peter Struycken Lichtkunstwerk NAI 1994, 1999 c/o Beeldrecht Amstelveen 237tl; 240tr, 241tr, 241br, 244tc, 247b, 250bc, 251br, 253tl, 256tl, 256cr, 263crb, 267bl, 270tr, 270br, 271tl, 271br, 274-275c, 276cra, 279br, 281b, 286b, 288tr, 288clb, 290tr, 291tr, 296tr, 296br, 301tc, 303tr, 308b, 309cr, 311cra, 314bl, 317b, 324br, 327b, 328clb, 342cla, 343tl, 349tl, 352cla, 356cl, 356bl, 357cr,

357bc, 359b, 362bl, 366tr, 367tr, 368c, 369bc, 375c, 376bl, 380cr, 384br, 390tl, 395tr, 402cl, 438cra, 438bl, 440bl; **Drents Museum, Assen:** 46br, 312bl, Badende kinderen bij stroompje c.1935 © von Duelman-Krumpelmann 315br; **Dro-vorm:** Mirande Phernambucq 146cla, 147br.

Robert Eckhardt: 292bl, 372c; **Eetbar Dit:** 402br; **Efteling Village Bosrijk:** 392cla; **Joop van de Ende Producties:** 420br; **Escher in Het Paleis, The Hague:** 222cla; **Mary Evans Picture Library:** 44bc.**Gert Fopma:** 275br, 277bl; **Foto Natura:** 168bl (B van Biezen), 295b (J Vermeer), 313tr and 314tc (F de Nooyer), 332t (J Sleurink); **Fotolia:** Jenifoto 98; **Frans Hals Museum, Haarlem:** 69tc, 190tr, 190cl, 190br, 191tl, 191tr, 191br, 191bl;

Gemeentearchief Amsterdam: 103tl, 103cl, 104clb, 105br, 106bl, 107tr, 107cr, 109r, 109tr, 109cr; **Gemeentemuseum, The Hague:** © Piet Mondrian/Holtzman Trust Victory Boogie-Woogie (unfinished), 1942-44, 1999 c/o Beeldrecht Amstelveen 228cl; **Getty Images:** altrendo travel 316 Hans Georg Eiben/The Image Bank 386-7; Vincent Jannink 347bl; Frans Lemmens/The Image Bank 174; Martin Rose 152cr. **Groninger Museum, Groningen:** 261tr, 288cl, 288cb, 289tl, 289cr, 289bl.**Tom Haartsen, J Holtkamp collection:** 32br, 32-33c; **Vanessa Hamilton:** 105c; **Harbour Crane:** 389tl; **Robert Harding Picture Library:** age fotostock 14br, 134; Ashley Cooper 171tc; Image Broker 16tr; Ingolf Pompe/LOOK 120; Roy Rainford 20; **Martine Hauwert:** 439tl; **Jan Den Hengst:** 95br; **Herberg Onder de Linden:** 412tc; **Het Arresthuis:** 388cr; **Hollandse Hoogte:** 307b, 420t; P. Babeliowsky 299tl, 299cra; Gé Dubbelman 300bc; B. van Flymen 36br, 304cra, 304bl; Vincent van den Hoogen 368cr; Rob Huibers 210br; Jaco Klamer 321c; M. Kooren 22bl, 22tl, 39tr, 45cra, 45br, 63bc; M. Pellanders 63br; Berry Stokvis 185bc; Lex Verspeek 182bl; G. Wessel 278tl, 298clb, 299br; **Hortus Botanicus, Leiden:** 218cla; **Hotel Droog:** 396bc; **Hotel Modez:** 400tc; Hotelsuites.nl: 401bc; **Hulton Getty Collection:** 70t.

Iconografisch Bureau: 107tl; **Internationaal Bloembollencentrum:** 35cr, 216br, 217tr, 217clb, 217cl, 217cla, 217bl; **Internationaal Instituut Voor Sociale Geschiedenis, Amsterdam:** 59crb. **Wim Janszen:** 262cl, 266cl, 270cl; **Wubbe de Jong:** 63clb, 113tl; **Joods Historisch Museum, Amsterdam:** 71br; **De Jopenkerk:** 409tr; **Jopie Huisman Museum, Workum:** 302cla.

Hugo Kaagman: © Hugo Kaagman Delft blue plane-tail decoration 1996-1997, 1999 c/o Beeldrecht Amstelveen 33tr; **Anne Kalkhoven:** 287bl, 315tr, 348tl; **Jan Van De Kam:** 23b, 41tr, 41cra, 41crb, 41br, 173tr, 173cb, 173crb, 264cl, 264bc, 265tr, 265cr, 266cla, 266cra, 266br, 266bl, 267tl, 267cla, 267cra, 267tr, 267crb, 267cr, 267br, 272tr, 273tl, 273tc, 273tr, 273cr, 273crb, 273bc, 273clb, 273bl, 273br, 273tl, 273tr, 273clb, 273bl, 274br, 275cra, 275cra, 277tr, 278br, 282cl, 297tr, 318br, 332c, 332br, 346tl, 352br, 354tr, 354cla, 354br, 354-355c, 355tr, 355crb, 355bl, 362tr, 362cla, 363ca, 363cr, 369cl, 372cla, 373tr, 375bl, © Joep Nicolas, Pieke 1995-1996, 1999 c/o Beeldrecht Amstelveen 376tr; 376cla, 376br, 377br, © Mari Andriessen Maastreechter Gees 1961-1962, 1999 c/o Beeldrecht Amstelveen 380bl, 381cl, 382bl, 383cr, 384tc, 384cla, 384crb, 385bc; **Klompenmuseum:** 313bl; S **Koninklijke Bibliotheek, The Hague:** 56cl; **Koninklijk Instituut voor de Tropen, Amsterdam:** 60tr, 60-61c; **Koninklijk Paleis, Amsterdam**/RVD: 69cr, 92cla, 92clb, 93crb; **Corine Koolstra:** © Suze Boschma-Berkhout Bartje, 1999 c/o Beeldrecht Amstelveen 312c; **Peter Koomen:** 182cr; **René Krekels, Nijmegen:** 27crb; **Kröller-müller Museum, Otterlo:** © Jean Dubuffet Jardin d'Émail 1973-

4, 1999 c/o Beeldrecht Amstelveen 342tr; 342br; 343c.

Andries a la Lande Cremer: 269b, 282tr; **Leeuwarder Courant**: Niels Westra 298bl; **Frans Lemmens**: 34c; **Claude Lévesque**: 356-357c; **De Librije**: 414tc; **Lucius Seafood Restaurant**: 406bc.

Marker Wadden: 168br; **Mauritshuis, The Hague**: 8-9, 226tr, 226c, 226bl, 227tc, 227crb, 227cra, 227bc, 231tl; **Multatuli Museum, Amsterdam**: 61tr; **Musée de la Chartreuse, Douai**: 54clb; **Museum Boerhaave, Leiden**: 54bc, 55tl, 55clb; **Museum Boijmans-van Beuningen, Rotterdam**: Hubert van Eyck, Three Marys at the Tomb, 1425-1435, Acquired with the collection of D.G. van Beuningen 1958, Museum Boijmans Van Beuningen 238cla, 238-9 all; **Museum Bredius, The Hague**: 224bl; **Museum Lambert van Meerten, Delft**: 233bl; **Museum de Fundatie, Paleis a/d Blijmarkt**: Gerlinde Schrijver 320bl; **Museum Nairac, Barneveld**: 341br; **Museum Het Rembrandthuis, Amsterdam**: 79bc, 82br; **Museum Schokland**: 330tr, 330cra. **Natura Artis Magistra**: 143cra; **Nederlands Architectuur Instituut**: 109cl, 146-147c; **Nederlands Scheepvaartmuseum, Amsterdam**: 136bl, 136cla, 137b, 137crb, 137t; **Nemo Science Museum**: DigiDaan 140tr, 140cla, 140clb, 140br; **Niedersächsische Staats- und Universitätsbibliothek, Göttingen**: 48-49c; **Flip de Nooyer**: 272-273c; **North Sea Jazz Festival/rob Drexhage**: 37br. **Onze-lieve-vrouwebasiliek, Maastricht**: 381tr. **Paleis Het Loo, Nationaal Museum, Apeldoorn**: E. Boeijinga 338tr; A. Meine Jansen 338cla, 339tl, 338bl; R. Mulder 338cla; **Openbare Bibliotheek Amsterdam**: 441tl; **De Paviljoens, Almere**: © Robert Morris Observatorium, 1977, 1999 c/o Beeldrecht Amstelveen 333br; **Paul Paris**: 28tr, 71bl, 172-173c, 173tl, 194br, 198tr, 249tr, 257br, 267cl, 272cla, 283cra, 286tr, 290clb, 292tr, 297bc, 303br, 305br, 309tr, 310clb, 311br, 335b, 352bl, 372tr; **Dick Polman**: 278c; **Robert Poutsma**: 24bl, 71tl, 146tr, 146br, 147tr, 147cr, 148cr, 148br, 166cl, 179tl, 344cr, 416br, 417tl, 418c; **Prinsenhof**: 399bc; **Projectbureau Ijburg**: 171t; PTT

Range Pictures: 52cla; **Herman Reis**: 23c, 24c, 25tr, 29cl, 56bl, 215br, 240b, 241tr, 274cla, 276br, 315cl, 323bl, **Rijksmuseum, Amsterdam**: 30tr, 30cl, 30bl, 30-31c, 31tr, 31cr, 31bl, 42, 44tr, 57t, 57crb, 61tl, 68cla, 70c, 126cl, 126bc, 127tl, 127c, 127br, 128tr, 128bl, 129tr, 129b, 199bl; **Rijksmuseum Muiderslot, Muiden**: 55cr; **Rijksmuseum van Oudheden, Leiden**: 46clb, 47tl, 47bc, 48bc, 48crb, 218tr; **Rijksmuseum voor Volkenkunde, Leiden**: 60bl, 61crb; **Rijkswaterstaat**: 250clb, 251tl, 251cr, 276tl; **La Rive**: 408bl.

Herman Scholten: 29bl, 176cla, 179bl, 182tl, 184ca, 194tl, 199tr, 203tr, 206cla, 210tr, 235tc, 244b, 250cla, 252tr, 252bl, 253cra, 258c, 258bl, 262b, 284cla, 284b, 285br, 287tr, 296clb, 300tr, 300cl, 328tr, 360tr, 361tr; 377bc, 382tl; **Schoolmuseum, Rotterdam/Wolters-noordhoff, Groningen**: 50-51c, 53tl, 58-59c; **Science Center NEMO**: 141br, 141cra; **Singer Museum**: Particuliere Collection

195bl; **Sint-jan, Den Bosch**:E Van Mackelenbergh 364cla, 364bc, 365tl; **Spaarnestad Fotoarchief**: 59tr, 61bc, 62clb, 62br, 63tc, 103bc, 147bl; **Spoorwegmuseum, Utrecht**: 205crb; **Stedelijk Museum, Amsterdam**: © Gerrit Rietveld Steltman chair 1963, 1999 c/o Beeldrecht Amstelveen 70bl; 132tr, © Marc Chagall Portrait of the Artist with Seven Fingers 1912, 1999 c/o Beeldrecht Amstelveen 132cla; © Gerrit Rietveld Red Blue Chair c.1918, 1999 c/o Beeldrecht Amstelveen 132bl; © Piet Mondrian/Holtzman Trust Composition in Red, Black, Blue, Yellow and Grey 1920, 1999 c/o Beeldrecht Amstelveen 132br; 133tl, © Karel Appel Foundation Man and Animals 1949, 1999 c/o Beeldrecht Amstelveen 133ca; © Jasper Johns Untitled 1965, 1999 c/o Beeldrecht Amstelveen 133bc; 133br, Tanzende 1911 © Ernst Ludwig Kirchner 133tl; **Stedelijk Museum De Lakenhal, Leiden**: 50cl, 108bc, 220b; **Stedelijk Museum, Zwolle**: 320tr; **Stempels**: 389bc, 397tc; **Stichting Leidens Ontzet**: 39tl; **Stichting Paardenreddingboot Ameland**: 279tr; **Stichting Vesting Bourtange**: 293tr; **Stichting4-Stromenland, Tiel**: 38bl; **Studio Putto, Derijp**: 22bl, 24c, 37tr, 45bl, 45crb, 48br, 88tr, 117bl, 177tr, 177cr; **Studiopress**: Guy van Grinsven 178tr.

Tony Stone Images: 104tr, 183cla; **Sven Torfinn**: 363tl, 363br; **TPG Nederland**: 440crb, 441bc; **Hans Tulleners**: 103cr, 104cr, 106c. **Van Gogh Museum, Amsterdam**: 70br, 130cla, 130clb, 131t, 131tr, 131cr; **Gerard op het Veld**: 34tr, 146c, 302tr, 340cra, 345bl, 346br, 360bl, 369tr, 372bl, 373br, 375tr, 383tr, 383bl; **Vereniging De Friesche Elf Steden**: 296br; **Govert Vetten**: 22tr, 73bl, 83br, 124clb, 146-147c, 199br, 200tr, 264cla, 416c, 428br; **de Verkadefabriek**: 415br; **Villa Augustus**: 398tl; **Volkskrant**: Wim Ruigrok 26tr; **Sietske de Vries, Amsterdam**: 34cl; **Willeke Vrij**: 35tr. **Wacon-Images/Ronald Dendekker**: 151tl; **Waalse Kerk**: 76cl. **Pim Westerweel**: 166cr, 167cr, 168crb, 199cra, 263cra, 263b, 266clb, 333tr, 345cr, 353cr, 366bl; **West-Fries Museum, Hoorn**: 60cla. **Zeeuws Museum, Middelburg**: Anda van Riet 254br 254cra; **Zuiderzeemuseum, Enkhuizen**: 169tr, photo Petra Stavast © Hugo Kaagman The Blue Fishvendor (www.kaagman.nl) stencils and spraypaint 181tl.

Front endpaper

Alamy Images: Hemis Rtc; Peter Horree Rc; Joana Kruse Lcl; frans lemmens Rcr, Rbl, Lbl; David Noton Photography Lc. **Corbis**: Frans Lemmens Ltc; Jean-Pierre Lescourret Ltl. **Dreamstime.com**: Rob Van Esch Lbr; Robertlindeboom Rtr; Pieter Snijder Rclb. **Getty Images**: altrendo travel Rcb; The Image Bank/Frans Lemmens Ltr.

Cover
Front and spine - Corbis: SOPA RF / SOPA.

All other images © Dorling Kindersley.
For further **information see: www.dkimages.com**

Phrase Book

In Emergency

Help!	**Help!**	*Help*
Stop!	**Stop!**	*Stop*
Call a doctor	**Haal een dokter**	*Haal uhn dok-tur*
Call an ambulance	**Bel een ambulance**	*Bell uhn ahm-bew-luhns-uh*
Call the police	**Roep de politie**	*Roop duh poe-leet-see*
Call the fire brigade	**Roep de brandweer**	*Roop duh brahnt-vheer*
Where is the nearest telephone?	**Waar is de dichtstbijzijnde telefoon?**	*Vhaar iss duh dikhst-baiy-zaiyn-duh tay-luh-foan*
Where is the nearest hospital?	**Waar is het dichtstbijzijnde ziekenhuis?**	*Vhaar iss het dikhst-baiy-zaiyn-duh zee-kuh-houws*

Communication Essentials

Yes	**Ja**	*Yaa*
No	**Nee**	*Nay*
Please	**Alstublieft**	*Ahls-tew-bleeft*
Thank you	**Dank u**	*Dahnk-ew*
Excuse me	**Pardon**	*Pahr-don*
Hello	**Hallo**	*Hallo*
Goodbye	**Dag**	*Dahgh*
Good night	**Slaap lekker**	*Slaap lek-kah*
morning	**Morgen**	*Mor-ghuh*
afternoon	**Middag**	*Mid-dahgh*
evening	**Avond**	*Ah-vohnd*
yesterday	**Gisteren**	*Ghis-tern*
today	**Vandaag**	*Vahn-daagh*
tomorrow	**Morgen**	*Mor-ghuh*
here	**Hier**	*Heer*
there	**Daar**	*Daar*
What?	**Wat?**	*Vhat*
When?	**Wanneer?**	*Vhan-eer*
Why?	**Waarom?**	*Vhaar-om*
Where?	**Waar?**	*Vhaar*
How?	**Hoe?**	*Hoo*

Useful Phrases

How are you?	**Hoe gaat het ermee?**	*Hoo ghaat het er-may*
Very well, thank you	**Heel goed, dank u**	*Hayl ghoot, dahnk ew*
How do you do?	**Hoe maakt u het?**	*Hoo maakt ew het*
See you soon	**Tot ziens**	*Tot zeens*
That's fine	**Prima**	*Pree-mah*
Where is/are?	**Waar is/zijn?**	*Vhaar iss/zayn…*
How far is it to…?	**Hoe ver is het naar…?**	*Hoo vehr iss het naar…*
How do I get to…?	**Hoe kom ik naar…?**	*Hoo kom ik naar…*
Do you speak English?	**Spreekt u engels?**	*Spraykt ew eng-uhls*
I don't understand	**Ik snap het niet**	*Ik snahp het neet*
Could you speak slowly?	**Kunt u langzamer praten?**	*Kuhnt ew lahng-zahmer praa-tuh*
I'm sorry	**Sorry**	*Sorry*

Useful Words

big	**groot**	*ghroaht*
small	**klein**	*klaiyn*
hot	**warm**	*vharm*
cold	**koud**	*khowt*
good	**goed**	*ghoot*
bad	**slecht**	*slekht*
enough	**genoeg**	*ghuh-noohkh*
well	**goed**	*ghoot*
open	**open**	*open*
closed	**gesloten**	*ghuh-slow-tuh*
left	**links**	*links*
right	**rechts**	*rekhts*
straight on	**rechtdoor**	*rehkht dohr*
near	**dichtbij**	*dikht baiy*
far	**ver weg**	*vehr vhekh*
up	**omhoog**	*om-hoakh*
down	**naar beneden**	*naar buh-nay-duh*
early	**vroeg**	*vroohkh*
late	**laat**	*laat*
entrance	**ingang**	*in-ghahng*
exit	**uitgang**	*ouht-ghang*
toilet	**wc**	*vhay say*
occupied	**bezet**	*buh-zett*
free (unoccupied)	**vrij**	*vraiy*
free (no charge)	**gratis**	*ghraah-tiss*

Making a Telephone Call

I'd like to place a long-distance call	**Ik wil graag interlokaal telefoneren**	*Ik vhil ghraakh inter-loh-kaahl tay-luh-foe-neh-ruh*
I'd like to call collect	**Ik wil "collect call" bellen**	*Ik vhil "collect call" bel-luh*
I'll try again later	**Ik probeer het later nog wel eens**	*Ik pro-beer het laater nokh vhel ayns*
Can I leave a message?	**Kunt u een boodschap doorgeven?**	*Kuhnt ew uhn boat-skhahp dohr-ghay-vuh*
Could you speak up a little please?	**Wilt u wat harder praten?**	*Vhilt ew vhat hahr-der praah-tuh*
Local call	**Lokaal gesprek**	*Low-kaahl ghuh-sprek*

Shopping

How much does this cost?	**Hoeveel kost dit?**	*Hoo-vayl kost dit*
I would like	**Ik wil graag**	*Ik vhil ghraakh*
Do you have…?	**Heeft u…?**	*Hayft ew…*
I'm just looking	**Ik kijk alleen even**	*Ik kaiyk alleyn ay-vuh*
Do you take credit cards?	**Neemt u credit cards aan?**	*Naymt ew credit cards aan*
Do you take traveller's cheques?	**Neemt u reischeques aan?**	*Naymt ew raiys-sheks aan*
What time do you open?	**Hoe laat gaat u open?**	*Hoo laat ghaat ew opuh*
What time do you close?	**Hoe laat gaat u dicht?**	*Hoo laat ghaat ew dikht*
This one	**Deze**	*Day-zuh*
That one	**Die**	*Dee*
expensive	**duur**	*dewr*
cheap	**goedkoop**	*ghoot-koap*
size	**maat**	*maat*
white	**wit**	*vhit*
black	**zwart**	*zvhahrt*
red	**rood**	*roat*
yellow	**geel**	*ghayl*
green	**groen**	*ghroon*
blue	**blauw**	*blah-ew*

Types of Shops

antique shop	**antiekwinkel**	*ahn-teek-vhin-kul*
bakery	**bakker**	*bah-ker*
bank	**bank**	*bahnk*
bookshop	**boekwinkel**	*book-vhin-kul*
butcher	**slager**	*slaakh-er*
cake shop	**banketbakkerij**	*bahnk-et-bahk-er-aiy*
cheese shop	**kaaswinkel**	*kaas-vhin-kul*
chip shop	**patatzaak**	*pah-taht-zaak*
chemist (dispensing)	**apotheek**	*ah-poe-taiyk*
delicatessen	**delicatessen**	*daylee-kah-tes-suh*
department store	**warenhuis**	*vhaar-uh-houws*
fishmonger	**viswinkel**	*viss-vhin-kul*
greengrocer	**groenteboer**	*ghroon-tuh-boor*
hairdresser	**kapper**	*kah-per*
market	**markt**	*mahrkt*
newsagent	**krantenwinkel**	*krahn-tuh-vhin-kul*
post office	**postkantoor**	*pohst-kahn-tor*
shoe shop	**schoenenwinkel**	*sghoo-nuh-vhin-kul*
supermarket	**supermarkt**	*sew-per-mahrkt*
tobacconist	**sigarenwinkel**	*see-ghaa-ruh-vhin-kul*
travel agent	**reisburo**	*raiys-bew-roa*

Sightseeing

art gallery	**gallerie**	*ghaller-ee*
bus station	**busstation**	*buhs-stah-shown*
bus ticket	**strippenkaart**	*strip-puh-kaahrt*
cathedral	**kathedraal**	*kah-tuh-draal*
church	**kerk**	*kehrk*
closed on public holidays	**op feestdagen gesloten**	*op fayst-daa-ghuh ghuh-slow-tuh*
day return	**dagretour**	*dahgh-ruh-tour*
garden	**tuin**	*touwn*
library	**bibliotheek**	*bee-bee-yo-tayk*
museum	**museum**	*mew-zay-uhm*
railway station	**station**	*stah-shown*
return ticket	**retourtje**	*ruh-tour-tyuh*
single journey	**enkeltje**	*eng-kuhl-tyuh*
tourist information	**VVV**	*fay fay fay*
town hall	**stadhuis**	*staht-houws*
train	**trein**	*traiyn*

Staying in a Hotel

Do you have a vacant room?	**Zijn er nog kamers vrij?**	*Zaiyn er nokh kaa-mers vray*
double room with double bed	**een twees persoonskamer met een twee persoonsbed**	*uhn tvhay-per soans-kaa-mer met uhn tvhay-per-soans beht*
twin room	**een kamer met een lits-jumeaux**	*uhn kaa-mer met uhn lee-zjoo-moh*
single room	**eenpersoons-kamer**	*ayn-per-soans-kaa-mer*
room with a bath	**kamer met bad**	*kaa-mer met baht*
shower	**douche**	*doosh*
porter	**kruier**	*krouw-yuh*
I have a reservation	**Ik heb gereserveerd**	*Ik hehp ghuh-ray-sehr-veert*

Eating Out

Have you got a table?	**Is er een tafel vrij?**	*Iss ehr uhn tah-fuhl vraiy*
I want to reserve a table	**Ik wil een tafel reserveren**	*Ik vhil uhn tah-fuhl ray-sehr-veer-uh*
The bill, please	**Mag ik afrekenen**	*Mukh ik ahf-ray-kuh-nuh*
I am a vegetarian	**Ik ben vegetariër**	*Ik ben fay-ghuh-taahr-ee-er*
waitress/waiter	**serveerster/ober**	*Sehr-veer-ster/oh-ber*
menu	**de kaart**	*duh kaahrt*
cover charge	**het couvert**	*het koo-vehr*
wine list	**de wijnkaart**	*duh vhaiyn-kaart*
glass	**het glas**	*het ghlahss*
bottle	**de fles**	*duh fless*
knife	**het mes**	*het mess*
fork	**de vork**	*duh fork*
spoon	**de lepel**	*duh lay-pul*
breakfast	**het ontbijt**	*het ont-baiyt*
lunch	**de lunch**	*duh lernsh*
dinner	**het diner**	*het dee-nay*
main course	**het hoofdgerecht**	*het hoaft-ghuh-rekht*
starter, first course	**het voorgerecht**	*het vohr-ghuh-rekht*
dessert	**het nagerecht**	*het naa-ghuh-rekht*
dish of the day	**het dagmenu**	*het dahgh-munh-ew*
bar	**het cafe**	*het kaa-fay*
café	**het eetcafe**	*het ayt-kaa-fay*
rare	**rare**	*'rare'*
medium	**medium**	*'medium'*
well done	**doorbakken**	*dohr-bah-kuh*

Menu Decoder

aardappels	aard-uppuhls	potatoes
azijn	aah-zaiyn	vinegar
biefstuk	beef-stuhk	steak
bier, pils	beer, pilss	beer
boter	boater	butter
brood/broodje	broat/broat-yuh	bread/roll
cake, taart, gebak	"cake", taahrt, ghuh-bahk	cake, pastry
carbonade	kahr-bow-naa-duh	pork chop
chocola	show-coa-laa	chocolate
citroen	see-troon	lemon
cocktail	cocktail	cocktail
droog	droakh	dry
eend	aynt	duck
ei	aiy	egg
garnalen	ghahr-naah-luh	prawns
gebakken	ghuh-bah-ken	fried
gegrild	ghuh-ghrillt	grilled
gekookt	ghuh-koakt	boiled
gepocheerd	ghuh-posh-eert	poached
gerookt	ghuh-roakt	smoked
geroosterd brood	ghuh-roas-tert broat	toast
groenten	ghroon-tuh	vegetables
ham	hahm	ham
haring	haa-ring	herring
hutspot	huht-spot	hot pot
ijs	aiyss	ice, ice cream
jenever	yuh-nay-vhur	gin
kaas	kaas	cheese
kabeljauw	kah-buhl-youw	cod
kip	kip	chicken
knoflook	knoff-loak	garlic
koffie	coffee	coffee
kool, rode of witte	coal, roe-duh off vhit-uh	cabbage, red or white
kreeft	krayft	lobster
kroket	crow-ket	ragout in bread-crumbs, deep fried
lamsvlees	lahms-flayss	lamb
lekkerbekje	lek-kah-bek-yuh	fried fillet of haddock
mineraalwater	meener-aahl-vhaater	mineral water

mosterd	moss-tehrt	mustard
niet scherp	neet skehrp	mild
olie	oh-lee	oil
paling	paa-ling	eel
pannekoek	pah-nuh-kook	pancake
patat frites	pah-taht freet	chips
peper	pay-per	pepper
poffertjes	poffer-tyuhs	tiny buckwheat pancakes
rijst	raiyst	rice
rijsttafel	raiys-tah-ful	Indonesian meal
rode wijn	roe-duh vhaiyn	red wine
rookworst	roak-vhorst	smoked sausage
rundvlees	ruhnt-flayss	beef
saus	souwss	sauce
schaaldieren	skaahl-deeh-ruh	shellfish
scherp	skehrp	hot (spicy)
schol	sghol	plaice
soep	soup	soup
stamppot	stahm-pot	sausage stew
suiker	souw-ker	sugar
thee	tay	tea
tosti	toss-tee	cheese on toast
uien	ouw-yuh	onions
uitsmijter	ouht-smaiy-ter	fried egg on bread with ham
varkensvlees	vahr-kuhns-flayss	pork
vers fruit	fehrss frouwt	fresh fruit
verse jus	vehr-suh zjhew	fresh orange juice
vis	fiss	fish/seafood
vlees	flayss	meat
water	vhaa-ter	water
witte wijn	vhih-tuh vhaiyn	white wine
worst	vhorst	sausage
zout	zouwt	salt

Numbers

1	een	ayn
2	twee	tvhay
3	drie	dree
4	vier	feer
5	vijf	faiyf
6	zes	zess
7	zeven	zay-vuh
8	acht	ahkht
9	negen	nay-guh
10	tien	teen
11	elf	elf
12	twaalf	tvhaalf
13	dertien	dehr-teen
14	veertien	feer-teen
15	vijftien	faiyf-teen
16	zestien	zess-teen
17	zeventien	zayvuh-teen
18	achtien	ahkh-teen
19	negentien	nay-ghuh-teen
20	twintig	tvhin-tikh
21	eenentwintig	aynuh-tvhin-tukh
30	dertig	dehr-tukh
40	veertig	feer-tukh
50	vijftig	faiyf-tukh
60	zestig	zess-tukh
70	zeventig	zay-vuh-tukh
80	tachtig	tahkh-tukh
90	negentig	nayguh-tukh
100	honderd	hohn-durt
1000	duizend	douw-zuhnt
1,000,000	miljoen	mill-yoon

Time

one minute	een minuut	uhn meen-ewt
one hour	een uur	uhn ewr
half an hour	een half uur	uhn hahlf ewr
half past one	half twee	hahlf tvhay
a day	een dag	uhn dahgh
a week	een week	uhn vhayk
a month	een maand	uhn maant
a year	een jaar	uhn jaar
Monday	maandag	maan-dahgh
Tuesday	dinsdag	dins-dahgh
Wednesday	woensdag	vhoons-dahgh
Thursday	donderdag	donder-dahgh
Friday	vrijdag	vraiy-dahgh
Saturday	zaterdag	zaater-dahgh
Sunday	zondag	zon-dahgh

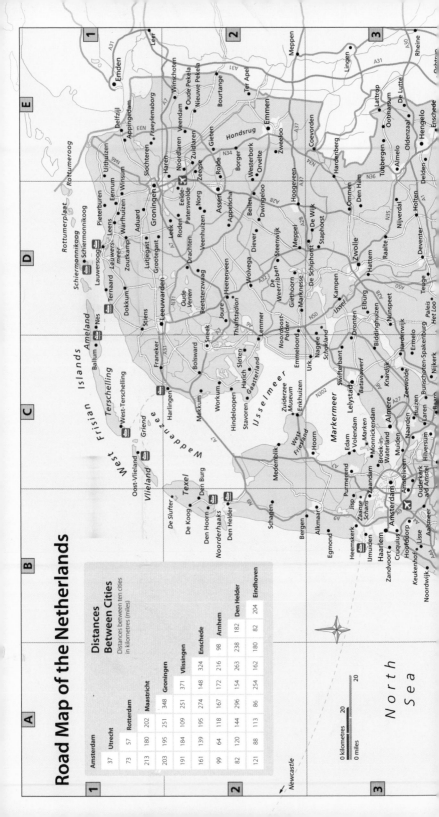

Road Map of the Netherlands

Distances Between Cities

Distances between ten cities in kilometres (miles)

Amsterdam									
37	Utrecht								
73	57	Rotterdam							
213	180	202	Maastricht						
203	195	251	348	Groningen					
191	184	109	251	371	Vlissingen				
161	139	195	274	148	324	Enschede			
99	64	118	167	172	216	98	Arnhem		
82	120	144	296	263	238	182	Den Helder	
121	88	113	254	162	180	82	204	Eindhoven

North Sea

Newcastle

0 kilometres 20
0 miles 20